the Accursed Vampire

THE CURSE AT WITCH CAMP

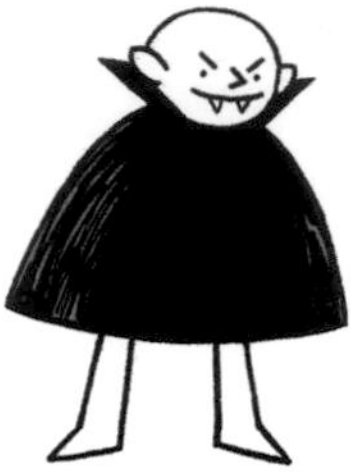

Quill Tree Books is an imprint of HarperCollins Publishers.
HarperAlley is an imprint of HarperCollins Publishers.

The Accursed Vampire : The Curse at Witch Camp

For information address HarperCollins Children's Books,
a division of HarperCollins Publishers,
195 Broadway, New York, NY 10007.
www.harperalley.com

Library of Congress Control Number: 2022941741
ISBN 978-0-06-295438-1 (trade bdg.)
ISBN 978-0-06-295437-4 (paperback)

The art for this book was rendered digitally.
Typography by Catherine San Juan
22 23 24 25 26 GPS 10 9 8 7 6 5 4 3 2 1

First Edition

the Accursed Vampire

THE CURSE AT WITCH CAMP

Madeline McGrane

Quill Tree Books
Imprints of HarperCollinsPublishers

HARPER alley

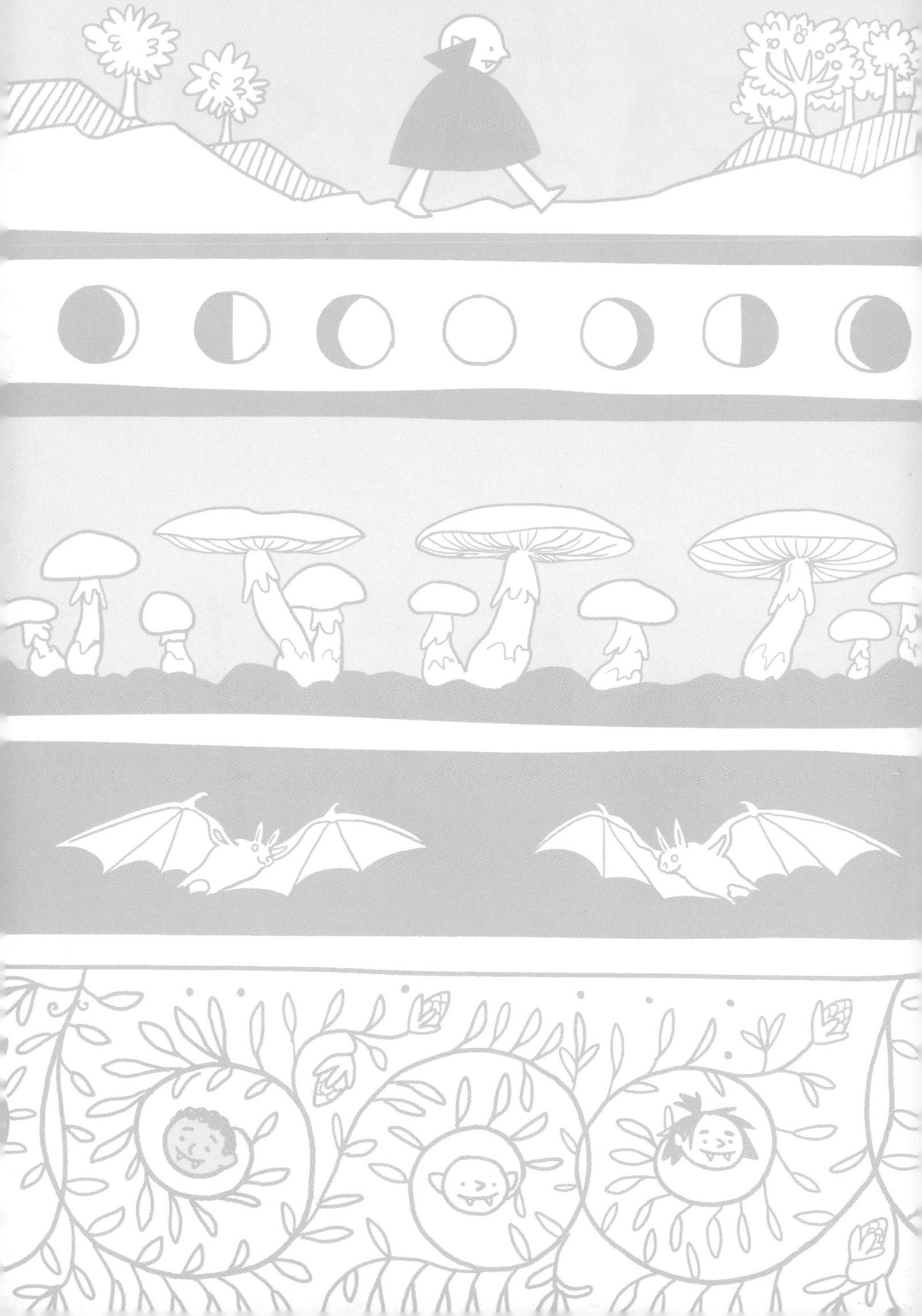

CHAPTER ONE

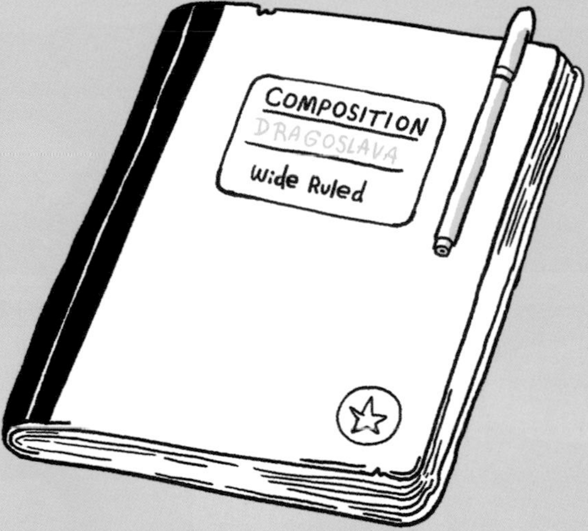
COMPOSITION
DRAGOSLAVA
Wide Ruled

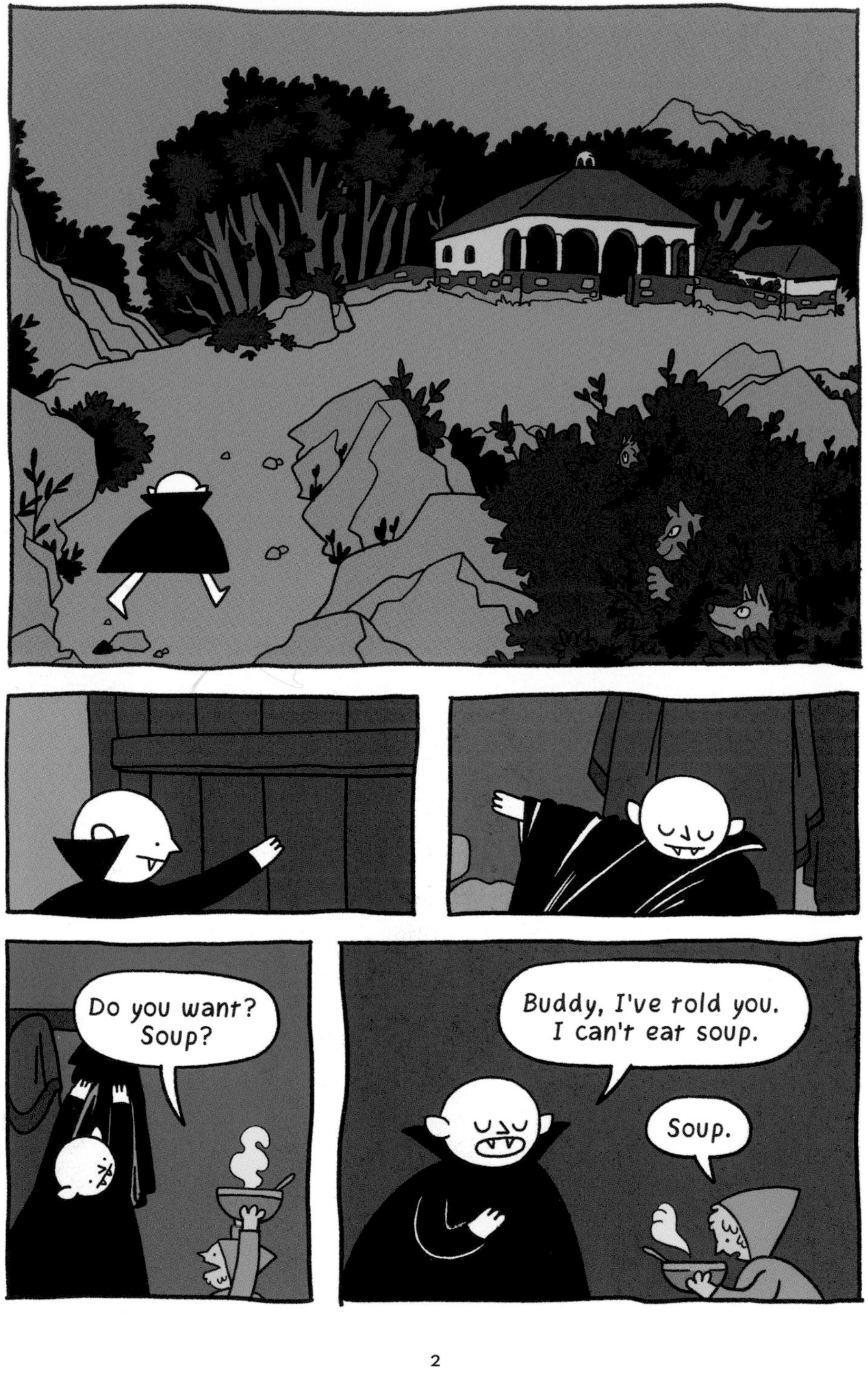
Do you want? Soup?
Buddy, I've told you. I can't eat soup.
Soup.

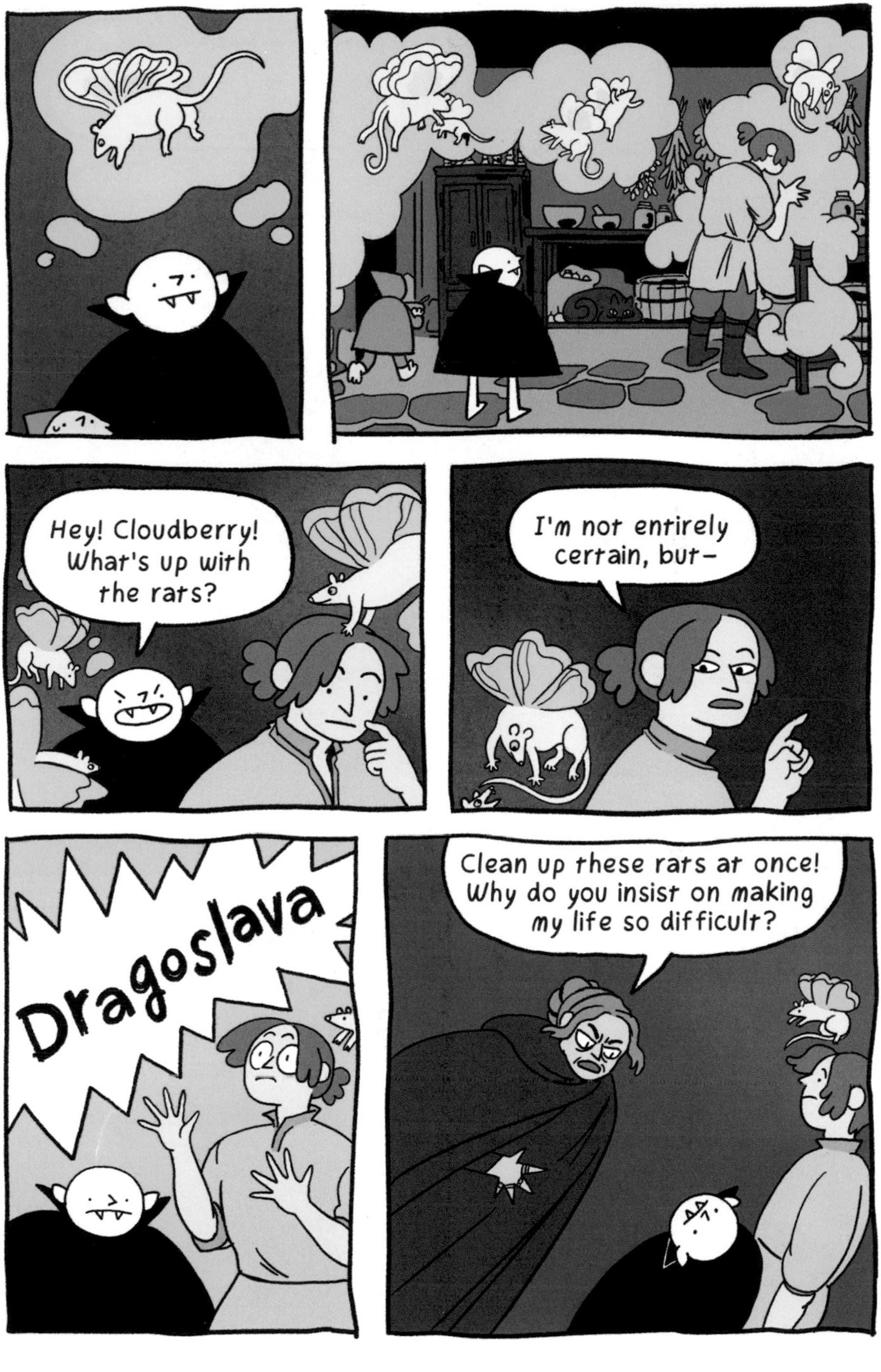
Hey! Cloudberry! What's up with the rats?
I'm not entirely certain, but–
Dragoslava
Clean up these rats at once! Why do you insist on making my life so difficult?

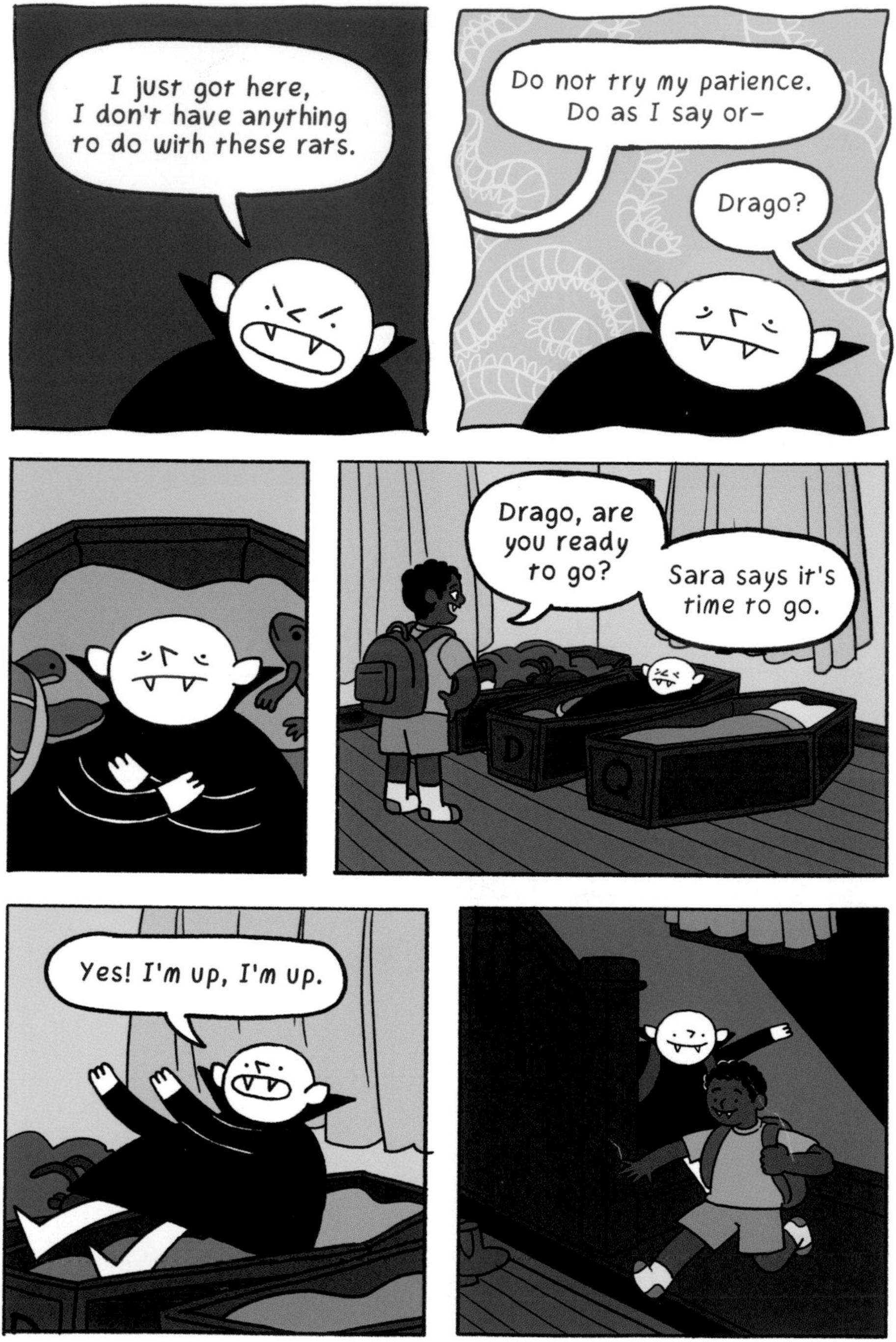
I just got here, I don't have anything to do with these rats.
Do not try my patience. Do as I say or–
Drago?
Drago, are you ready to go?
Sara says it's time to go.
D
Q
Yes! I'm up, I'm up.

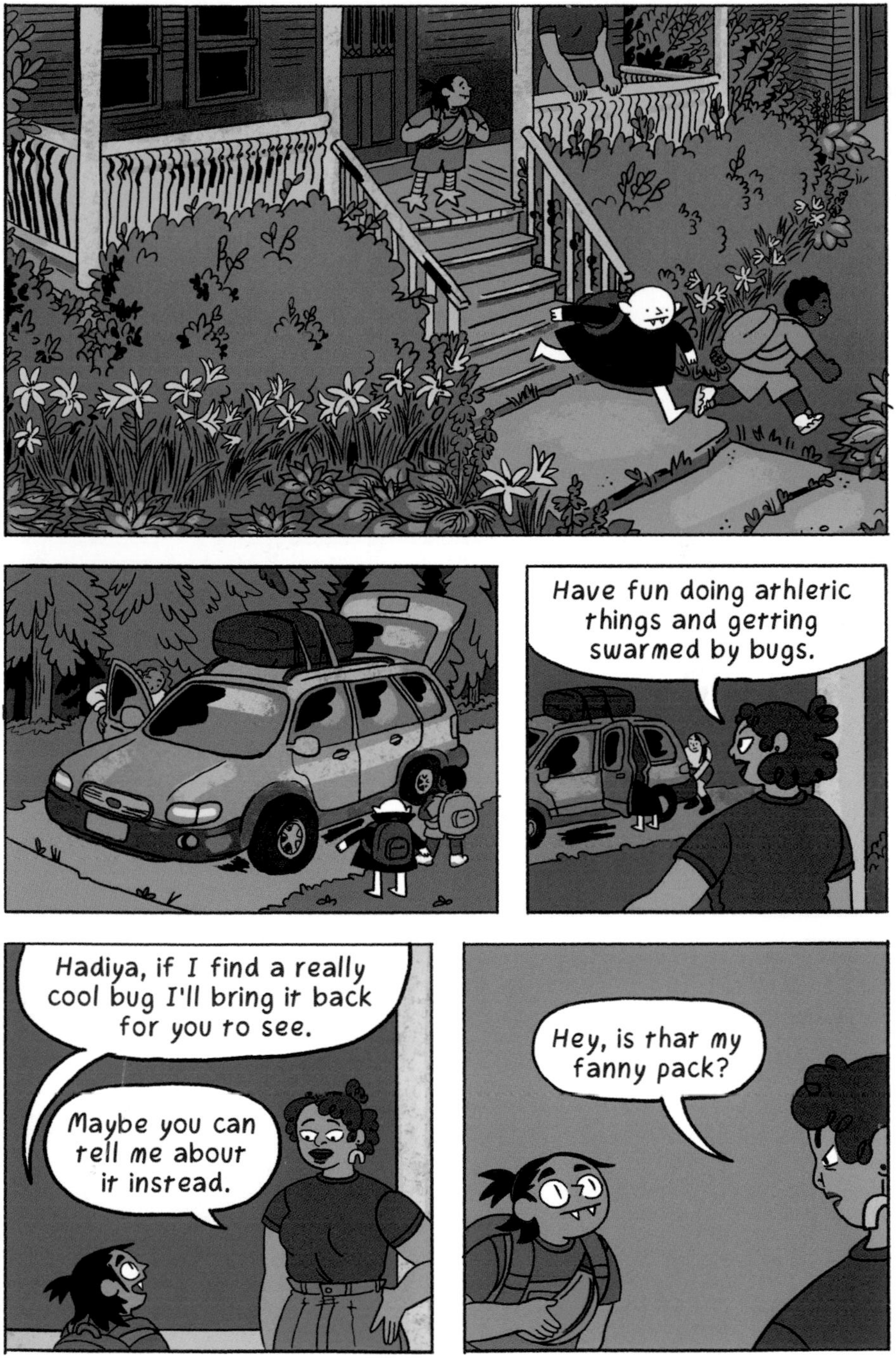
Have fun doing athletic things and getting swarmed by bugs.
Hadiya, if I find a really cool bug I'll bring it back for you to see.
Maybe you can tell me about it instead.
Hey, is that my fanny pack?

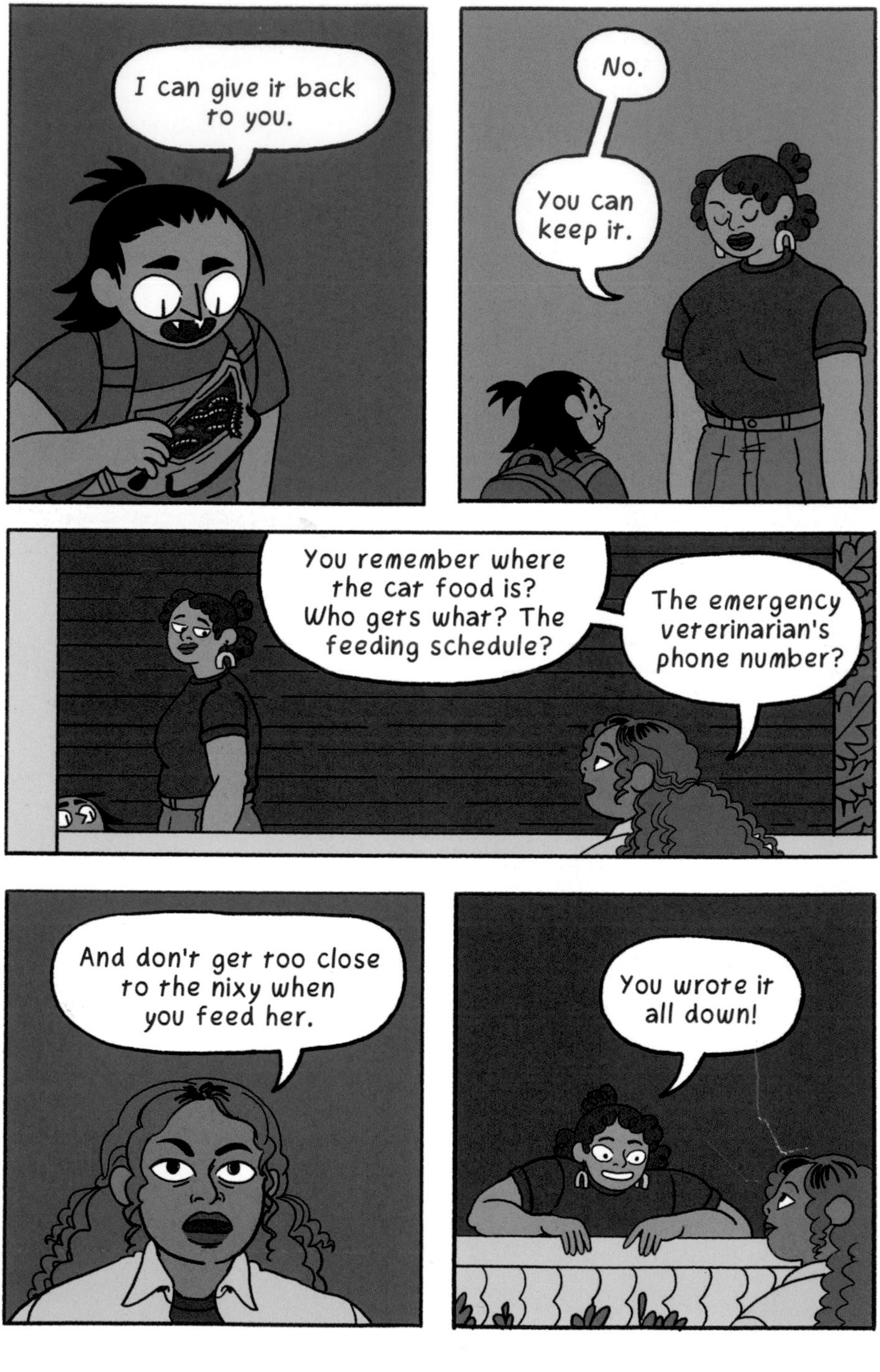
I can give it back to you.
No.
You can keep it.
You remember where the cat food is? Who gets what? The feeding schedule?
The emergency veterinarian's phone number?
And don't get too close to the nixy when you feed her.
You wrote it all down!

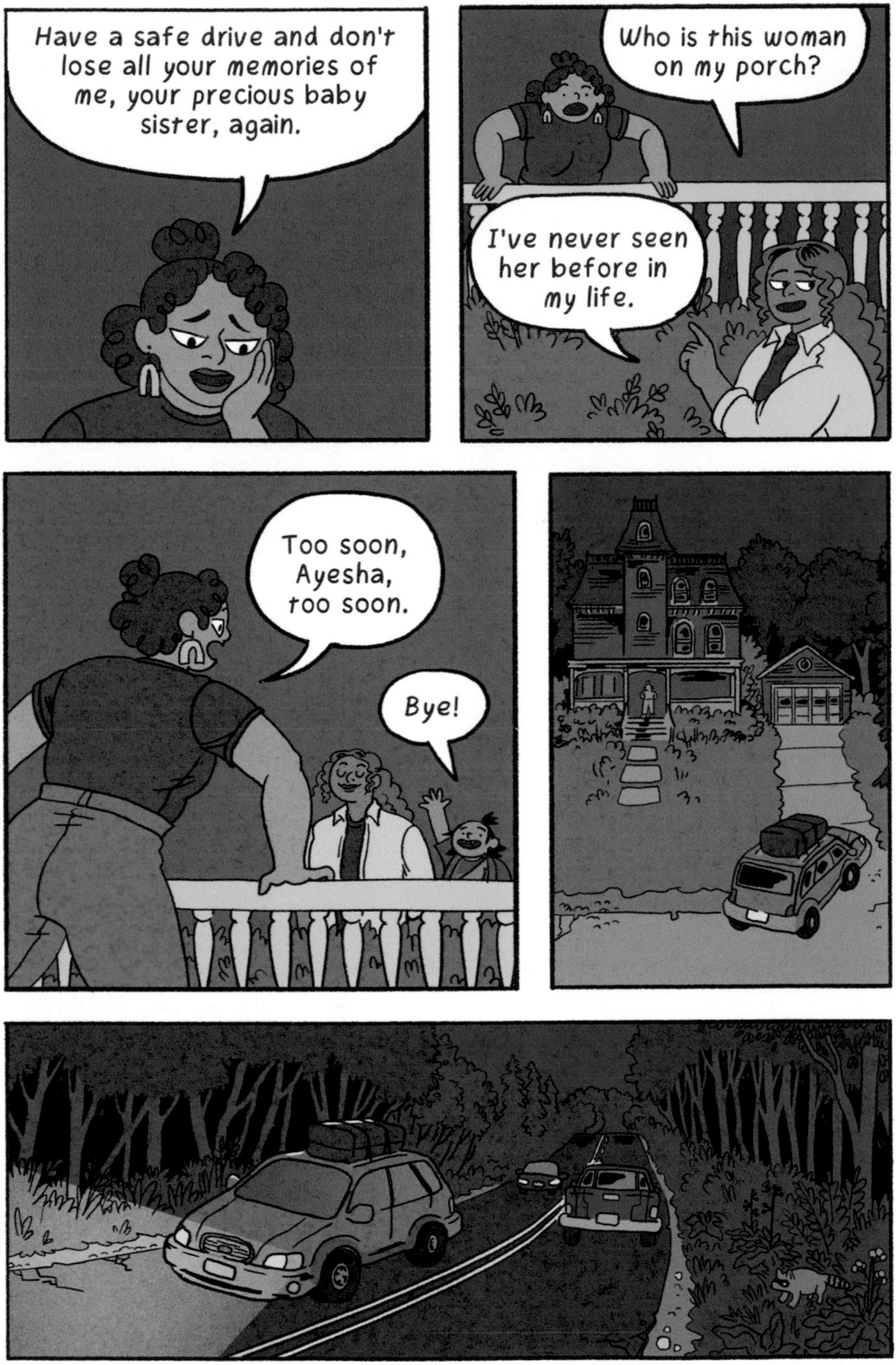
Have a safe drive and don't lose all your memories of me, your precious baby sister, again.
Who is this woman on my porch?
I've never seen her before in my life.
Too soon, Ayesha, too soon.
Bye!

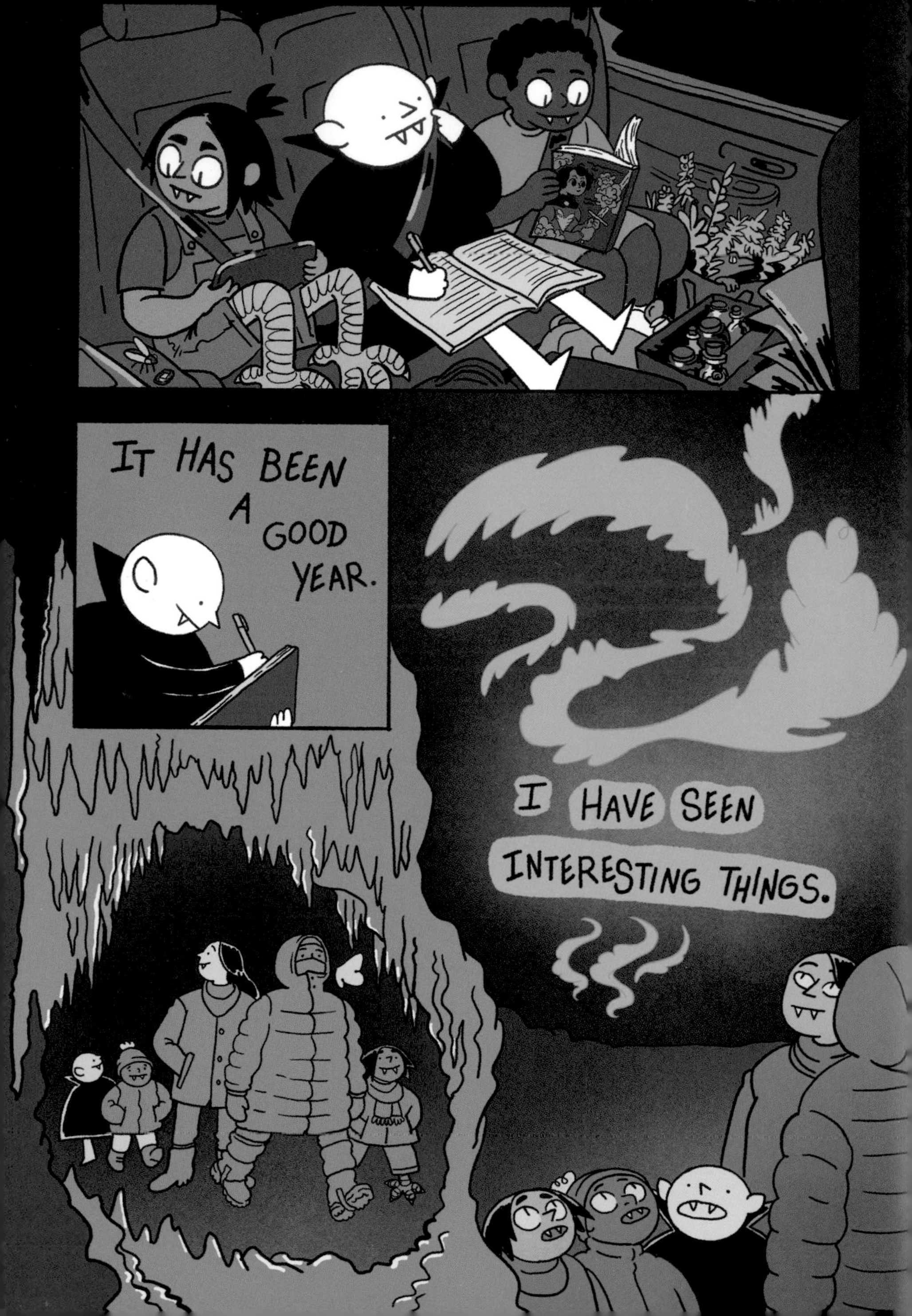
IT HAS BEEN A GOOD YEAR.
I HAVE SEEN INTERESTING THINGS.

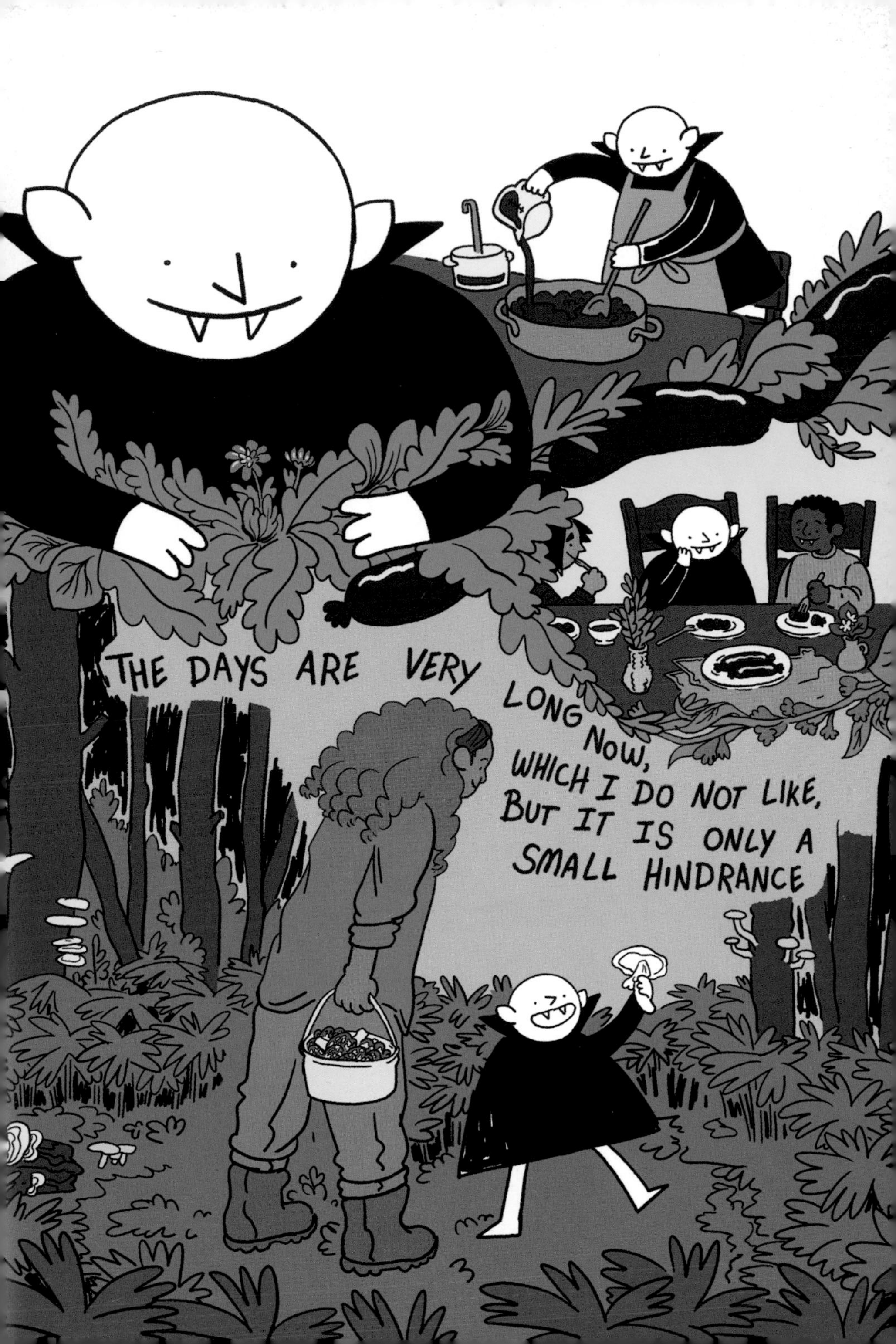
THE DAYS ARE VERY LONG NOW,
WHICH I DO NOT LIKE,
BUT IT IS ONLY A SMALL HINDRANCE

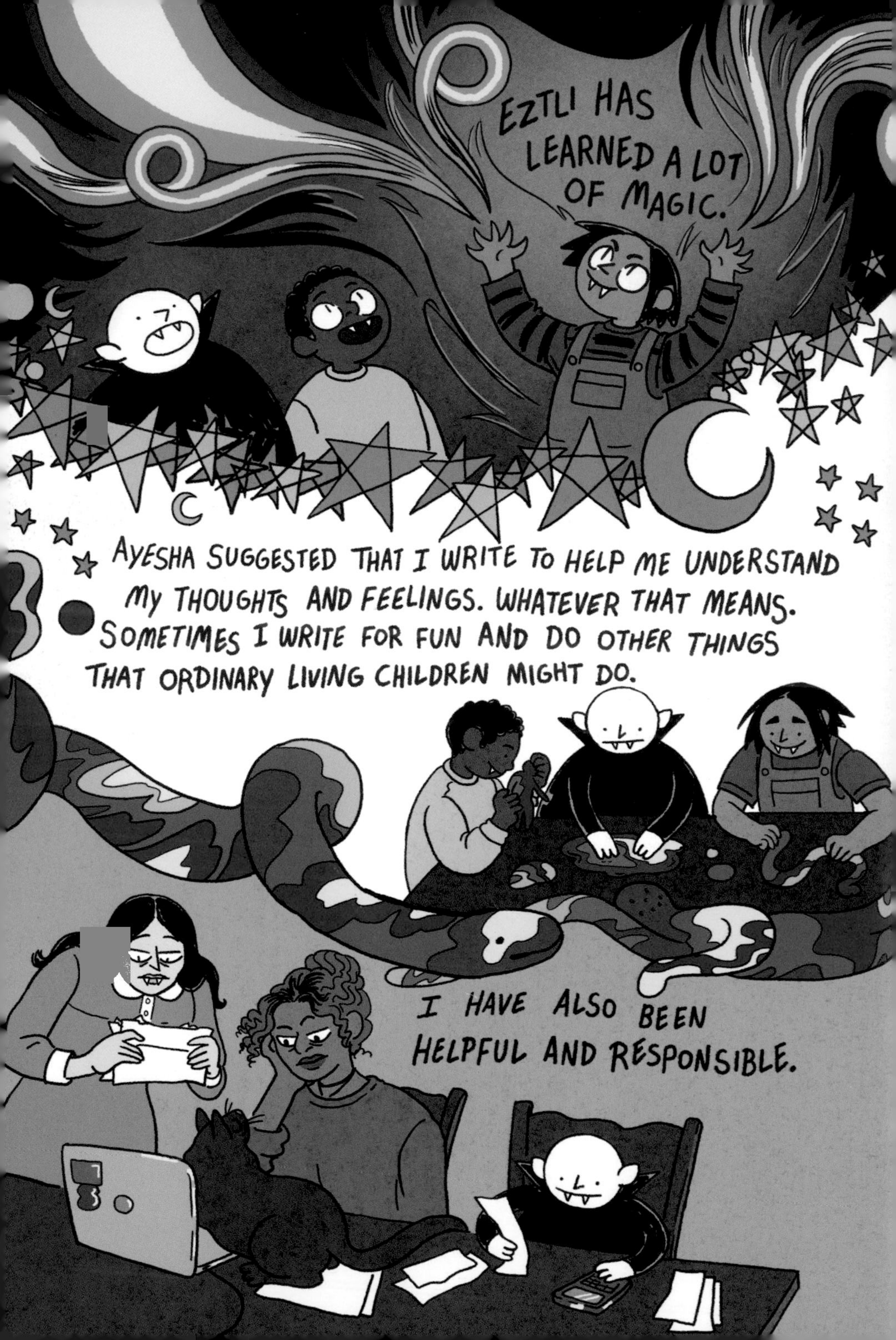
EZTLI HAS LEARNED A LOT OF MAGIC.
AYESHA SUGGESTED THAT I WRITE TO HELP ME UNDERSTAND MY THOUGHTS AND FEELINGS. WHATEVER THAT MEANS. SOMETIMES I WRITE FOR FUN AND DO OTHER THINGS THAT ORDINARY LIVING CHILDREN MIGHT DO.
I HAVE ALSO BEEN HELPFUL AND RESPONSIBLE.

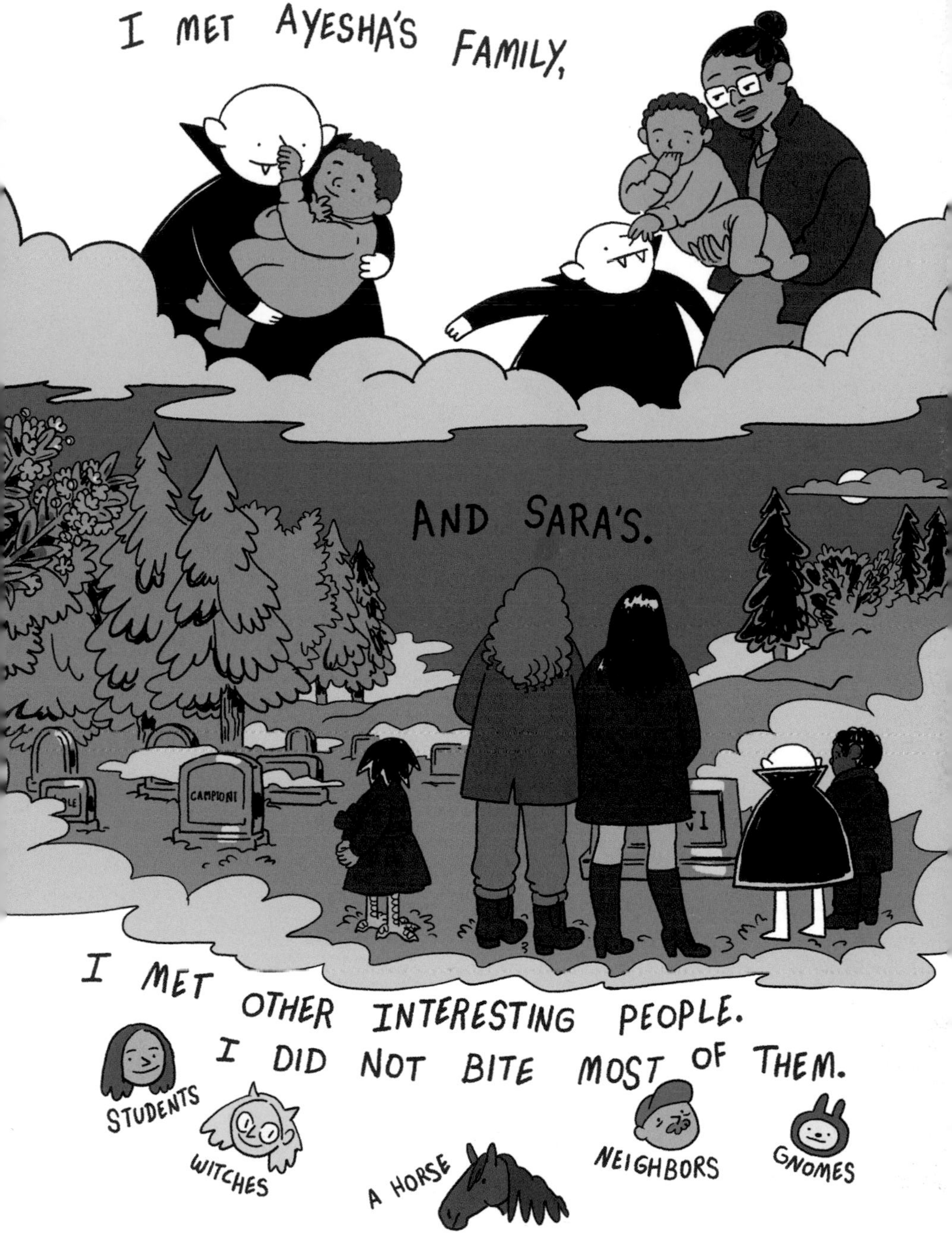
I MET AYESHA'S FAMILY,
AND SARA'S.
CAMPIONI
I MET OTHER INTERESTING PEOPLE.
I DID NOT BITE MOST OF THEM.
STUDENTS
WITCHES
A HORSE
NEIGHBORS
GNOMES

I AM GOING TO A SUMMER CAMP FOR YOUNG WITCHES FOR THREE WEEKS. I DON'T KNOW EXACTLY WHAT THAT MEANS.

PREVIOUSLY I HAVE USED CAMPING TO DESCRIBE WHEN I MUST BURROW INTO THE MUDDY, FETID EARTH TO ESCAPE THE CRUEL RAYS OF THE SUN.

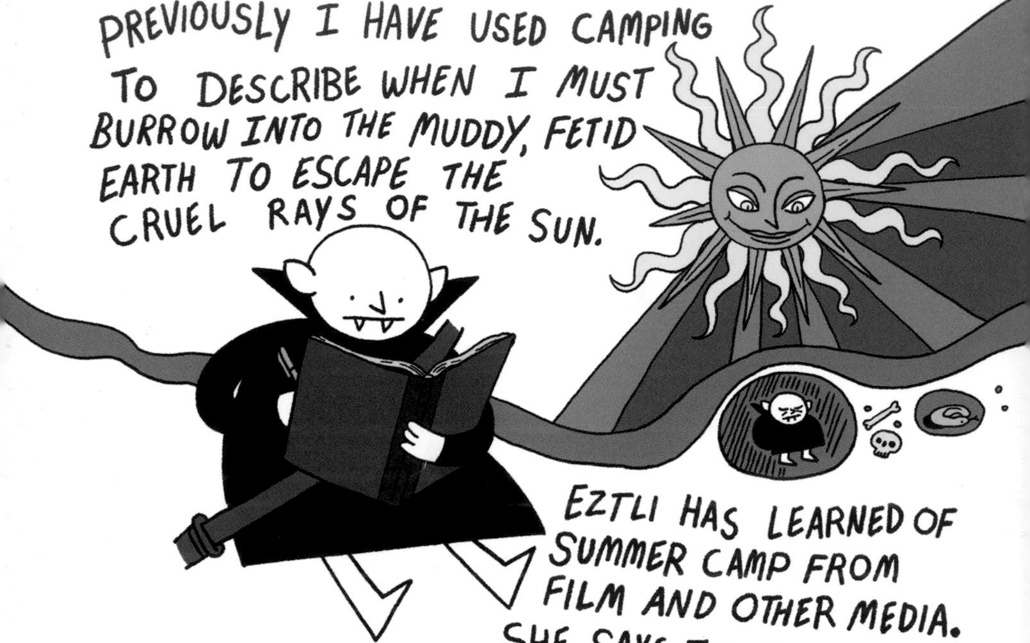

EZTLI HAS LEARNED OF SUMMER CAMP FROM FILM AND OTHER MEDIA. SHE SAYS IT MAY BE FUN. I REMAIN SKEPTICAL.

AYESHA IS GOING TO TEACH LIVING KIDS ABOUT MAGIC. SARA IS GOING TO MAKE FOOD FOR THE LIVING KIDS.

THEY CANNOT DRINK BLOOD.

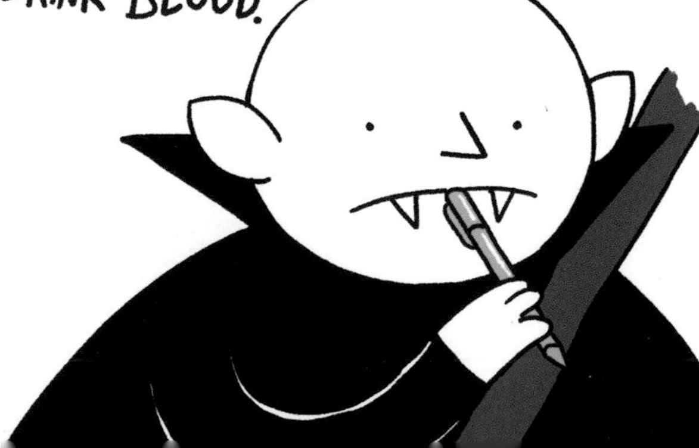

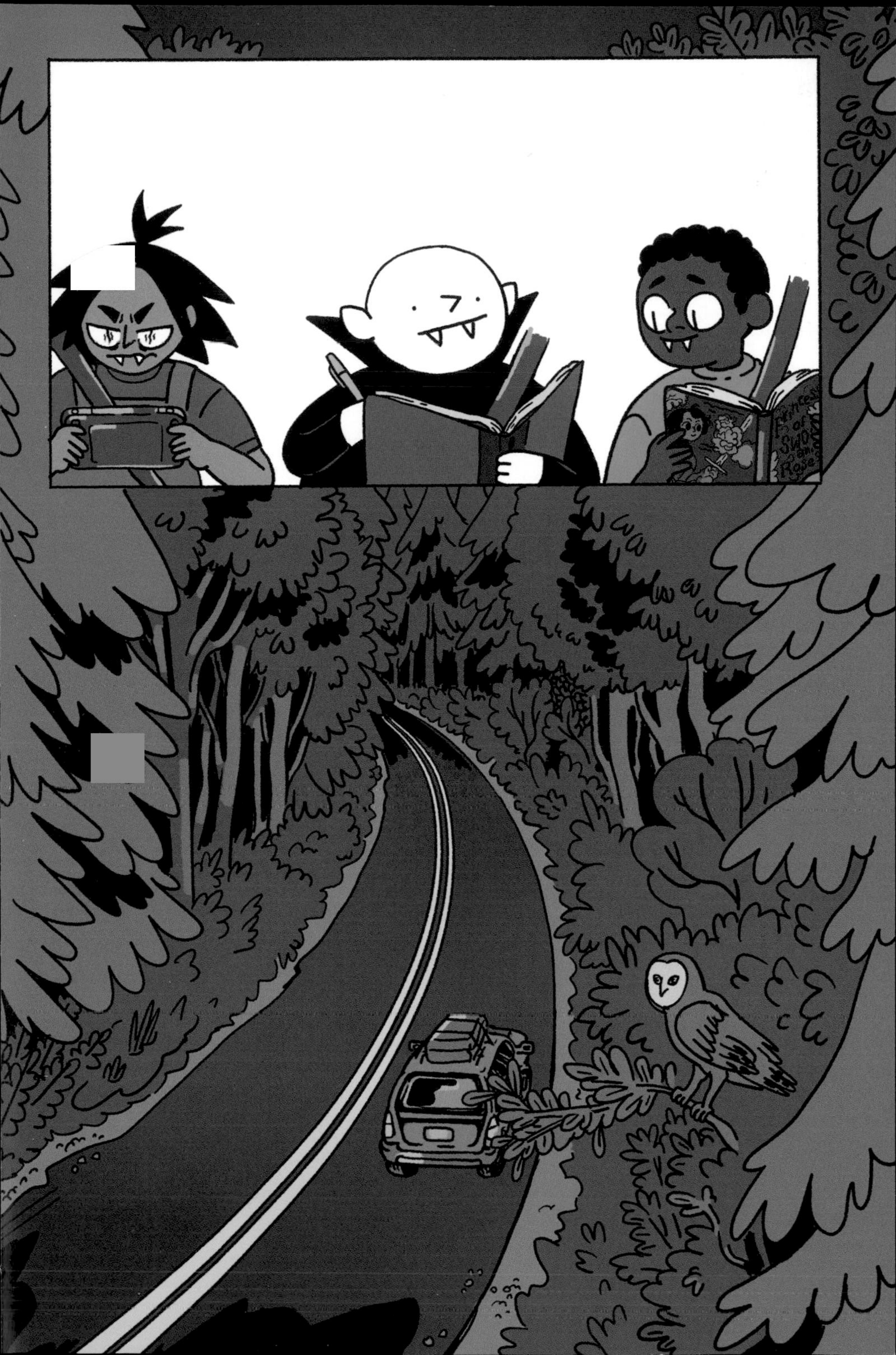

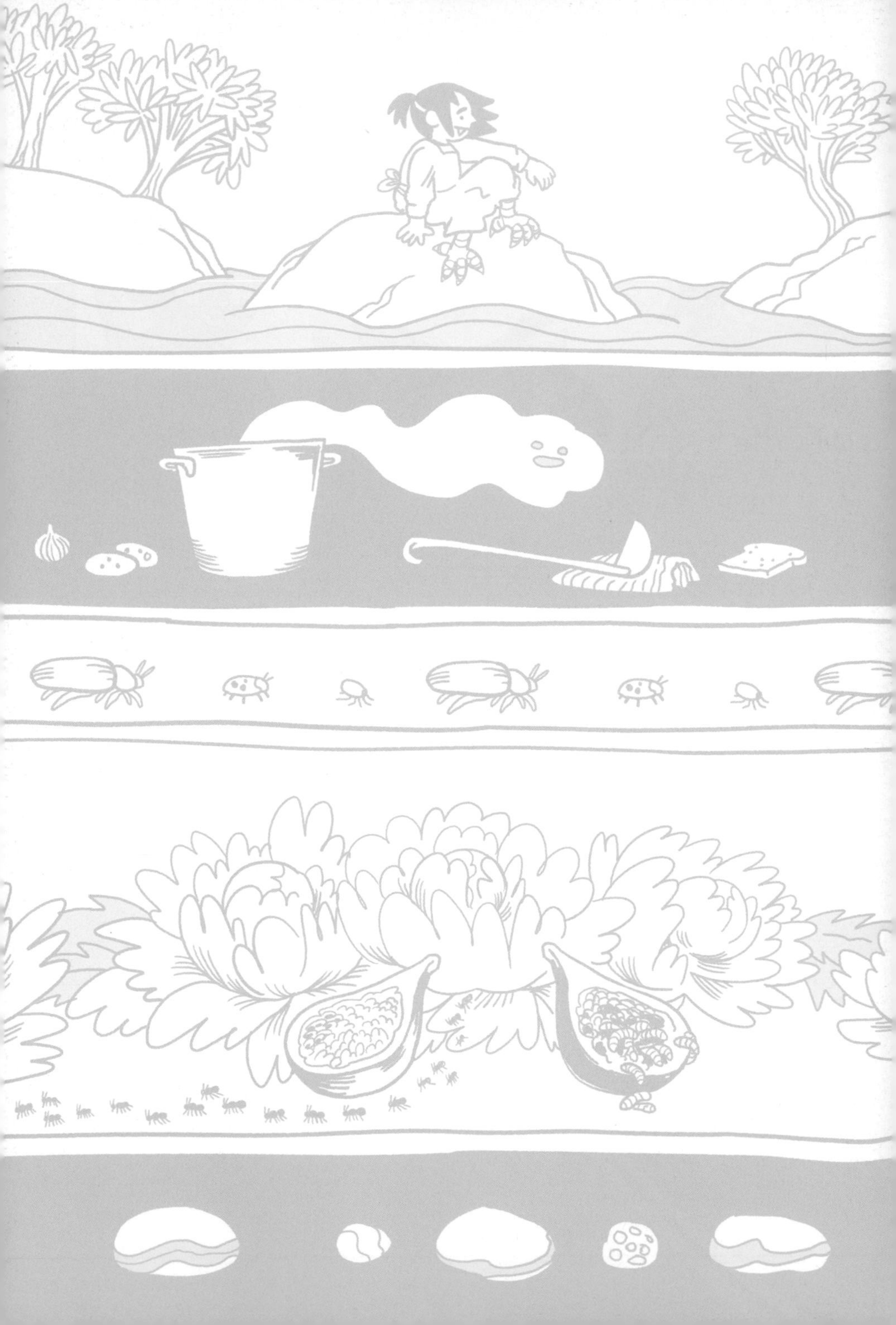

CHAPTER TWO

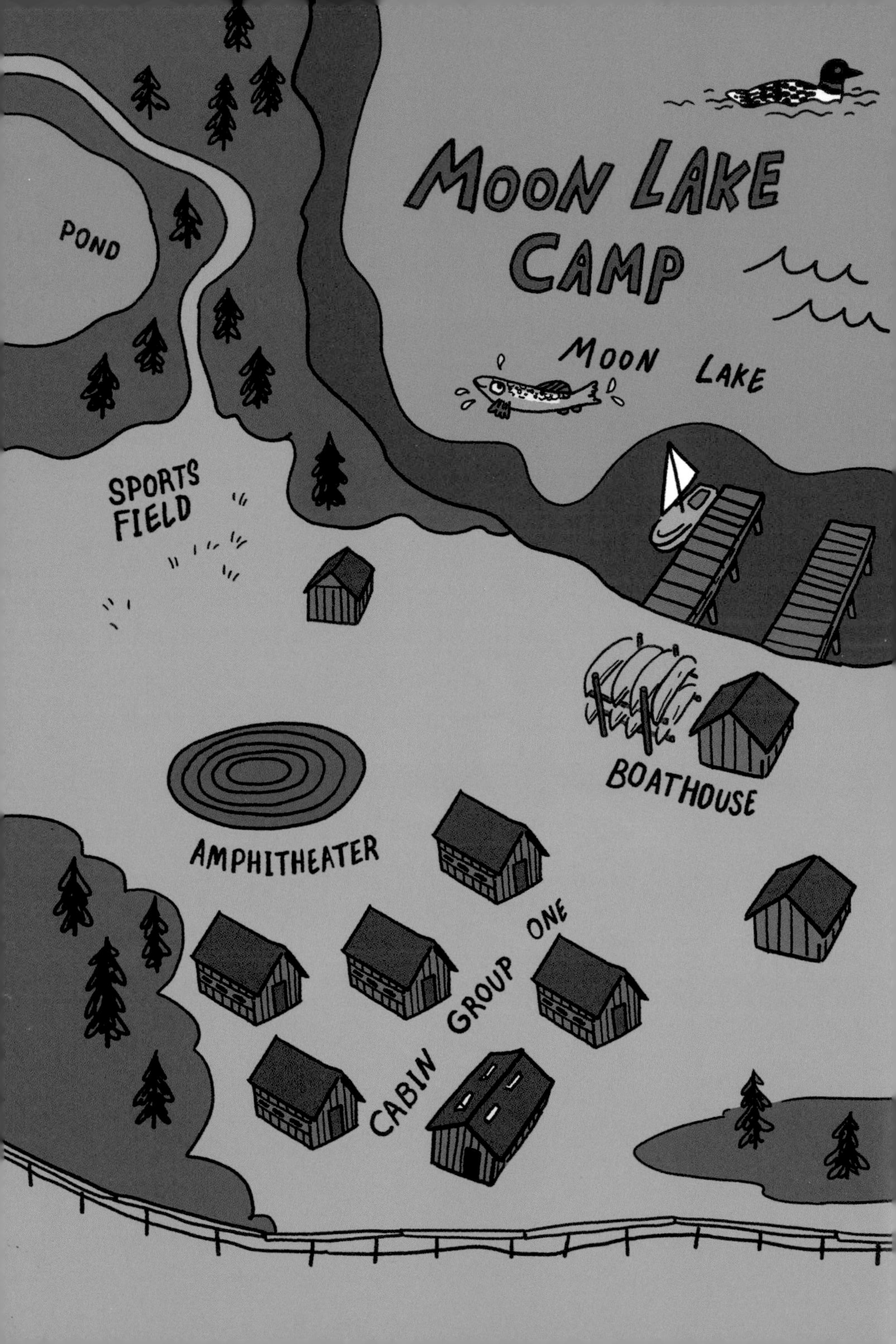
MOON LAKE CAMP
POND
MOON LAKE
SPORTS FIELD
BOATHOUSE
AMPHITHEATER
CABIN GROUP ONE

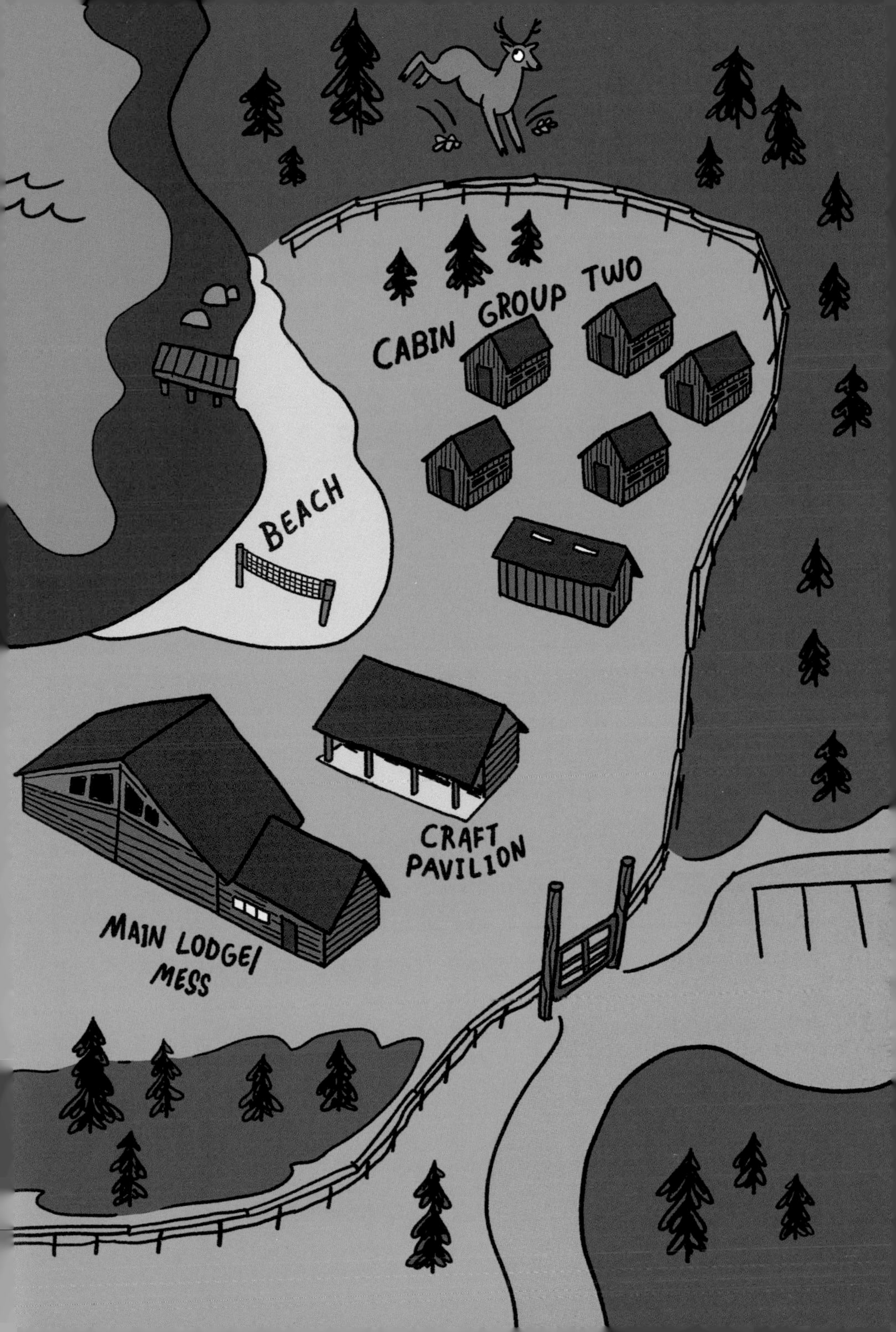
CABIN GROUP TWO
BEACH
CRAFT PAVILION
MAIN LODGE/ MESS

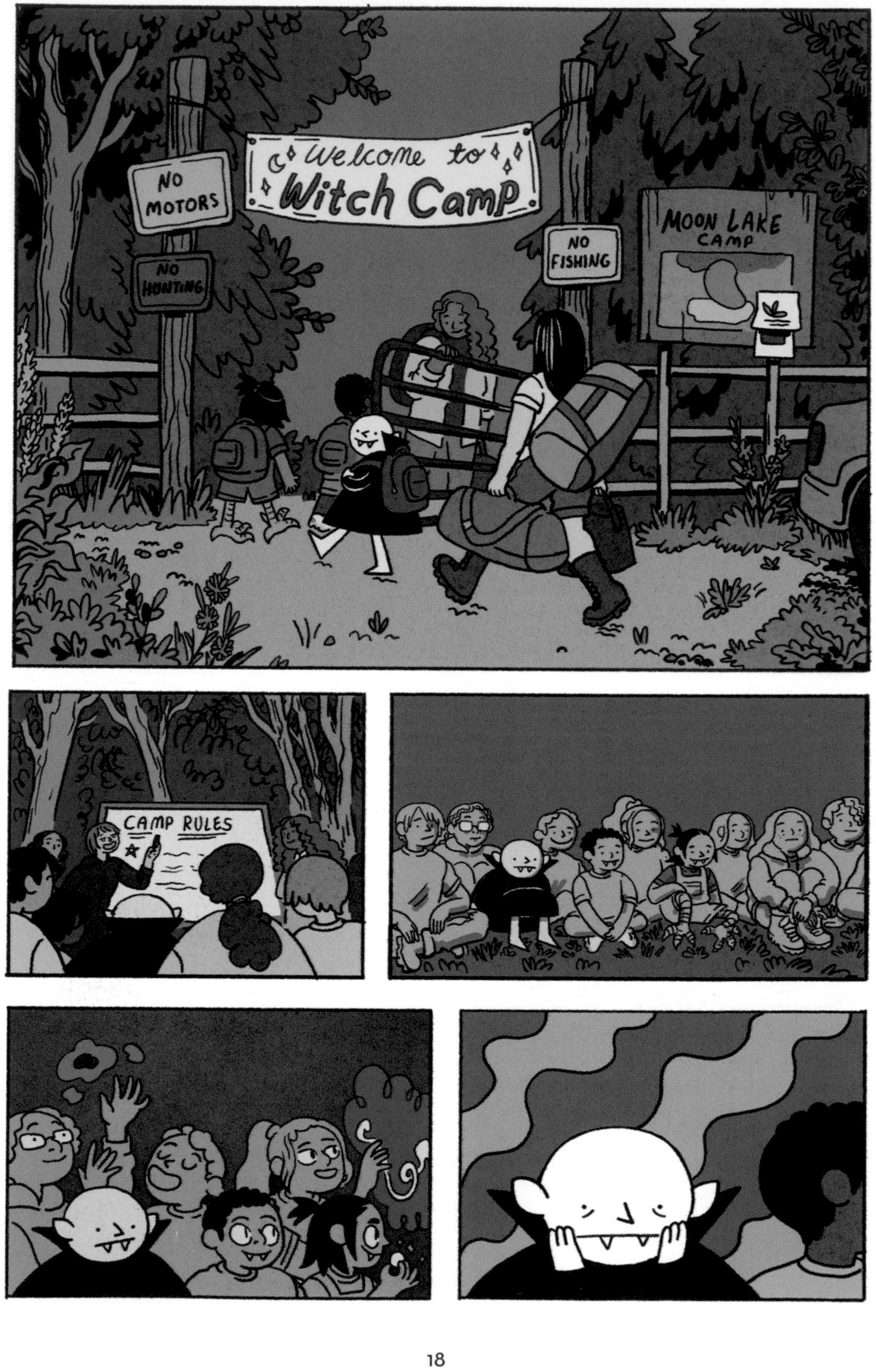
Welcome to Witch Camp
NO MOTORS
NO HUNTING
NO FISHING
MOON LAKE CAMP
CAMP RULES

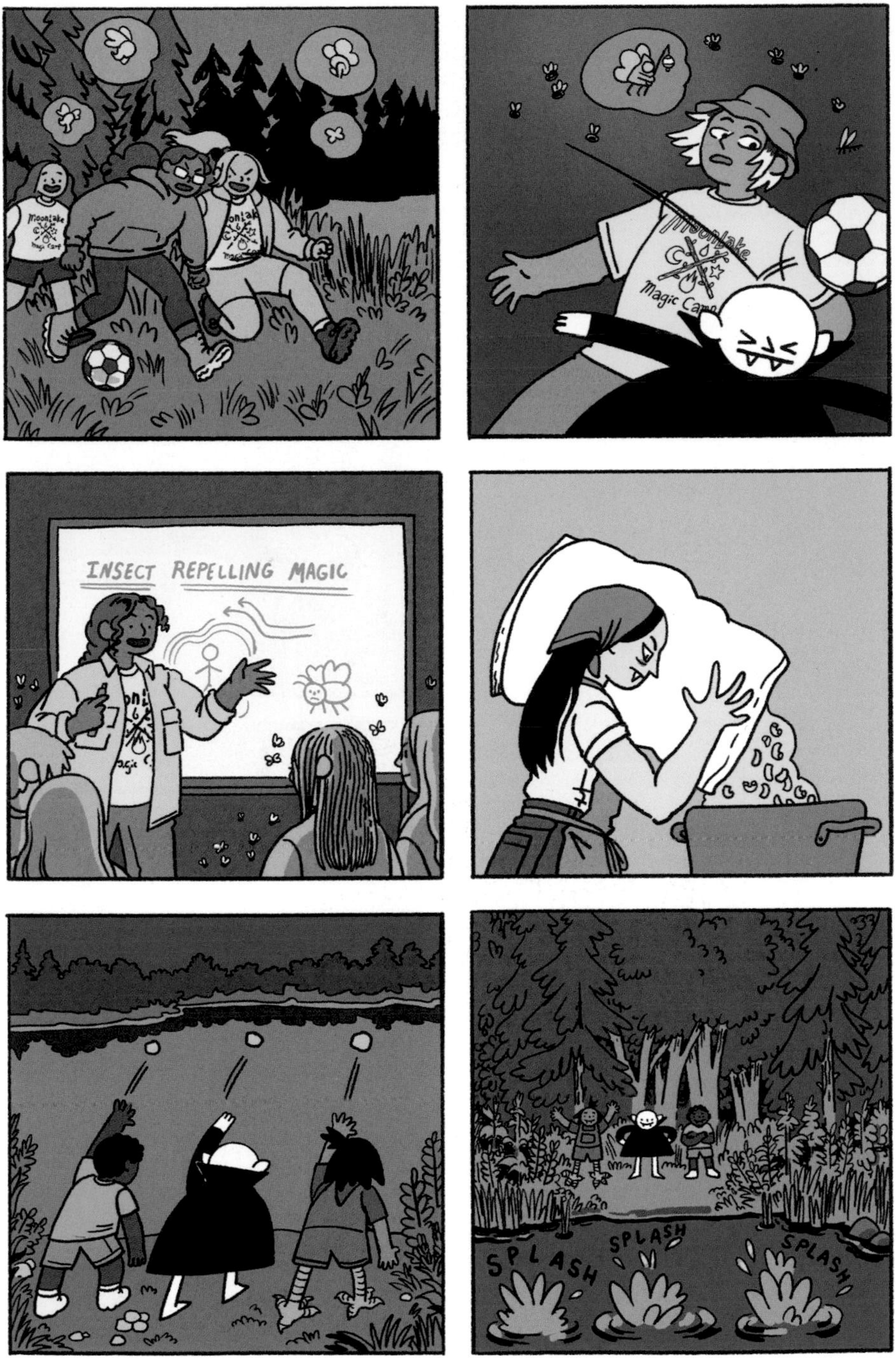
INSECT REPELLING MAGIC
SPLASH
SPLASH
SPLASH

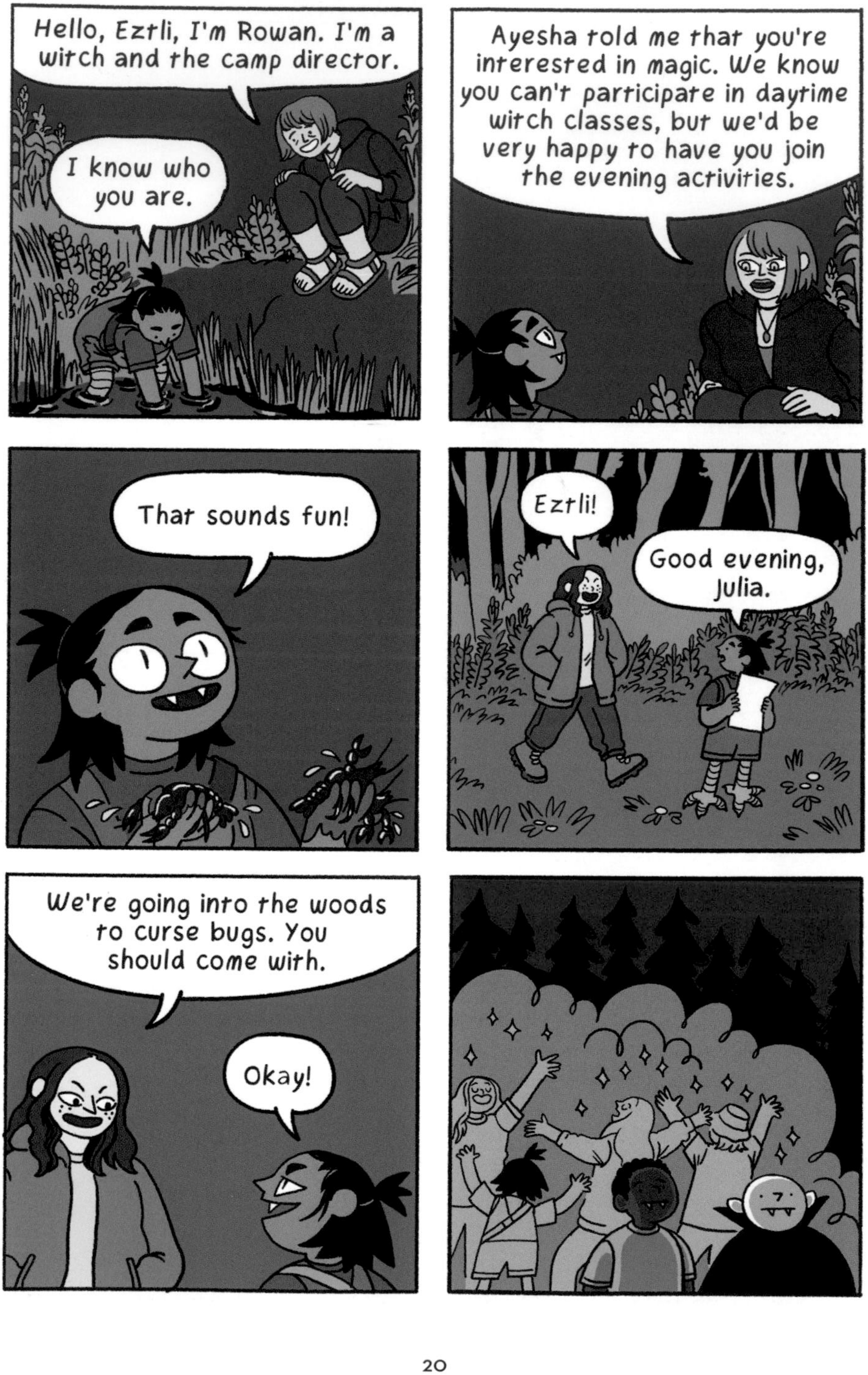
Hello, Eztli, I'm Rowan. I'm a witch and the camp director.
I know who you are.
Ayesha told me that you're interested in magic. We know you can't participate in daytime witch classes, but we'd be very happy to have you join the evening activities.
That sounds fun!
Eztli!
Good evening, Julia.
We're going into the woods to curse bugs. You should come with.
Okay!

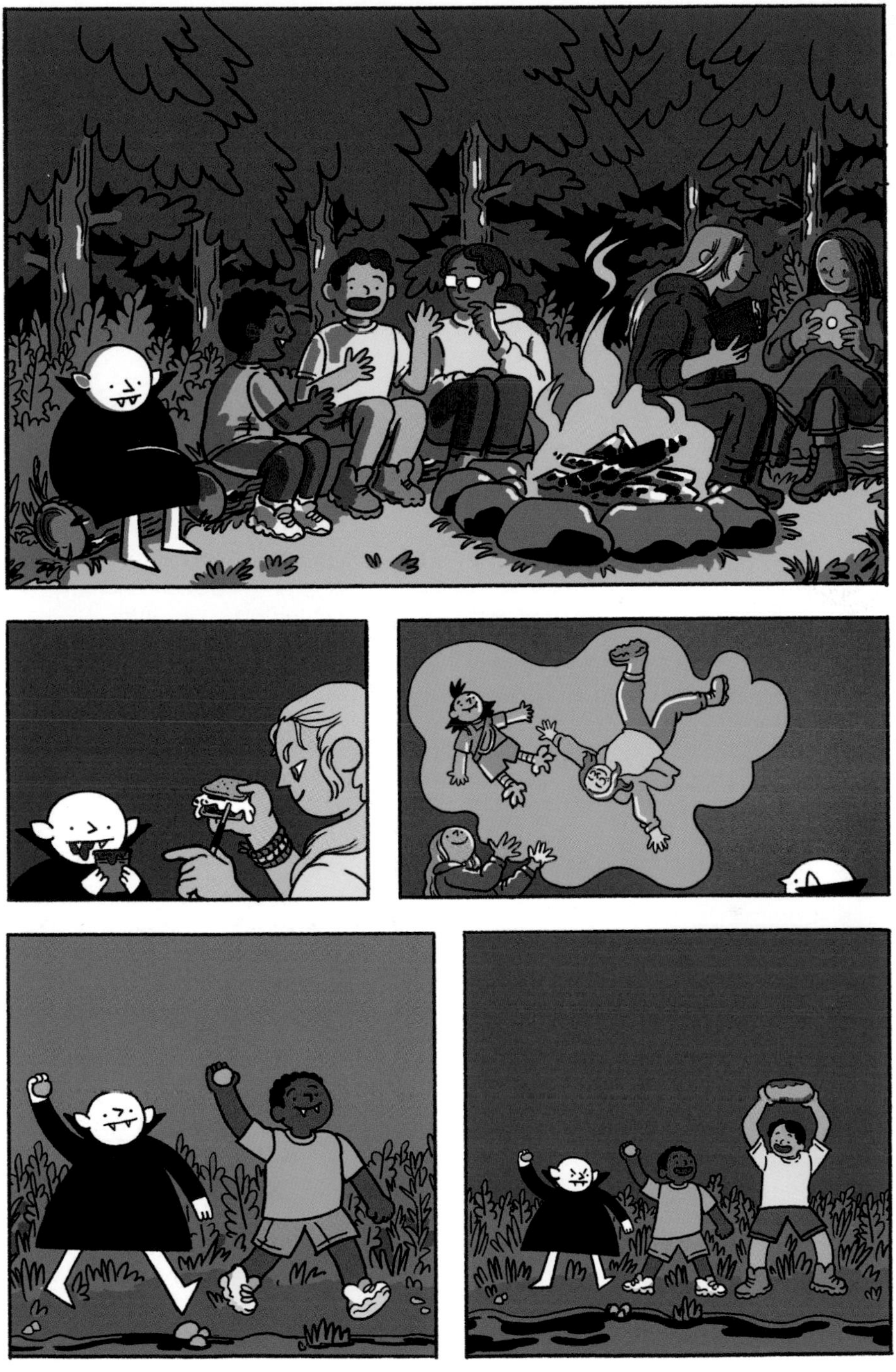

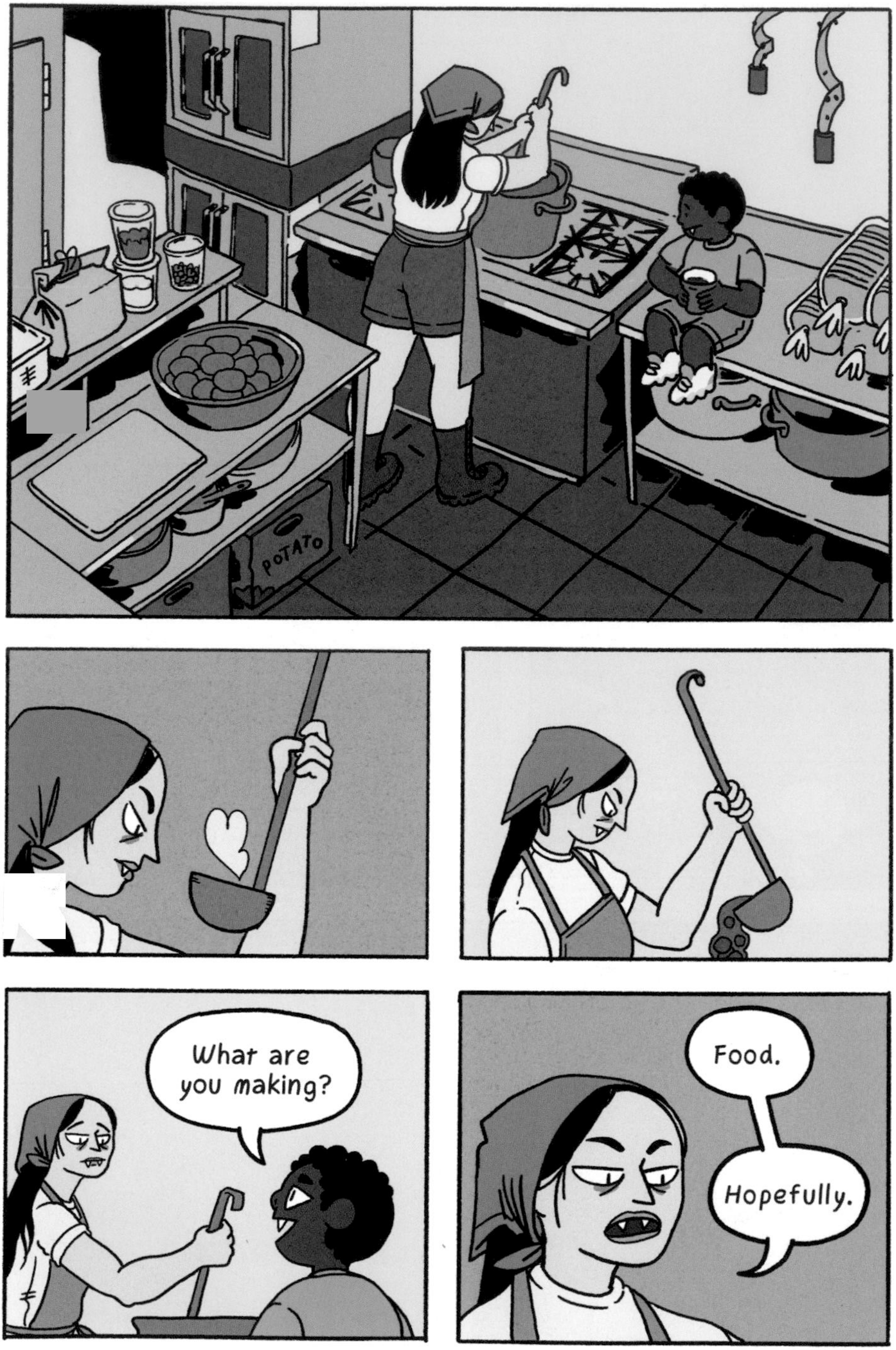
POTATO
What are you making?
Food.
Hopefully.

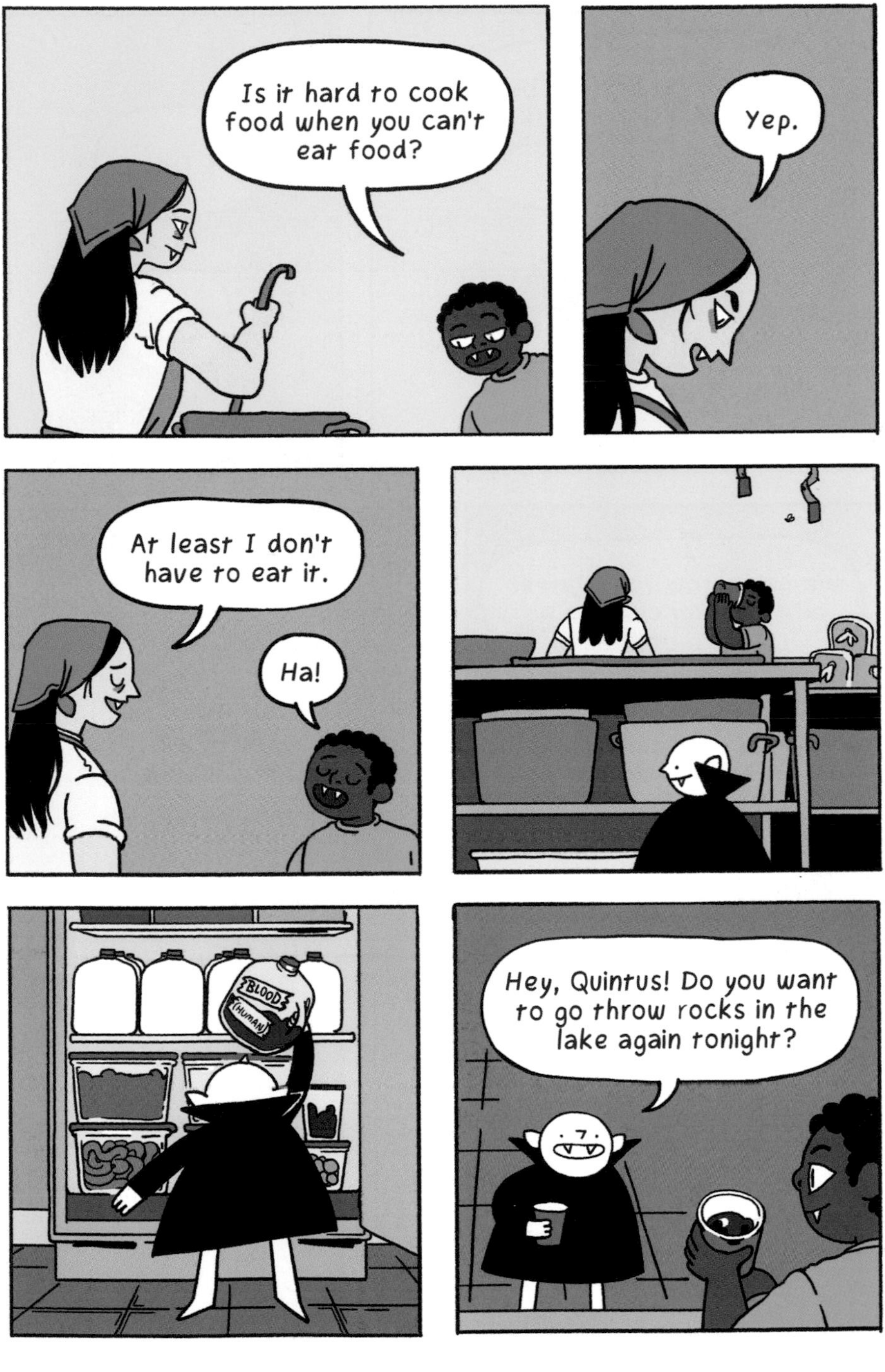
Is it hard to cook food when you can't eat food?
Yep.
At least I don't have to eat it.
Ha!
BLOOD
HUMAN
Hey, Quintus! Do you want to go throw rocks in the lake again tonight?

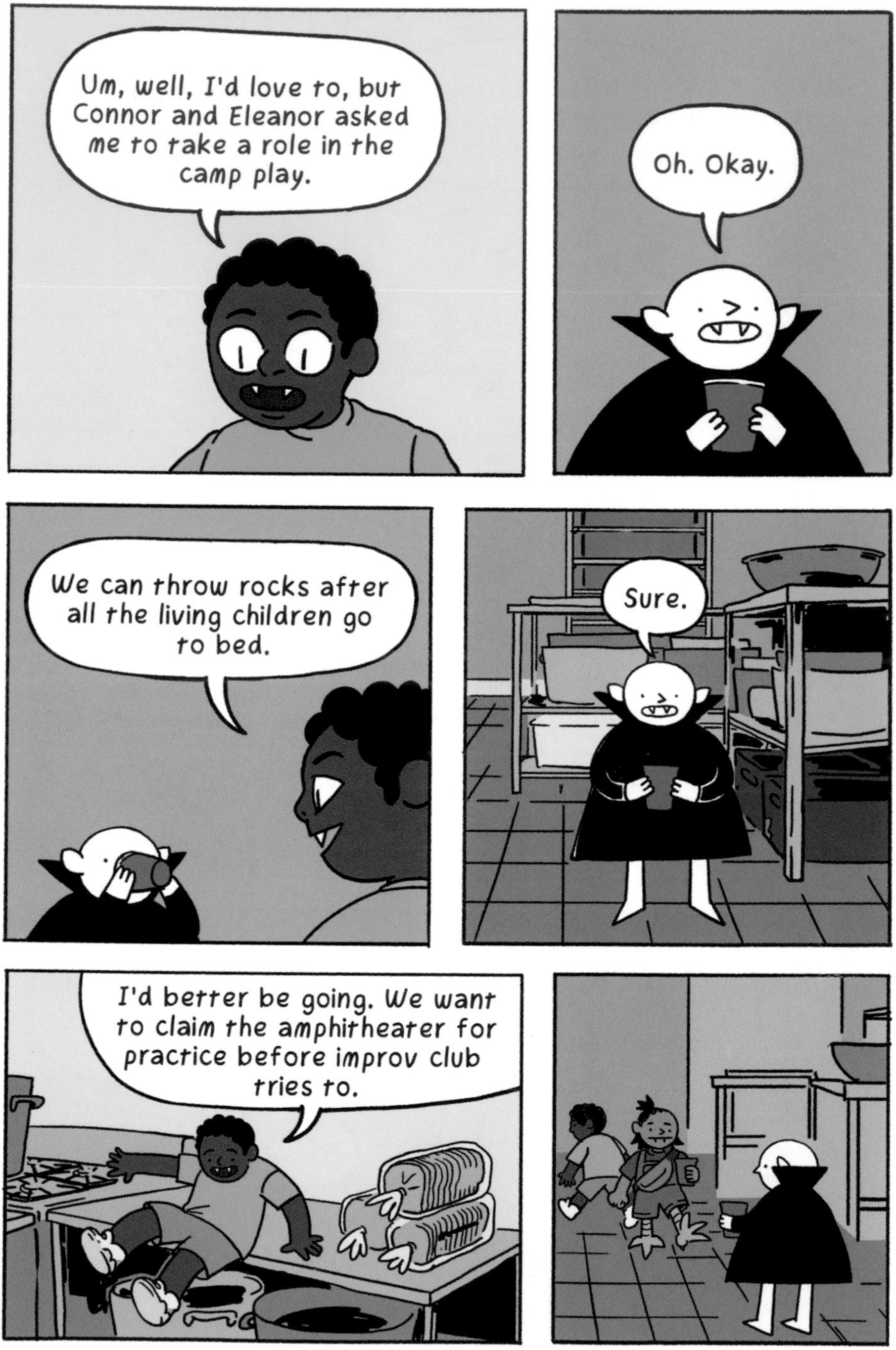
Um, well, I'd love to, but Connor and Eleanor asked me to take a role in the camp play.
Oh. Okay.
We can throw rocks after all the living children go to bed.
Sure.
I'd better be going. We want to claim the amphitheater for practice before improv club tries to.

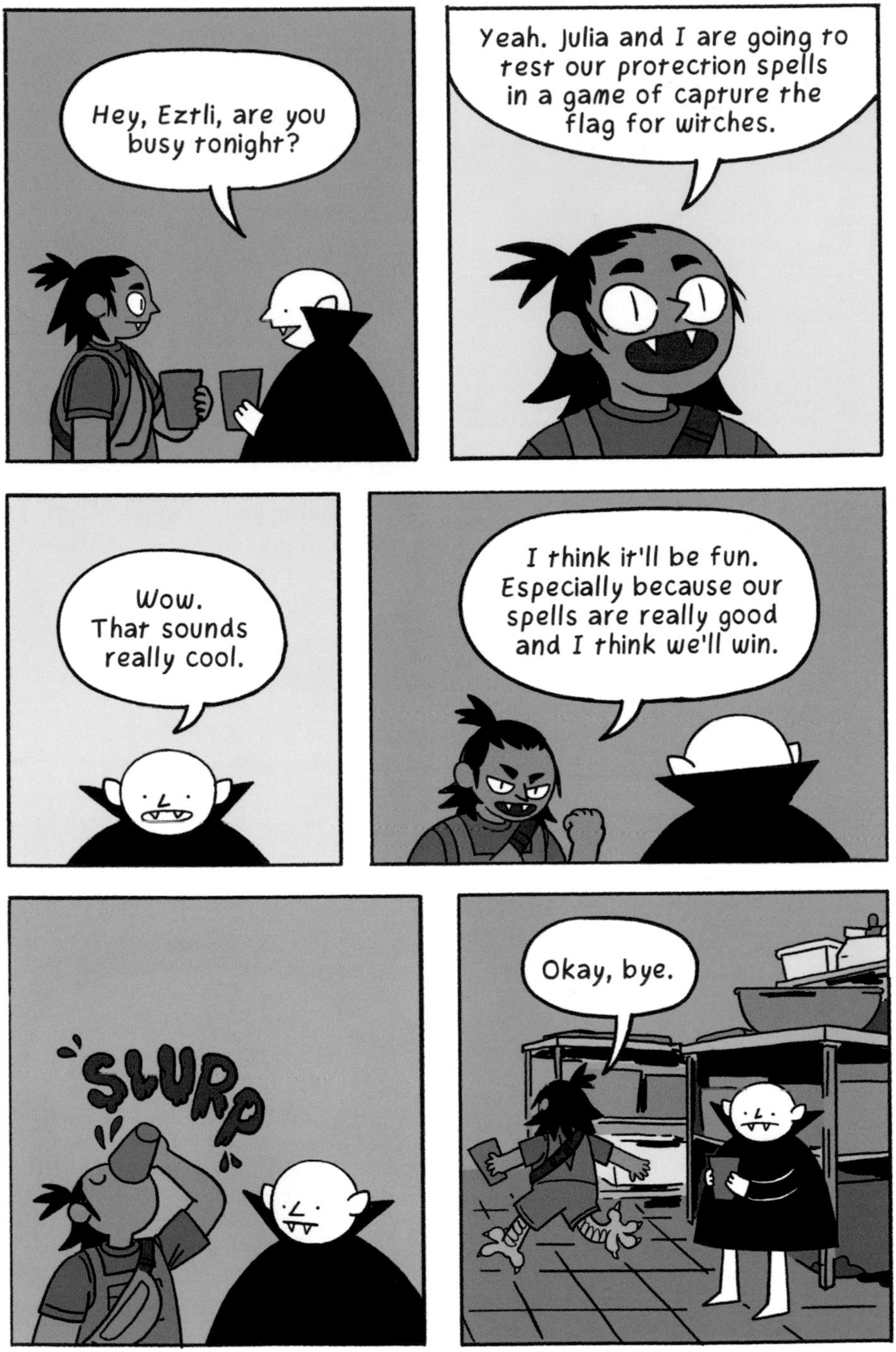
Hey, Eztli, are you busy tonight?
Yeah. Julia and I are going to test our protection spells in a game of capture the flag for witches.
Wow. That sounds really cool.
I think it'll be fun. Especially because our spells are really good and I think we'll win.
SLURP
Okay, bye.

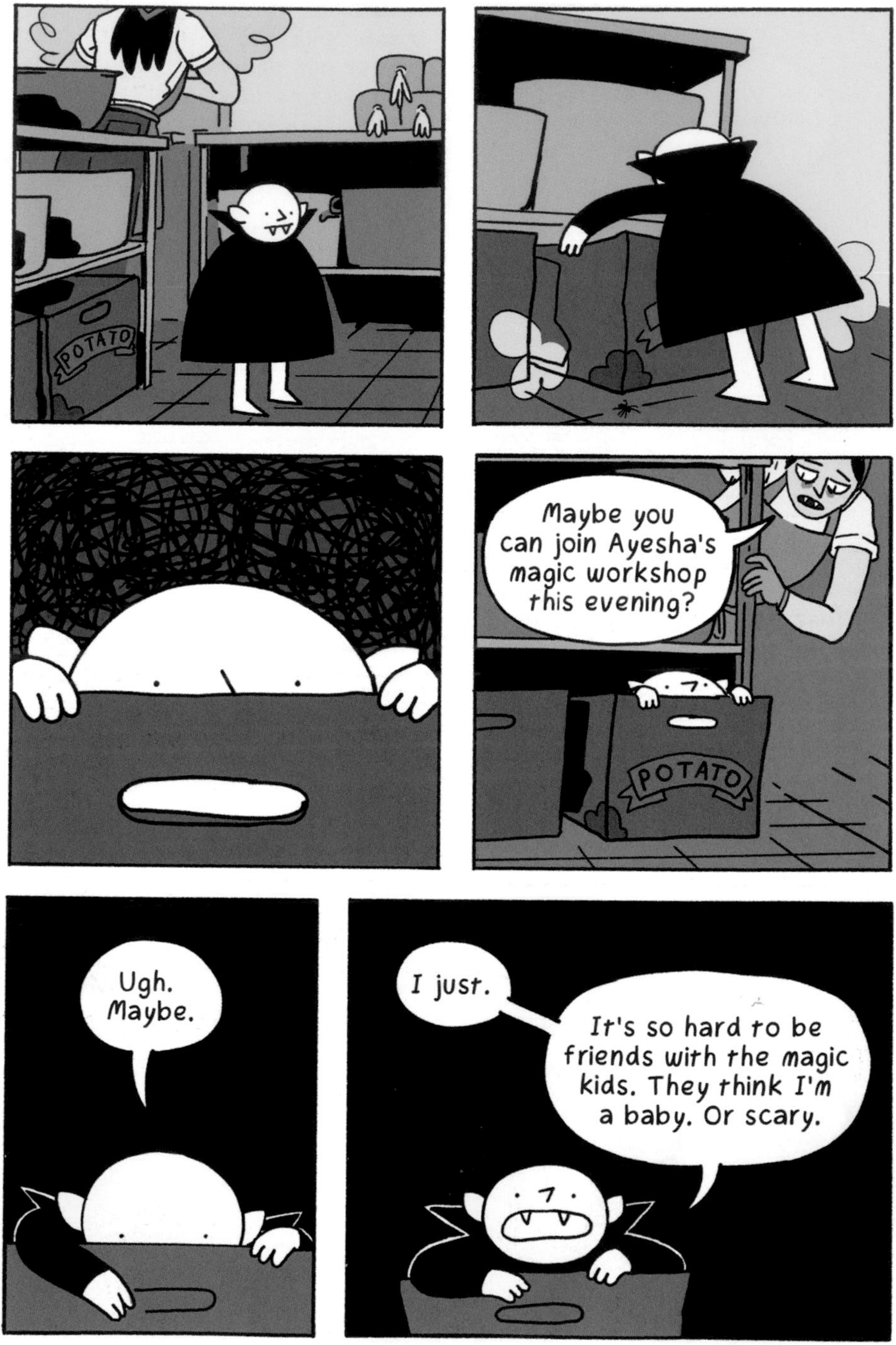
POTATO
Maybe you can join Ayesha's magic workshop this evening?
POTATO
Ugh. Maybe.
I just.
It's so hard to be friends with the magic kids. They think I'm a baby. Or scary.

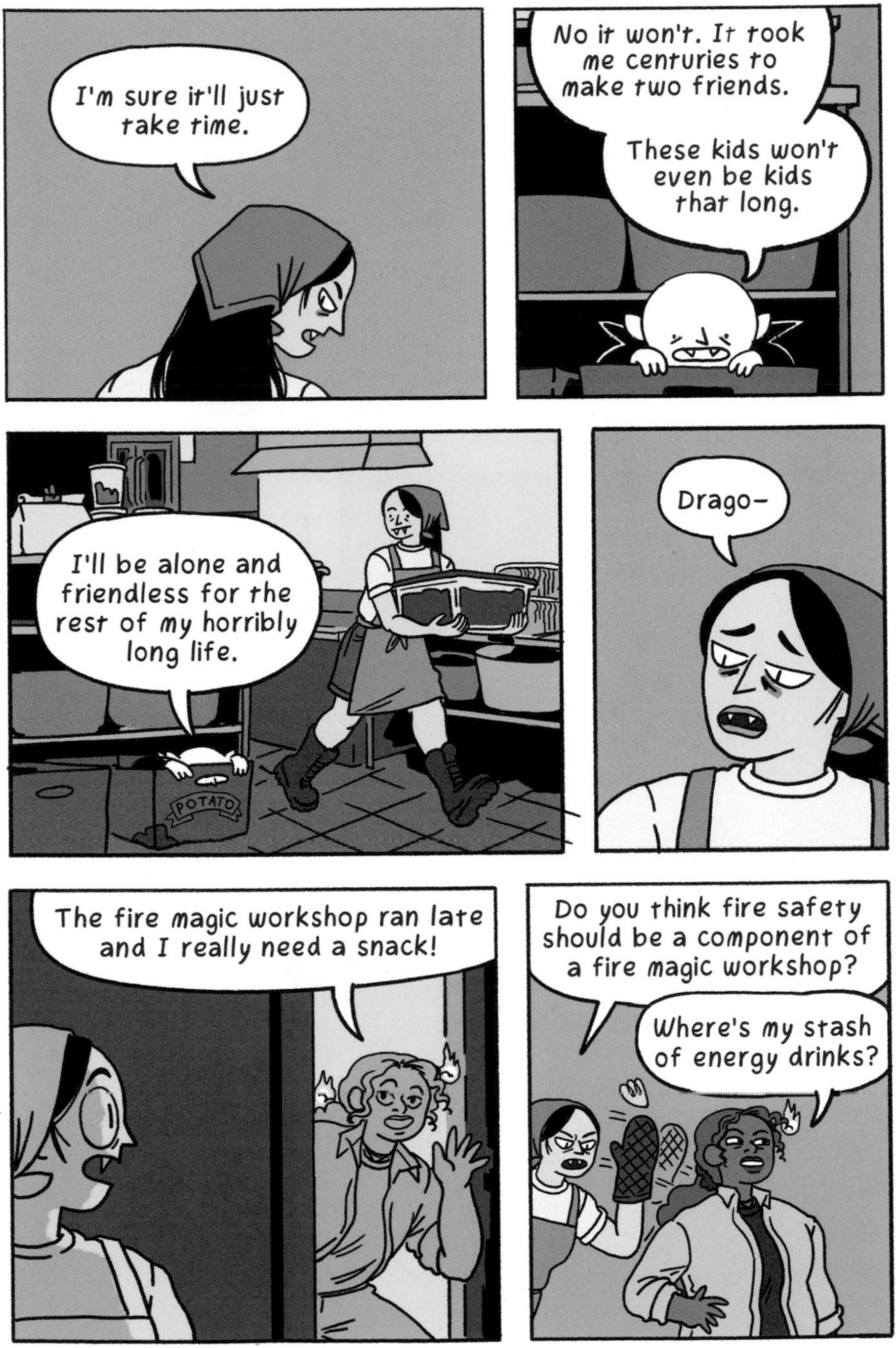
I'm sure it'll just take time.
No it won't. It took me centuries to make two friends.
These kids won't even be kids that long.
I'll be alone and friendless for the rest of my horribly long life.
POTATO
Drago–
The fire magic workshop ran late and I really need a snack!
Do you think fire safety should be a component of a fire magic workshop?
Where's my stash of energy drinks?

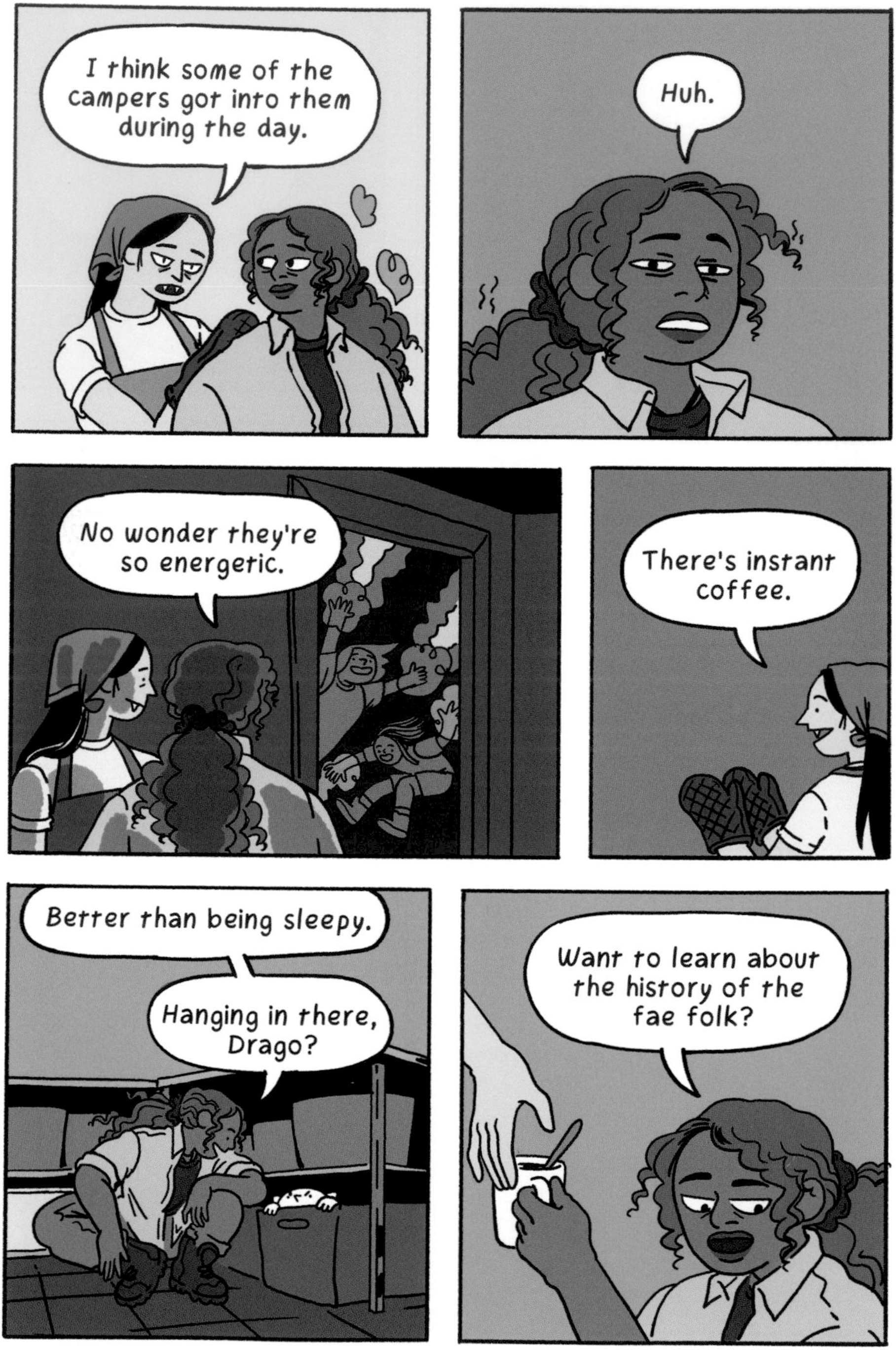
I think some of the campers got into them during the day.
Huh.
No wonder they're so energetic.
There's instant coffee.
Better than being sleepy.
Hanging in there, Drago?
Want to learn about the history of the fae folk?

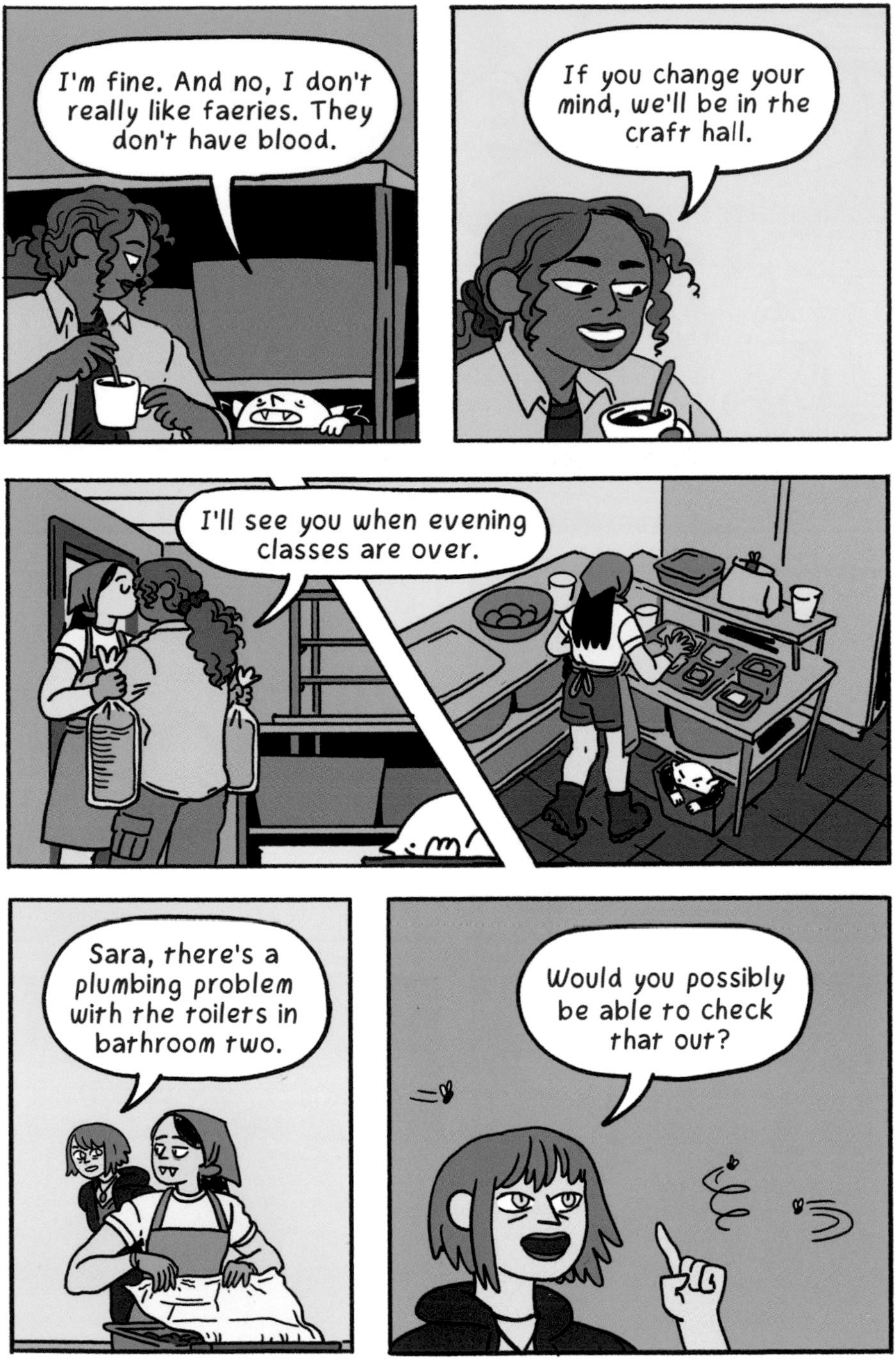
I'm fine. And no, I don't really like faeries. They don't have blood.
If you change your mind, we'll be in the craft hall.
I'll see you when evening classes are over.
Sara, there's a plumbing problem with the toilets in bathroom two.
Would you possibly be able to check that out?

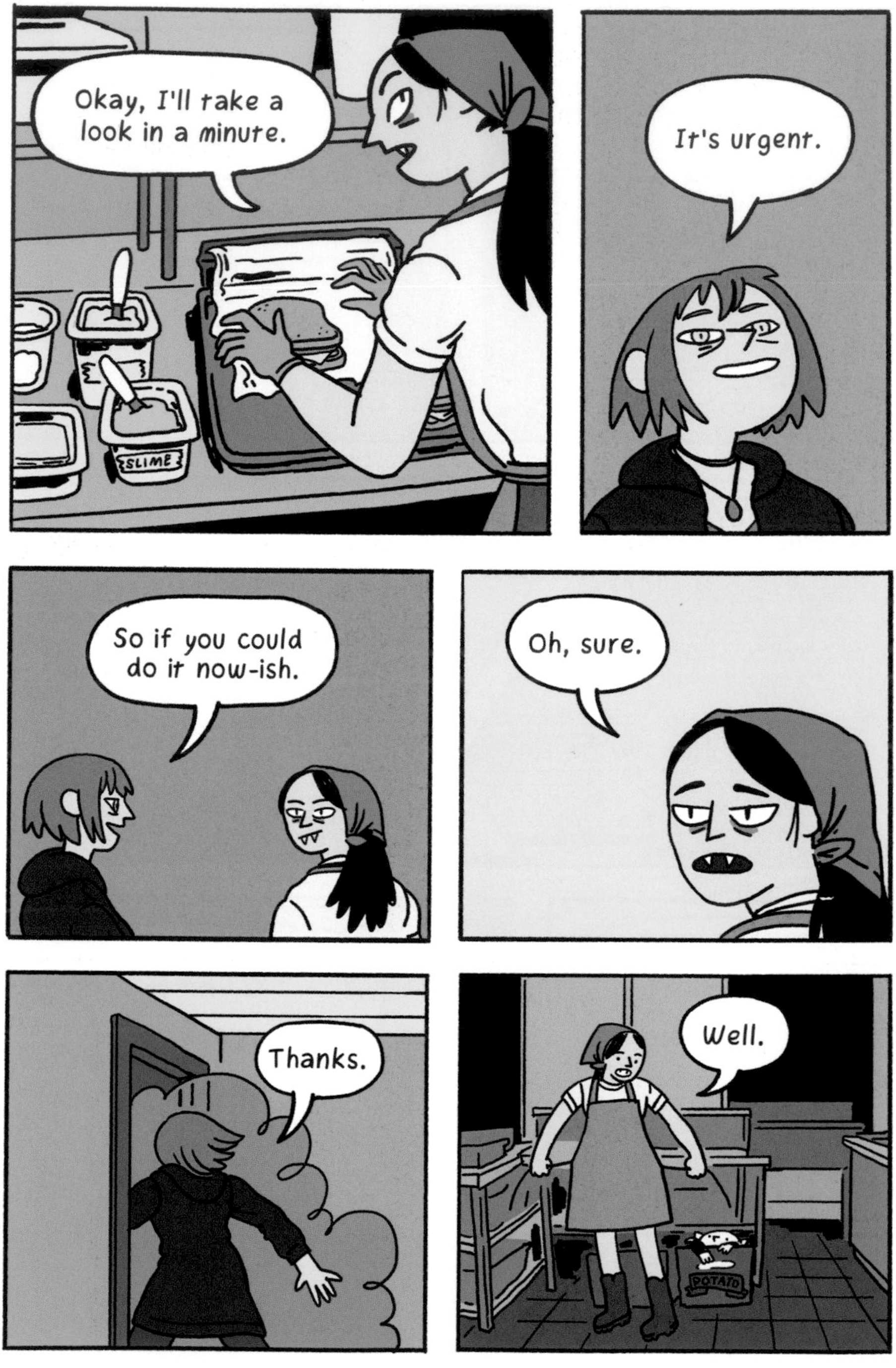
Okay, I'll take a look in a minute.
SLIME
It's urgent.
So if you could do it now-ish.
Oh, sure.
Thanks.
Well.
POTATO

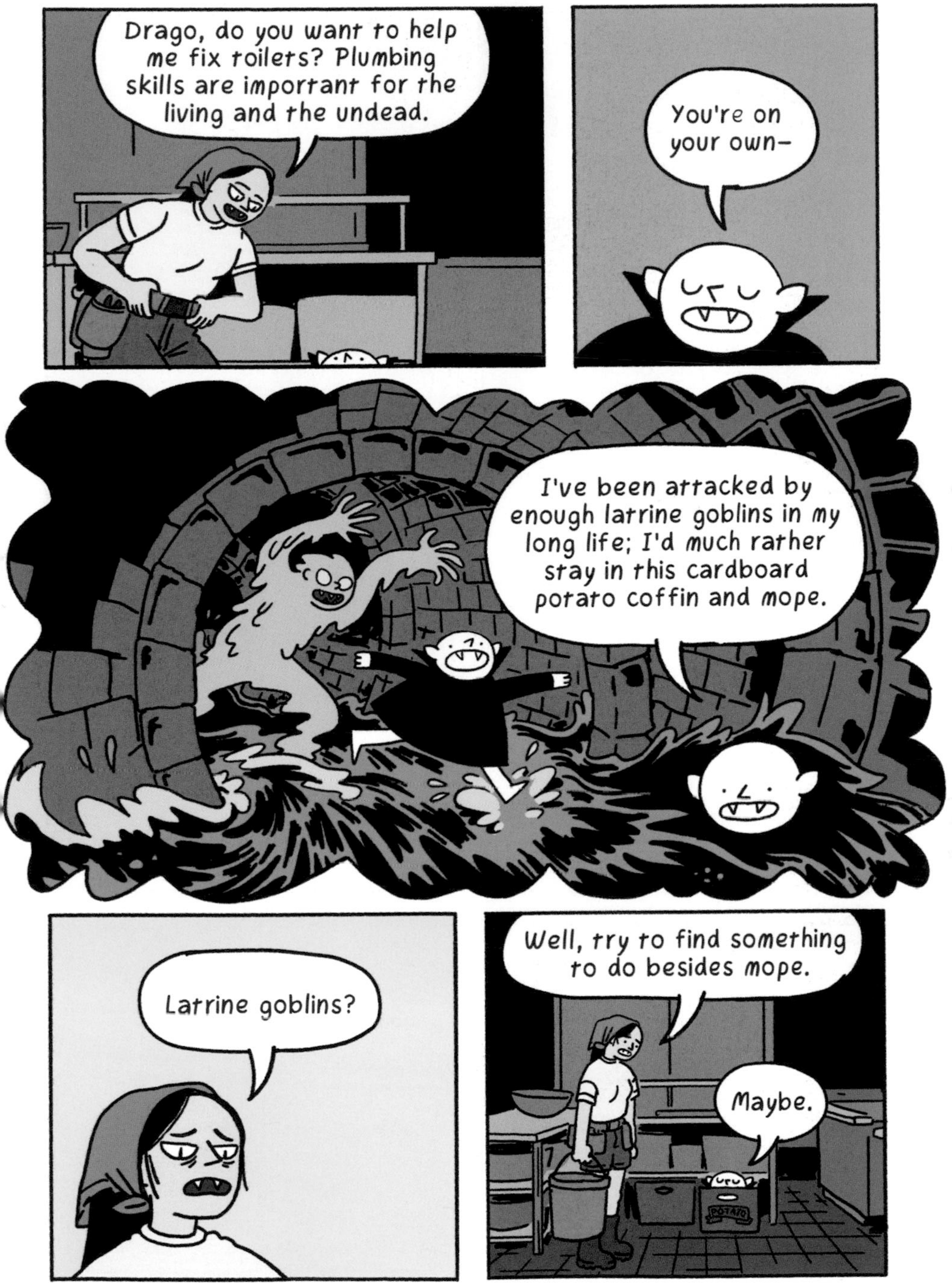
Drago, do you want to help me fix toilets? Plumbing skills are important for the living and the undead.
You're on your own–
I've been attacked by enough latrine goblins in my long life; I'd much rather stay in this cardboard potato coffin and mope.
Latrine goblins?
Well, try to find something to do besides mope.
Maybe.
POTATO

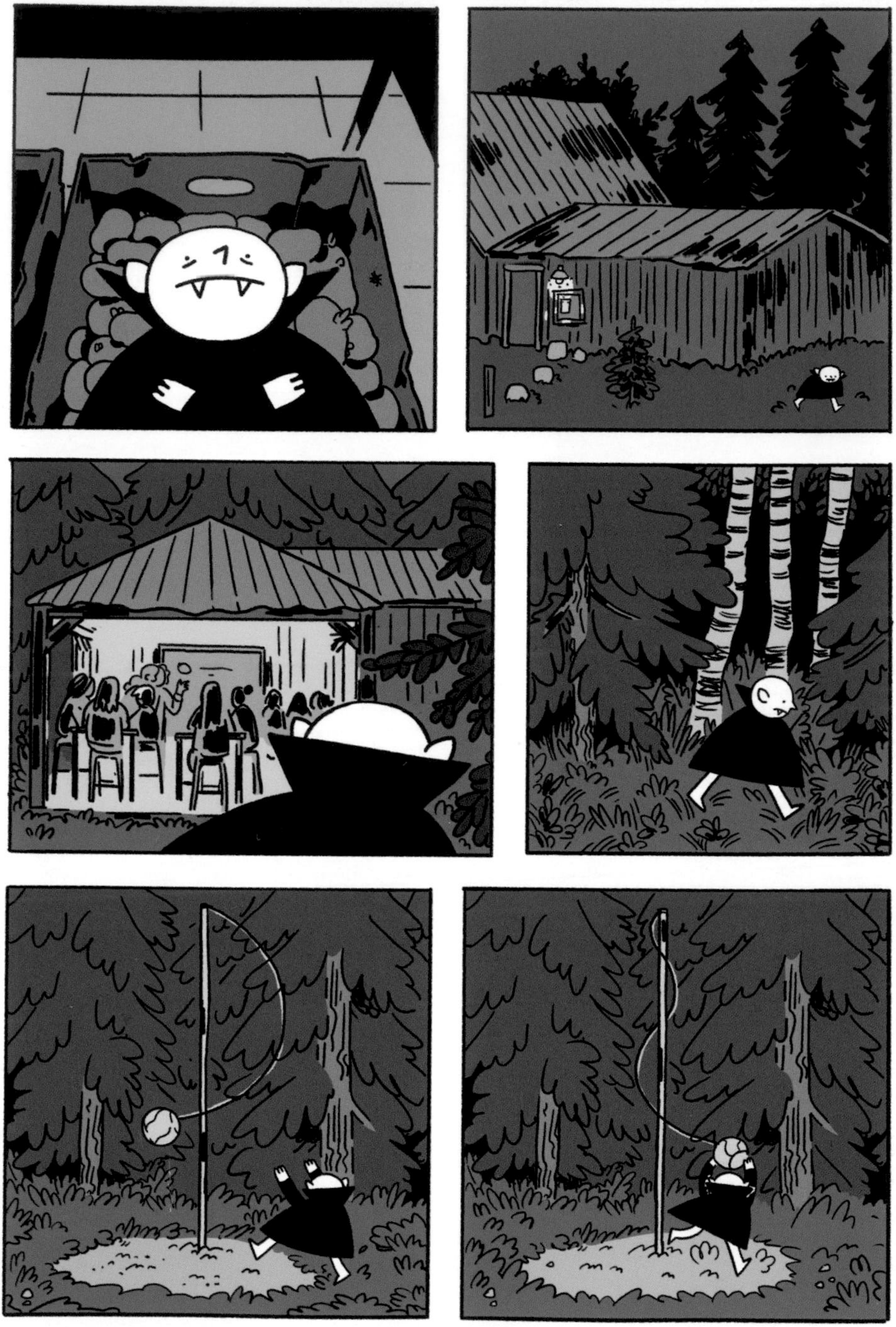

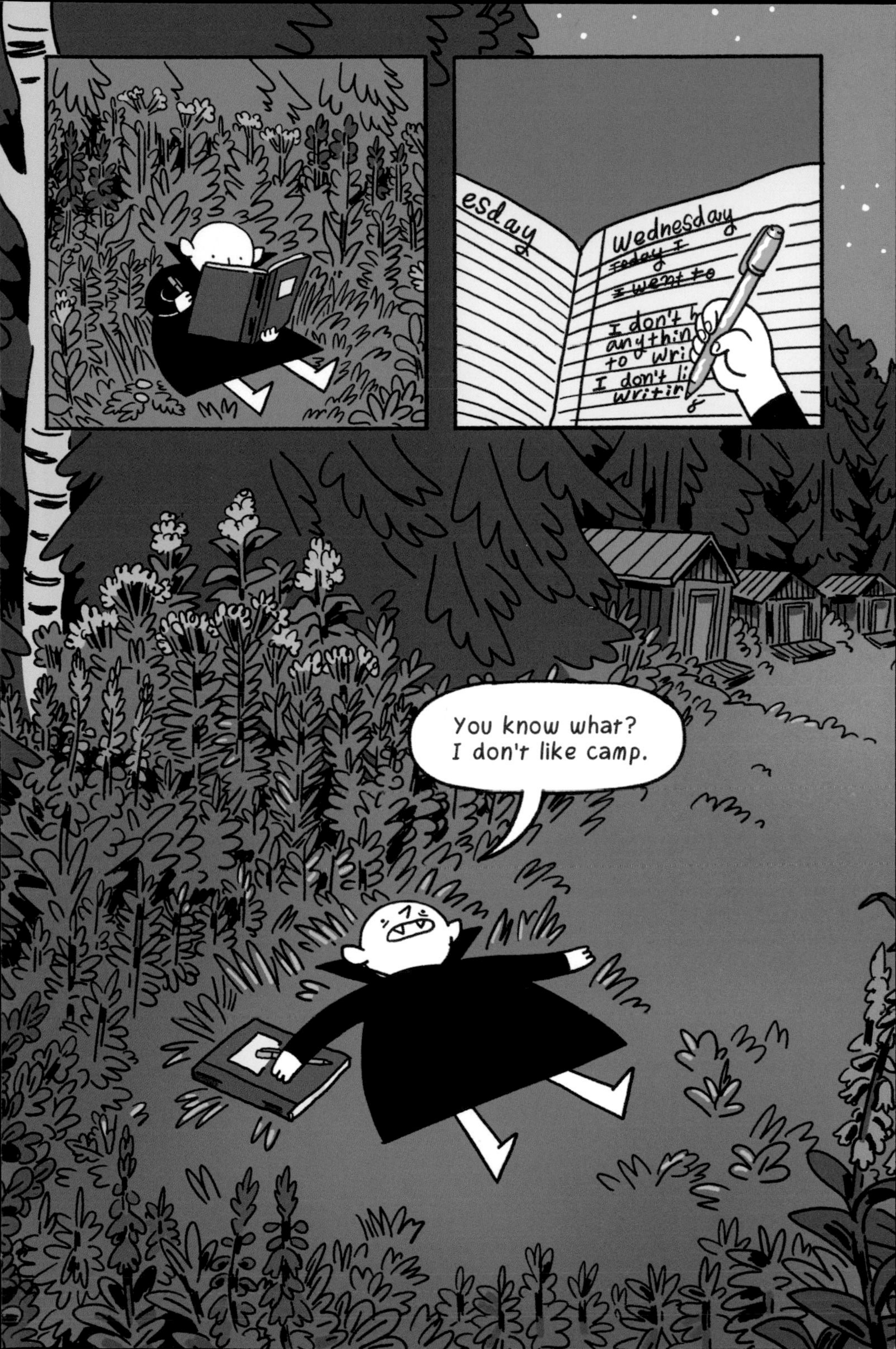
esday
Wednesday
Today I
I went to
I don't h
anythin
to wri
I don't li
writin
You know what? I don't like camp.

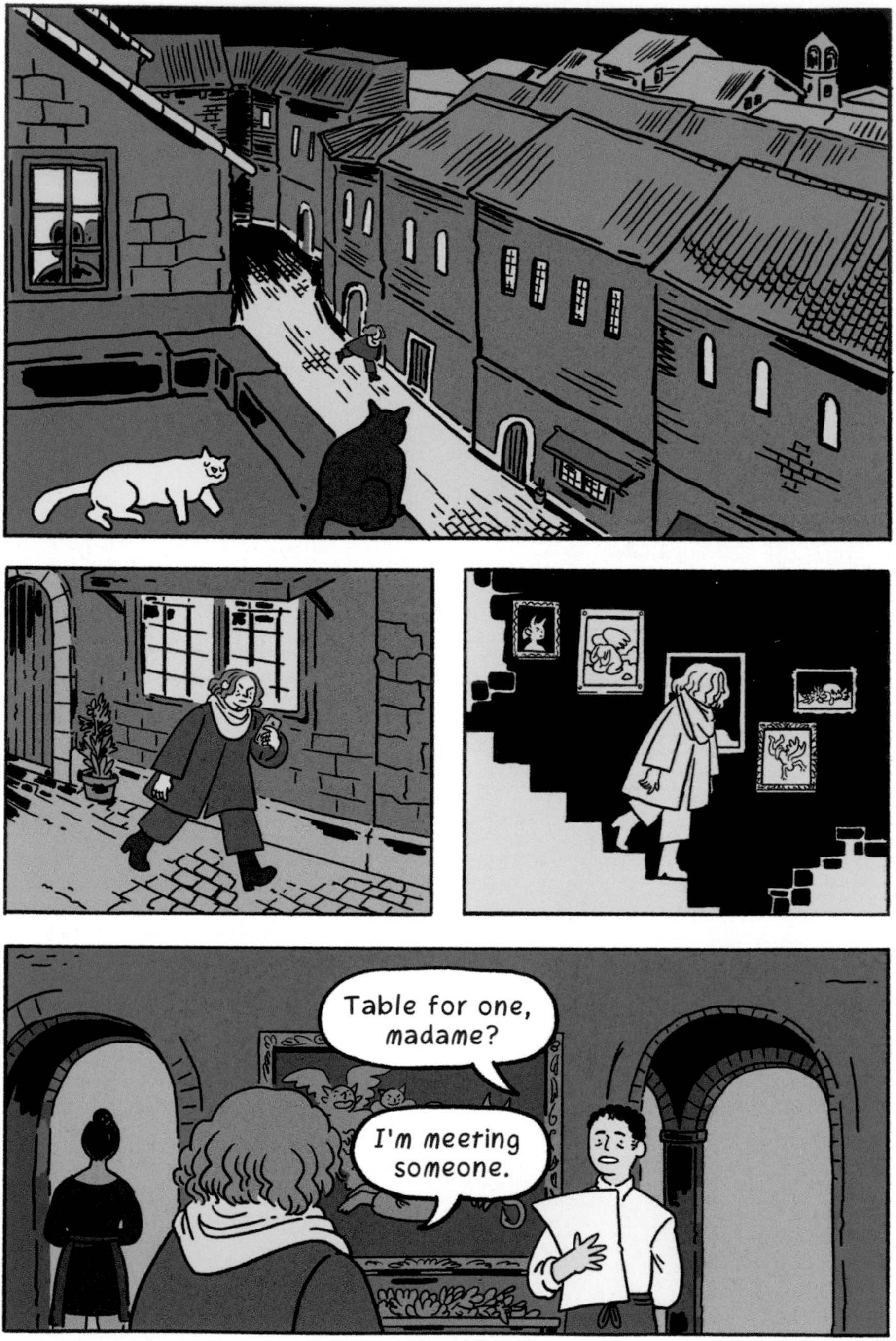
Table for one, madame?
I'm meeting someone.

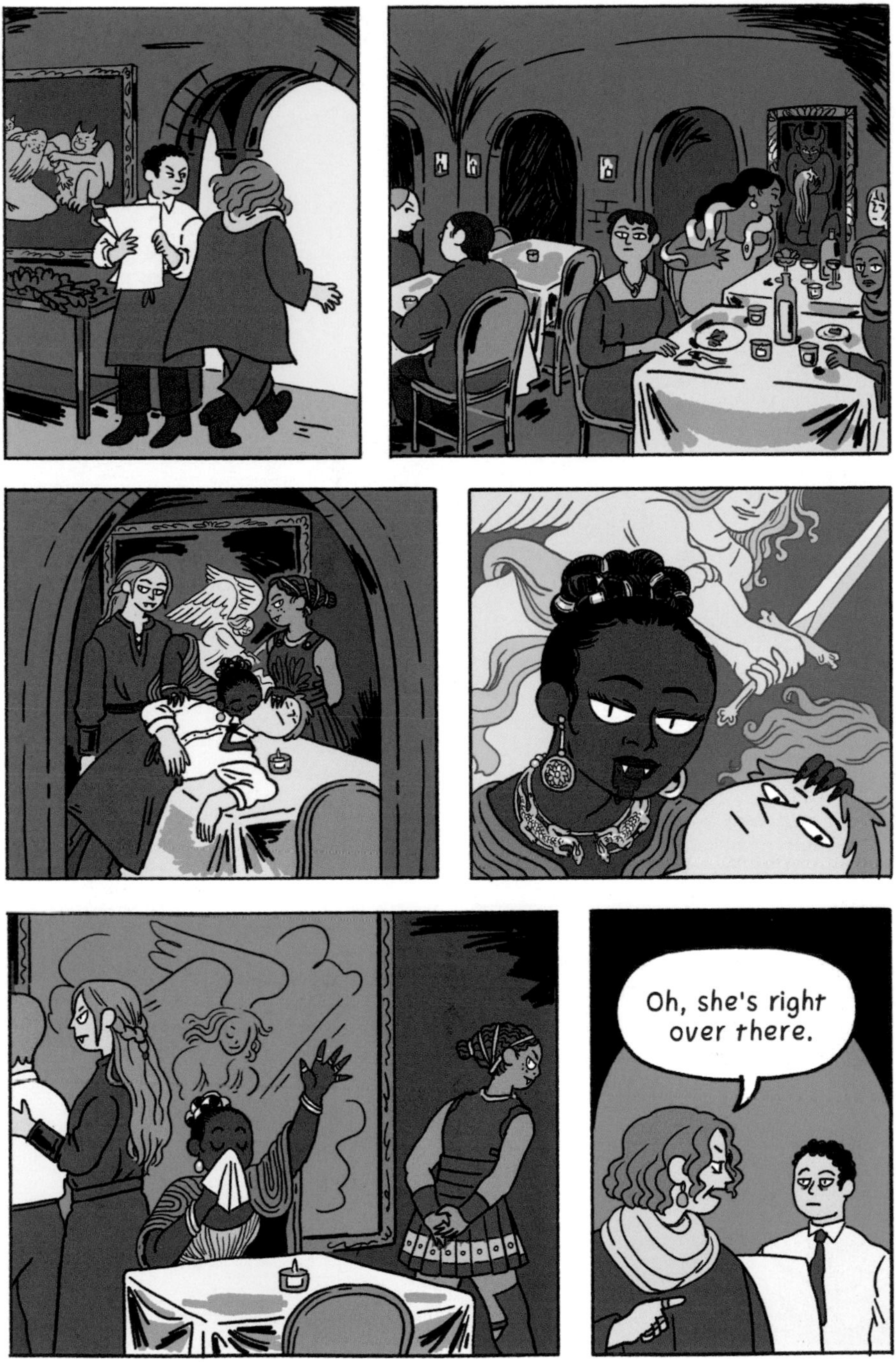
Oh, she's right over there.

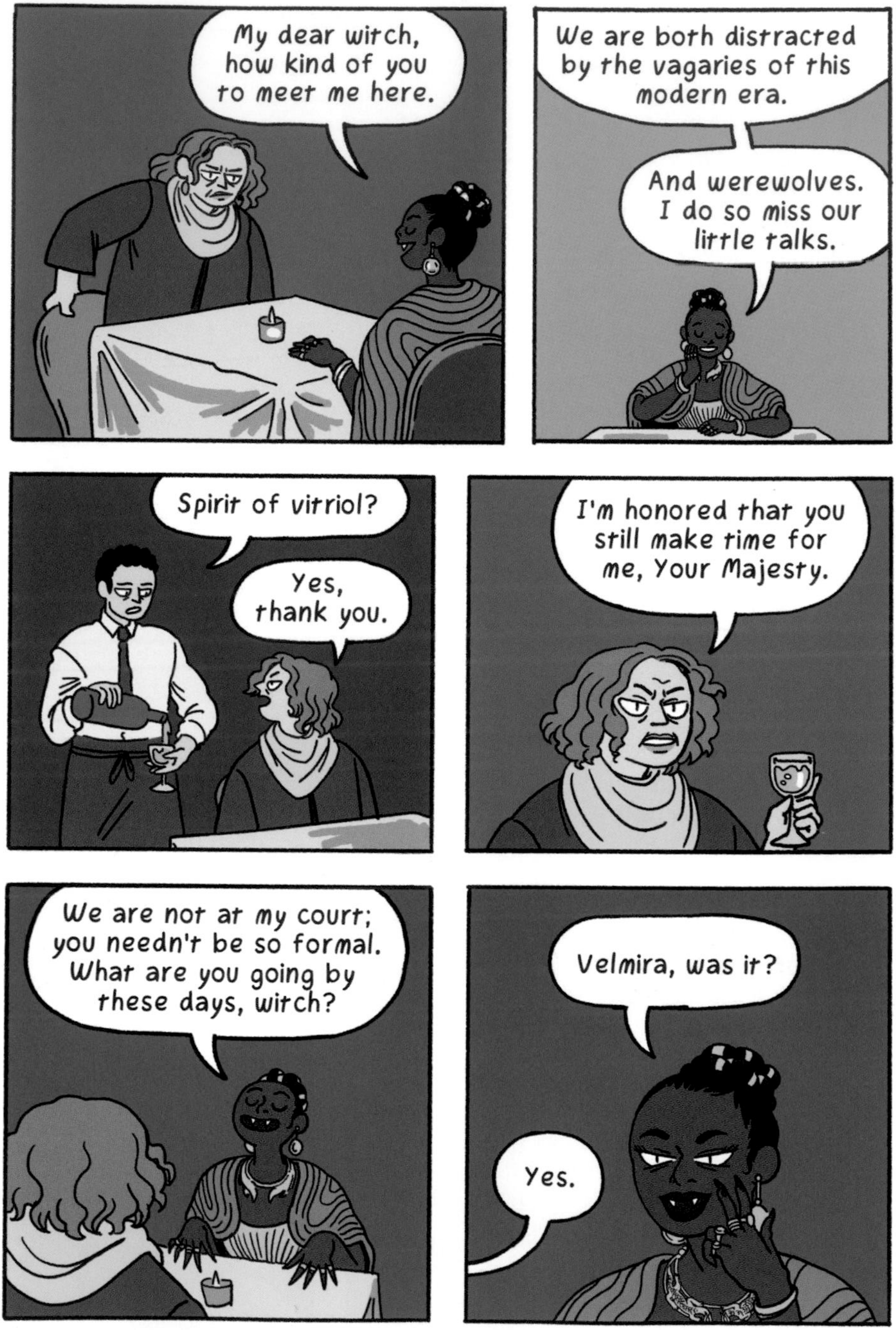
My dear witch, how kind of you to meet me here.
We are both distracted by the vagaries of this modern era.
And werewolves. I do so miss our little talks.
Spirit of vitriol?
Yes, thank you.
I'm honored that you still make time for me, Your Majesty.
We are not at my court; you needn't be so formal. What are you going by these days, witch?
Velmira, was it?
Yes.

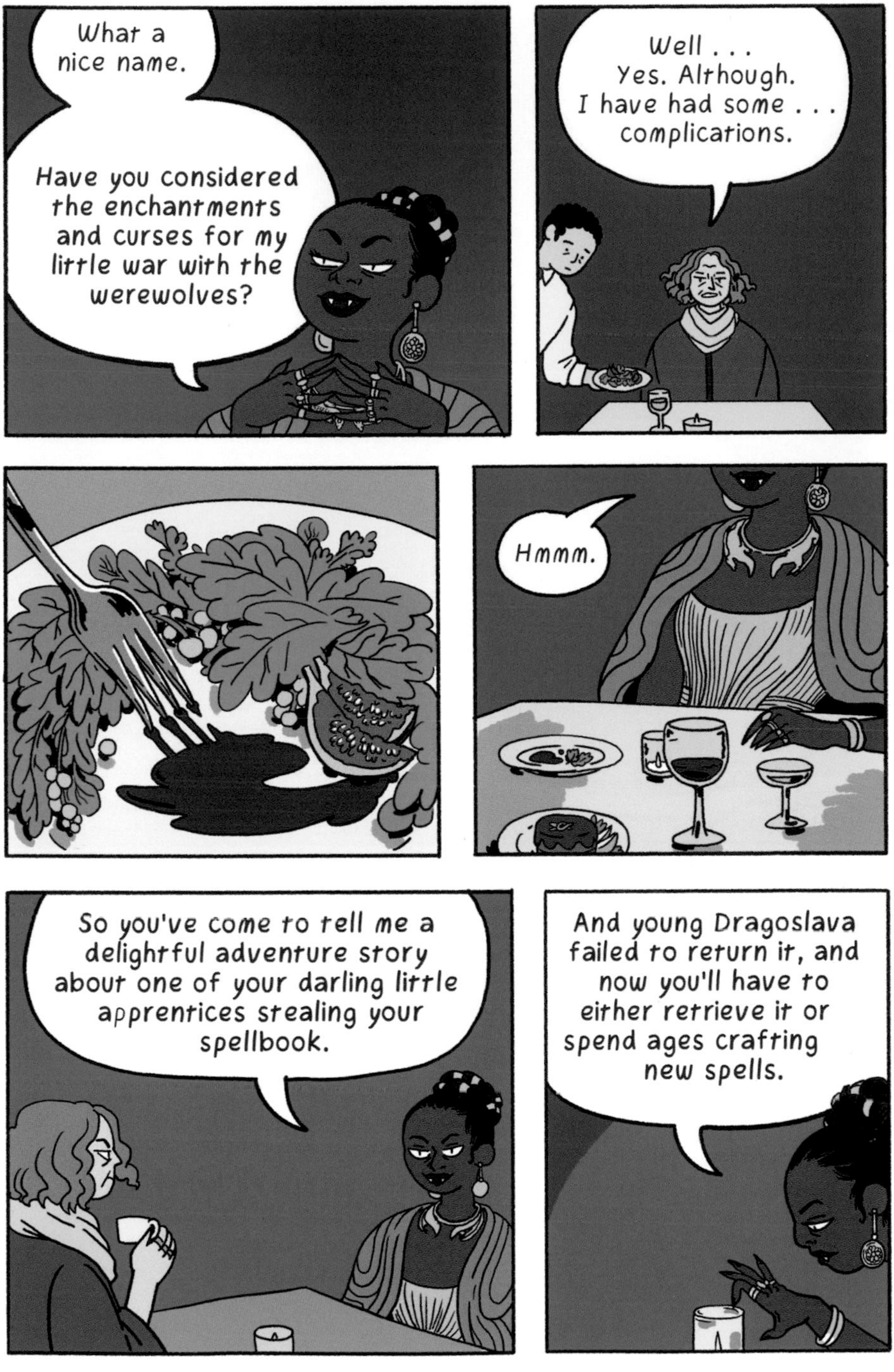
What a nice name.
Have you considered the enchantments and curses for my little war with the werewolves?
Well . . . Yes. Although. I have had some . . . complications.
Hmmm.
So you've come to tell me a delightful adventure story about one of your darling little apprentices stealing your spellbook.
And young Dragoslava failed to return it, and now you'll have to either retrieve it or spend ages crafting new spells.

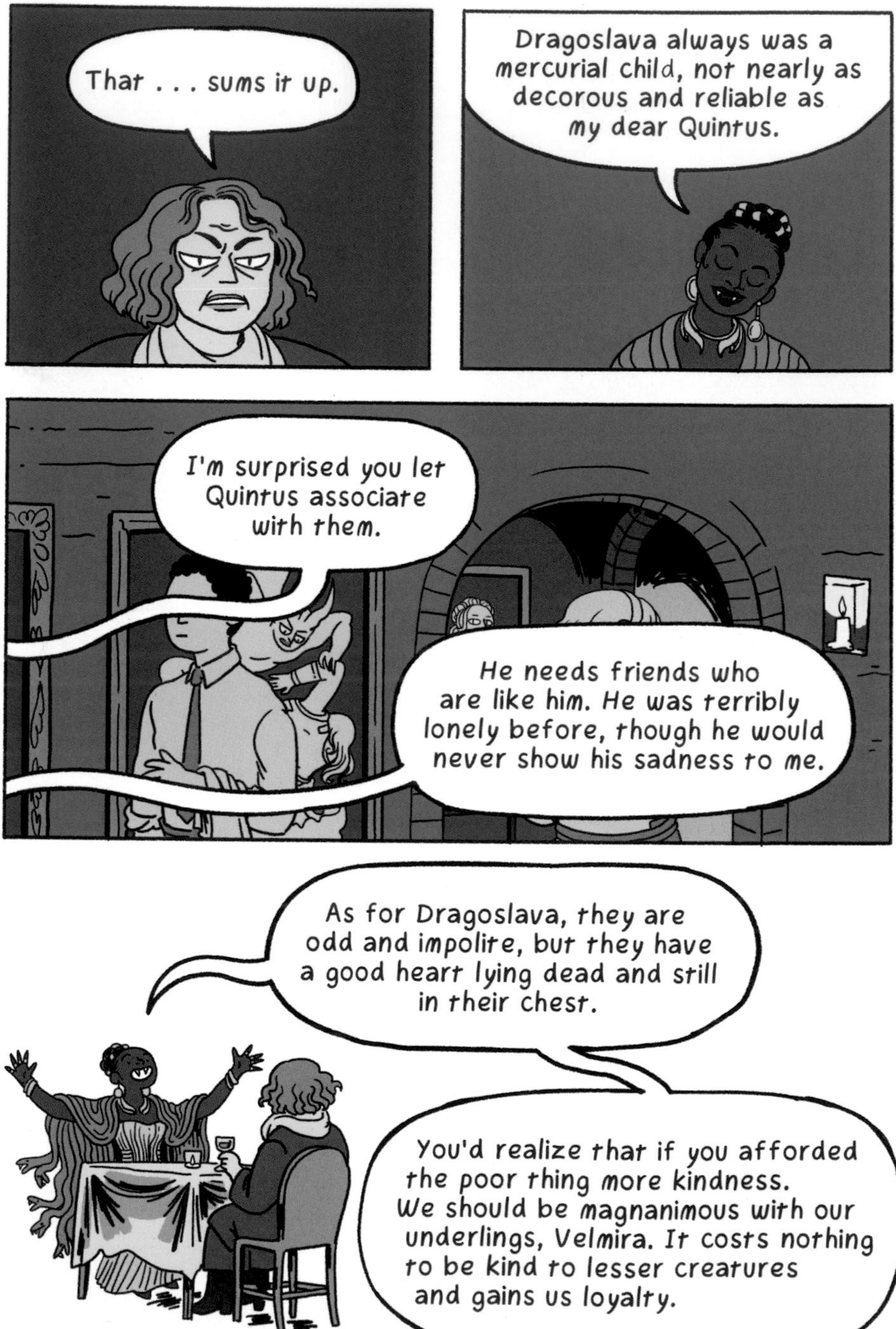
That . . . sums it up.
Dragoslava always was a mercurial child, not nearly as decorous and reliable as my dear Quintus.
I'm surprised you let Quintus associate with them.
He needs friends who are like him. He was terribly lonely before, though he would never show his sadness to me.
As for Dragoslava, they are odd and impolite, but they have a good heart lying dead and still in their chest.
You'd realize that if you afforded the poor thing more kindness. We should be magnanimous with our underlings, Velmira. It costs nothing to be kind to lesser creatures and gains us loyalty.

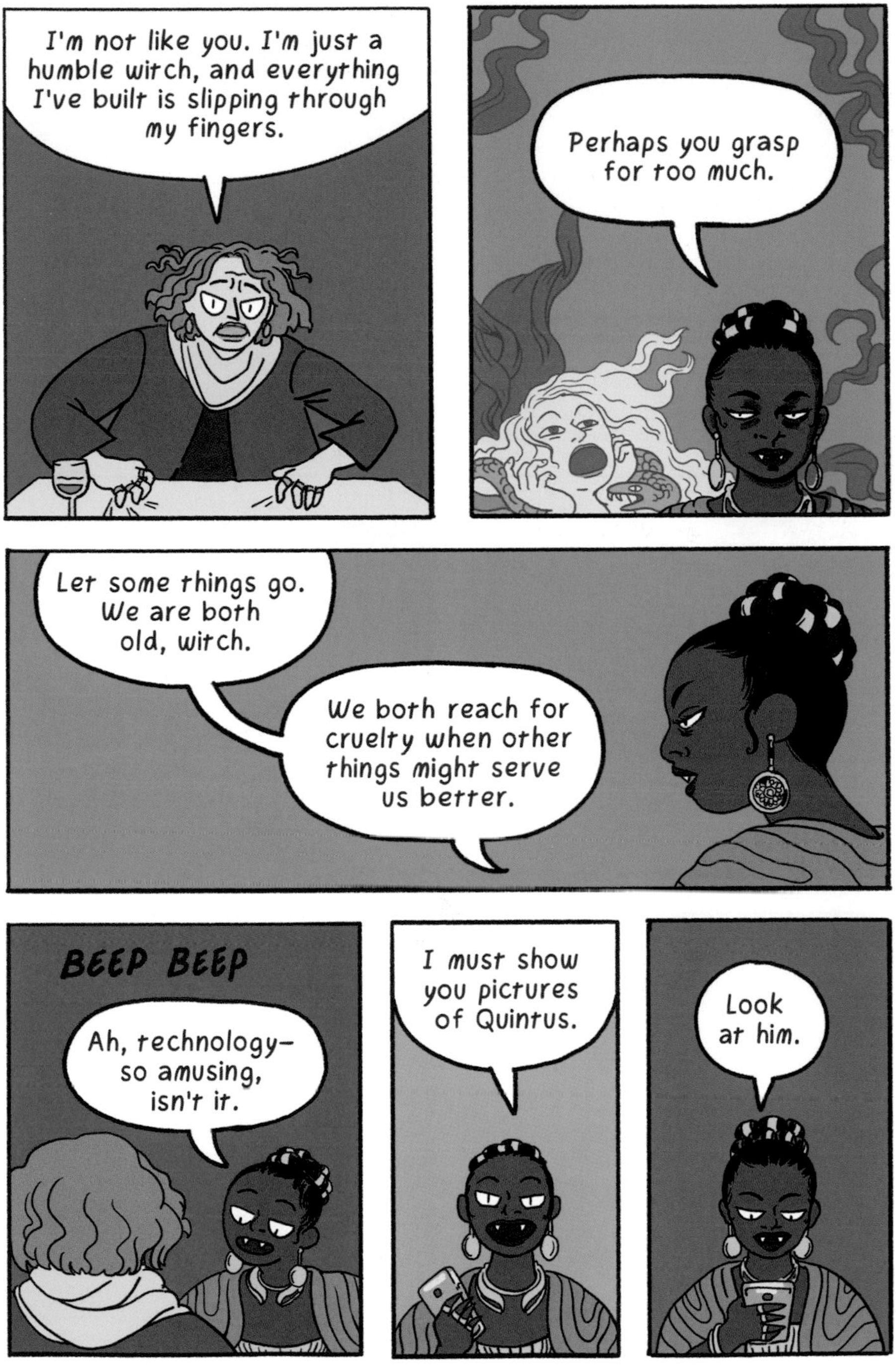
I'm not like you. I'm just a humble witch, and everything I've built is slipping through my fingers.
Perhaps you grasp for too much.
Let some things go. We are both old, witch.
We both reach for cruelty when other things might serve us better.
BEEP BEEP
Ah, technology– so amusing, isn't it.
I must show you pictures of Quintus.
Look at him.

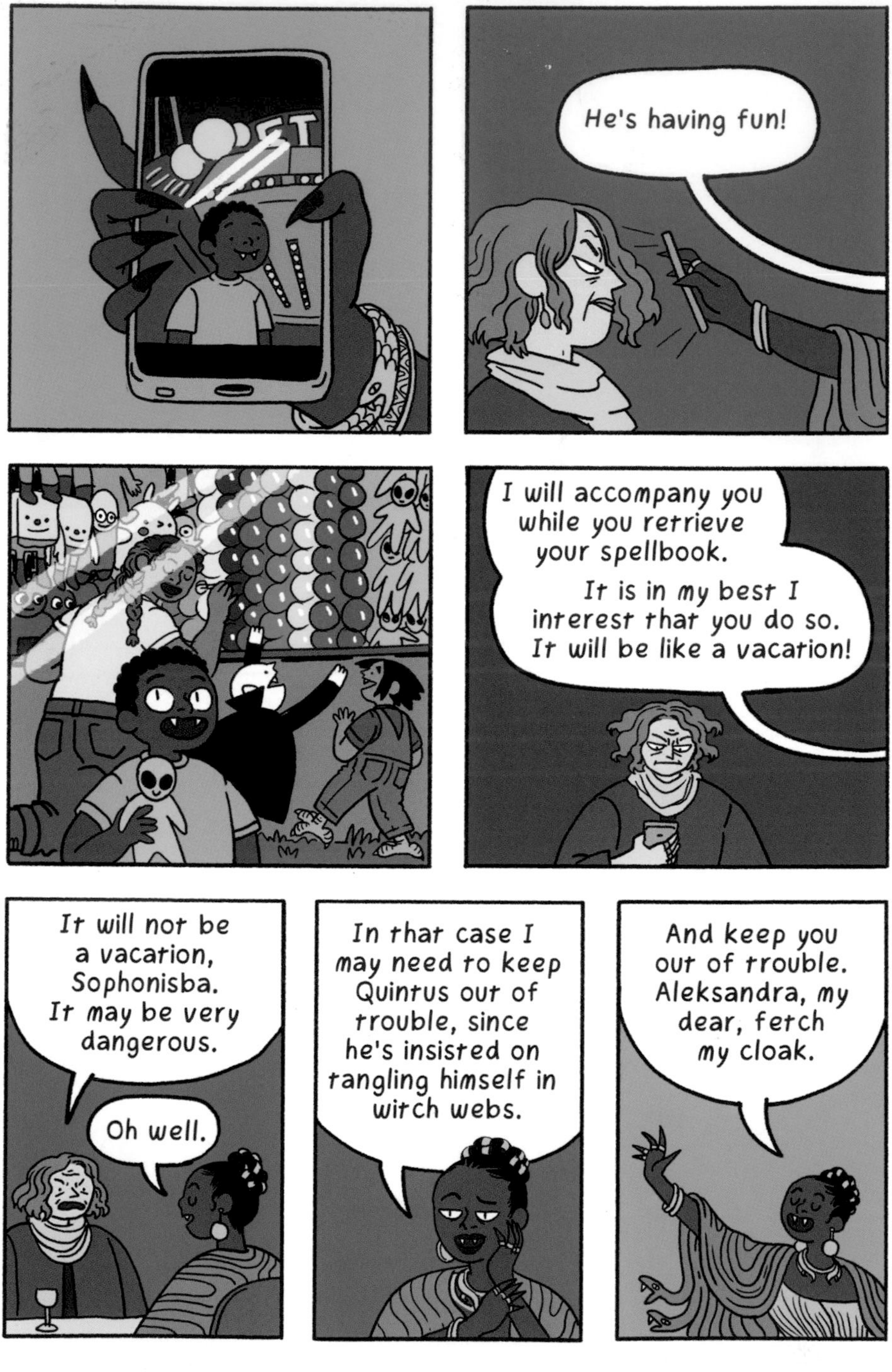

He's having fun!
I will accompany you while you retrieve your spellbook.
It is in my best I interest that you do so. It will be like a vacation!
It will not be a vacation, Sophonisba. It may be very dangerous.
Oh well.
In that case I may need to keep Quintus out of trouble, since he's insisted on tangling himself in witch webs.
And keep you out of trouble. Aleksandra, my dear, fetch my cloak.

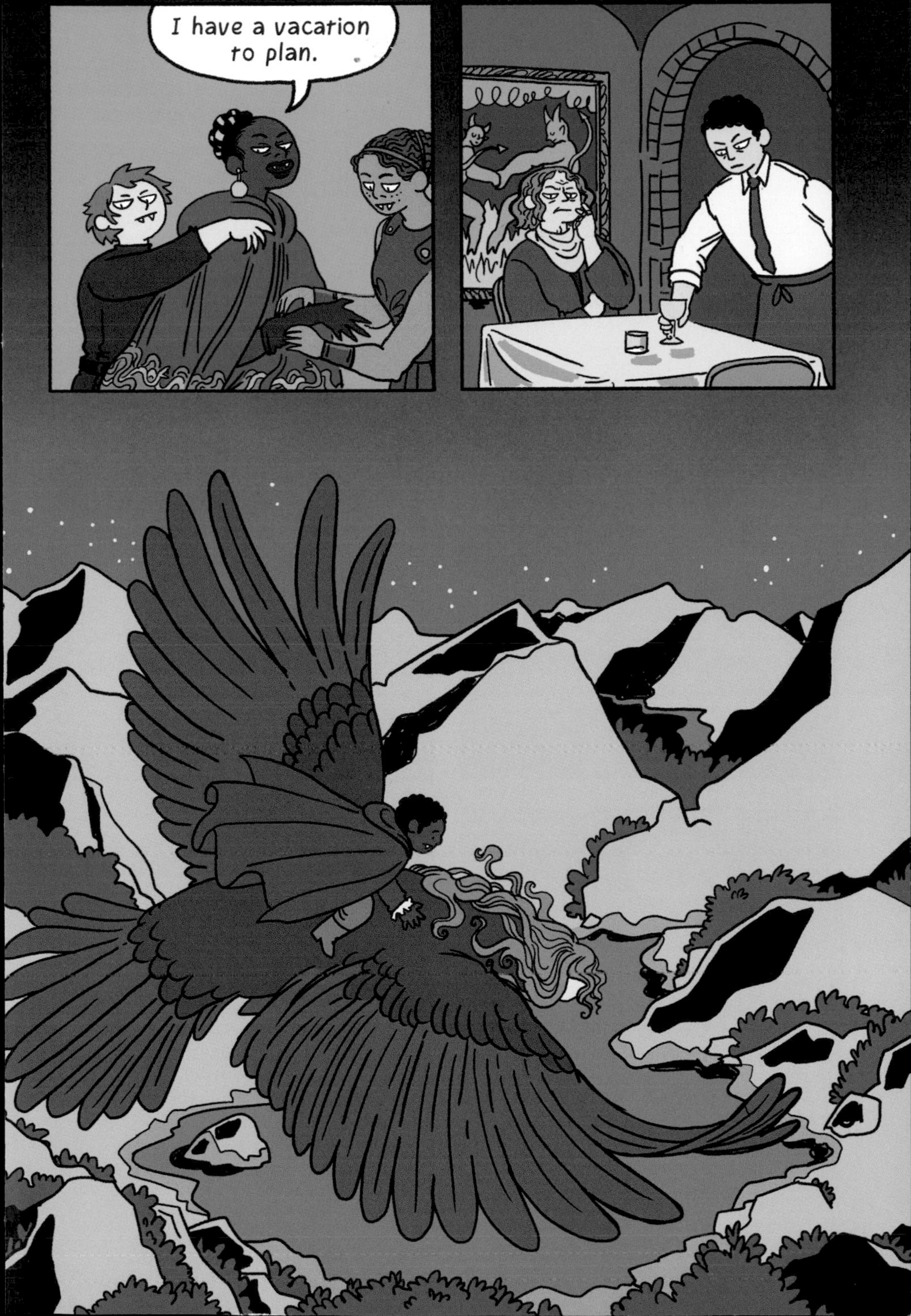
I have a vacation to plan.

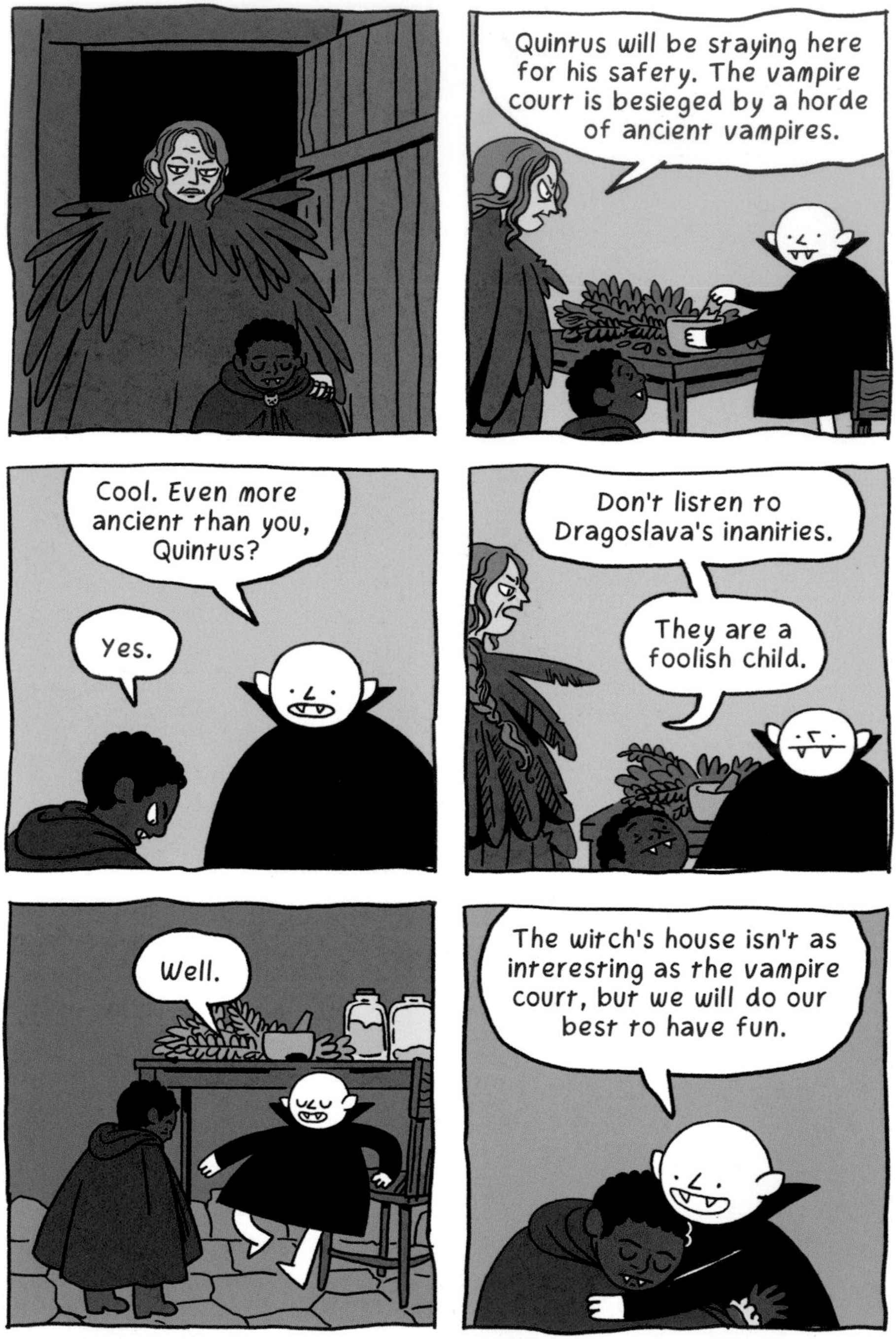
Quintus will be staying here for his safety. The vampire court is besieged by a horde of ancient vampires.
Cool. Even more ancient than you, Quintus?
Yes.
Don't listen to Dragoslava's inanities.
They are a foolish child.
Well.
The witch's house isn't as interesting as the vampire court, but we will do our best to have fun.

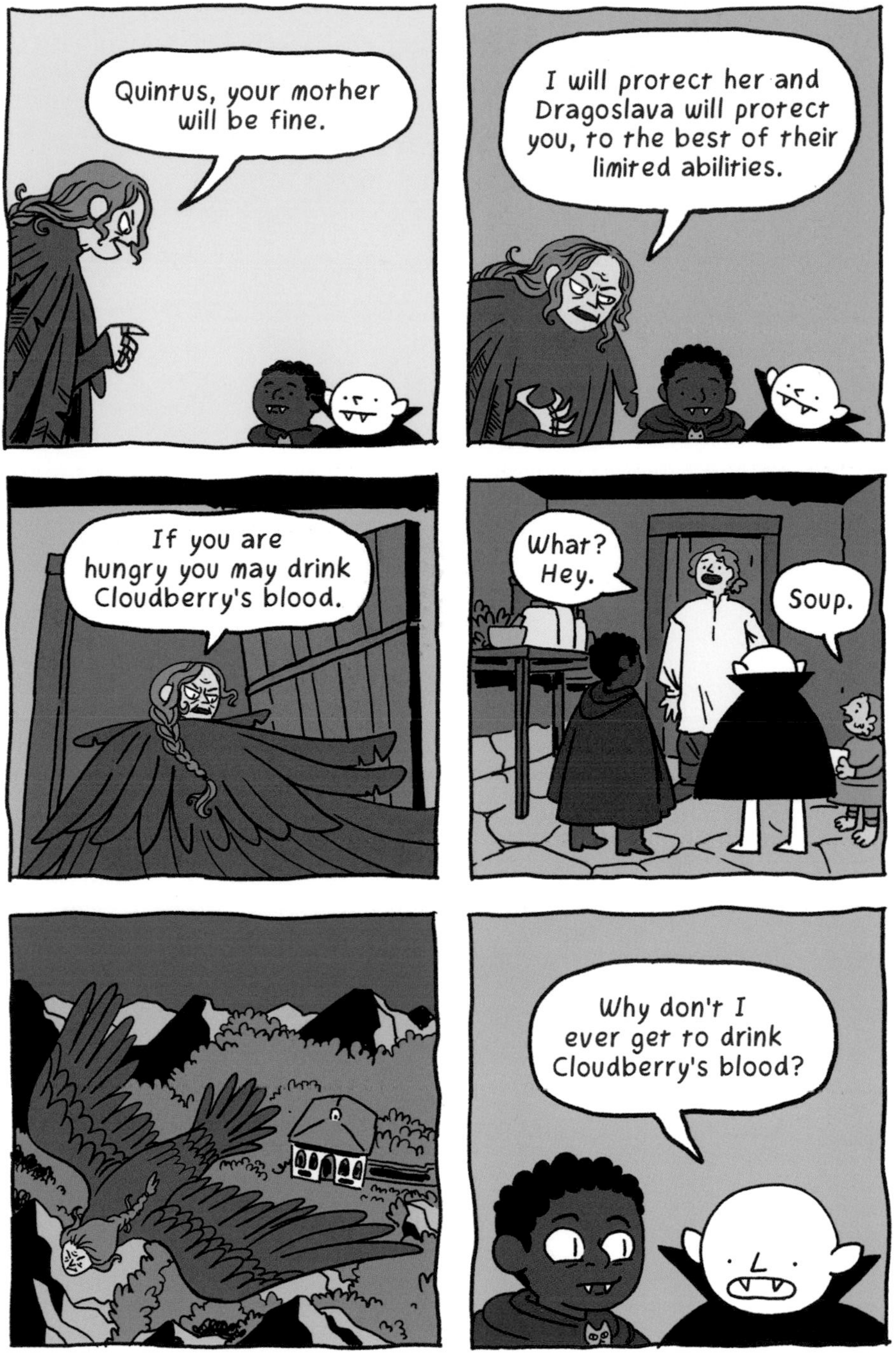
Quintus, your mother will be fine.
I will protect her and Dragoslava will protect you, to the best of their limited abilities.
If you are hungry you may drink Cloudberry's blood.
What? Hey.
Soup.
Why don't I ever get to drink Cloudberry's blood?

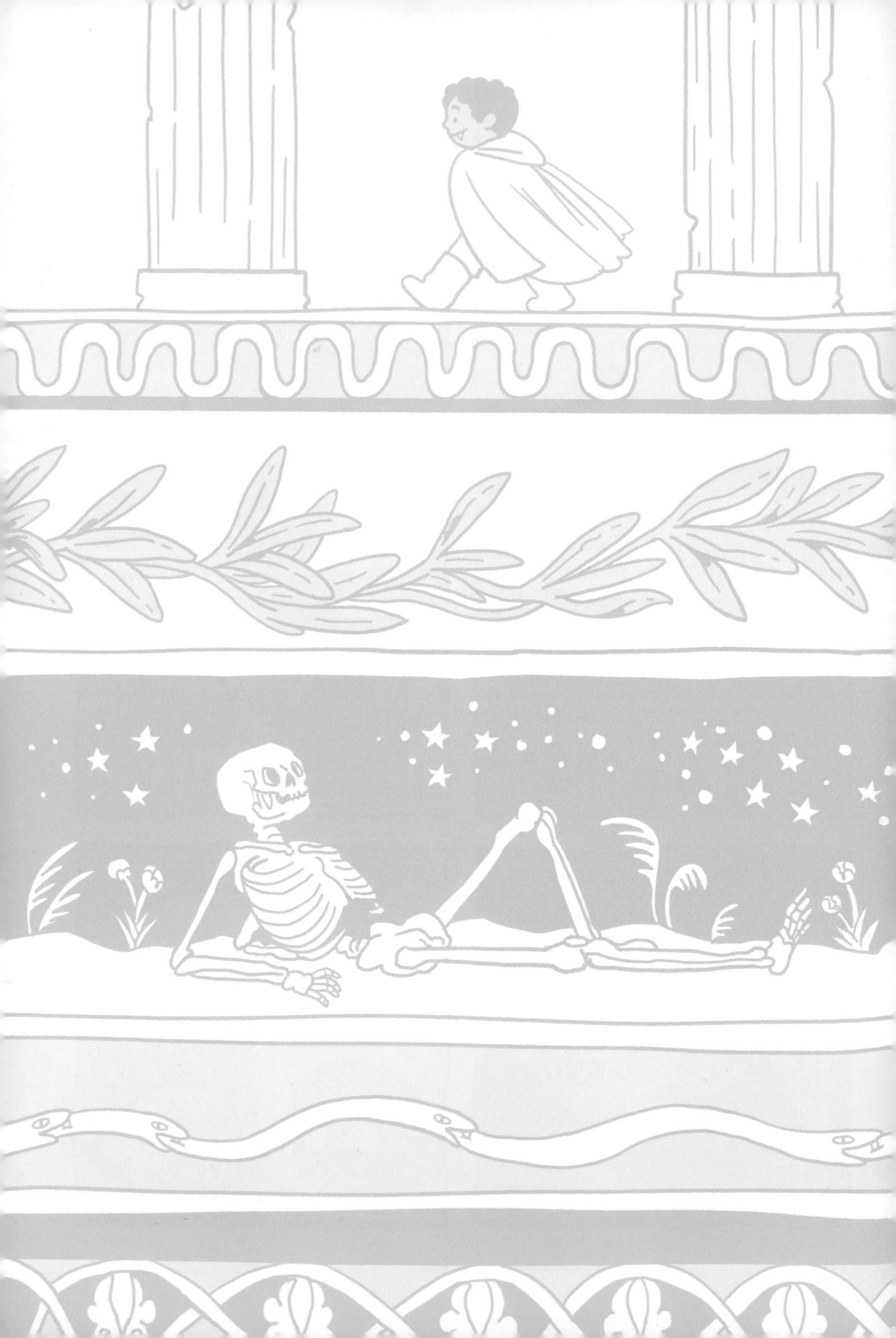

CHAPTER THREE

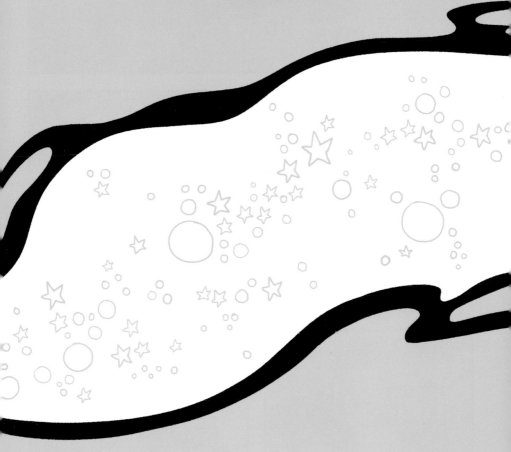

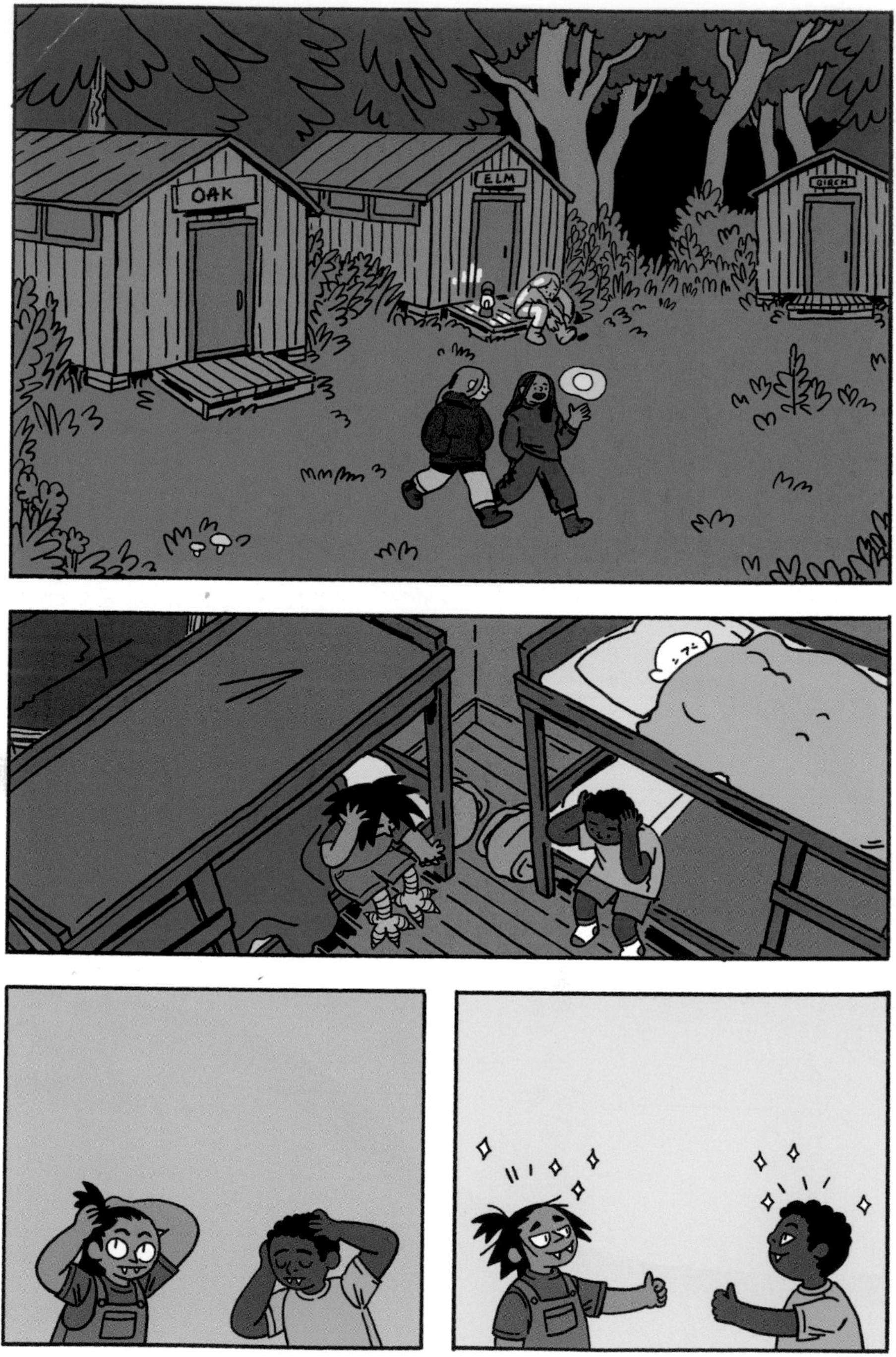
OAK
ELM

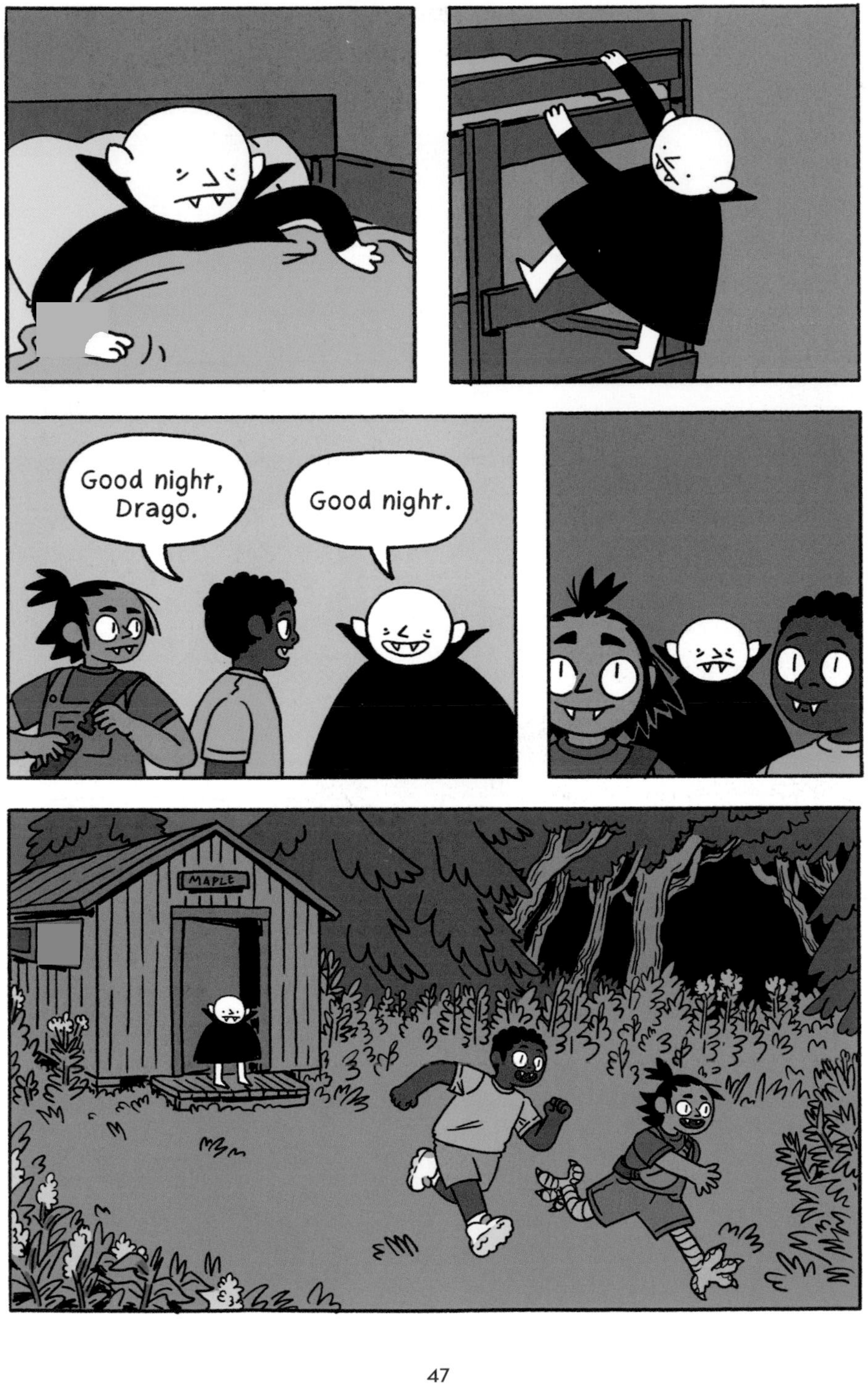
Good night, Drago.
Good night.
MAPLE

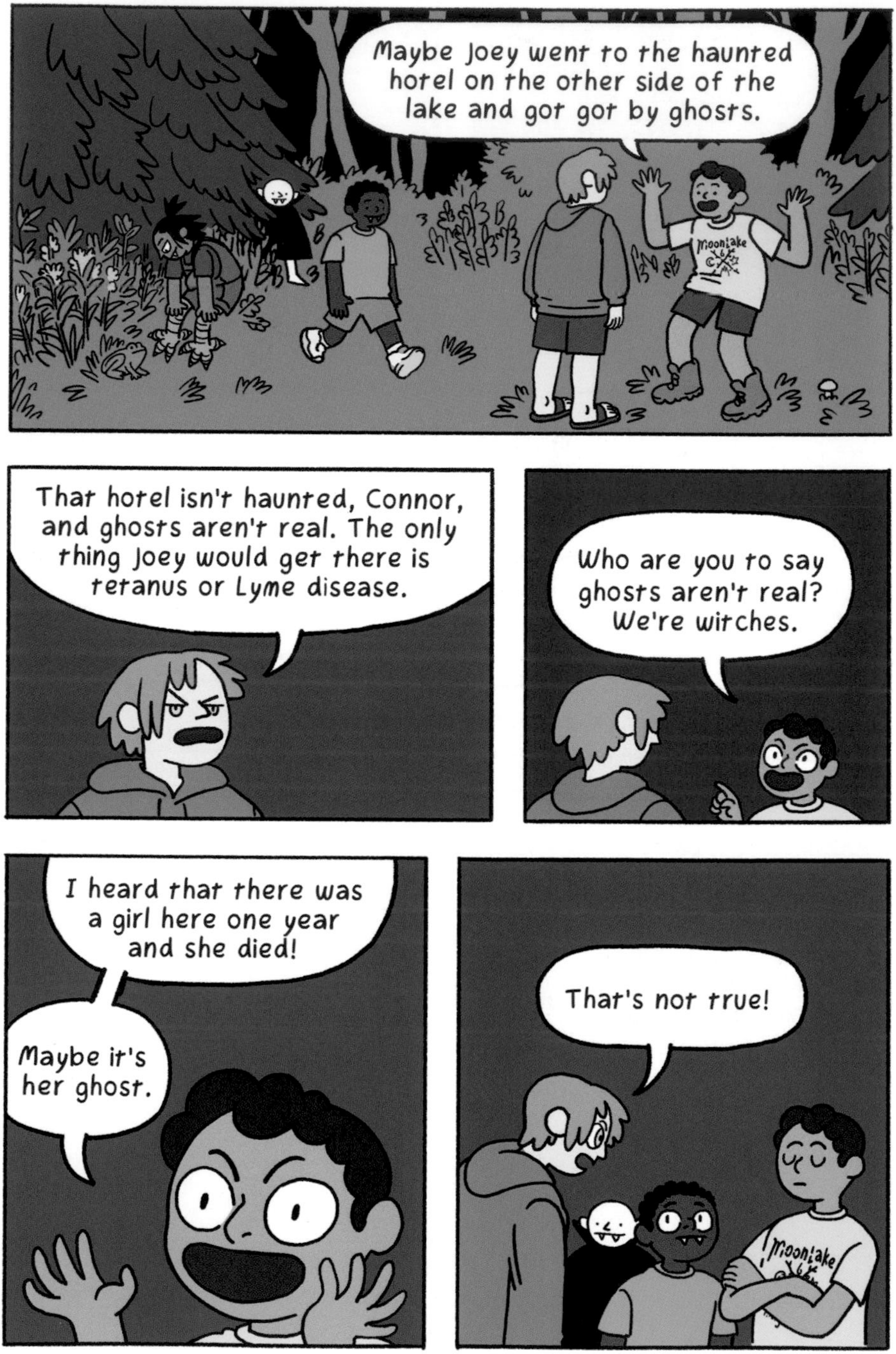

Maybe Joey went to the haunted hotel on the other side of the lake and got got by ghosts.
Moonlake
That hotel isn't haunted, Connor, and ghosts aren't real. The only thing Joey would get there is tetanus or Lyme disease.
Who are you to say ghosts aren't real? We're witches.
I heard that there was a girl here one year and she died!
Maybe it's her ghost.
That's not true!
Moonlake

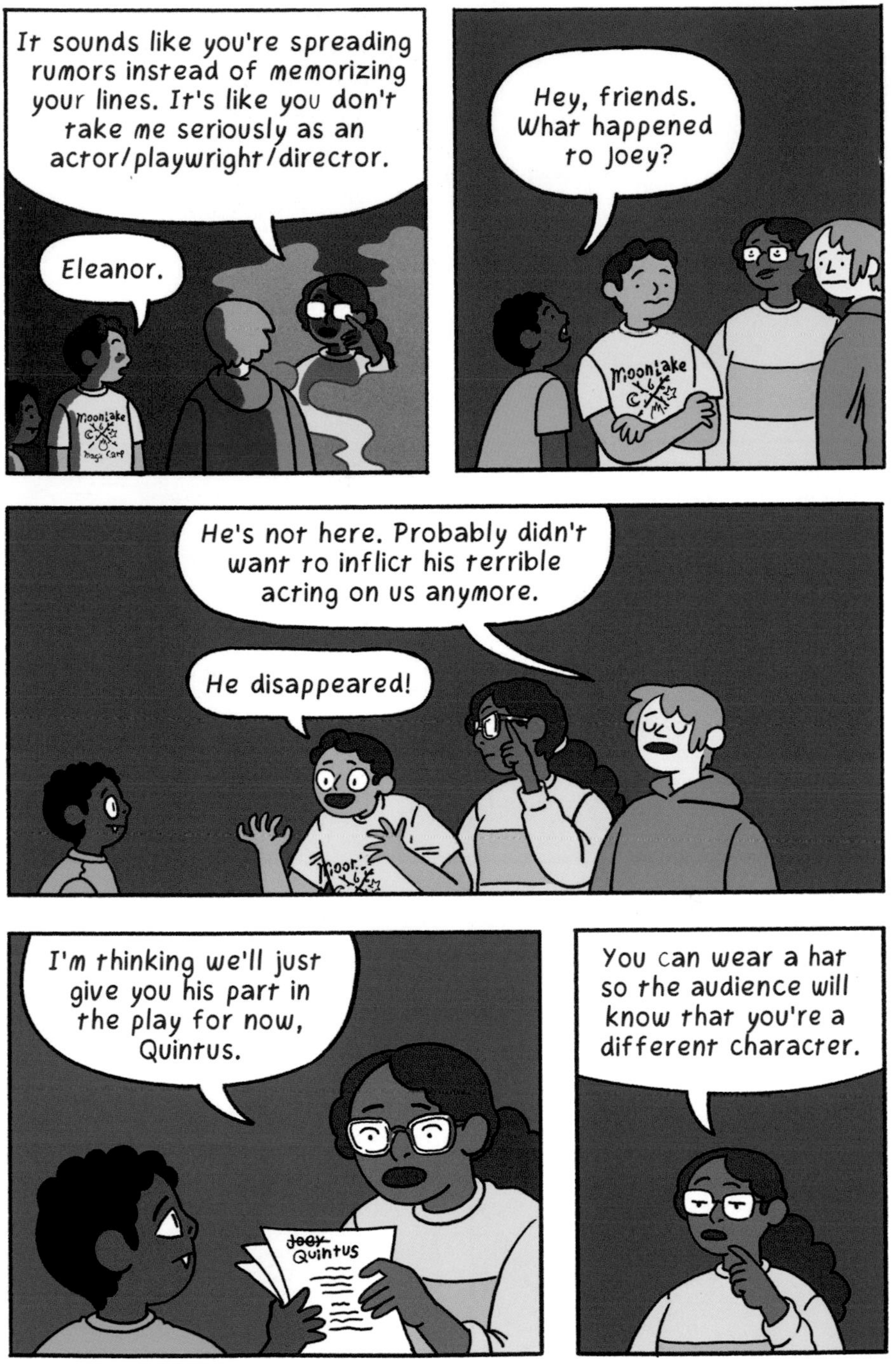
It sounds like you're spreading rumors instead of memorizing your lines. It's like you don't take me seriously as an actor/playwright/director.
Eleanor.
Hey, friends. What happened to Joey?
He's not here. Probably didn't want to inflict his terrible acting on us anymore.
He disappeared!
I'm thinking we'll just give you his part in the play for now, Quintus.
~~Joey~~
Quintus
You can wear a hat so the audience will know that you're a different character.

Okay.

Hey!

I made you guys friendship bracelets during craft time.

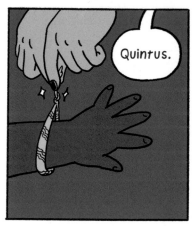

Quintus.

And here you go, Eztli.

Thank you!

Thanks. Blue is my sixth-favorite color.

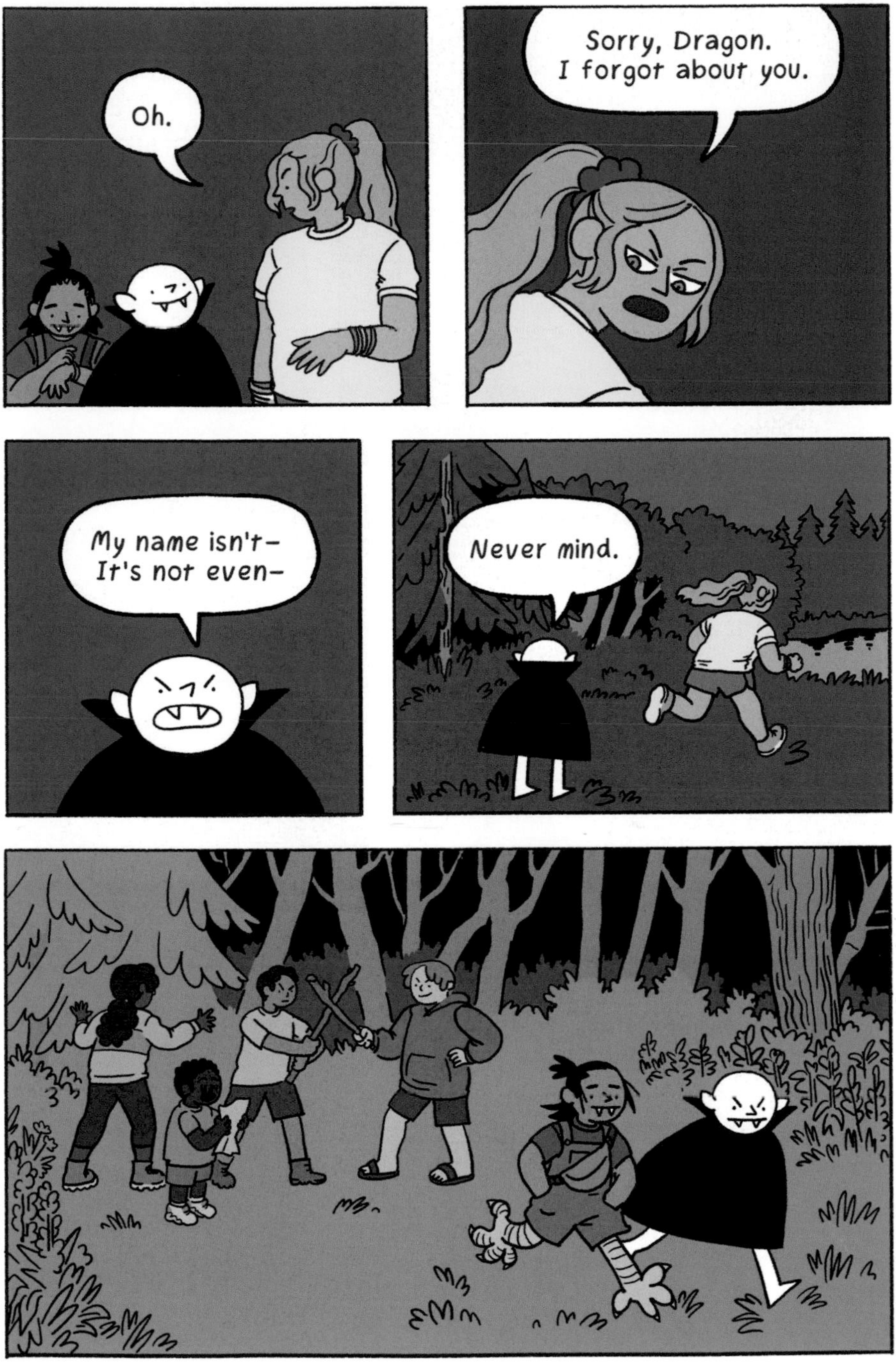
Oh.
Sorry, Dragon. I forgot about you.
My name isn't— It's not even—
Never mind.

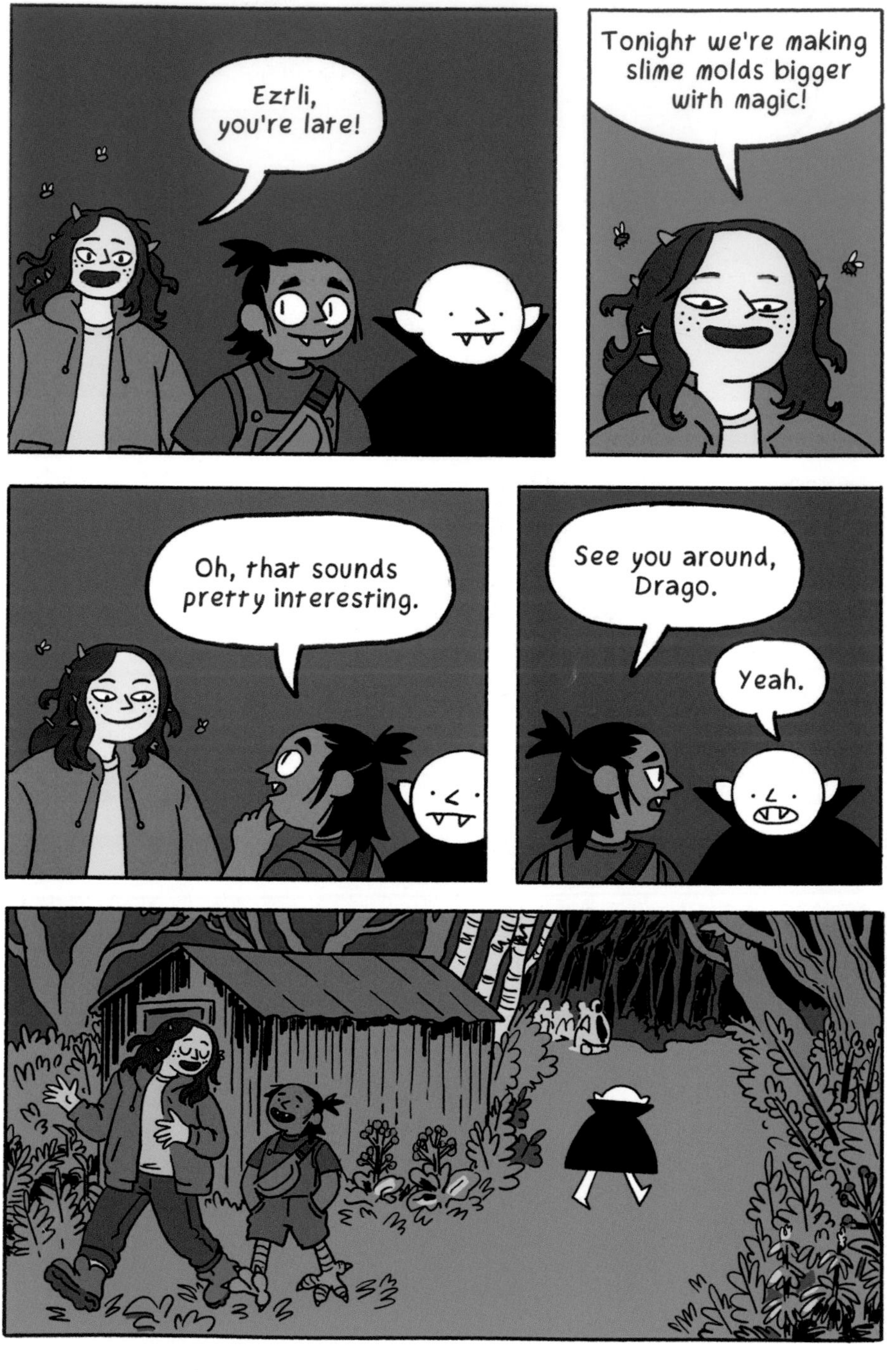
Eztli, you're late!
Tonight we're making slime molds bigger with magic!
Oh, that sounds pretty interesting.
See you around, Drago.
Yeah.

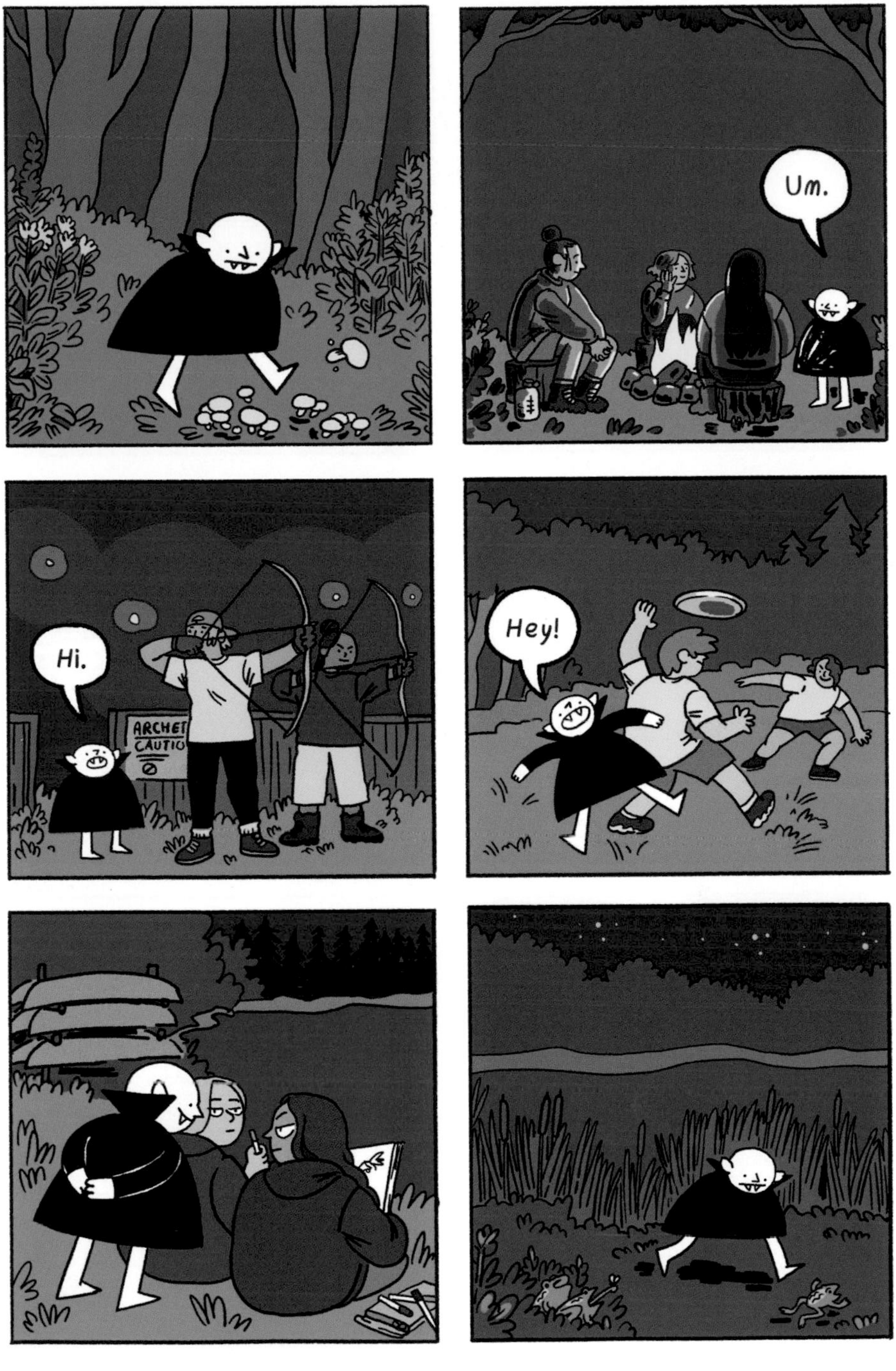
Um.
Hi.
Hey!

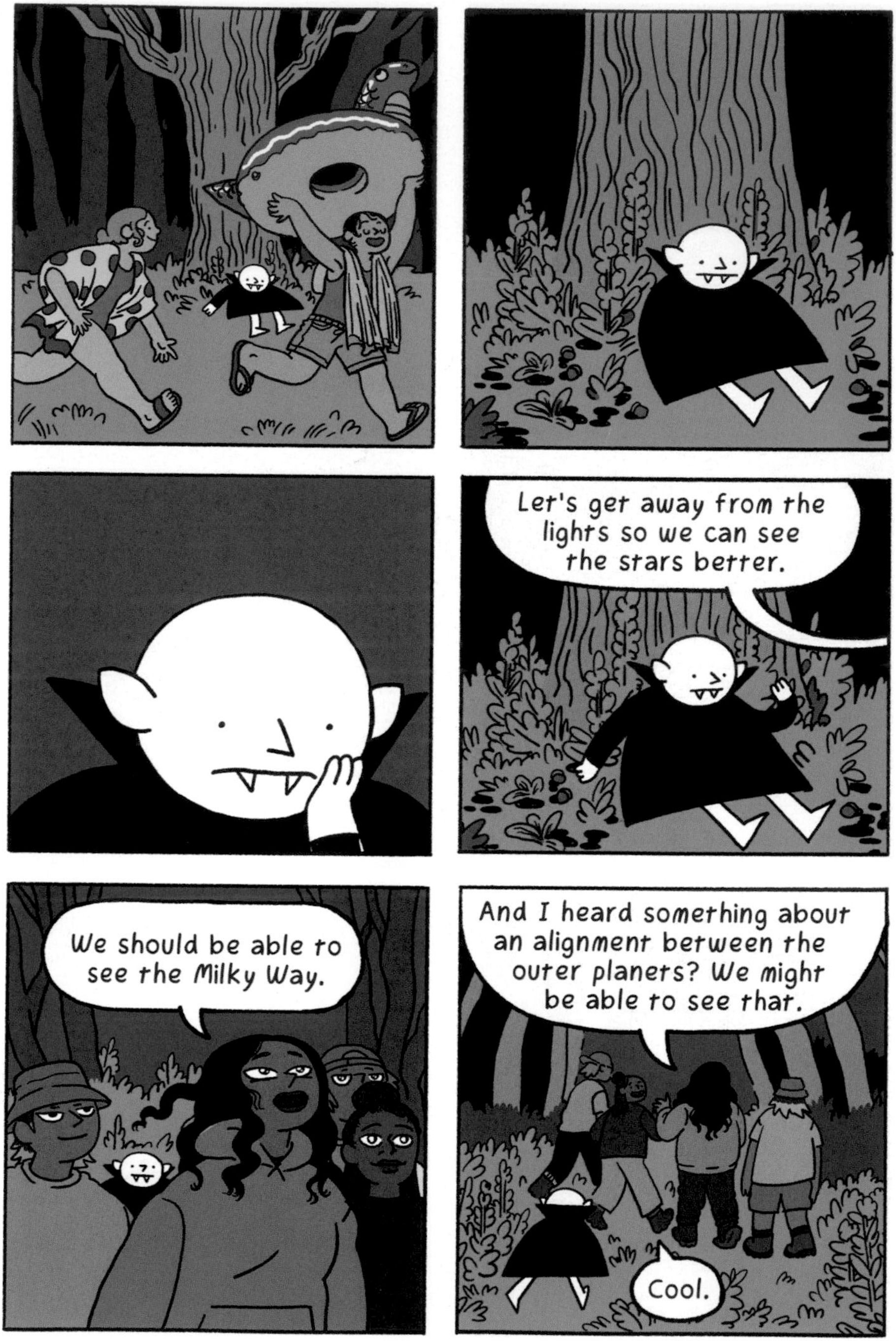
Let's get away from the lights so we can see the stars better.
We should be able to see the Milky Way.
And I heard something about an alignment between the outer planets? We might be able to see that.
Cool.

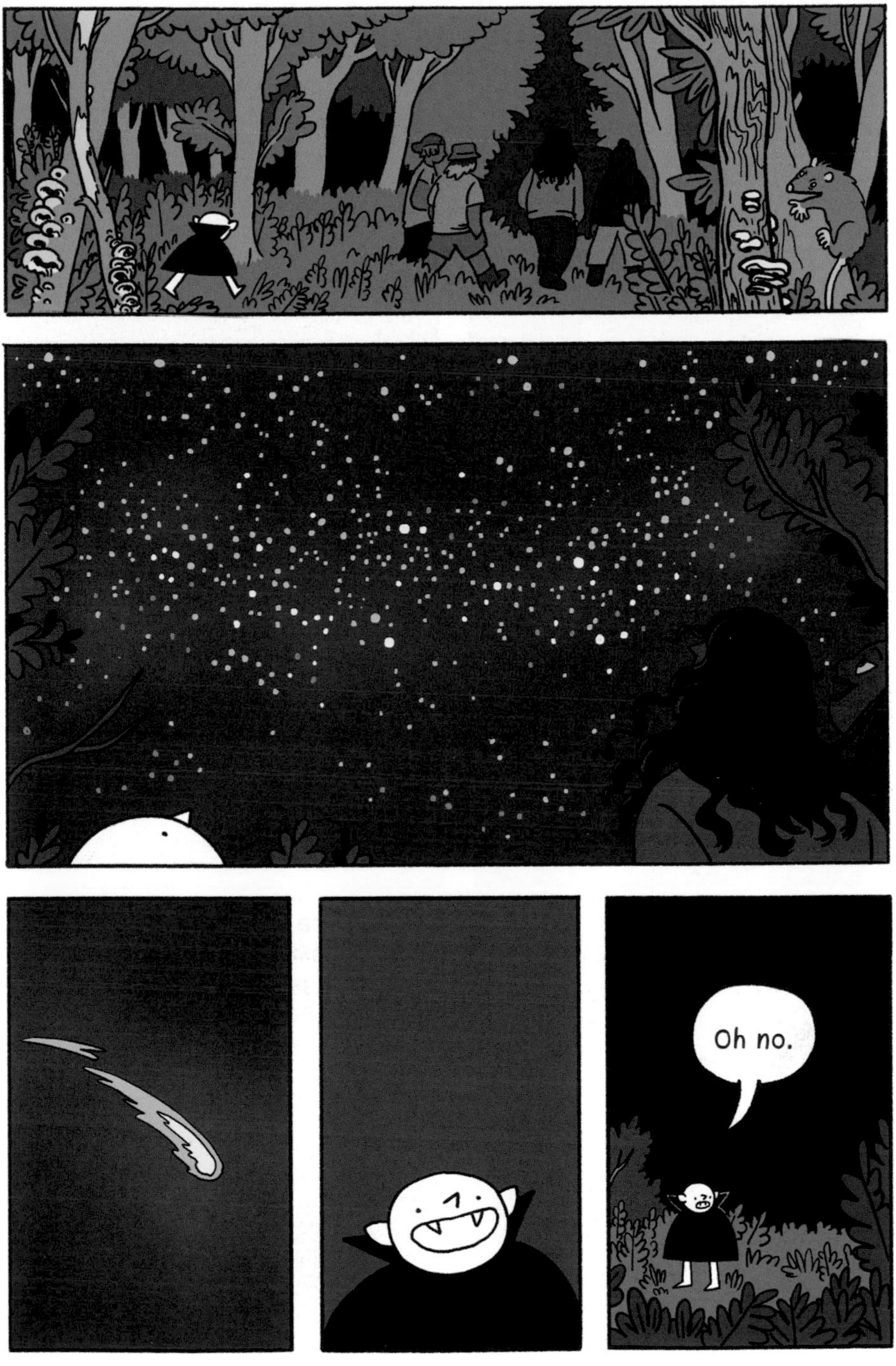
Oh no.

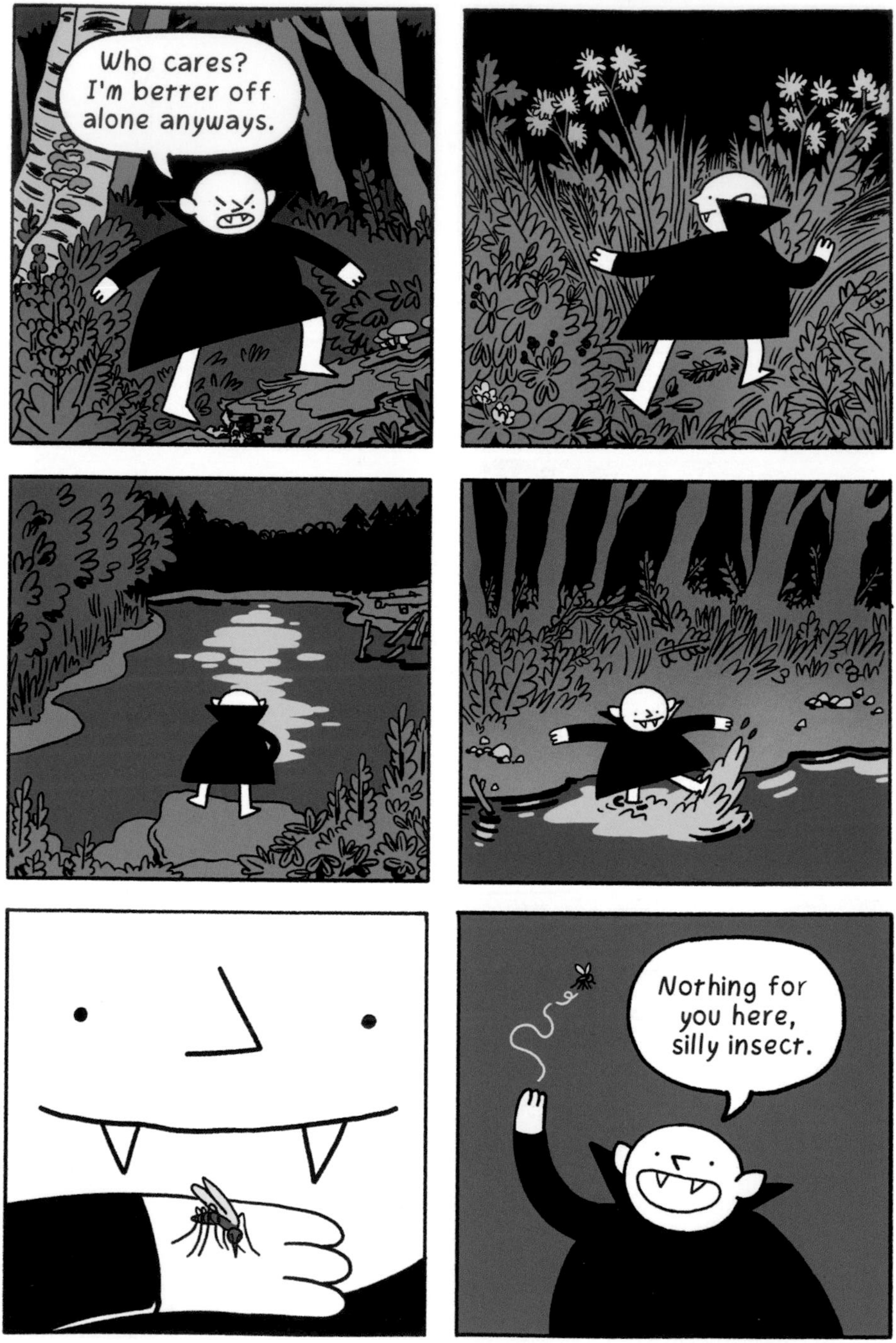
Who cares? I'm better off alone anyways.
Nothing for you here, silly insect.

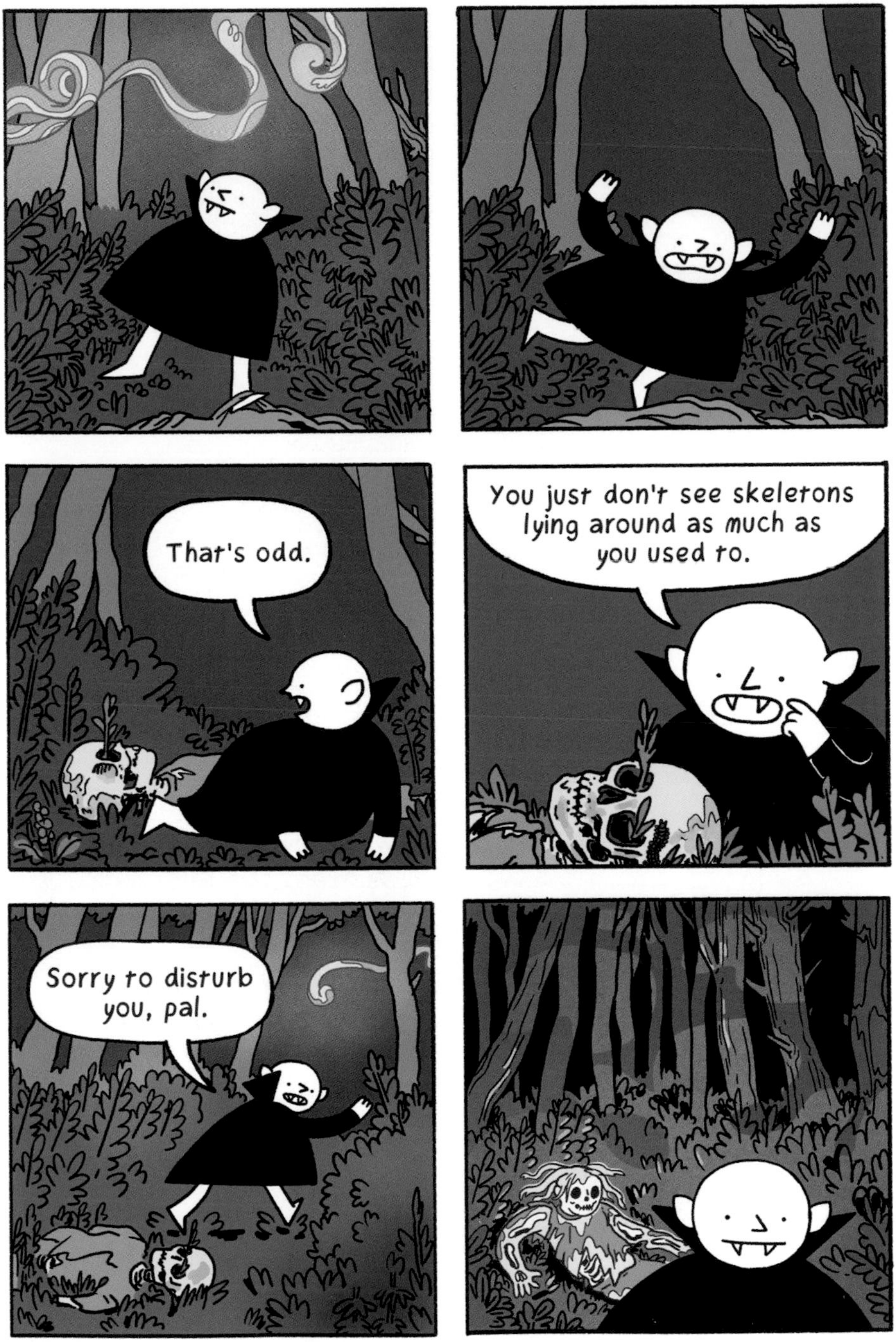
That's odd.
You just don't see skeletons lying around as much as you used to.
Sorry to disturb you, pal.

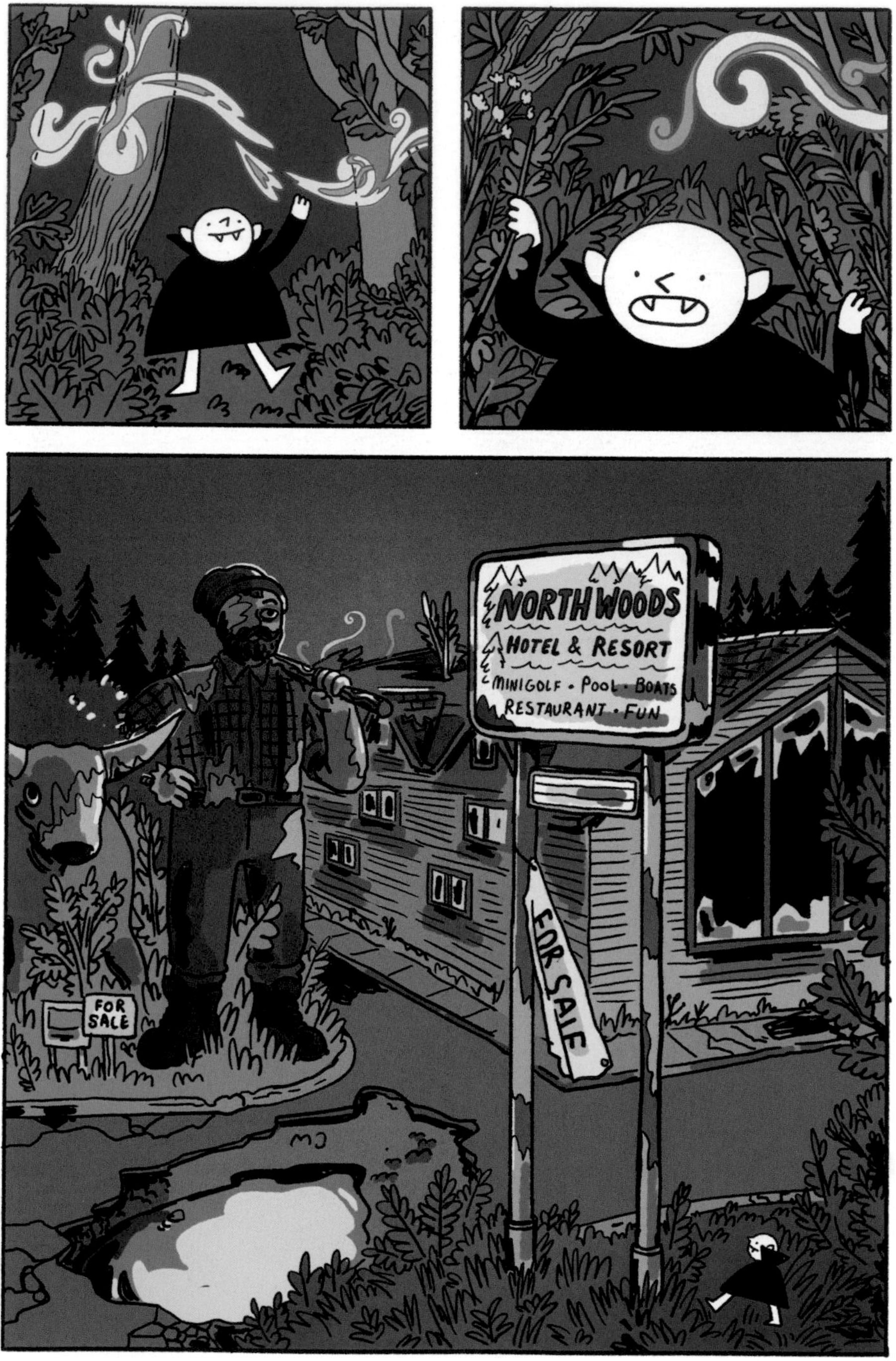
NORTH WOODS
HOTEL & RESORT
MINIGOLF • POOL • BOATS
RESTAURANT • FUN
FOR SALE
FOR SALE

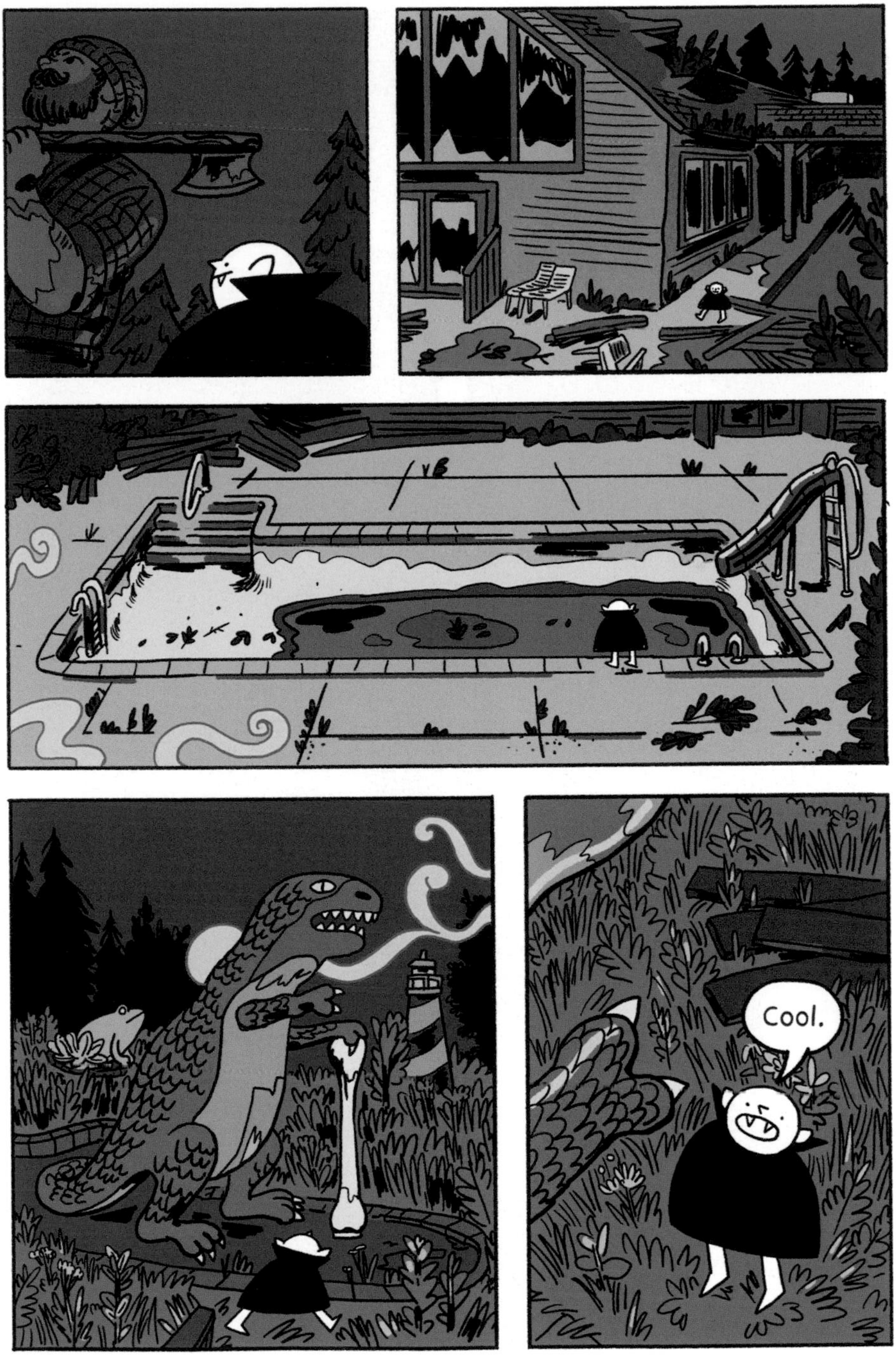
Cool.

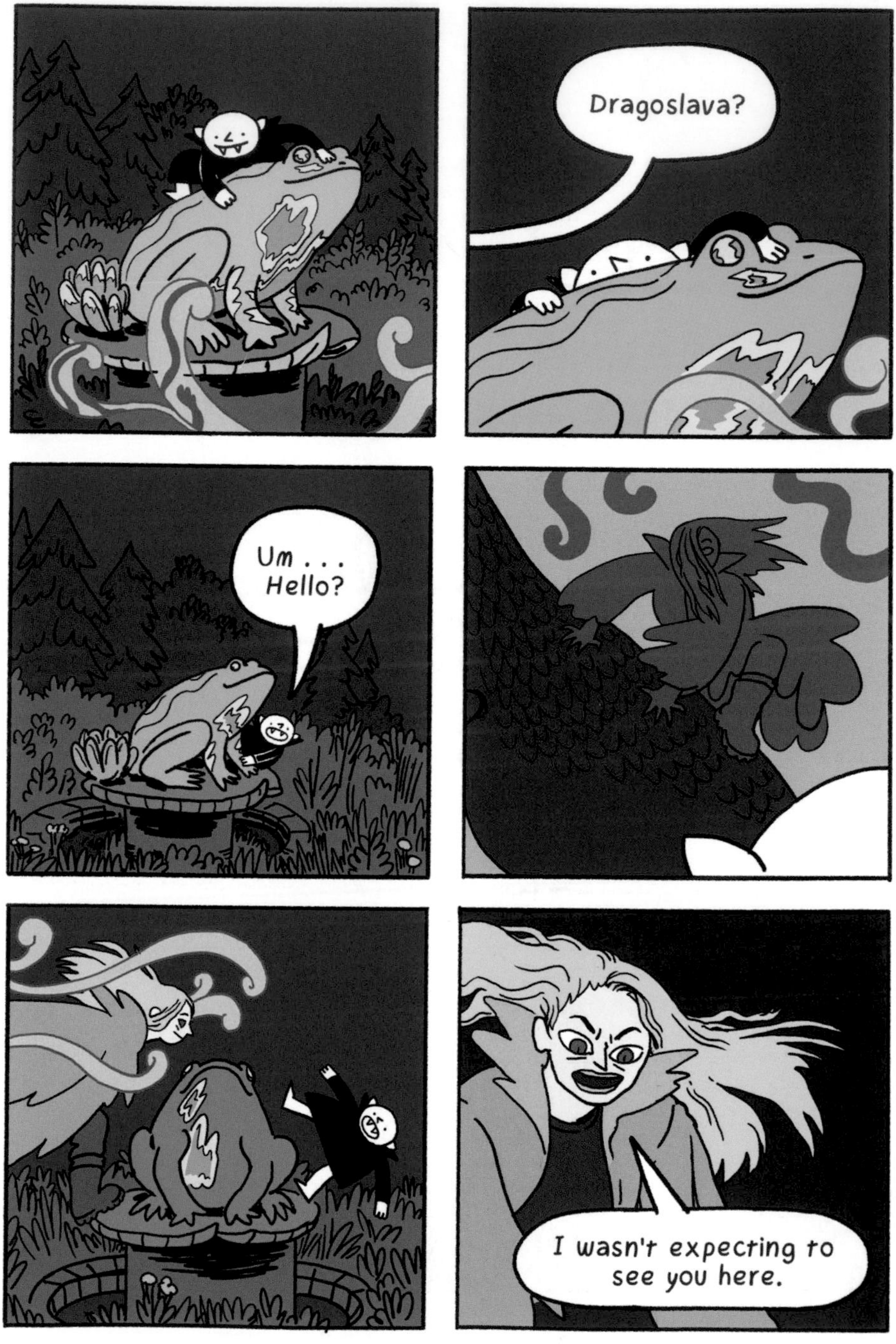
Dragoslava?
Um . . .
Hello?
I wasn't expecting to
see you here.

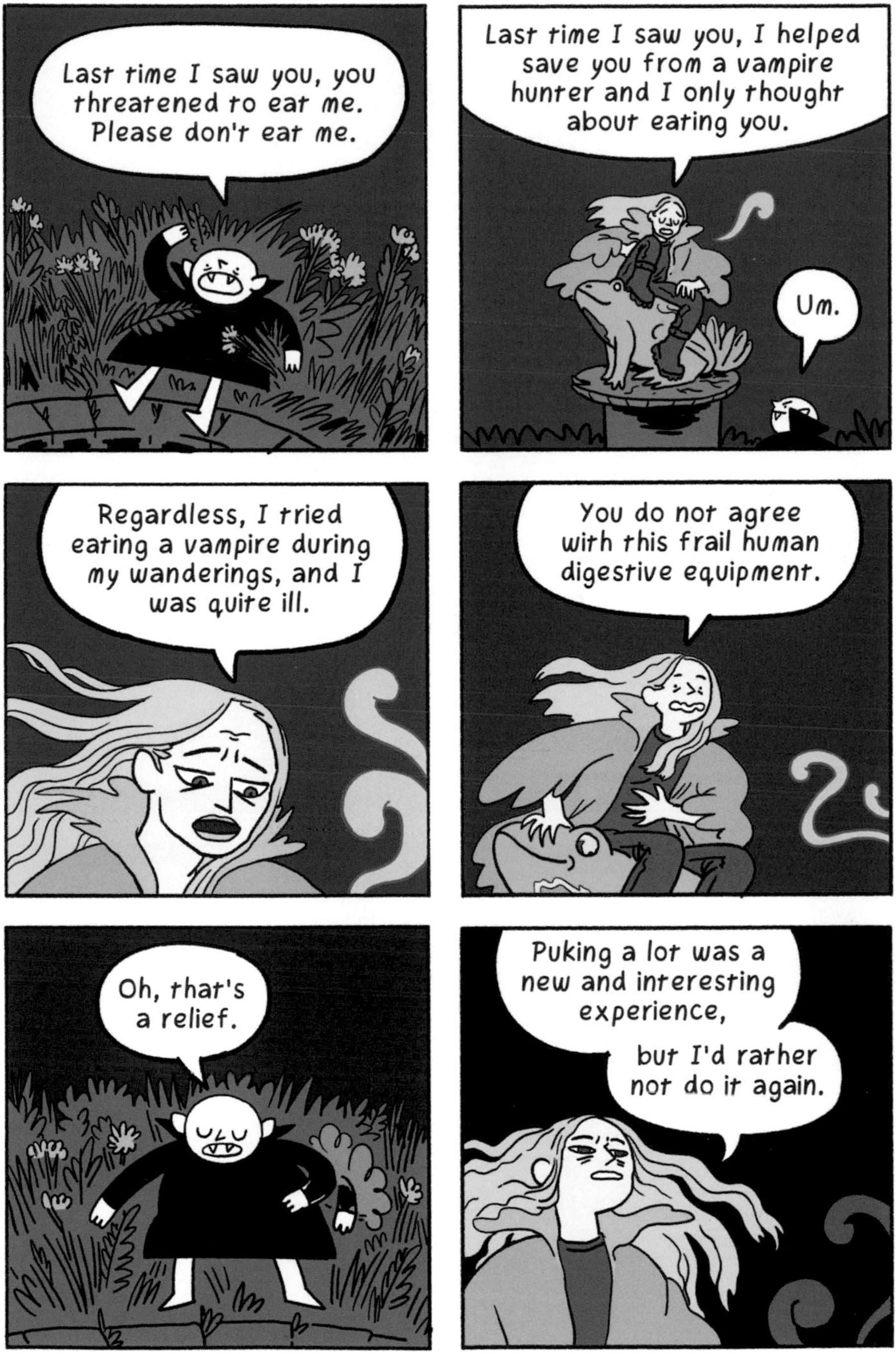
Last time I saw you, you threatened to eat me. Please don't eat me.
Last time I saw you, I helped save you from a vampire hunter and I only thought about eating you.
Um.
Regardless, I tried eating a vampire during my wanderings, and I was quite ill.
You do not agree with this frail human digestive equipment.
Oh, that's a relief.
Puking a lot was a new and interesting experience,
but I'd rather not do it again.

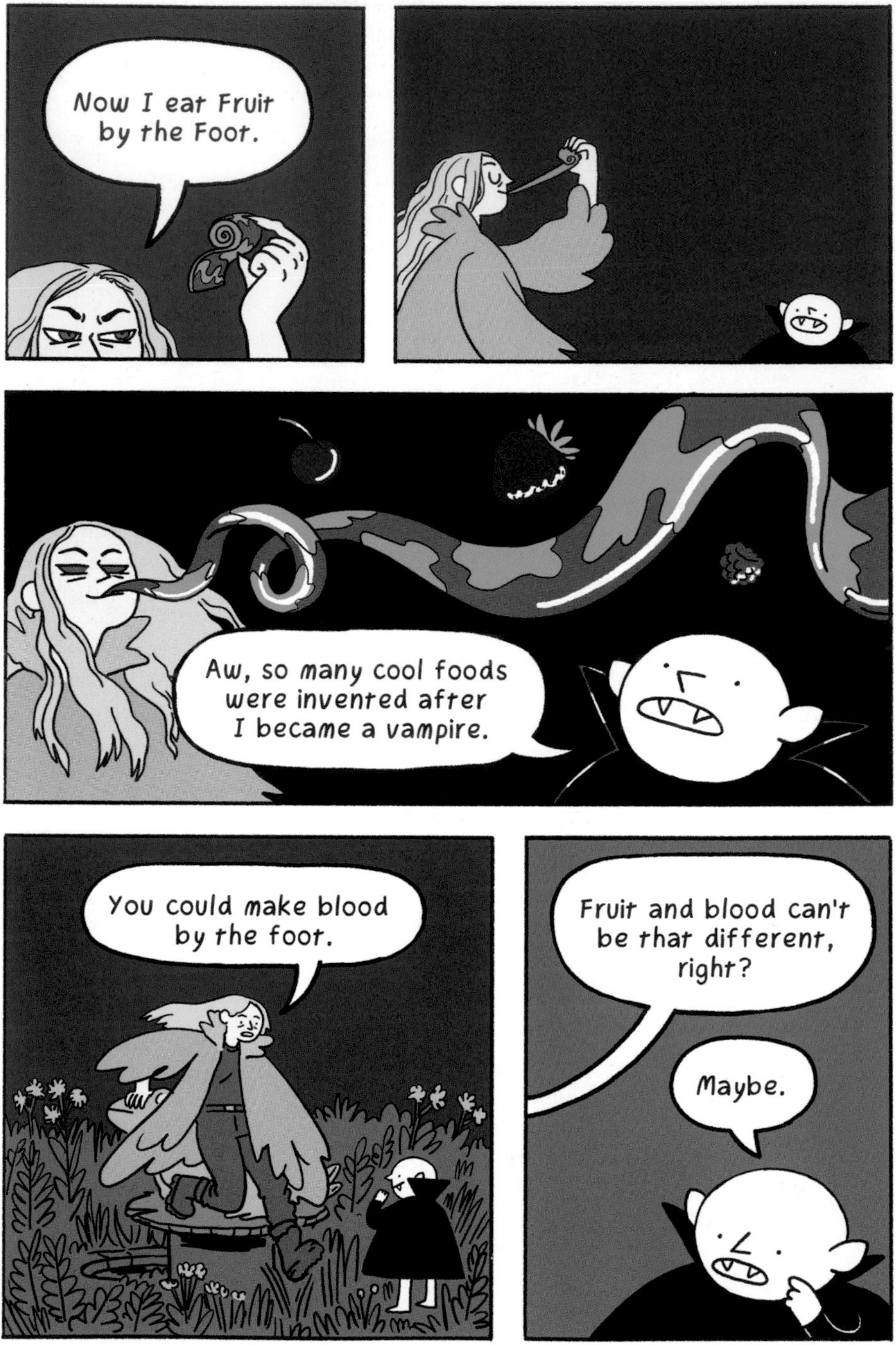
Now I eat Fruit by the Foot.
Aw, so many cool foods were invented after I became a vampire.
You could make blood by the foot.
Fruit and blood can't be that different, right?
Maybe.

So what are you doing here?

You know, just working on some complex magic.

There's going to be this alignment of planets and it's really going to give me the power I need for a particular spell.

Oh, more magic, cool.

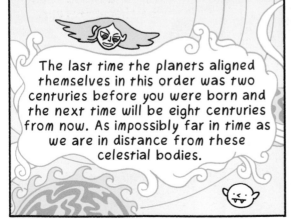

The last time the planets aligned themselves in this order was two centuries before you were born and the next time will be eight centuries from now. As impossibly far in time as we are in distance from these celestial bodies.

Yet you may well live to see that future day.

Oh. Um. Wow.

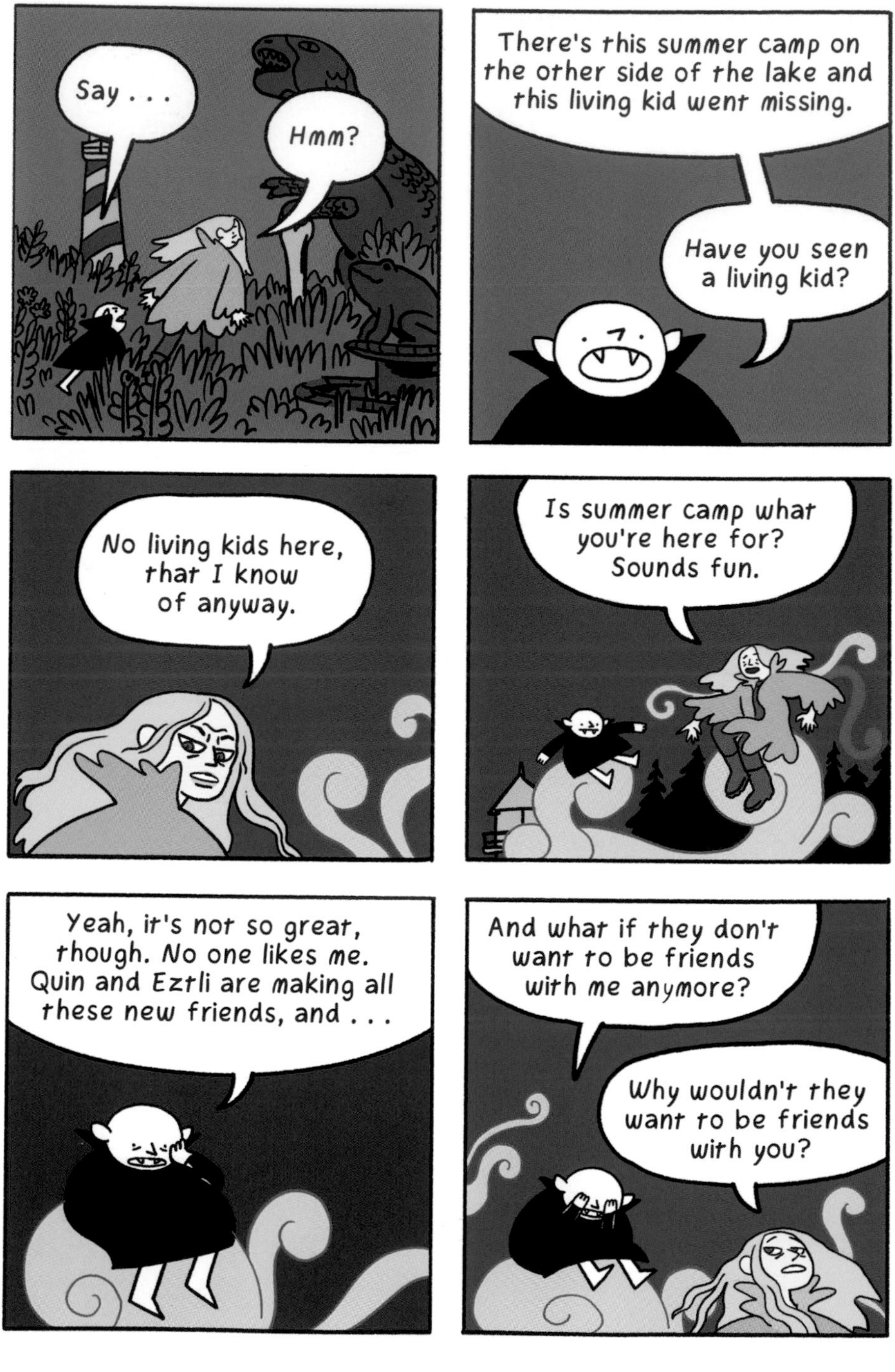
Say . . .
Hmm?
There's this summer camp on the other side of the lake and this living kid went missing.
Have you seen a living kid?
No living kids here, that I know of anyway.
Is summer camp what you're here for? Sounds fun.
Yeah, it's not so great, though. No one likes me. Quin and Eztli are making all these new friends, and . . .
And what if they don't want to be friends with me anymore?
Why wouldn't they want to be friends with you?

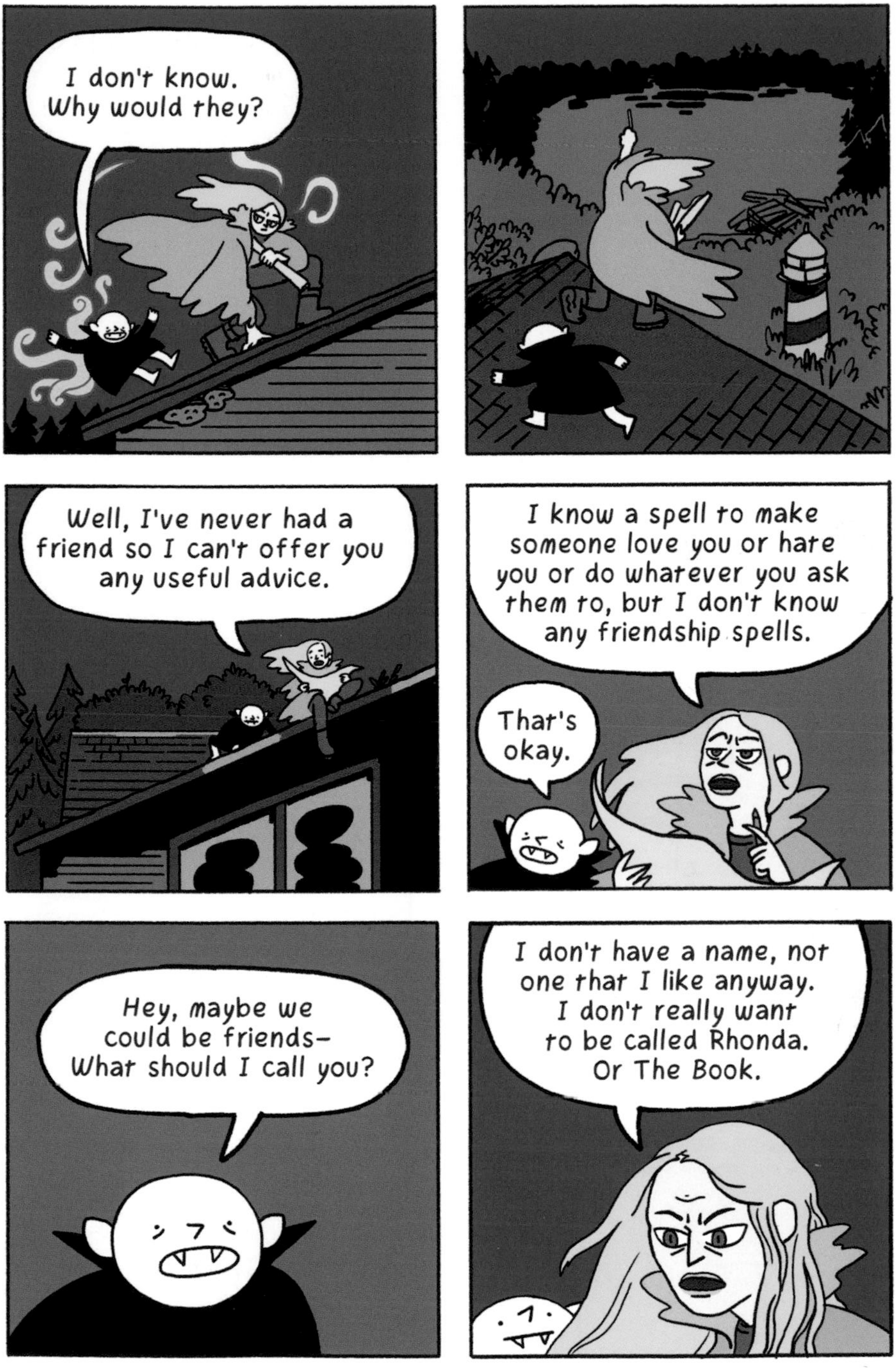

I don't know. Why would they?
Well, I've never had a friend so I can't offer you any useful advice.
I know a spell to make someone love you or hate you or do whatever you ask them to, but I don't know any friendship spells.
That's okay.
Hey, maybe we could be friends– What should I call you?
I don't have a name, not one that I like anyway. I don't really want to be called Rhonda. Or The Book.

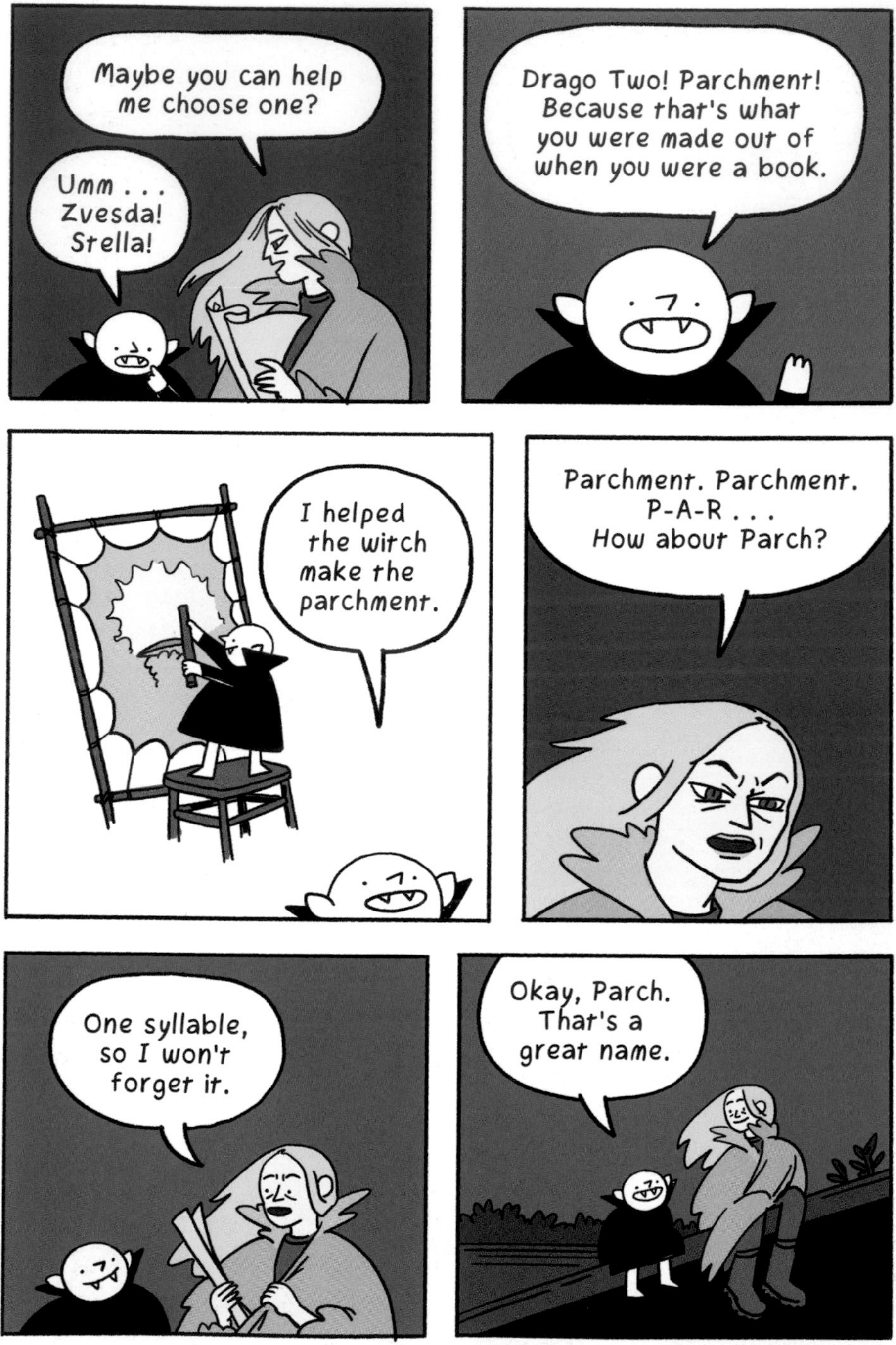
Maybe you can help me choose one?
Umm . . . Zvesda! Stella!
Drago Two! Parchment! Because that's what you were made out of when you were a book.
I helped the witch make the parchment.
Parchment. Parchment. P-A-R . . . How about Parch?
One syllable, so I won't forget it.
Okay, Parch. That's a great name.

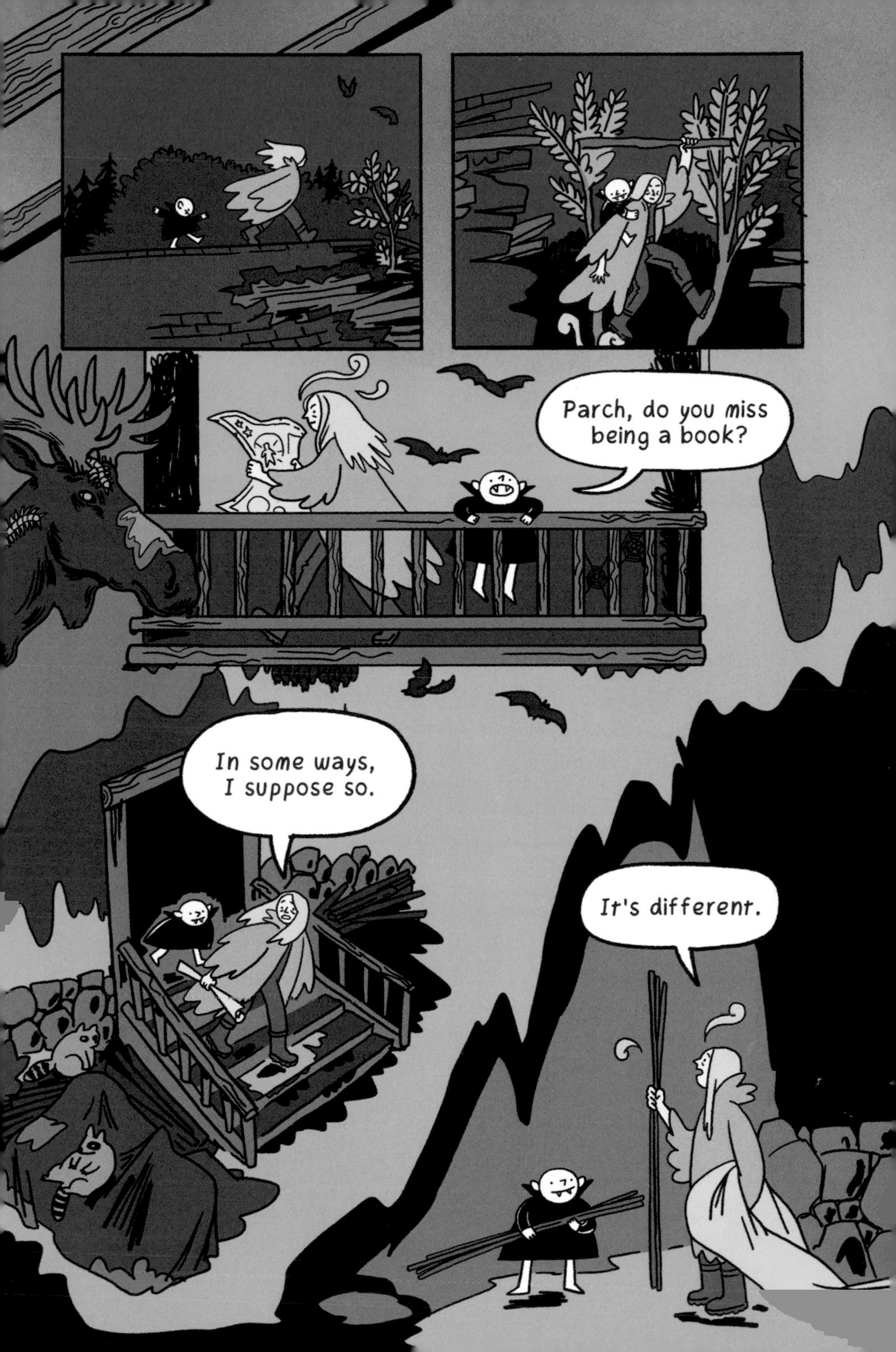

Parch, do you miss being a book?
In some ways, I suppose so.
It's different.

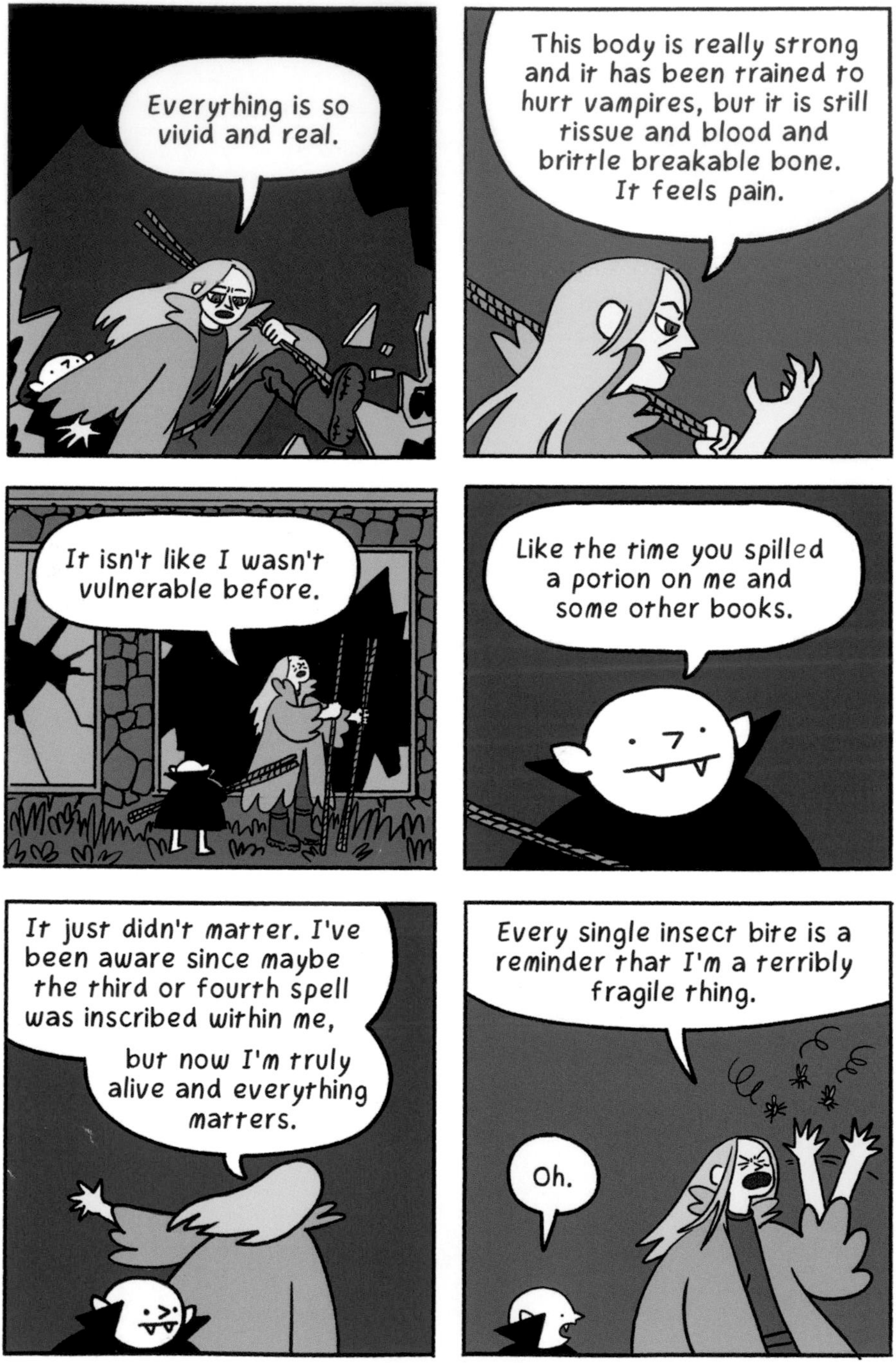
Everything is so vivid and real.
This body is really strong and it has been trained to hurt vampires, but it is still tissue and blood and brittle breakable bone. It feels pain.
It isn't like I wasn't vulnerable before.
Like the time you spilled a potion on me and some other books.
It just didn't matter. I've been aware since maybe the third or fourth spell was inscribed within me,
but now I'm truly alive and everything matters.
Every single insect bite is a reminder that I'm a terribly fragile thing.
Oh.

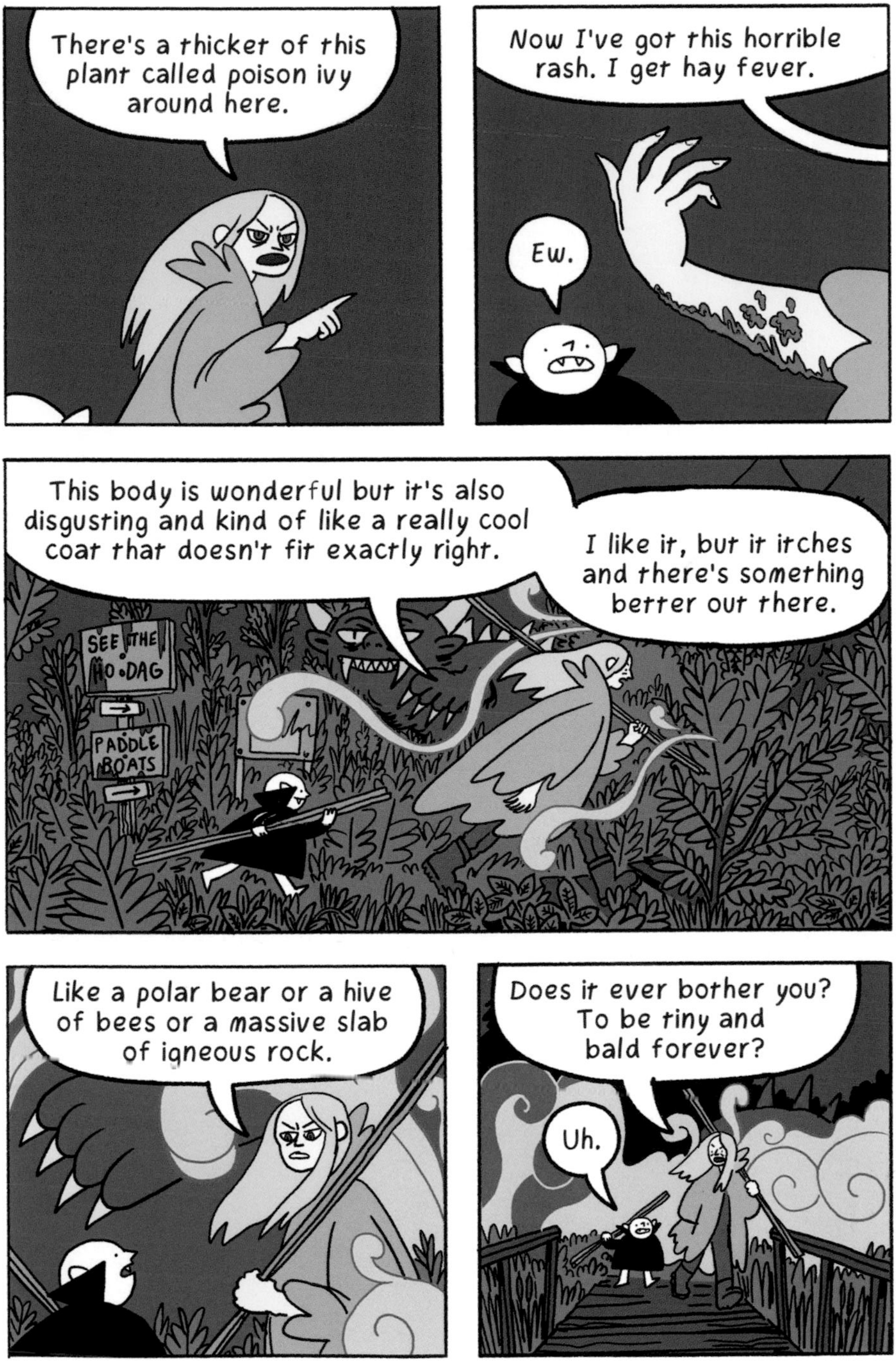
There's a thicket of this plant called poison ivy around here.
Now I've got this horrible rash. I get hay fever.
Ew.
This body is wonderful but it's also disgusting and kind of like a really cool coat that doesn't fit exactly right.
I like it, but it itches and there's something better out there.
SEE THE HO.DAG
PADDLE BOATS
Like a polar bear or a hive of bees or a massive slab of igneous rock.
Does it ever bother you? To be tiny and bald forever?
Uh.

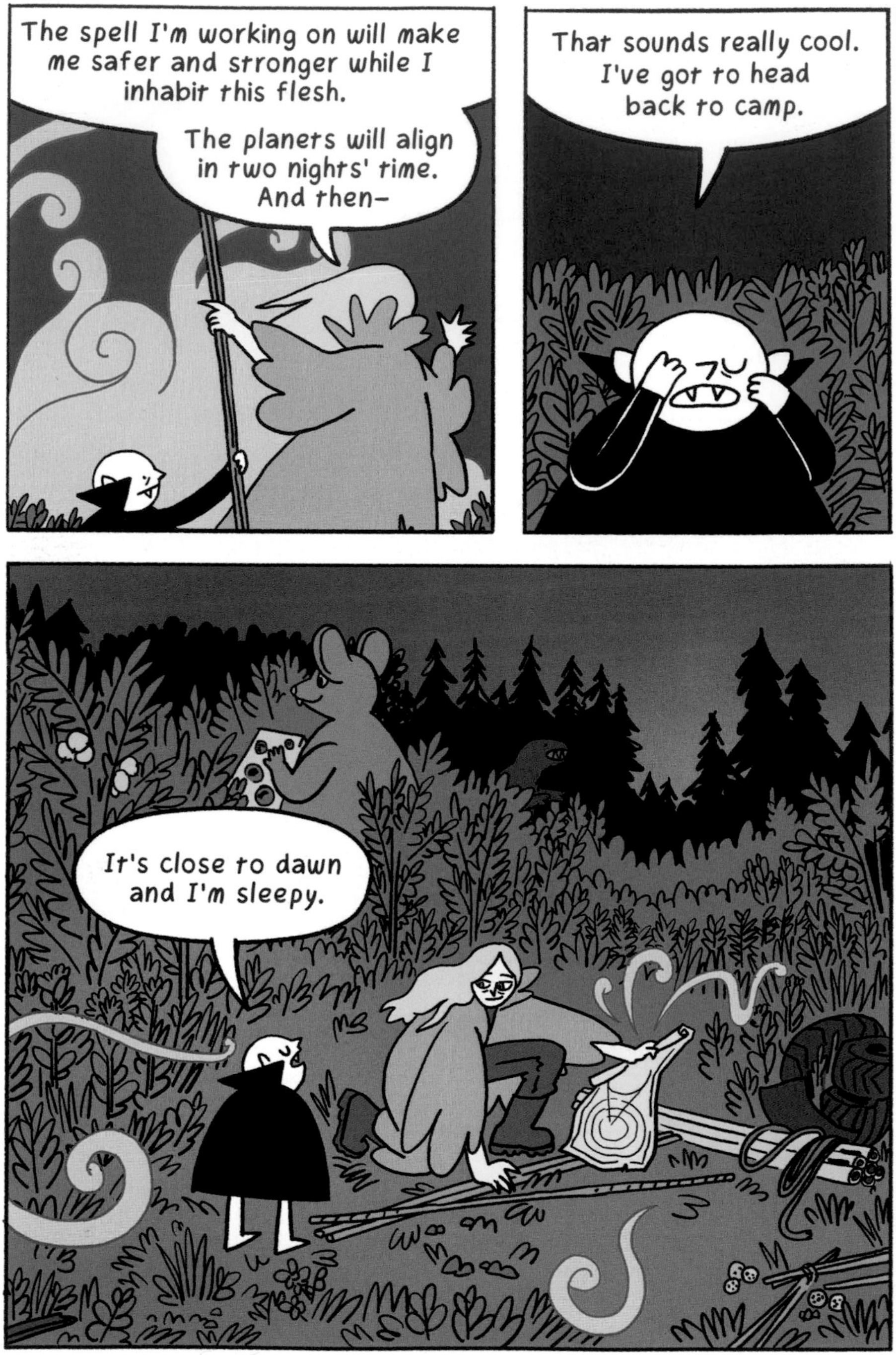
The spell I'm working on will make me safer and stronger while I inhabit this flesh.
The planets will align in two nights' time. And then-
That sounds really cool. I've got to head back to camp.
It's close to dawn and I'm sleepy.

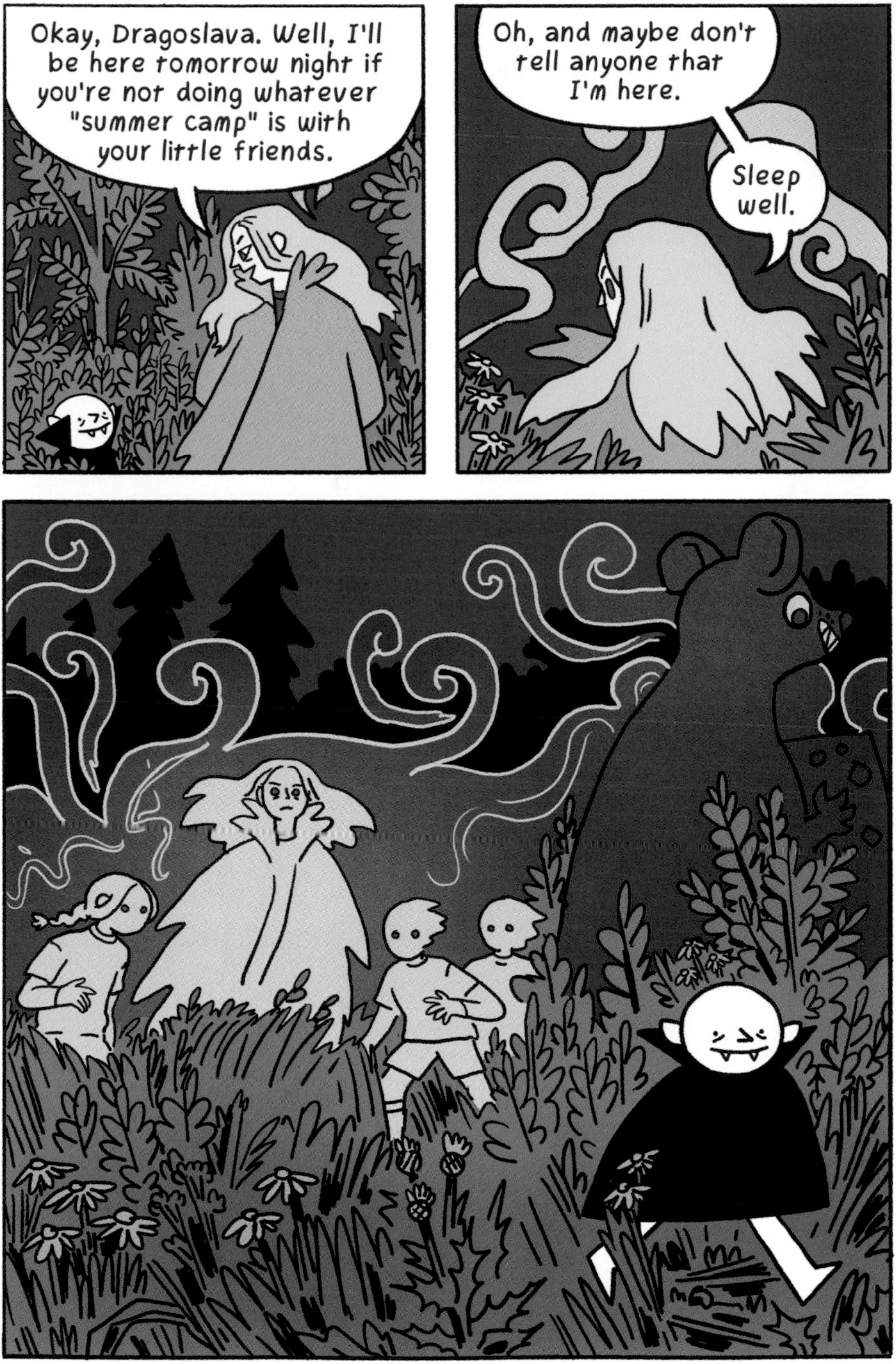
Okay, Dragoslava. Well, I'll be here tomorrow night if you're not doing whatever "summer camp" is with your little friends.
Oh, and maybe don't tell anyone that I'm here.
Sleep well.

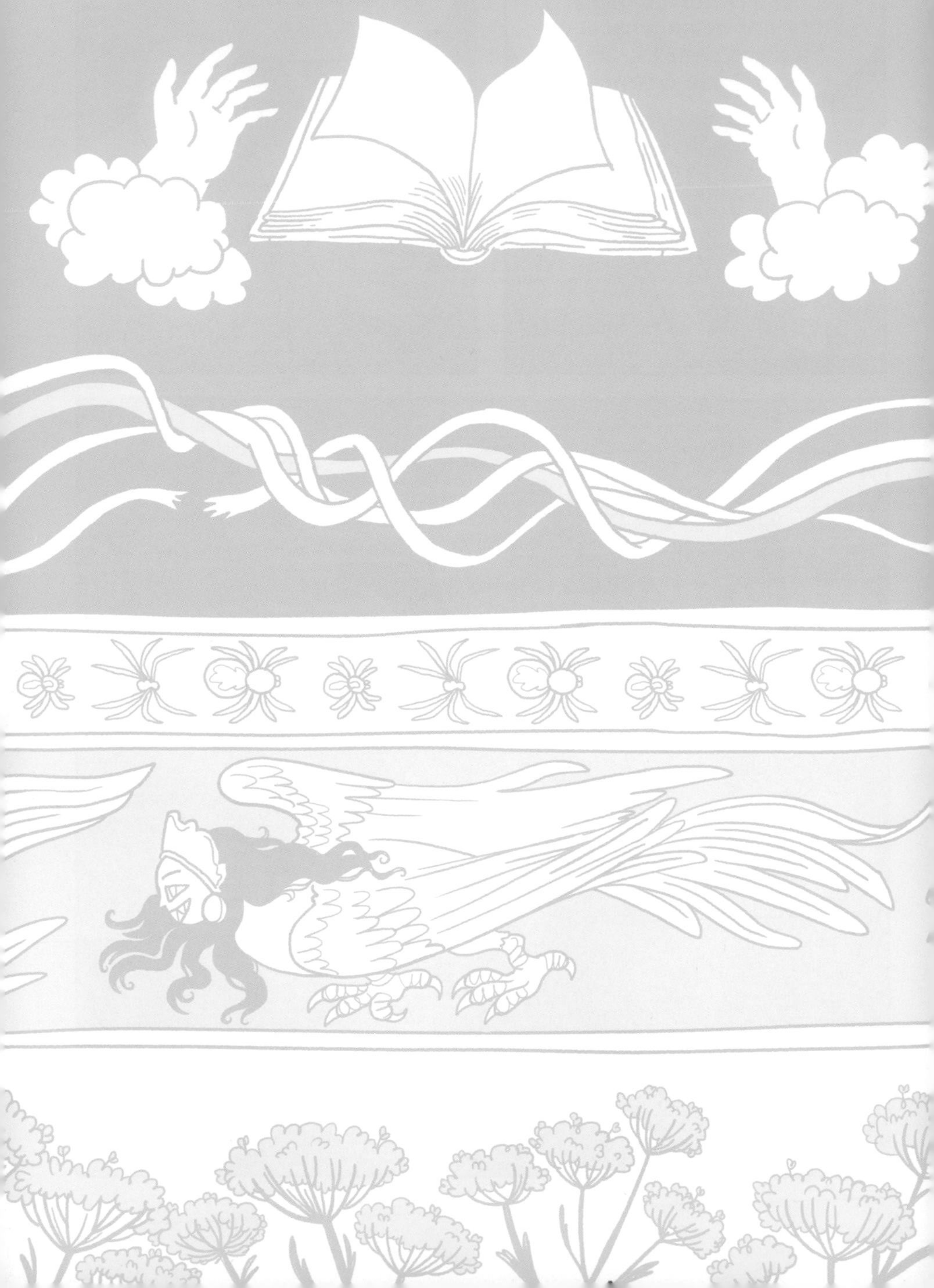

CHAPTER
FOUR

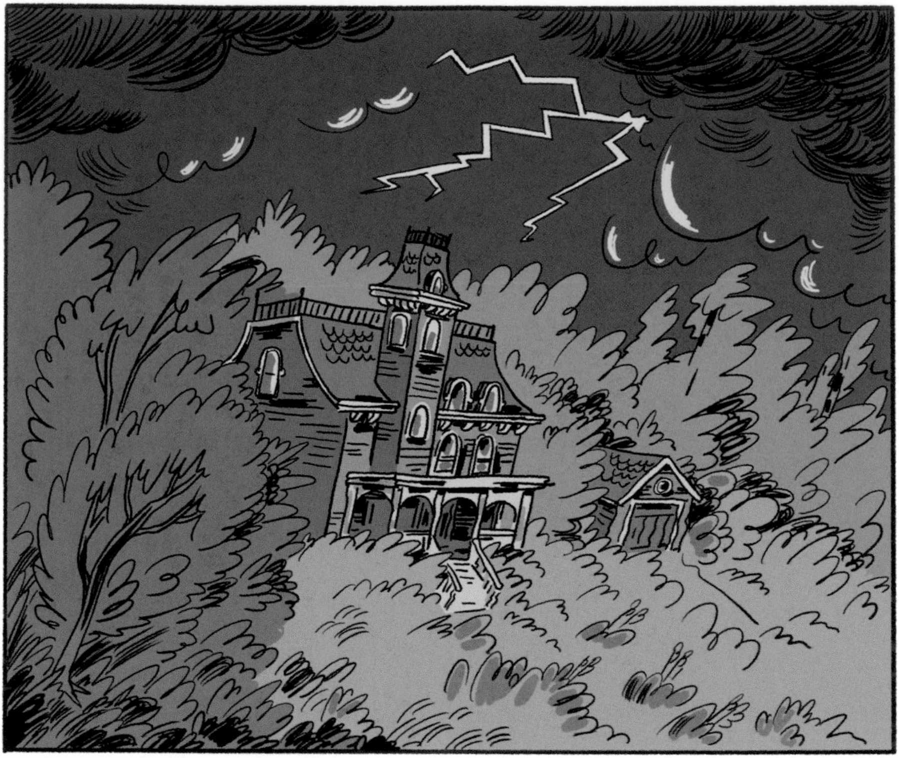

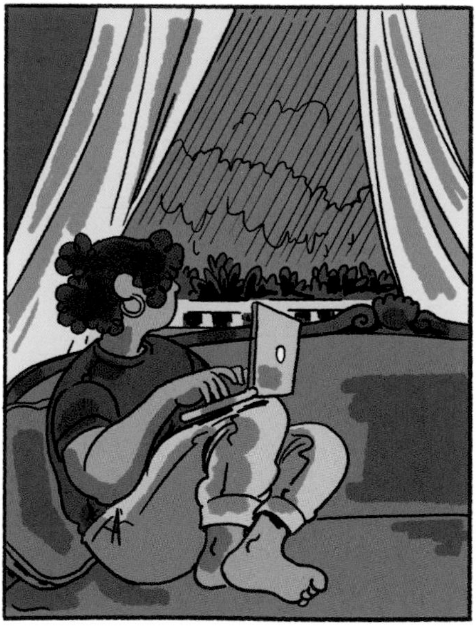

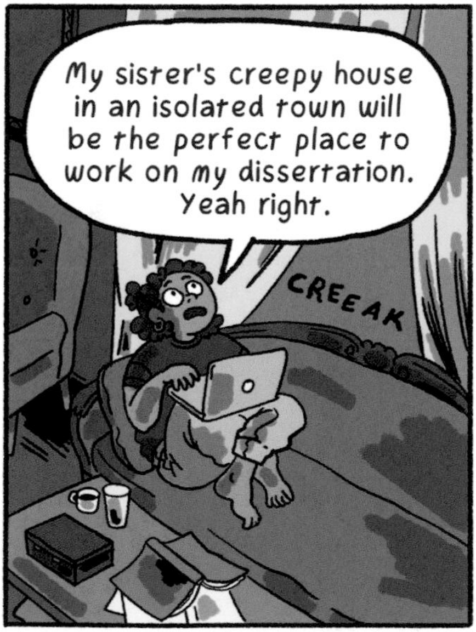
My sister's creepy house in an isolated town will be the perfect place to work on my dissertation. Yeah right.
CREEAK

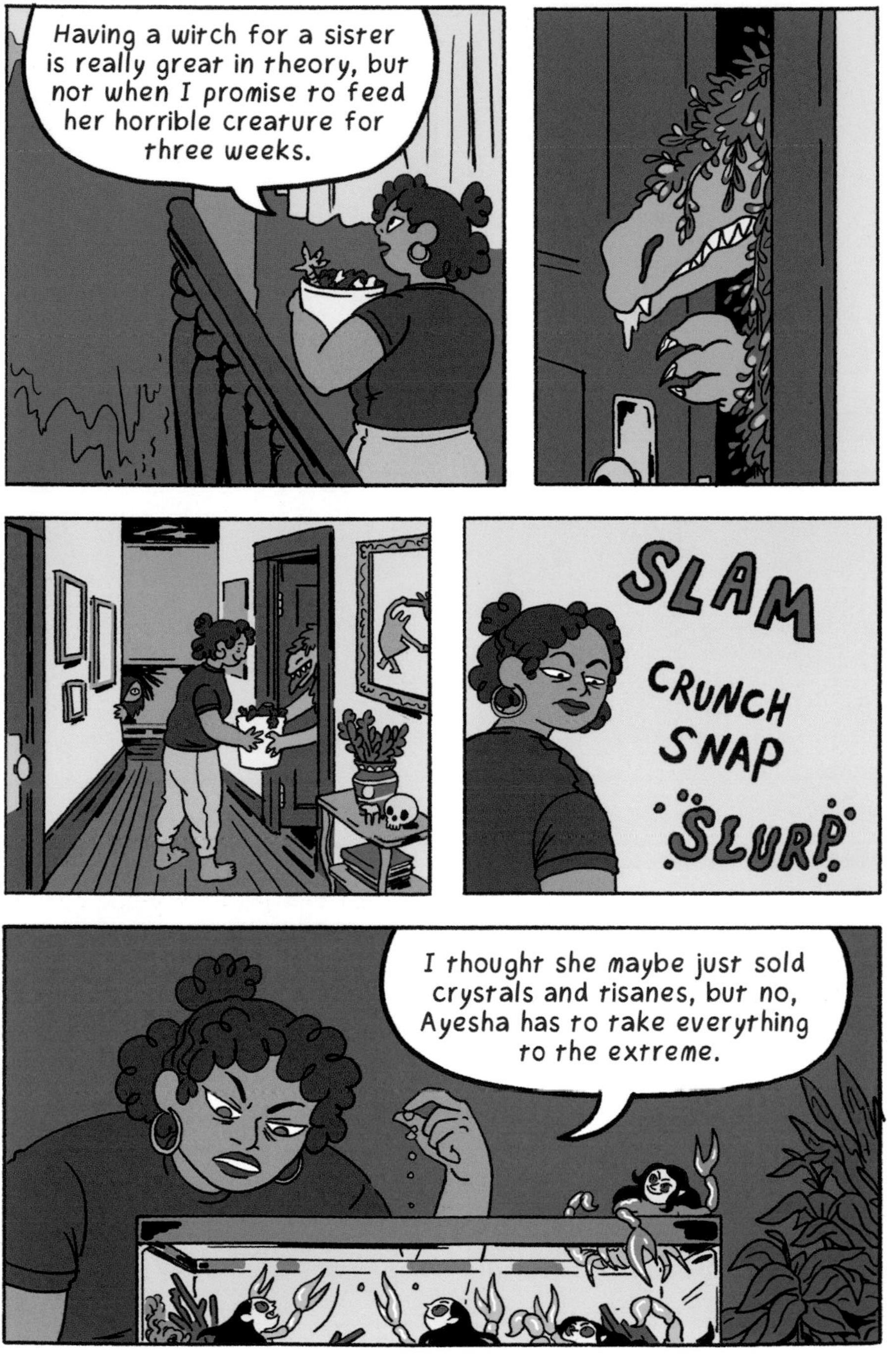
Having a witch for a sister is really great in theory, but not when I promise to feed her horrible creature for three weeks.
SLAM
CRUNCH
SNAP
SLURP
I thought she maybe just sold crystals and tisanes, but no, Ayesha has to take everything to the extreme.

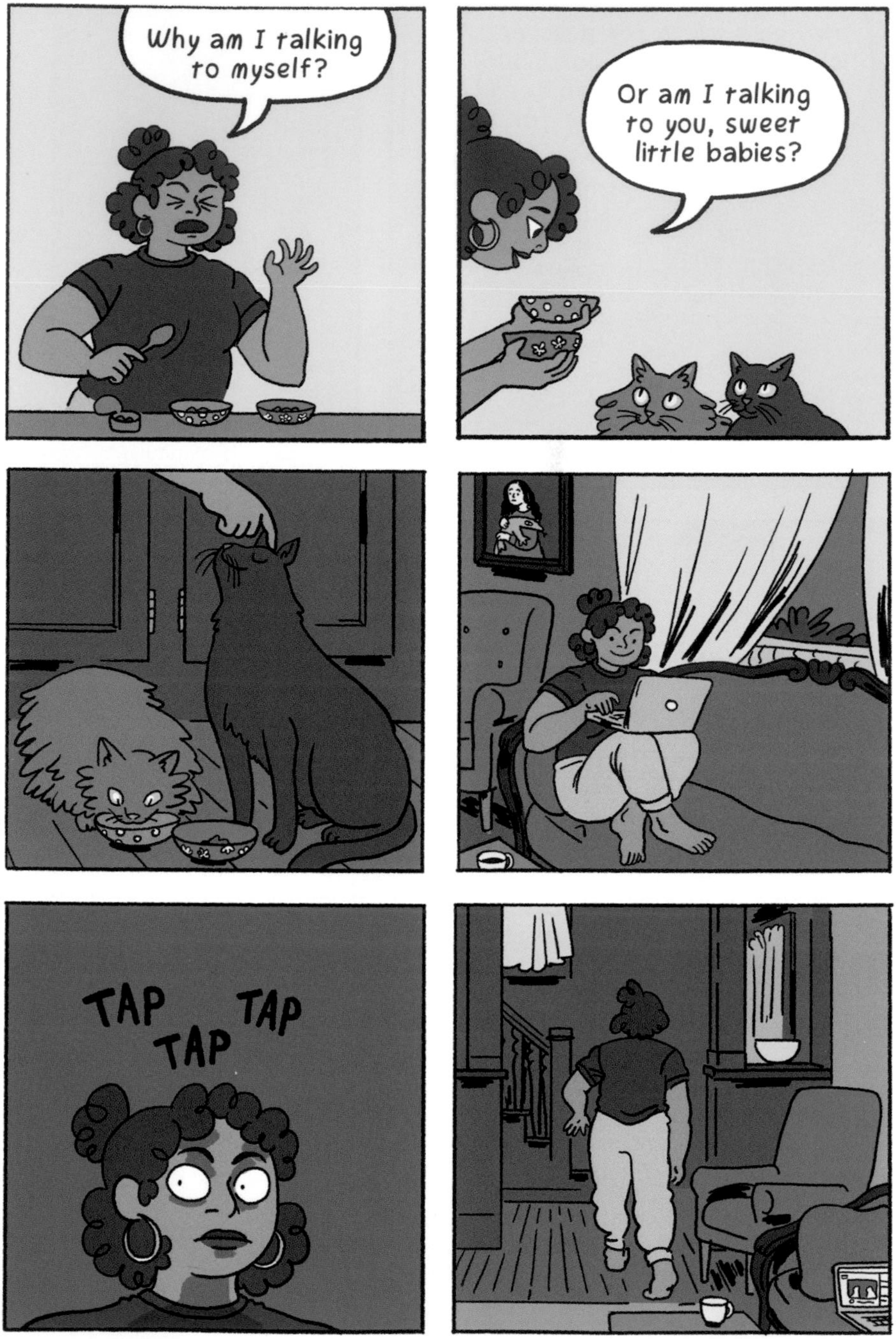
Why am I talking to myself?
Or am I talking to you, sweet little babies?
TAP
TAP
TAP

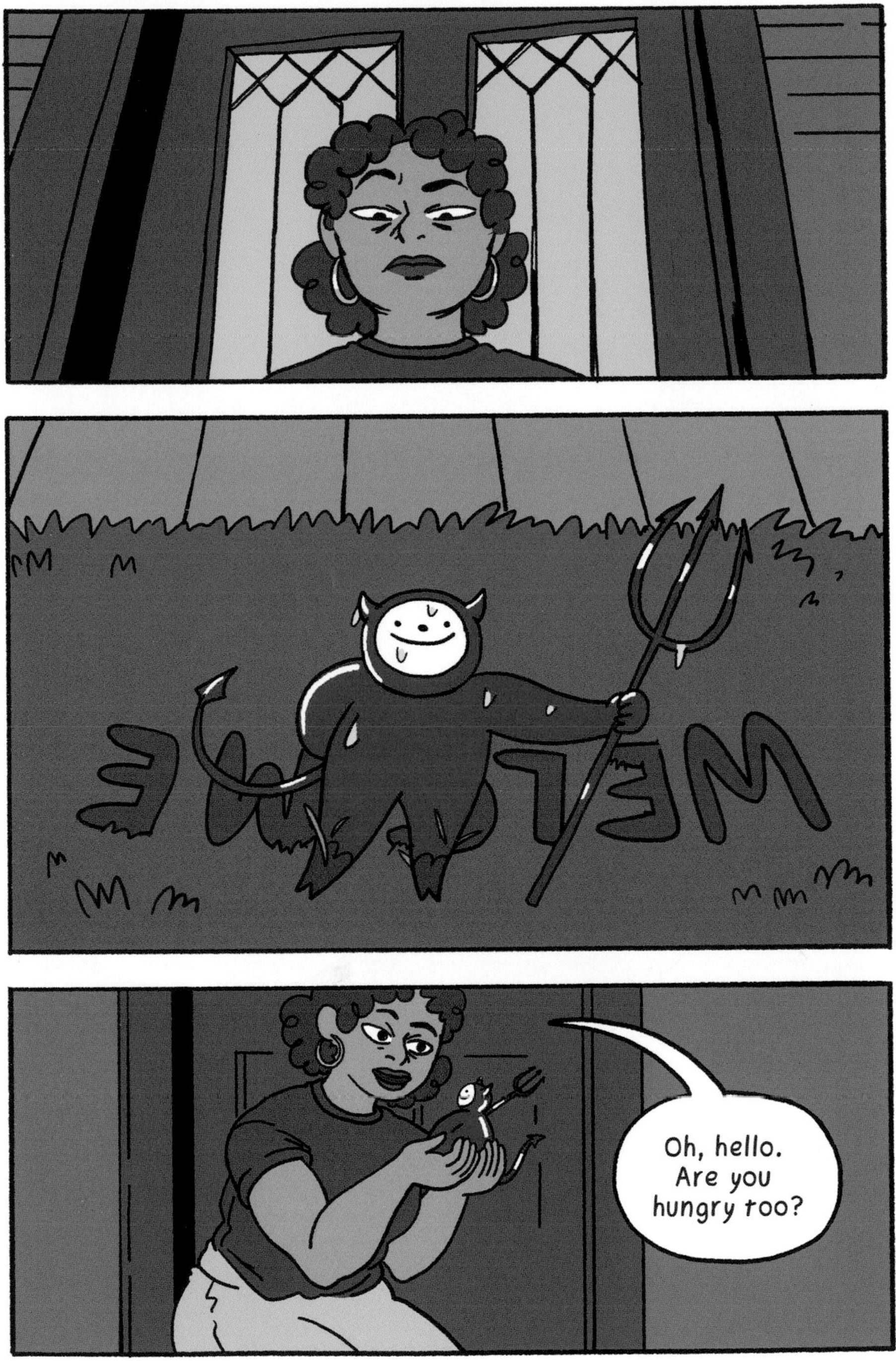
Oh, hello.
Are you
hungry too?

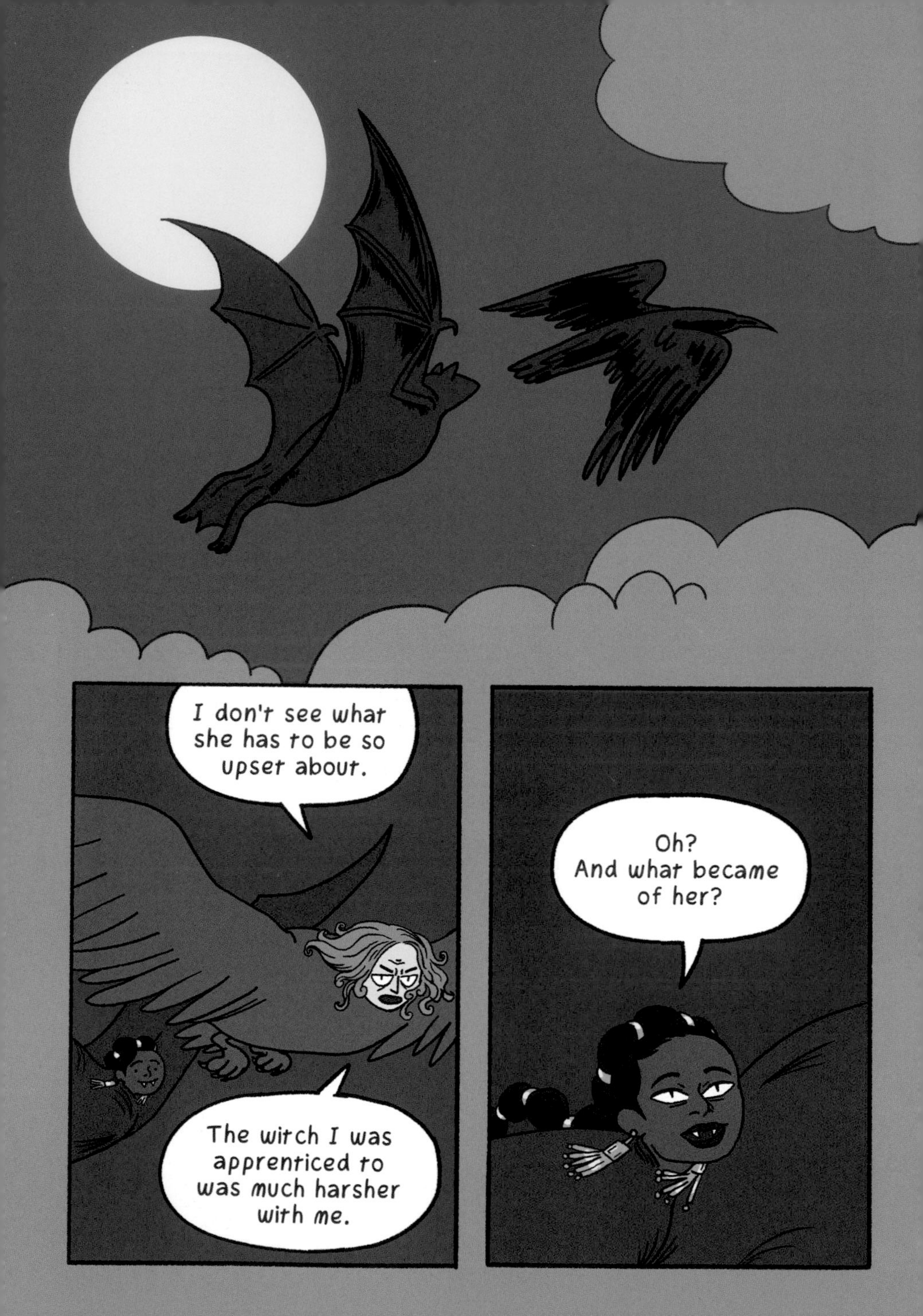
I don't see what she has to be so upset about.
The witch I was apprenticed to was much harsher with me.
Oh? And what became of her?

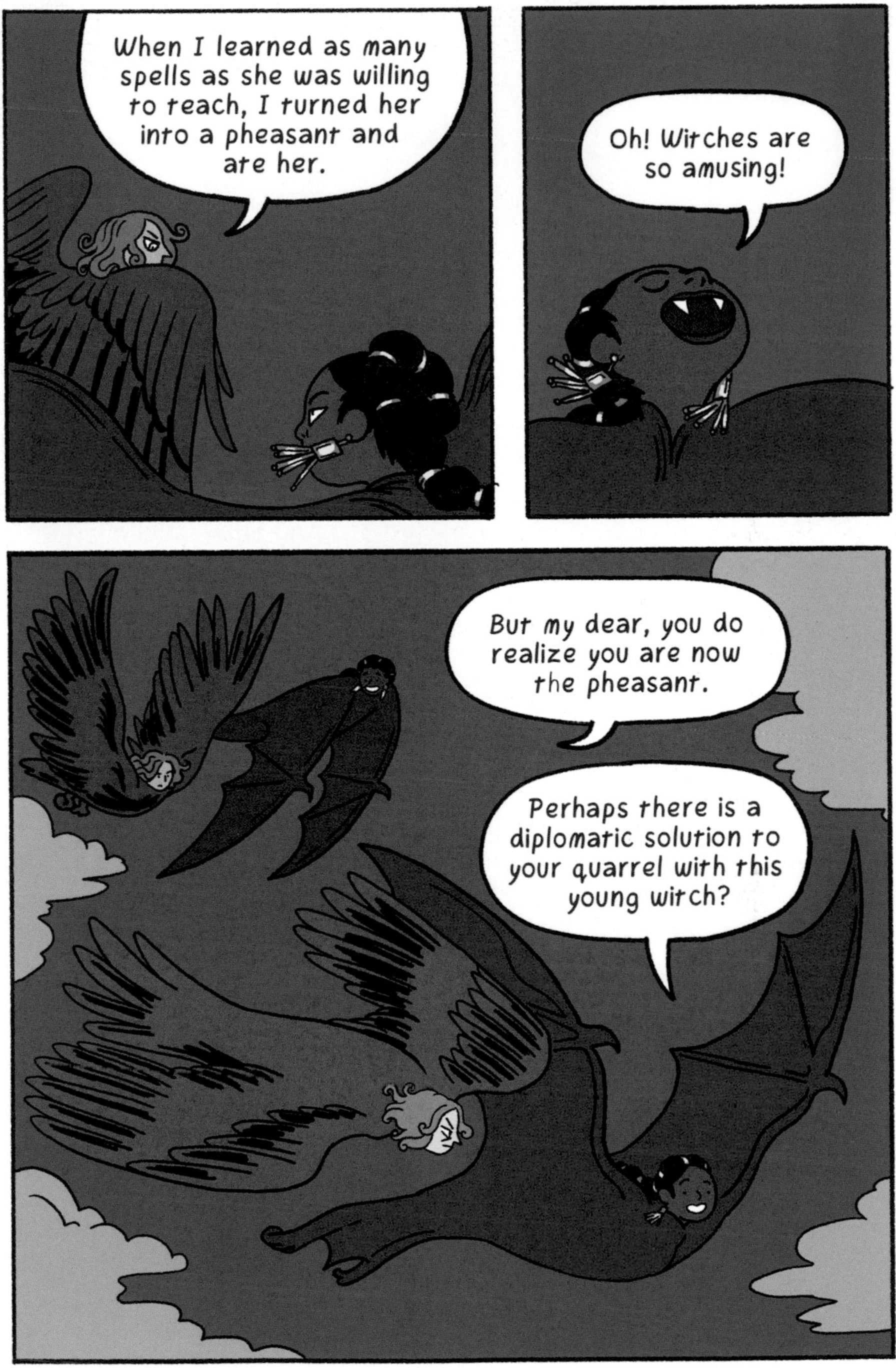
When I learned as many spells as she was willing to teach, I turned her into a pheasant and ate her.
Oh! Witches are so amusing!
But my dear, you do realize you are now the pheasant.
Perhaps there is a diplomatic solution to your quarrel with this young witch?

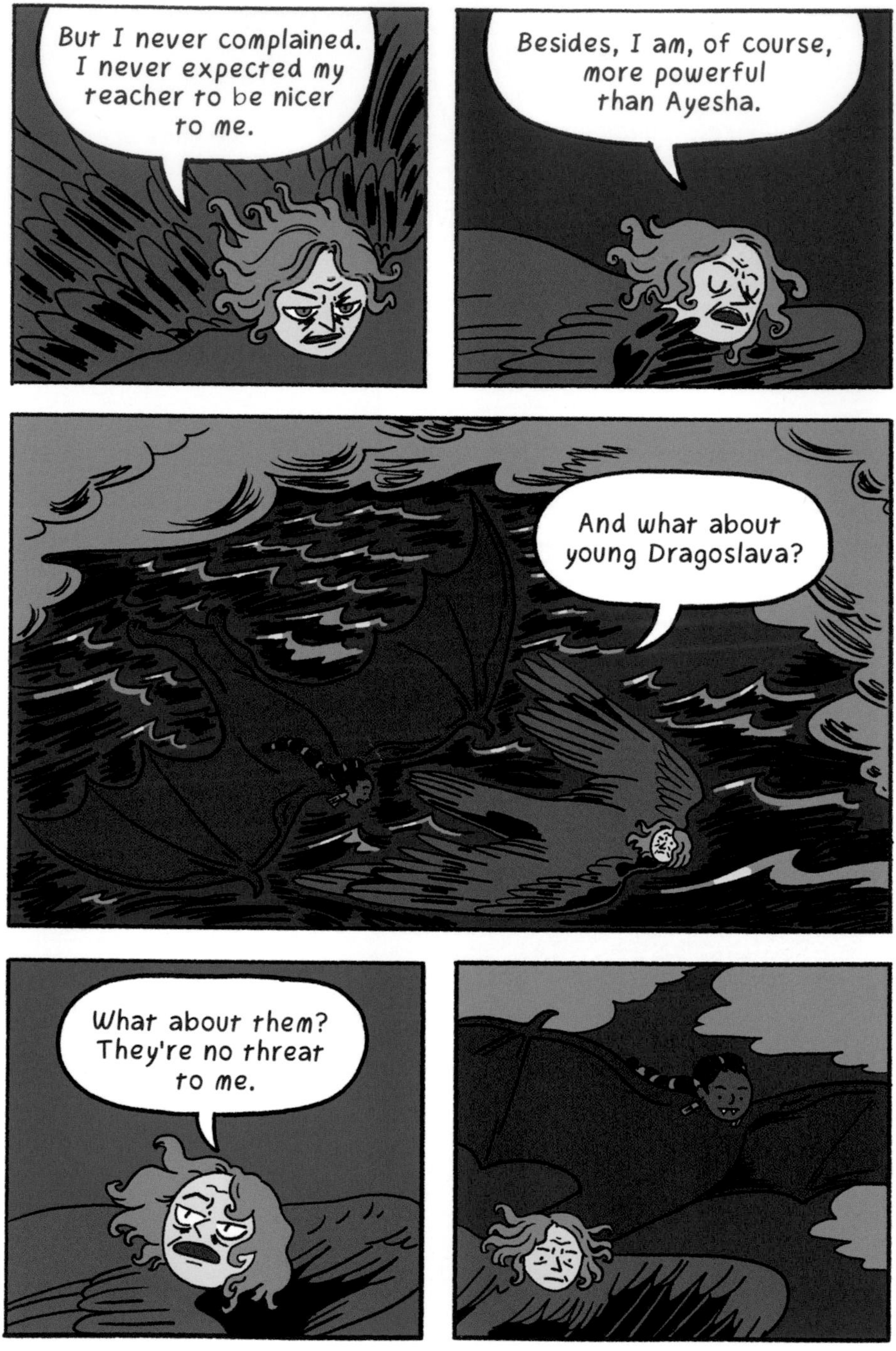
But I never complained. I never expected my teacher to be nicer to me.
Besides, I am, of course, more powerful than Ayesha.
And what about young Dragoslava?
What about them? They're no threat to me.

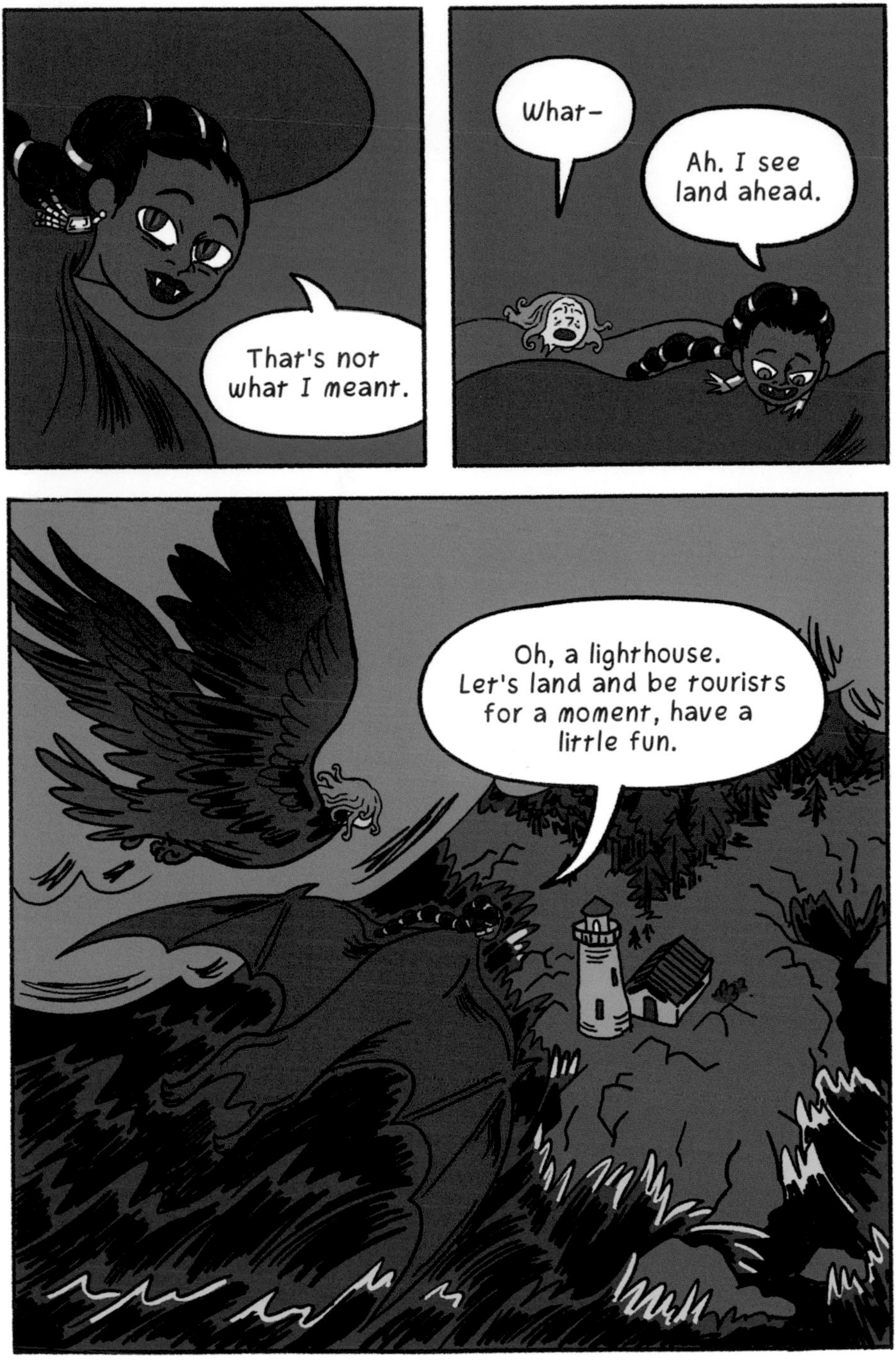
That's not what I meant.
What-
Ah. I see land ahead.
Oh, a lighthouse. Let's land and be tourists for a moment, have a little fun.

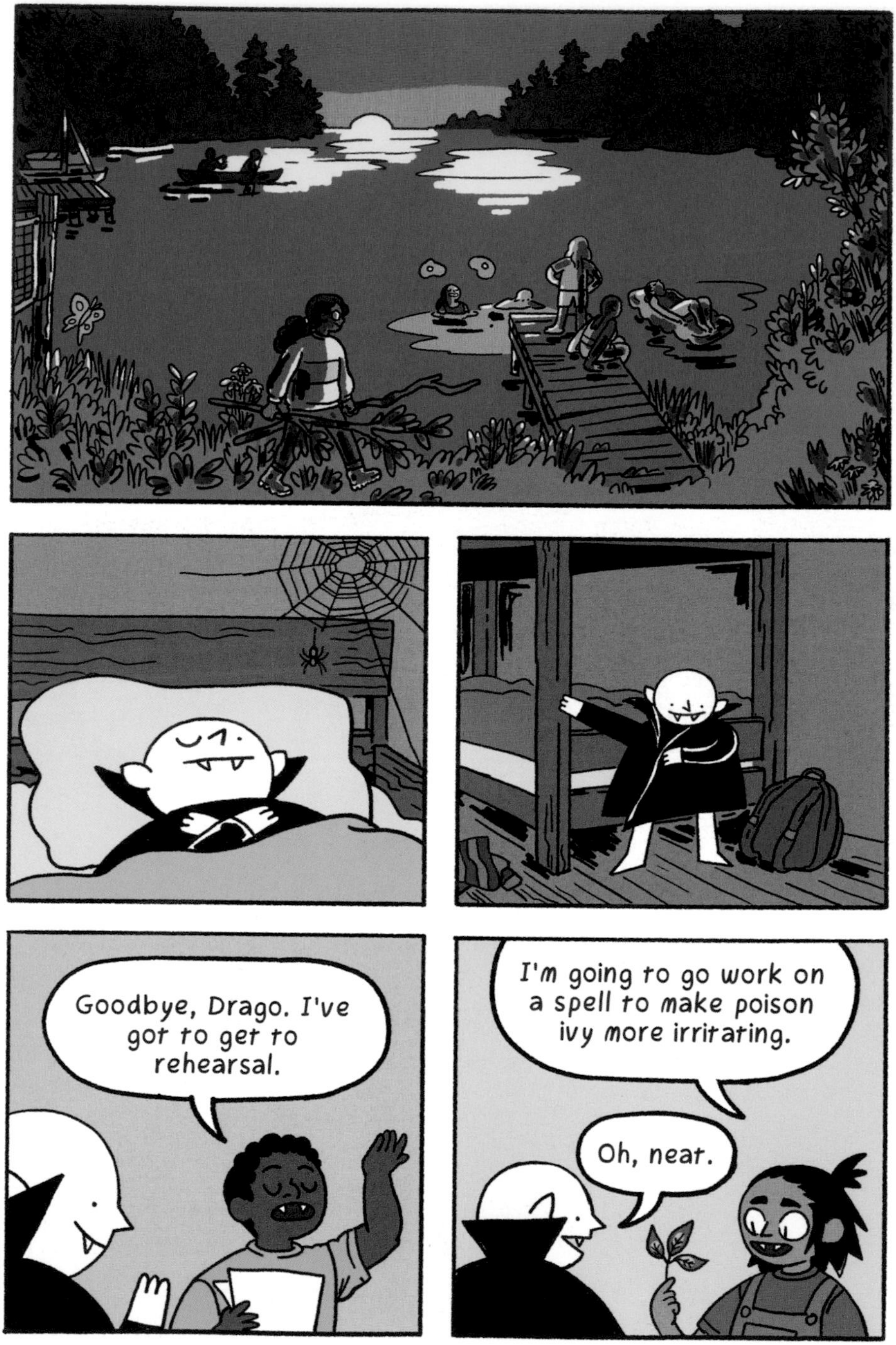

Goodbye, Drago. I've got to get to rehearsal.
I'm going to go work on a spell to make poison ivy more irritating.
Oh, neat.

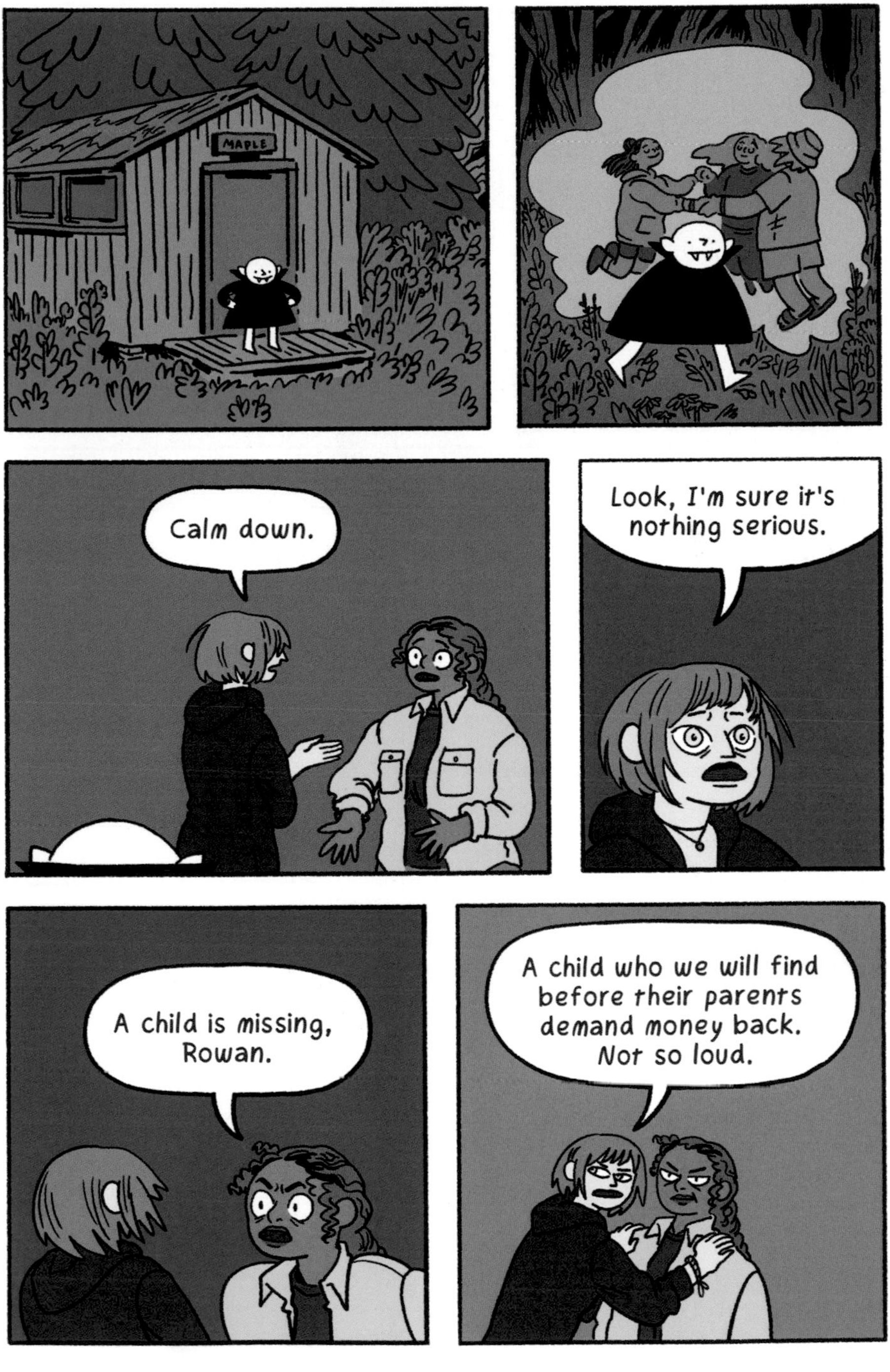
MAPLE
Calm down.
Look, I'm sure it's nothing serious.
A child is missing, Rowan.
A child who we will find before their parents demand money back. Not so loud.

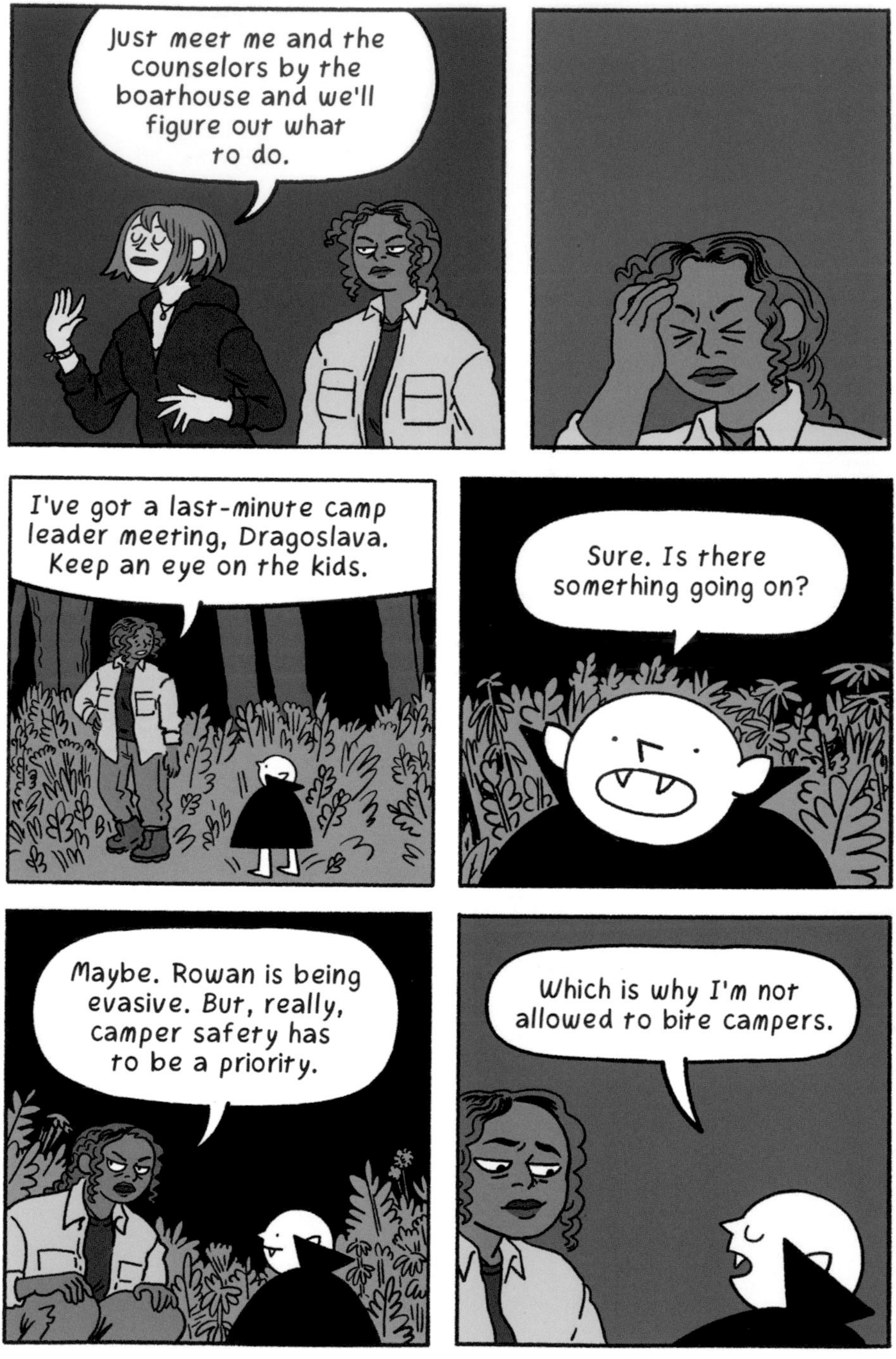
Just meet me and the counselors by the boathouse and we'll figure out what to do.
I've got a last-minute camp leader meeting, Dragoslava. Keep an eye on the kids.
Sure. Is there something going on?
Maybe. Rowan is being evasive. But, really, camper safety has to be a priority.
Which is why I'm not allowed to bite campers.

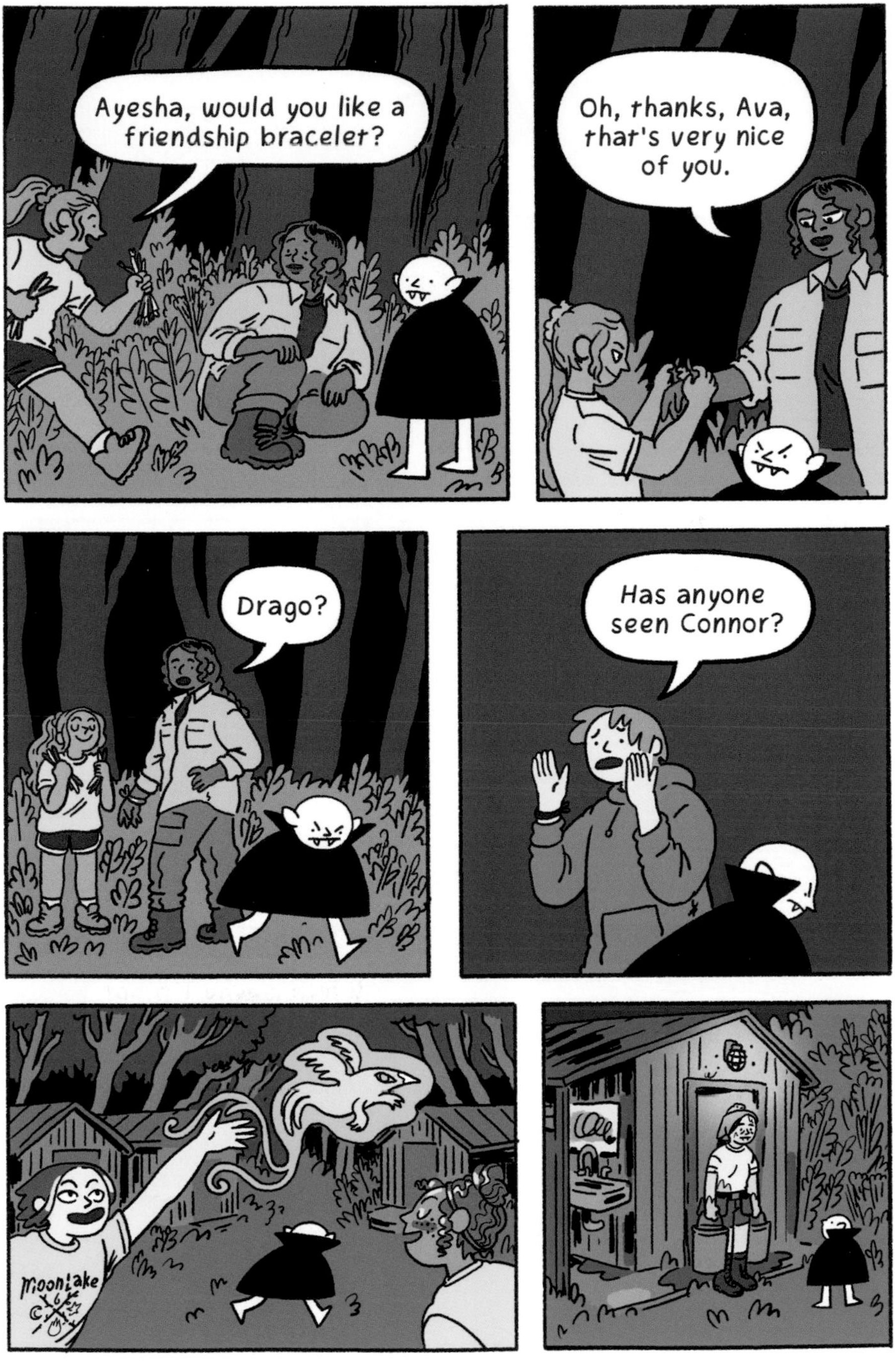
Ayesha, would you like a friendship bracelet?
Oh, thanks, Ava, that's very nice of you.
Drago?
Has anyone seen Connor?
MoonLake

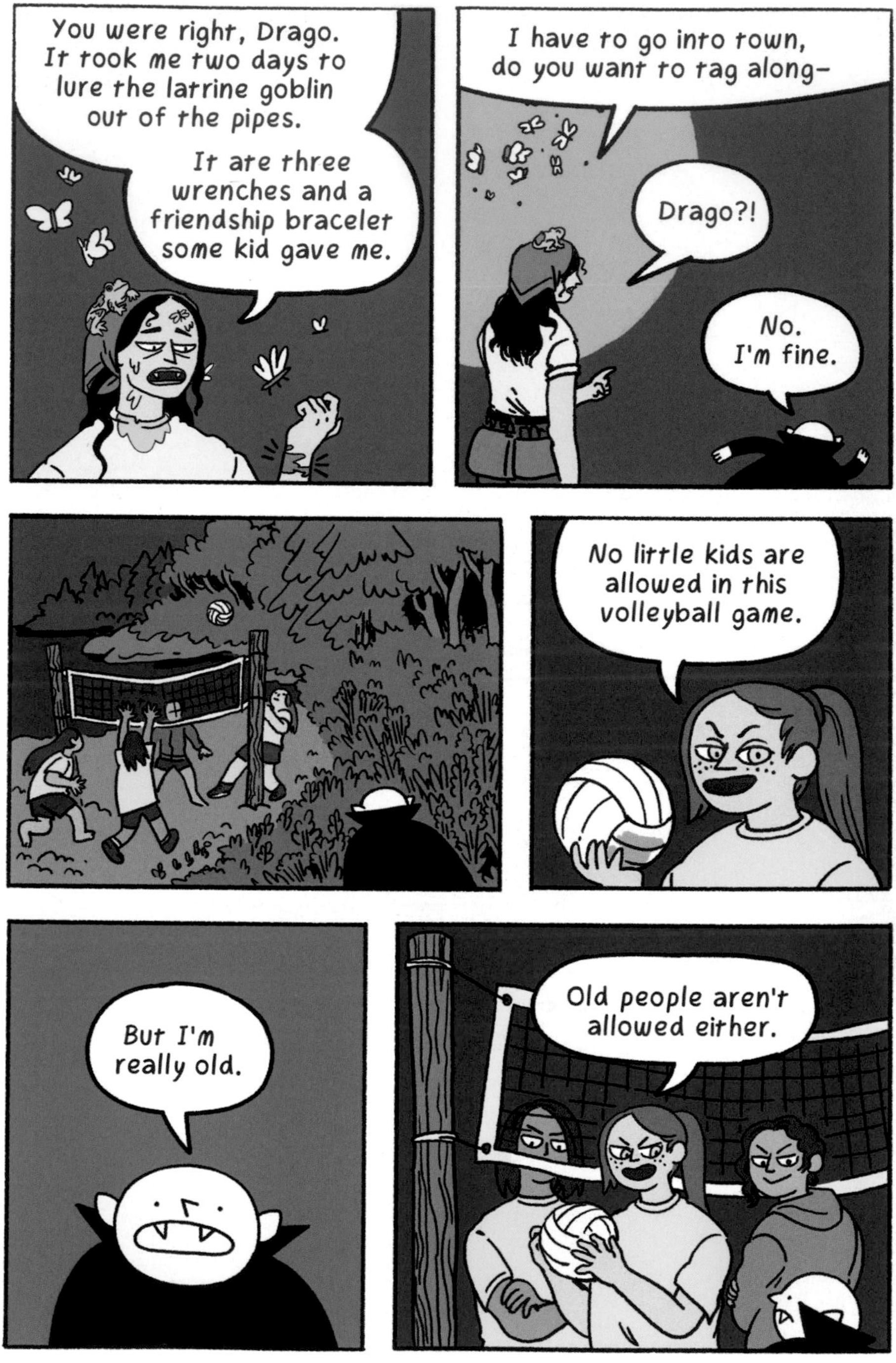
You were right, Drago. It took me two days to lure the latrine goblin out of the pipes.
It ate three wrenches and a friendship bracelet some kid gave me.
I have to go into town, do you want to tag along-
Drago?!
No. I'm fine.
No little kids are allowed in this volleyball game.
But I'm really old.
Old people aren't allowed either.

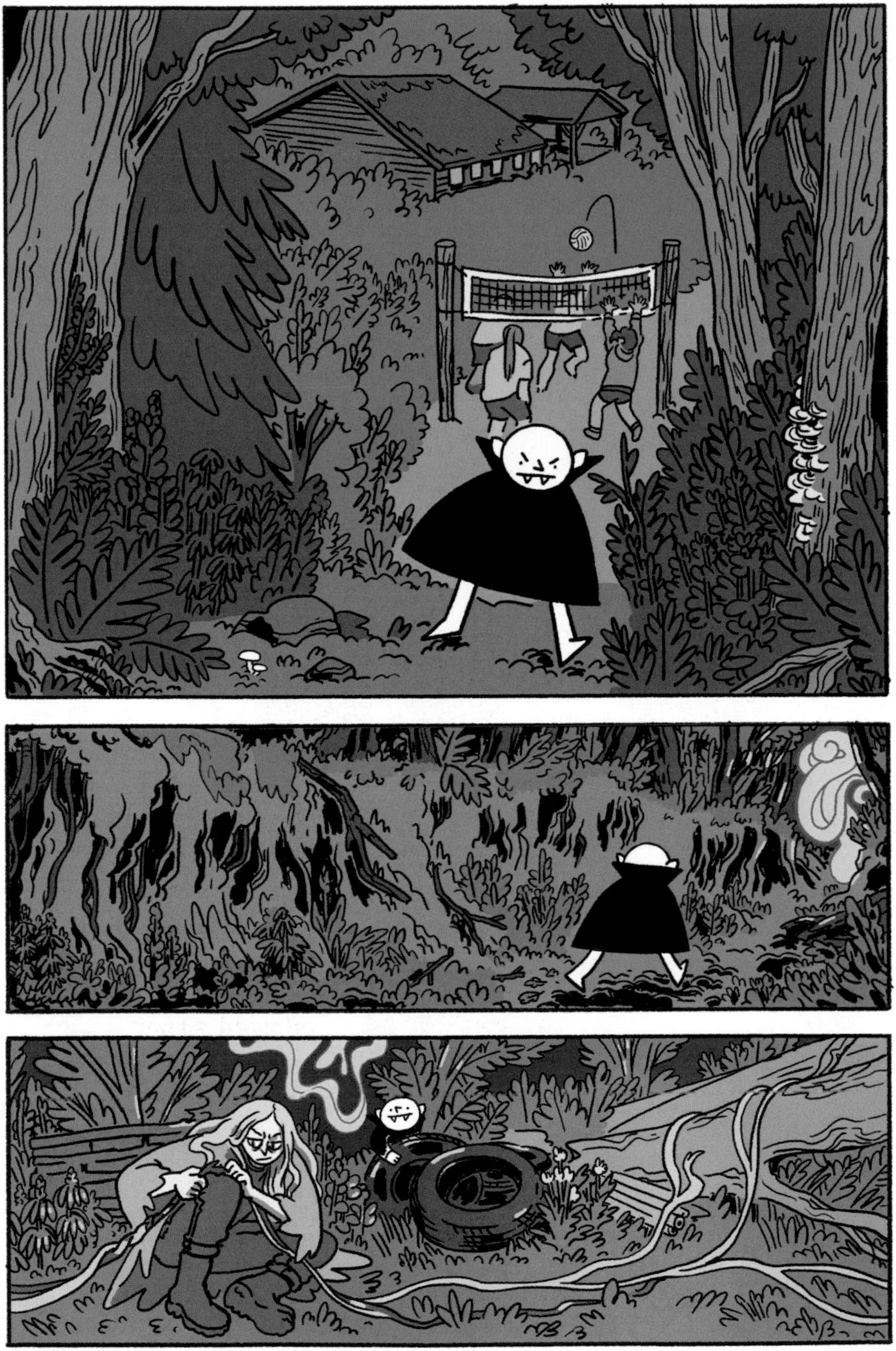

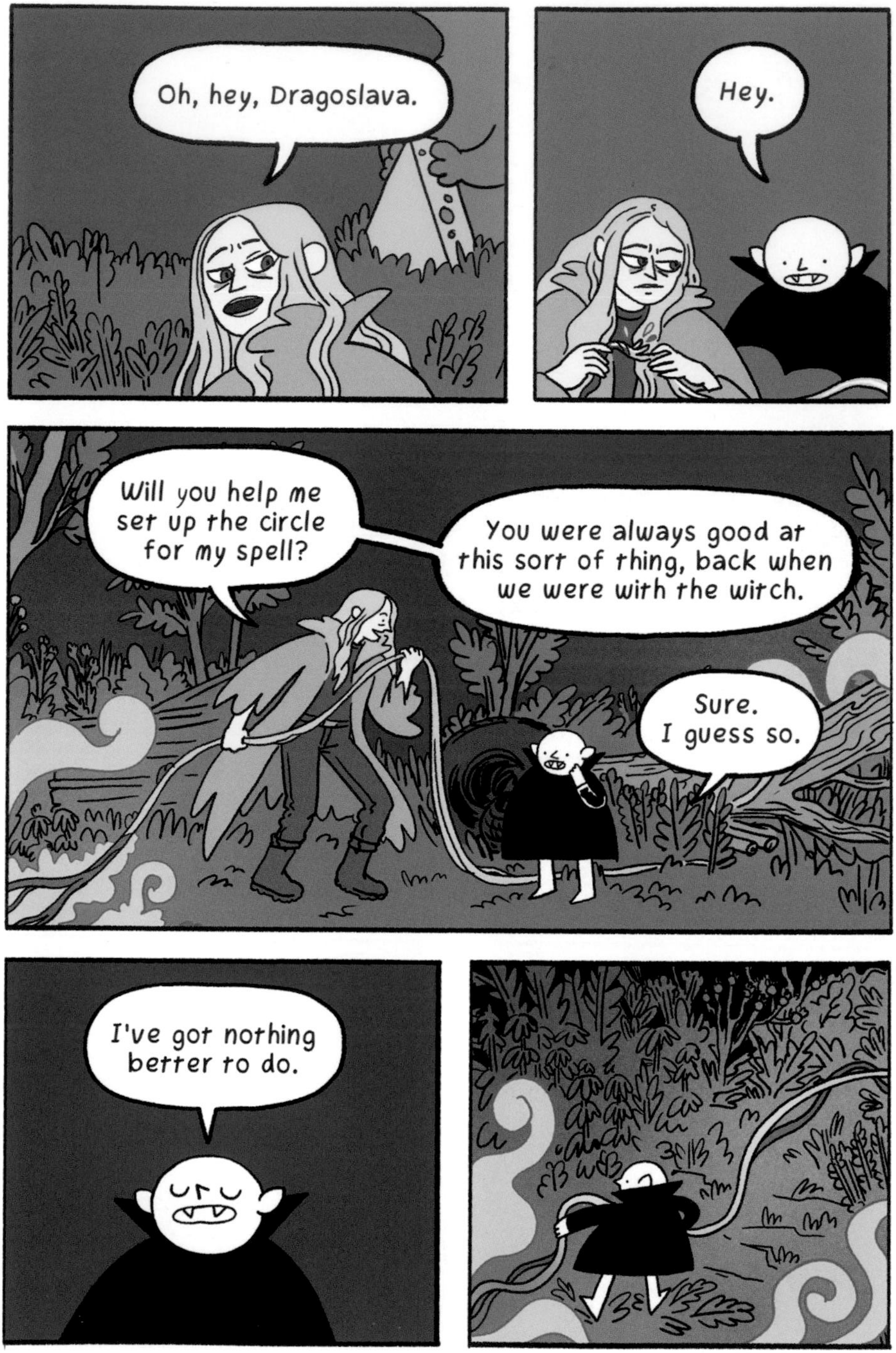
Oh, hey, Dragoslava.
Hey.
Will you help me set up the circle for my spell?
You were always good at this sort of thing, back when we were with the witch.
Sure. I guess so.
I've got nothing better to do.

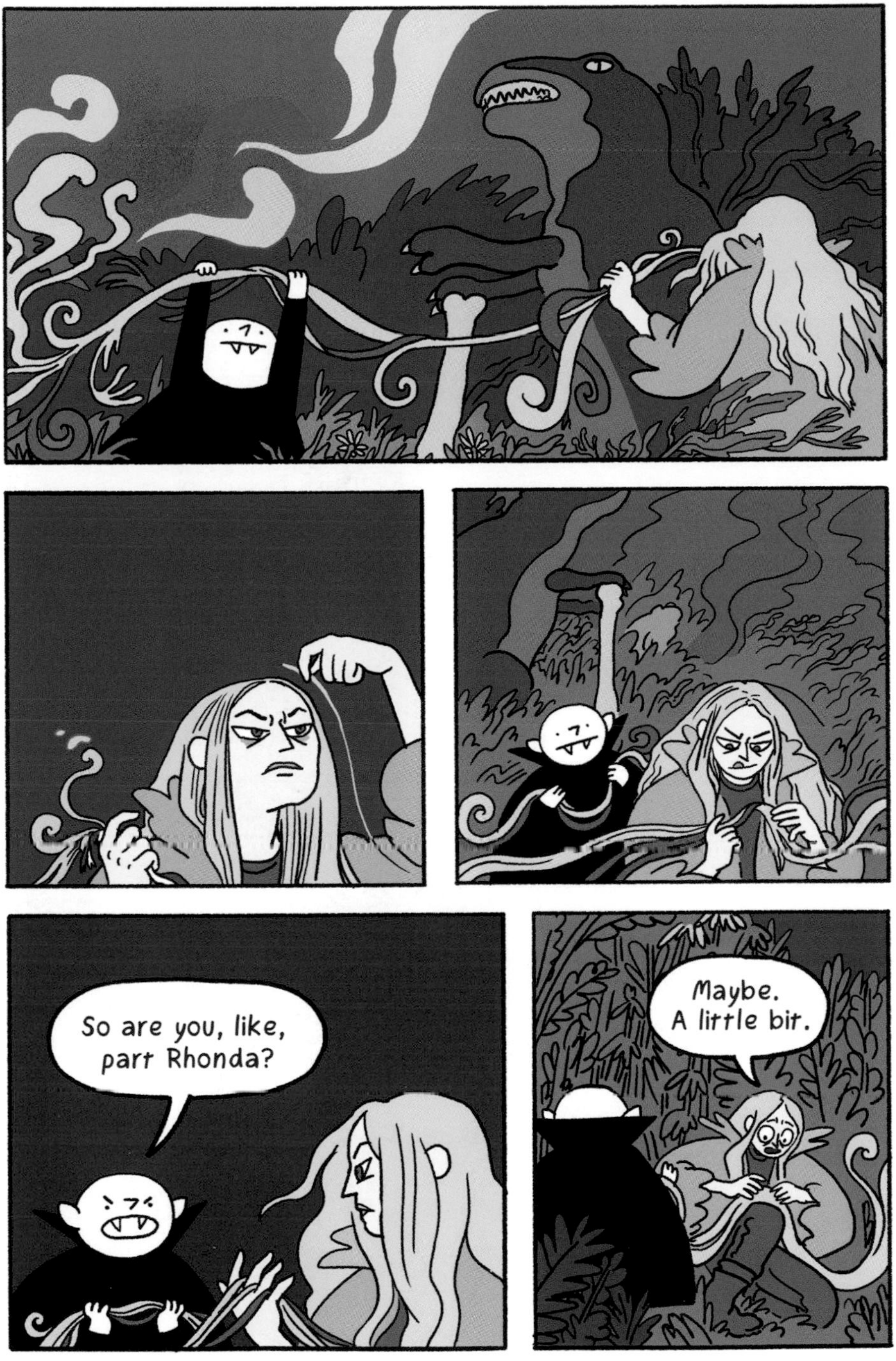
So are you, like, part Rhonda?
Maybe. A little bit.

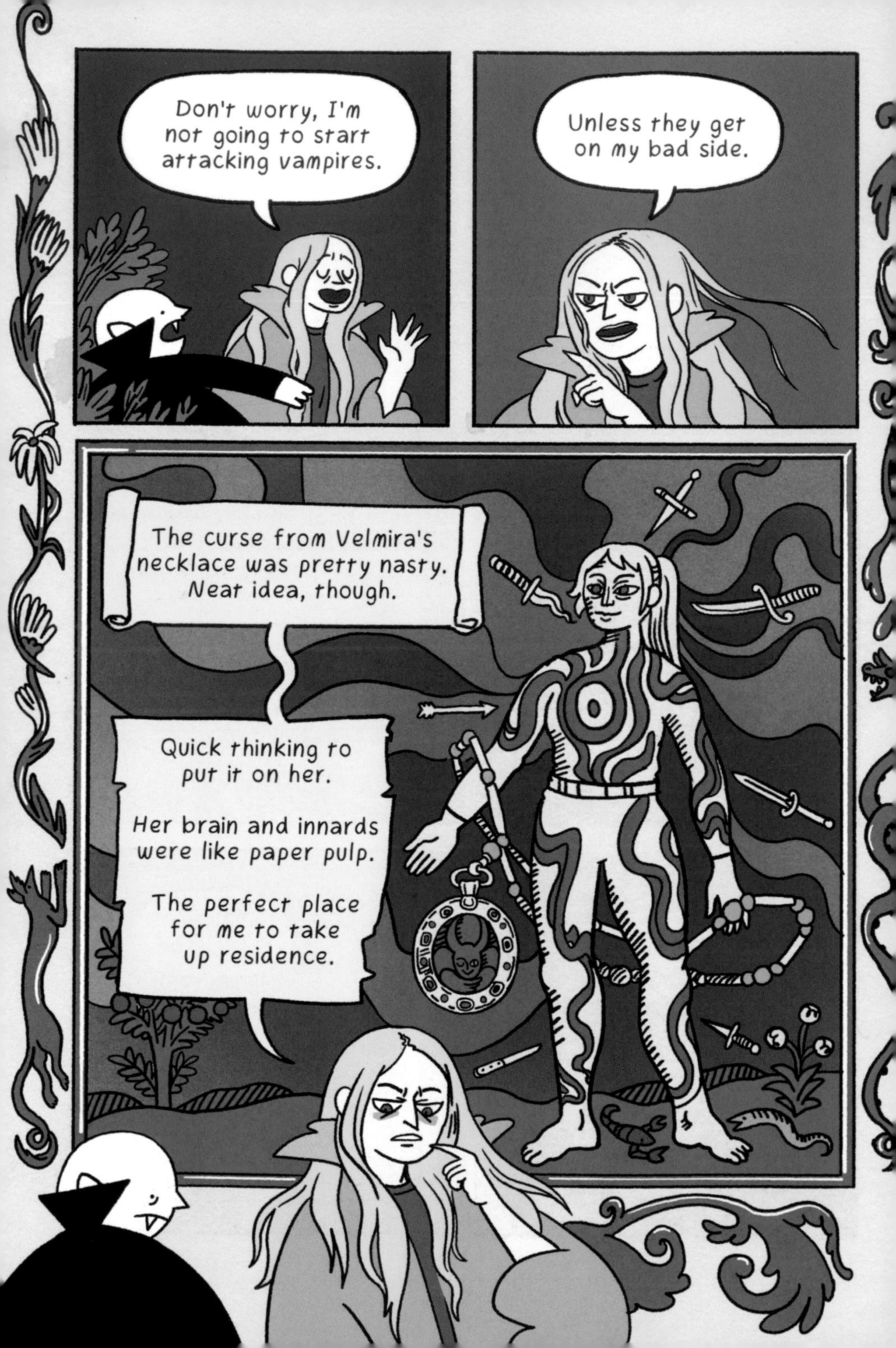

Don't worry, I'm not going to start attacking vampires.
Unless they get on my bad side.
The curse from Velmira's necklace was pretty nasty. Neat idea, though.
Quick thinking to put it on her.
Her brain and innards were like paper pulp.
The perfect place for me to take up residence.

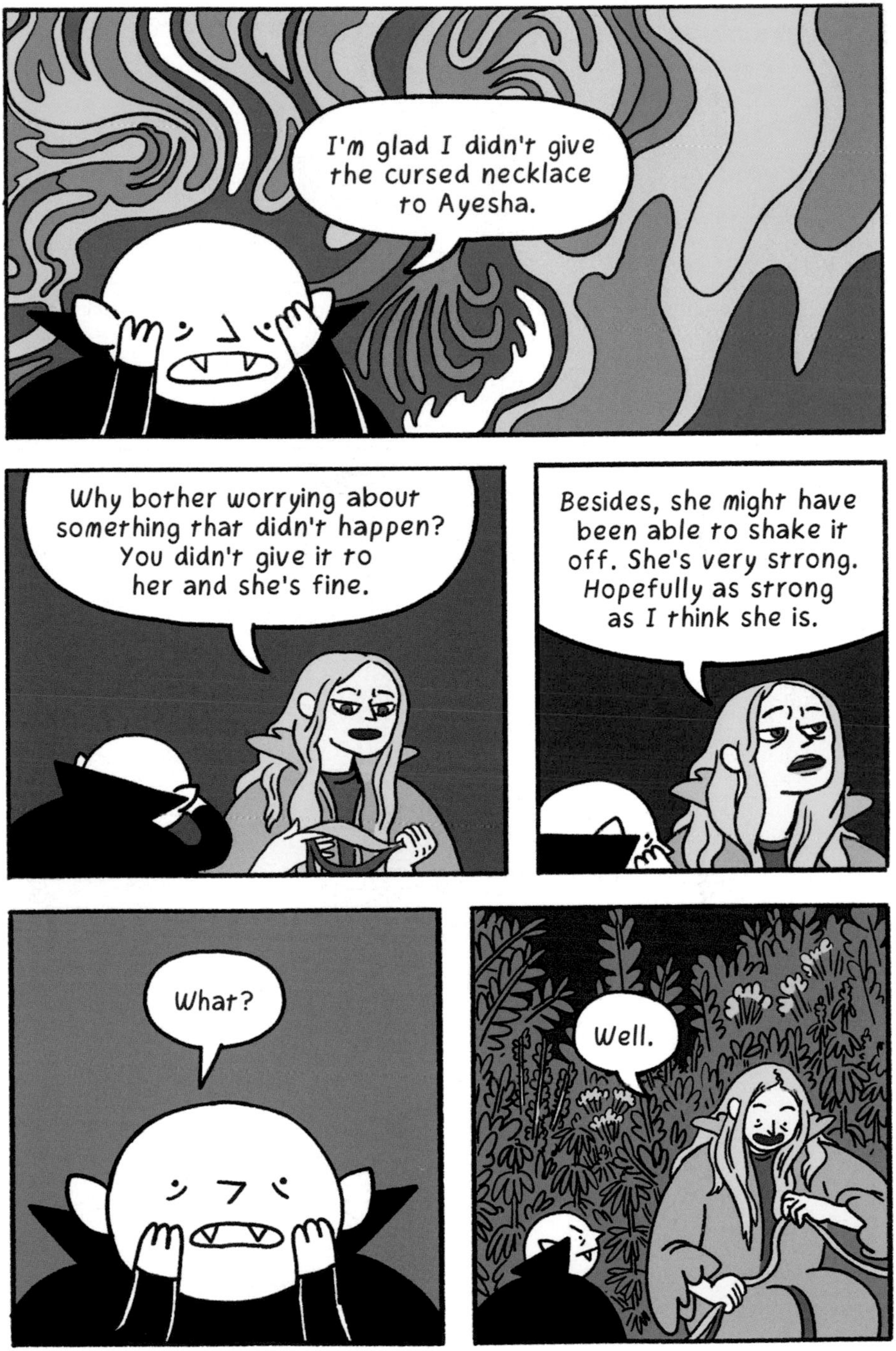
I'm glad I didn't give the cursed necklace to Ayesha.
Why bother worrying about something that didn't happen? You didn't give it to her and she's fine.
Besides, she might have been able to shake it off. She's very strong. Hopefully as strong as I think she is.
What?
Well.

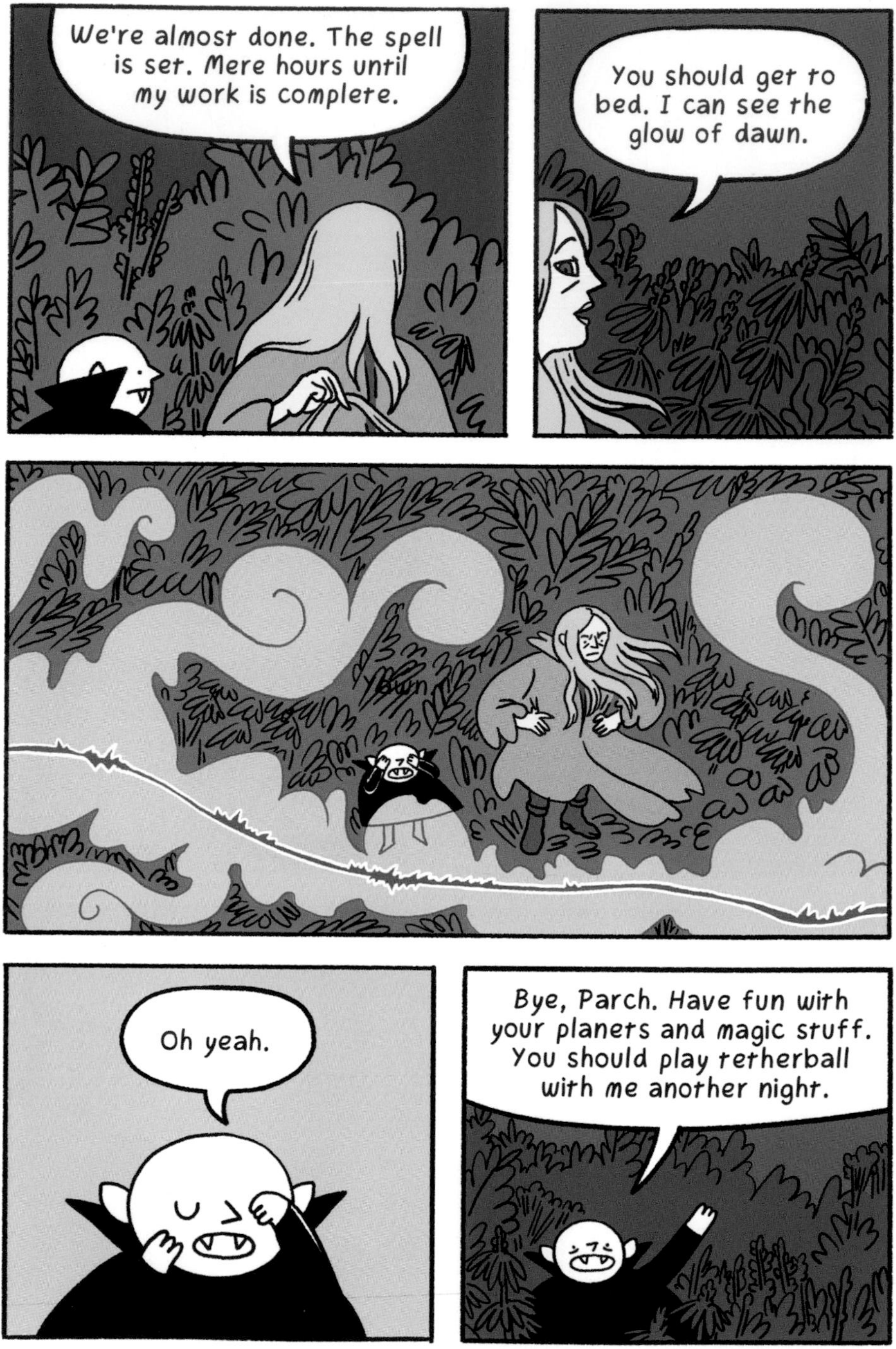
We're almost done. The spell is set. Mere hours until my work is complete.
You should get to bed. I can see the glow of dawn.
Yawn
Oh yeah.
Bye, Parch. Have fun with your planets and magic stuff. You should play tetherball with me another night.

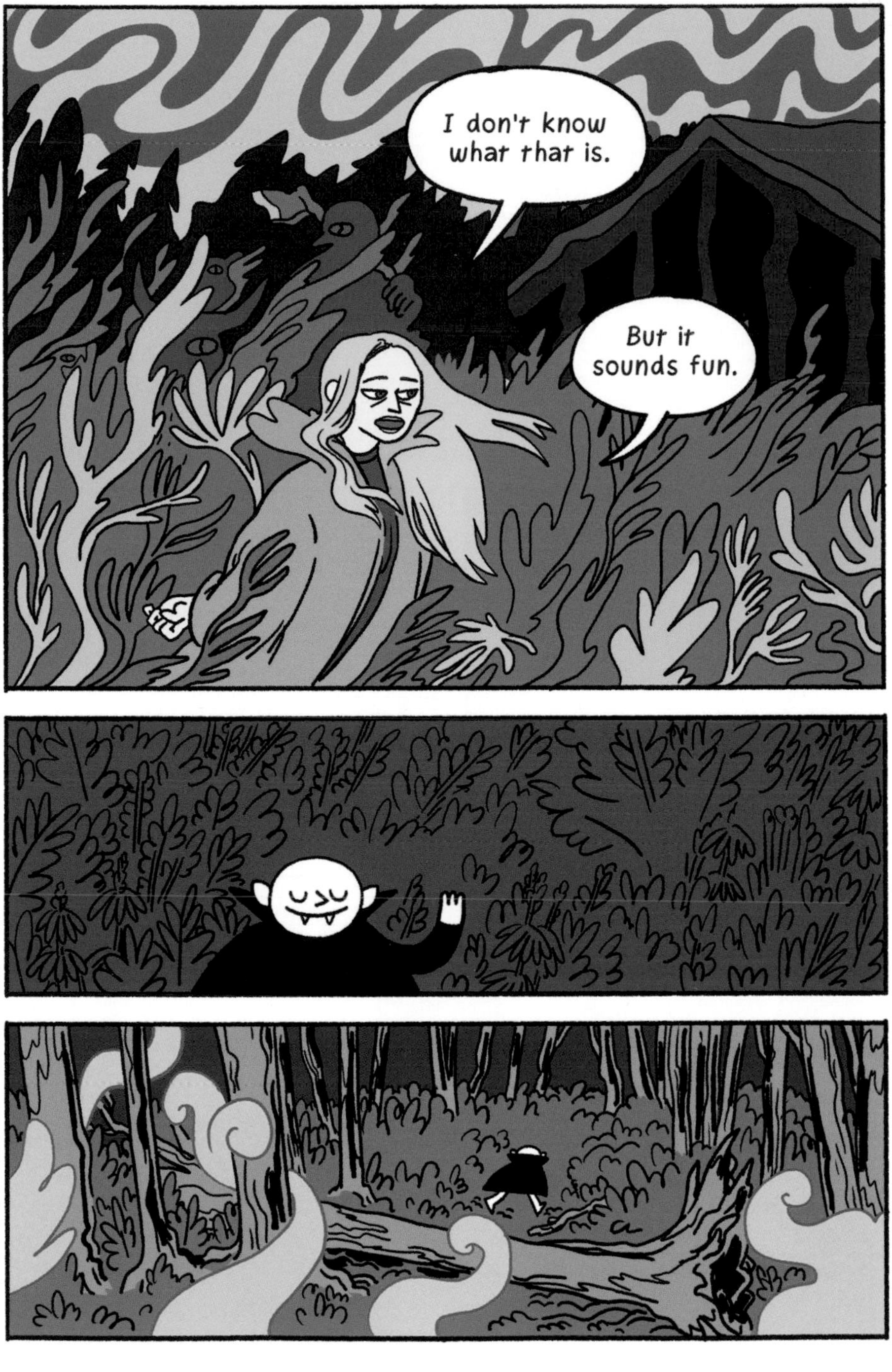
I don't know what that is.
But it sounds fun.

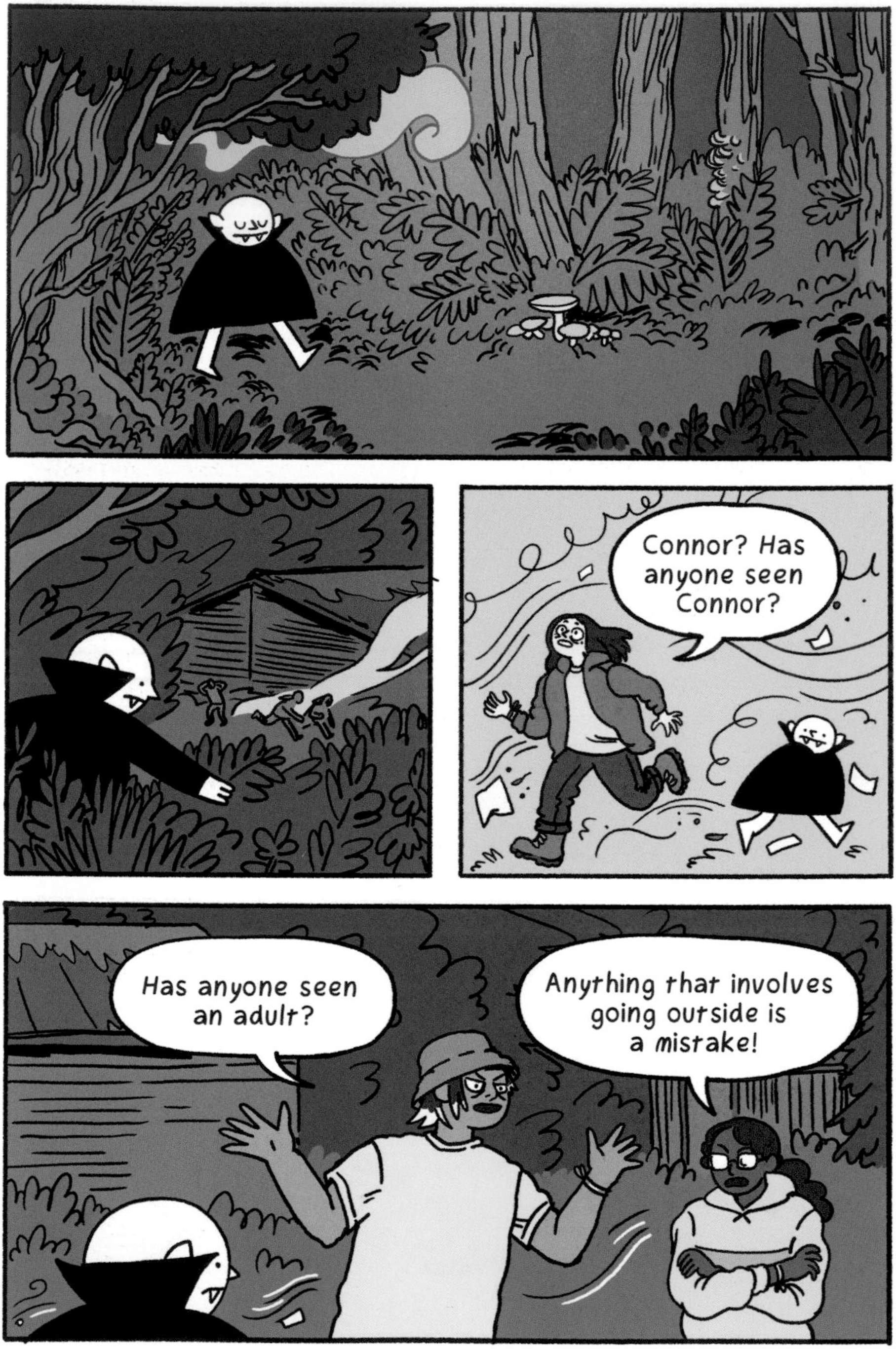
Connor? Has anyone seen Connor?
Has anyone seen an adult?
Anything that involves going outside is a mistake!

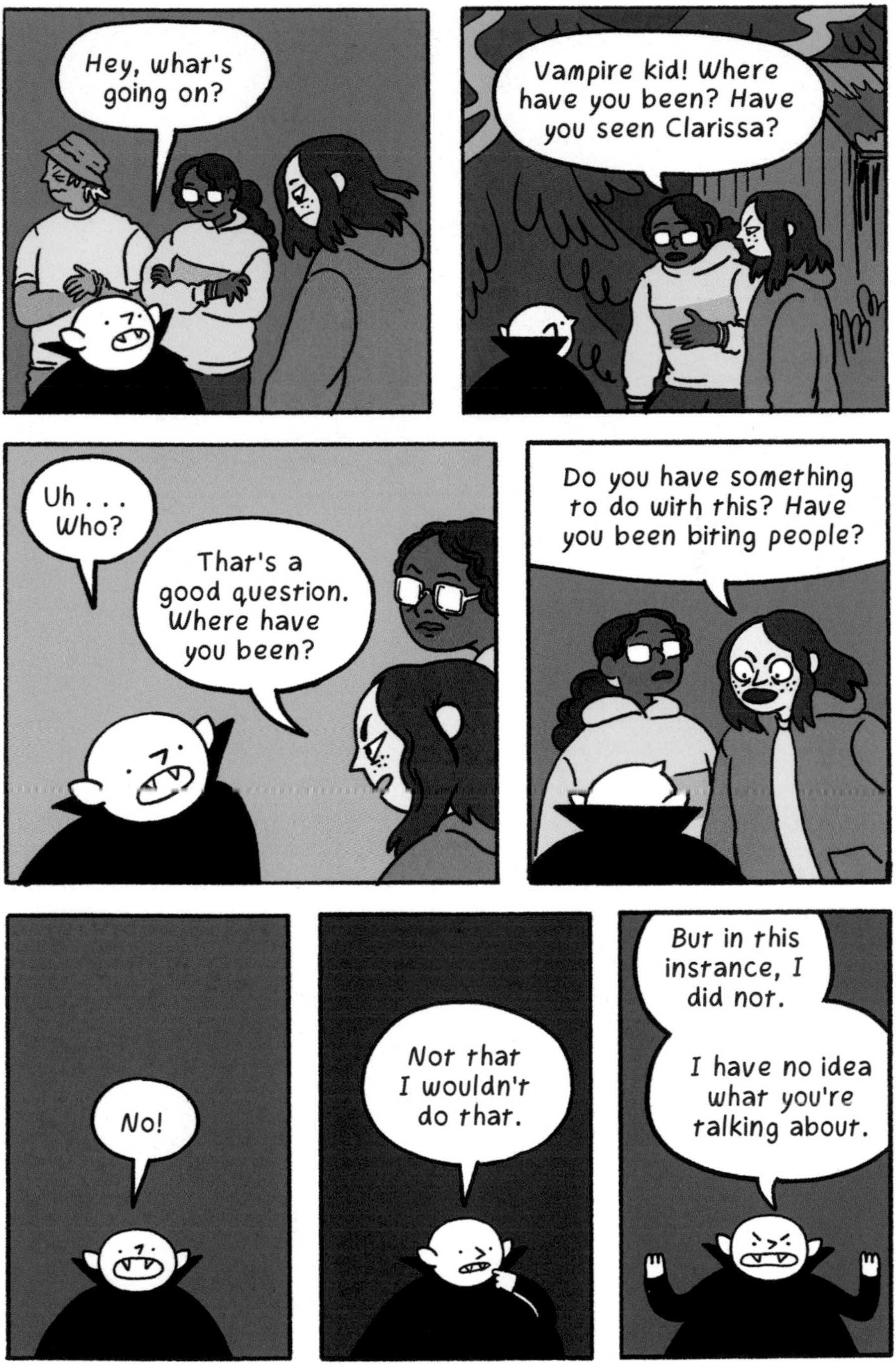
Hey, what's going on?
Vampire kid! Where have you been? Have you seen Clarissa?
Uh . . . Who?
That's a good question. Where have you been?
Do you have something to do with this? Have you been biting people?
No!
Not that I wouldn't do that.
But in this instance, I did not.
I have no idea what you're talking about.

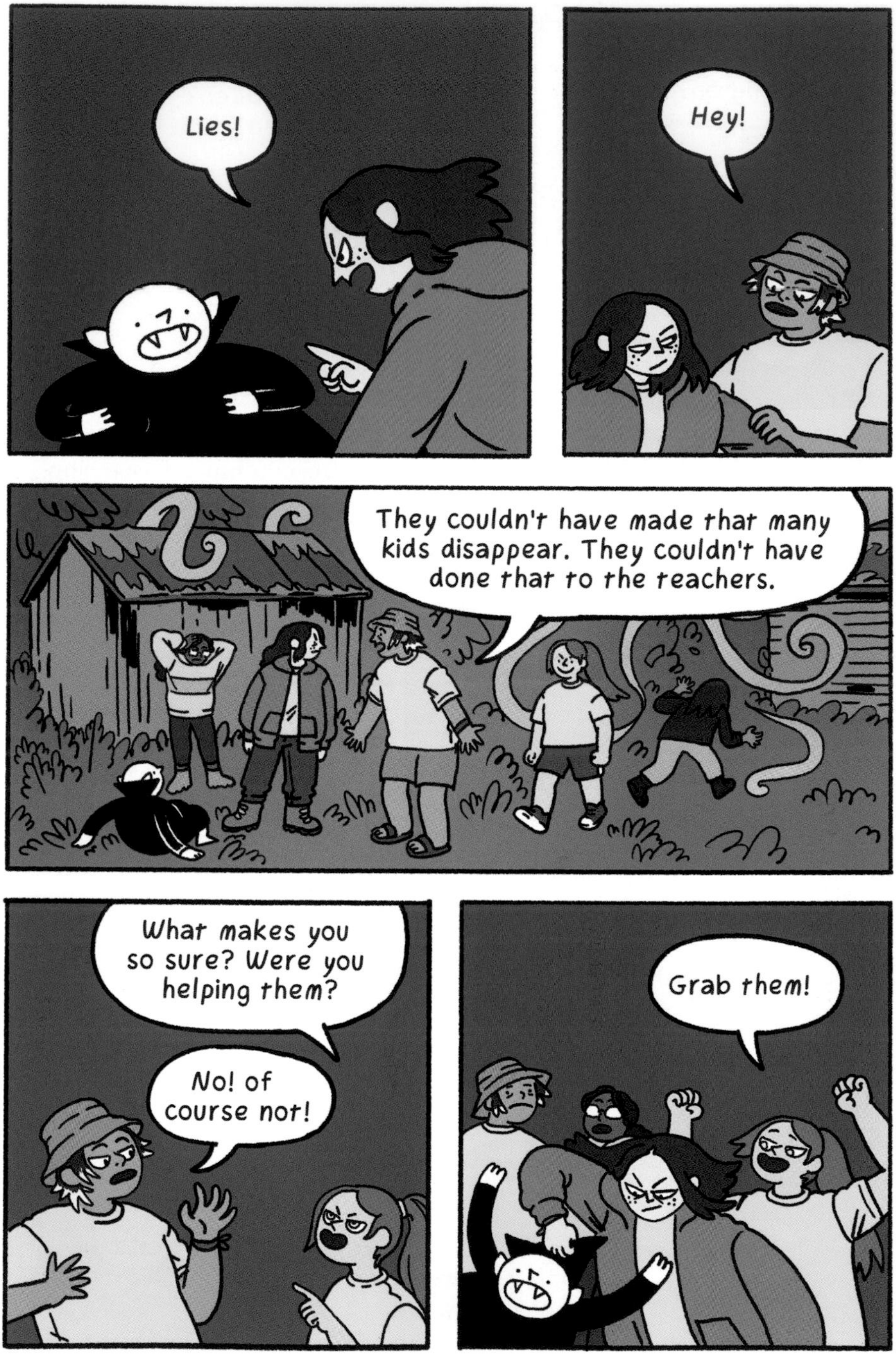
Lies!
Hey!
They couldn't have made that many kids disappear. They couldn't have done that to the teachers.
What makes you so sure? Were you helping them?
No! of course not!
Grab them!

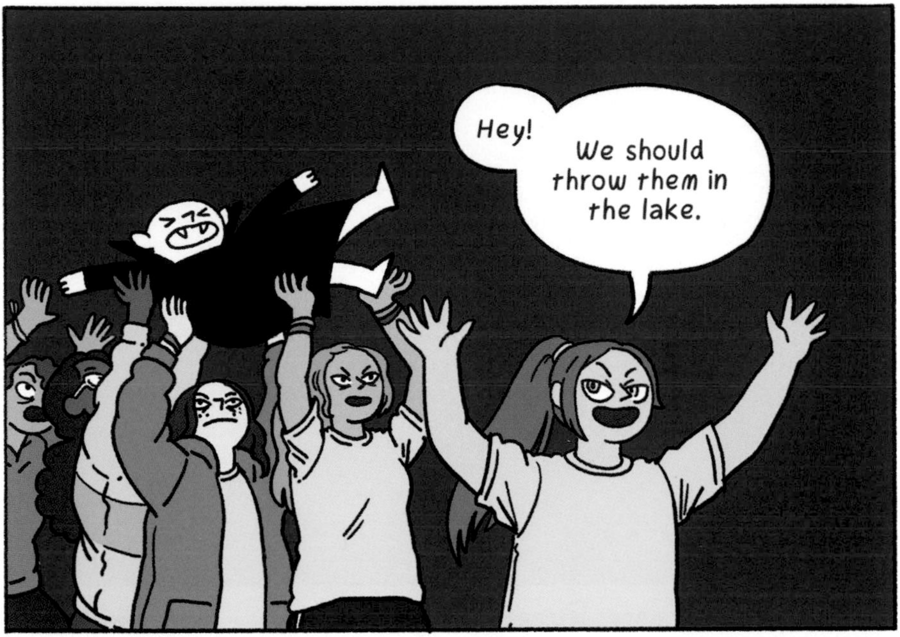
Hey!
We should throw them in the lake.

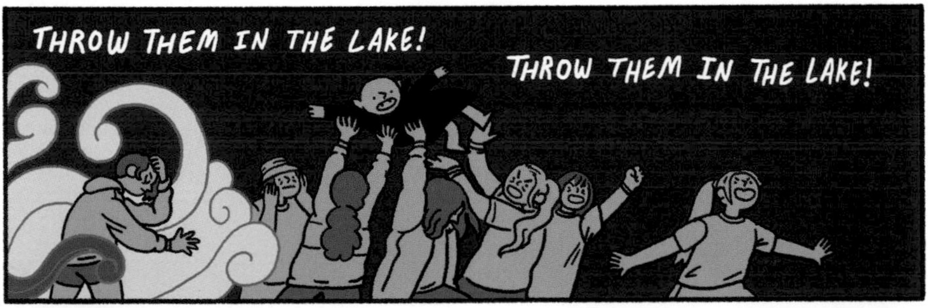
THROW THEM IN THE LAKE!
THROW THEM IN THE LAKE!

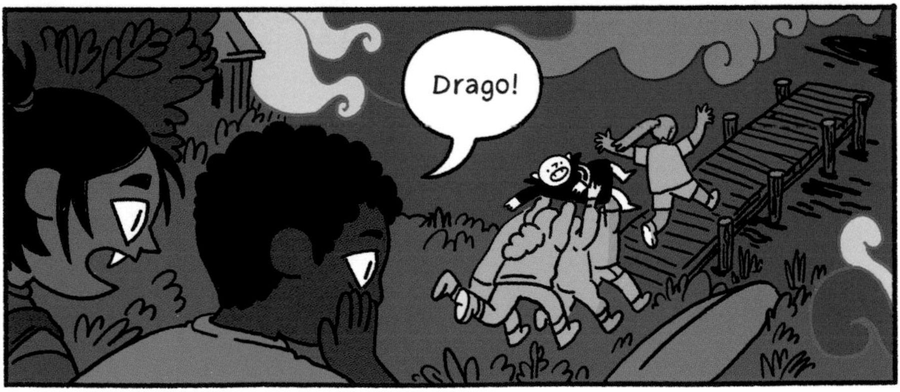
Drago!

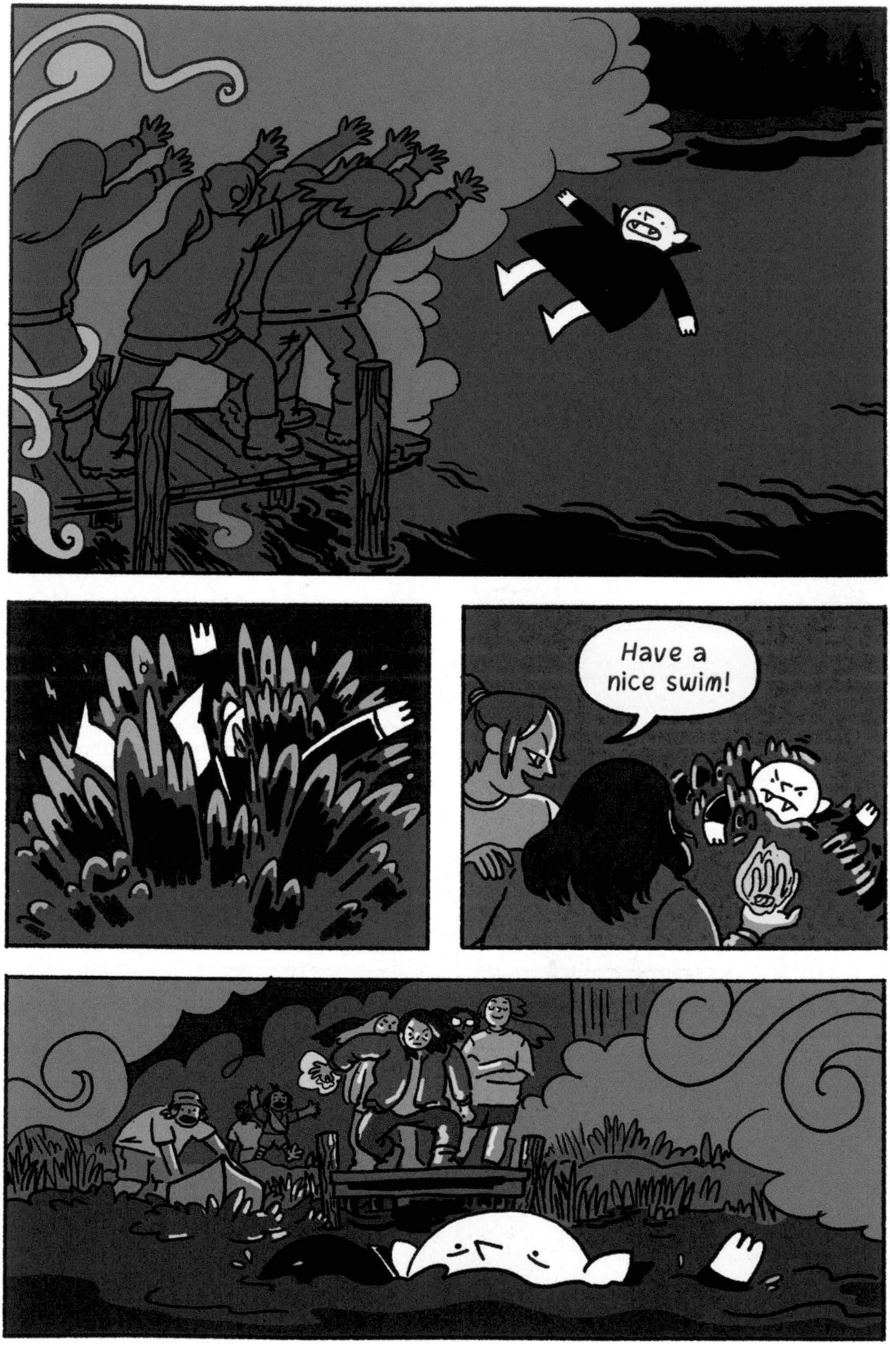
Have a nice swim!

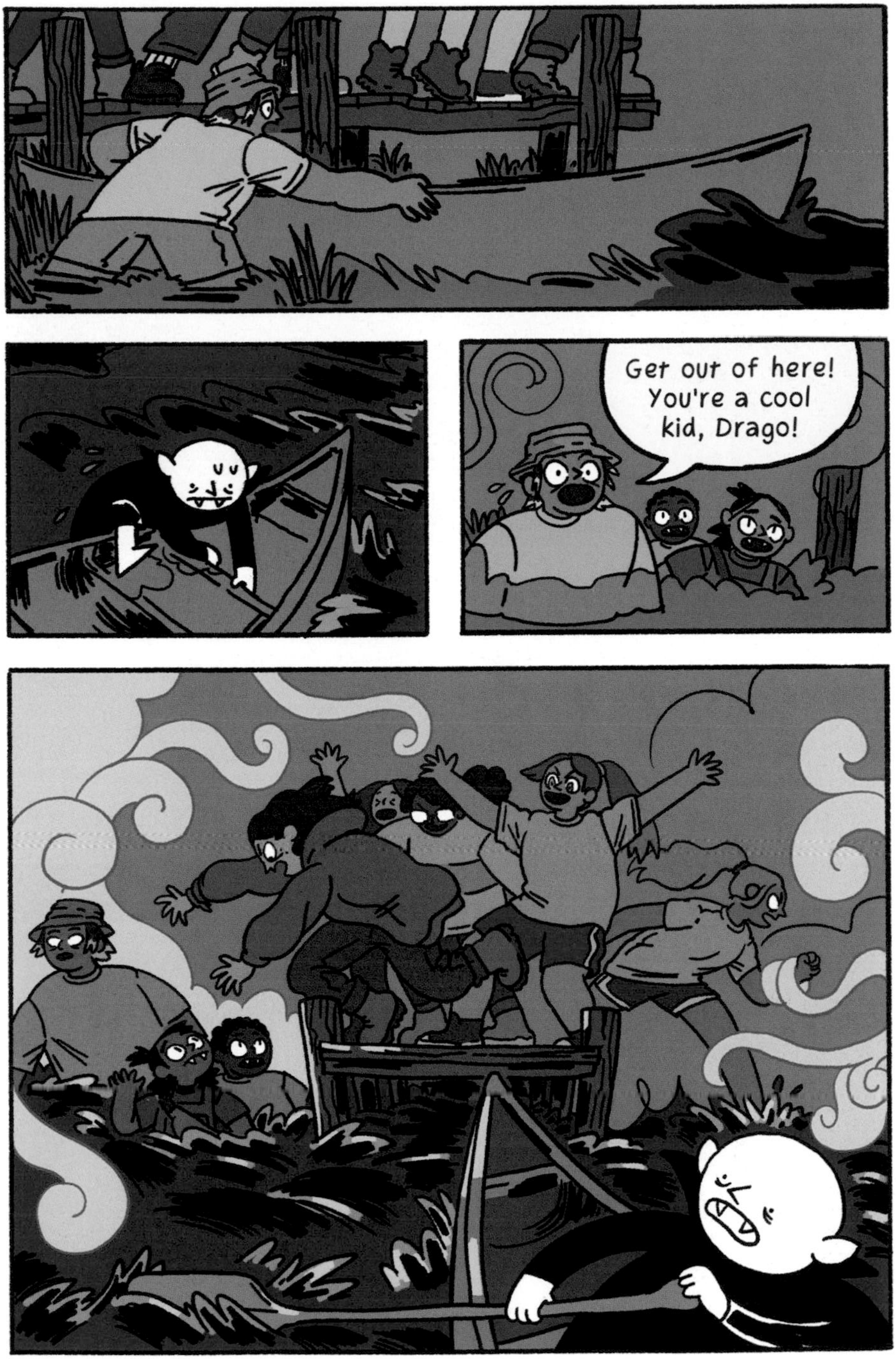

Get out of here! You're a cool kid, Drago!

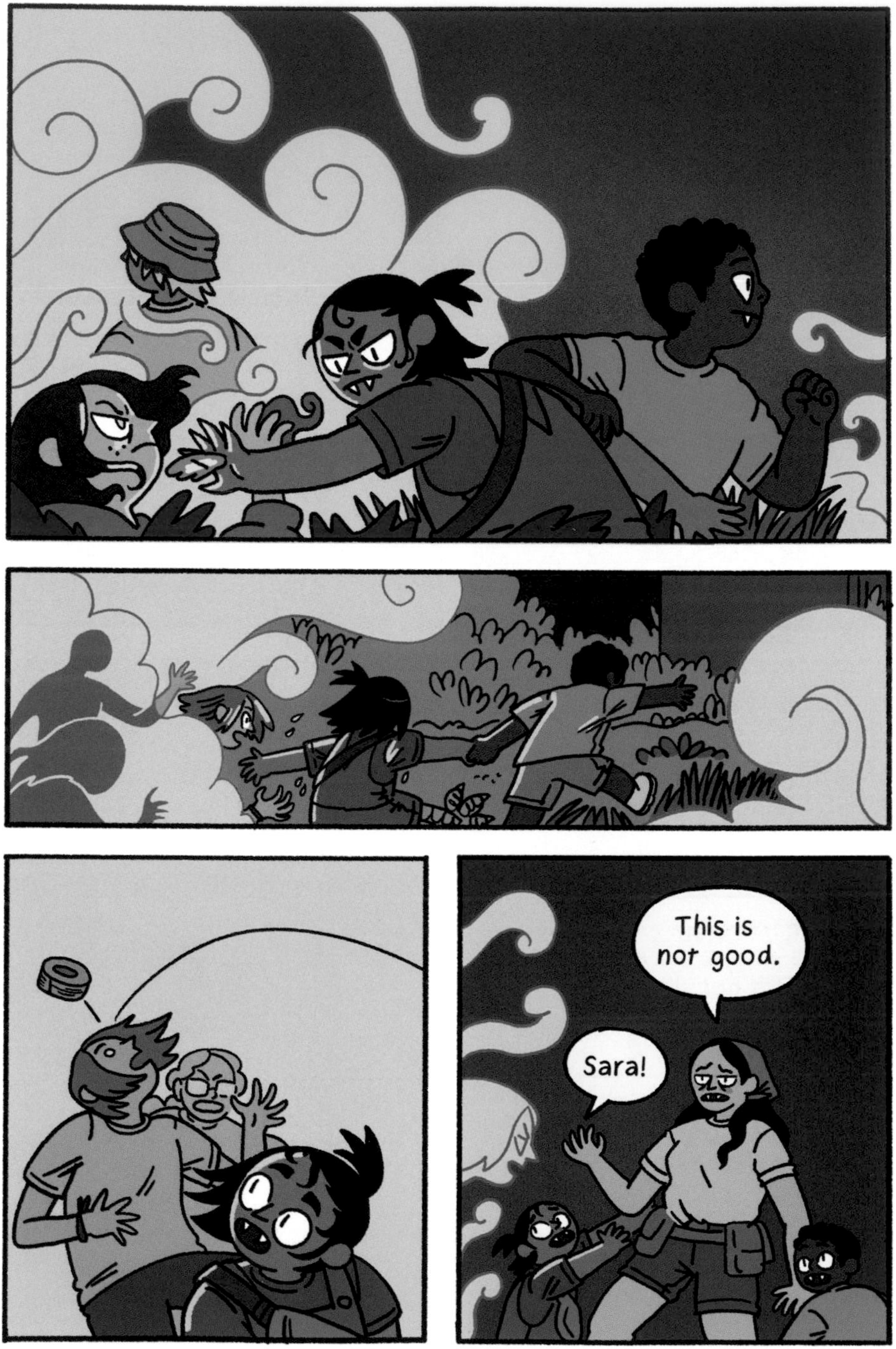
This is not good.
Sara!

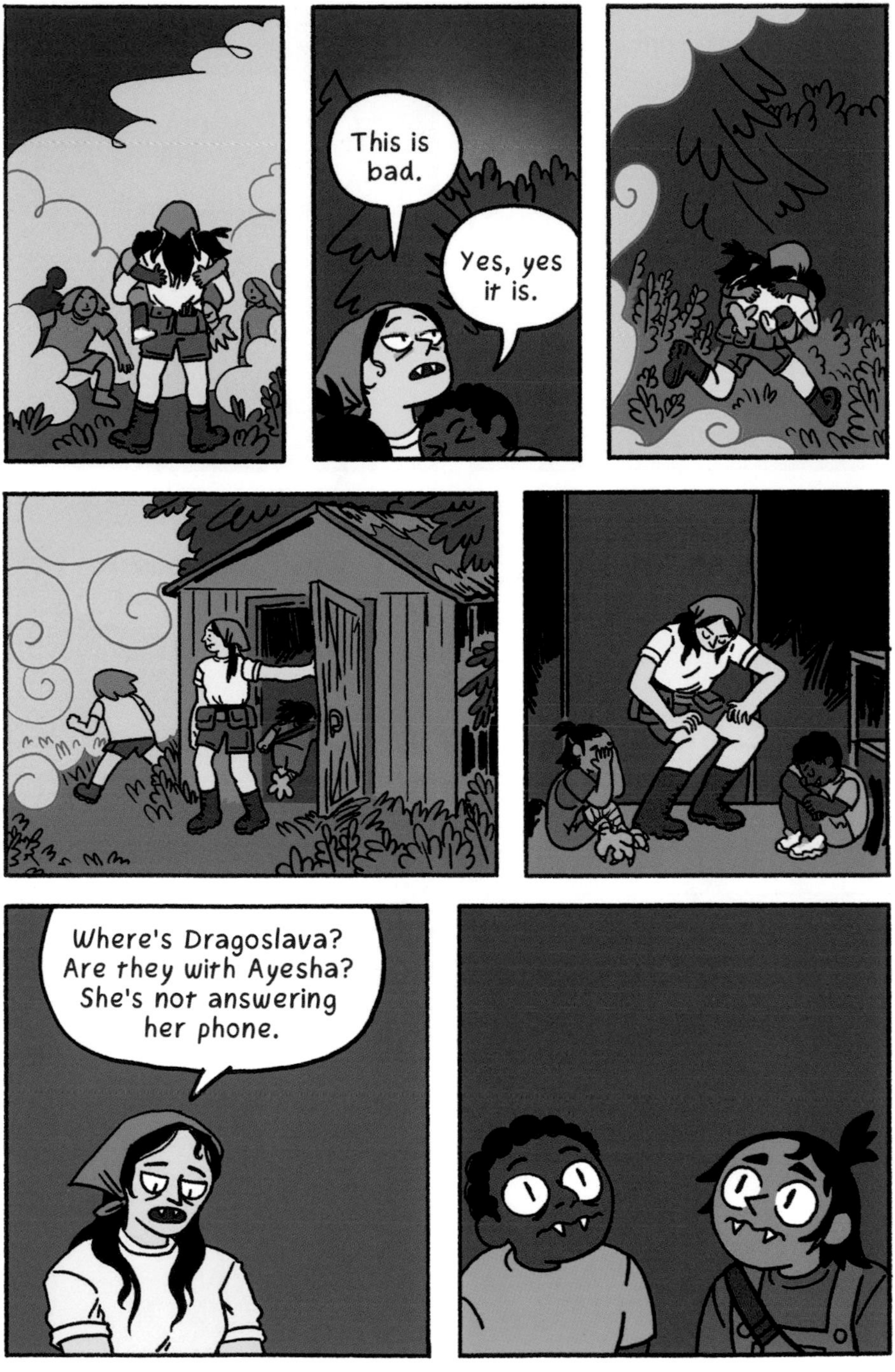
This is bad.
Yes, yes it is.
Where's Dragoslava? Are they with Ayesha? She's not answering her phone.

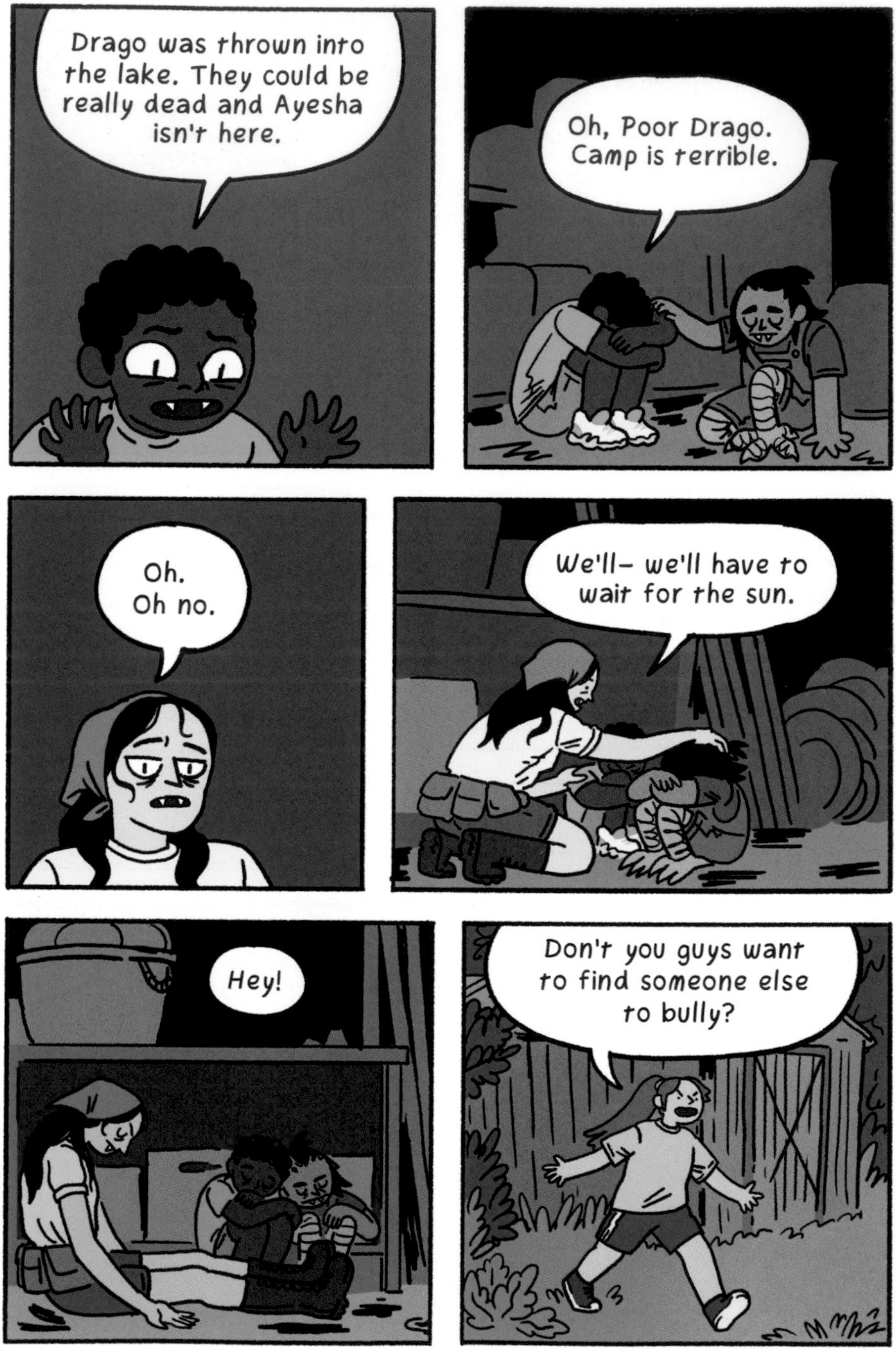
Drago was thrown into the lake. They could be really dead and Ayesha isn't here.
Oh, Poor Drago. Camp is terrible.
Oh. Oh no.
We'll- we'll have to wait for the sun.
Hey!
Don't you guys want to find someone else to bully?

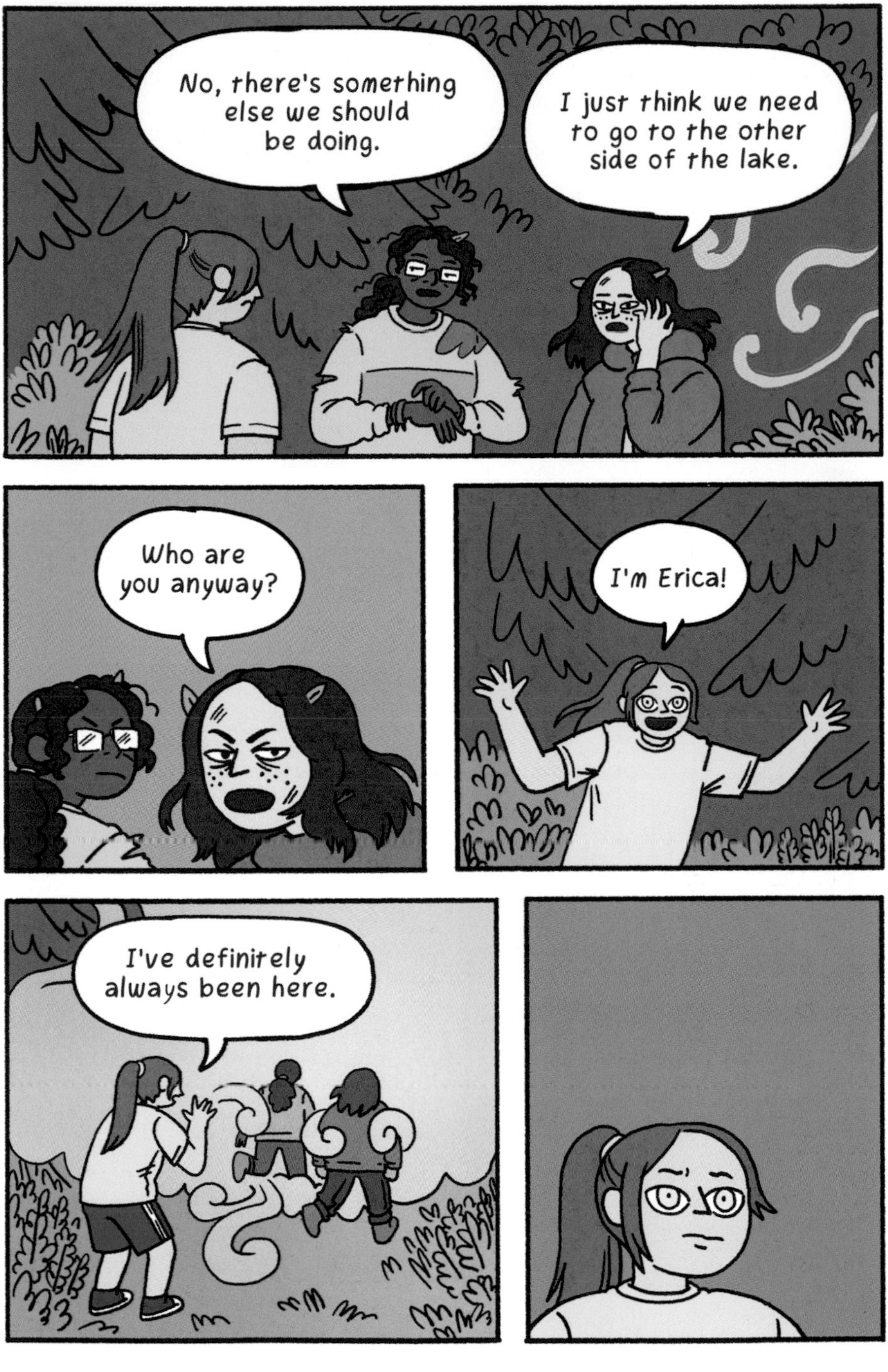
No, there's something else we should be doing.
I just think we need to go to the other side of the lake.
Who are you anyway?
I'm Erica!
I've definitely always been here.

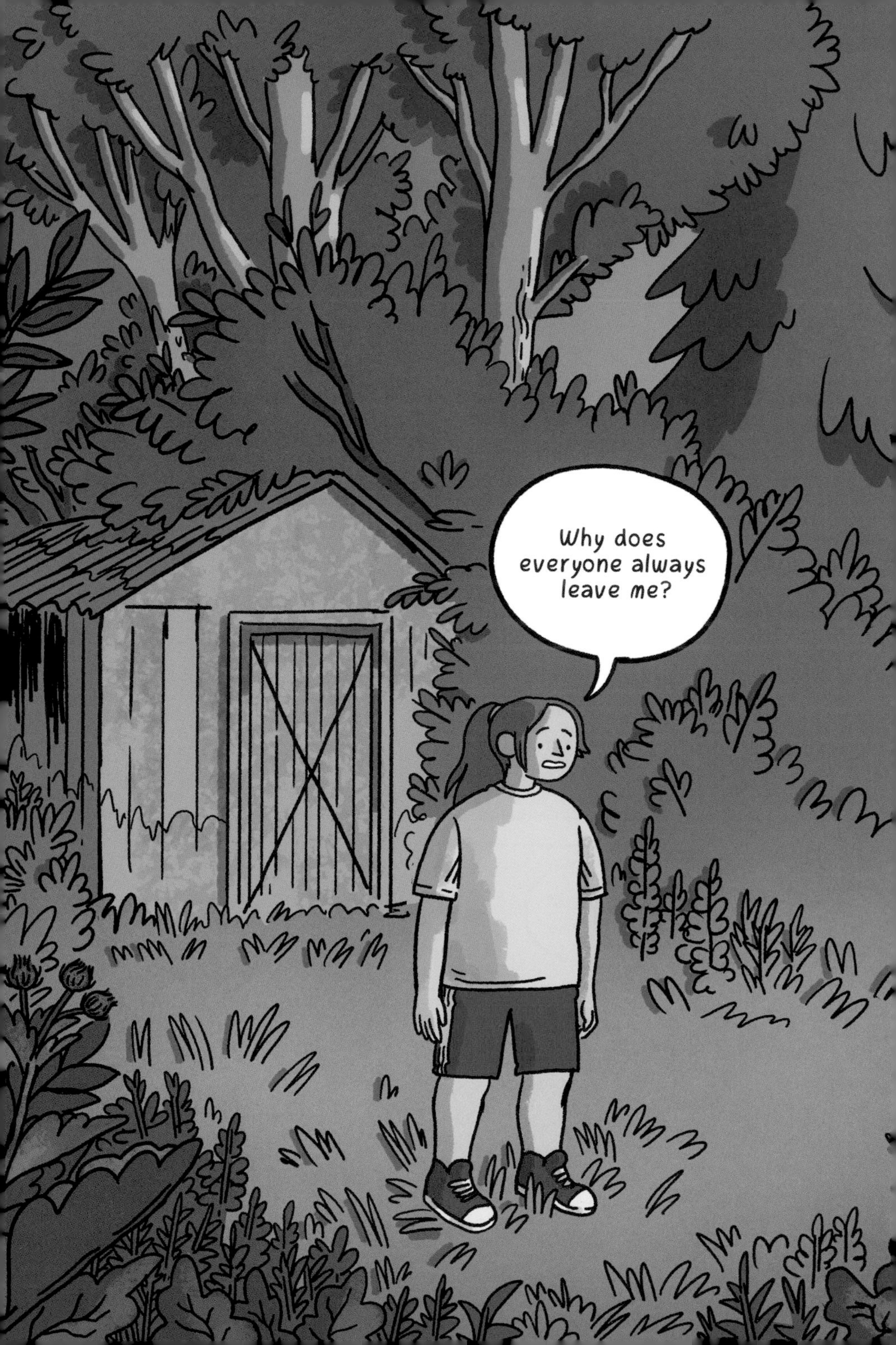
Why does everyone always leave me?

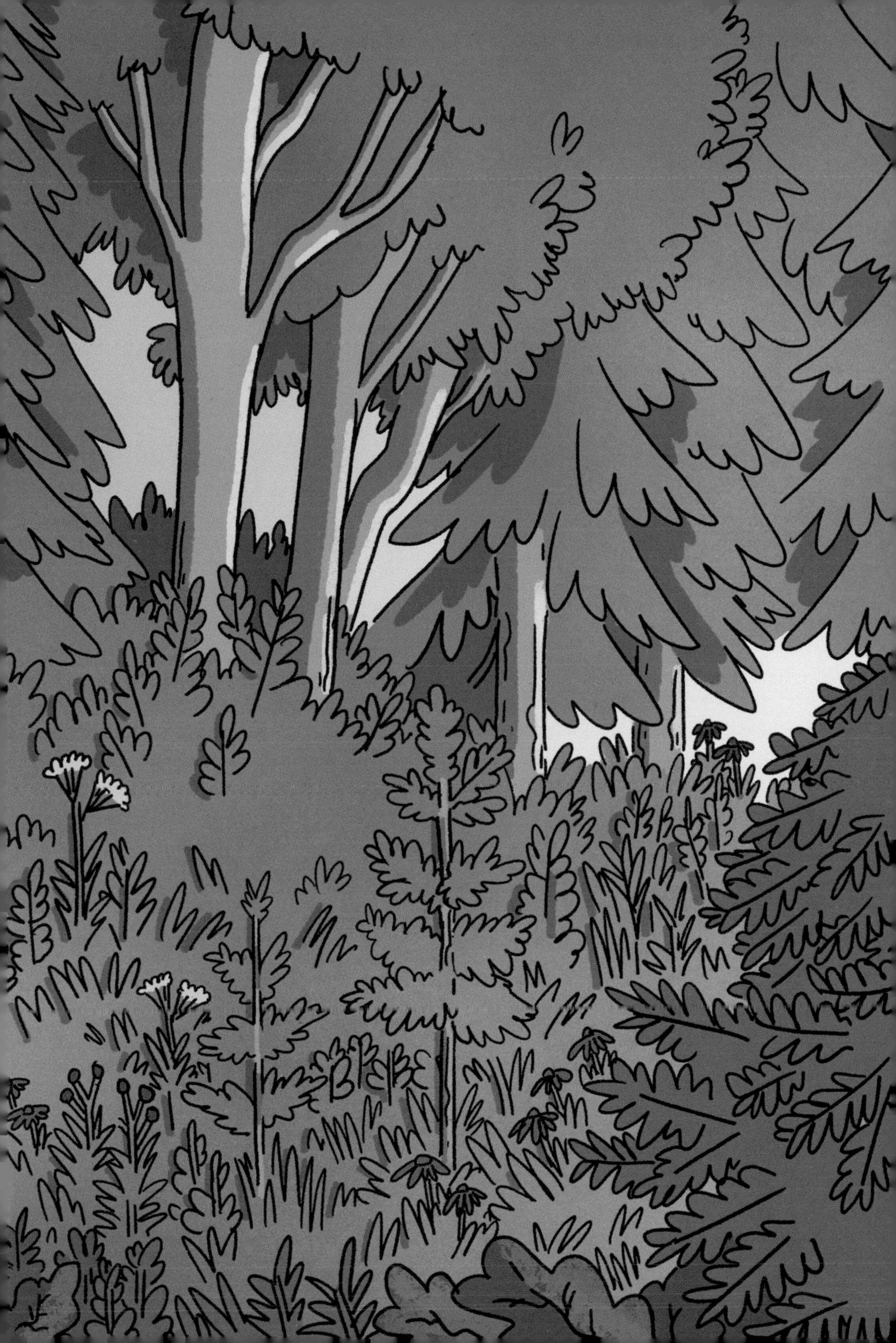

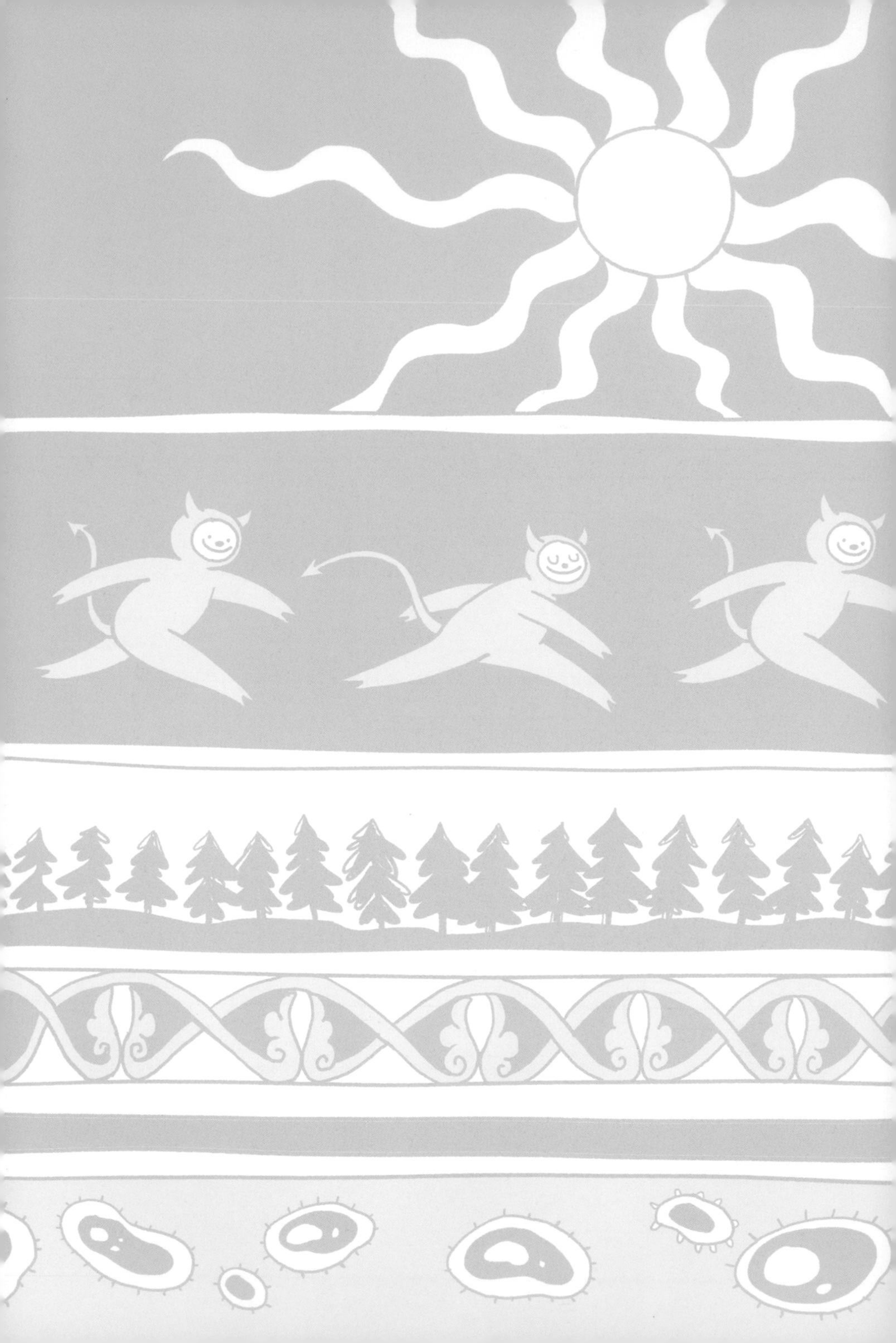

CHAPTER
FIVE

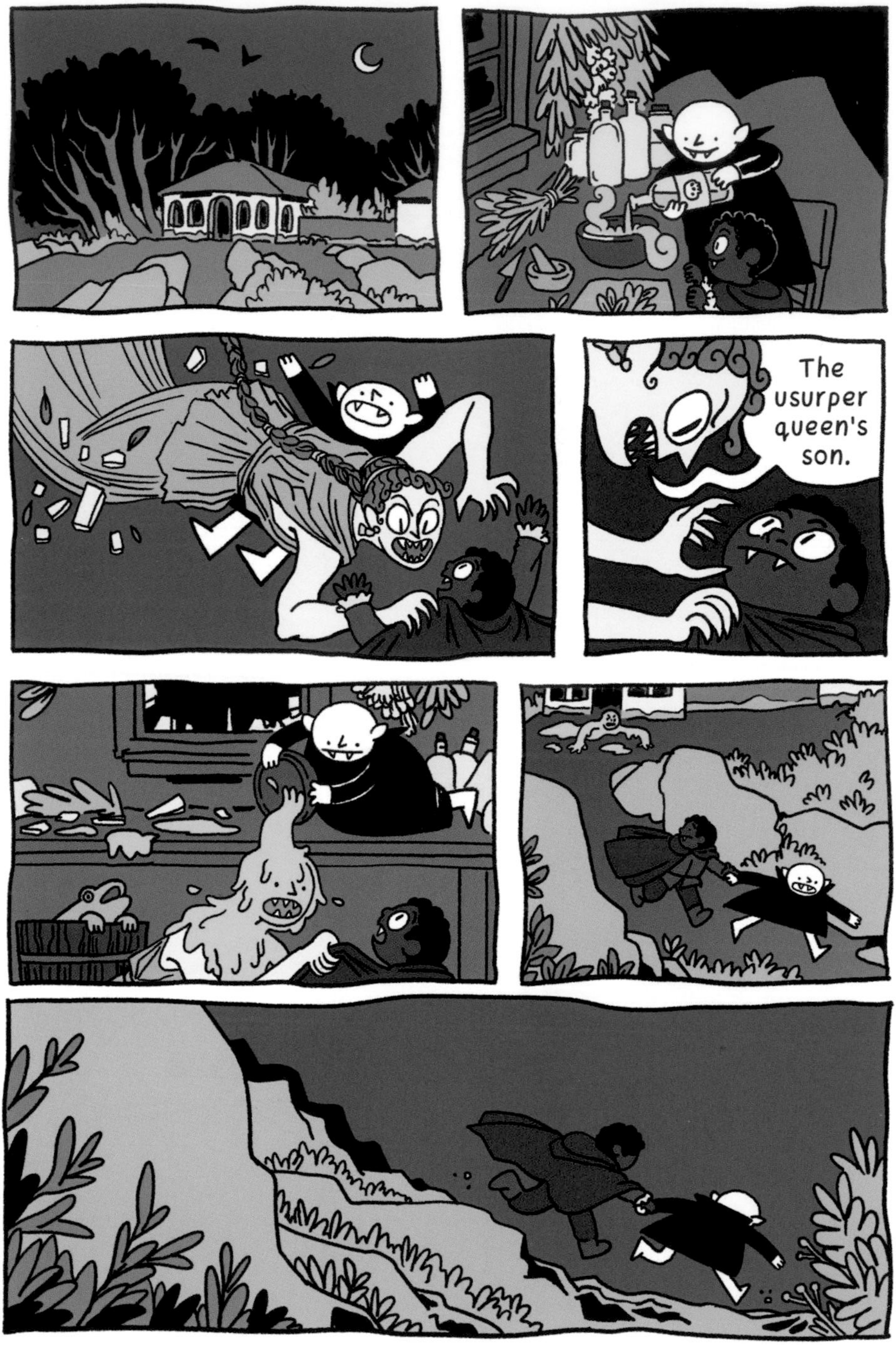
The usurper queen's son.

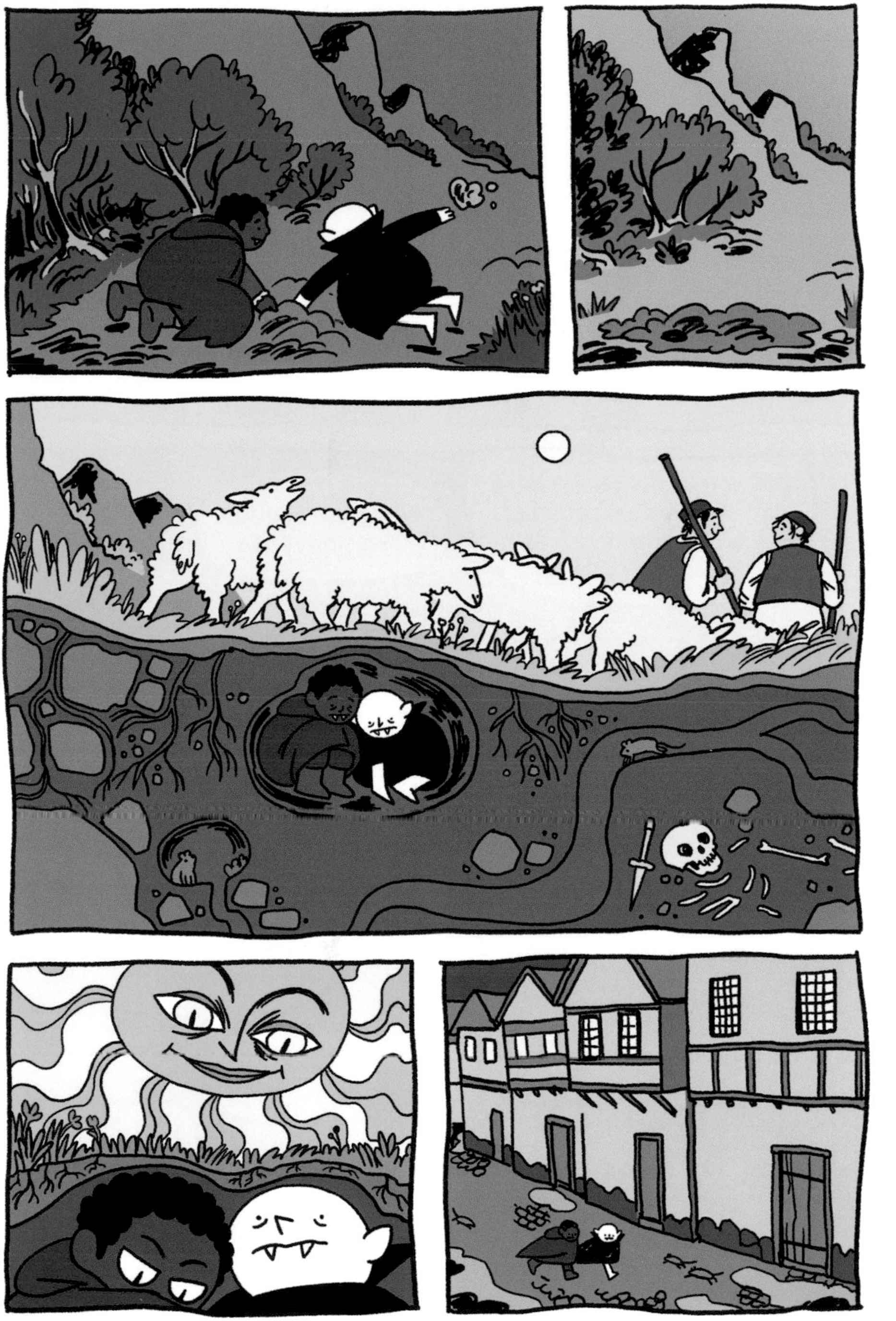

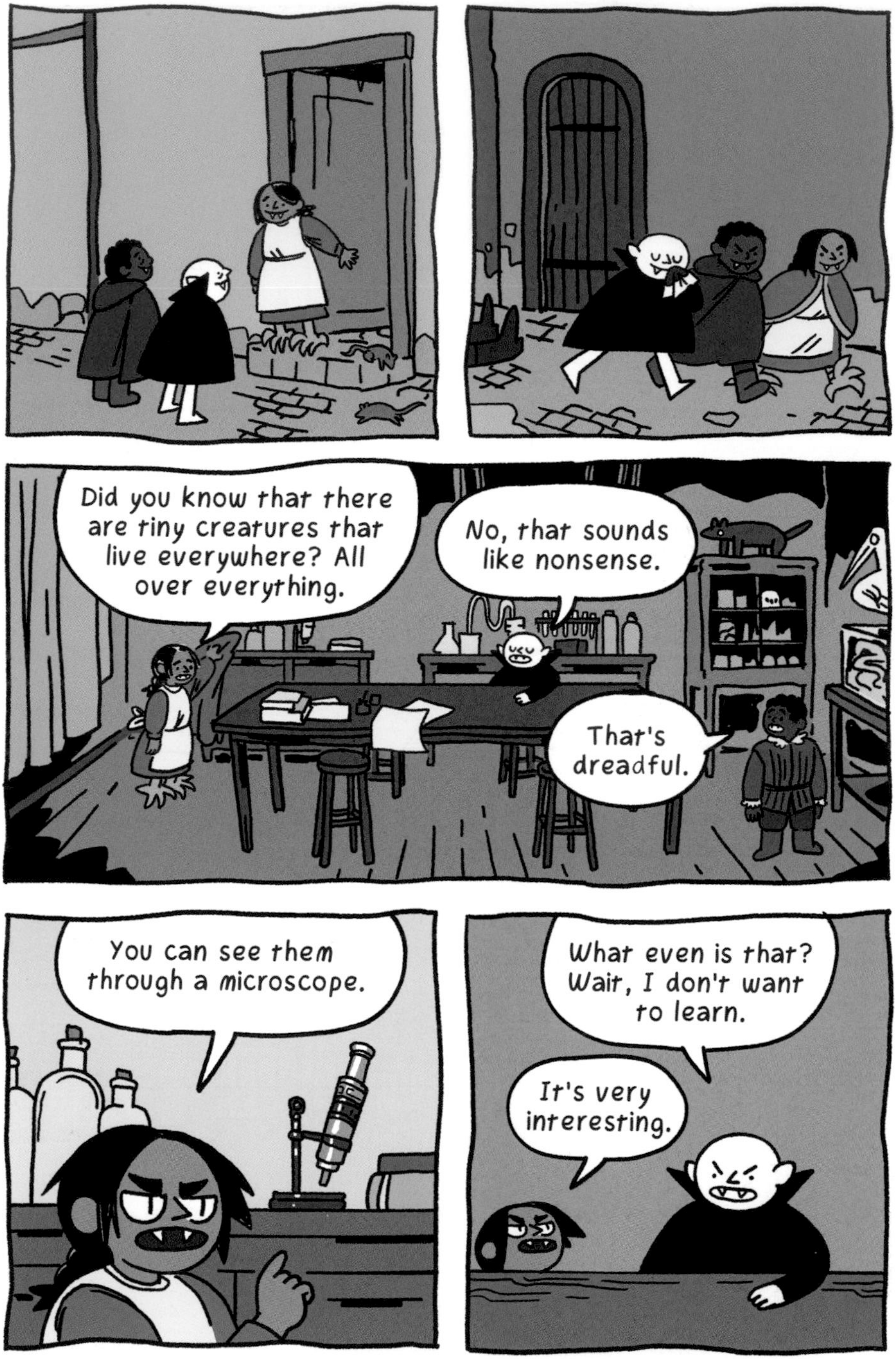
Did you know that there are tiny creatures that live everywhere? All over everything.
No, that sounds like nonsense.
That's dreadful.
You can see them through a microscope.
What even is that? Wait, I don't want to learn.
It's very interesting.

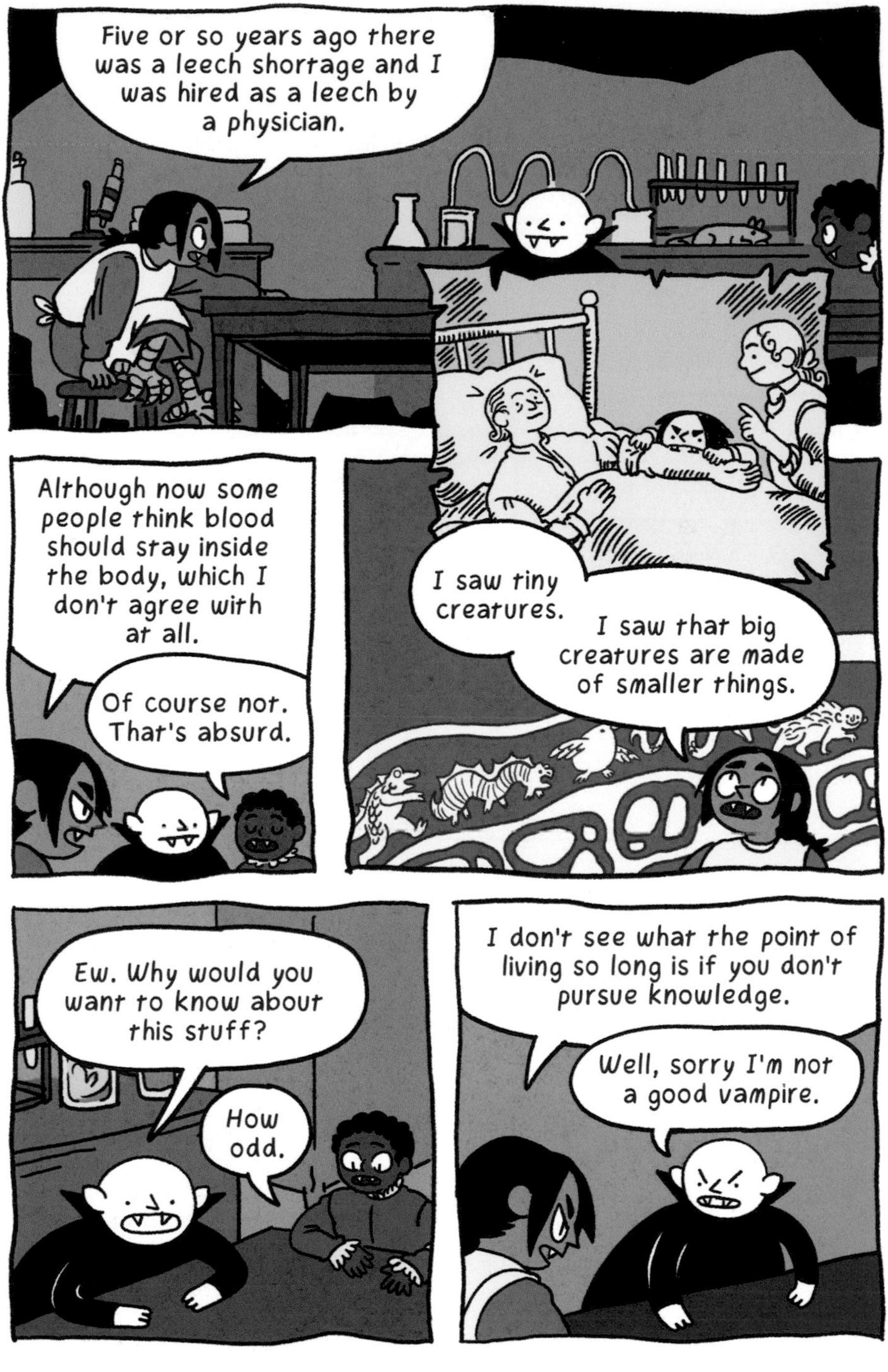
Five or so years ago there was a leech shortage and I was hired as a leech by a physician.
Although now some people think blood should stay inside the body, which I don't agree with at all.
Of course not. That's absurd.
I saw tiny creatures.
I saw that big creatures are made of smaller things.
Ew. Why would you want to know about this stuff?
How odd.
I don't see what the point of living so long is if you don't pursue knowledge.
Well, sorry I'm not a good vampire.

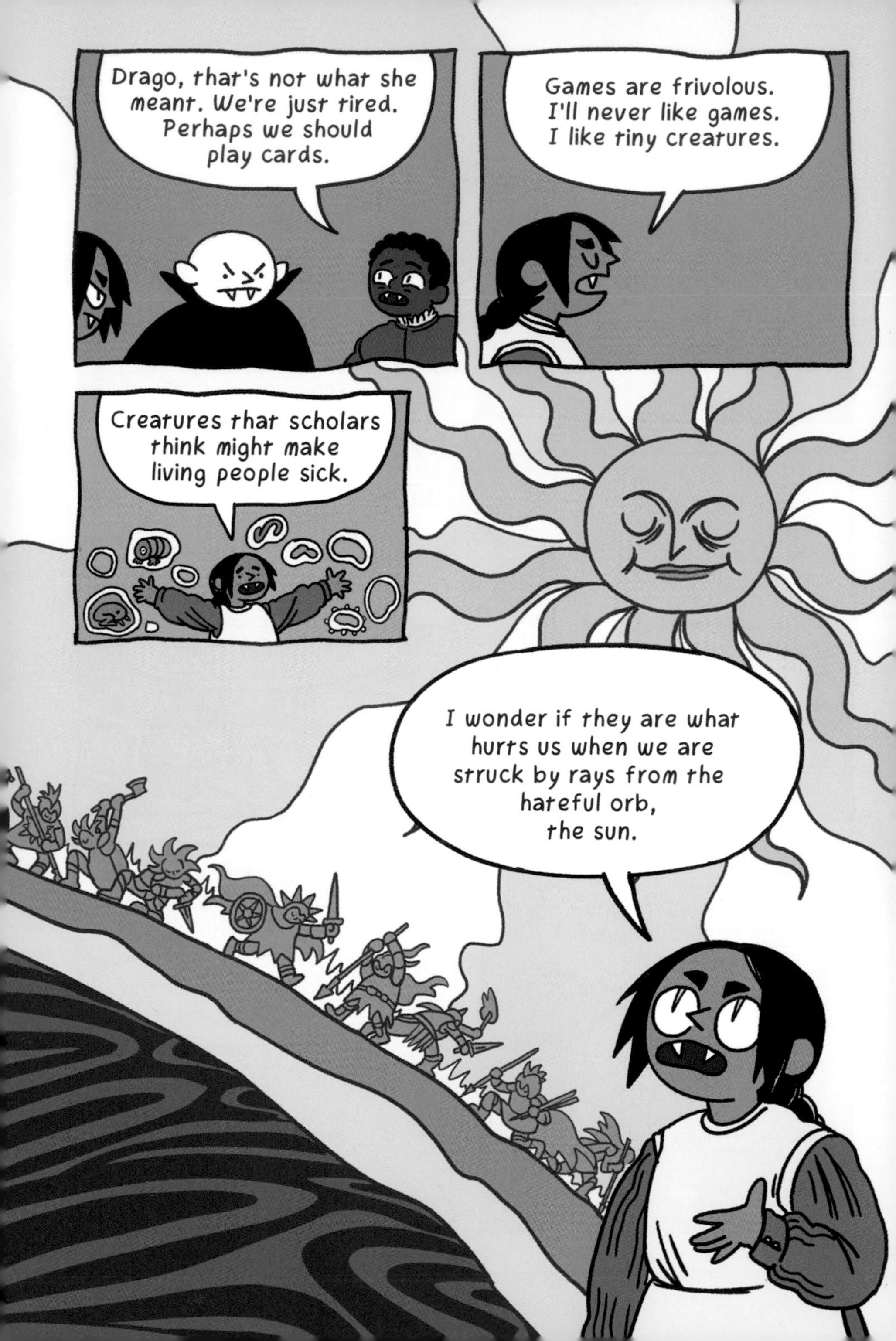
Drago, that's not what she meant. We're just tired. Perhaps we should play cards.
Games are frivolous. I'll never like games. I like tiny creatures.
Creatures that scholars think might make living people sick.
I wonder if they are what hurts us when we are struck by rays from the hateful orb, the sun.

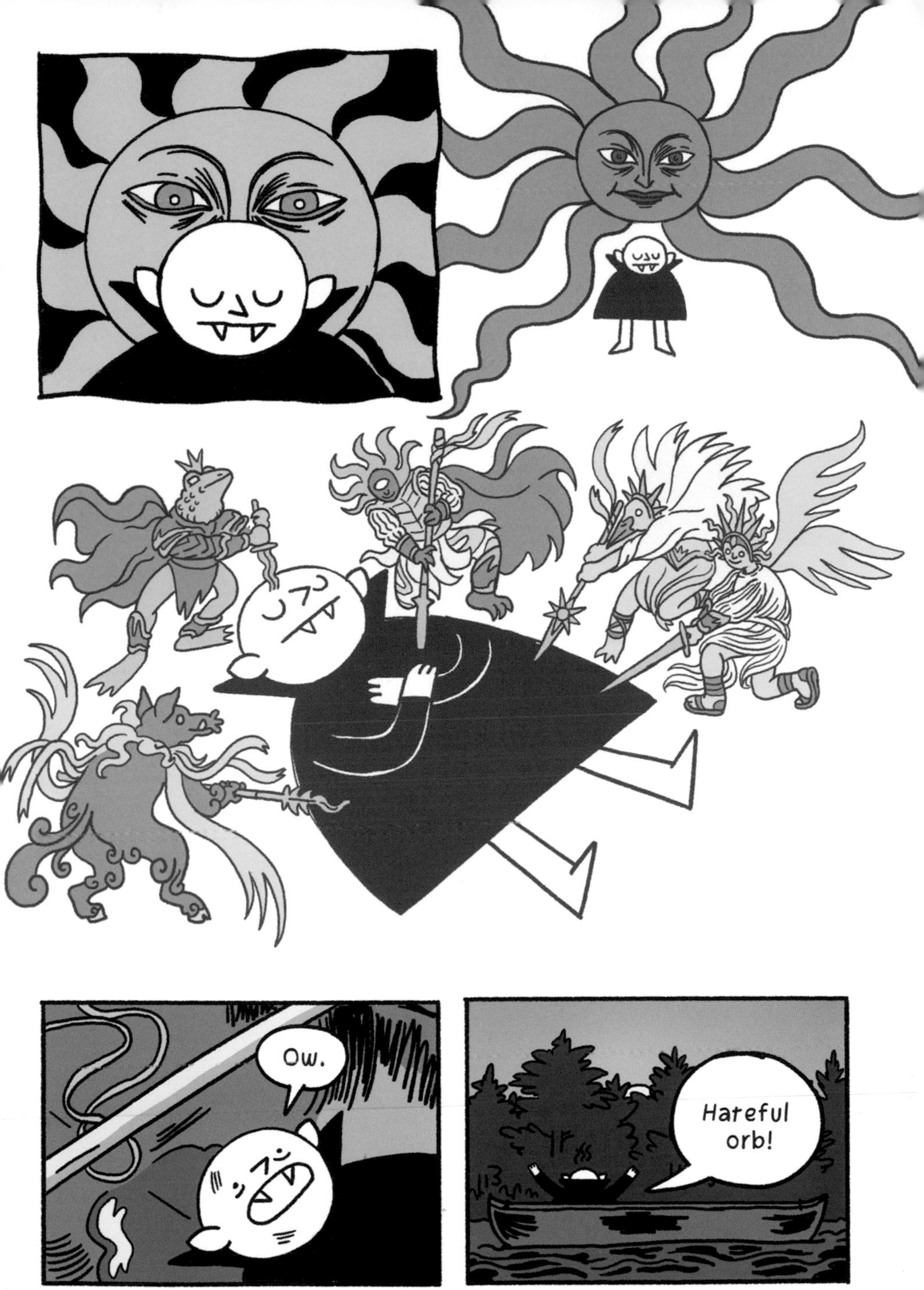
Ow.
Hateful orb!

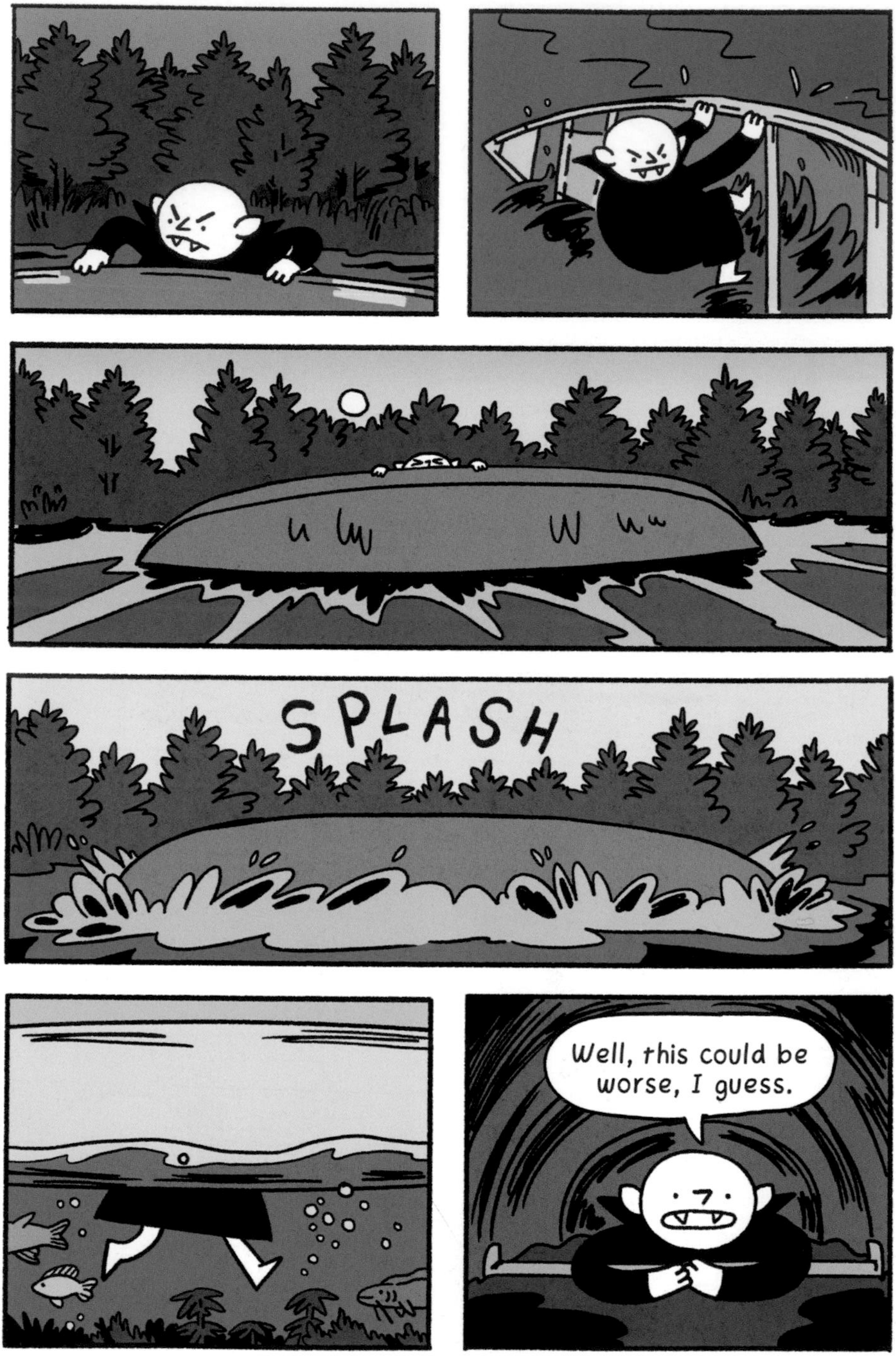
SPLASH
Well, this could be worse, I guess.

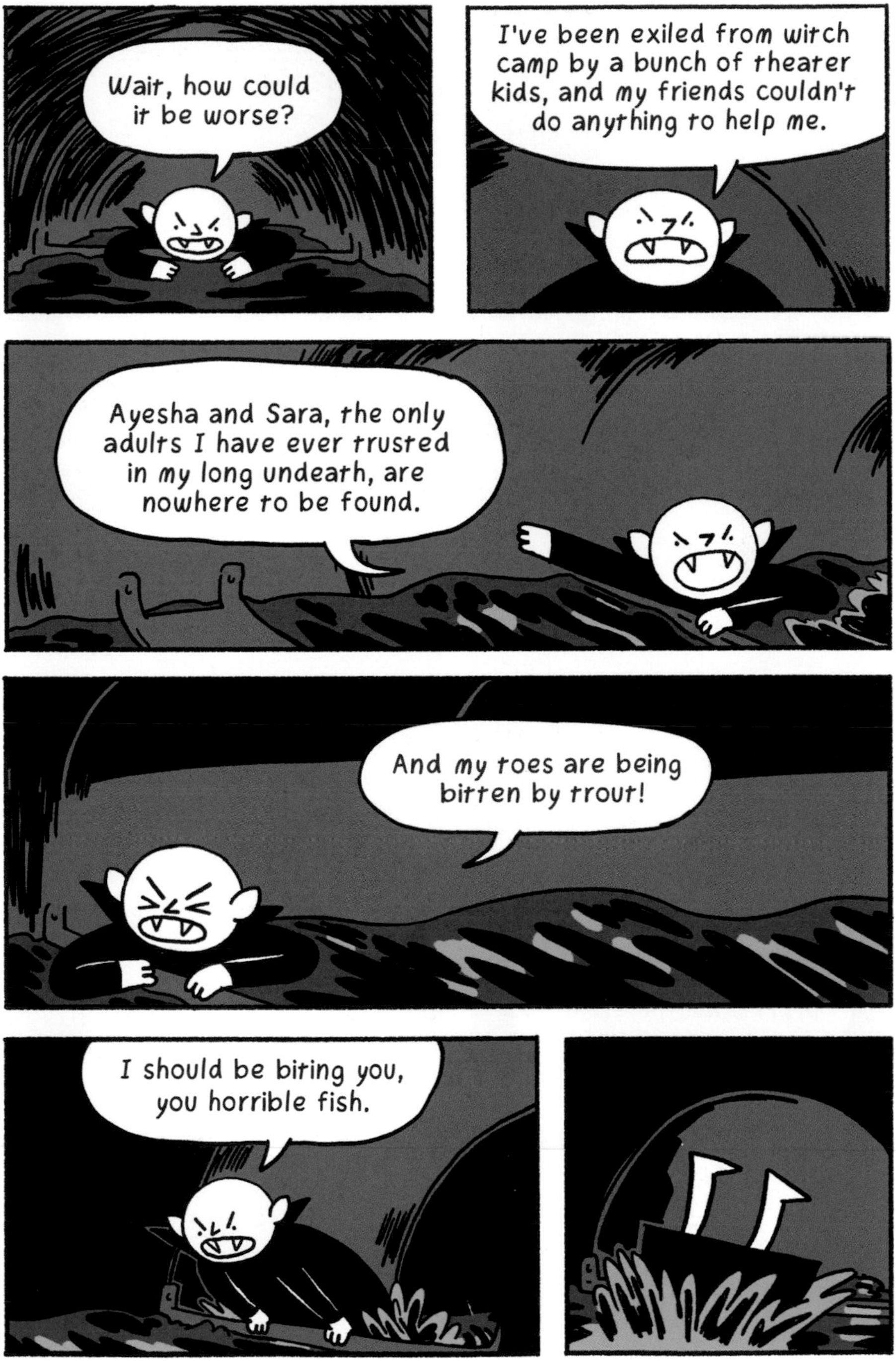

Wait, how could it be worse?
I've been exiled from witch camp by a bunch of theater kids, and my friends couldn't do anything to help me.
Ayesha and Sara, the only adults I have ever trusted in my long undeath, are nowhere to be found.
And my toes are being bitten by trout!
I should be biting you, you horrible fish.

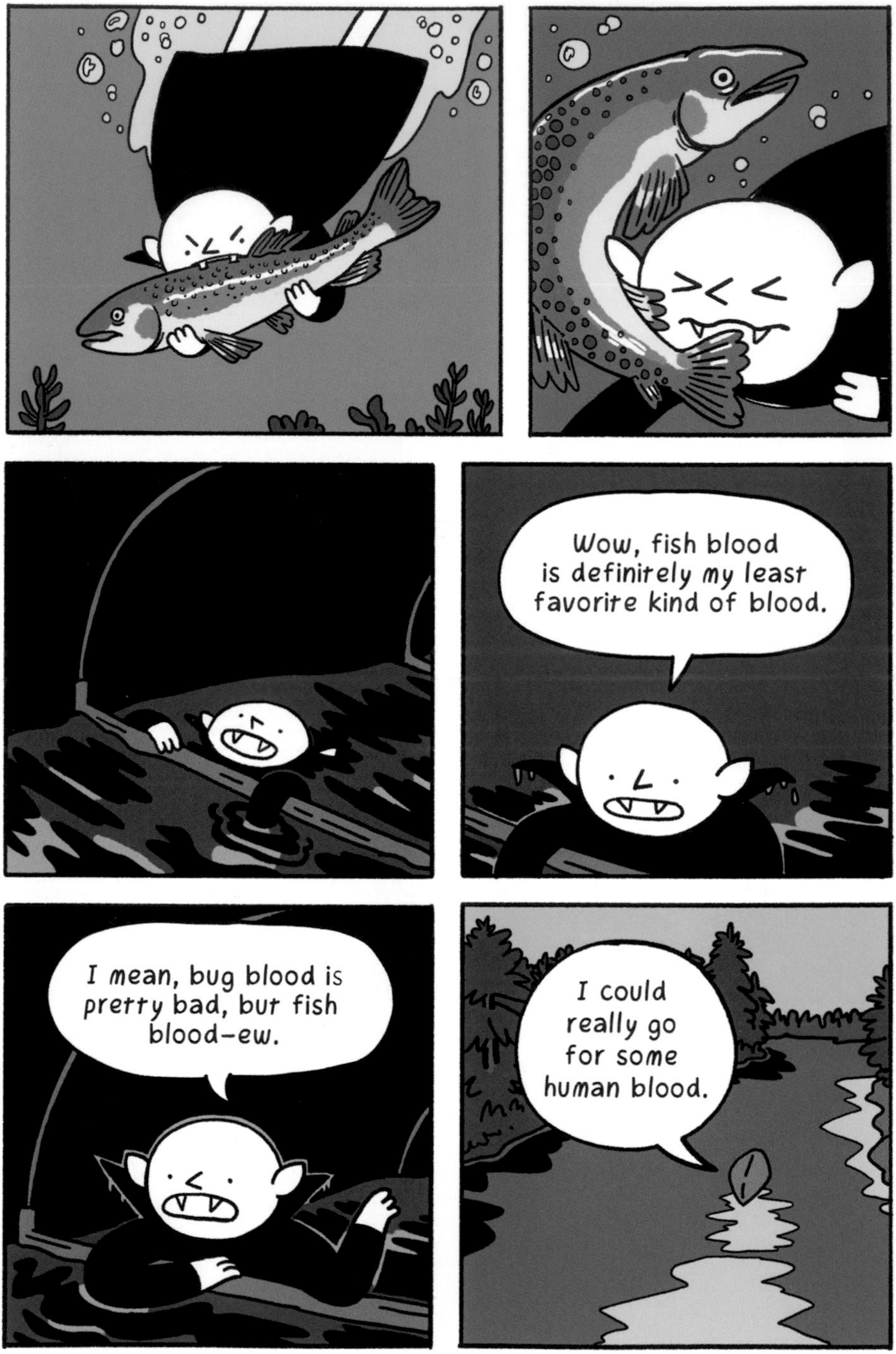
Wow, fish blood is definitely my least favorite kind of blood.
I mean, bug blood is pretty bad, but fish blood—ew.
I could really go for some human blood.

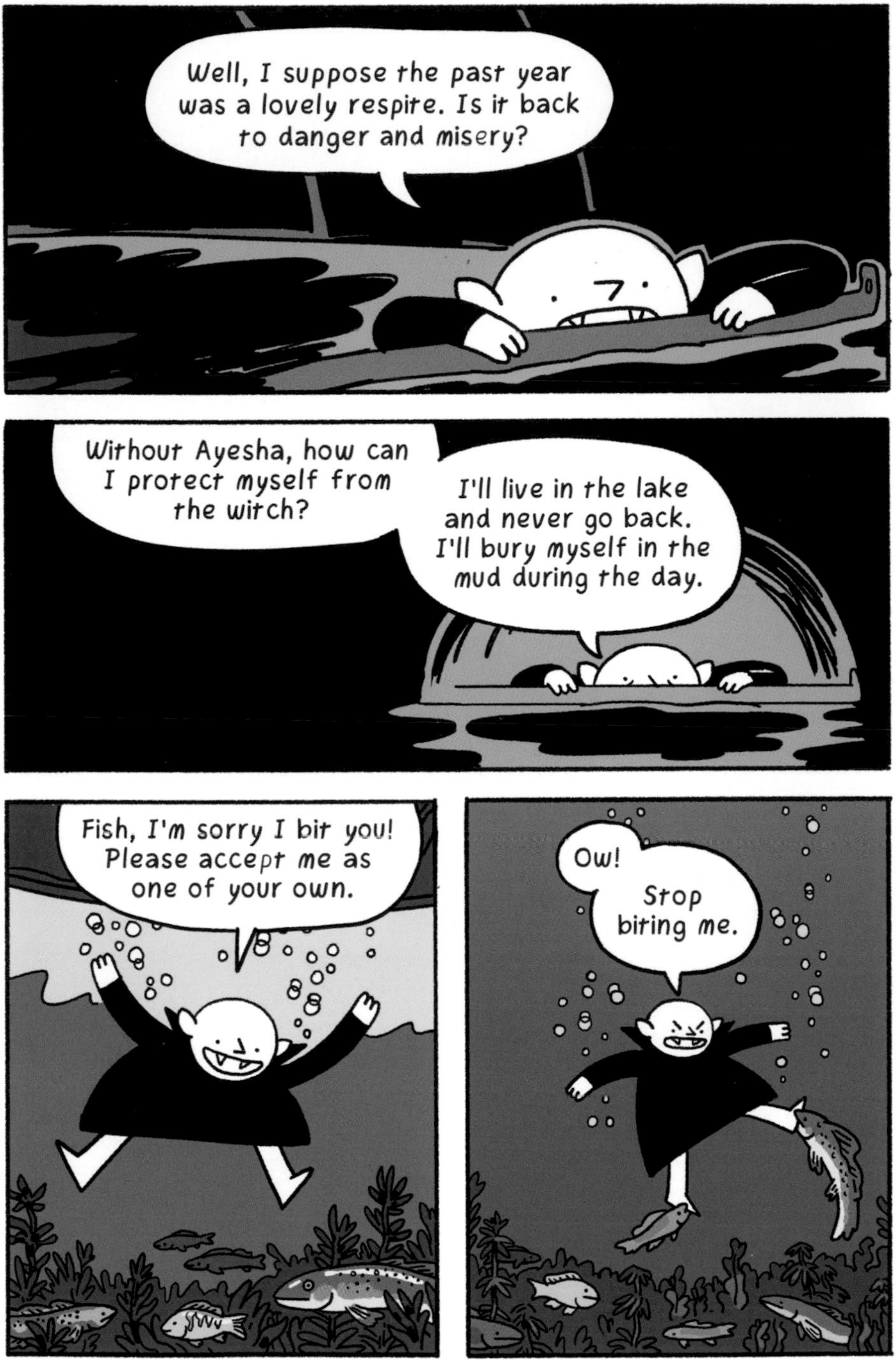
Well, I suppose the past year was a lovely respite. Is it back to danger and misery?
Without Ayesha, how can I protect myself from the witch?
I'll live in the lake and never go back. I'll bury myself in the mud during the day.
Fish, I'm sorry I bit you! Please accept me as one of your own.
Ow!
Stop biting me.

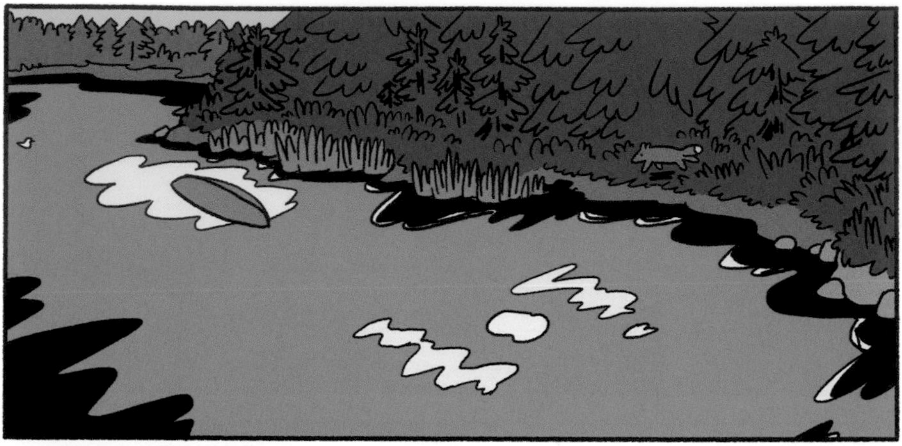

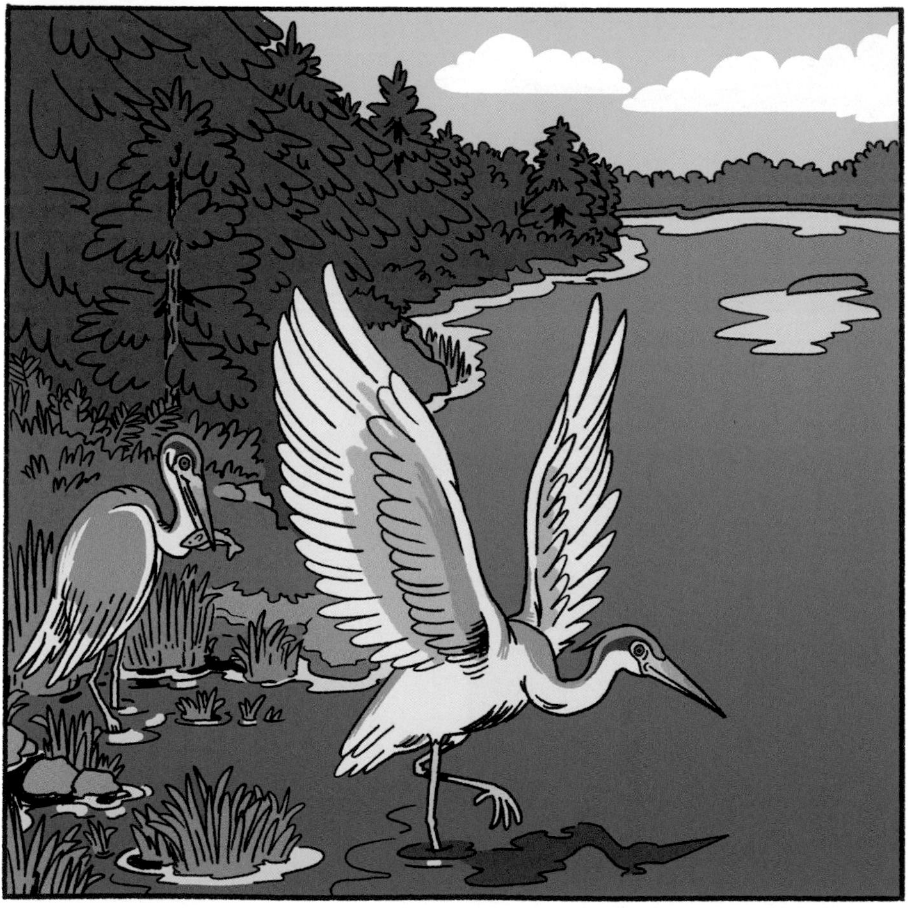

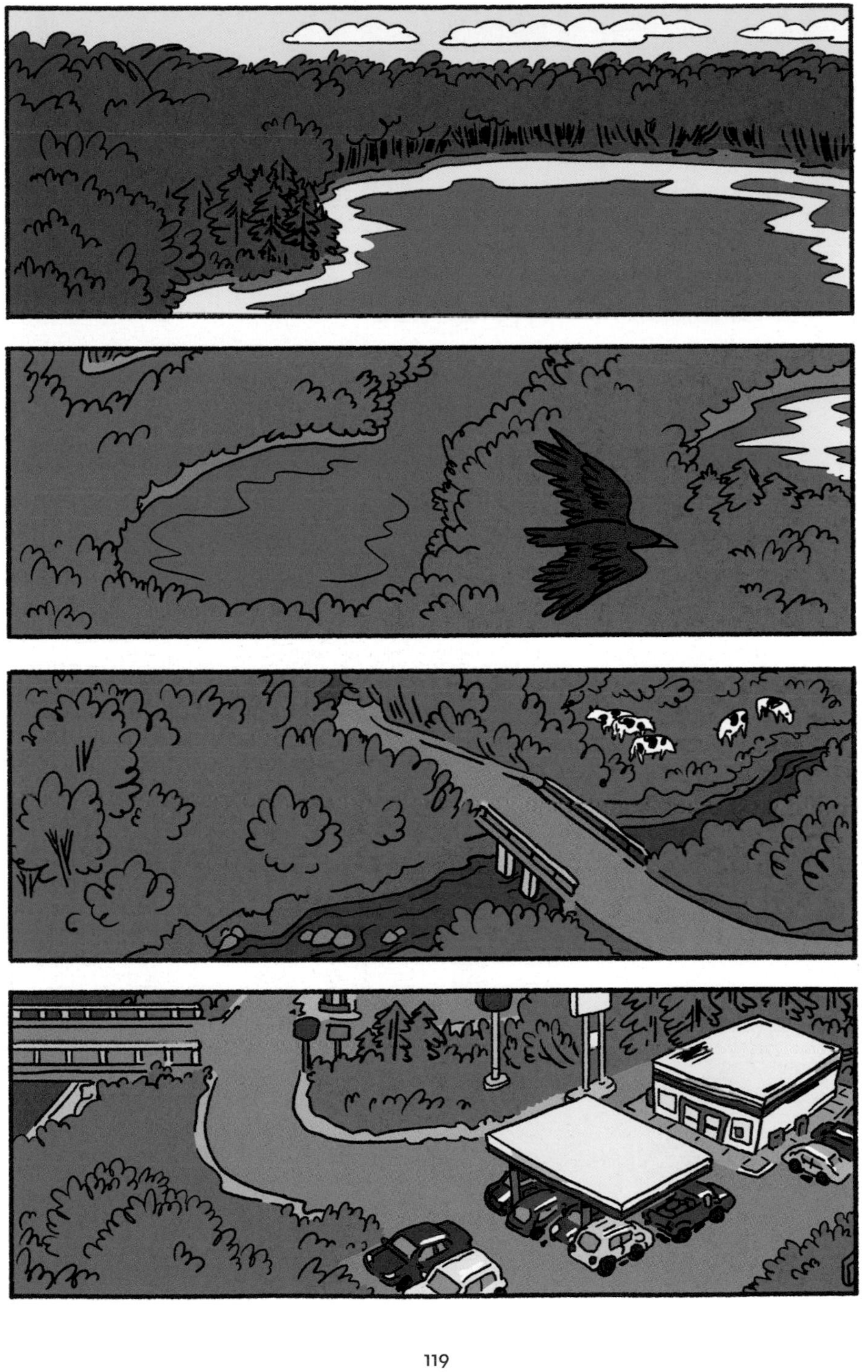

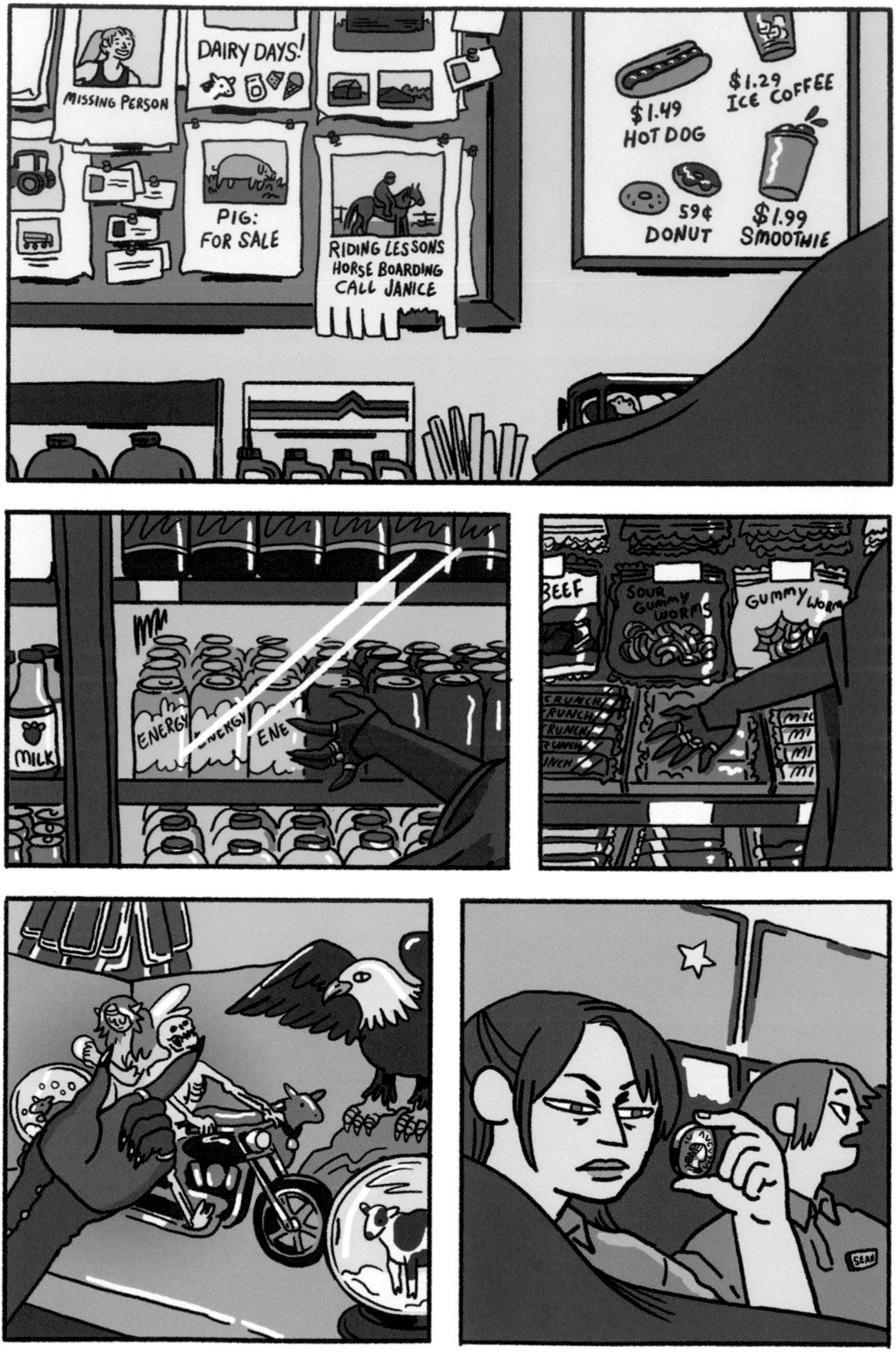

MISSING PERSON
DAIRY DAYS!
PIG: FOR SALE
RIDING LESSONS
HORSE BOARDING
CALL JANICE
$1.49
HOT DOG
$1.29
ICE COFFEE
59¢
DONUT
$1.99
SMOOTHIE
ENERGY
ENERGY
ENE
MILK
BEEF
SOUR GUMMY WORMS
GUMMY WORM
SEAN

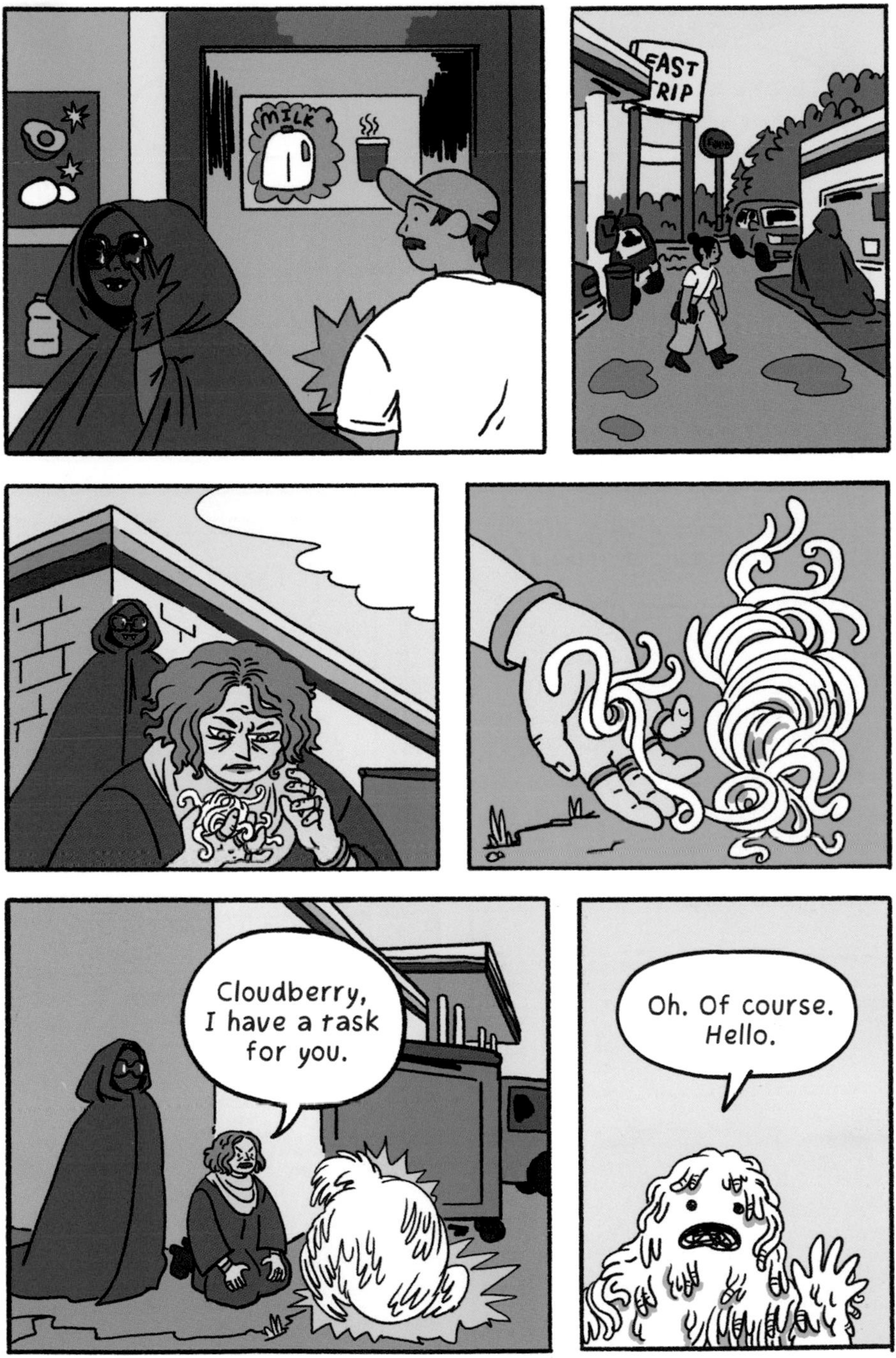
MILK
EAST
TRIP
Cloudberry, I have a task for you.
Oh. Of course. Hello.

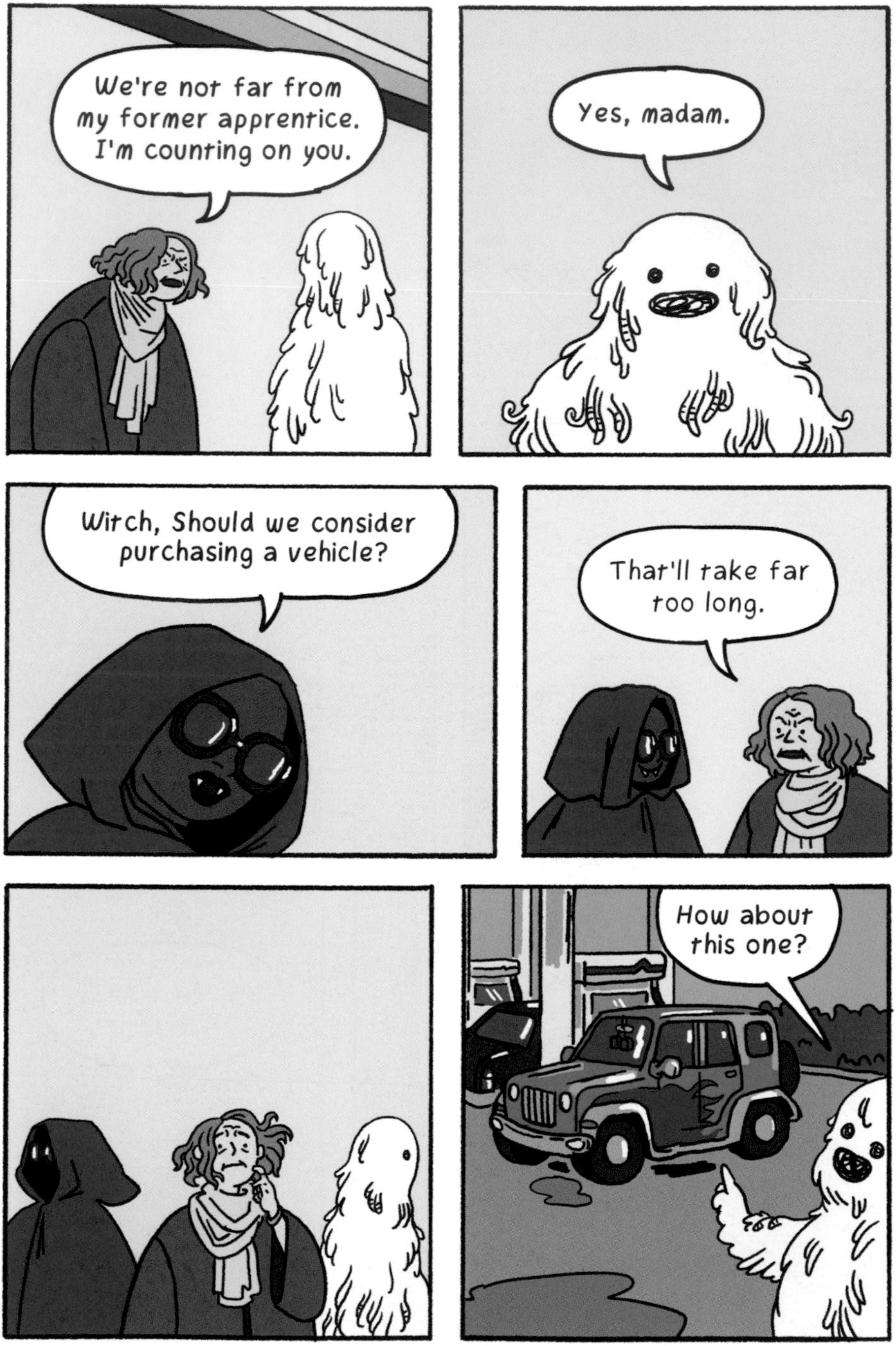
We're not far from my former apprentice. I'm counting on you.
Yes, madam.
Witch, Should we consider purchasing a vehicle?
That'll take far too long.
How about this one?

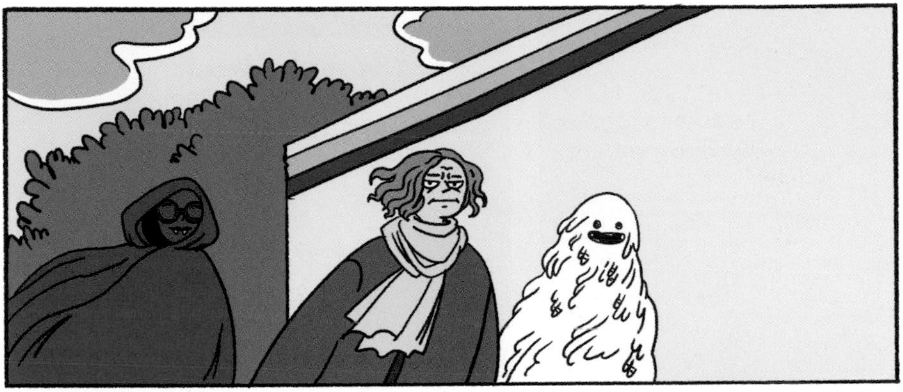

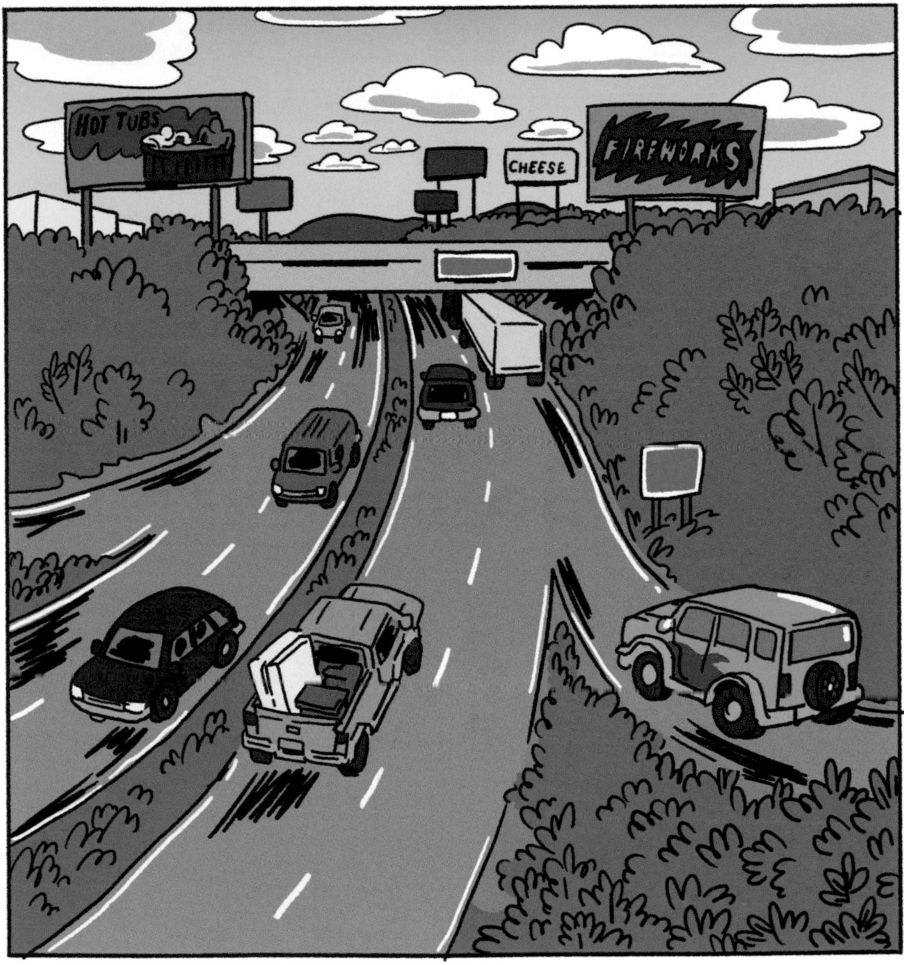
HOT TUBS
CHEESE
FIREWORKS

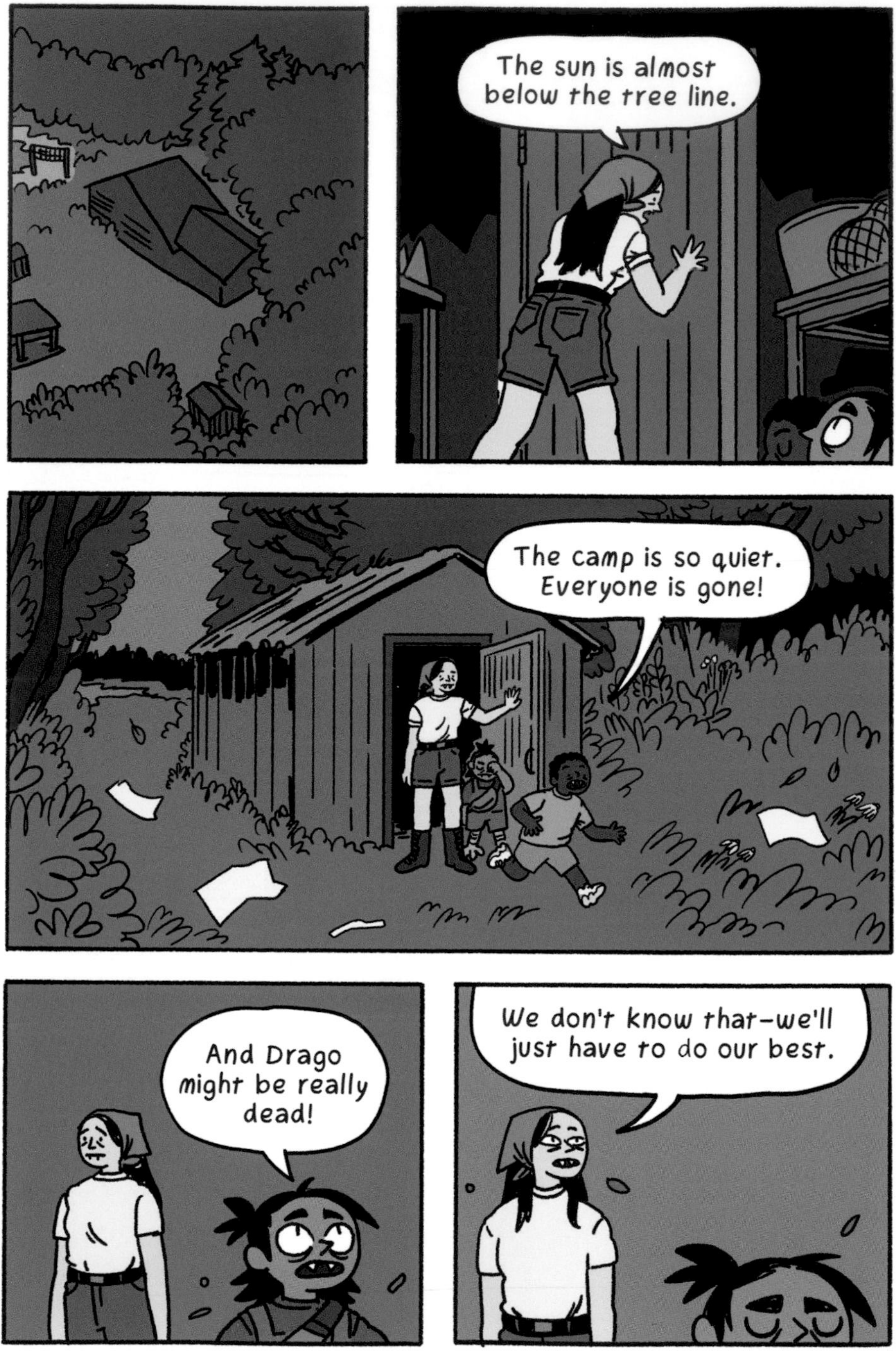
The sun is almost below the tree line.
The camp is so quiet. Everyone is gone!
And Drago might be really dead!
We don't know that–we'll just have to do our best.

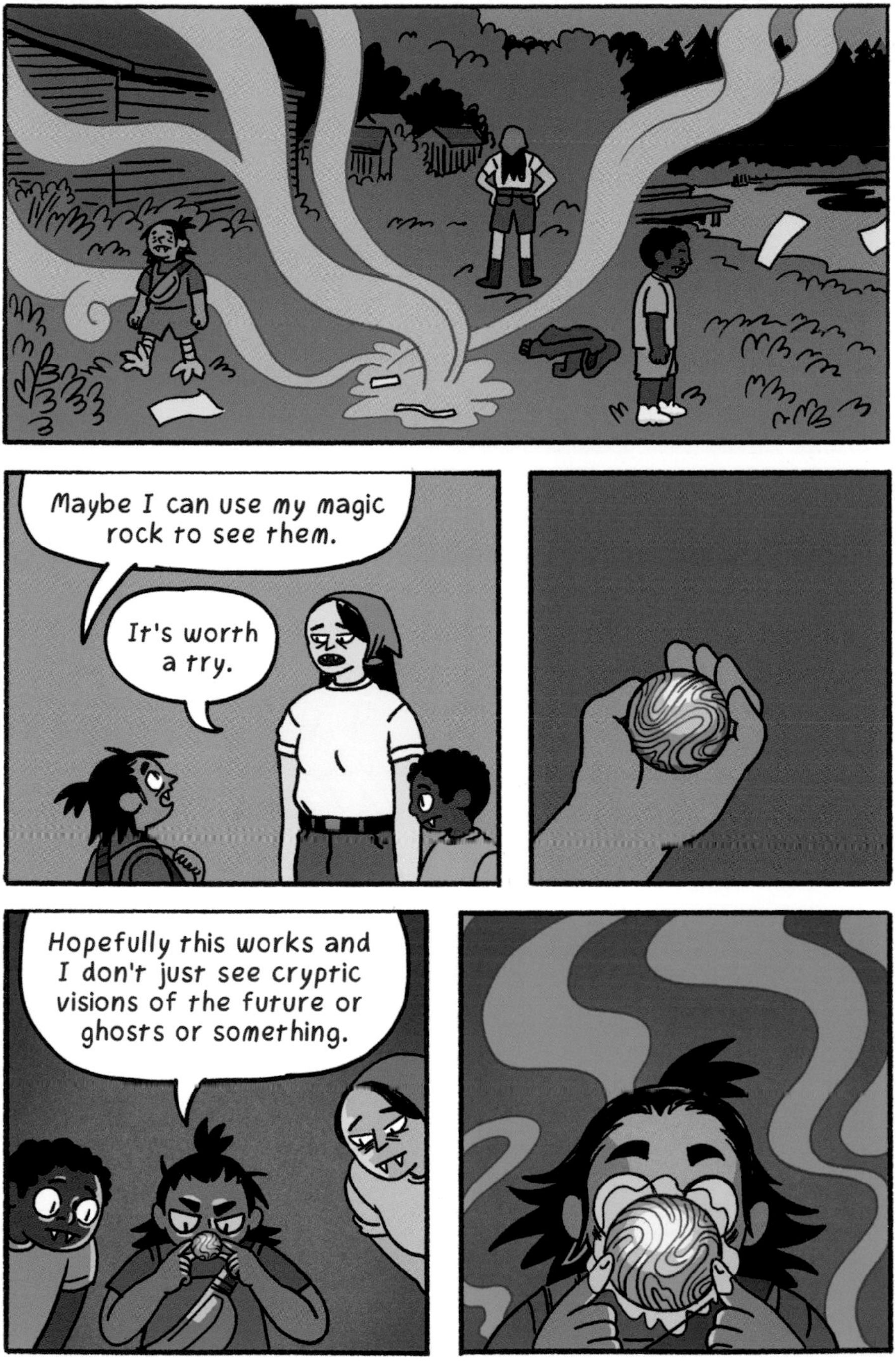
Maybe I can use my magic rock to see them.
It's worth a try.
Hopefully this works and I don't just see cryptic visions of the future or ghosts or something.

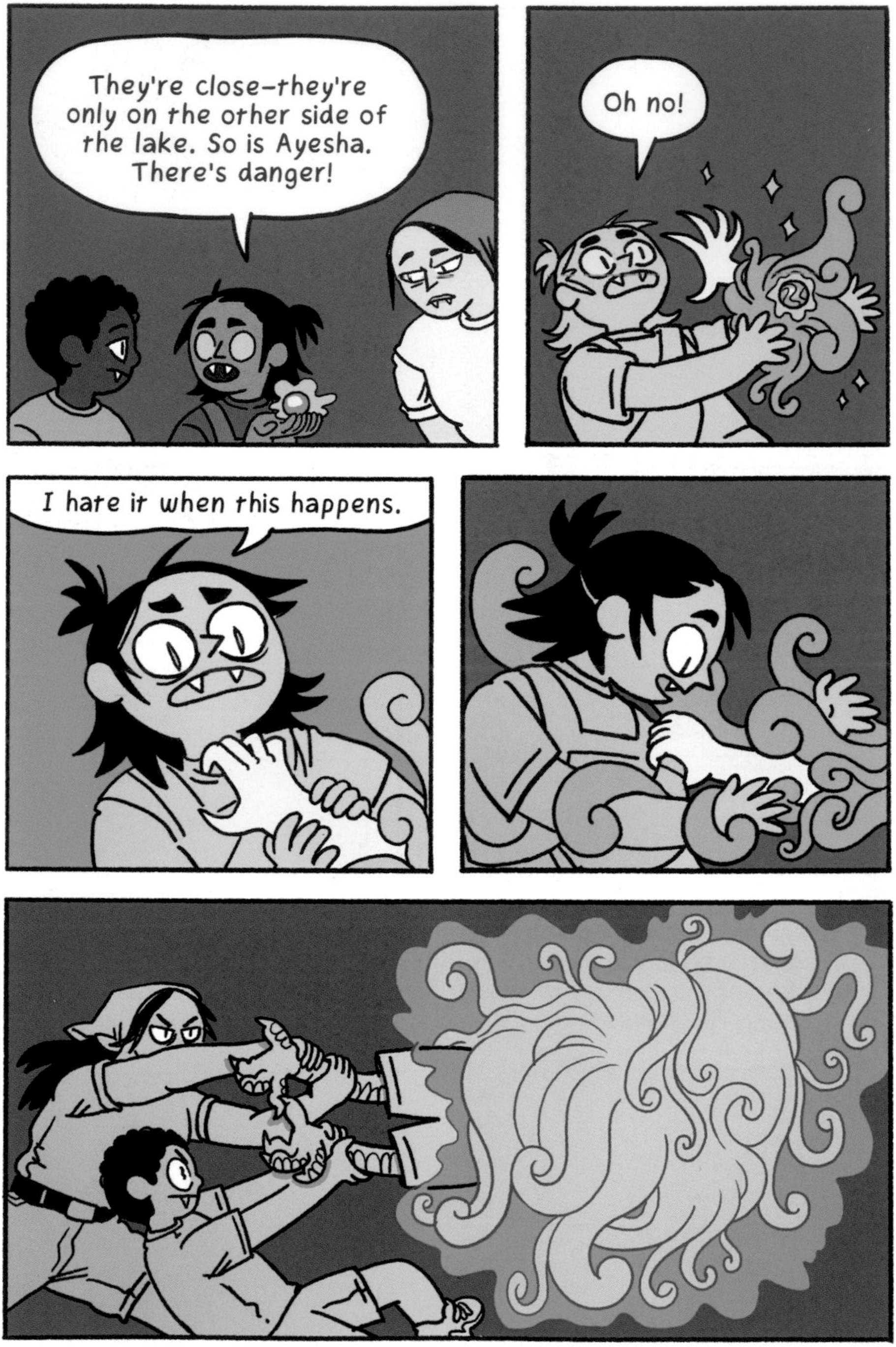
They're close–they're only on the other side of the lake. So is Ayesha. There's danger!
Oh no!
I hate it when this happens.

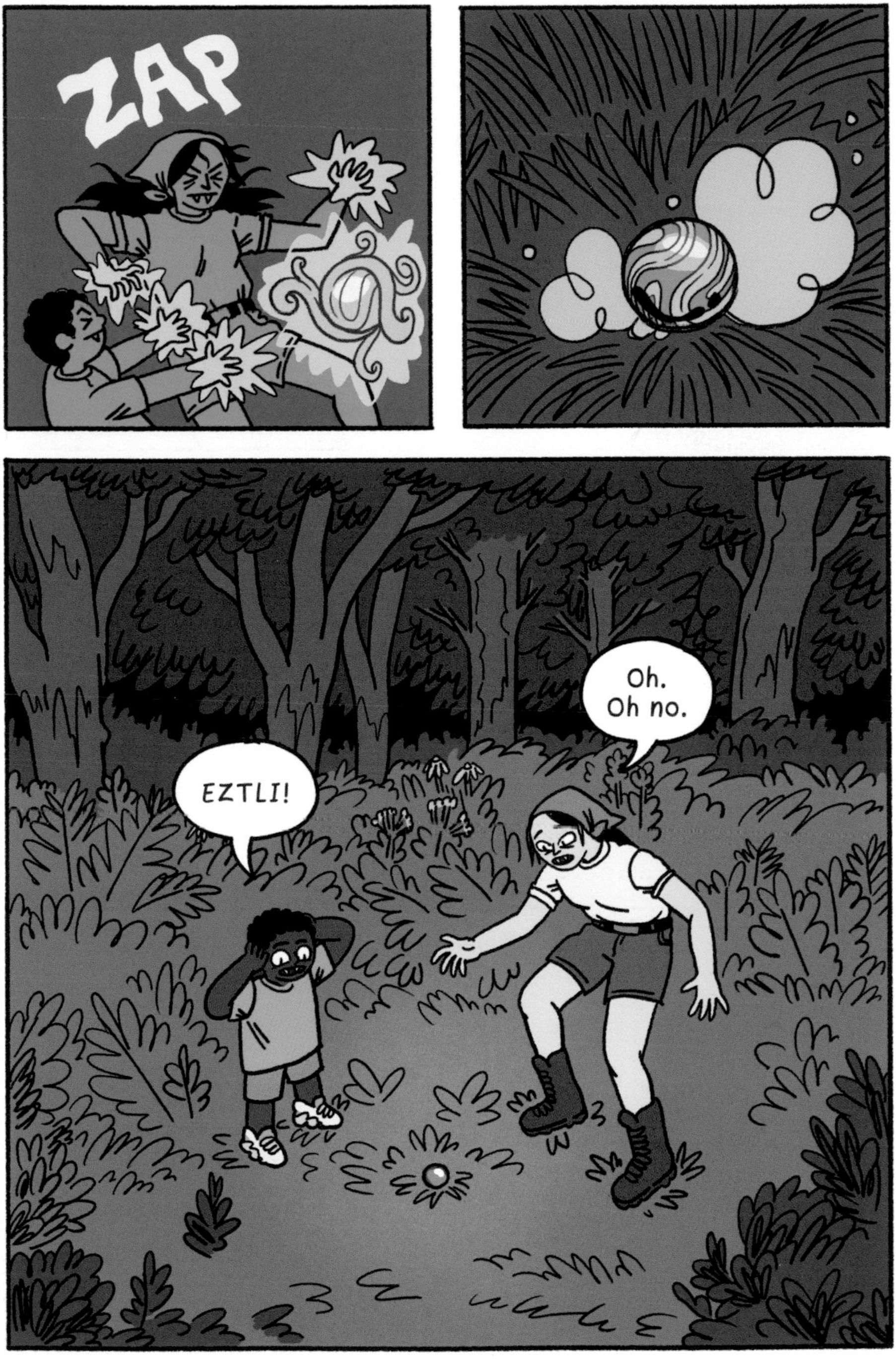
ZAP
EZTLI!
Oh.
Oh no.

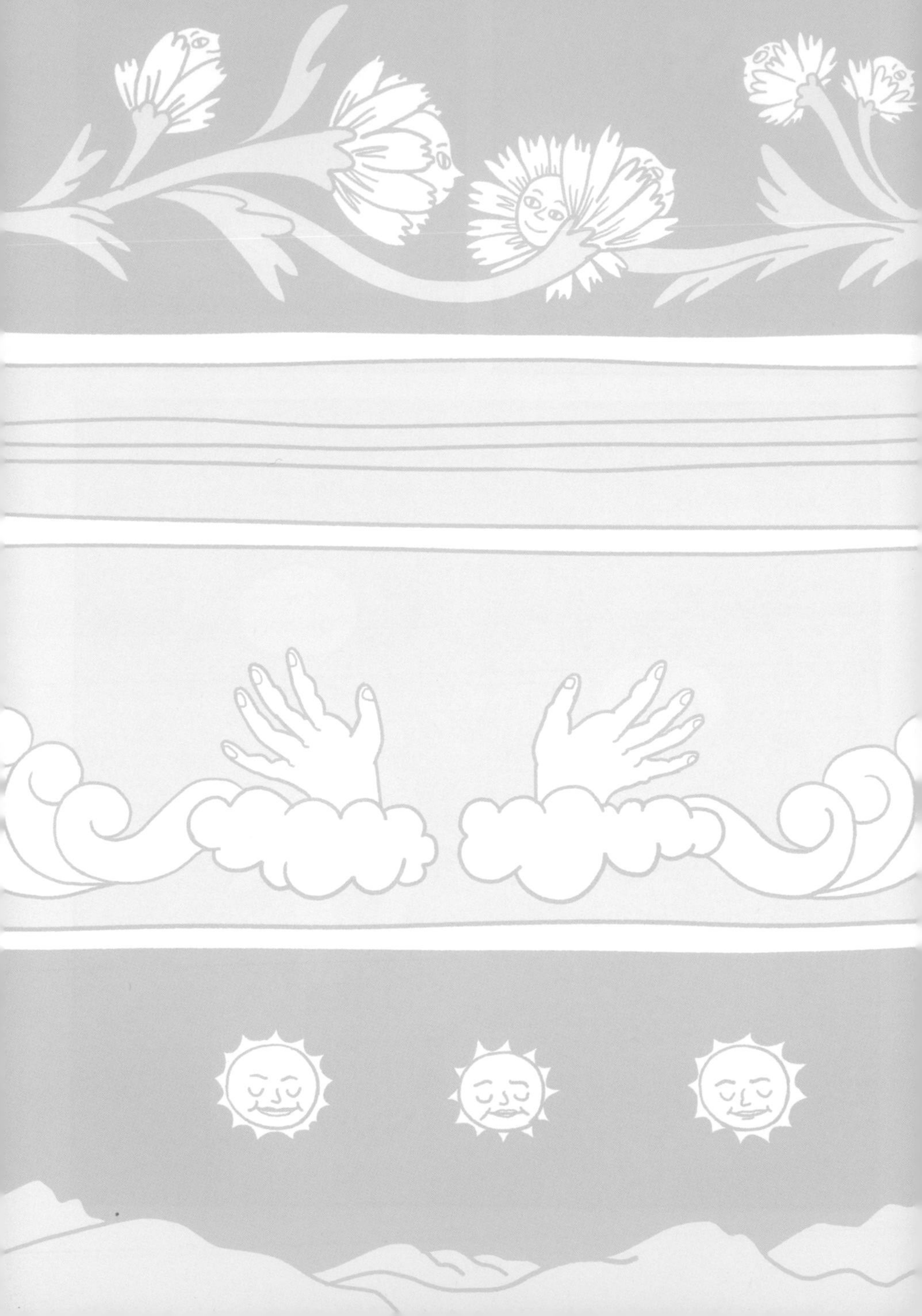

CHAPTER SIX

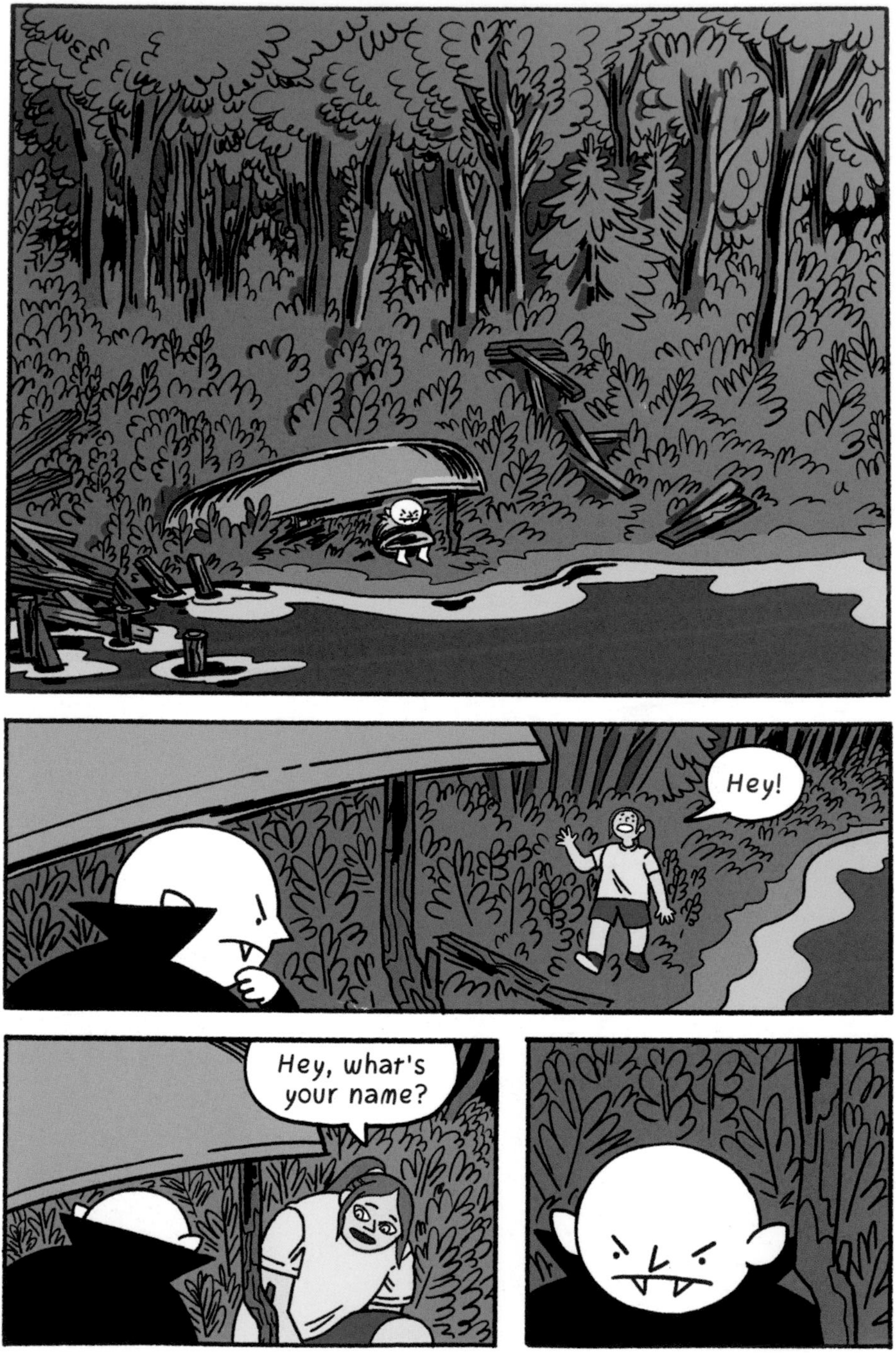
Hey!
Hey, what's your name?

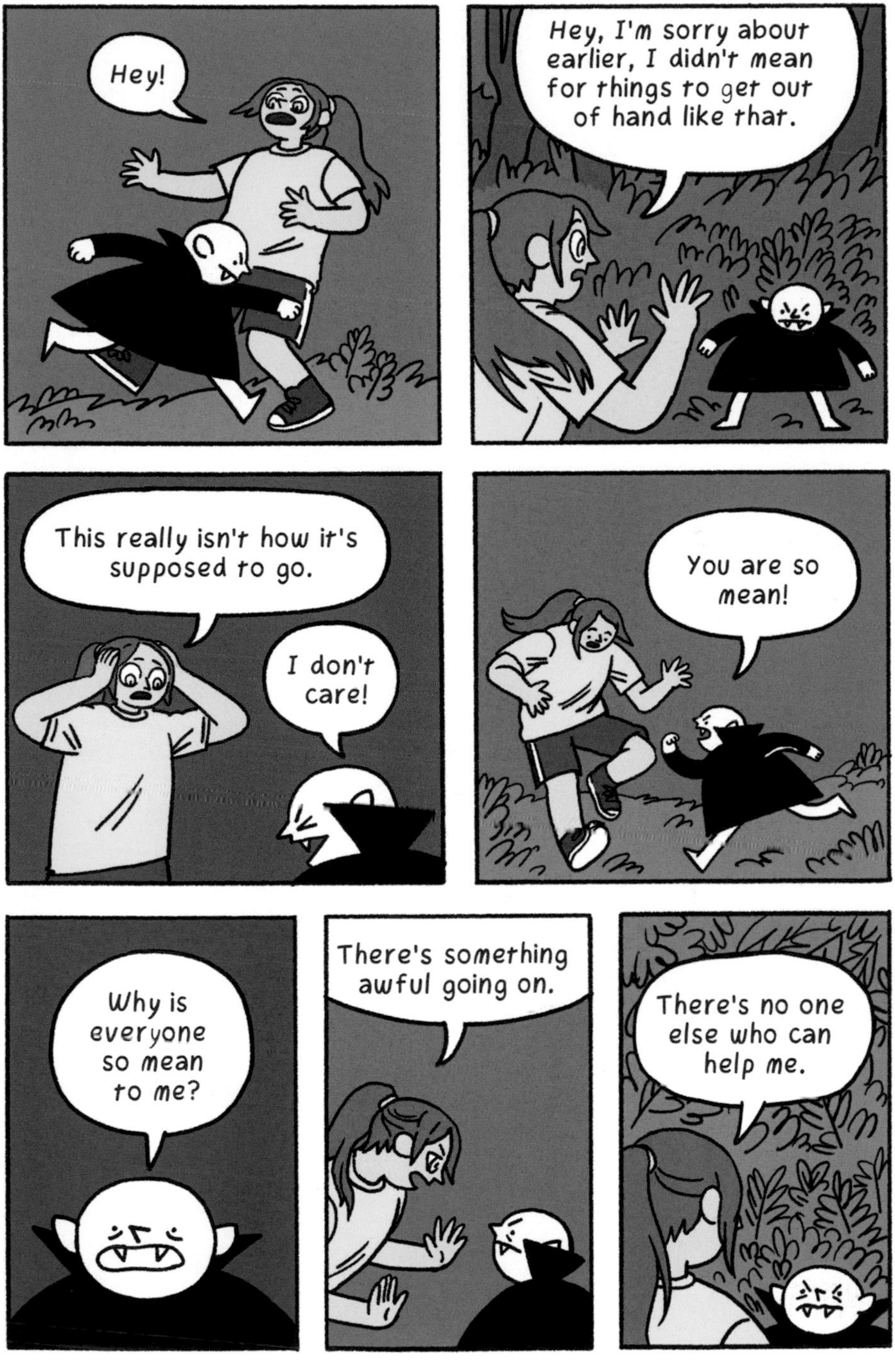
Hey!
Hey, I'm sorry about earlier, I didn't mean for things to get out of hand like that.
This really isn't how it's supposed to go.
I don't care!
You are so mean!
Why is everyone so mean to me?
There's something awful going on.
There's no one else who can help me.

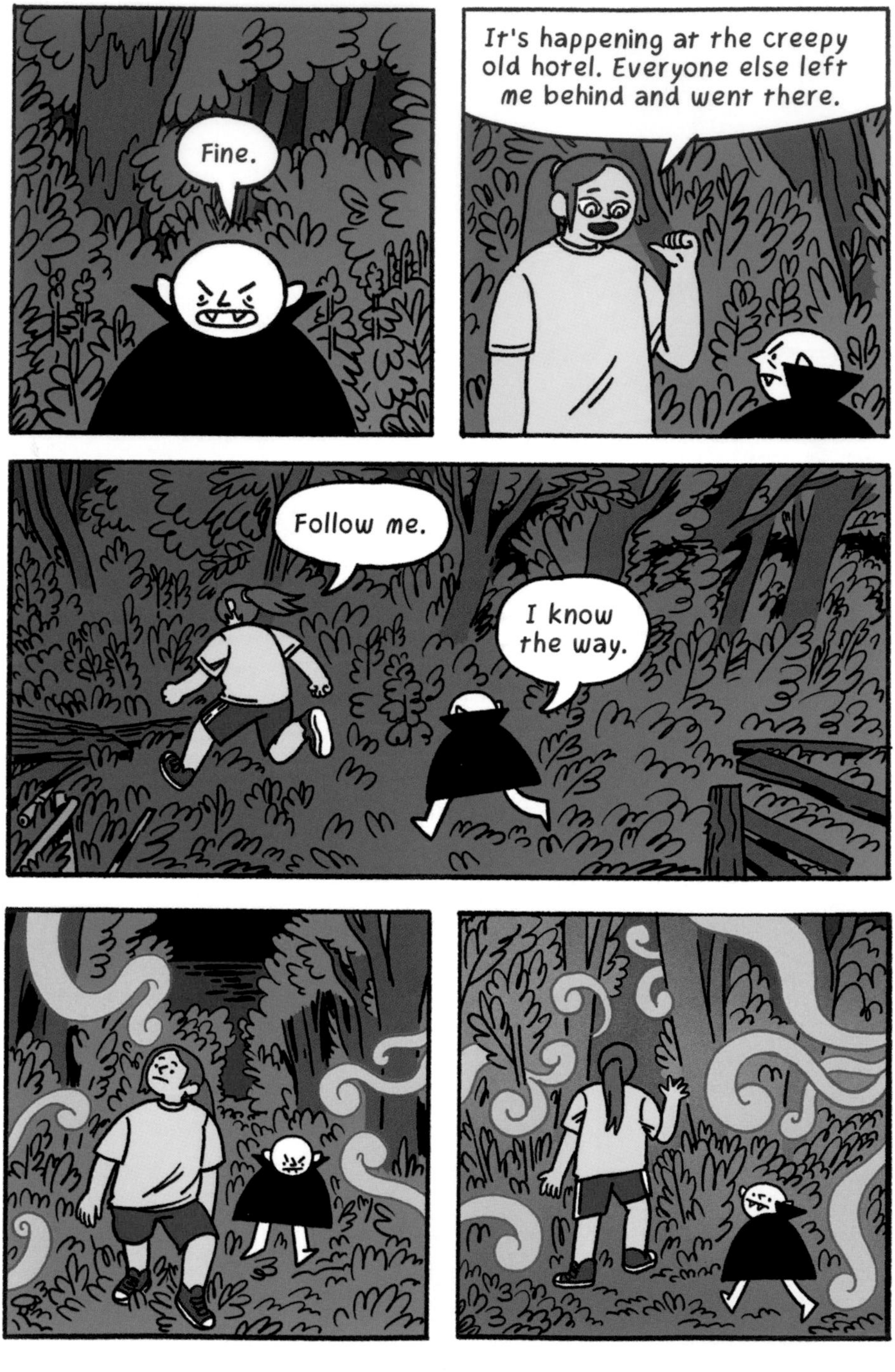
Fine.
It's happening at the creepy old hotel. Everyone else left me behind and went there.
Follow me.
I know the way.

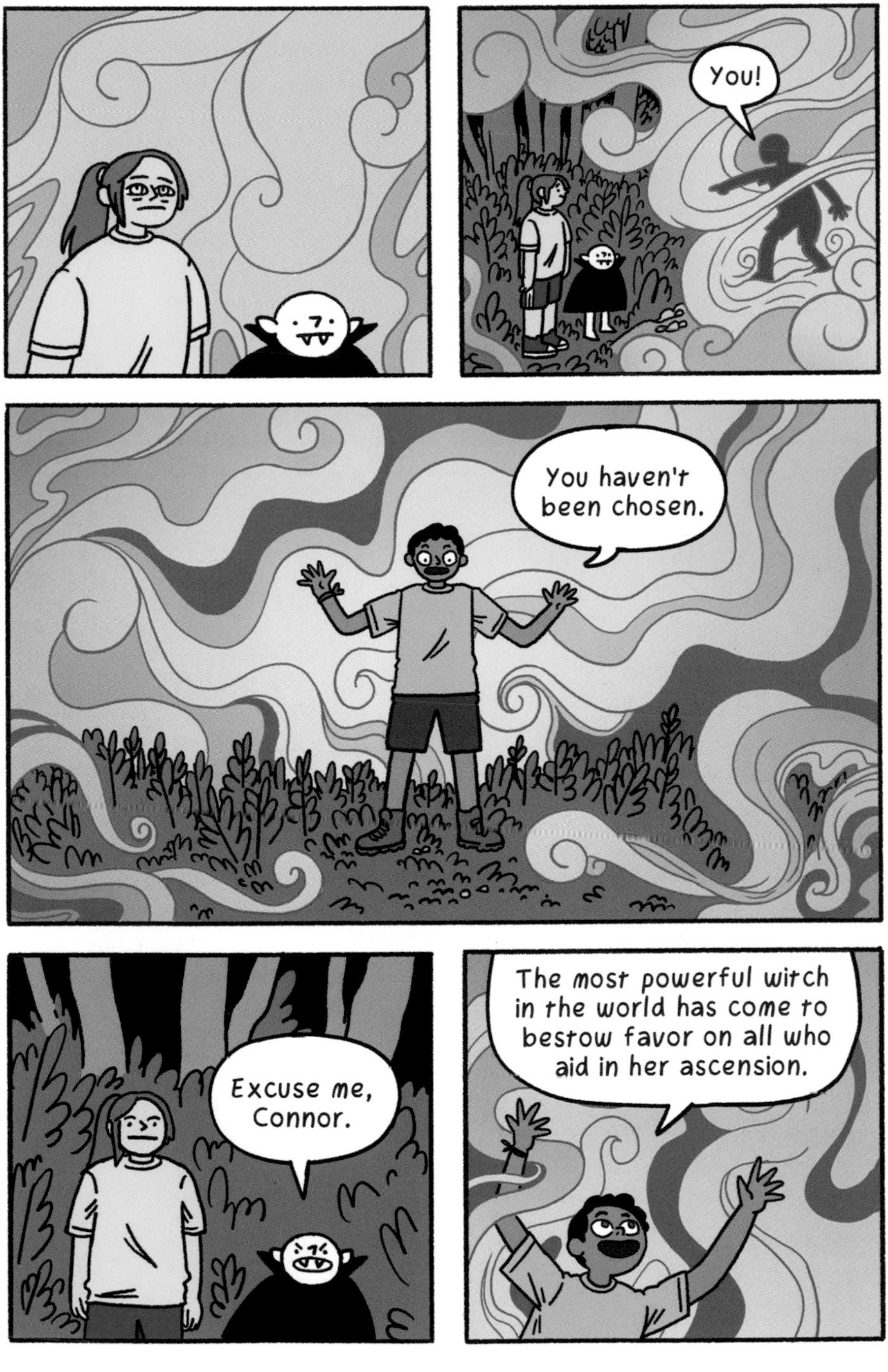
You!
You haven't been chosen.
Excuse me, Connor.
The most powerful witch in the world has come to bestow favor on all who aid in her ascension.

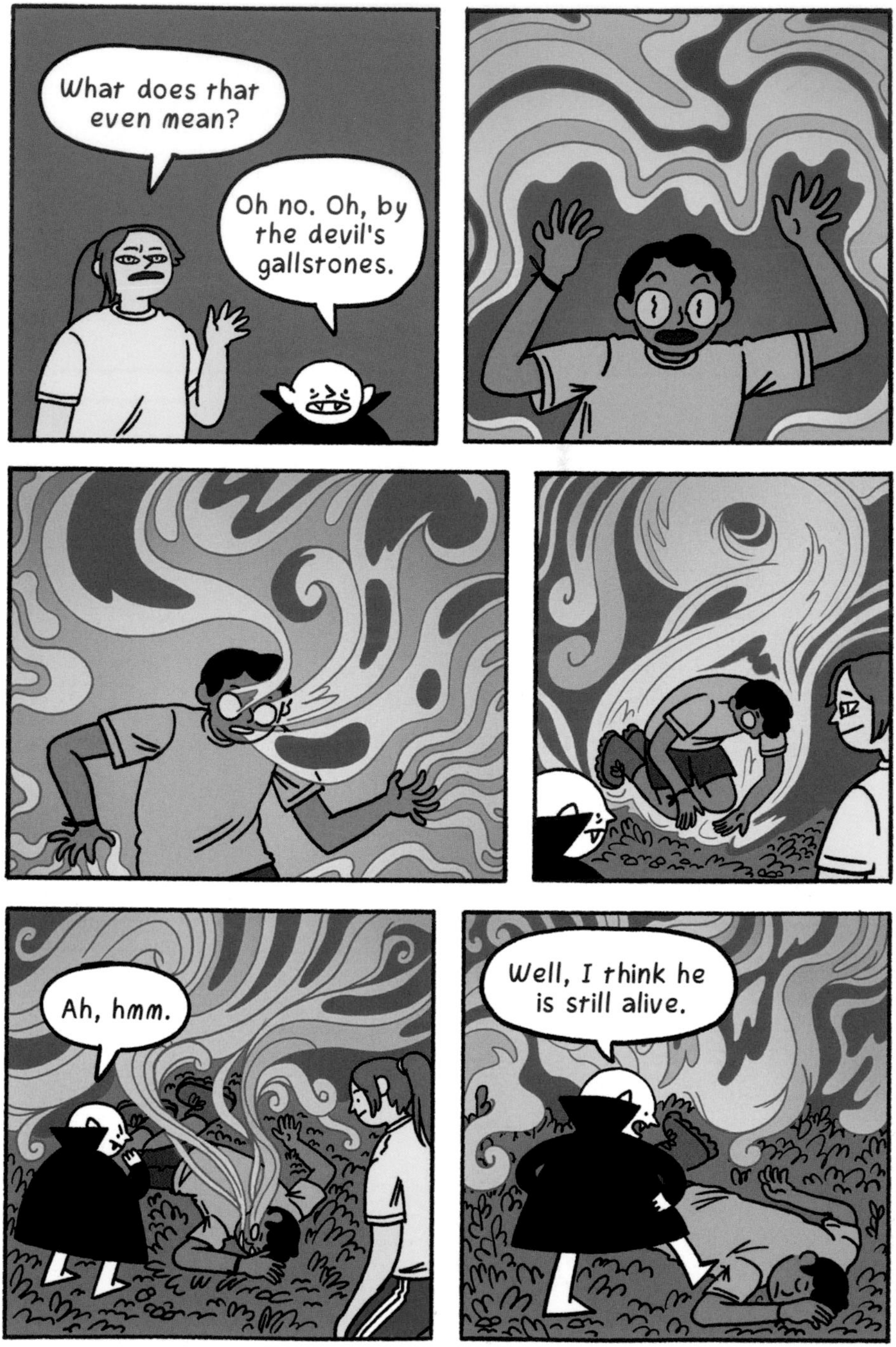
What does that even mean?
Oh no. Oh, by the devil's gallstones.
Ah, hmm.
Well, I think he is still alive.

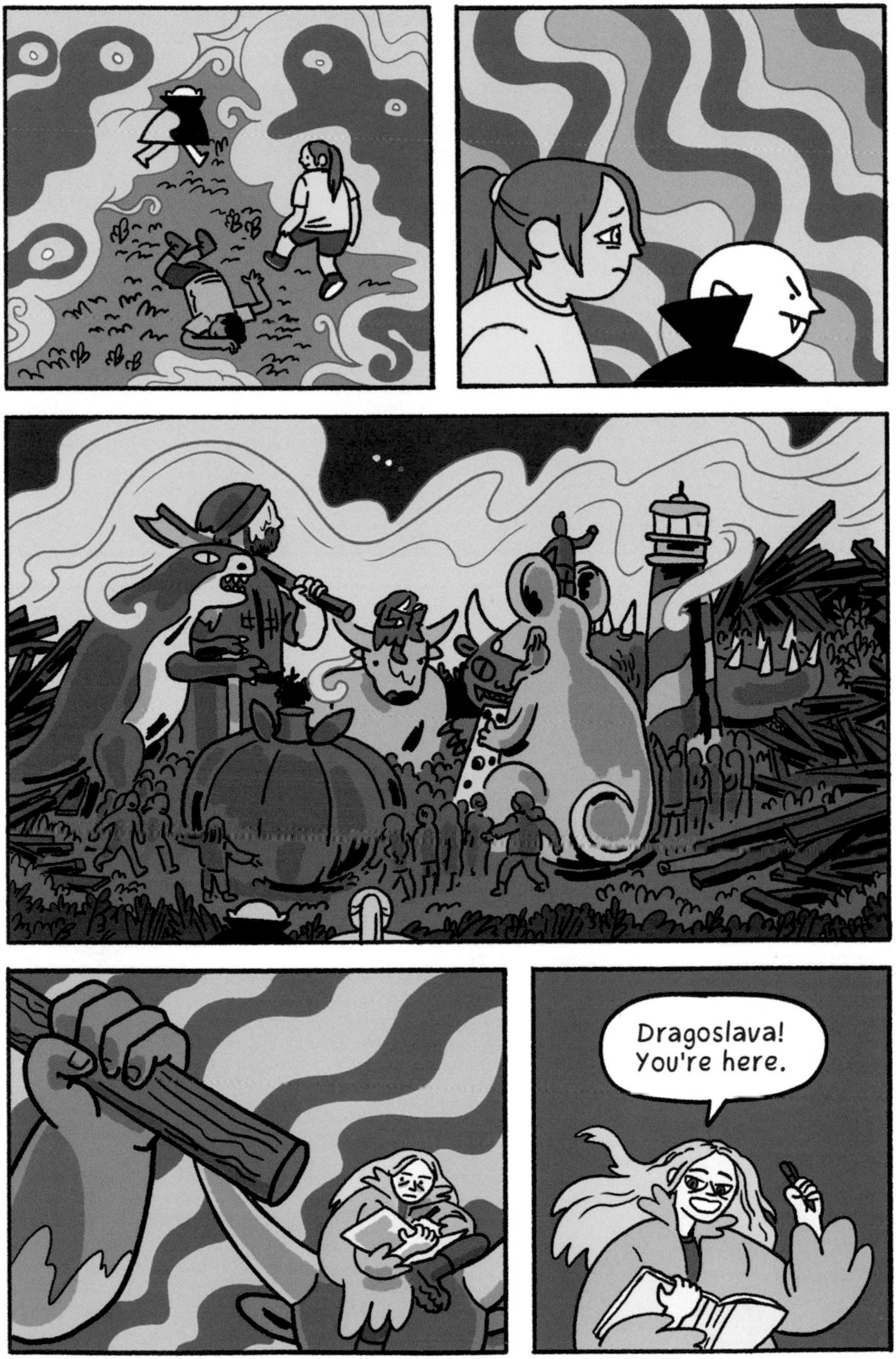
Dragoslava! You're here.

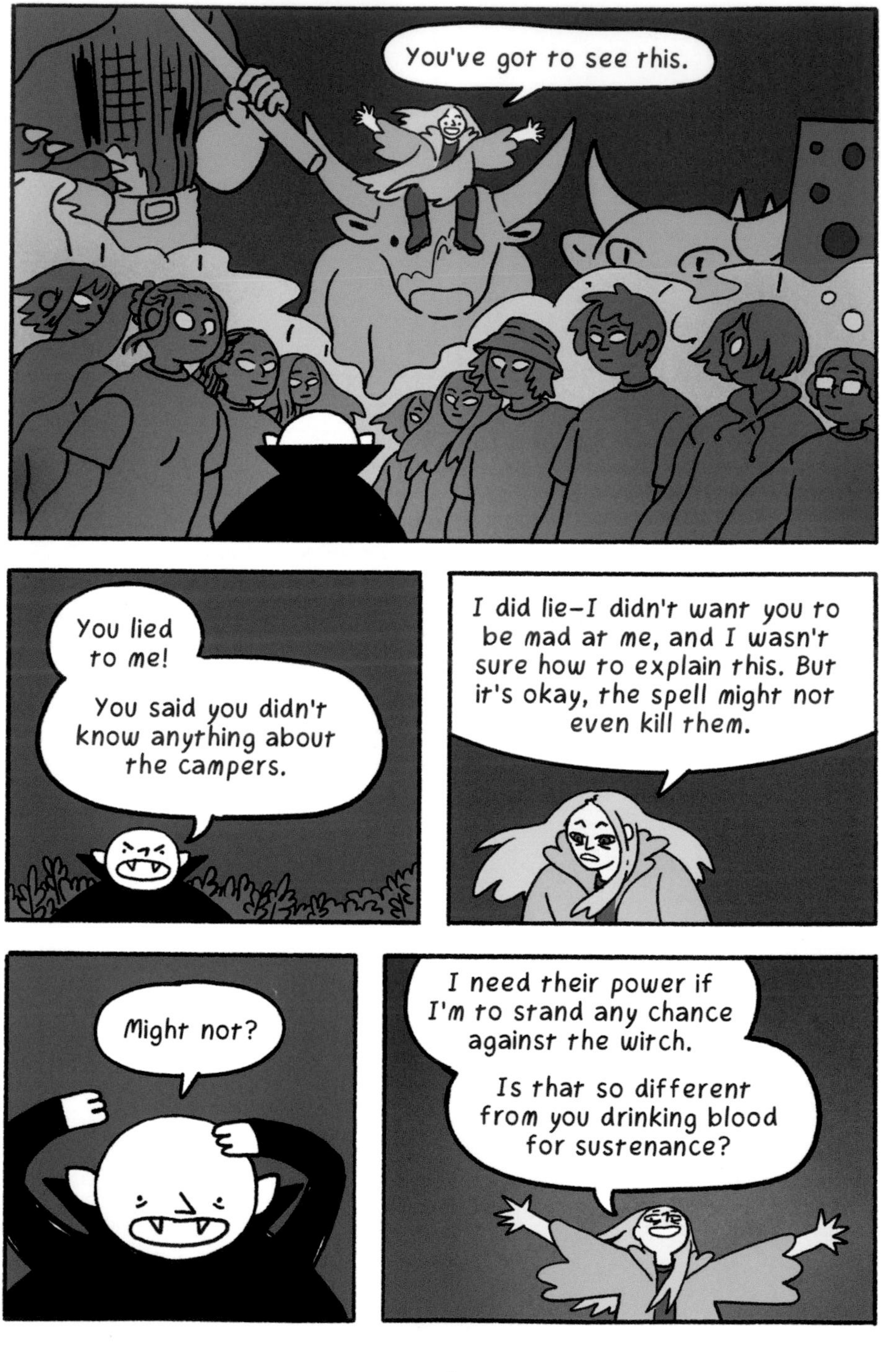
You've got to see this.
You lied to me!
You said you didn't know anything about the campers.
I did lie—I didn't want you to be mad at me, and I wasn't sure how to explain this. But it's okay, the spell might not even kill them.
Might not?
I need their power if I'm to stand any chance against the witch.
Is that so different from you drinking blood for sustenance?

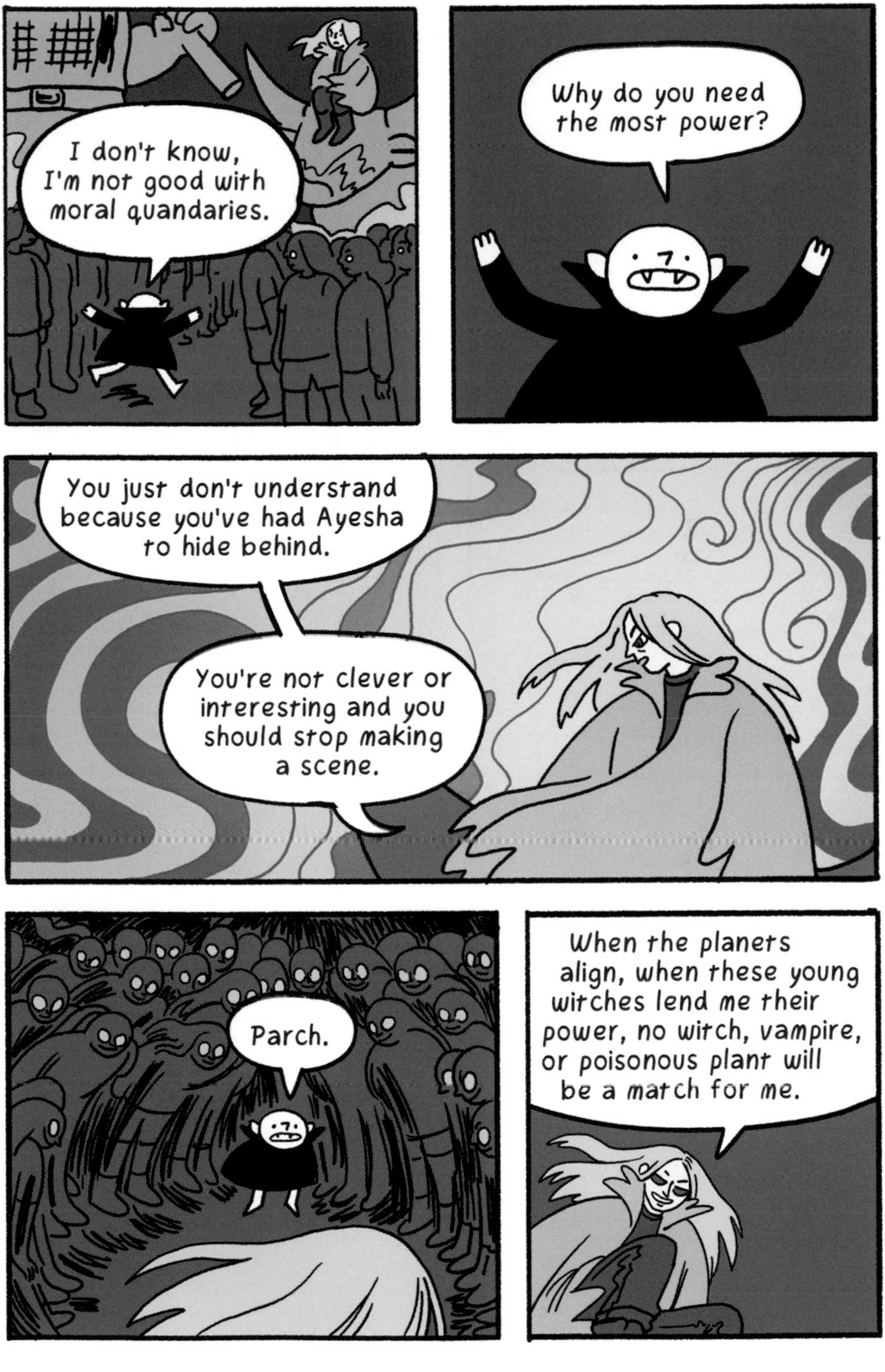
I don't know, I'm not good with moral quandaries.
Why do you need the most power?
You just don't understand because you've had Ayesha to hide behind.
You're not clever or interesting and you should stop making a scene.
Parch.
When the planets align, when these young witches lend me their power, no witch, vampire, or poisonous plant will be a match for me.

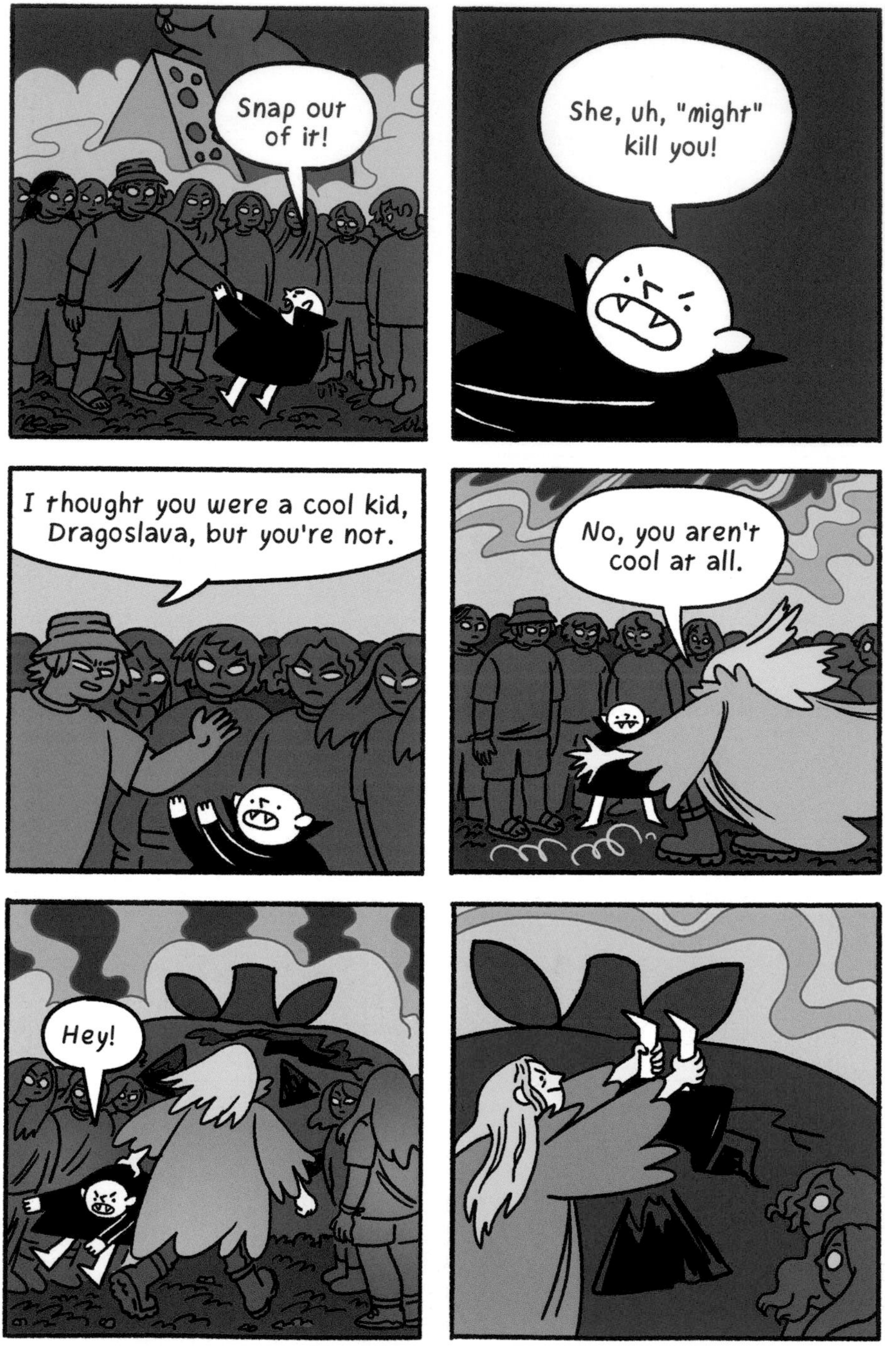

Snap out of it!
She, uh, "might" kill you!
I thought you were a cool kid, Dragoslava, but you're not.
No, you aren't cool at all.
Hey!

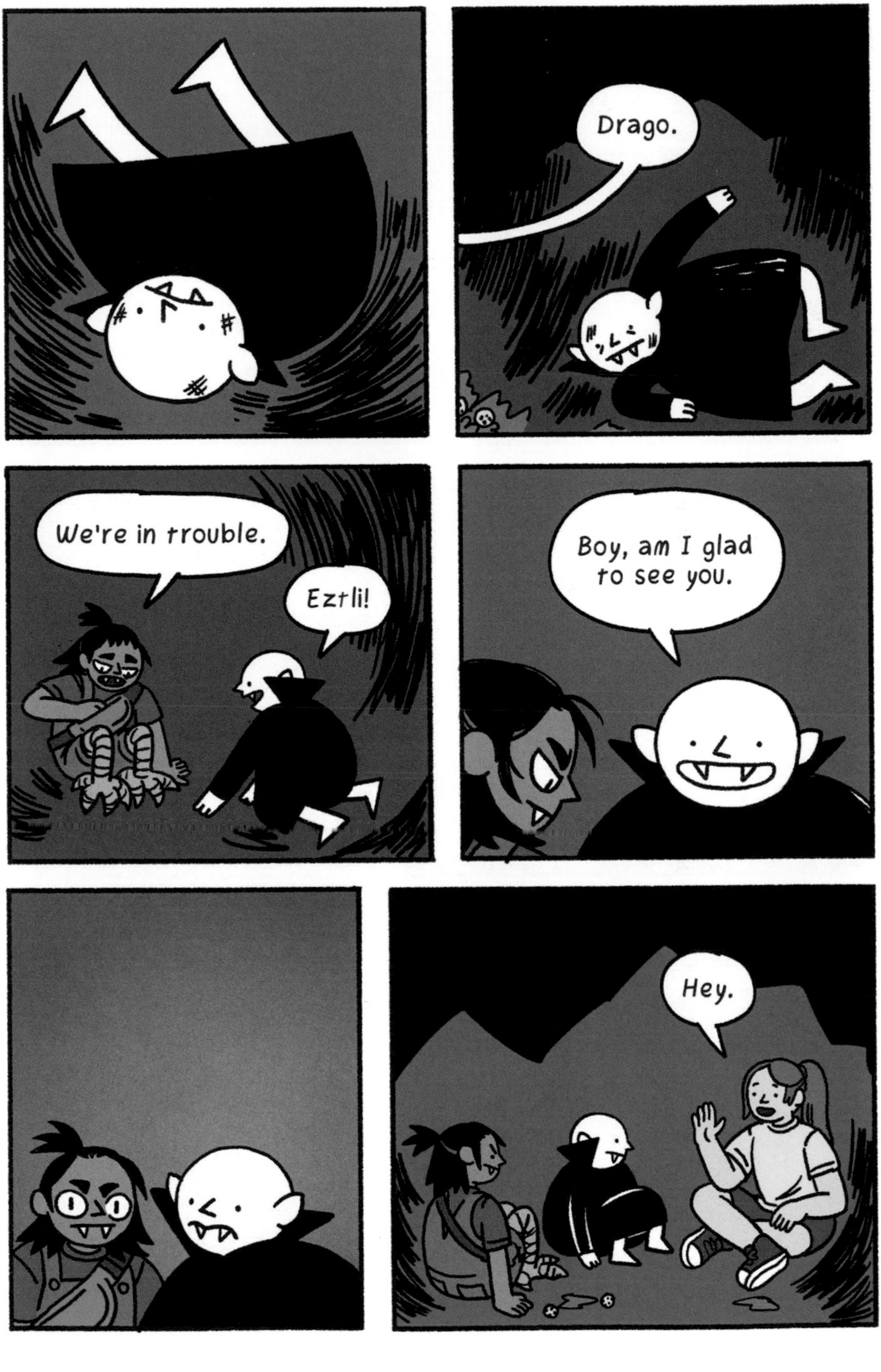
Drago.
We're in trouble.
Eztli!
Boy, am I glad to see you.
Hey.

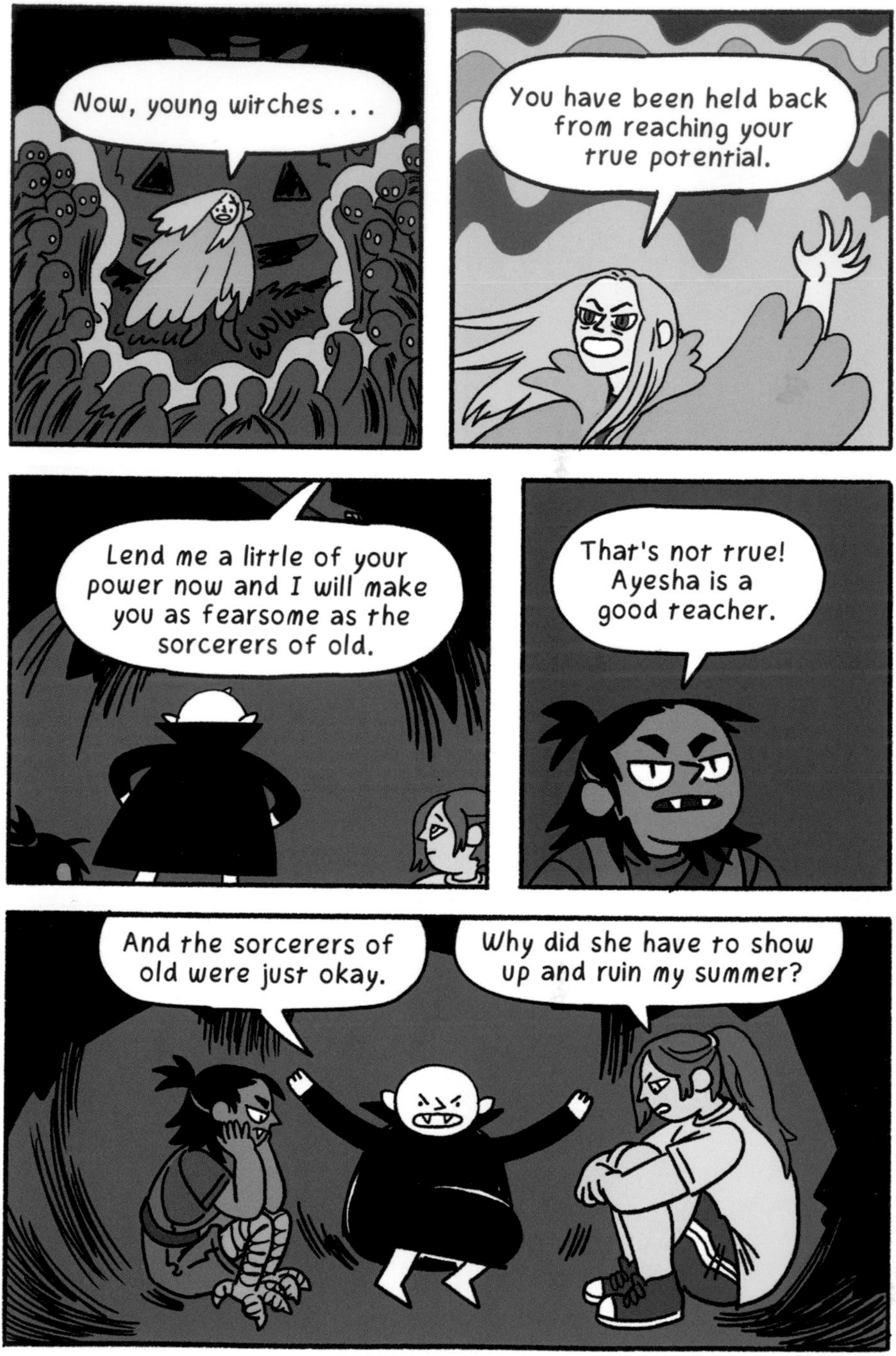
Now, young witches . . .
You have been held back from reaching your true potential.
Lend me a little of your power now and I will make you as fearsome as the sorcerers of old.
That's not true! Ayesha is a good teacher.
And the sorcerers of old were just okay.
Why did she have to show up and ruin my summer?

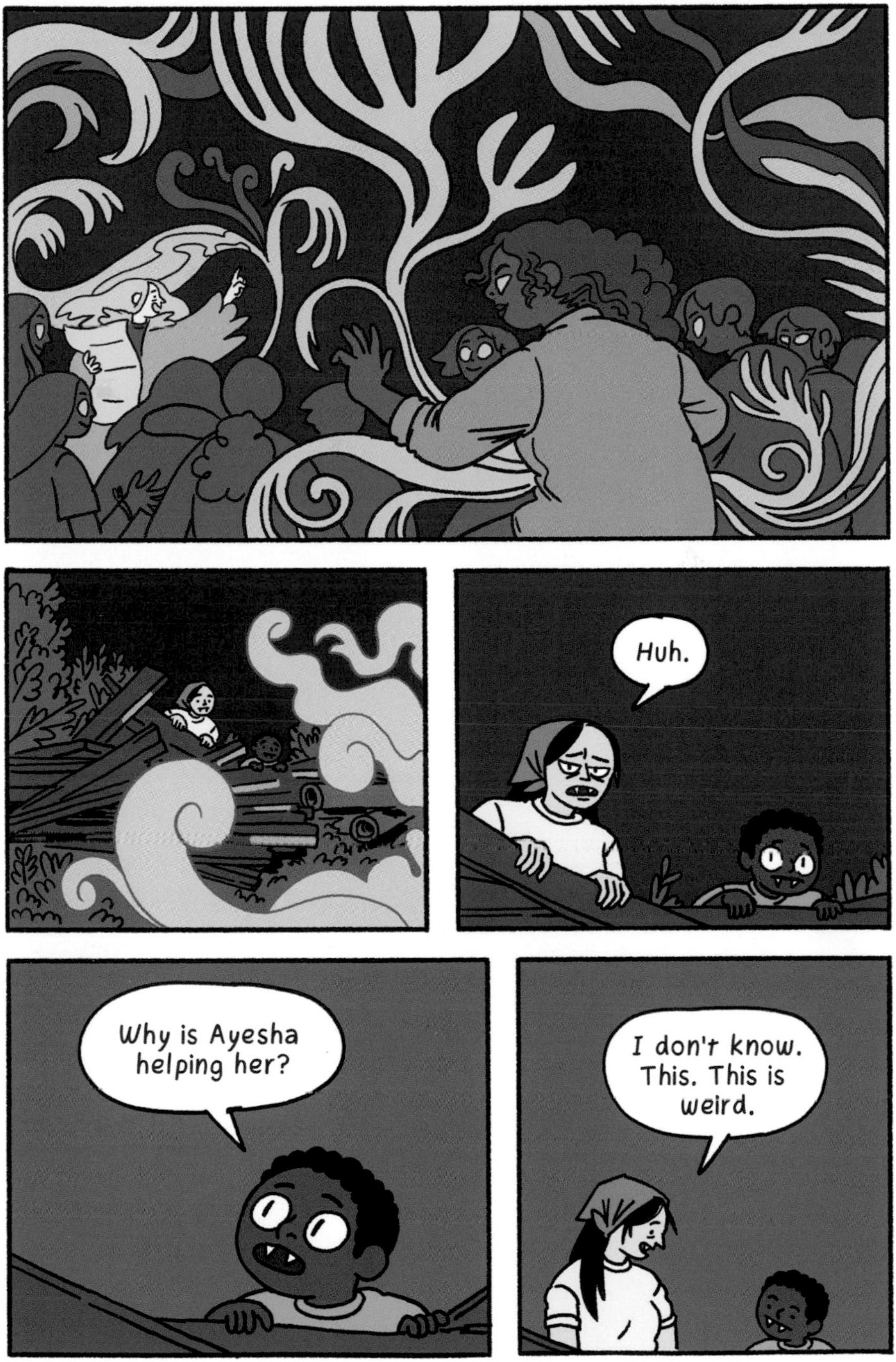
Huh.
Why is Ayesha helping her?
I don't know. This. This is weird.

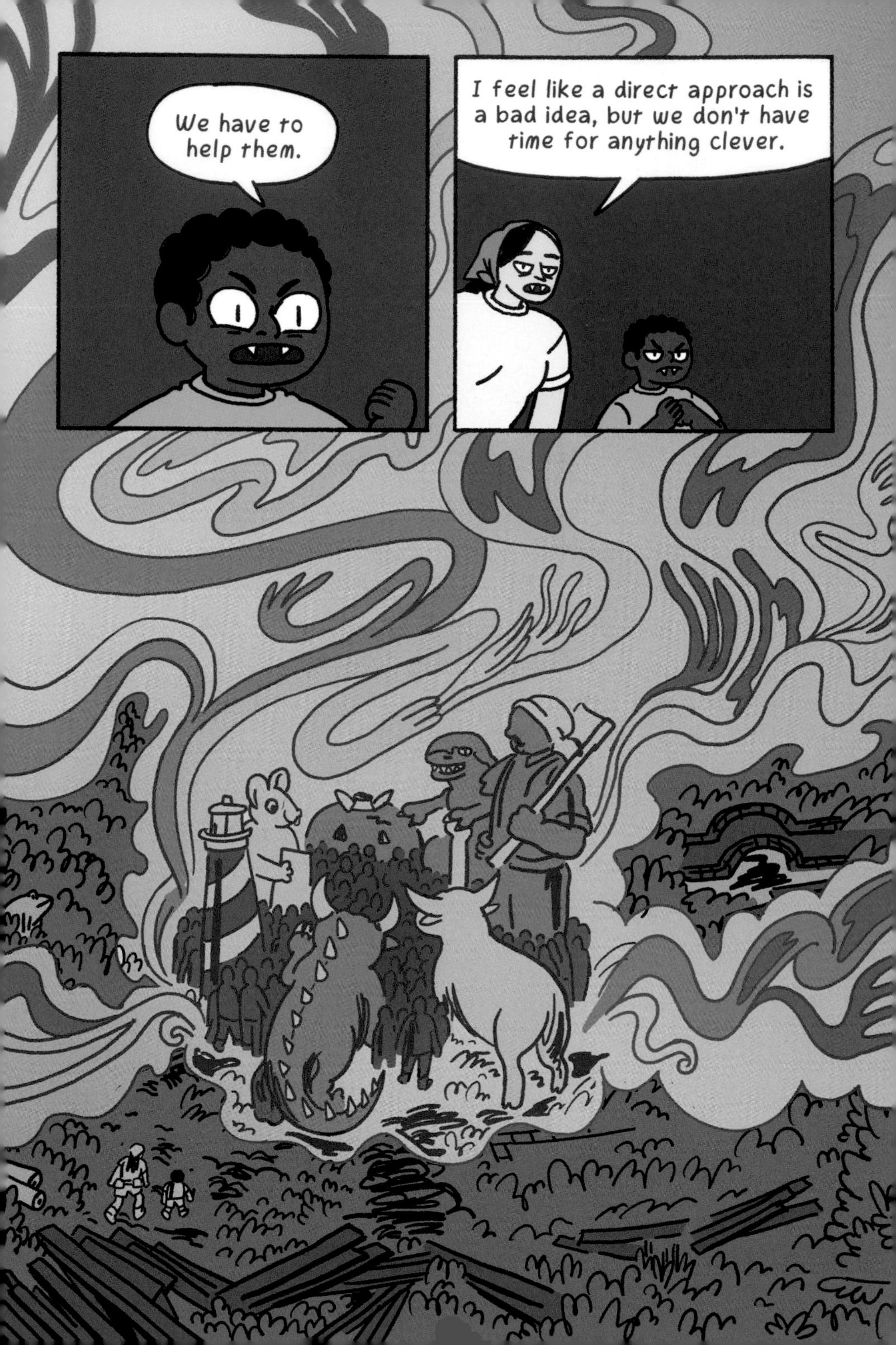
We have to help them.
I feel like a direct approach is a bad idea, but we don't have time for anything clever.

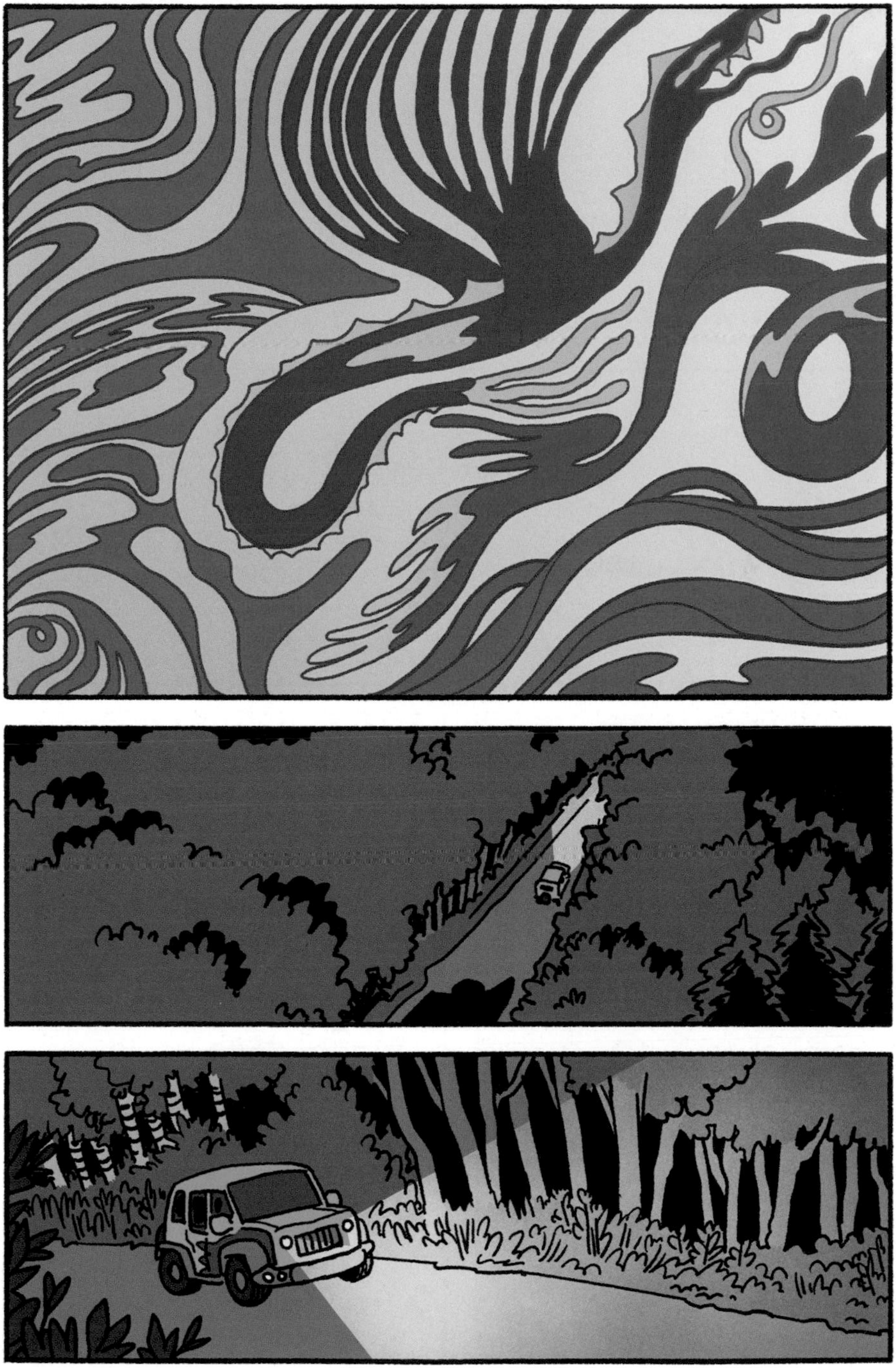

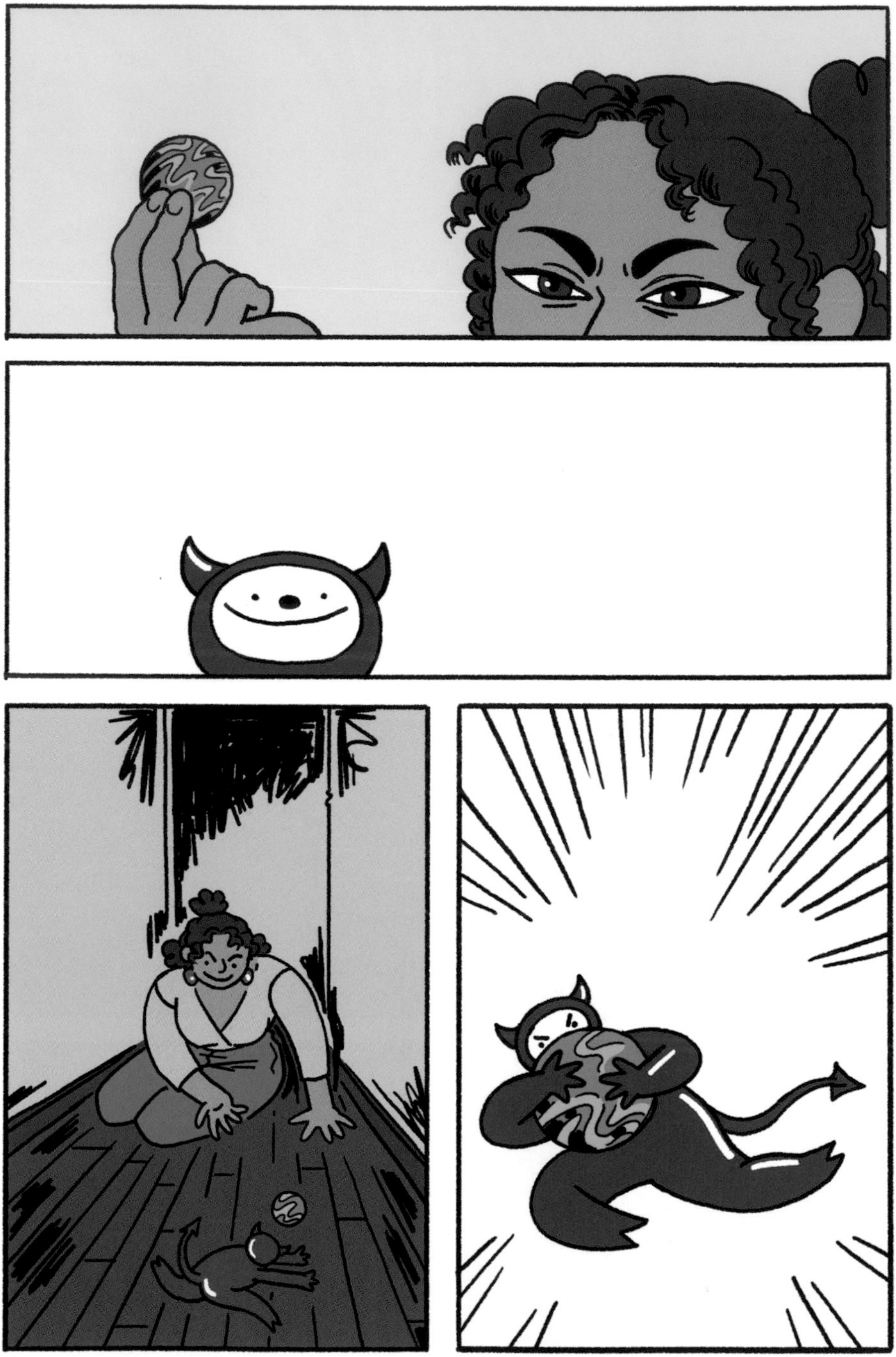

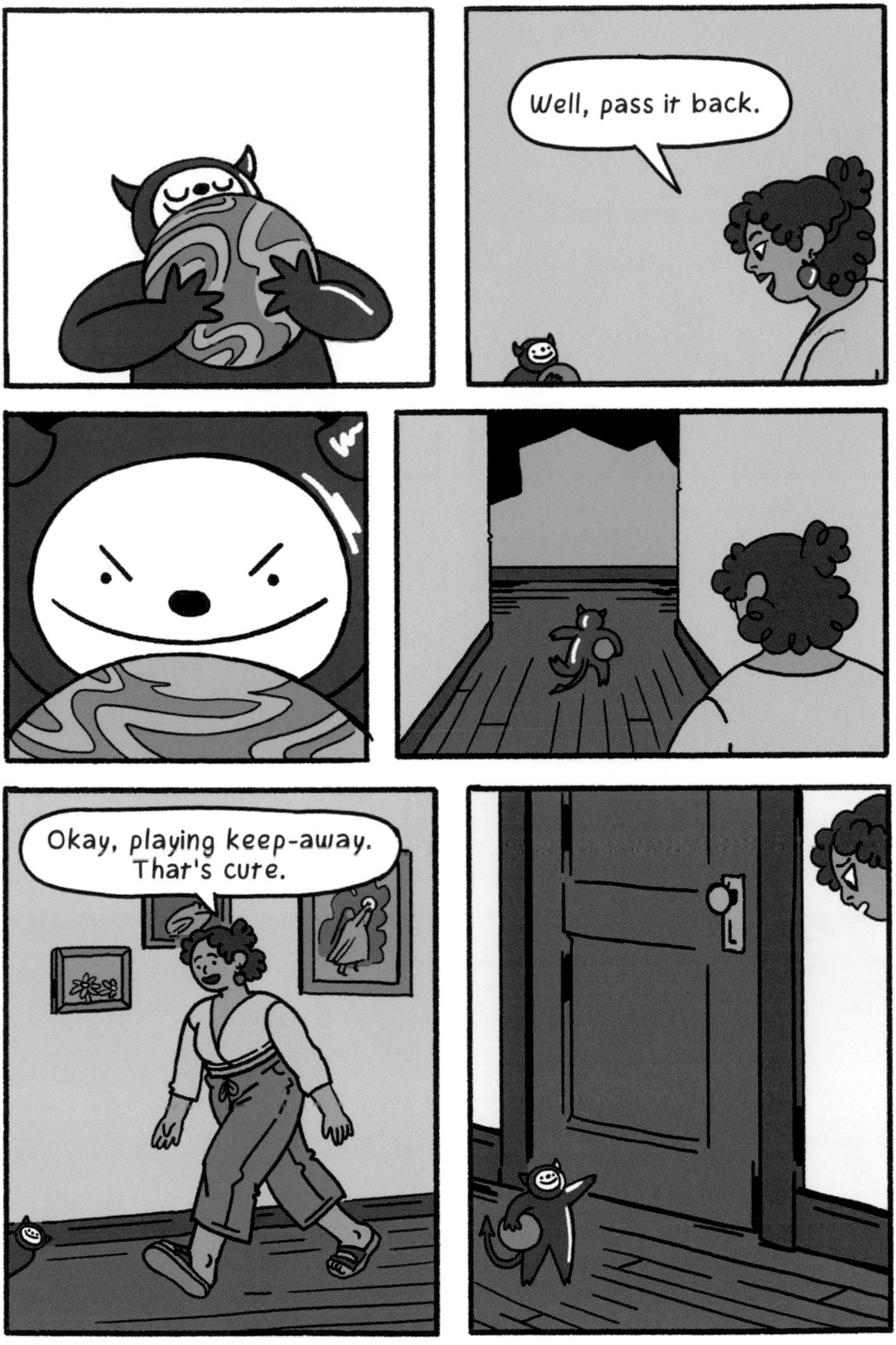
Well, pass it back.
Okay, playing keep-away. That's cute.

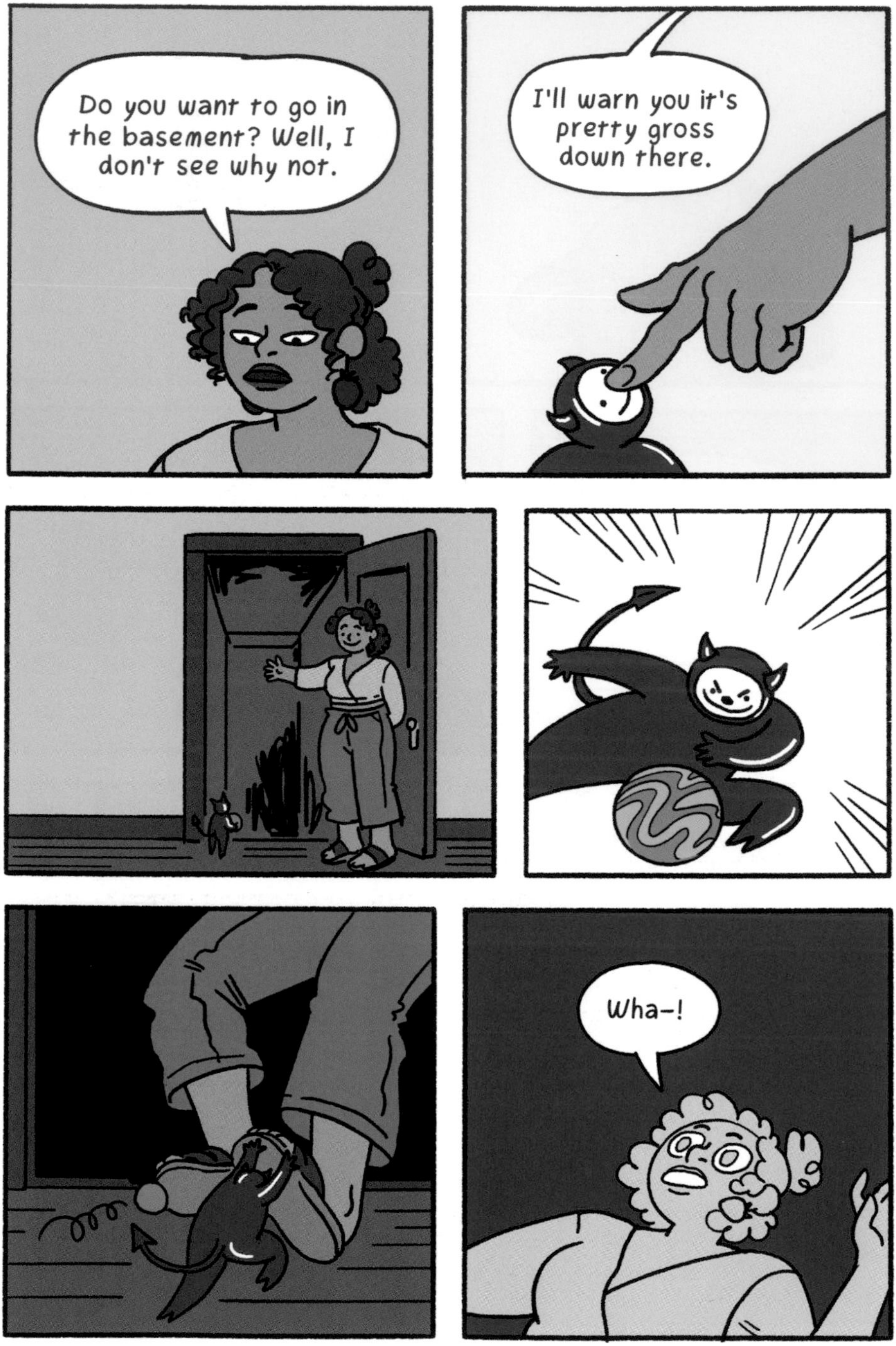
Do you want to go in the basement? Well, I don't see why not.
I'll warn you it's pretty gross down there.
Wha-!

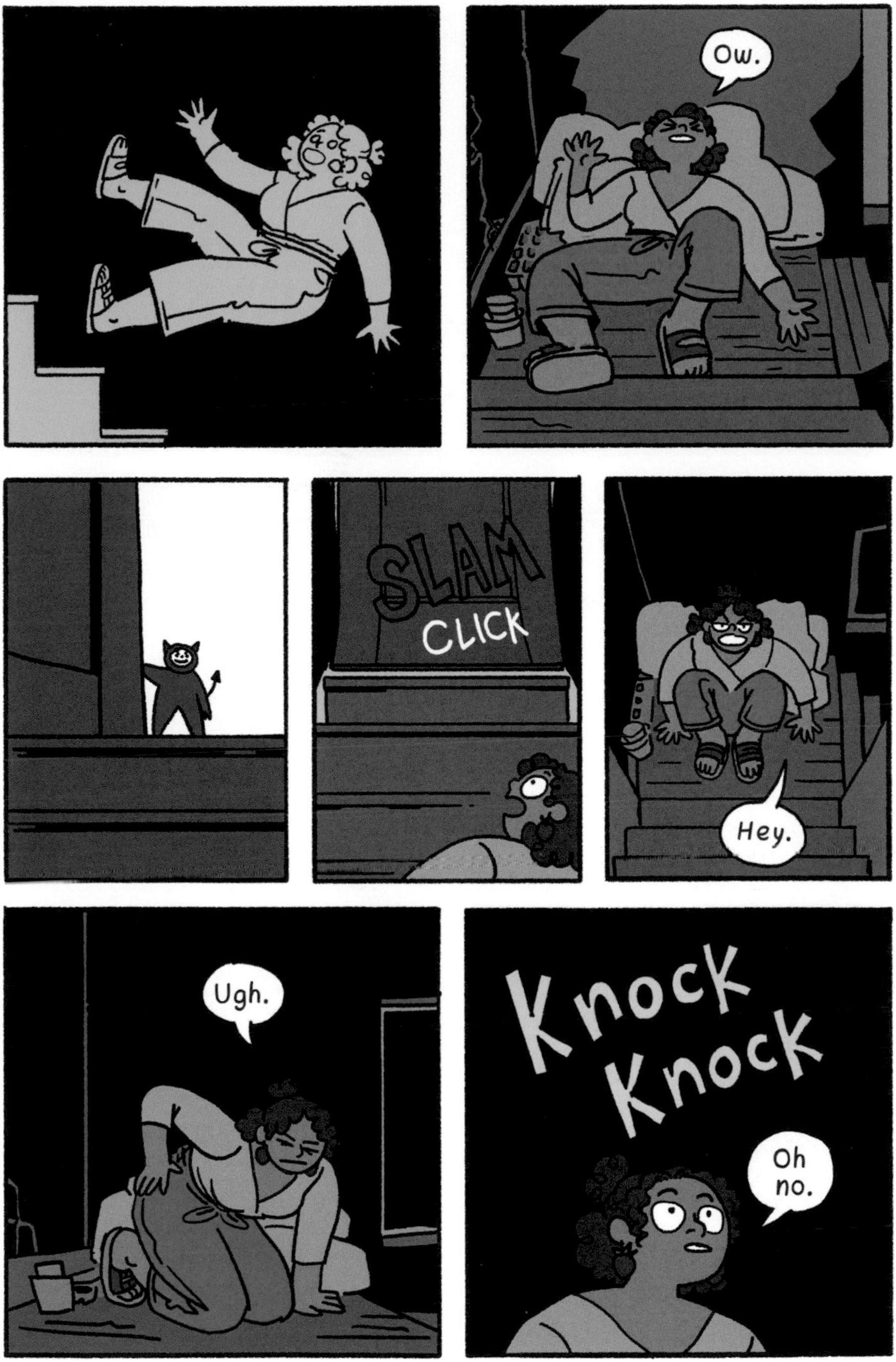
Ow.
SLAM
CLICK
Hey.
Ugh.
Knock Knock
Oh no.

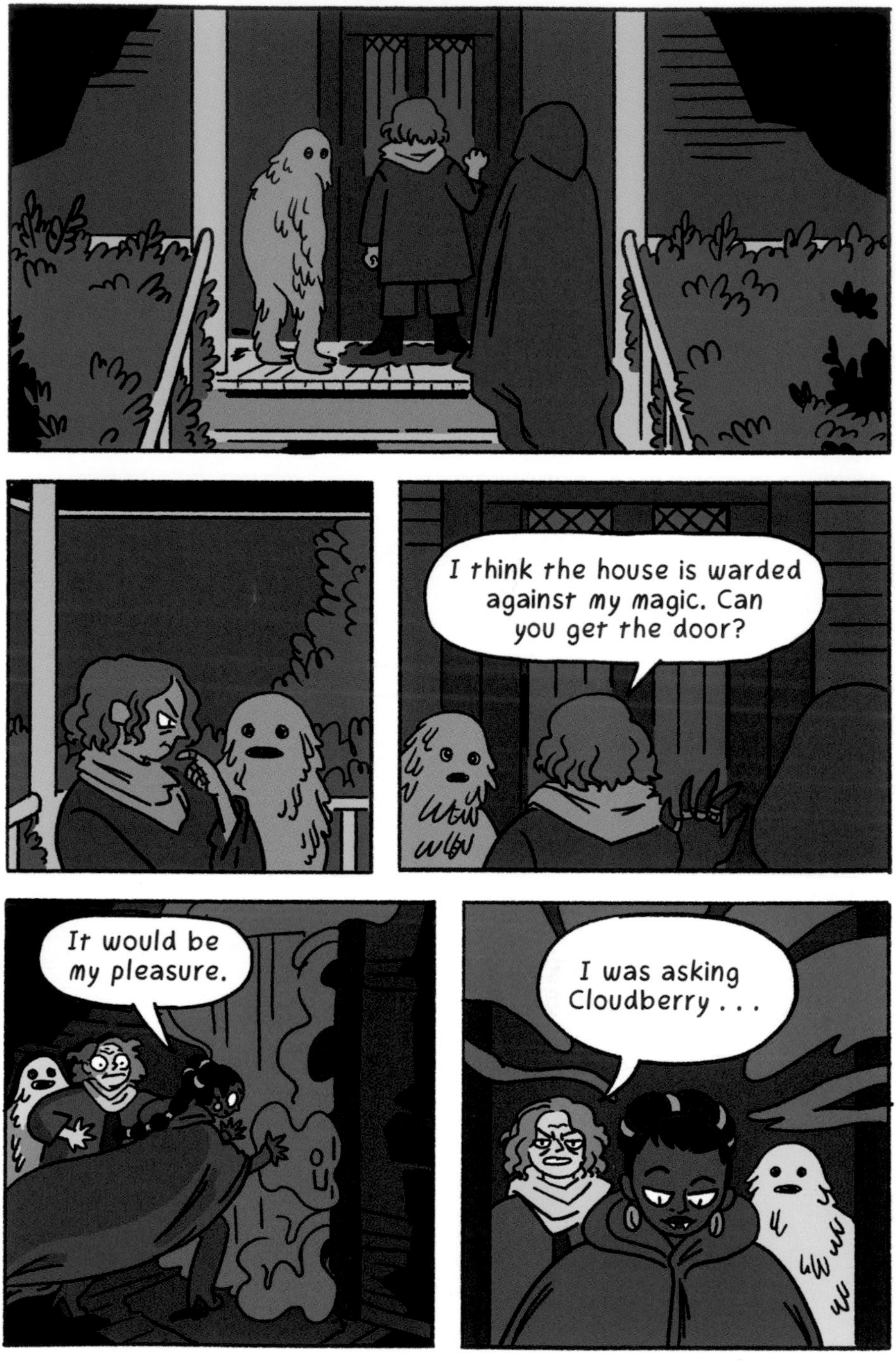
I think the house is warded against my magic. Can you get the door?
It would be my pleasure.
I was asking Cloudberry . . .

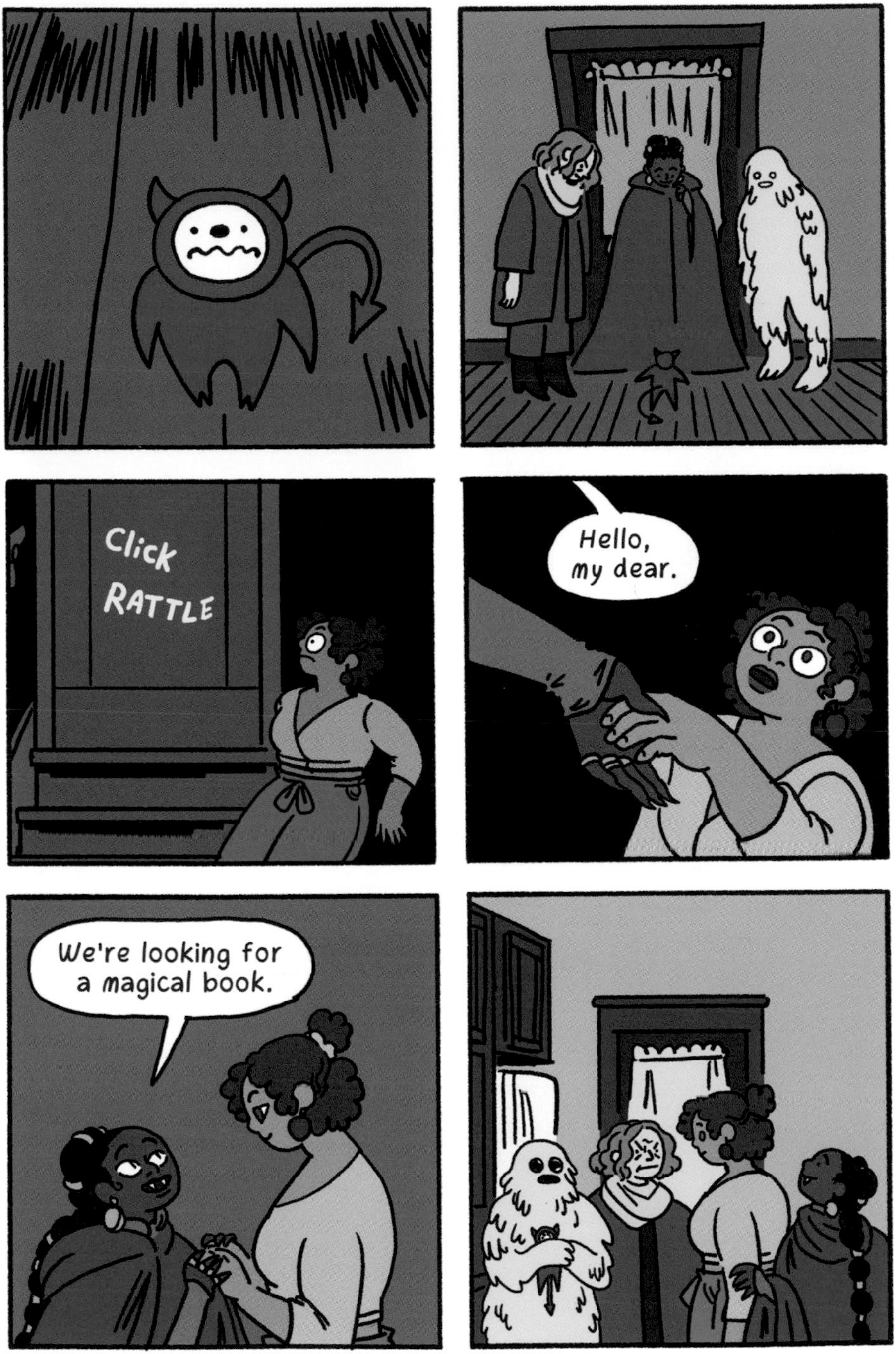
Click
RATTLE
Hello, my dear.
We're looking for a magical book.

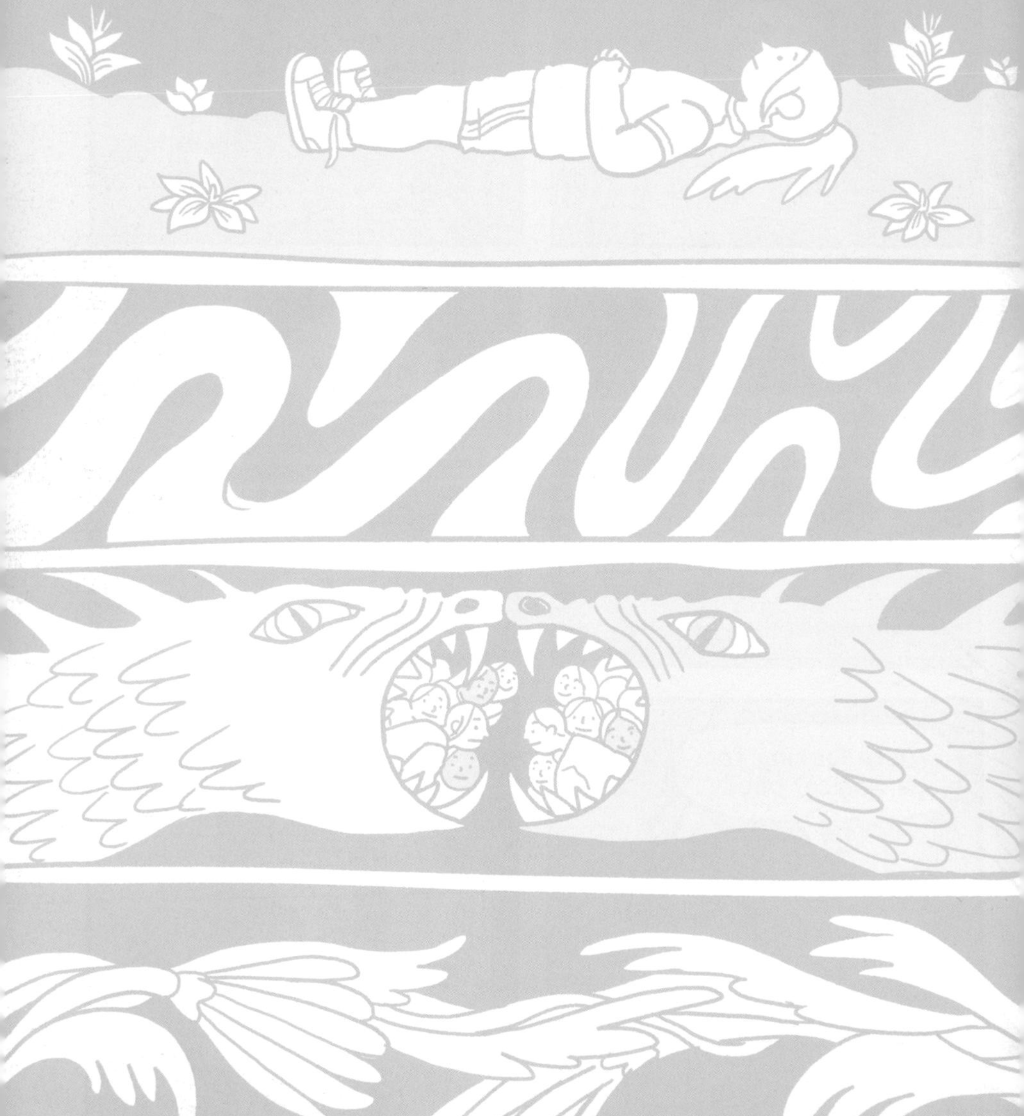

CHAPTER SEVEN

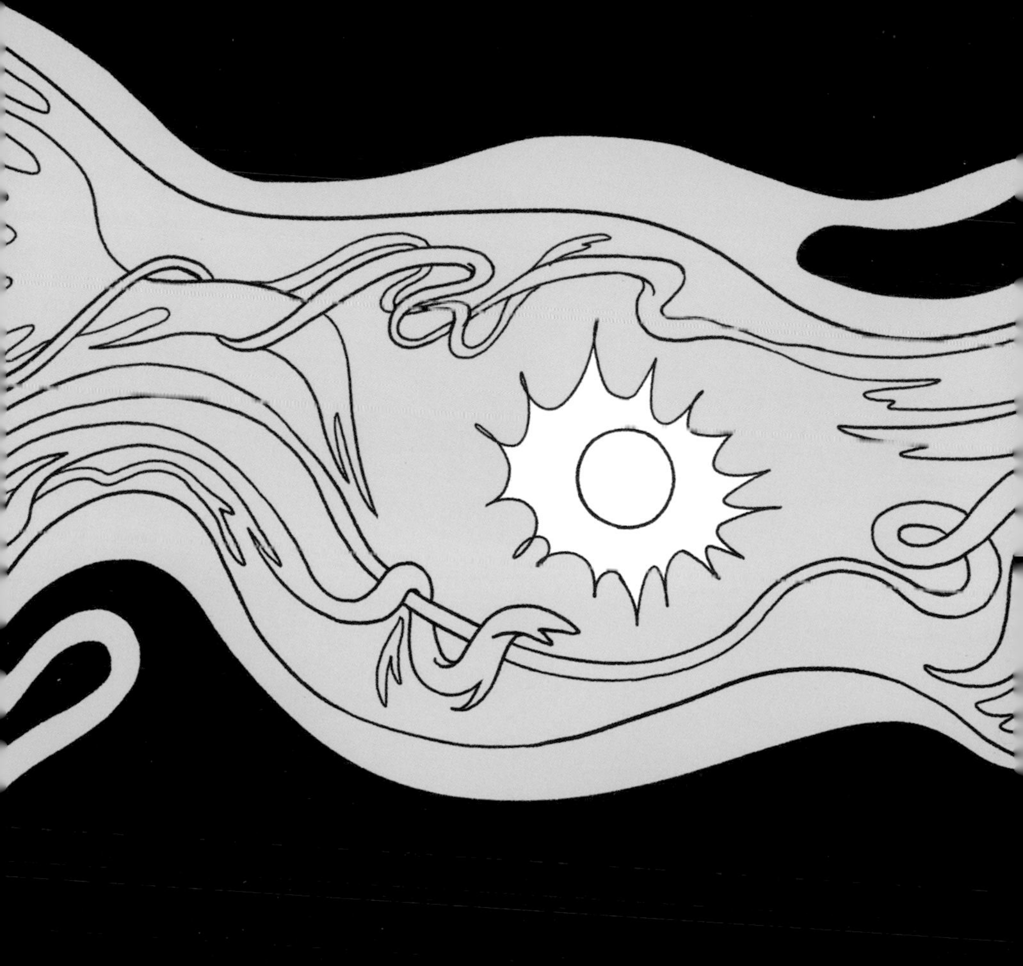

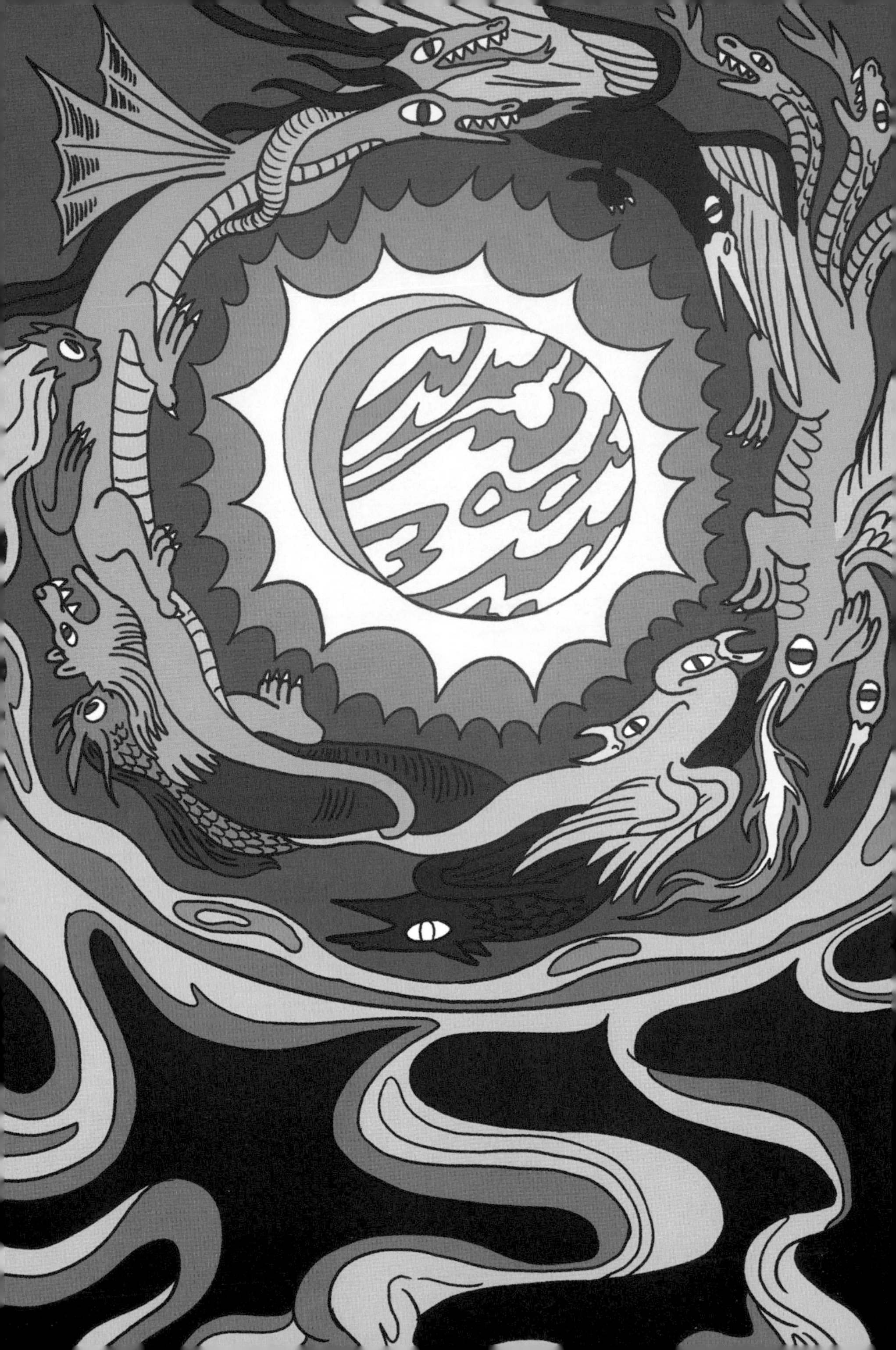

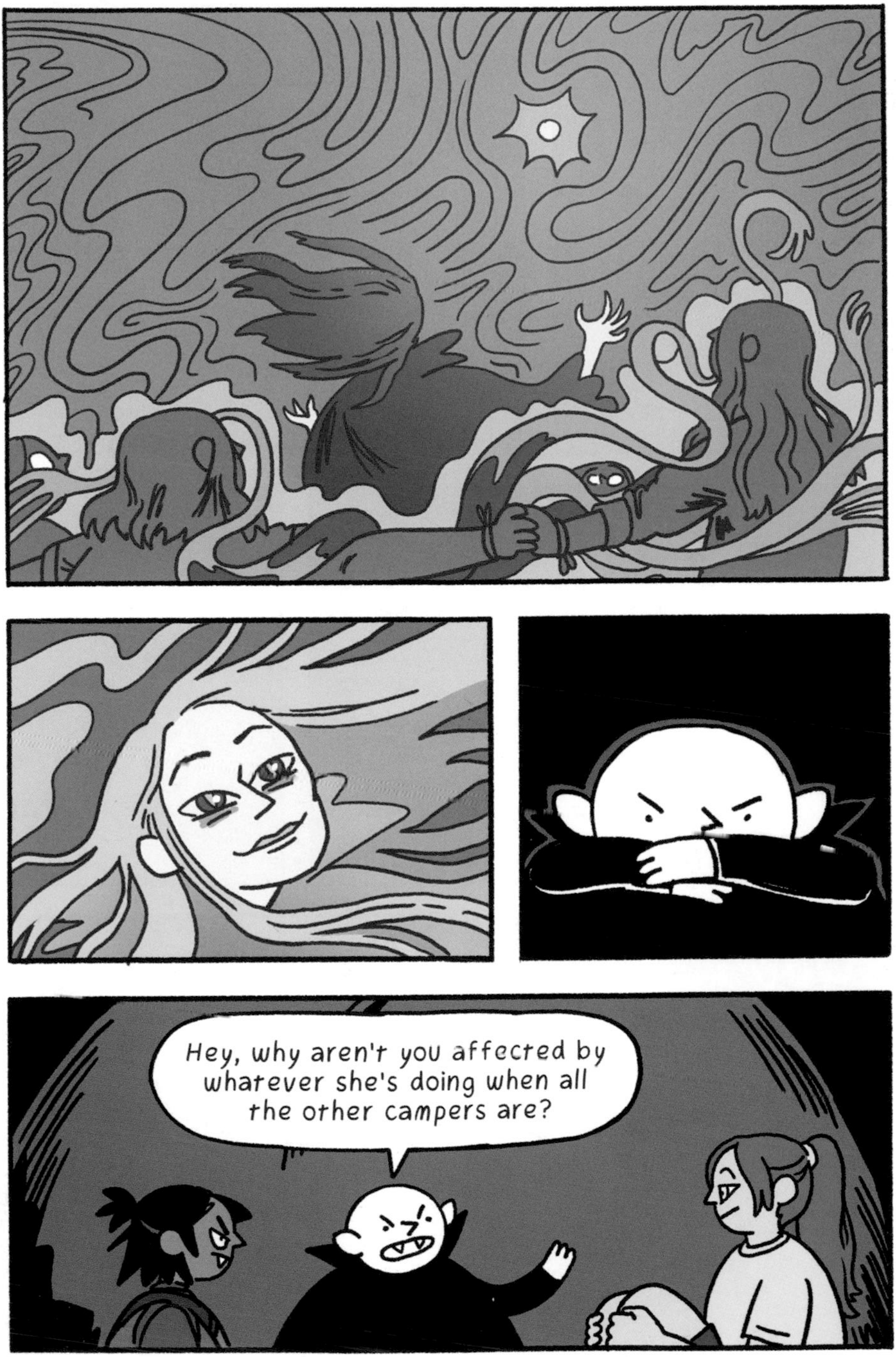
Hey, why aren't you affected by whatever she's doing when all the other campers are?

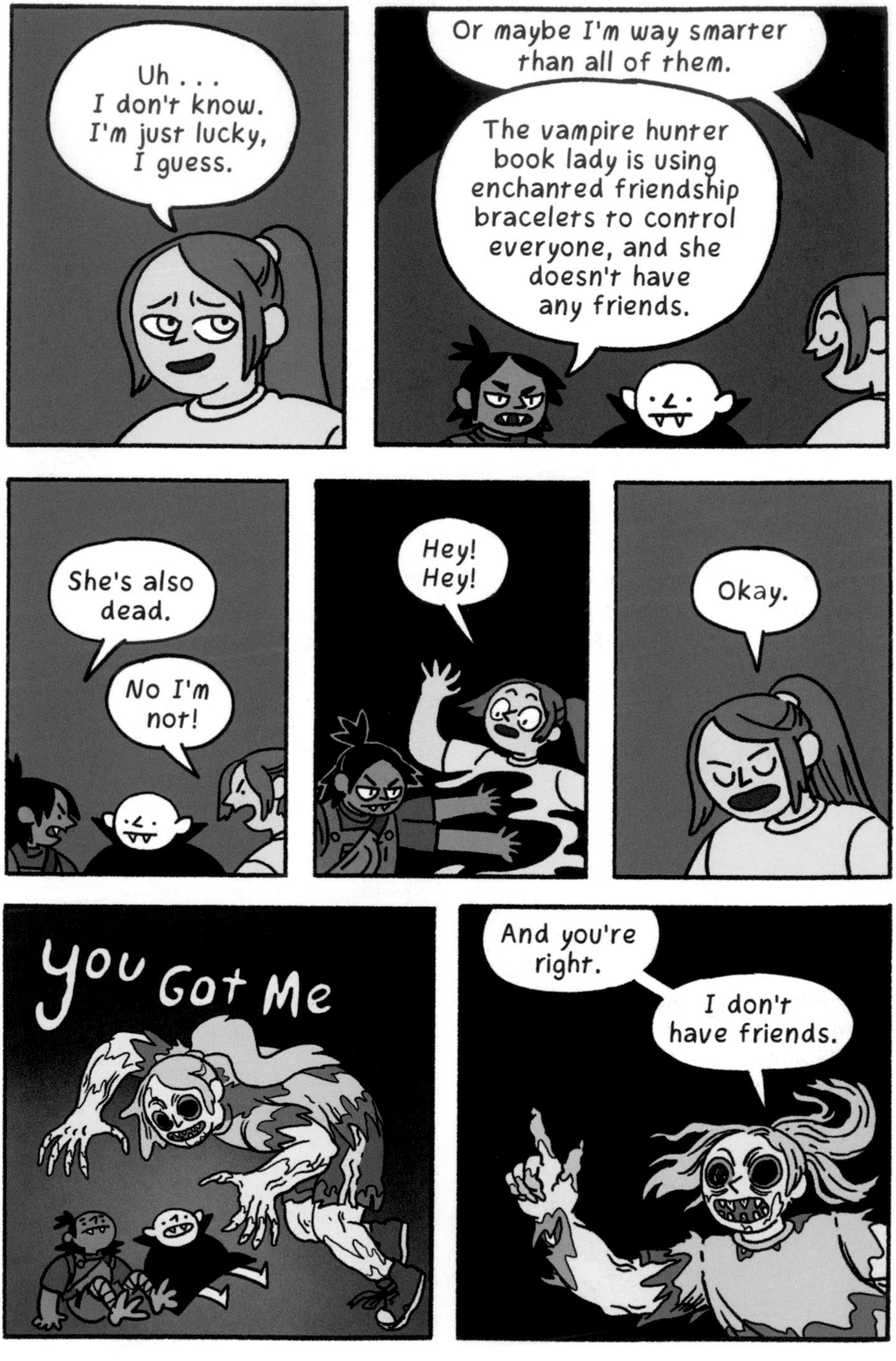
Uh . . . I don't know. I'm just lucky, I guess.
Or maybe I'm way smarter than all of them.
The vampire hunter book lady is using enchanted friendship bracelets to control everyone, and she doesn't have any friends.
She's also dead.
No I'm not!
Hey! Hey!
Okay.
You Got Me
And you're right.
I don't have friends.

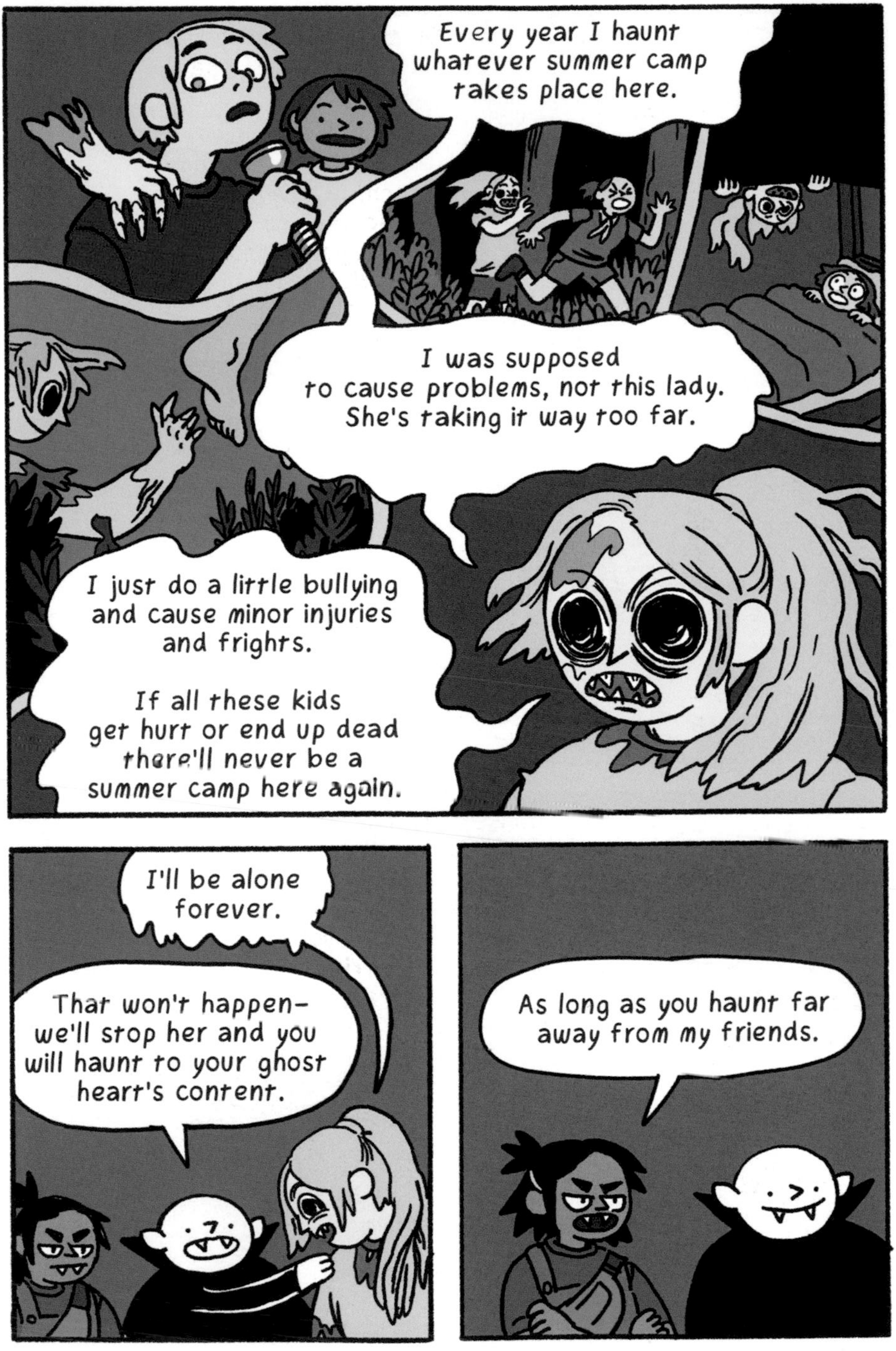
Every year I haunt whatever summer camp takes place here.
I was supposed to cause problems, not this lady. She's taking it way too far.
I just do a little bullying and cause minor injuries and frights.
If all these kids get hurt or end up dead there'll never be a summer camp here again.
I'll be alone forever.
That won't happen— we'll stop her and you will haunt to your ghost heart's content.
As long as you haunt far away from my friends.

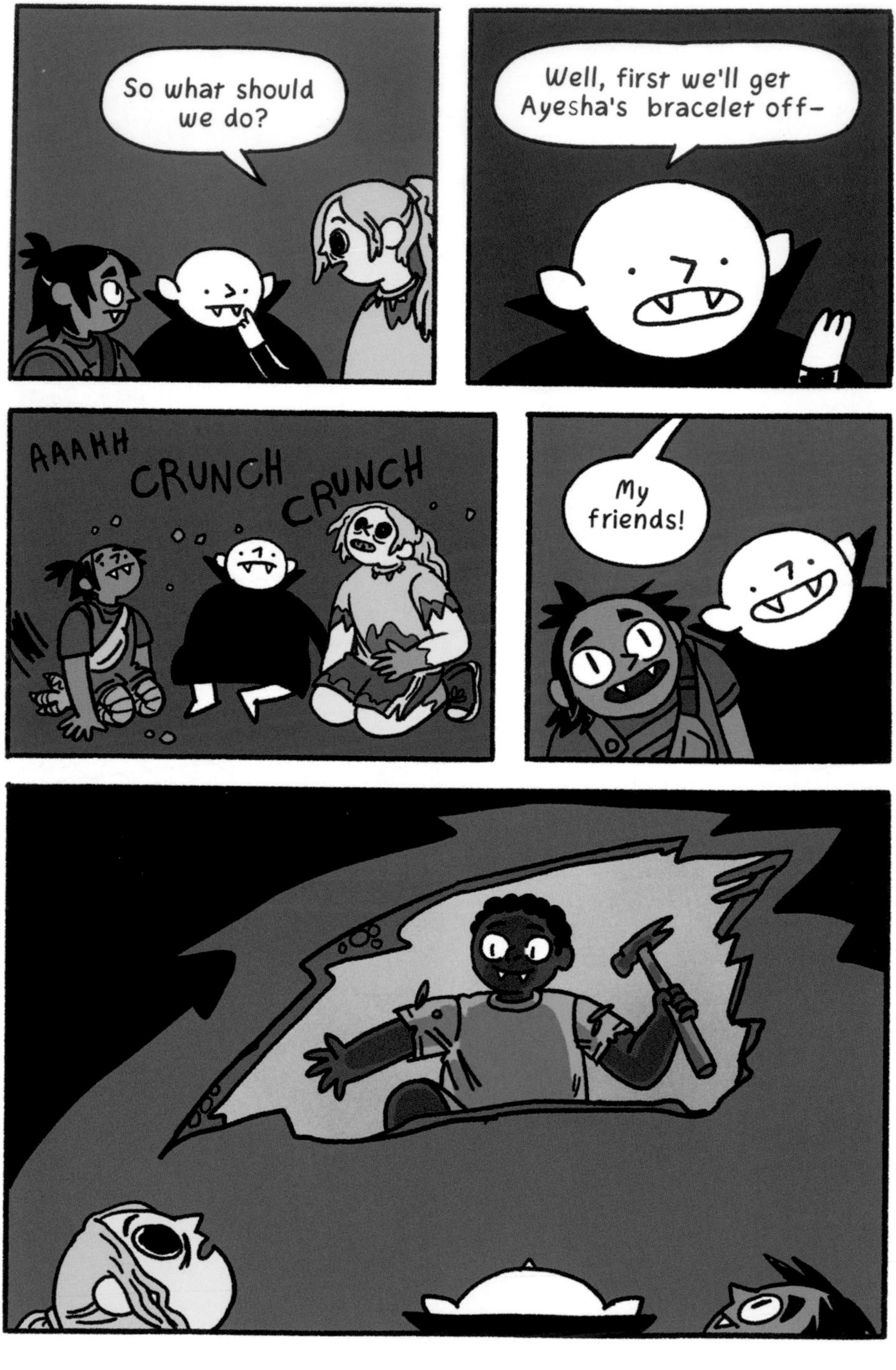
So what should we do?
Well, first we'll get Ayesha's bracelet off–
AAAHH
CRUNCH
CRUNCH
My friends!

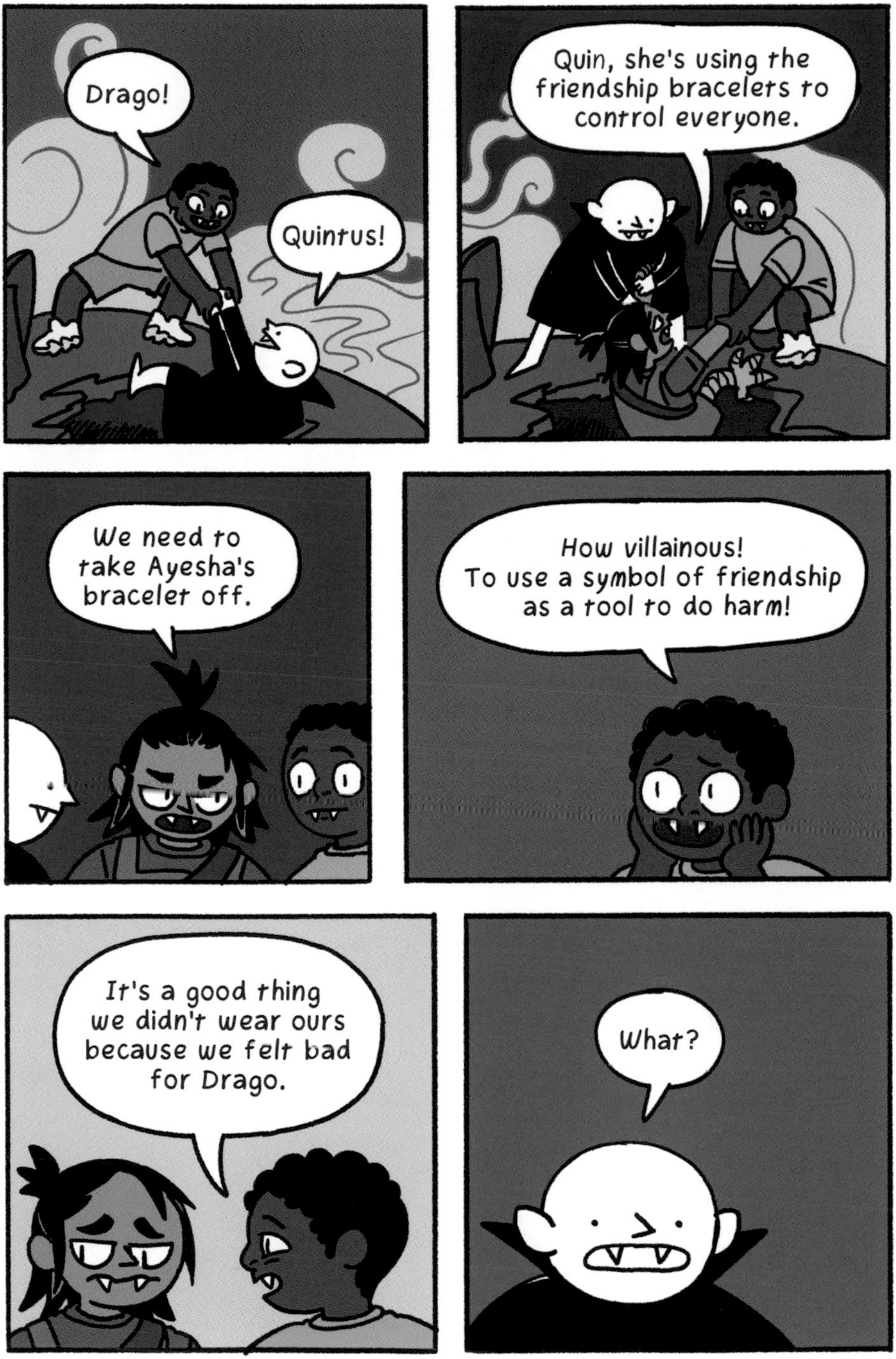
Drago!
Quintus!
Quin, she's using the friendship bracelets to control everyone.
We need to take Ayesha's bracelet off.
How villainous! To use a symbol of friendship as a tool to do harm!
It's a good thing we didn't wear ours because we felt bad for Drago.
What?

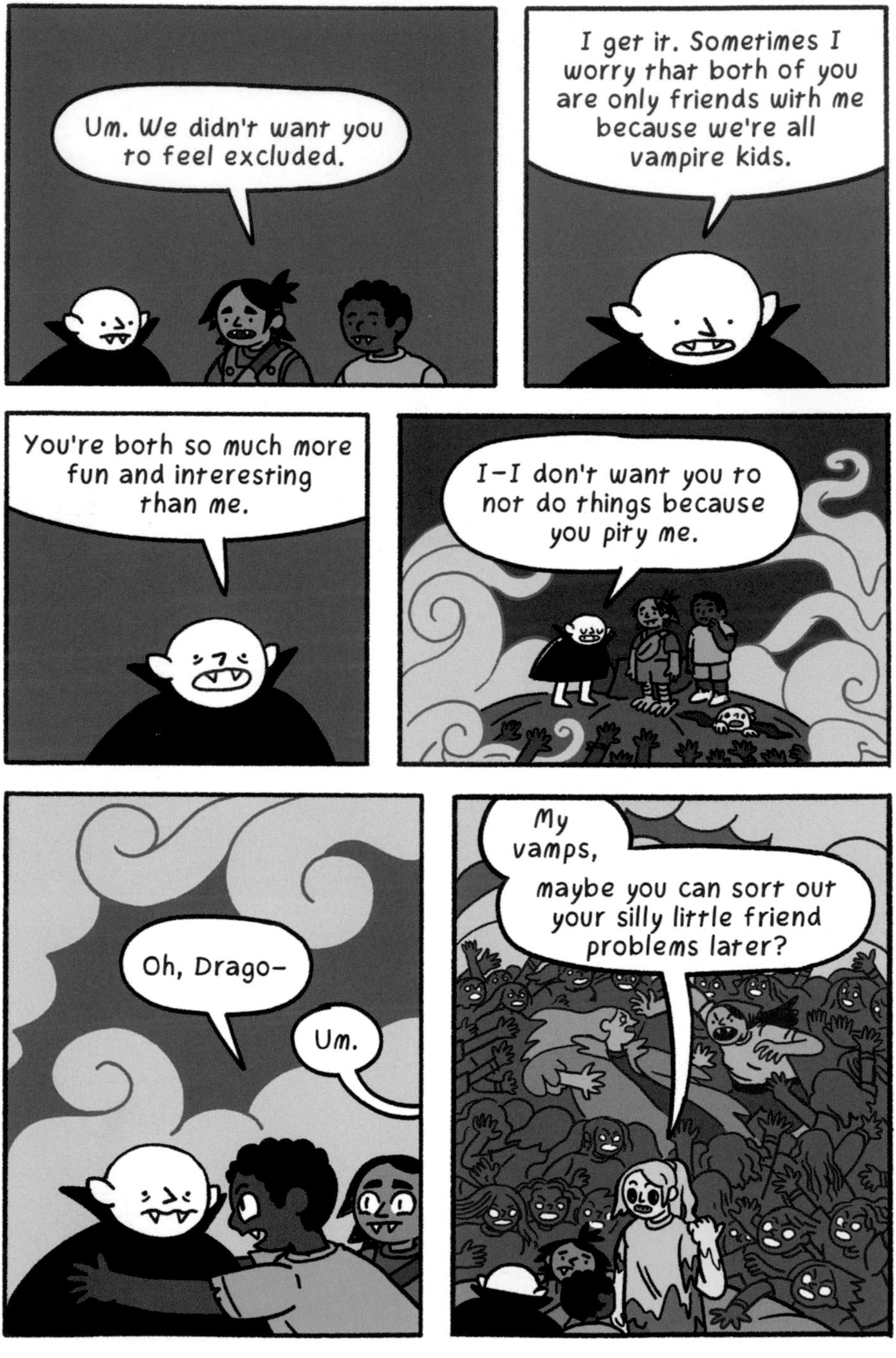
Um. We didn't want you to feel excluded.
I get it. Sometimes I worry that both of you are only friends with me because we're all vampire kids.
You're both so much more fun and interesting than me.
I-I don't want you to not do things because you pity me.
Oh, Drago-
Um.
My vamps,
maybe you can sort out your silly little friend problems later?

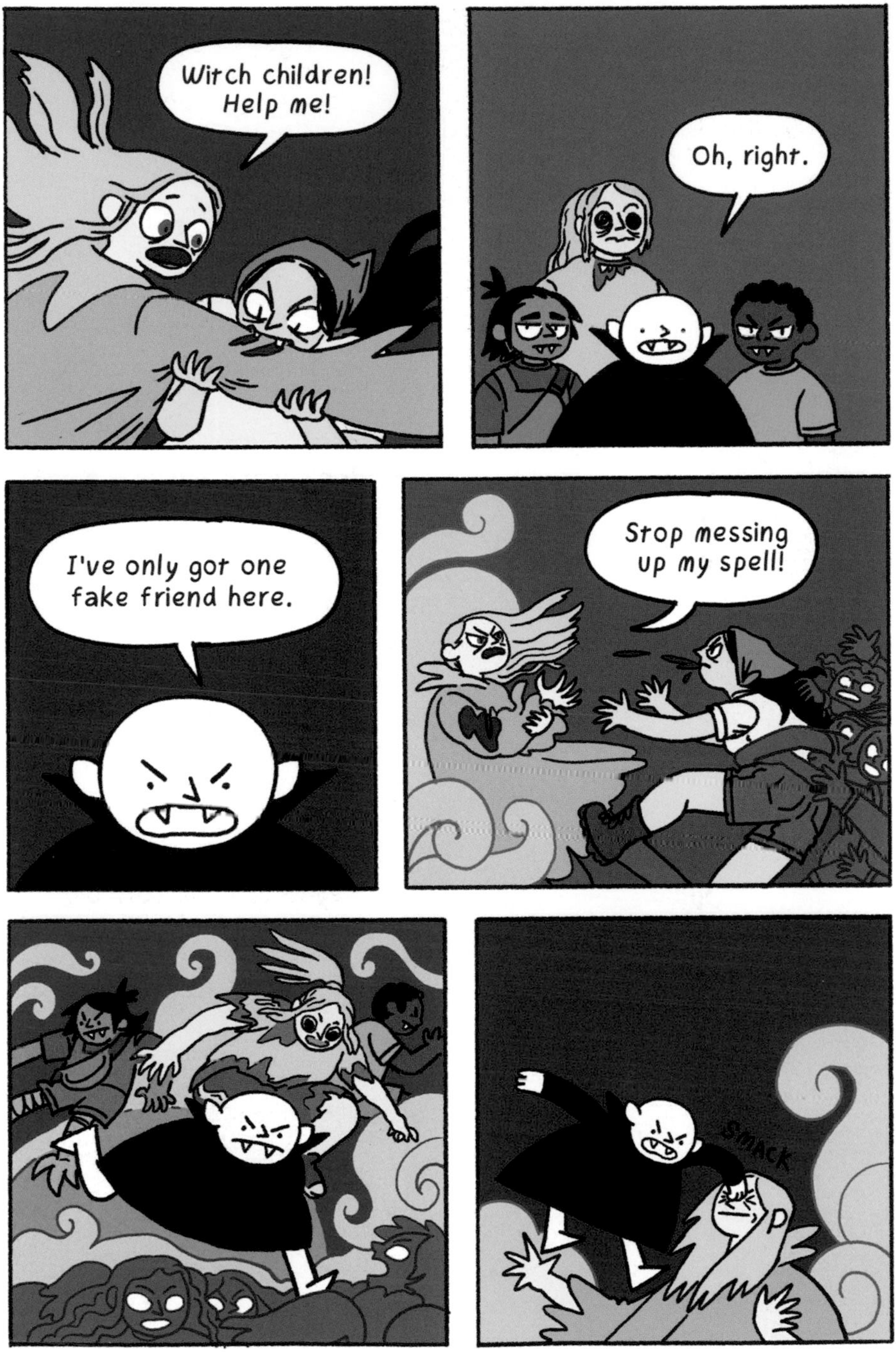
Witch children! Help me!
Oh, right.
I've only got one fake friend here.
Stop messing up my spell!
SMACK

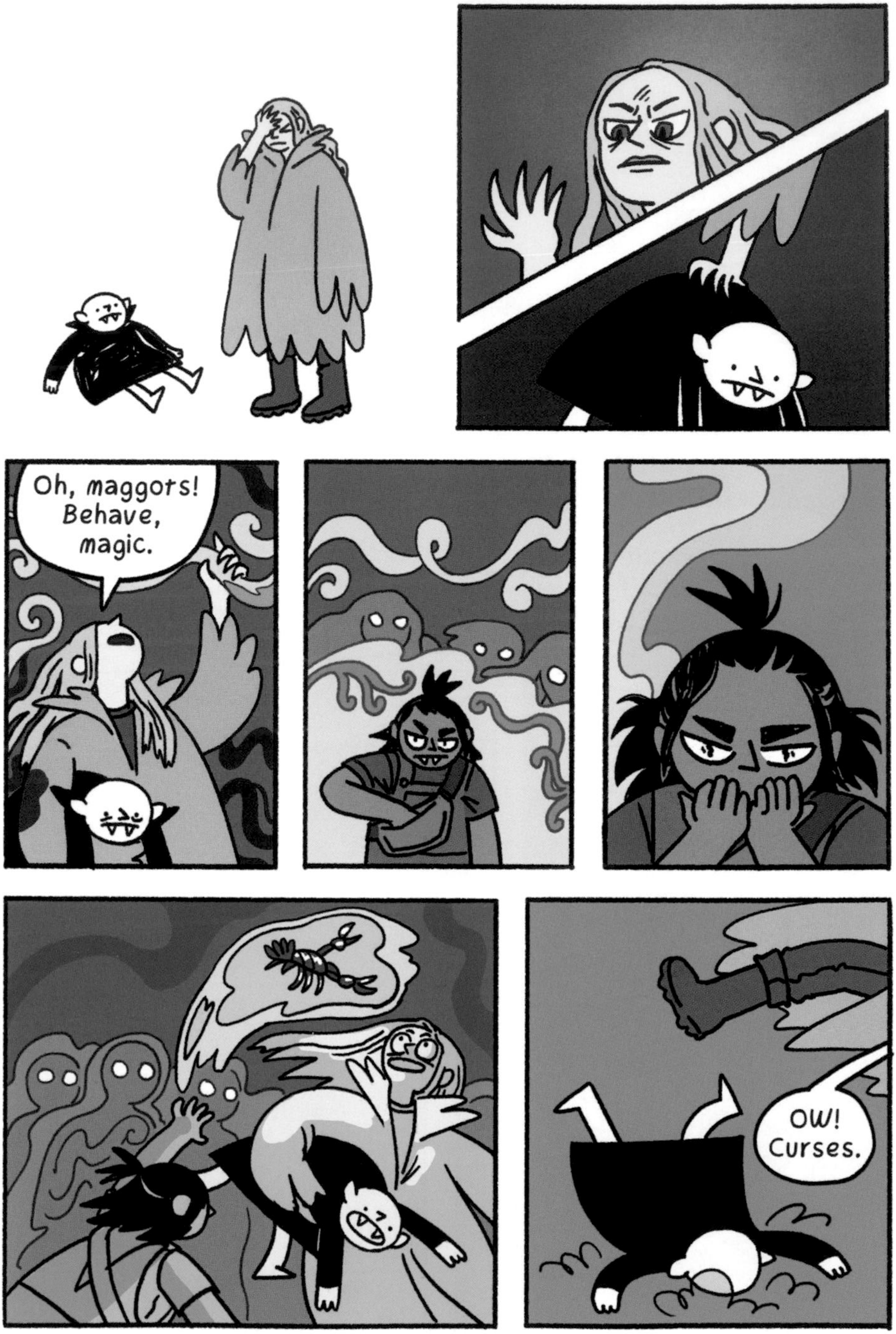
Oh, maggots!
Behave,
magic.
OW!
Curses.

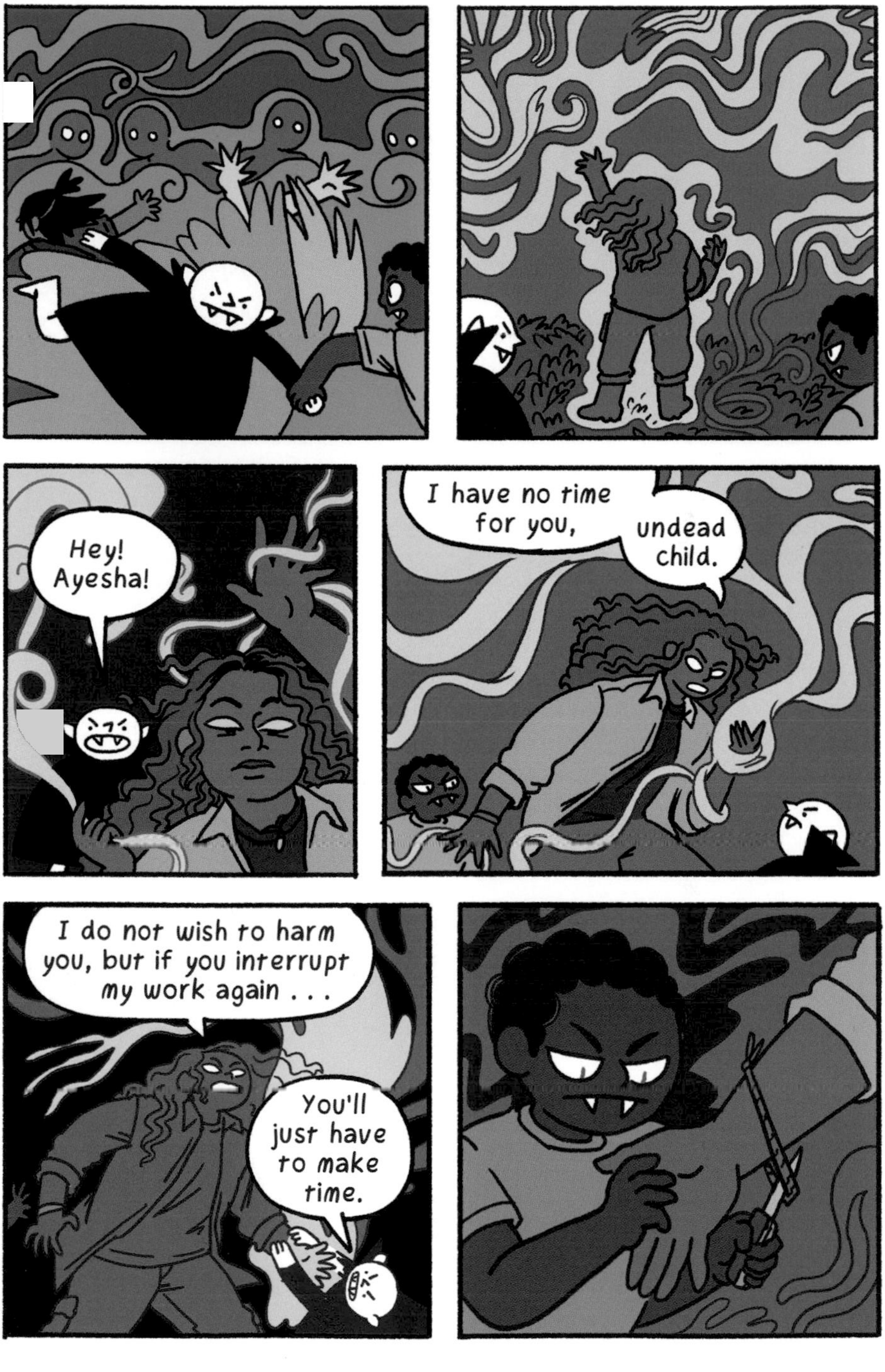
Hey!
Ayesha!
I have no time for you,
undead child.
I do not wish to harm you, but if you interrupt my work again . . .
You'll just have to make time.

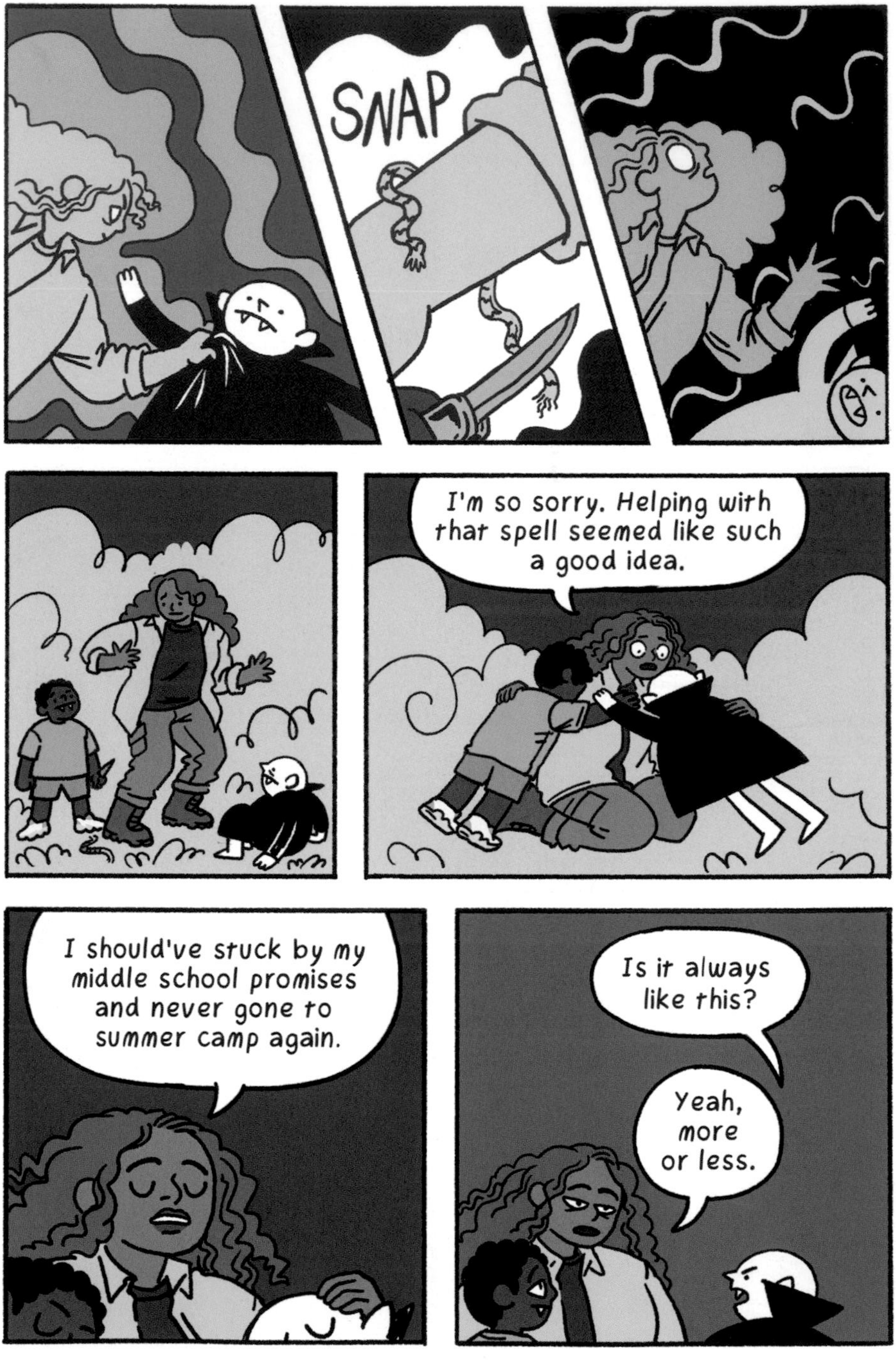
SNAP
I'm so sorry. Helping with that spell seemed like such a good idea.
I should've stuck by my middle school promises and never gone to summer camp again.
Is it always like this?
Yeah, more or less.

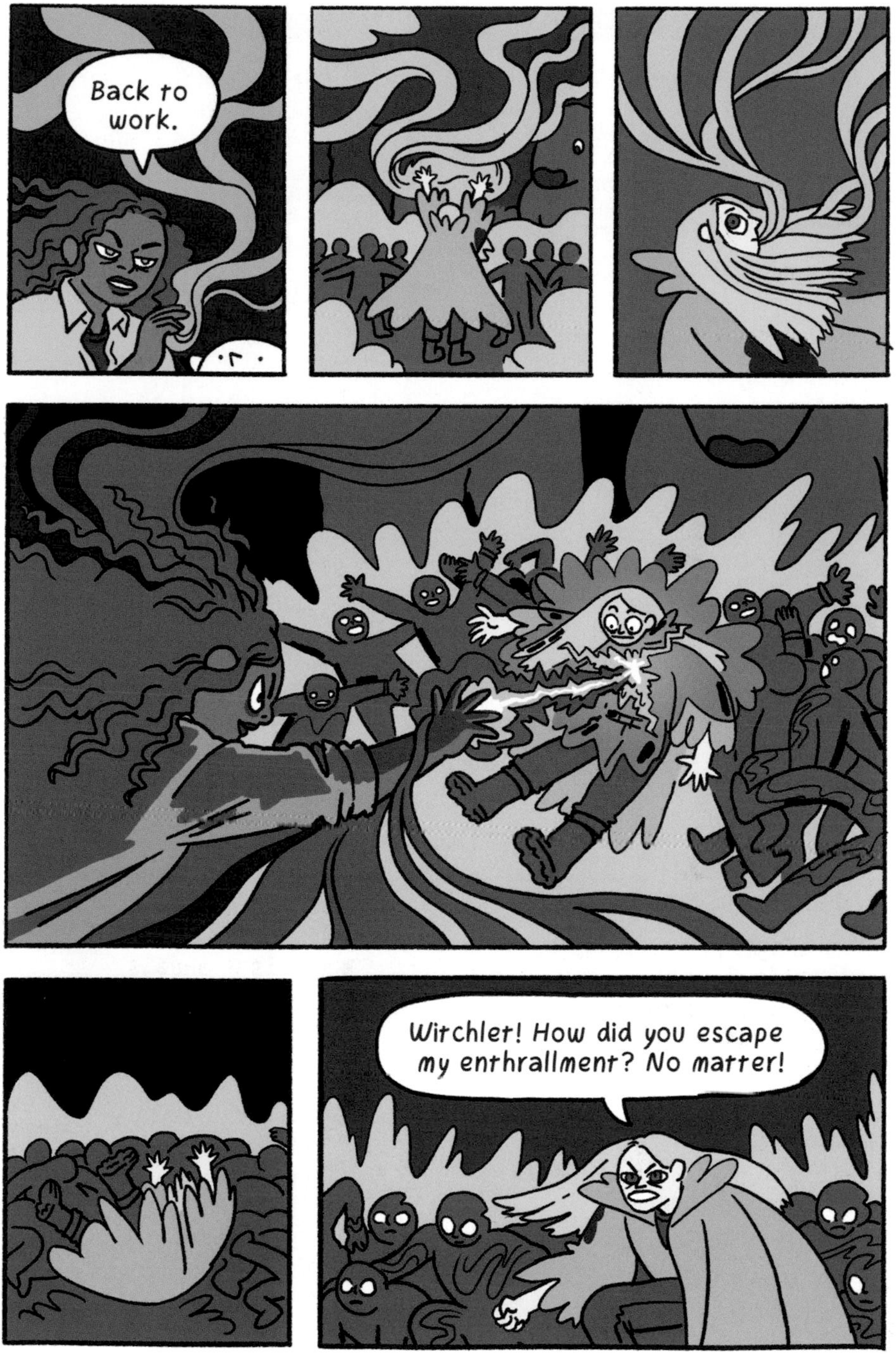
Back to work.
Witchlet! How did you escape my enthrallment? No matter!

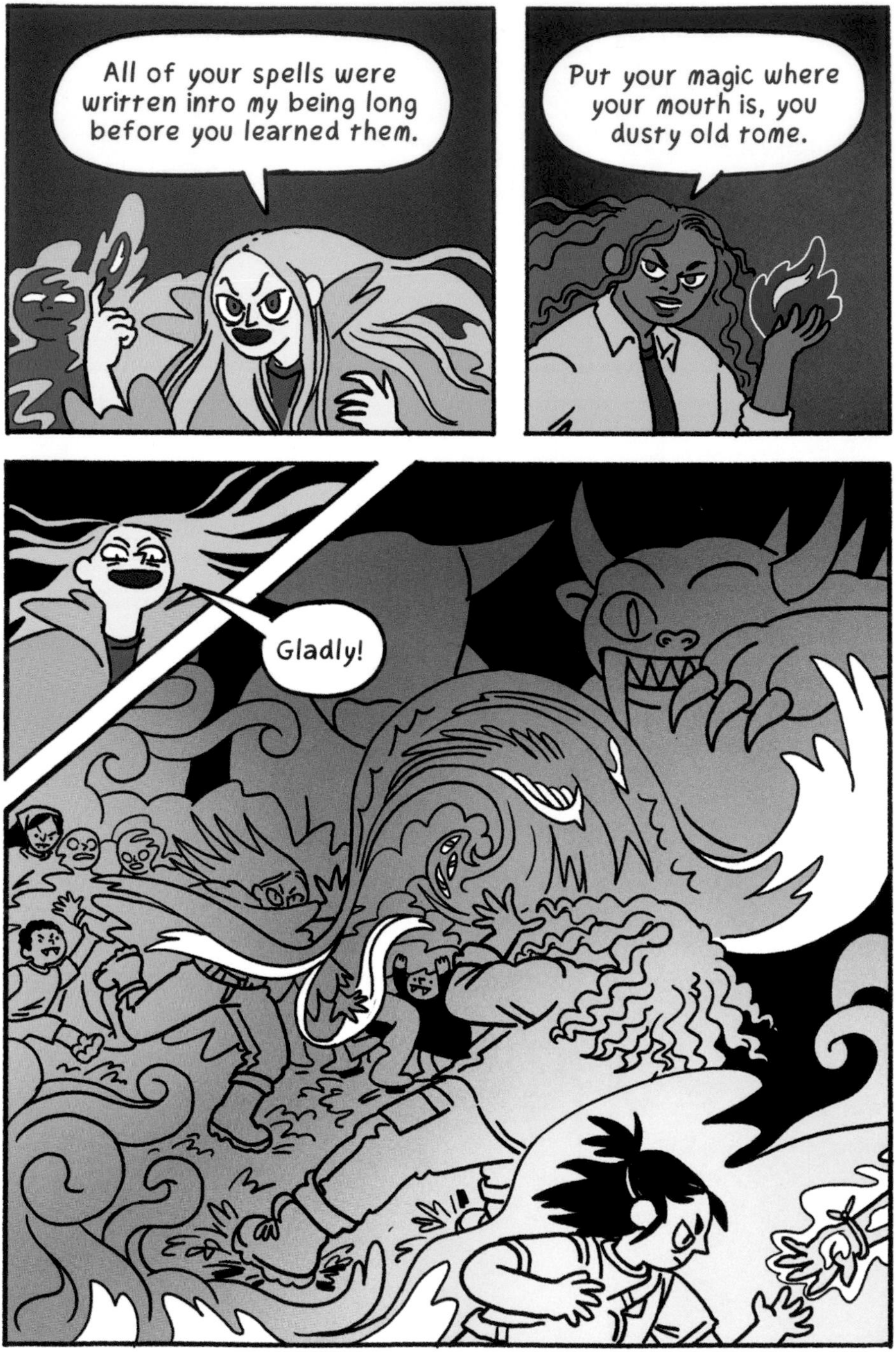
All of your spells were written into my being long before you learned them.
Put your magic where your mouth is, you dusty old tome.
Gladly!

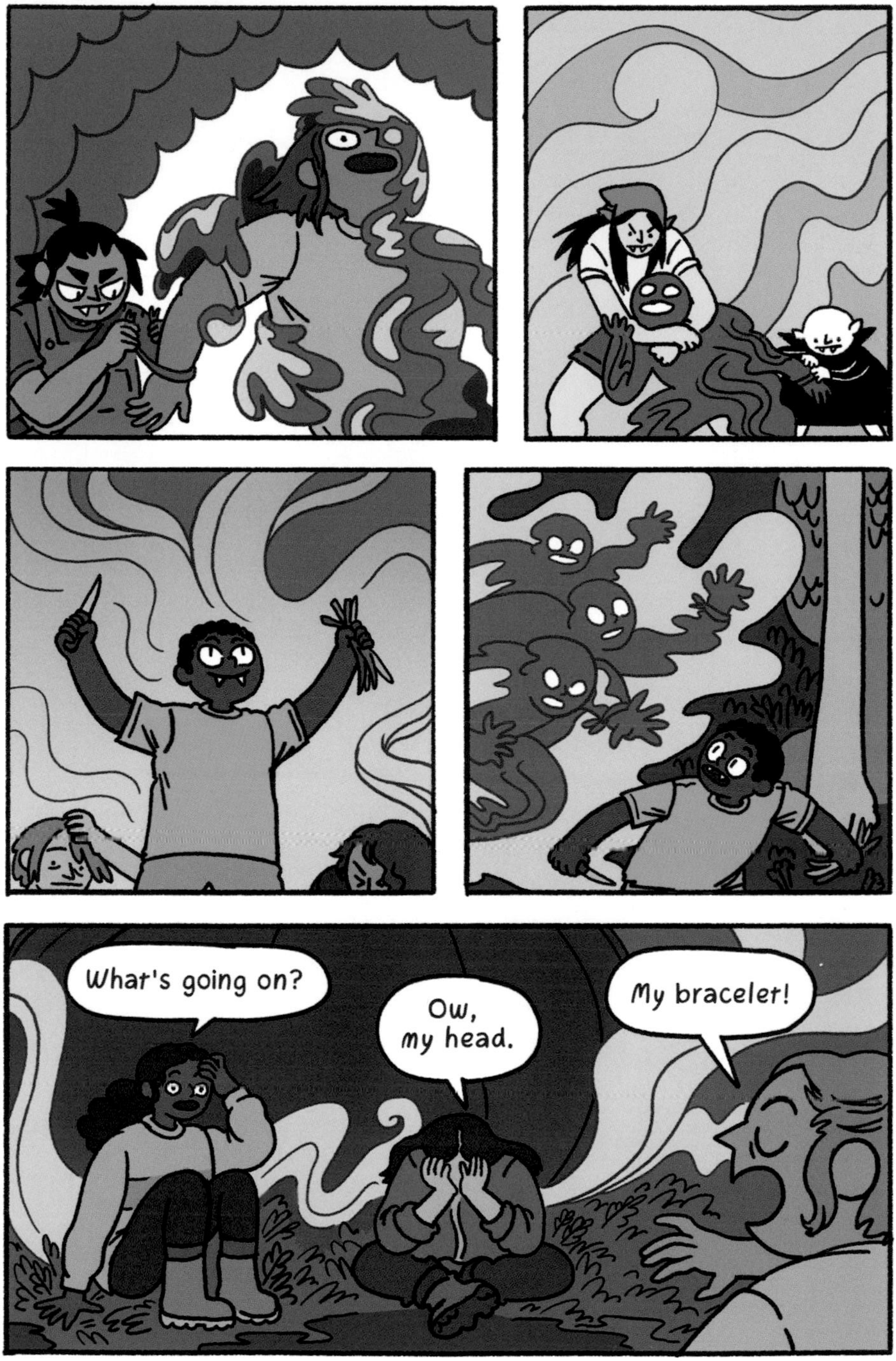
What's going on?
Ow, my head.
My braceler!

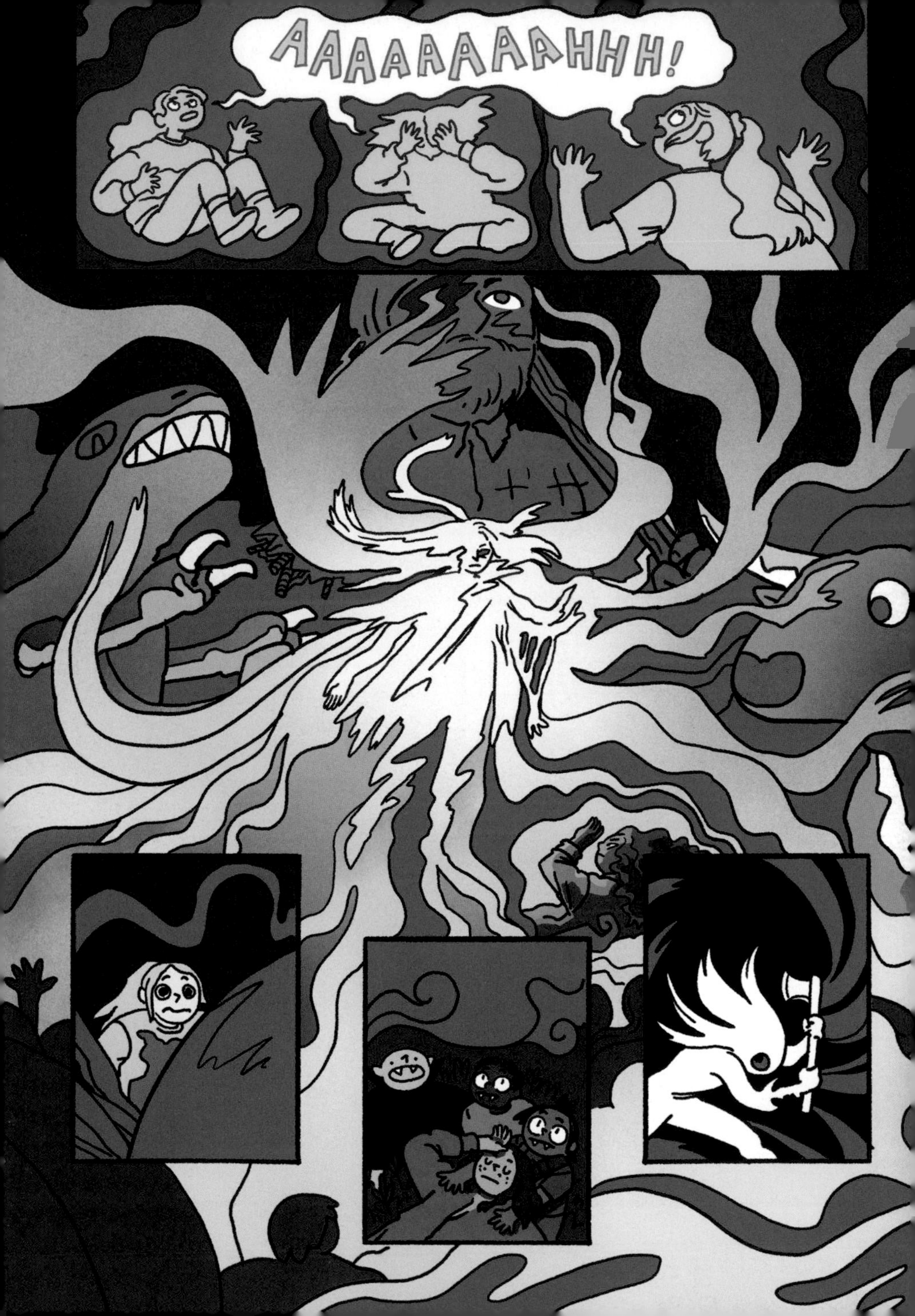
AAAAAAAAHHH!

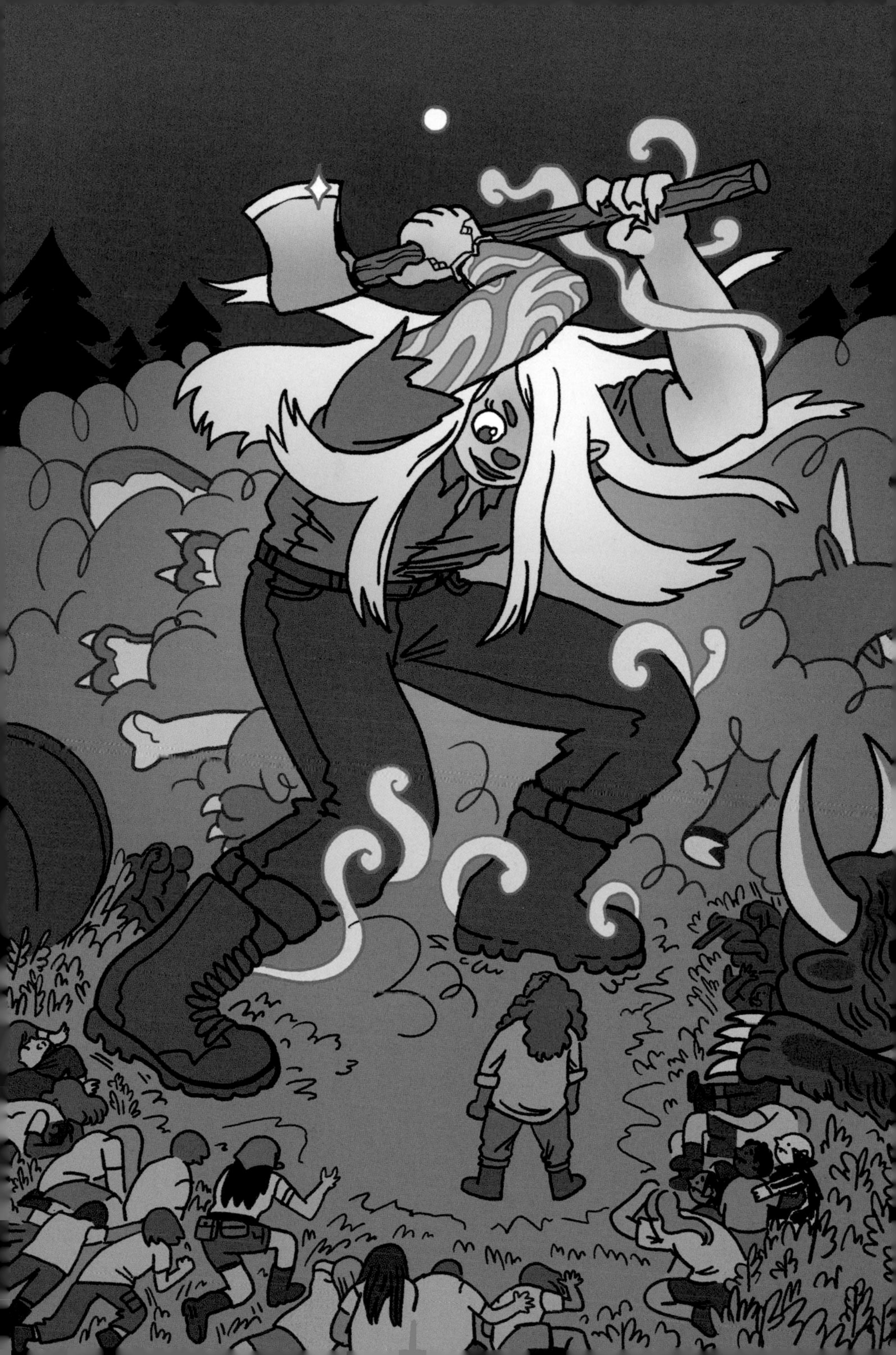

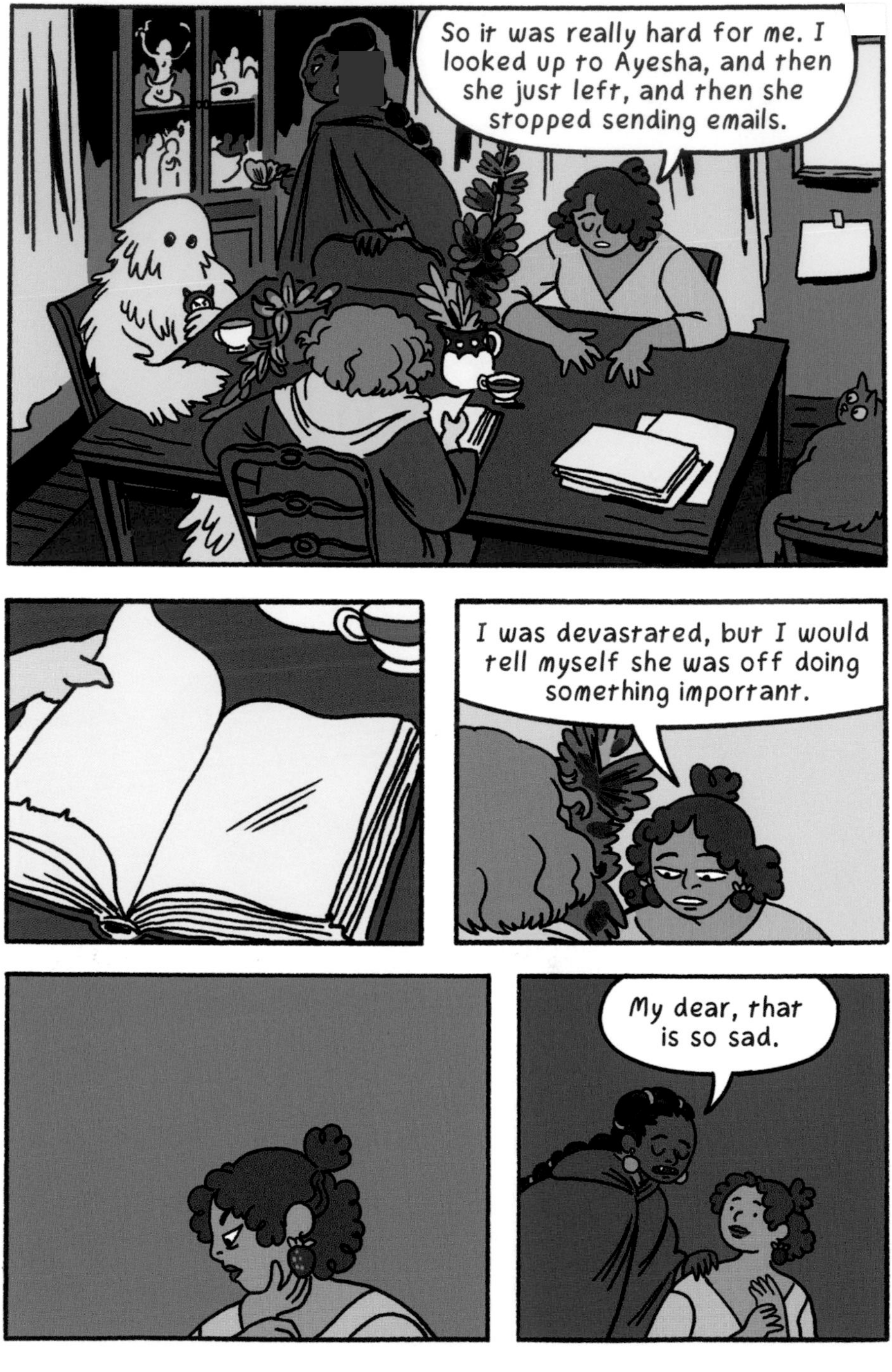
So it was really hard for me. I looked up to Ayesha, and then she just left, and then she stopped sending emails.
I was devastated, but I would tell myself she was off doing something important.
My dear, that is so sad.

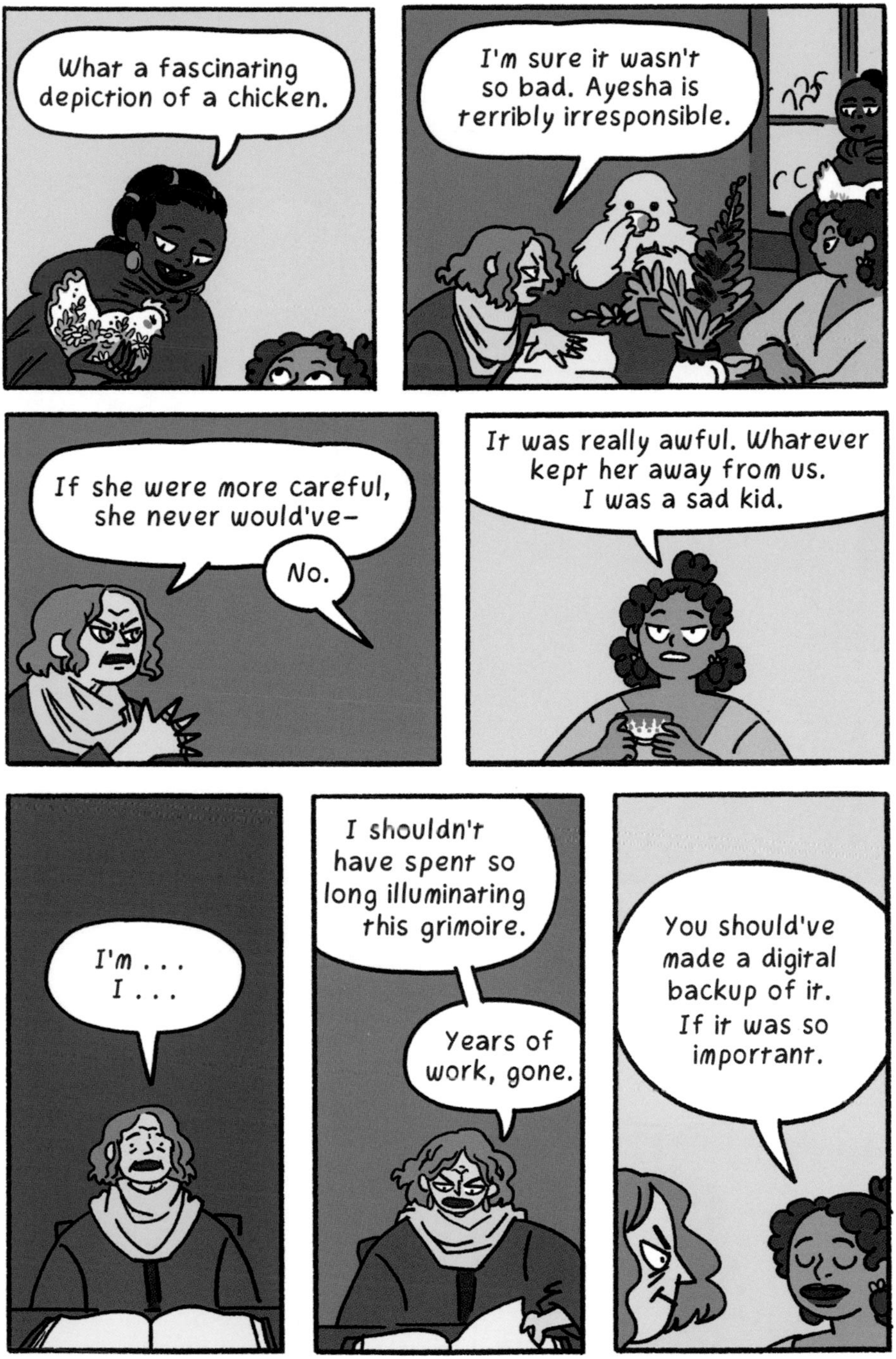
What a fascinating depiction of a chicken.
I'm sure it wasn't so bad. Ayesha is terribly irresponsible.
If she were more careful, she never would've—
No.
It was really awful. Whatever kept her away from us. I was a sad kid.
I'm . . .
I . . .
I shouldn't have spent so long illuminating this grimoire.
Years of work, gone.
You should've made a digital backup of it. If it was so important.

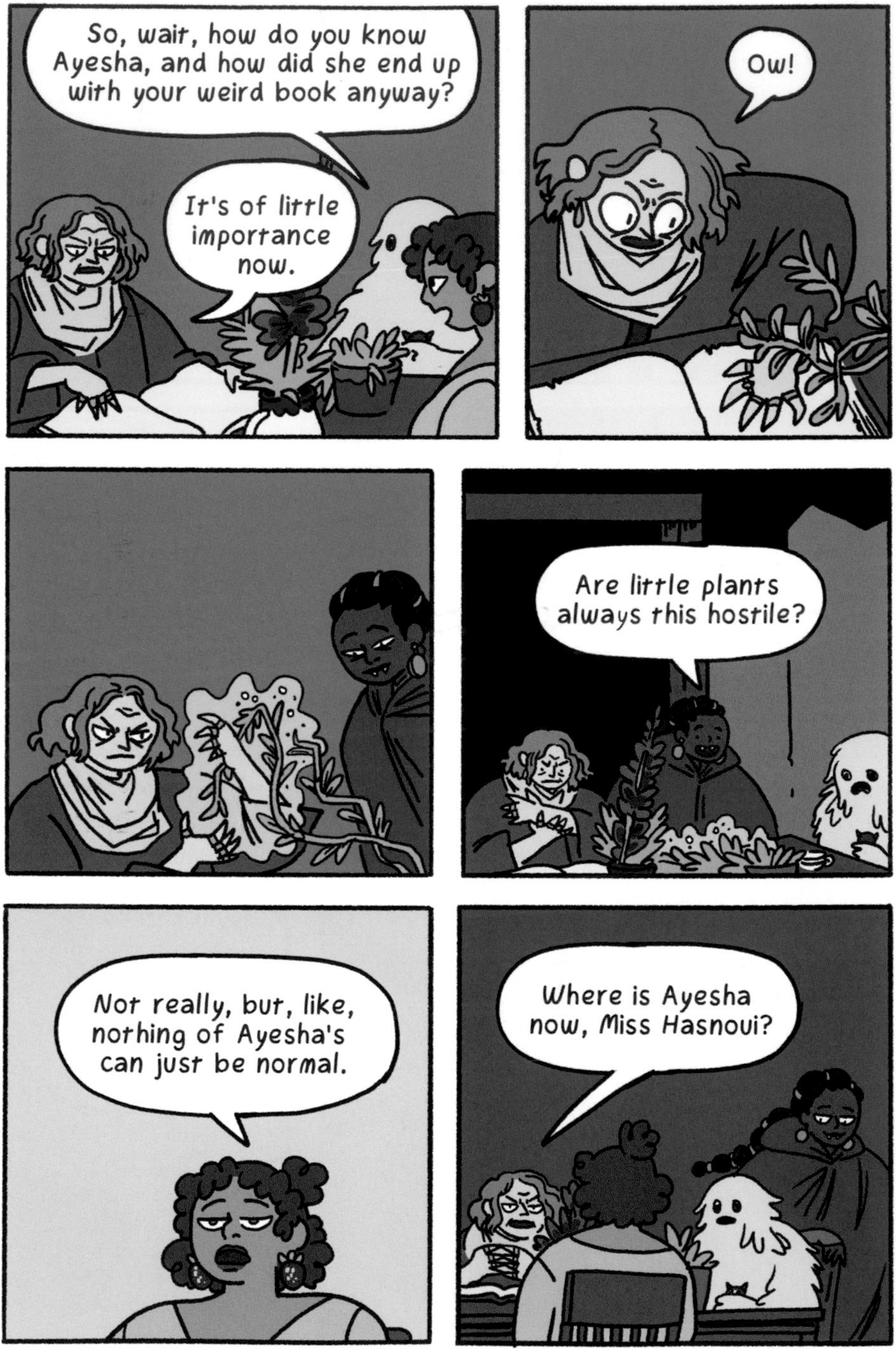

So, wait, how do you know Ayesha, and how did she end up with your weird book anyway?
It's of little importance now.
Ow!
Are little plants always this hostile?
Not really, but, like, nothing of Ayesha's can just be normal.
Where is Ayesha now, Miss Hasnoui?

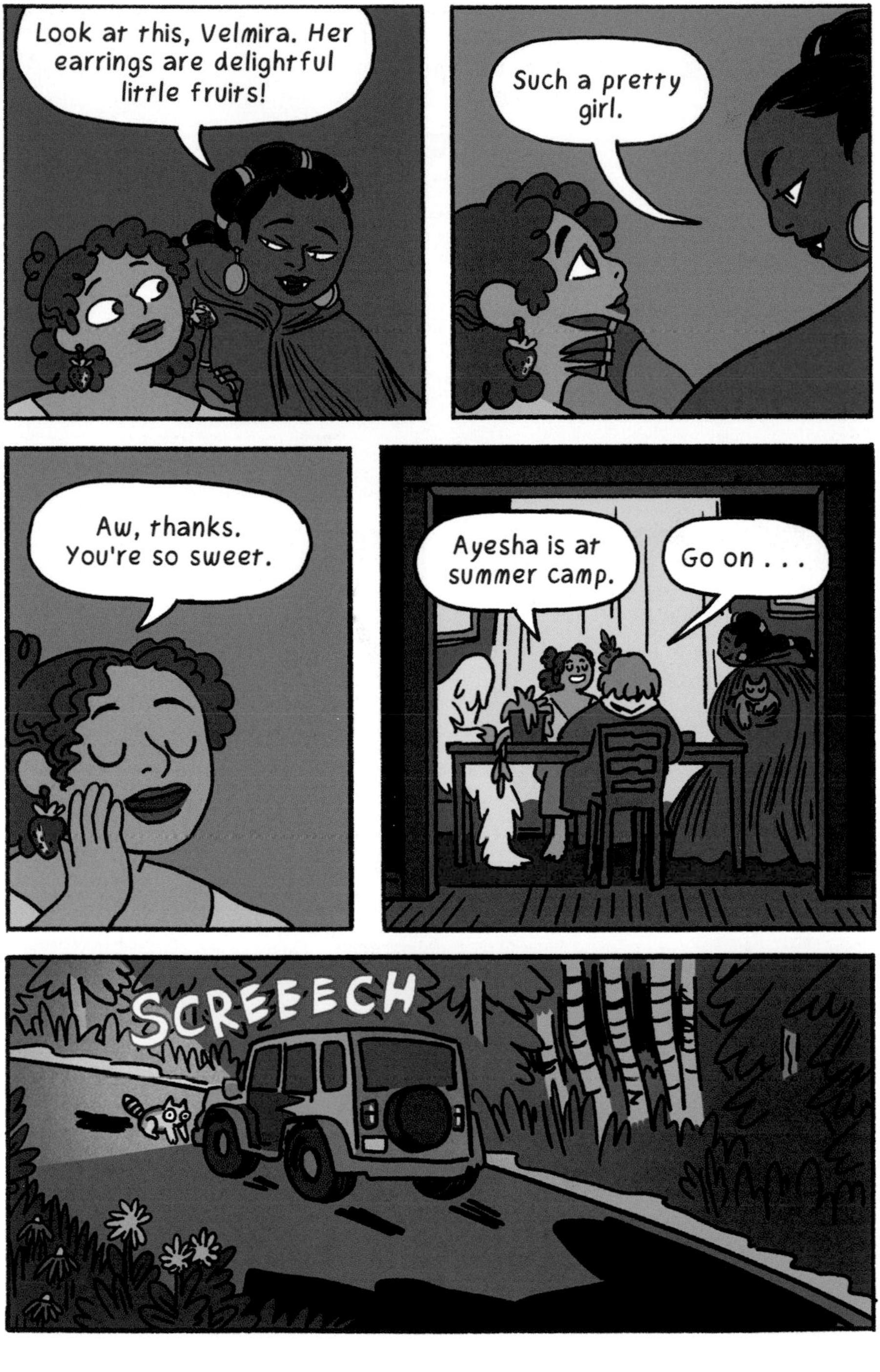
Look at this, Velmira. Her earrings are delightful little fruits!
Such a pretty girl.
Aw, thanks. You're so sweet.
Ayesha is at summer camp.
Go on . . .
SCREEECH

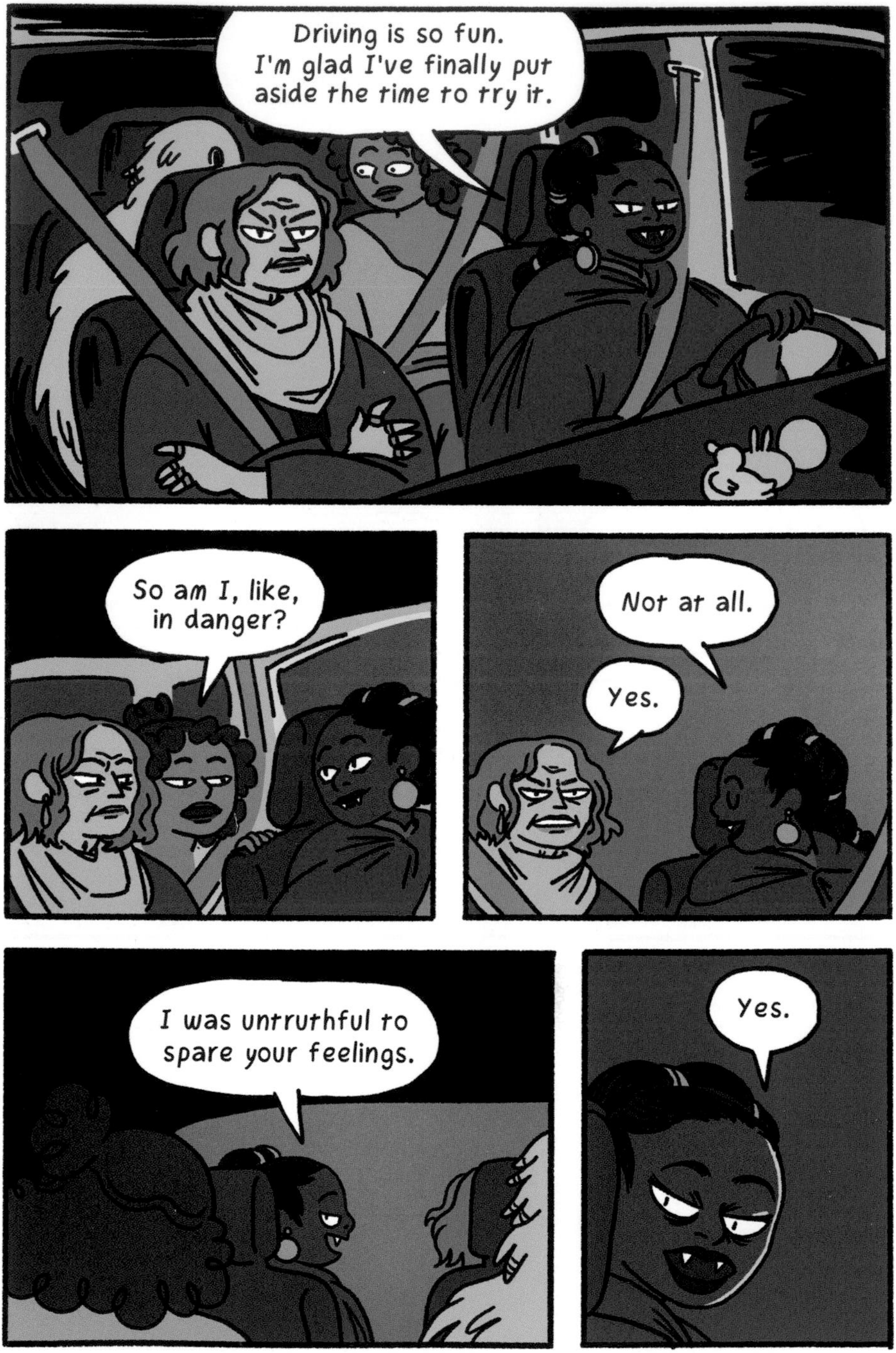
Driving is so fun. I'm glad I've finally put aside the time to try it.
So am I, like, in danger?
Not at all.
Yes.
I was untruthful to spare your feelings.
Yes.

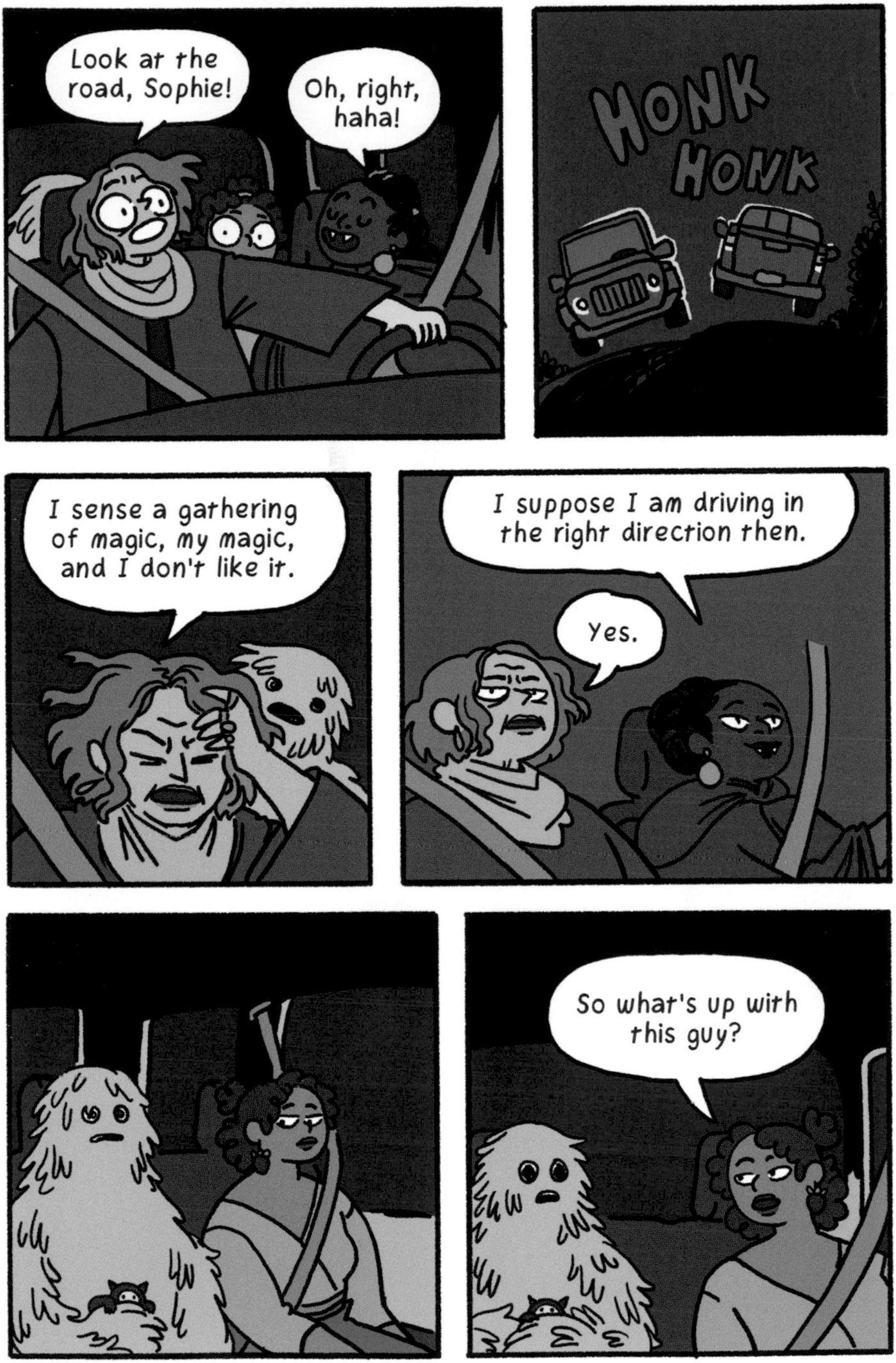
Look at the road, Sophie!
Oh, right, haha!
HONK
HONK
I sense a gathering of magic, my magic, and I don't like it.
I suppose I am driving in the right direction then.
Yes.
So what's up with this guy?

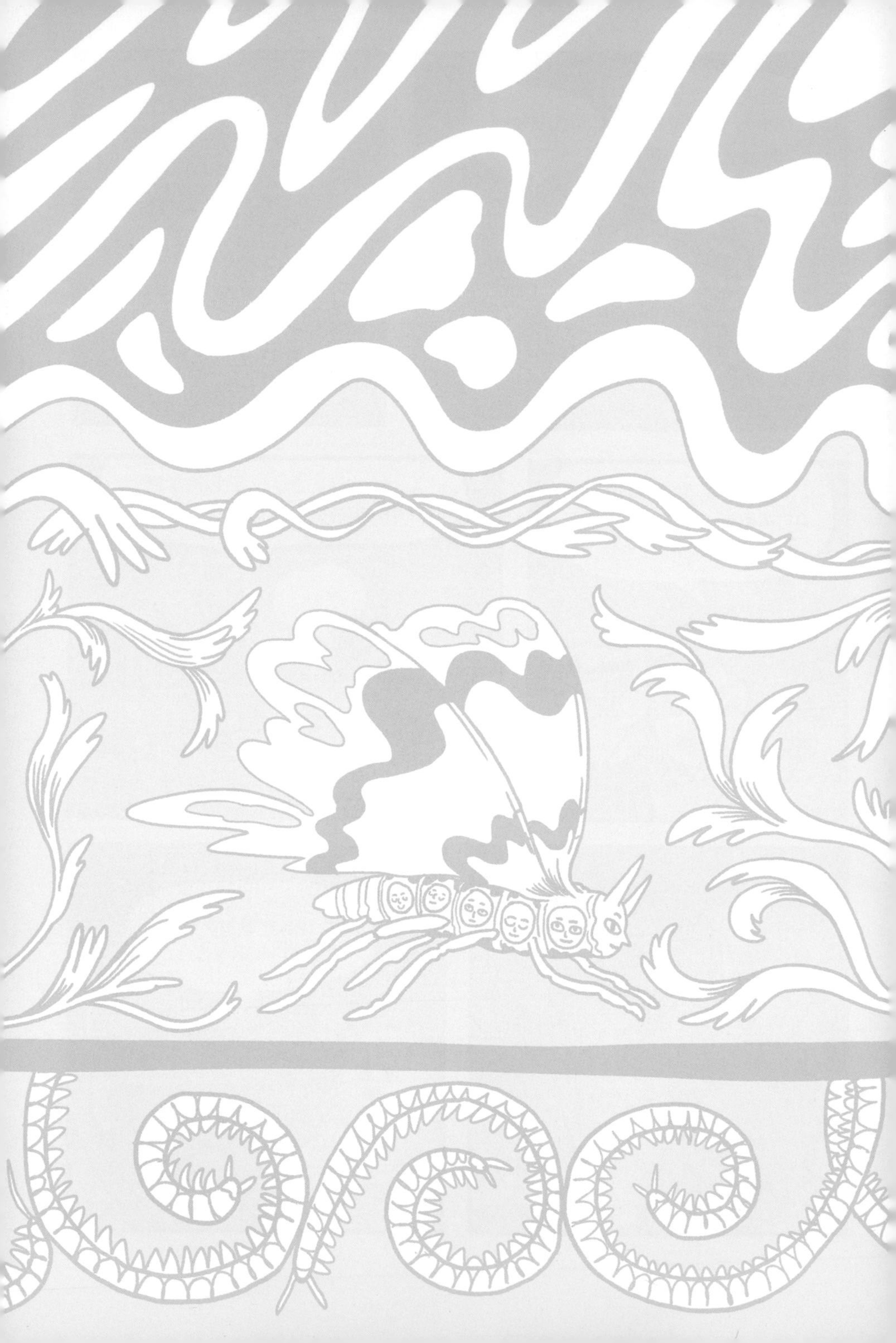

CHAPTER EIGHT

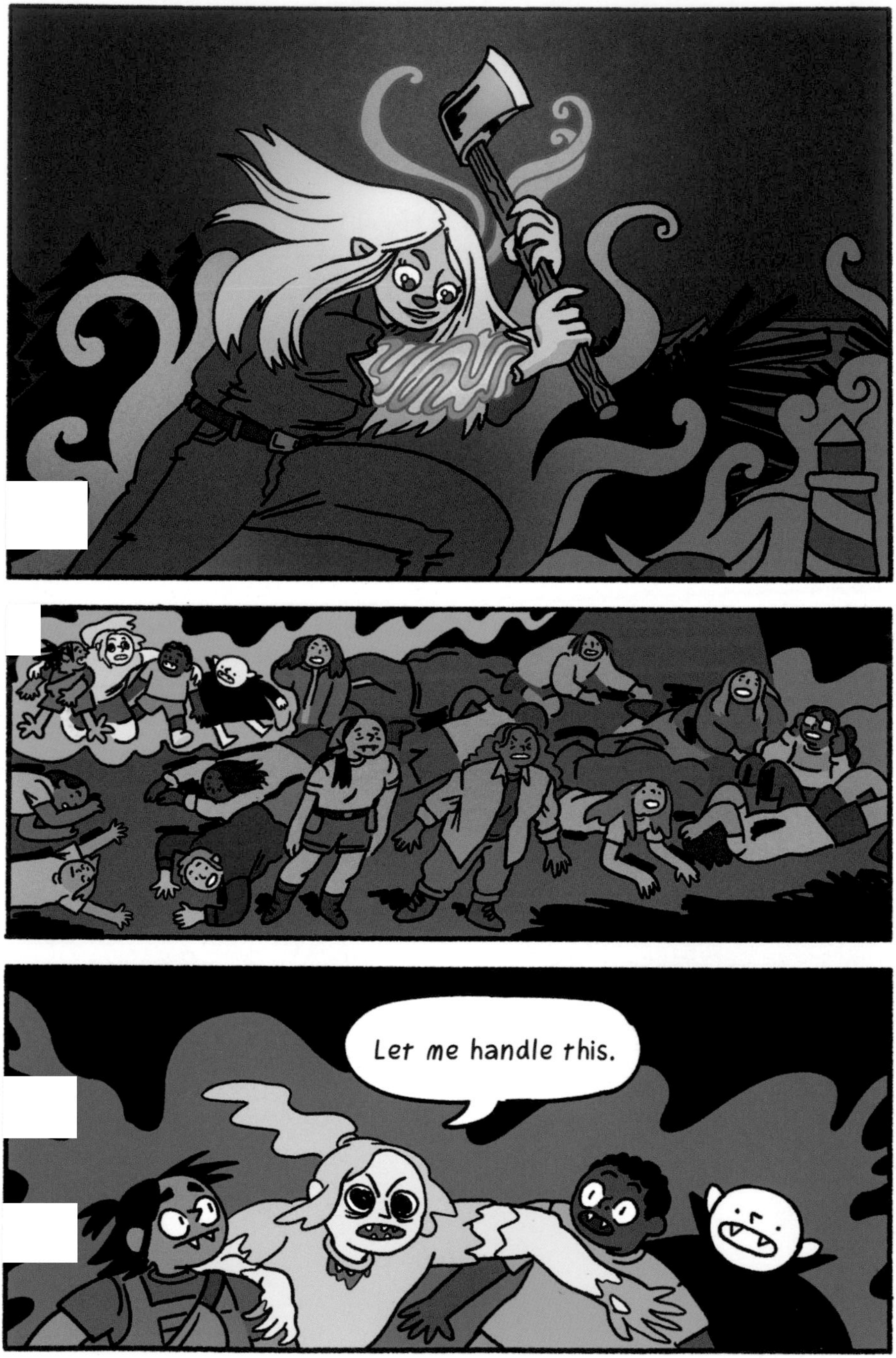
Let me handle this.

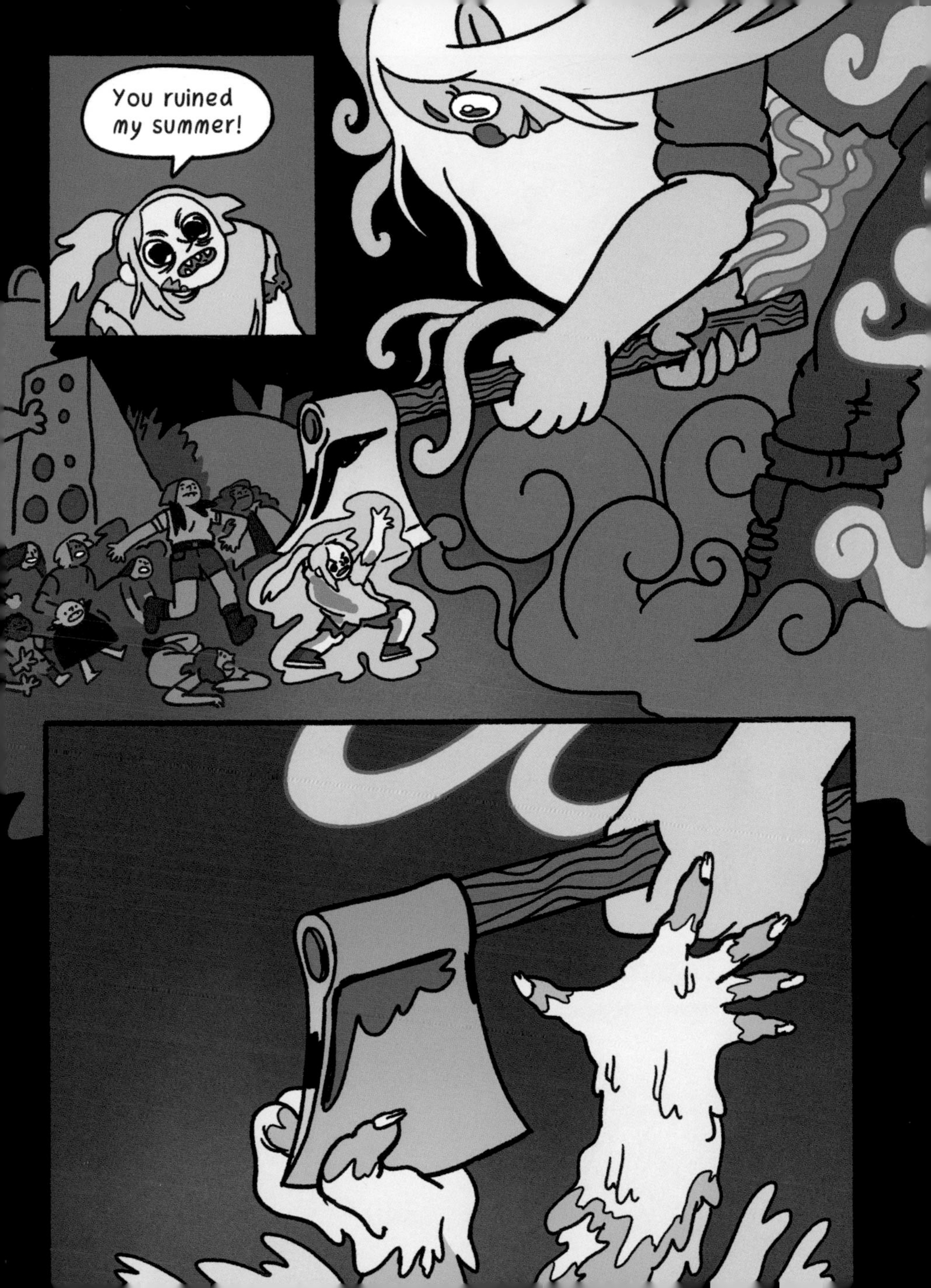
You ruined my summer!

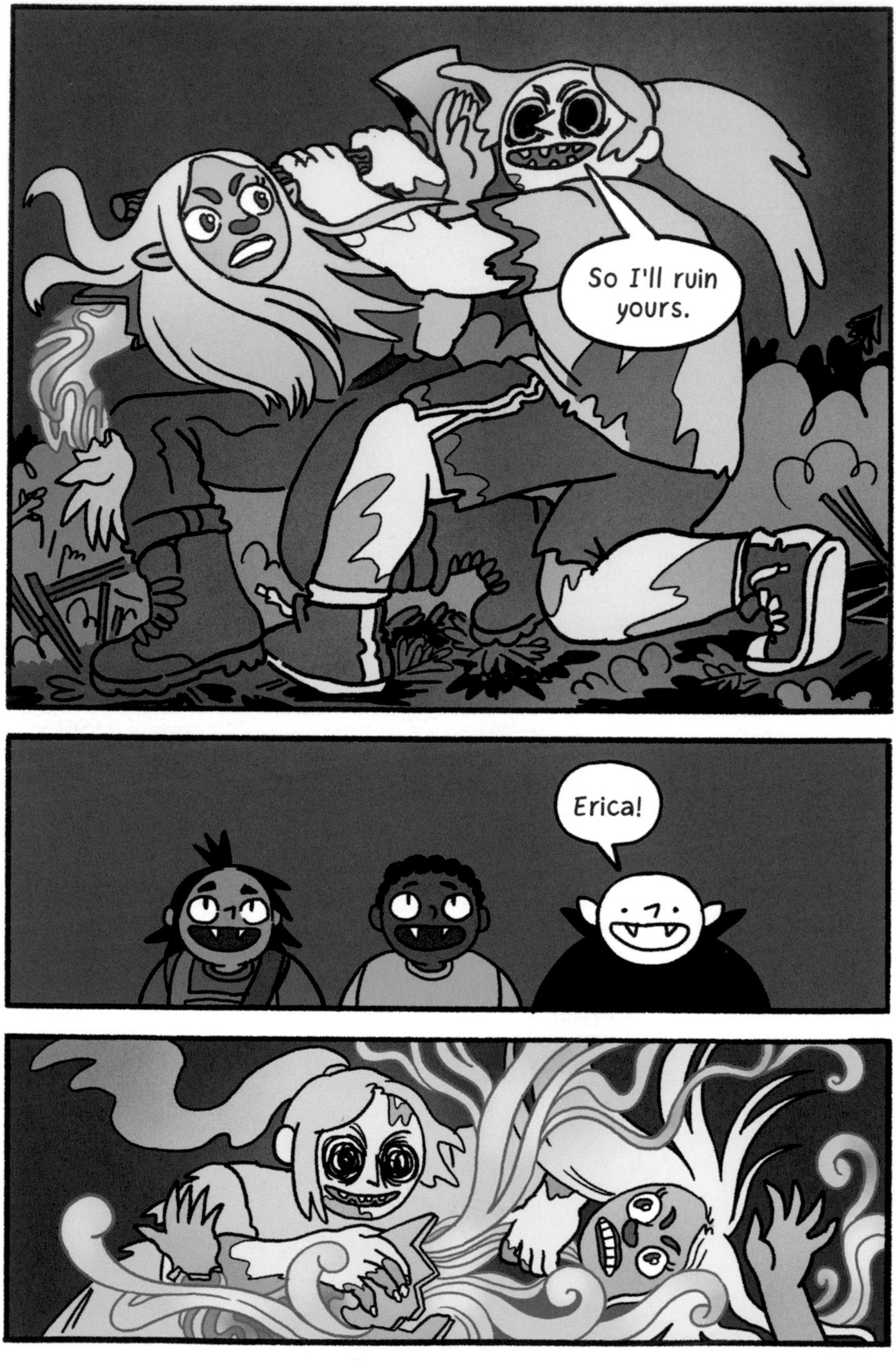
So I'll ruin yours.
Erica!

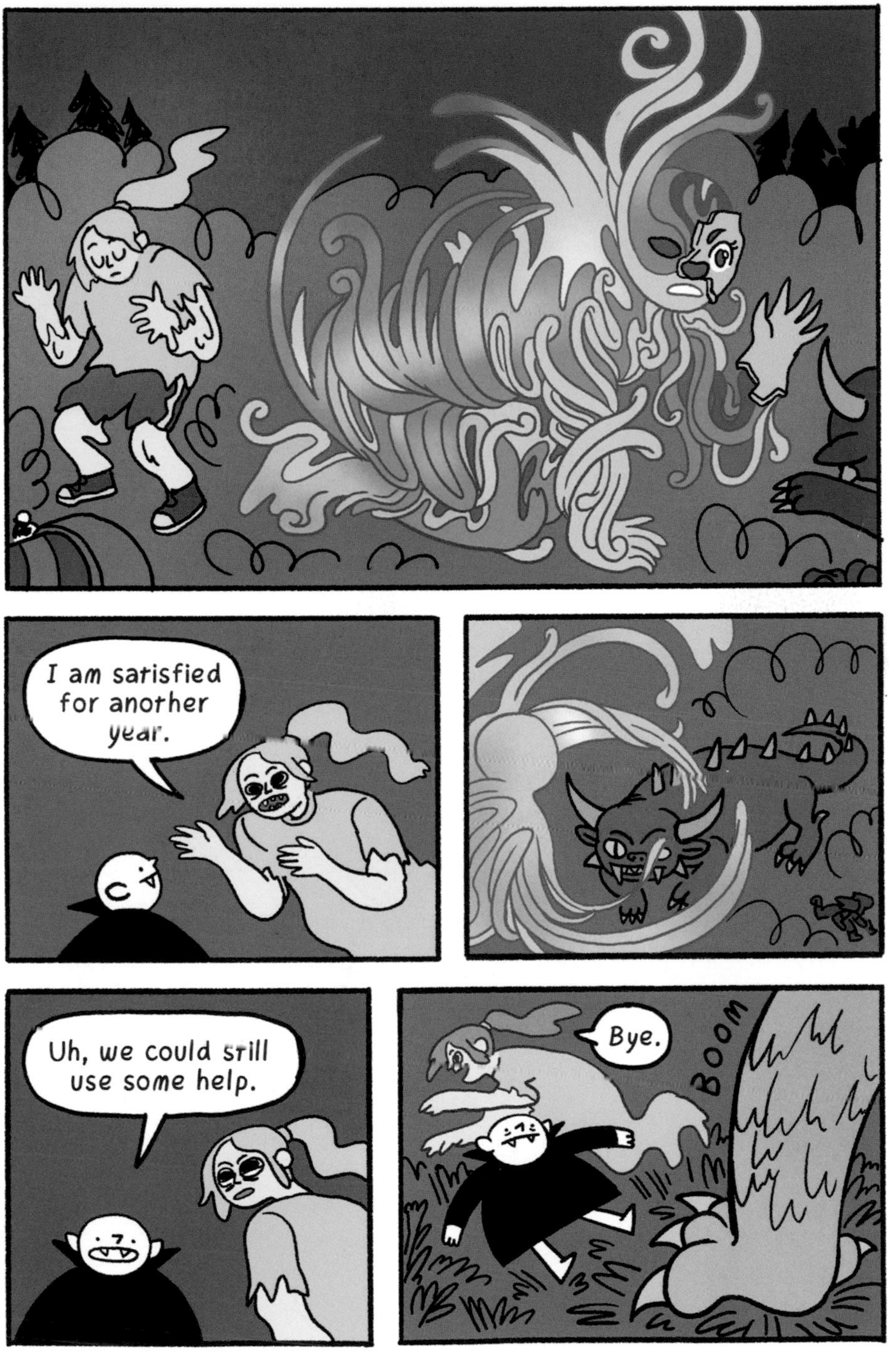
I am satisfied for another year.
Uh, we could still use some help.
Bye.
BOOM

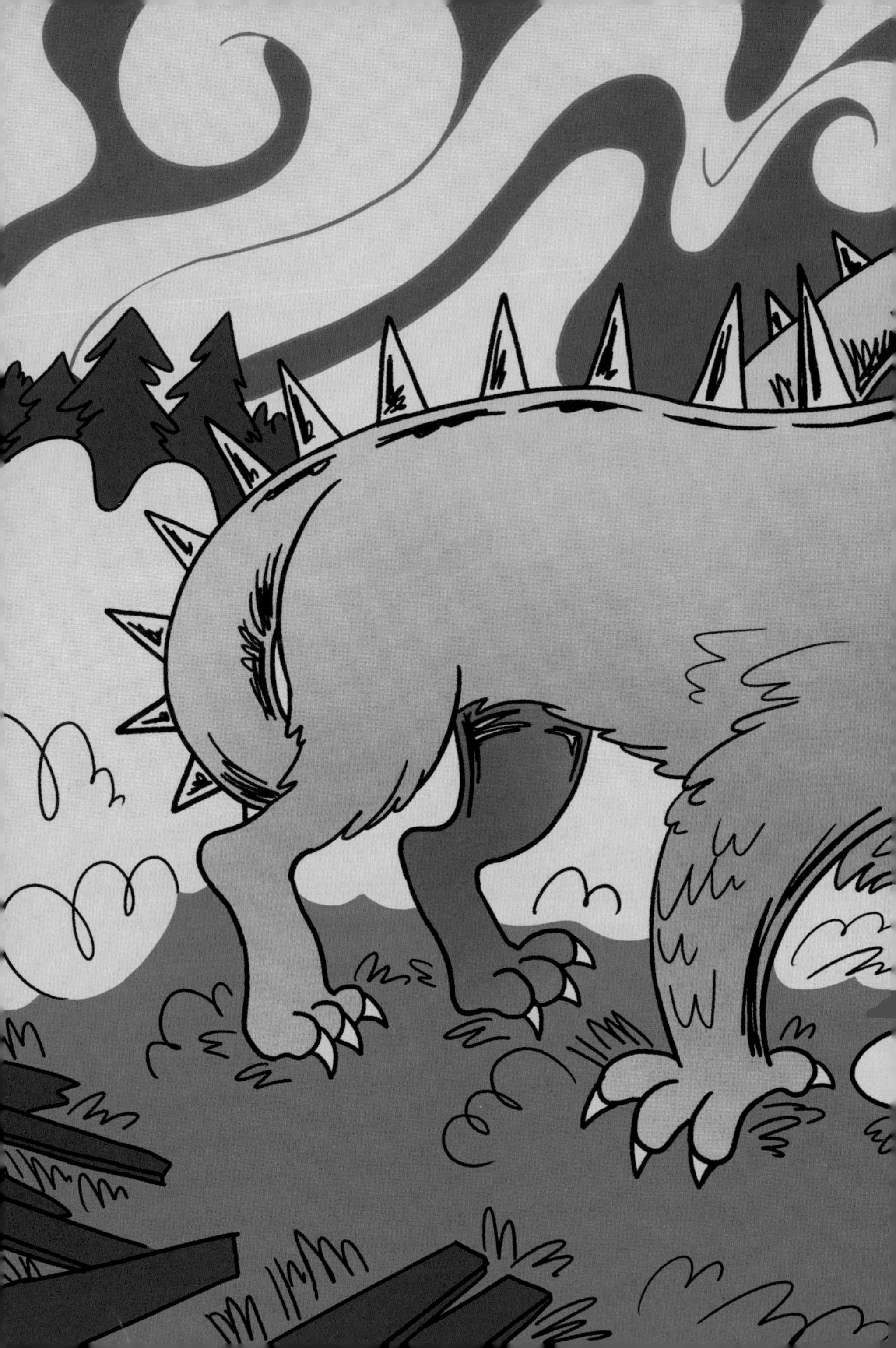

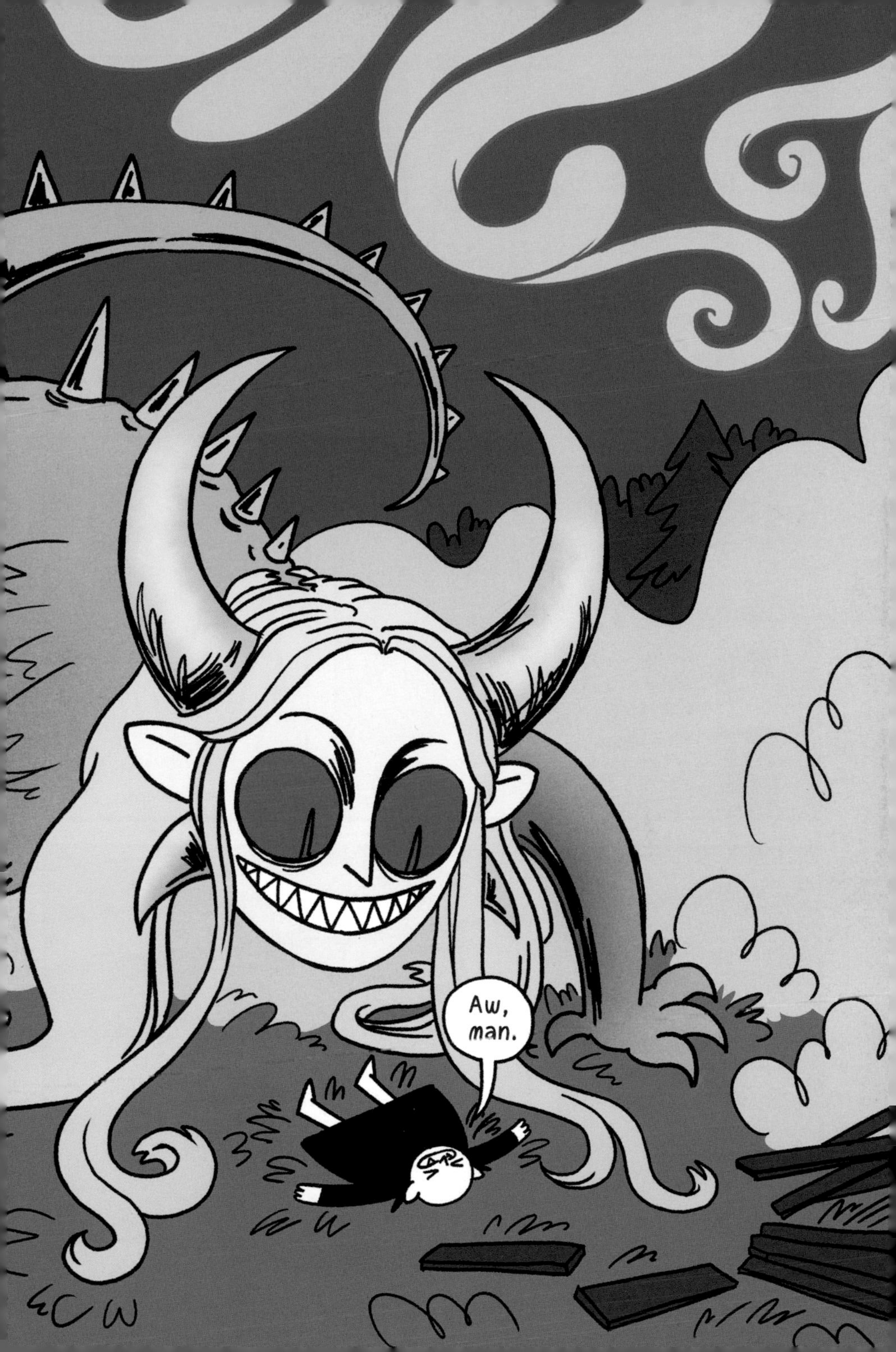
Aw, man.

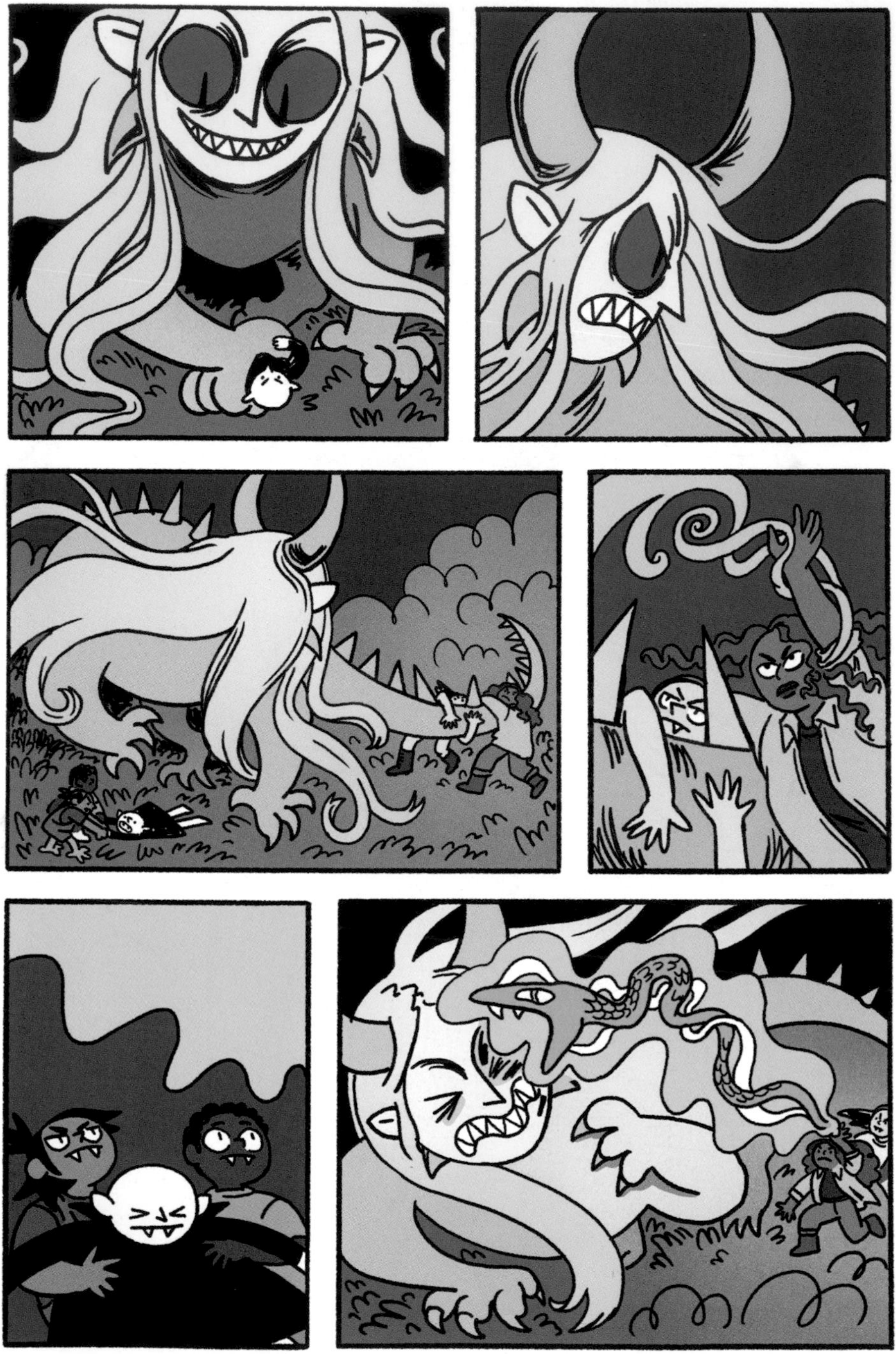

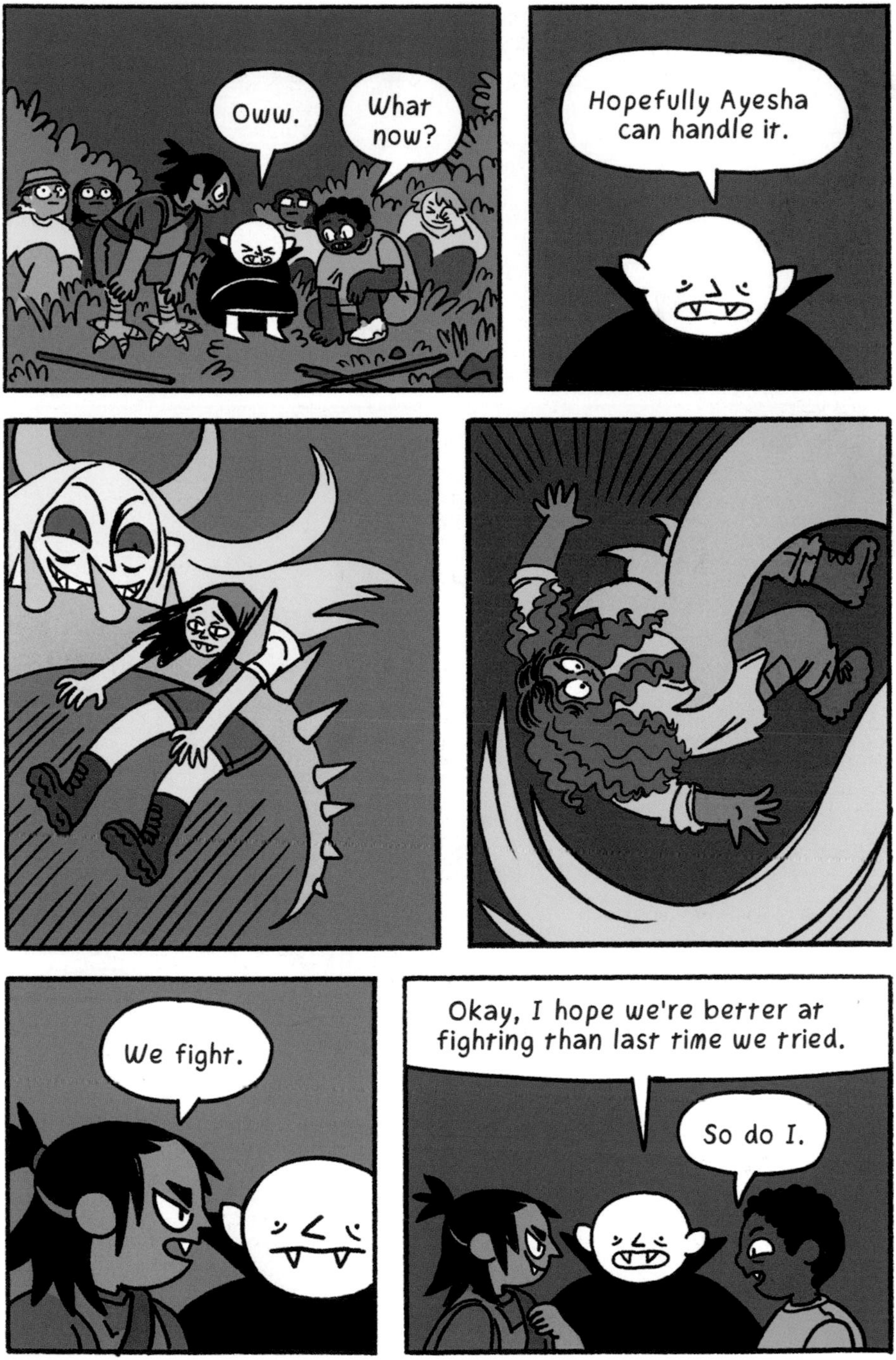
Oww.
What now?
Hopefully Ayesha can handle it.
We fight.
Okay, I hope we're better at fighting than last time we tried.
So do I.

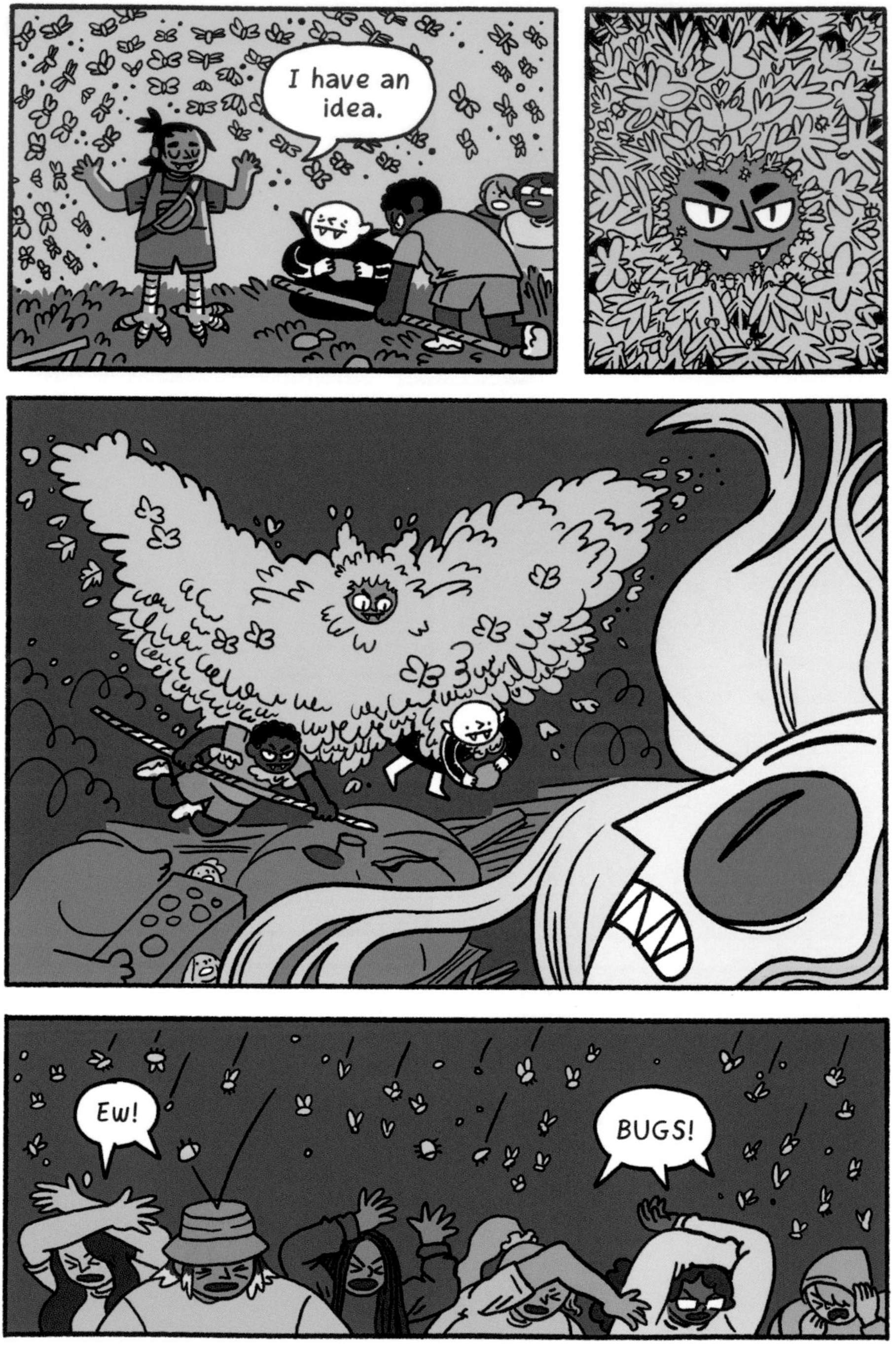

I have an idea.
Ew!
BUGS!

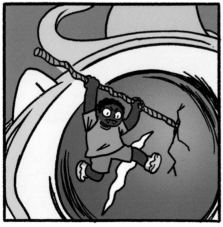

Ow.

Oh.

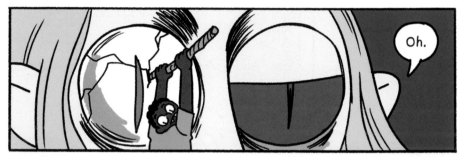

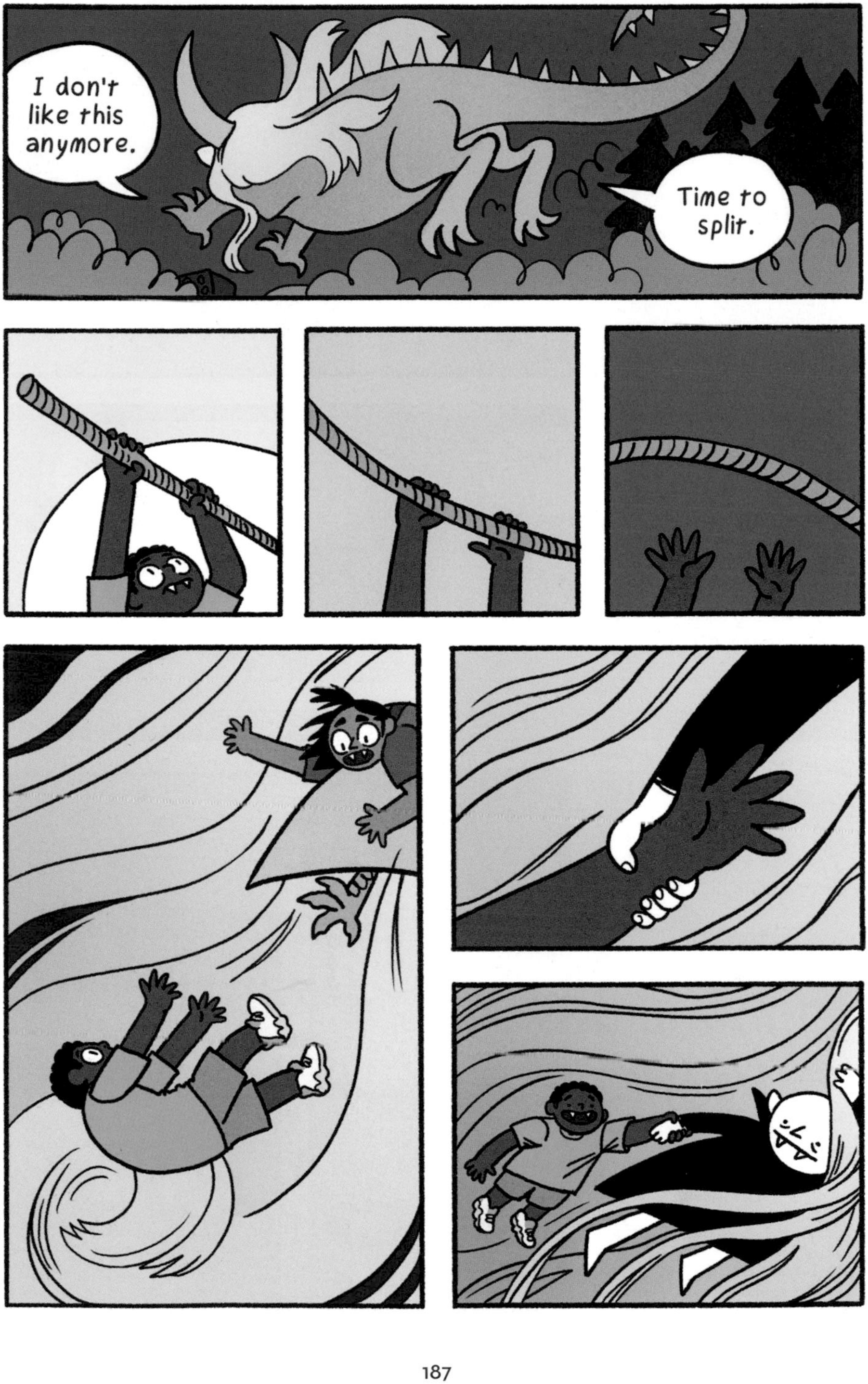
I don't like this anymore.
Time to split.

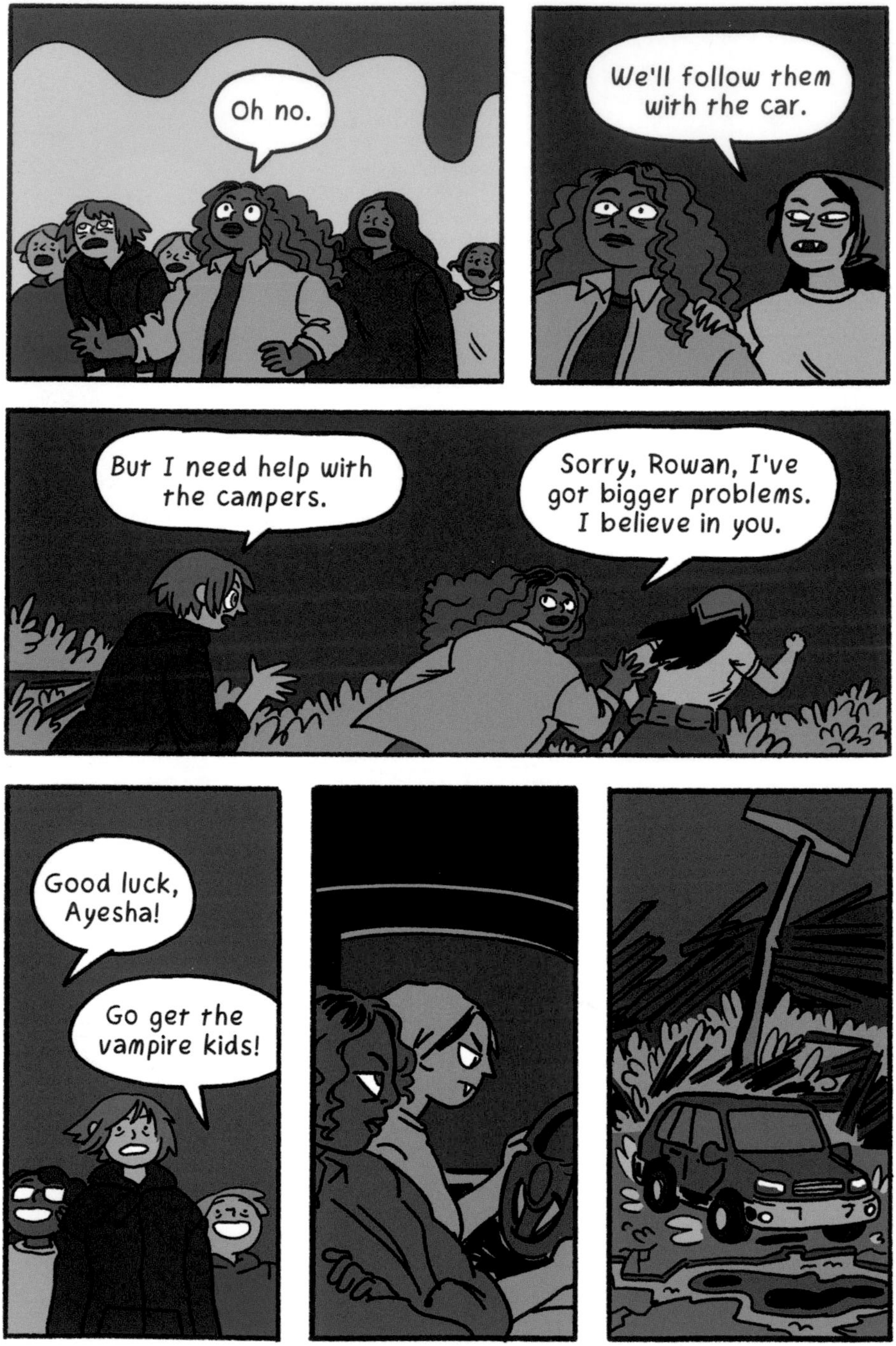
Oh no.
We'll follow them with the car.
But I need help with the campers.
Sorry, Rowan, I've got bigger problems. I believe in you.
Good luck, Ayesha!
Go get the vampire kids!

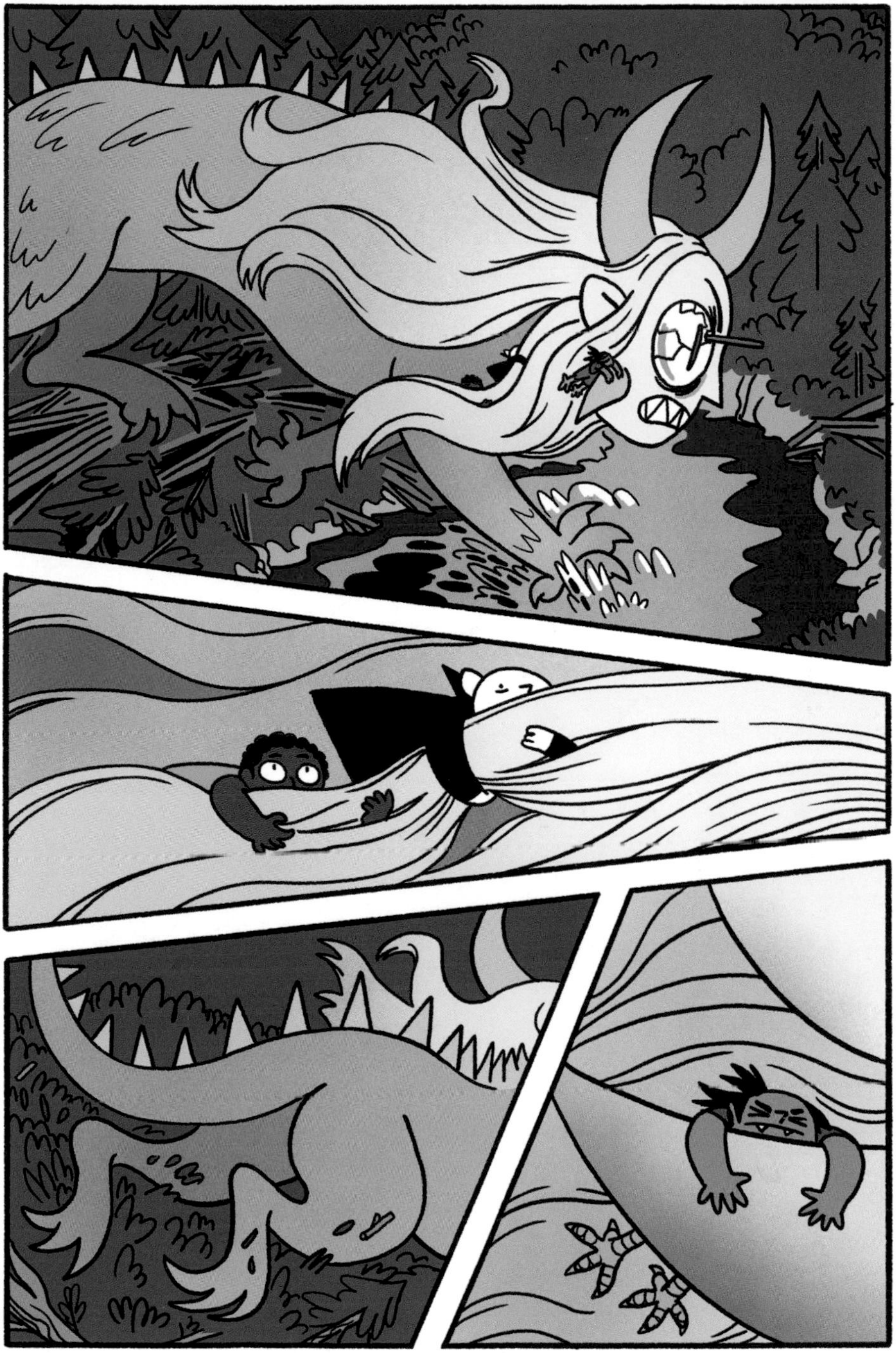

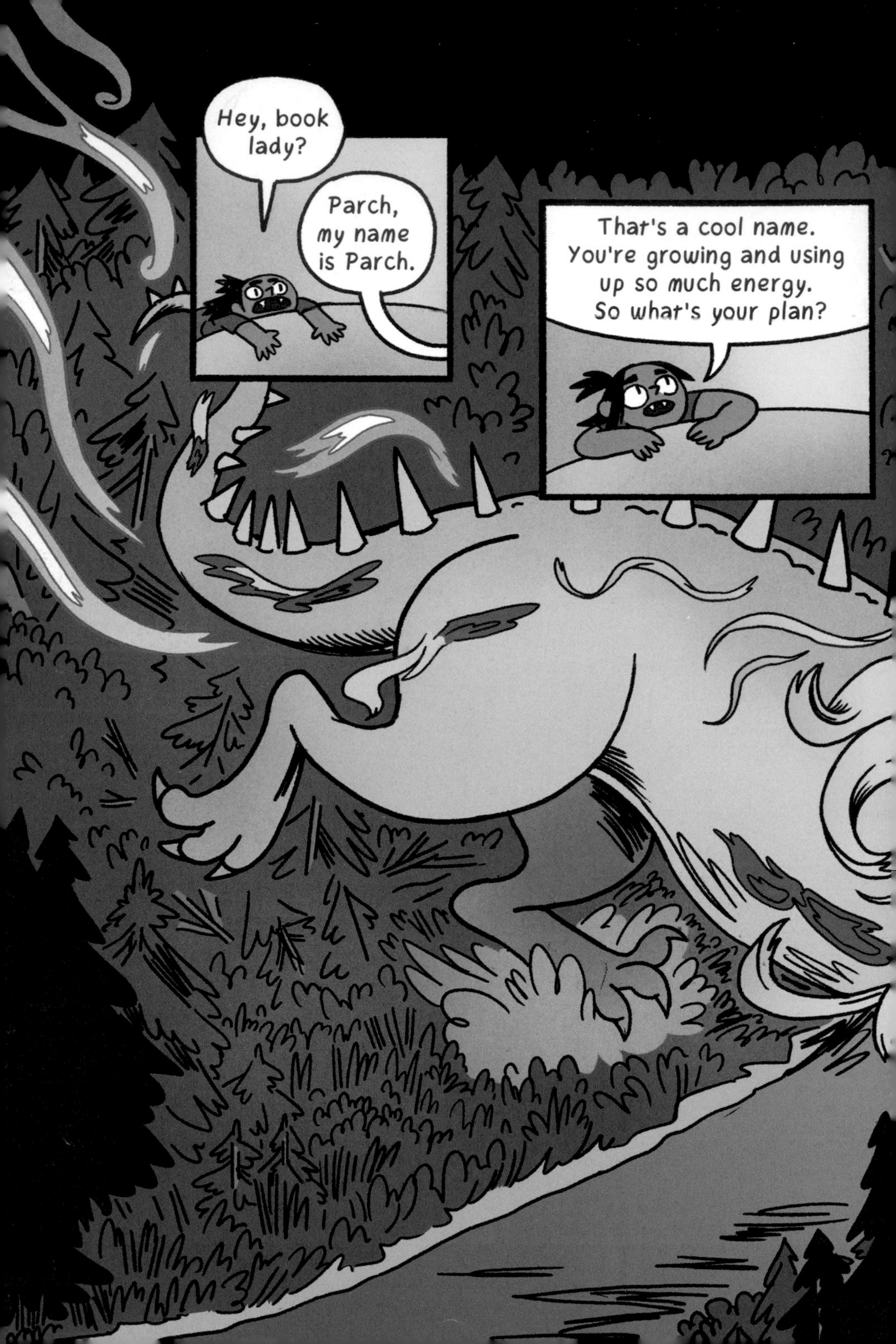
Hey, book lady?
Parch, my name is Parch.
That's a cool name. You're growing and using up so much energy. So what's your plan?

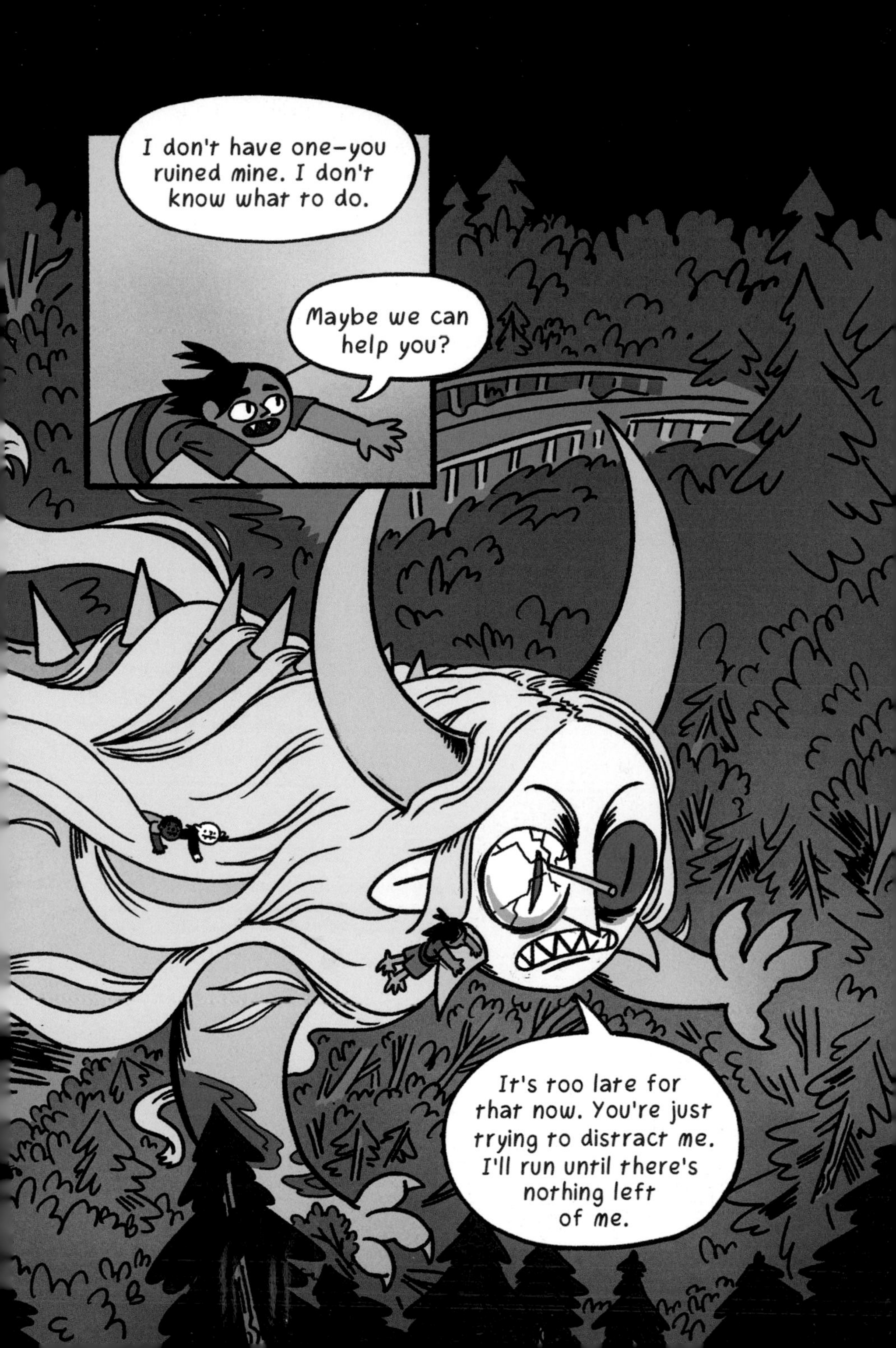
I don't have one—you ruined mine. I don't know what to do.
Maybe we can help you?
It's too late for that now. You're just trying to distract me. I'll run until there's nothing left of me.

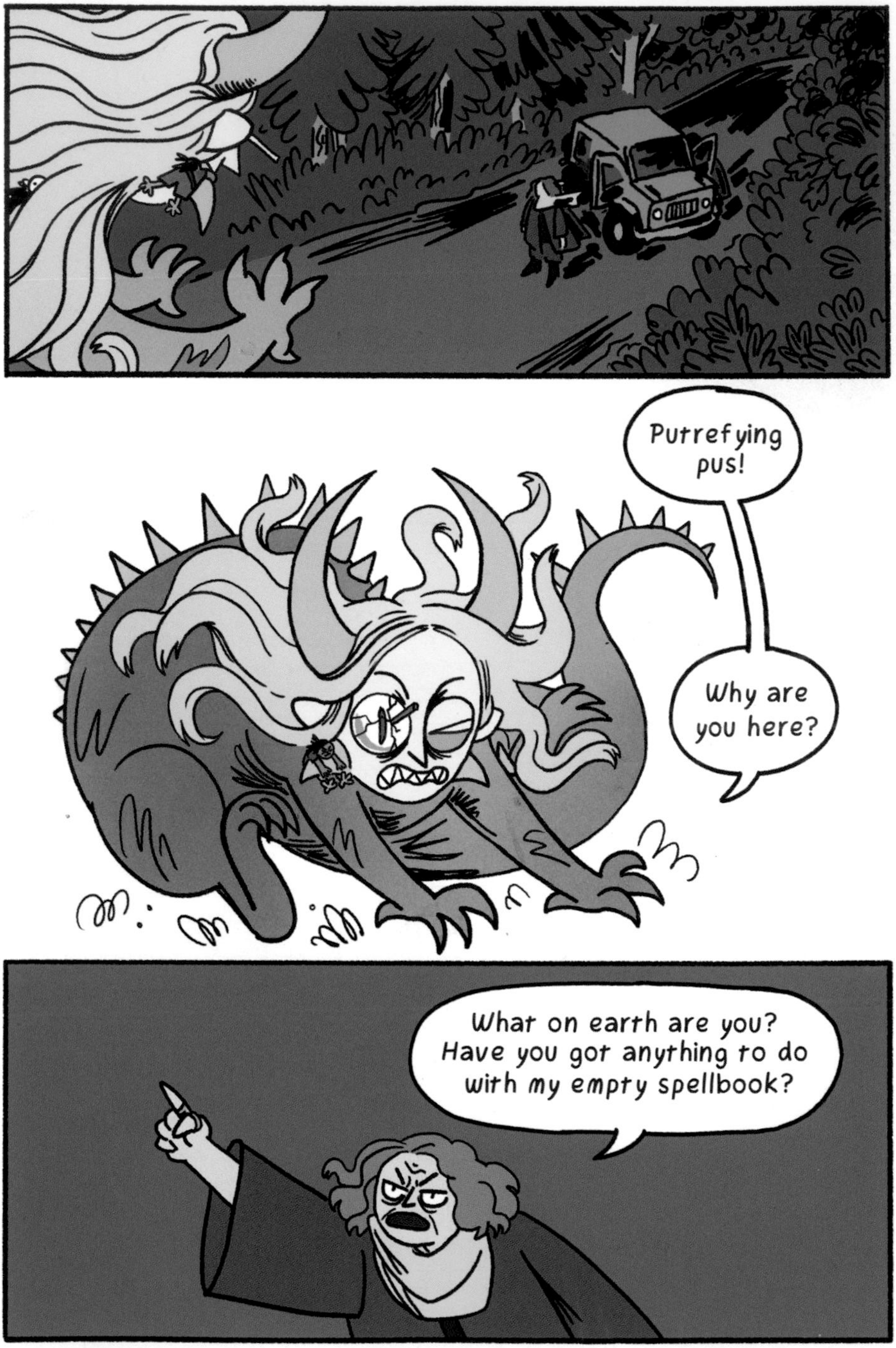
Putrefying pus!
Why are you here?
What on earth are you? Have you got anything to do with my empty spellbook?

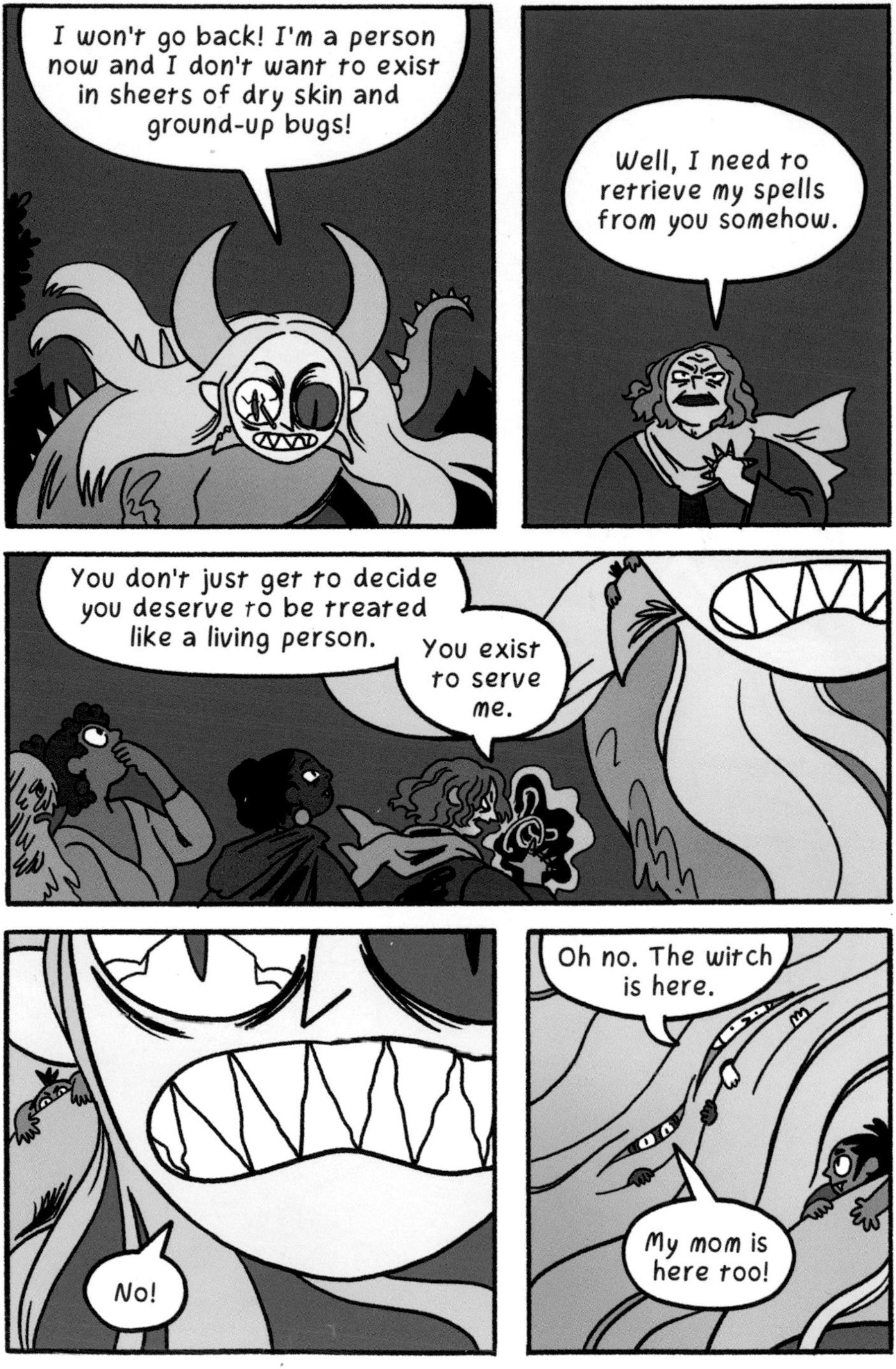
I won't go back! I'm a person now and I don't want to exist in sheets of dry skin and ground-up bugs!
Well, I need to retrieve my spells from you somehow.
You don't just get to decide you deserve to be treated like a living person.
You exist to serve me.
No!
Oh no. The witch is here.
My mom is here too!

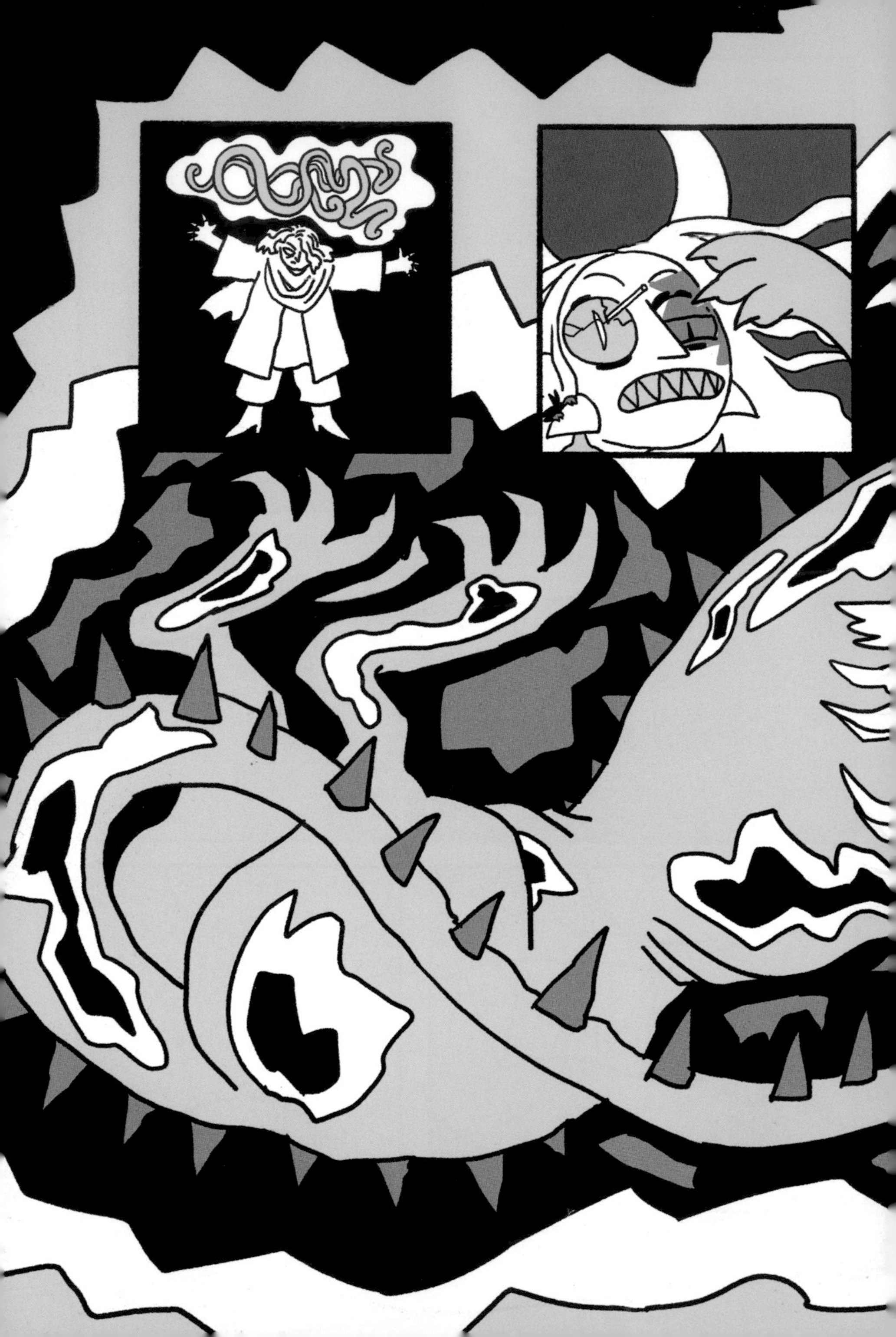

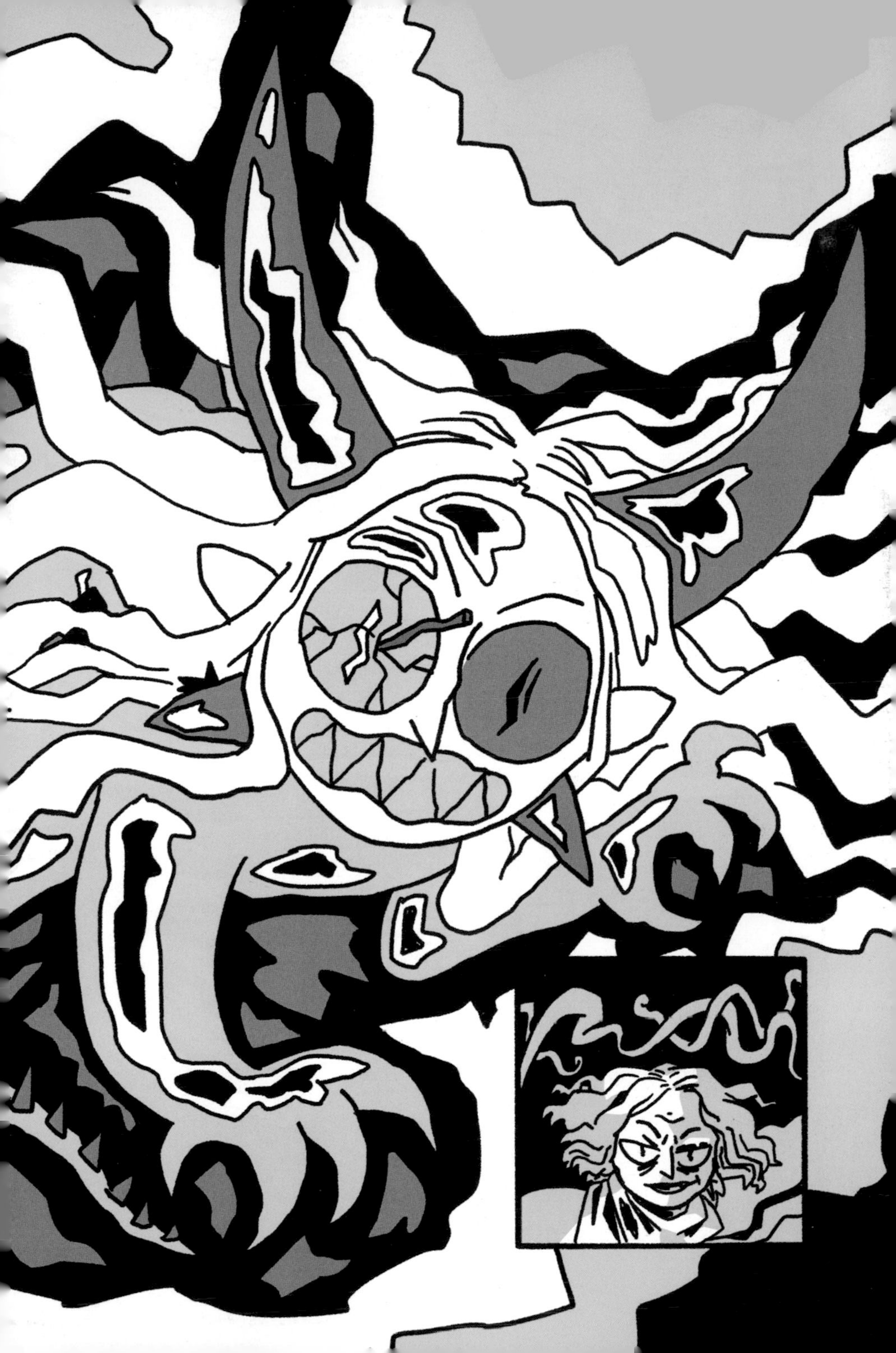

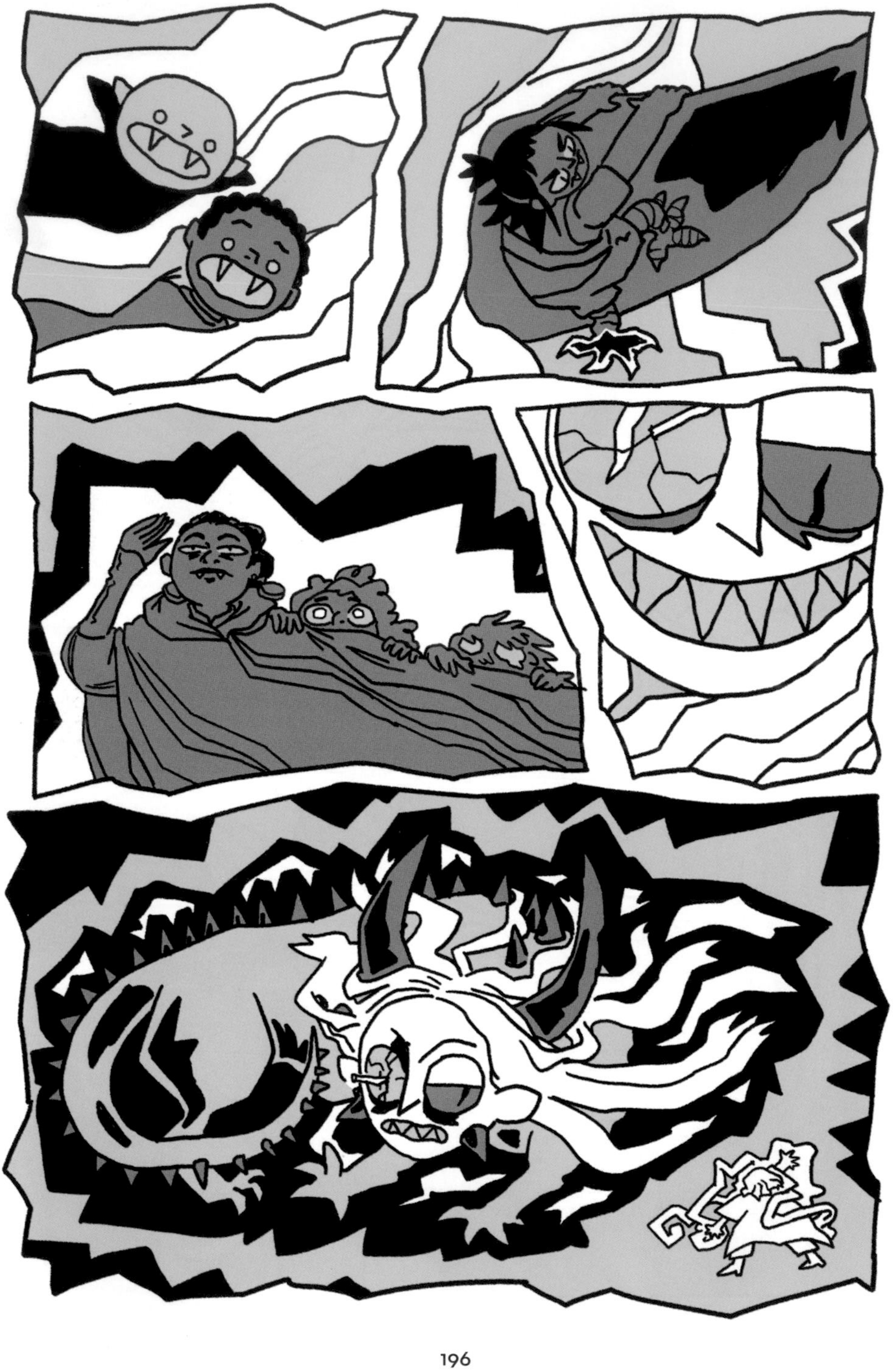

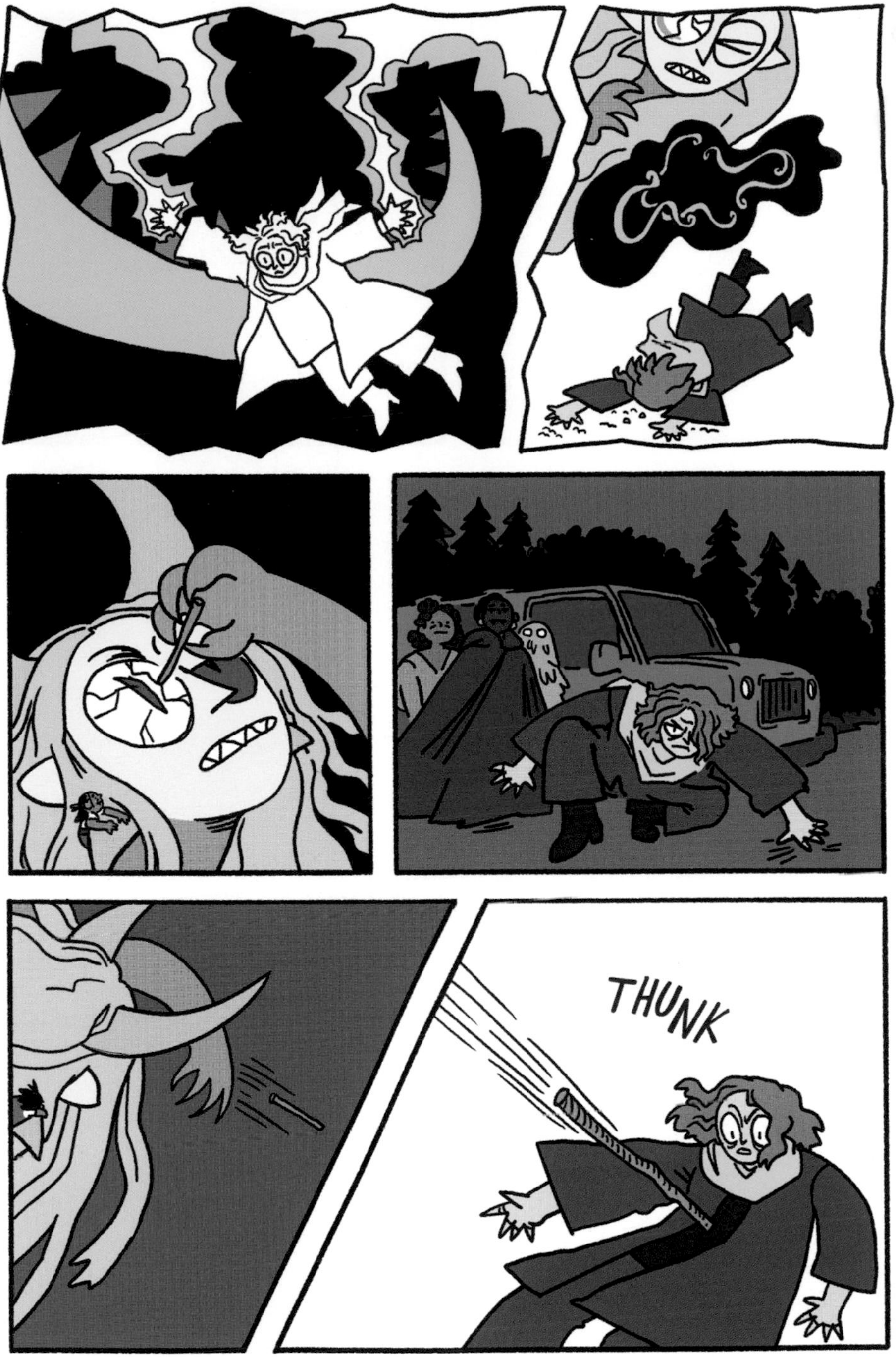
THUNK

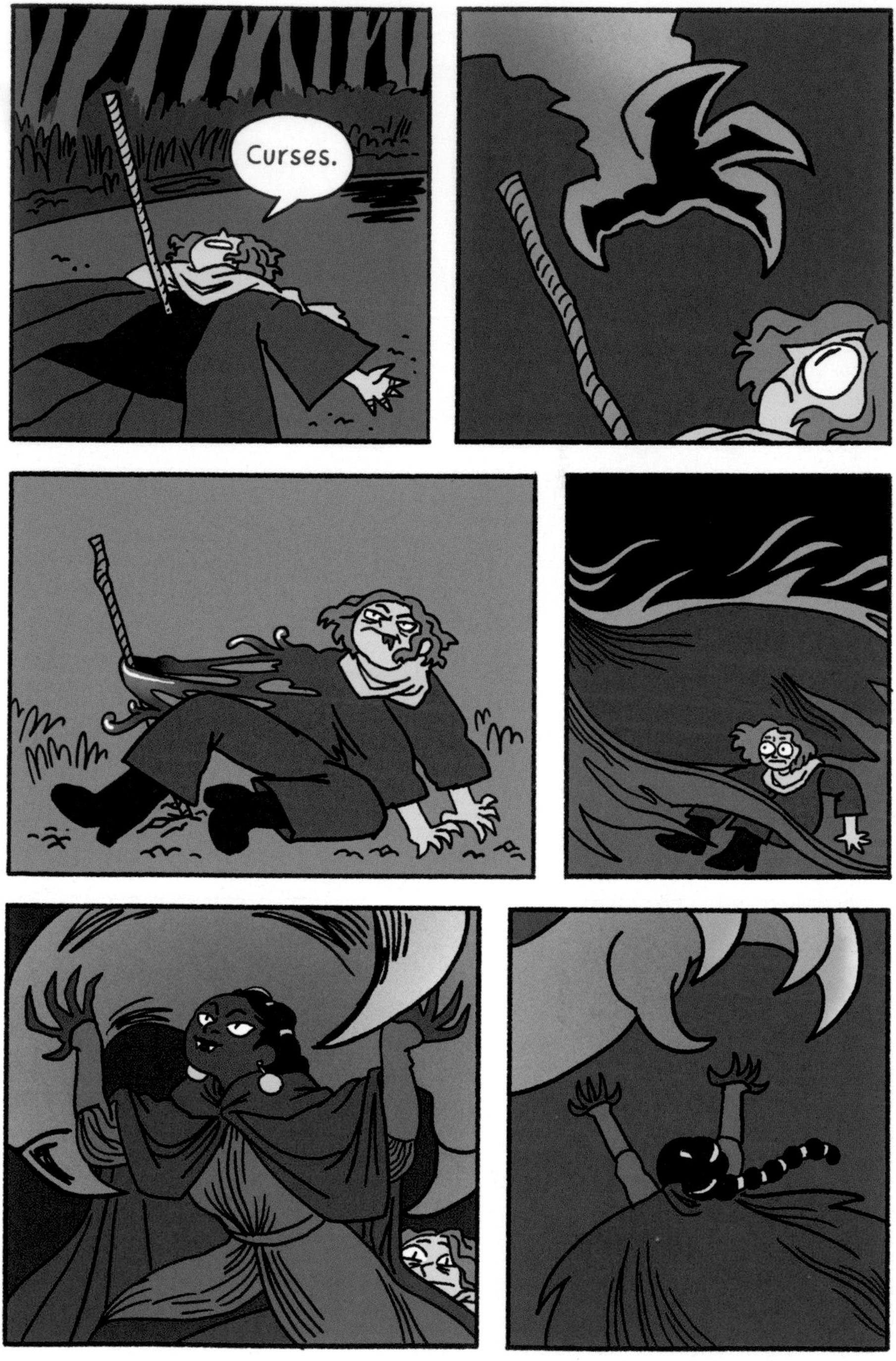
Curses.

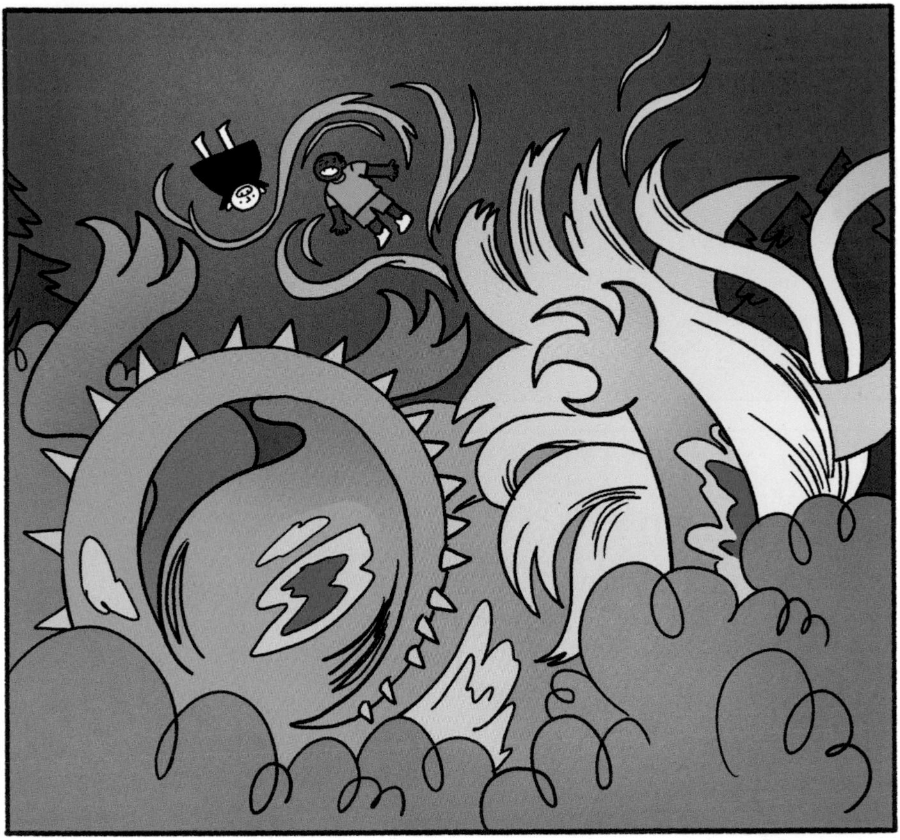

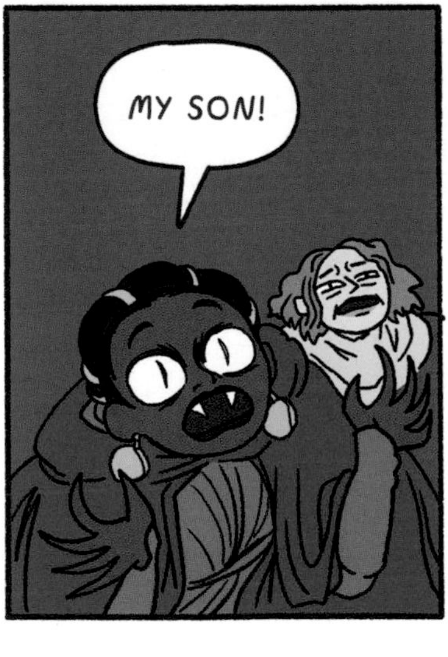
MY SON!

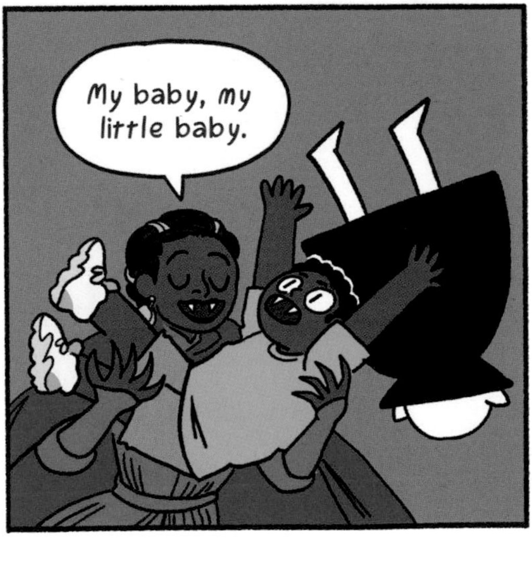
My baby, my little baby.

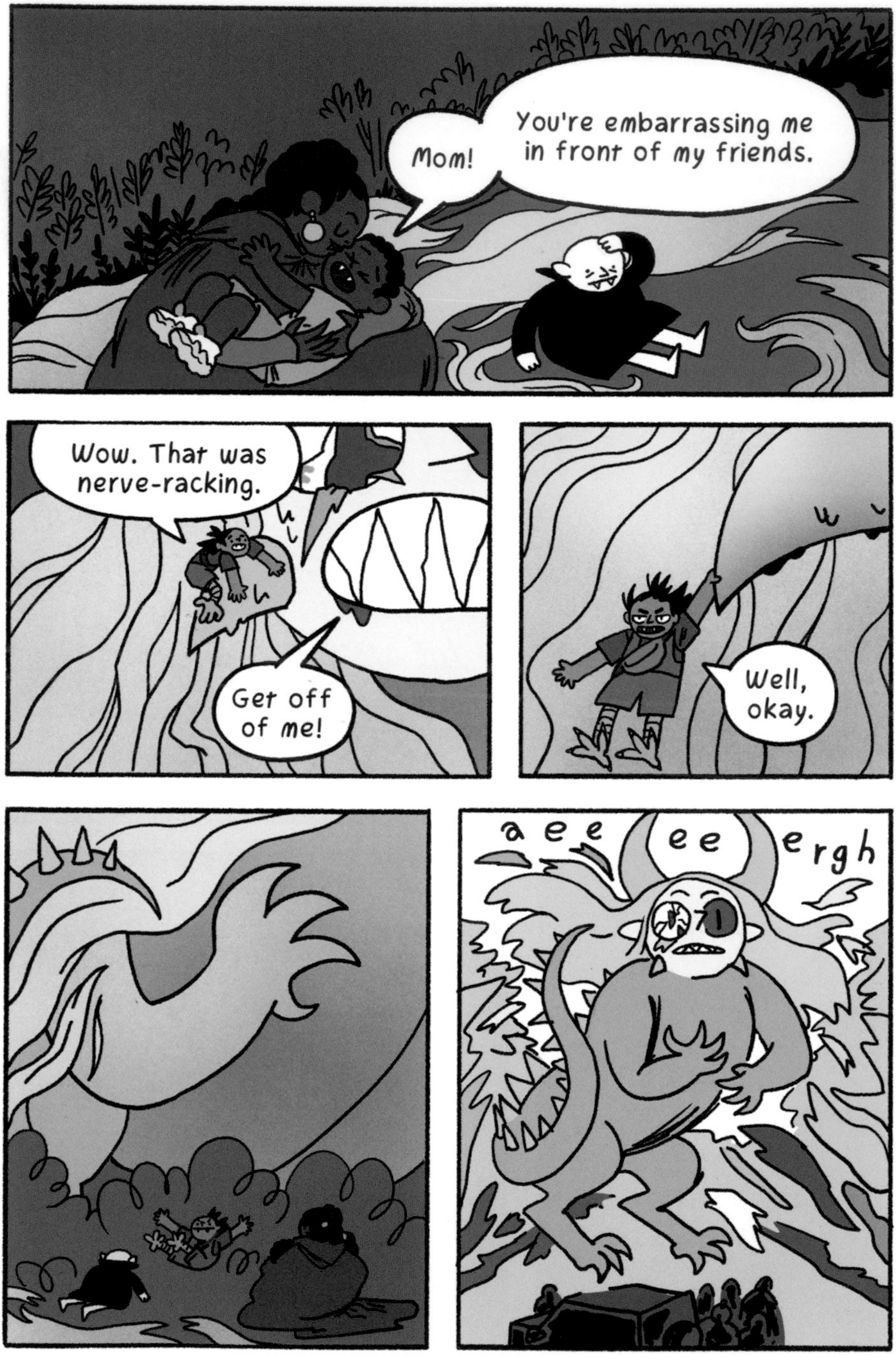
Mom!
You're embarrassing me in front of my friends.
Wow. That was nerve-racking.
Get off of me!
Well, okay.
a e e
ee
ergh

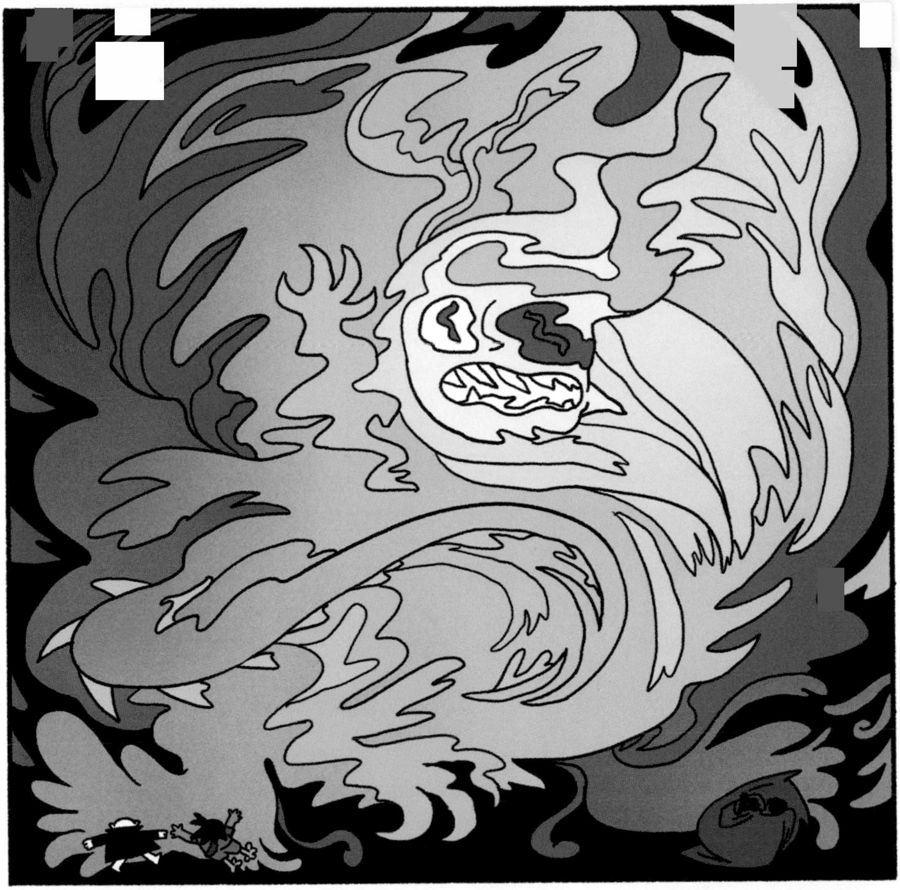

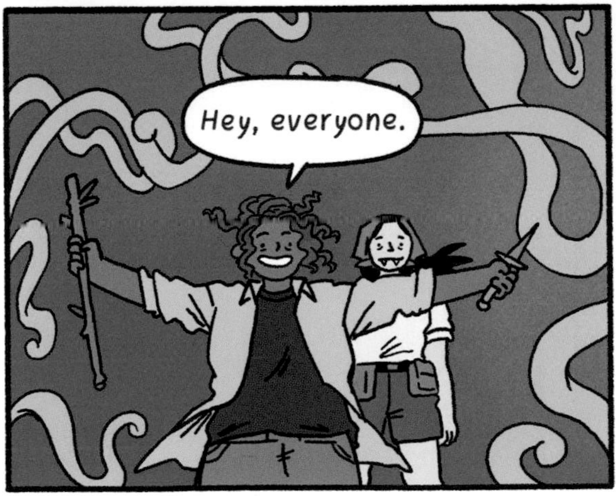
Hey, everyone.

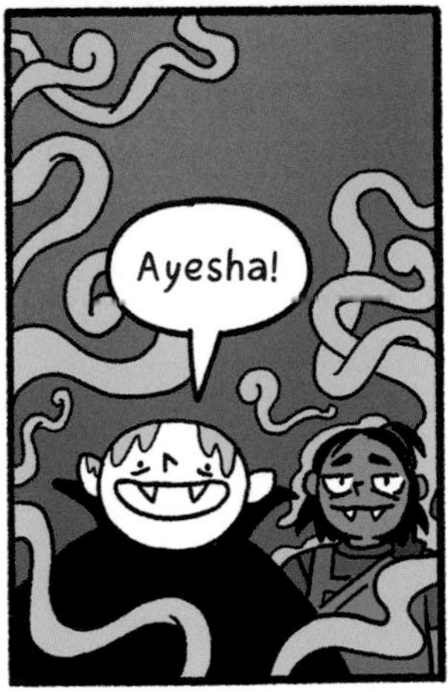
Ayesha!

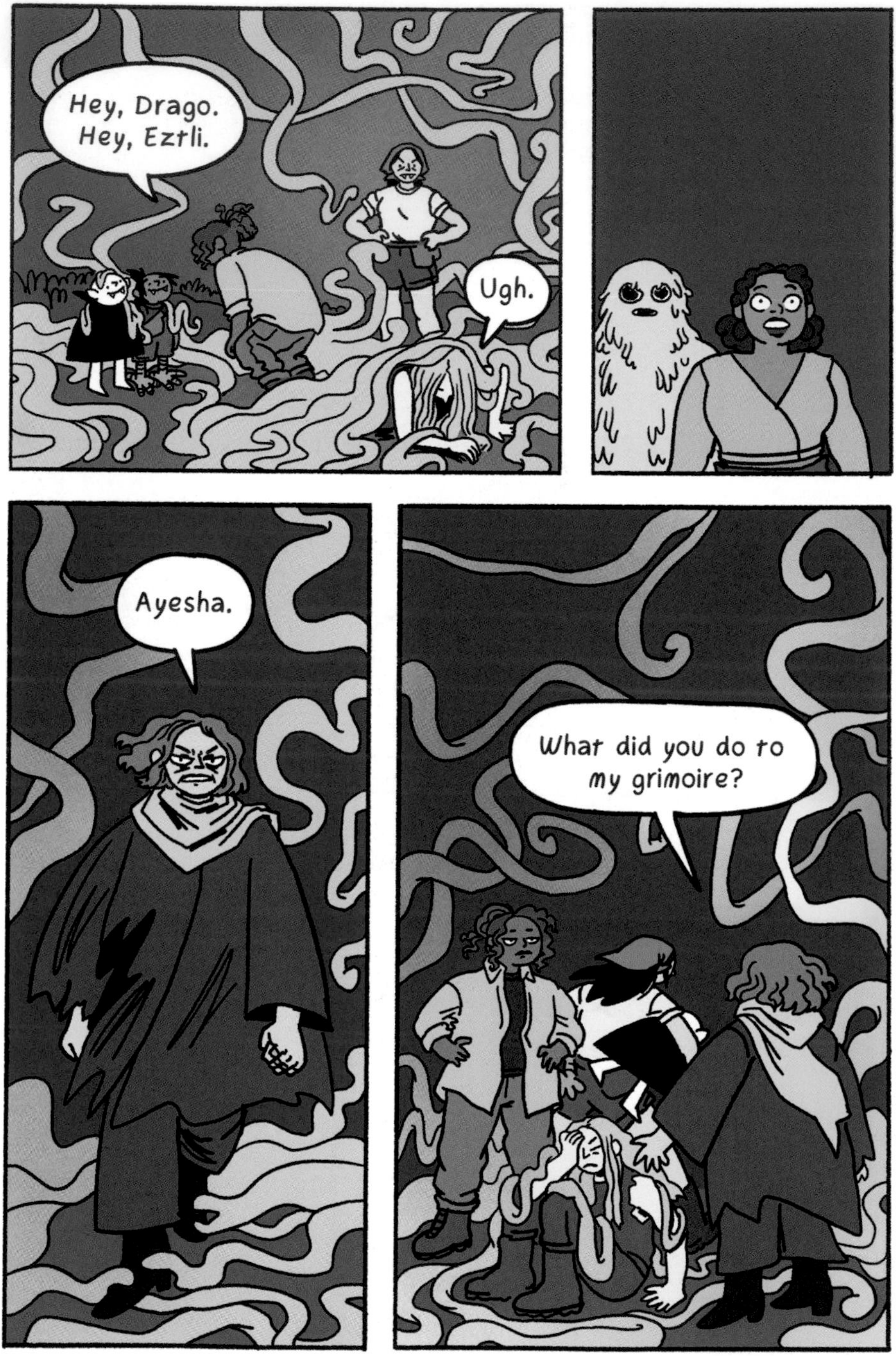
Hey, Drago.
Hey, Eztli.
Ugh.
Ayesha.
What did you do to my grimoire?

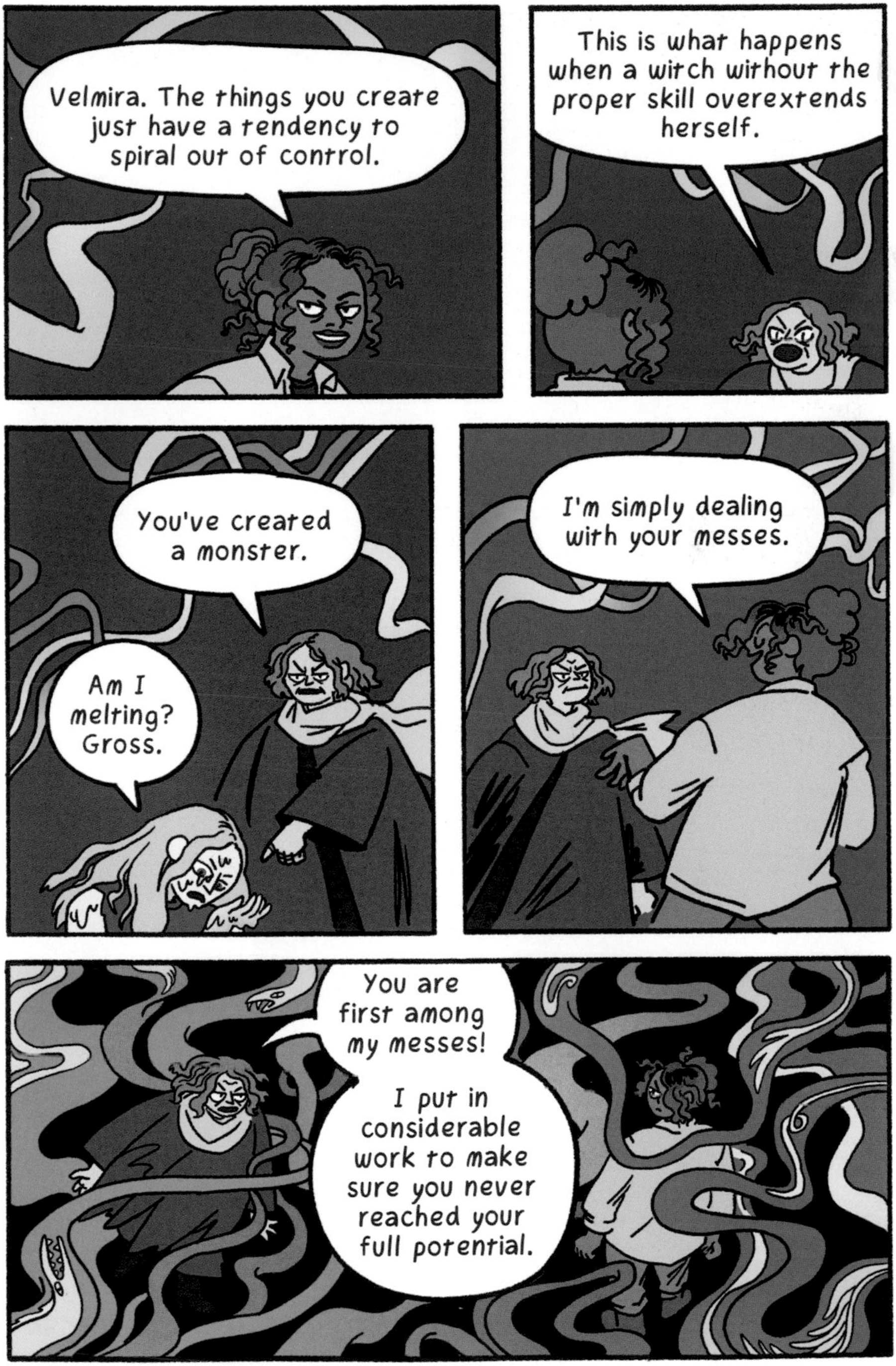
Velmira. The things you create just have a tendency to spiral out of control.
This is what happens when a witch without the proper skill overextends herself.
You've created a monster.
Am I melting? Gross.
I'm simply dealing with your messes.
You are first among my messes!
I put in considerable work to make sure you never reached your full potential.

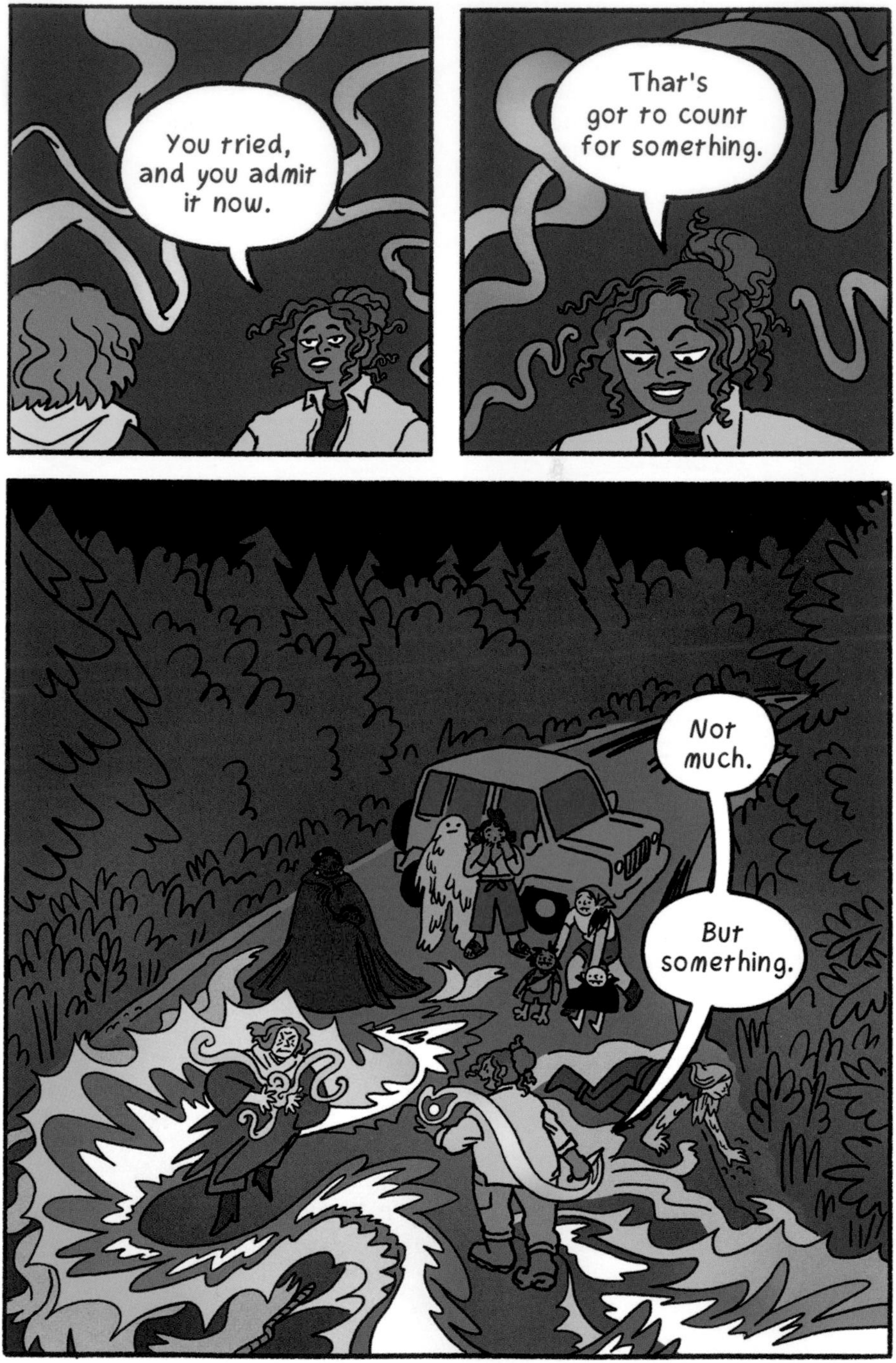
You tried, and you admit it now.
That's got to count for something.
Not much.
But something.

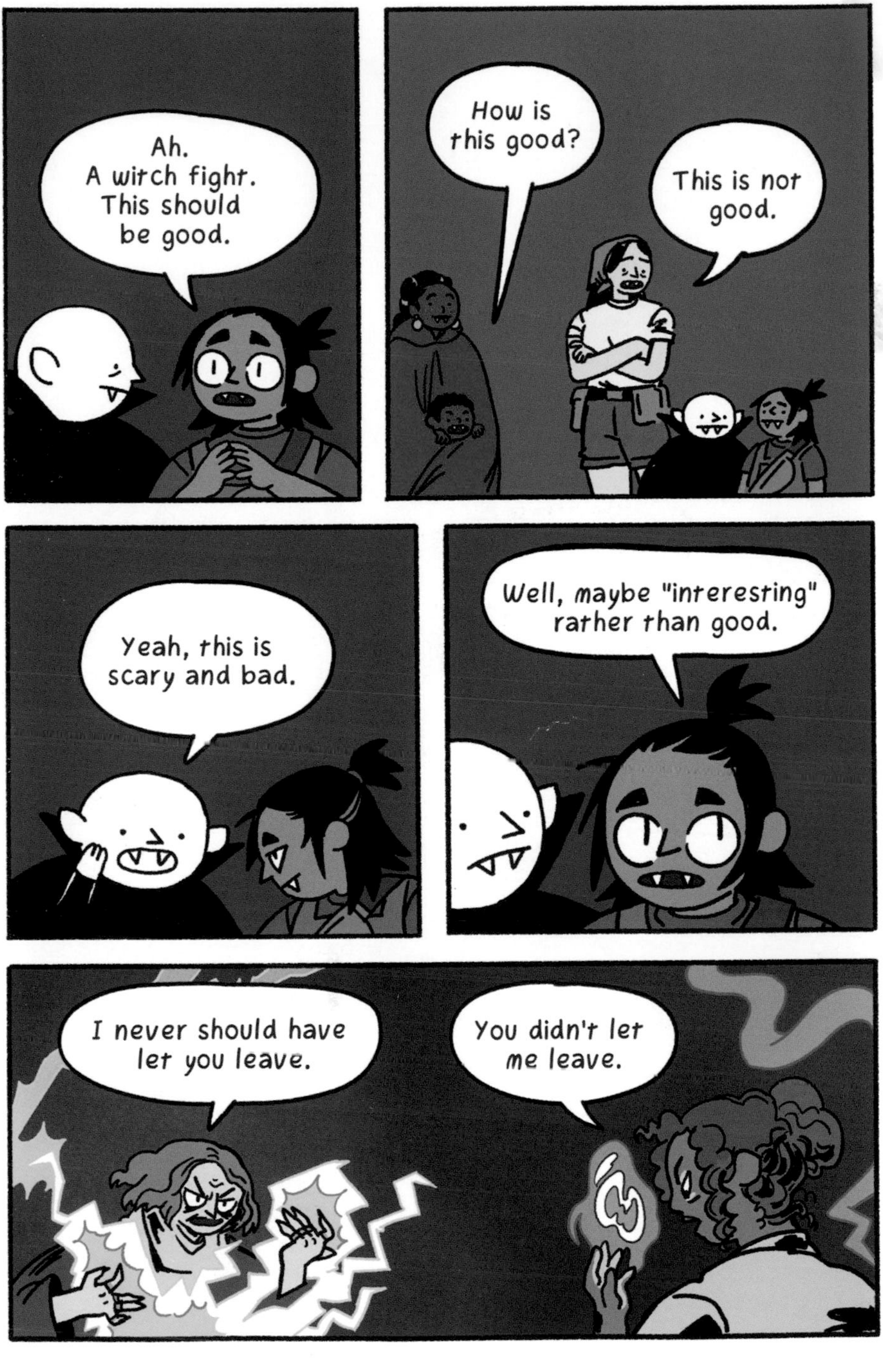
Ah.
A witch fight.
This should
be good.
How is
this good?
This is not
good.
Yeah, this is
scary and bad.
Well, maybe "interesting"
rather than good.
I never should have
let you leave.
You didn't let
me leave.

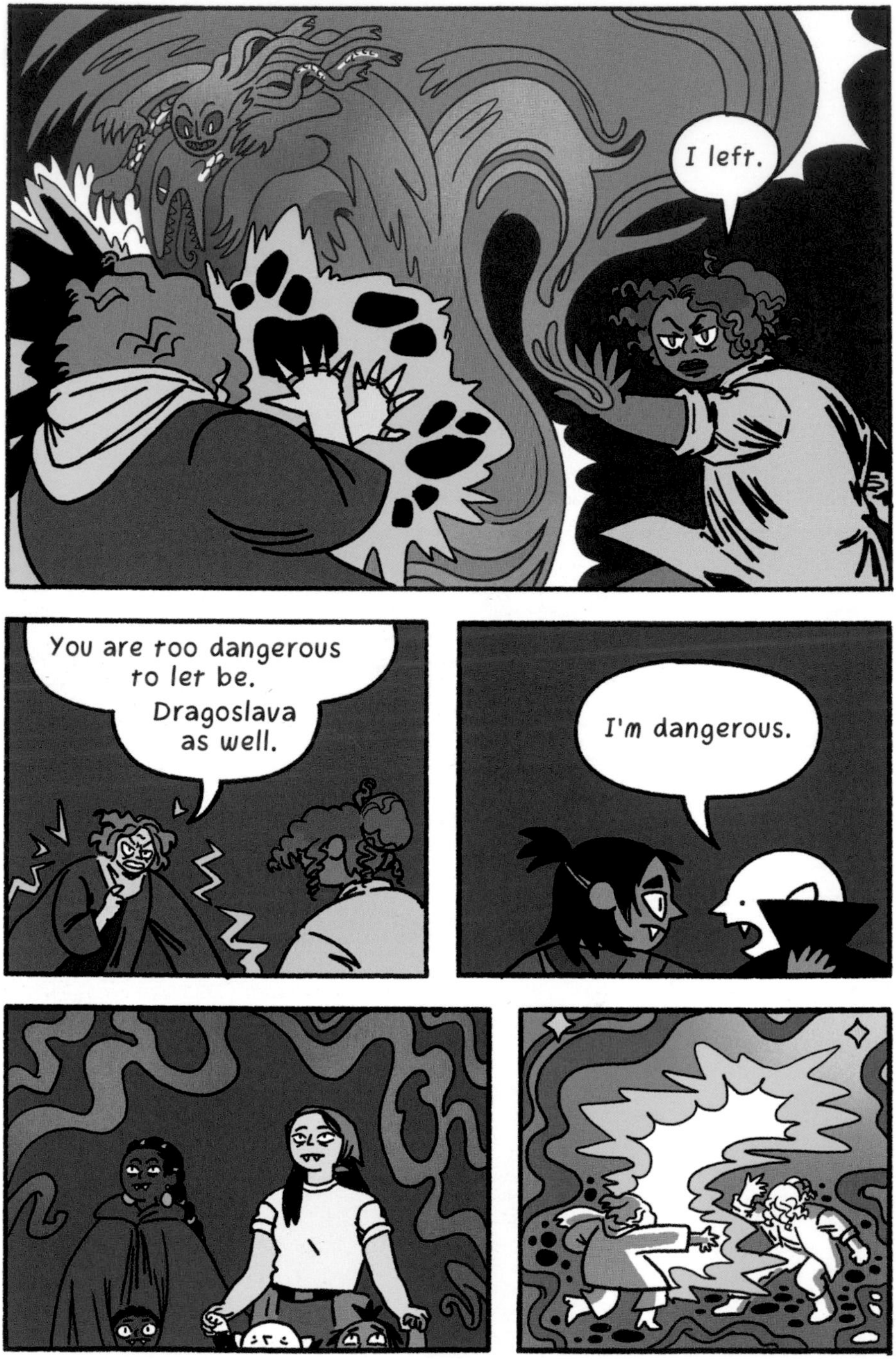
I left.
You are too dangerous to let be. Dragoslava as well.
I'm dangerous.

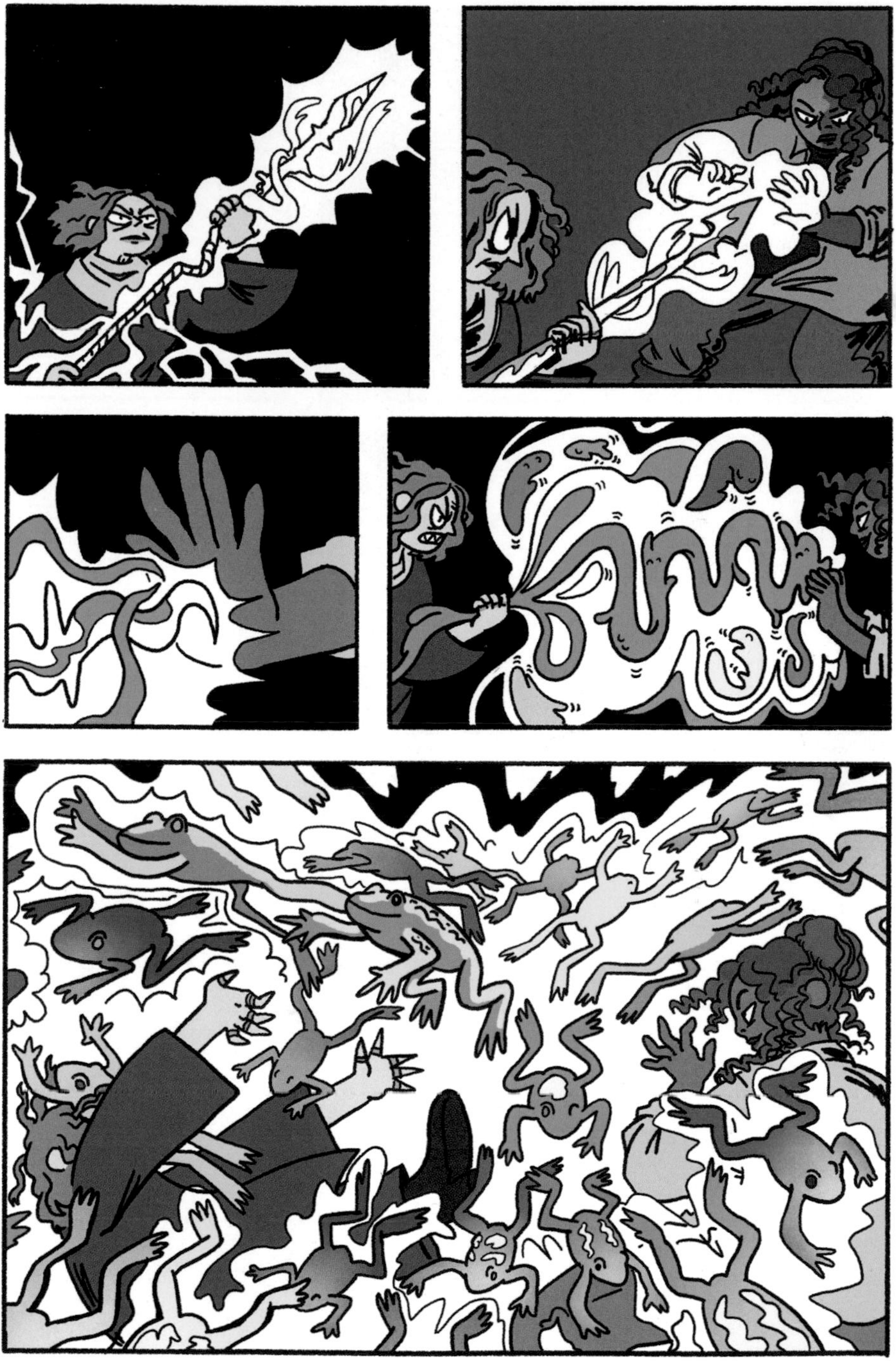

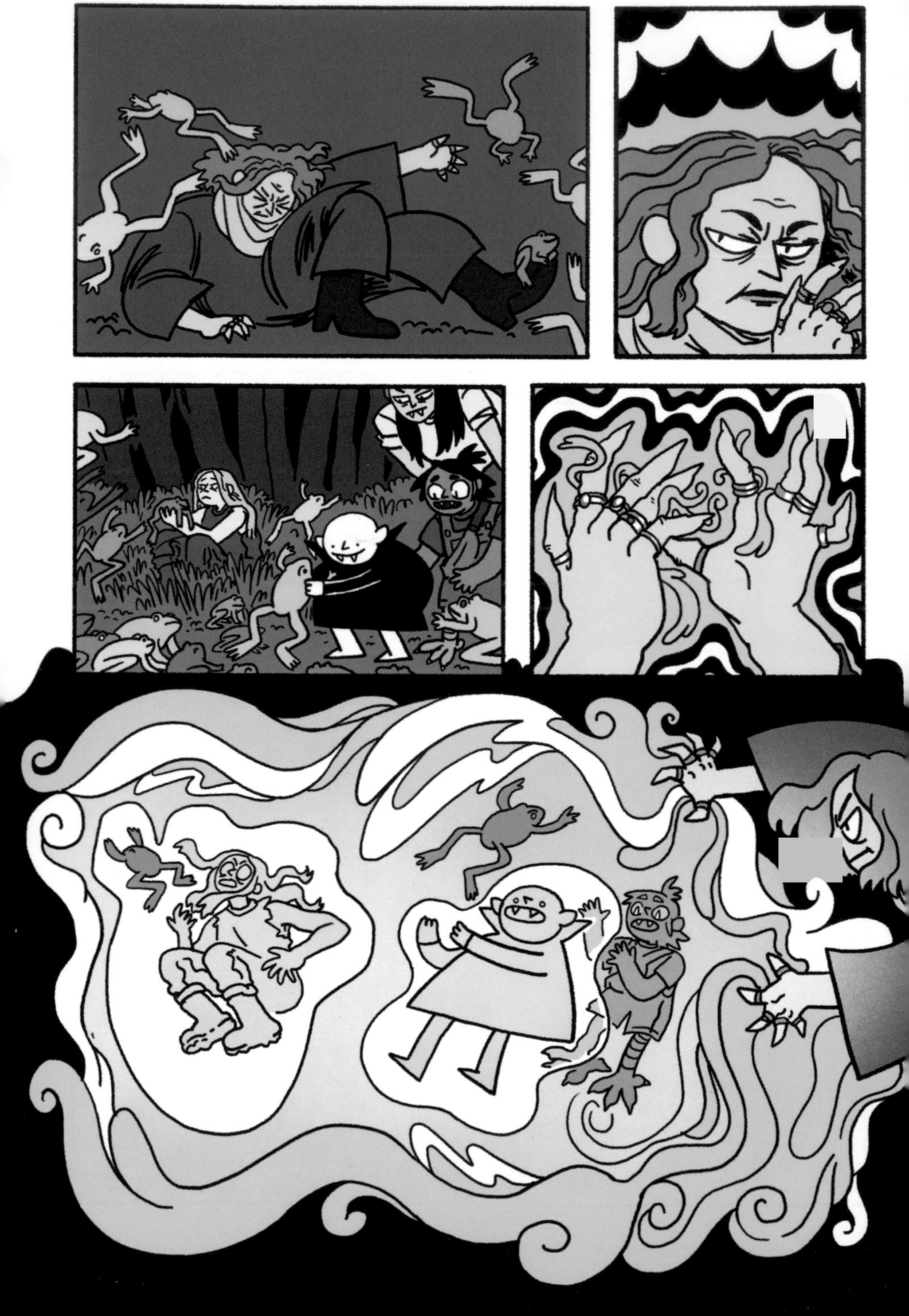

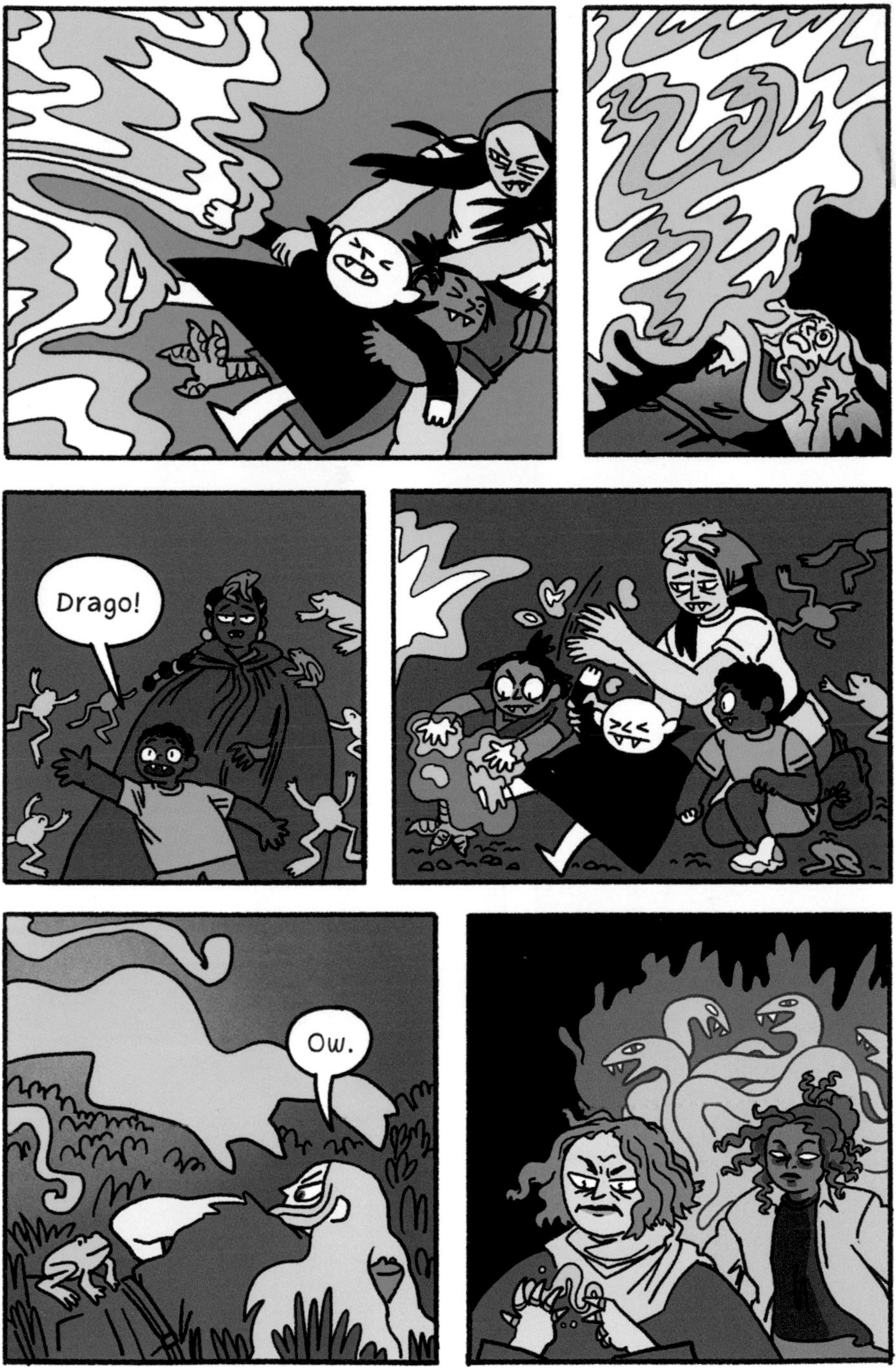
Drago!
Ow.

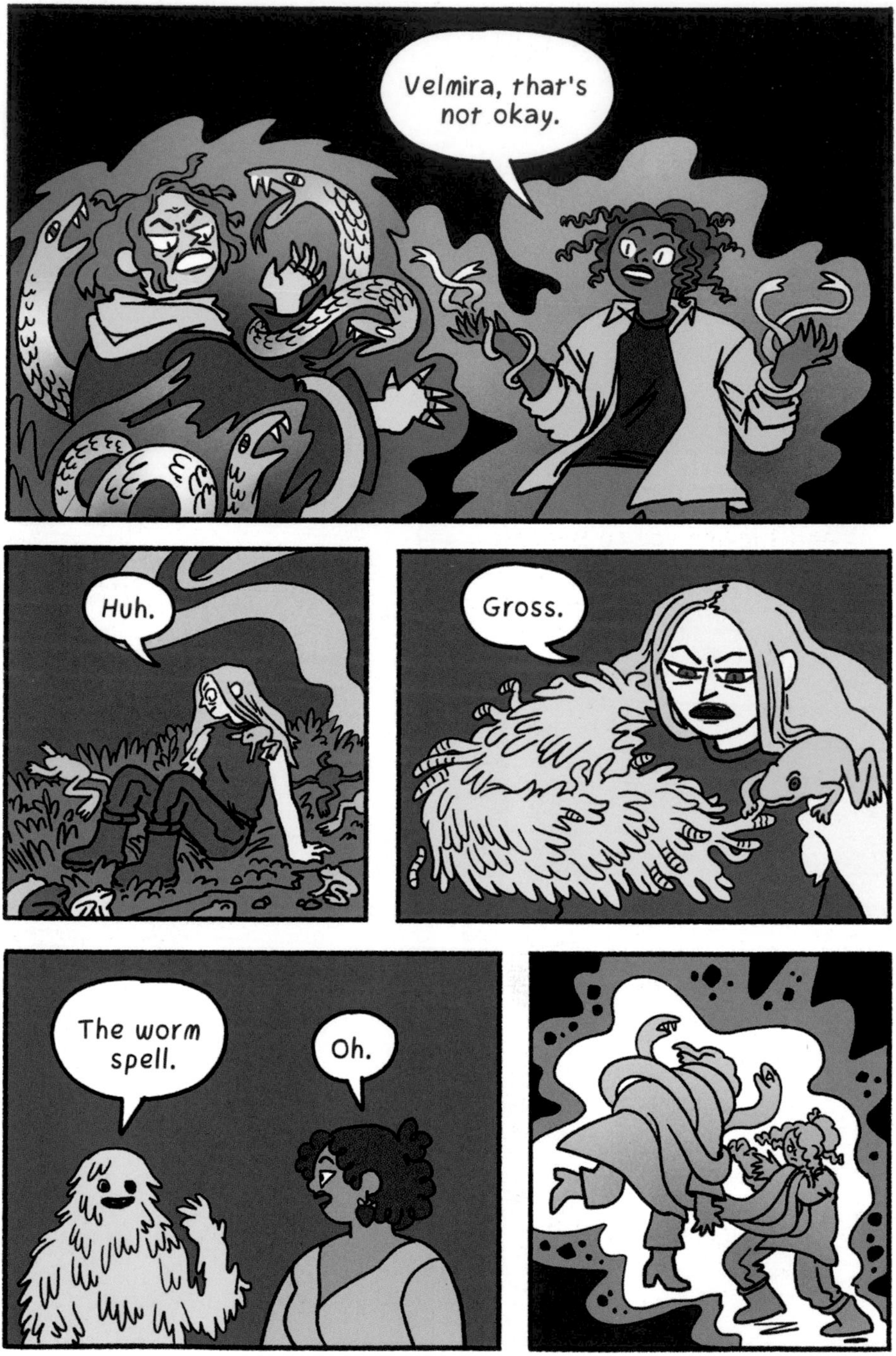

Velmira, that's not okay.
Huh.
Gross.
The worm spell.
Oh.

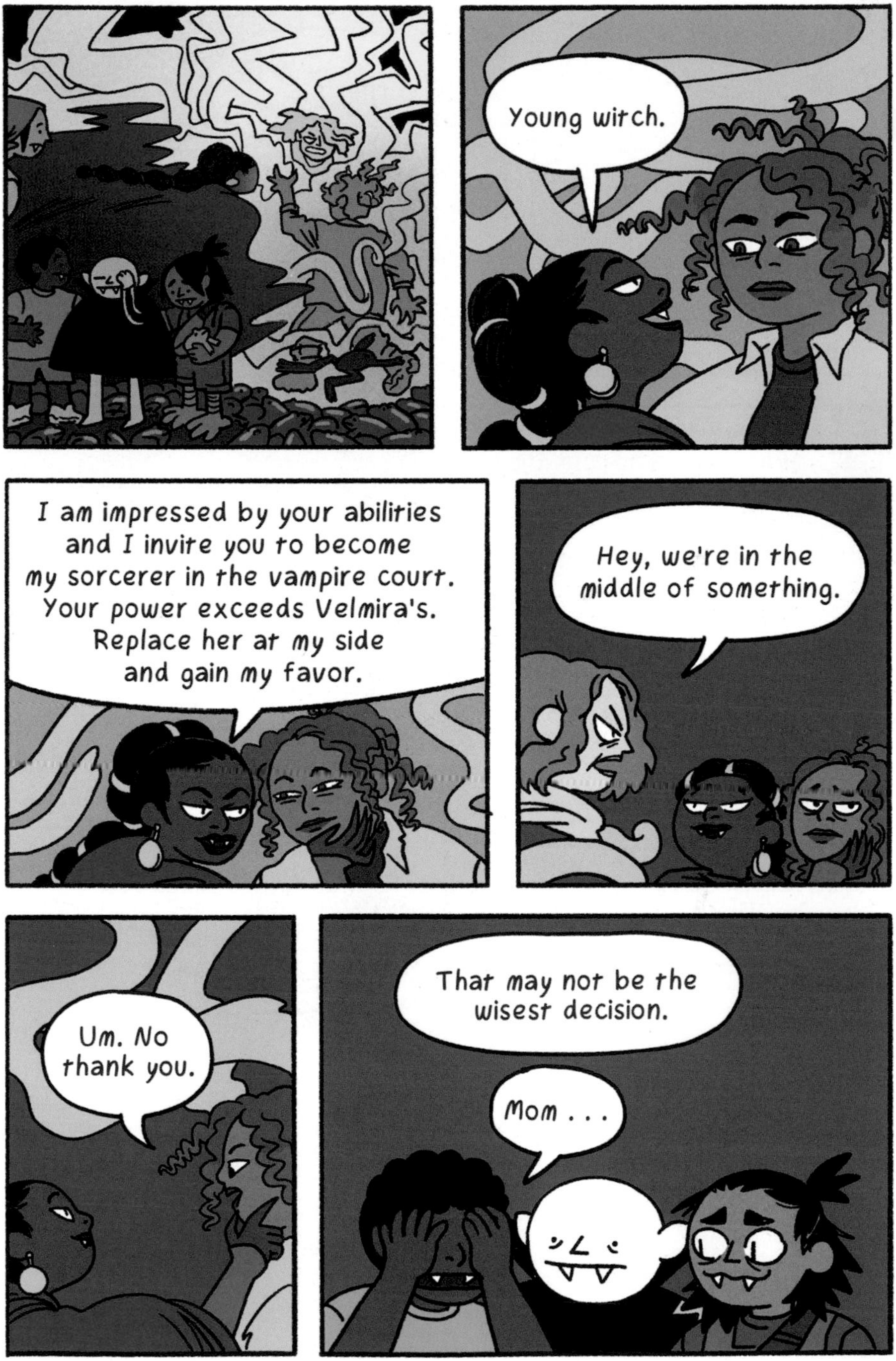
Young witch.
I am impressed by your abilities and I invite you to become my sorcerer in the vampire court. Your power exceeds Velmira's. Replace her at my side and gain my favor.
Hey, we're in the middle of something.
Um. No thank you.
That may not be the wisest decision.
Mom . . .

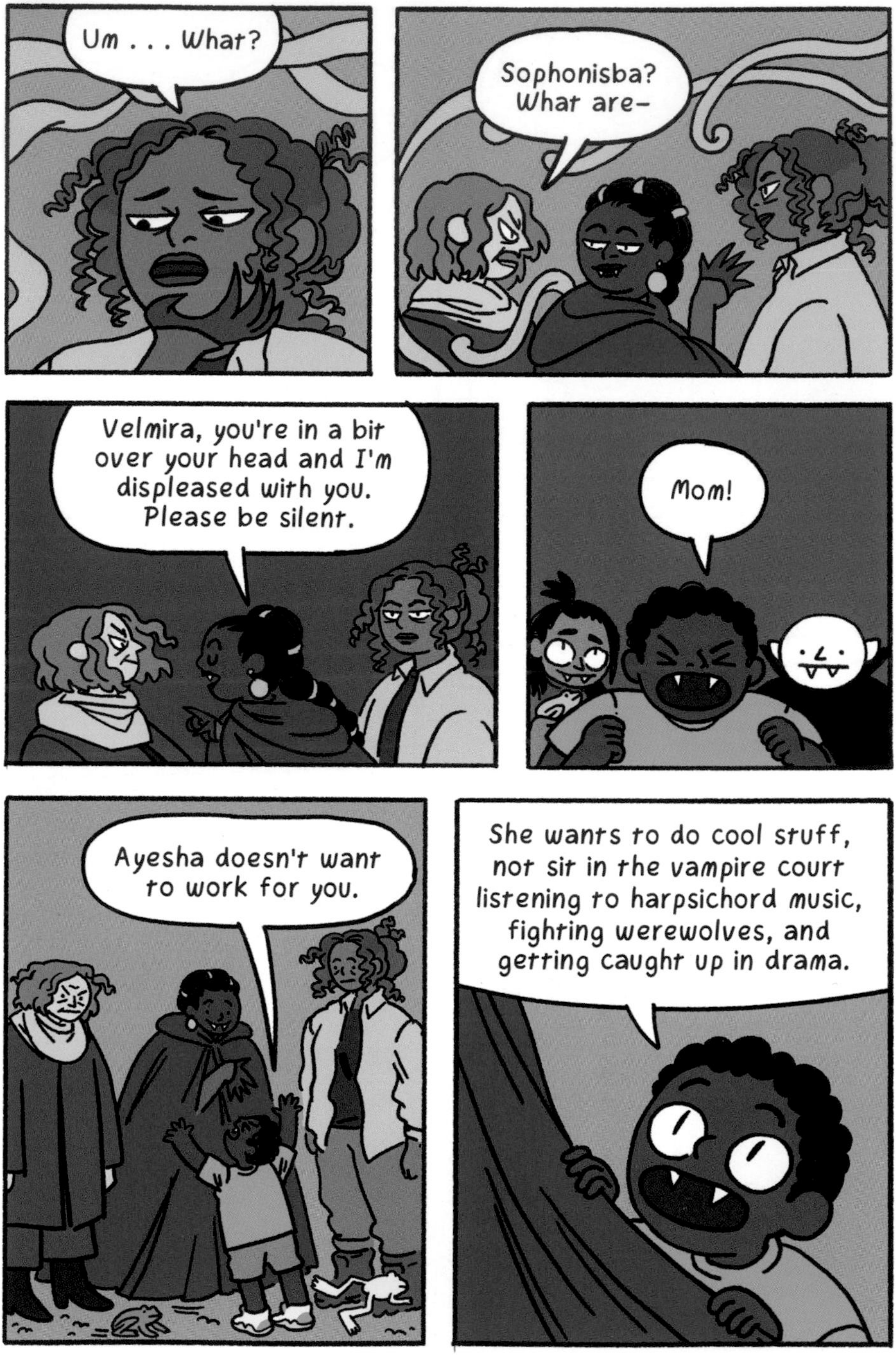
Um . . . What?
Sophonisba? What are–
Velmira, you're in a bit over your head and I'm displeased with you. Please be silent.
Mom!
Ayesha doesn't want to work for you.
She wants to do cool stuff, not sit in the vampire court listening to harpsichord music, fighting werewolves, and getting caught up in drama.

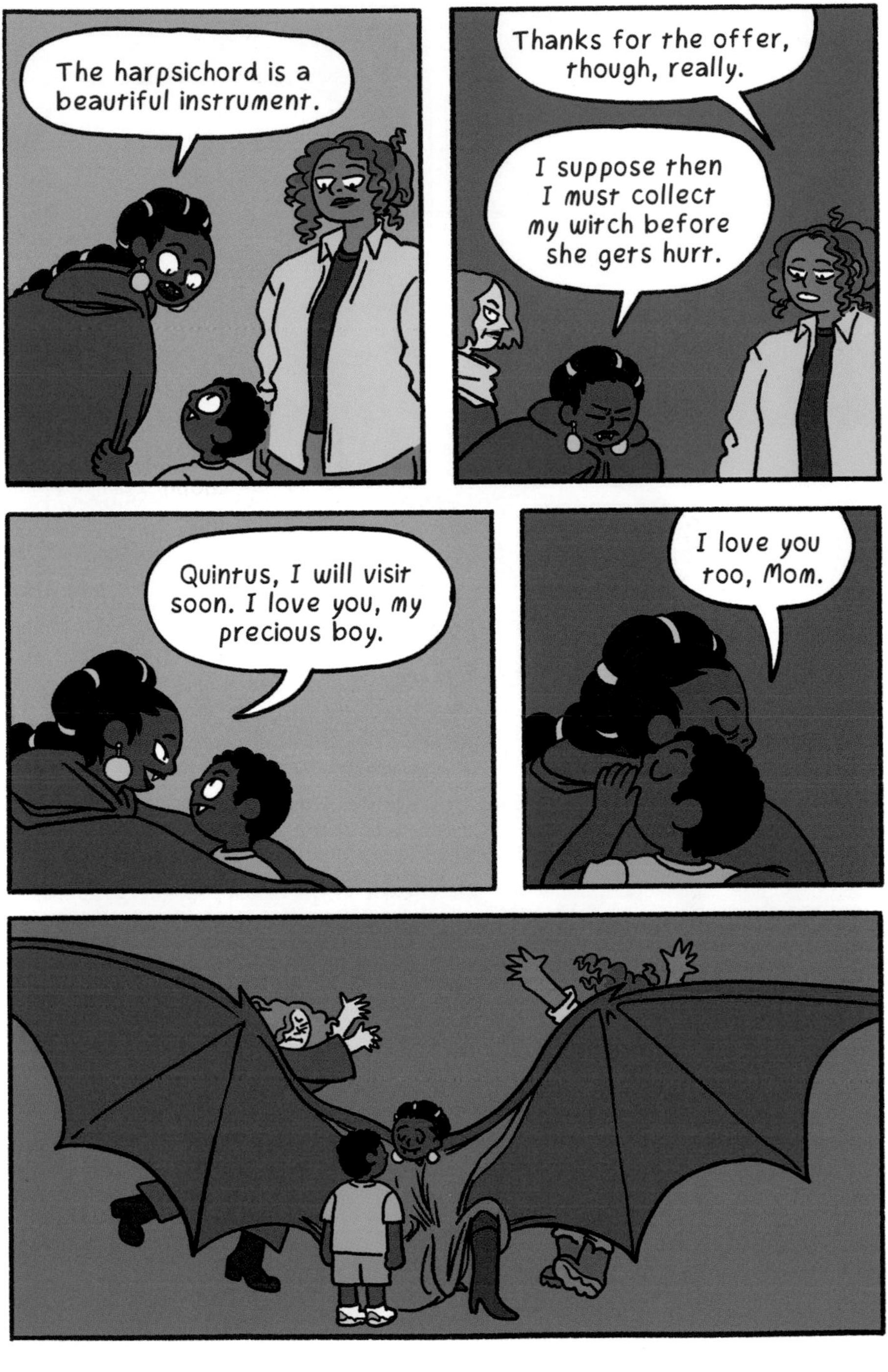
The harpsichord is a beautiful instrument.
Thanks for the offer, though, really.
I suppose then I must collect my witch before she gets hurt.
Quintus, I will visit soon. I love you, my precious boy.
I love you too, Mom.

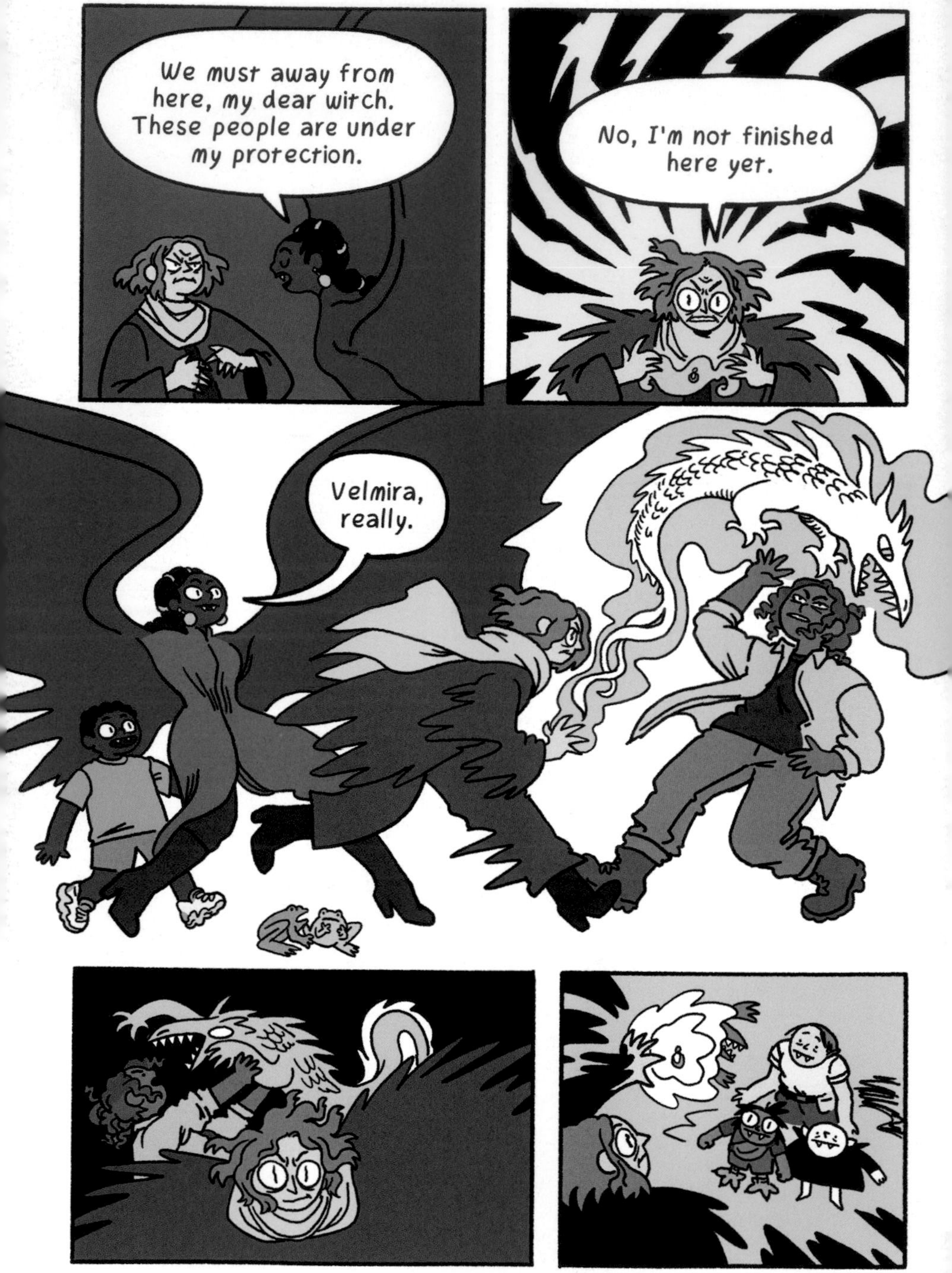
We must away from here, my dear witch. These people are under my protection.
No, I'm not finished here yet.
Velmira, really.

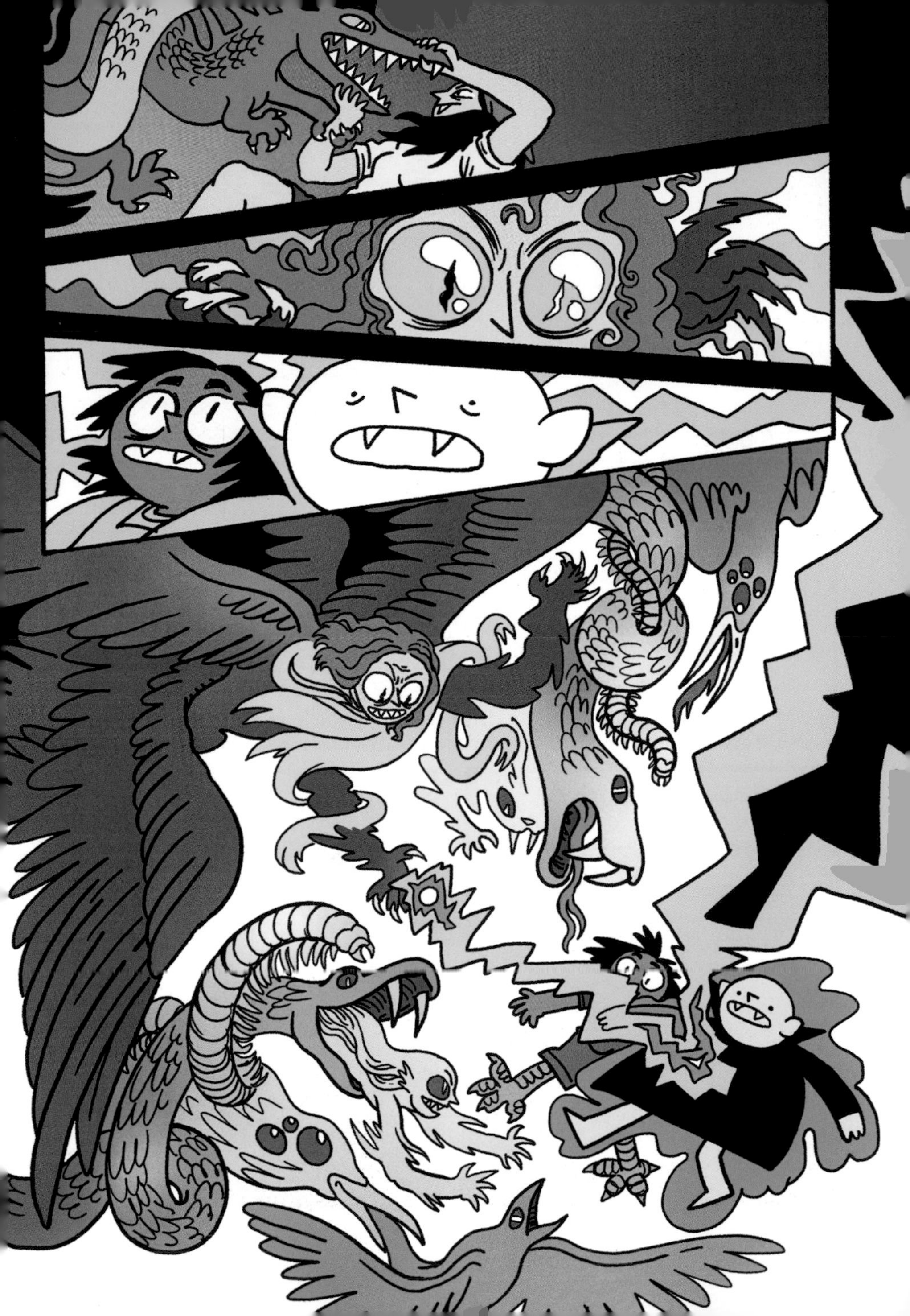

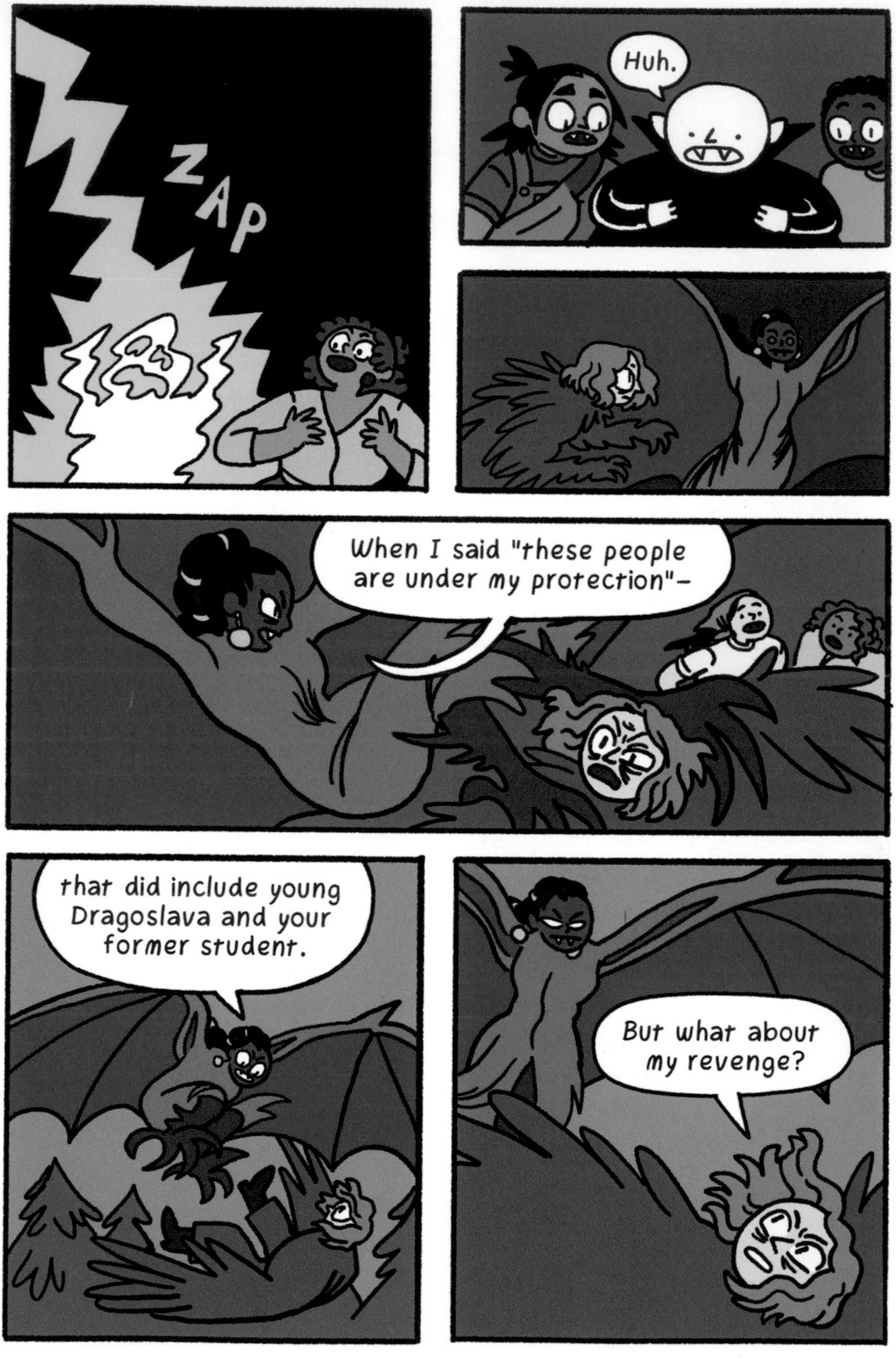
ZAP
Huh.
When I said "these people are under my protection"–
that did include young Dragoslava and your former student.
But what about my revenge?

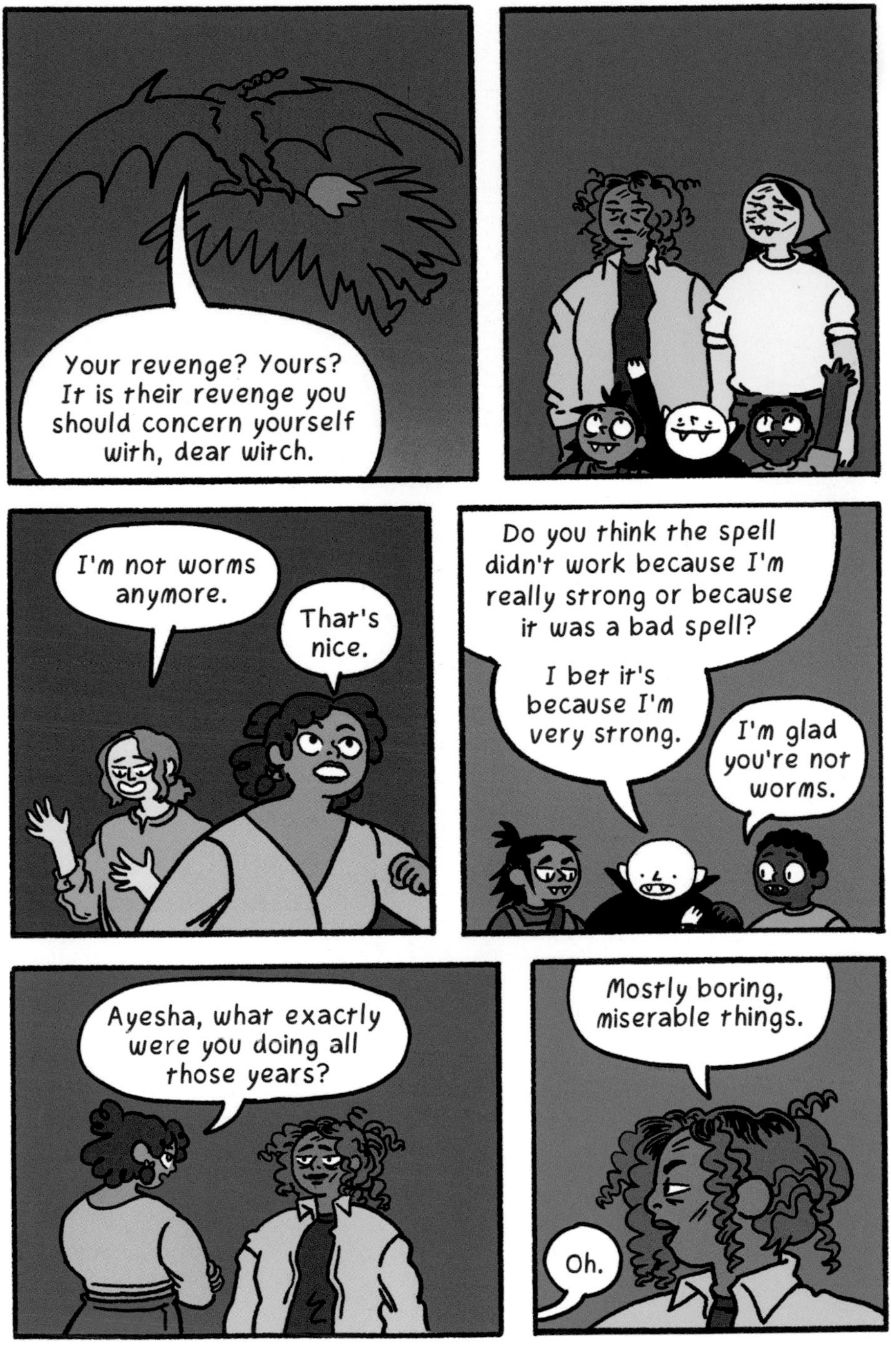
Your revenge? Yours? It is their revenge you should concern yourself with, dear witch.
I'm not worms anymore.
That's nice.
Do you think the spell didn't work because I'm really strong or because it was a bad spell?
I bet it's because I'm very strong.
I'm glad you're not worms.
Ayesha, what exactly were you doing all those years?
Mostly boring, miserable things.
Oh.

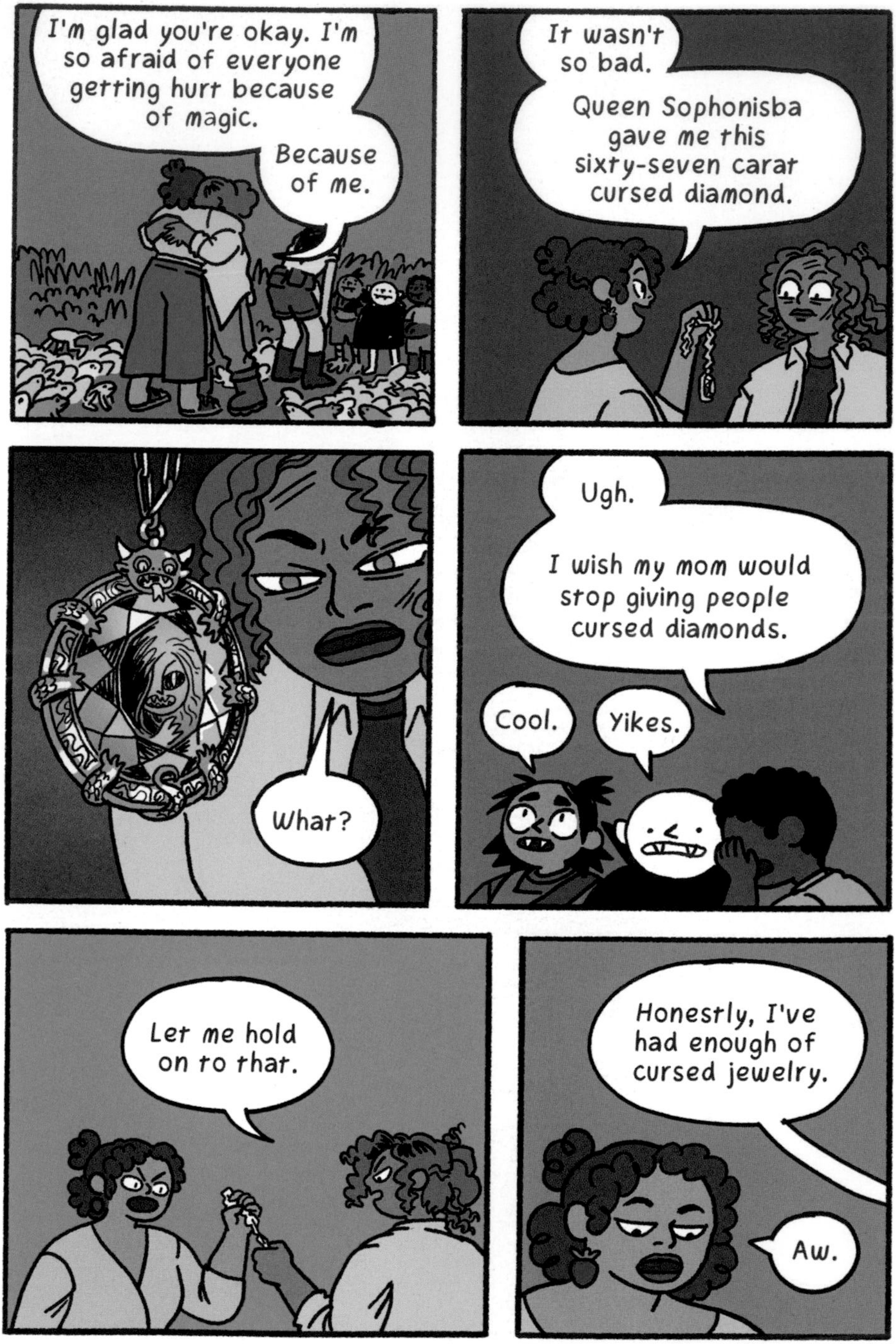

I'm glad you're okay. I'm so afraid of everyone getting hurt because of magic.
Because of me.
It wasn't so bad.
Queen Sophonisba gave me this sixty-seven carat cursed diamond.
What?
Ugh.
I wish my mom would stop giving people cursed diamonds.
Cool.
Yikes.
Let me hold on to that.
Honestly, I've had enough of cursed jewelry.
Aw.

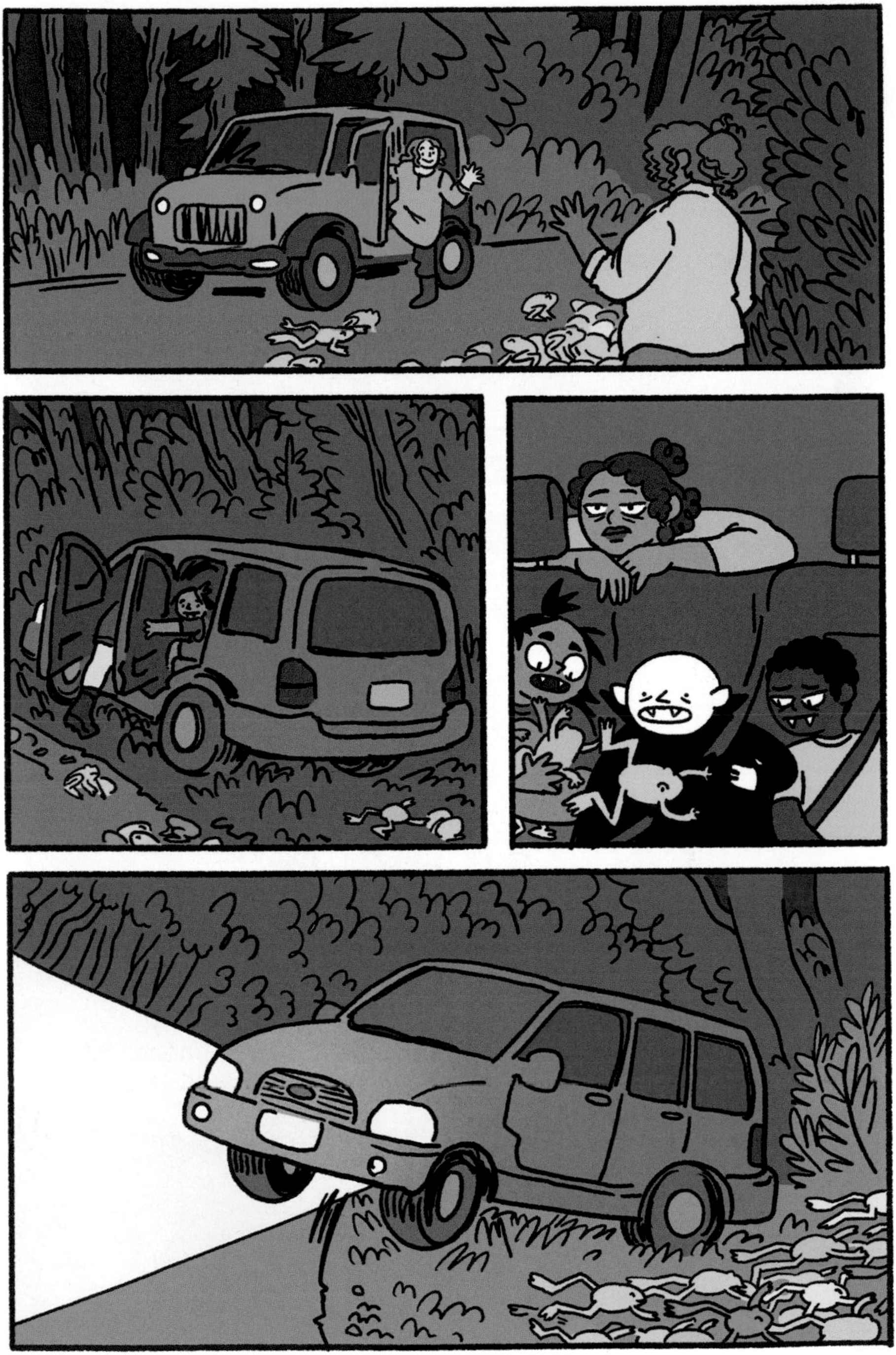

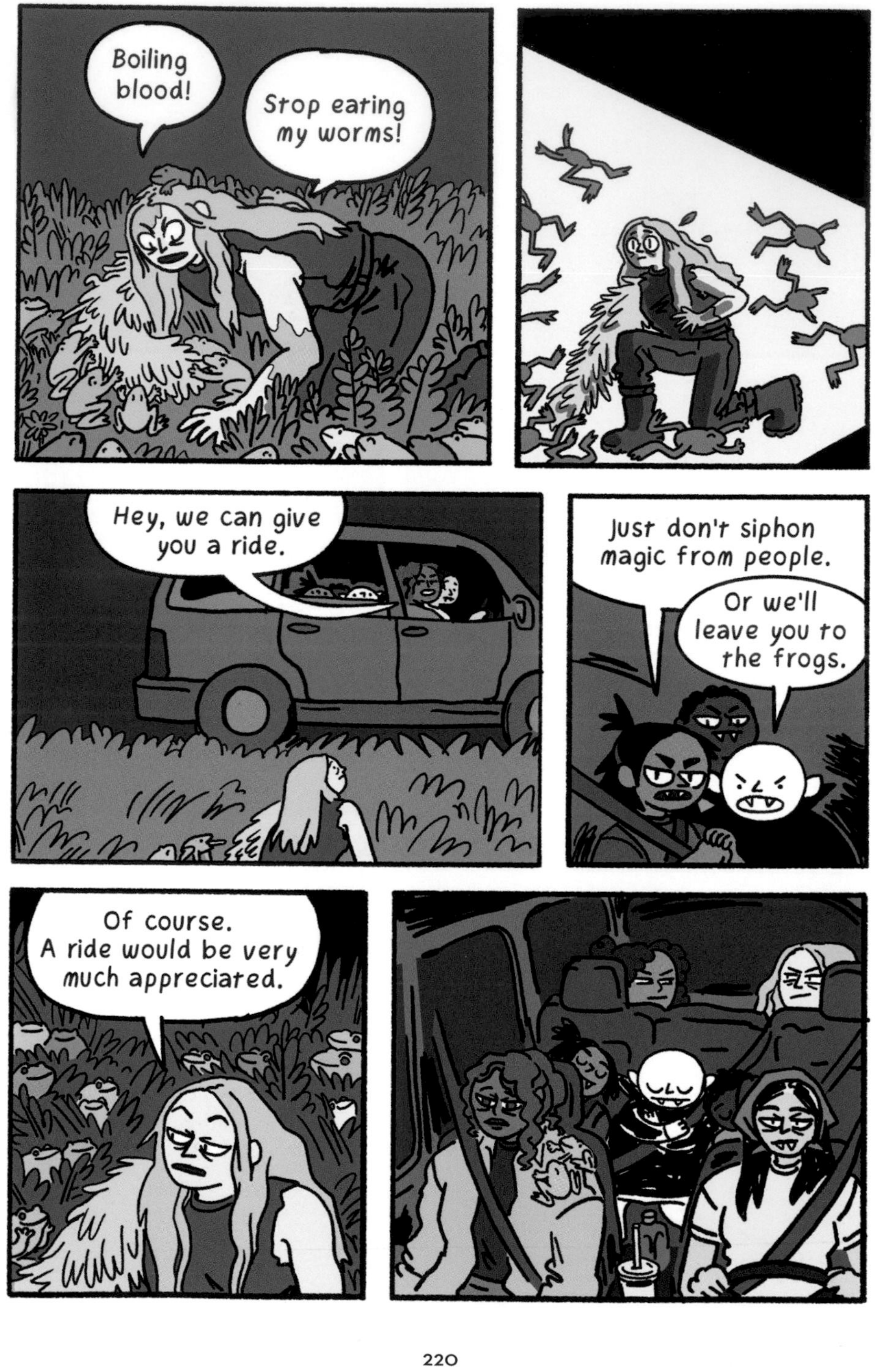
Boiling blood!
Stop eating my worms!
Hey, we can give you a ride.
Just don't siphon magic from people.
Or we'll leave you to the frogs.
Of course. A ride would be very much appreciated.

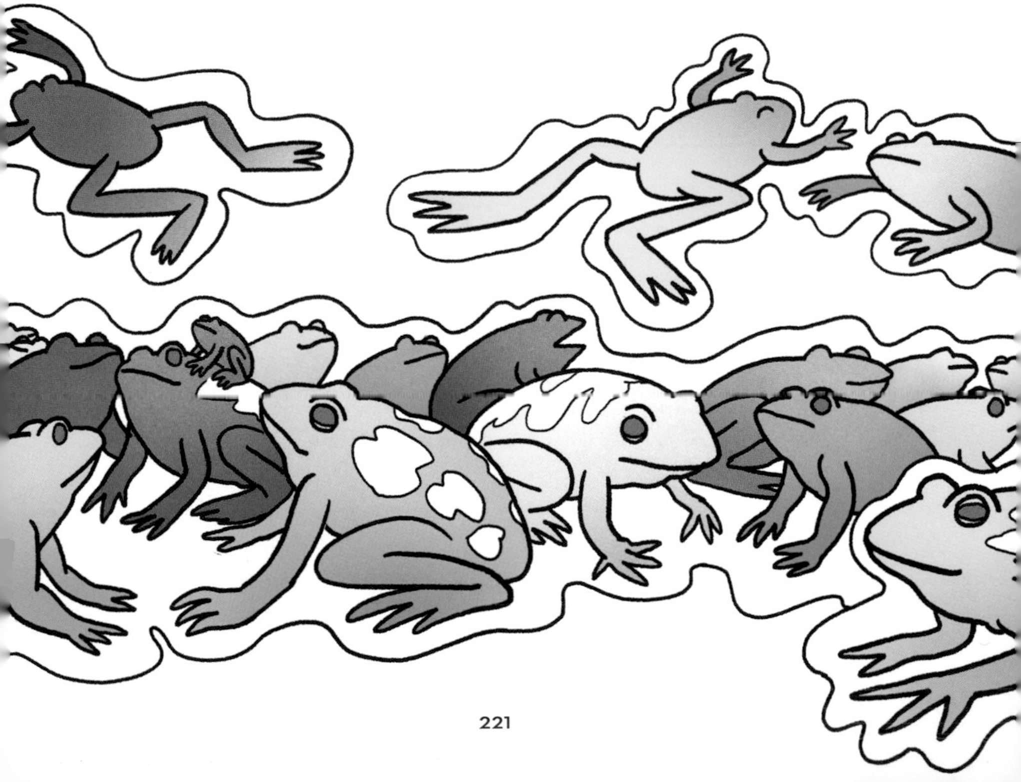

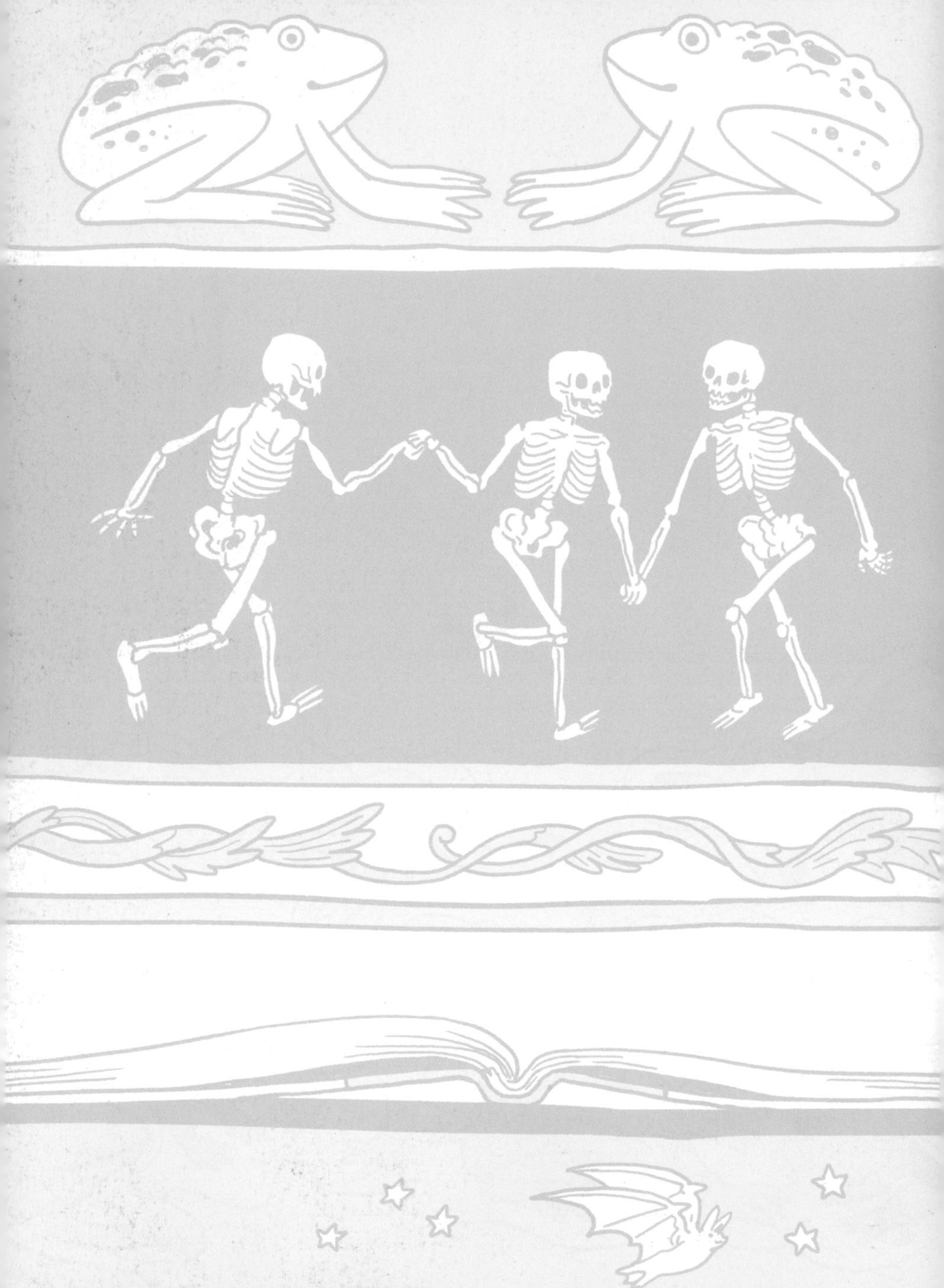

CHAPTER NINE

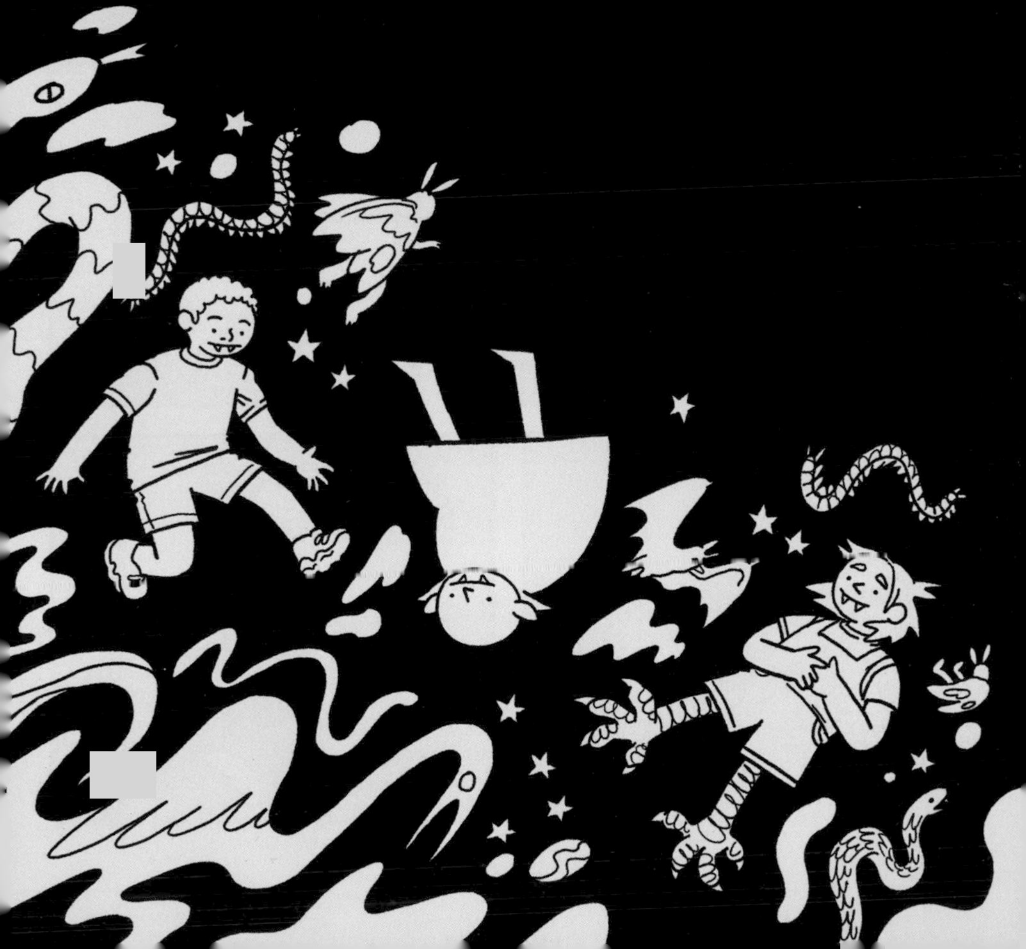

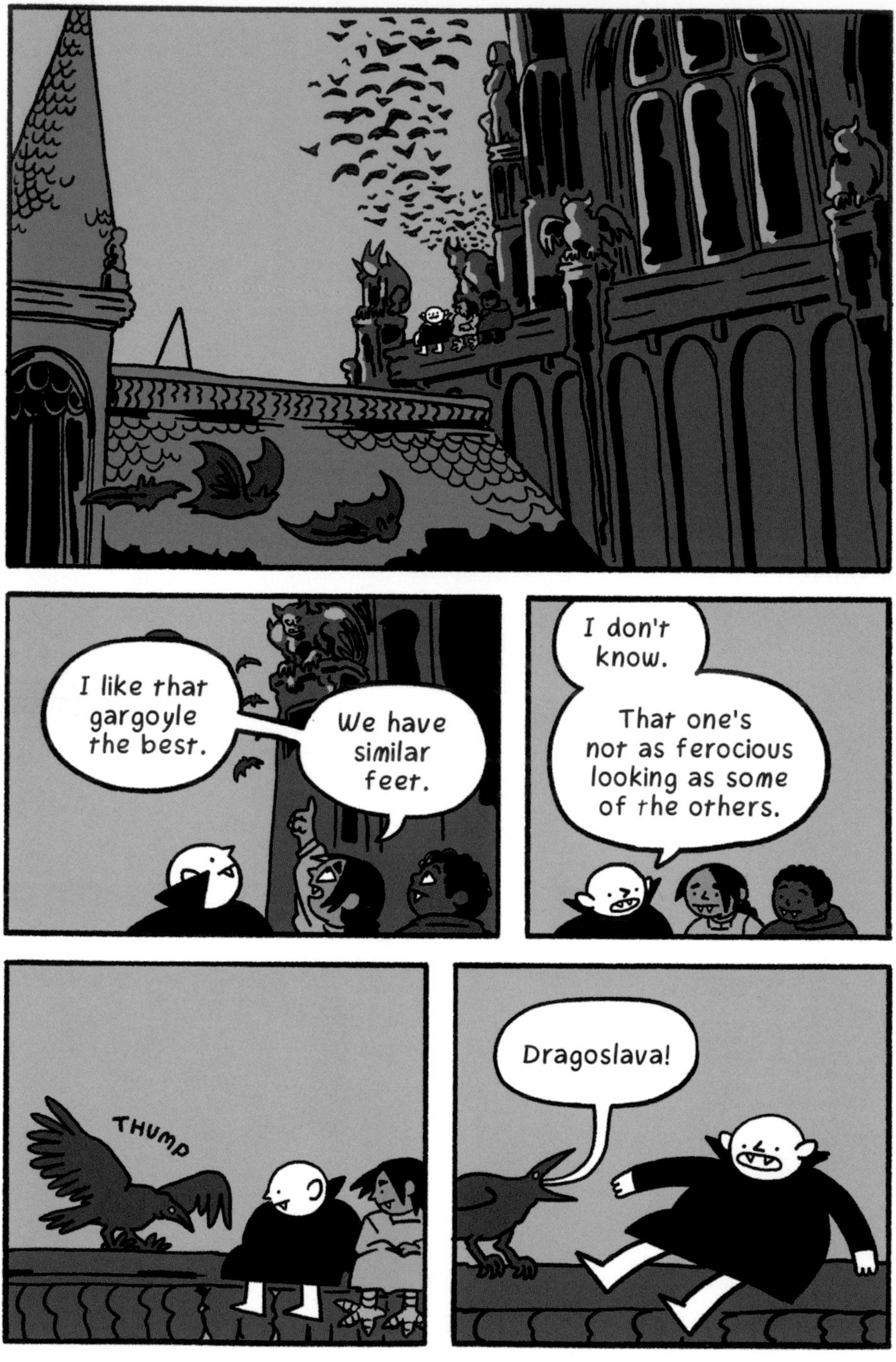
I like that gargoyle the best.
We have similar feet.
I don't know.
That one's not as ferocious looking as some of the others.
THUMP
Dragoslava!

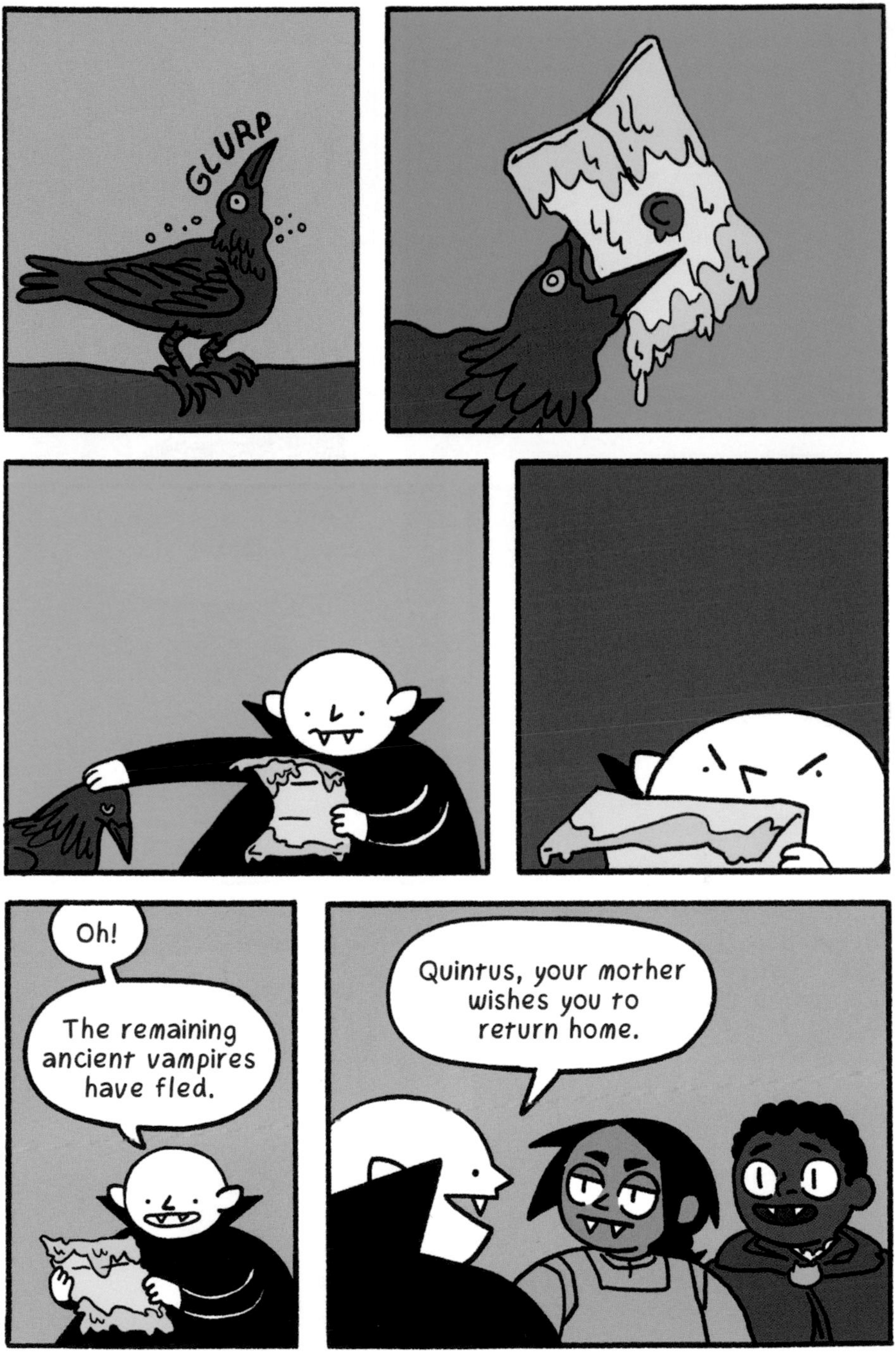
GLURP
Oh!
The remaining ancient vampires have fled.
Quintus, your mother wishes you to return home.

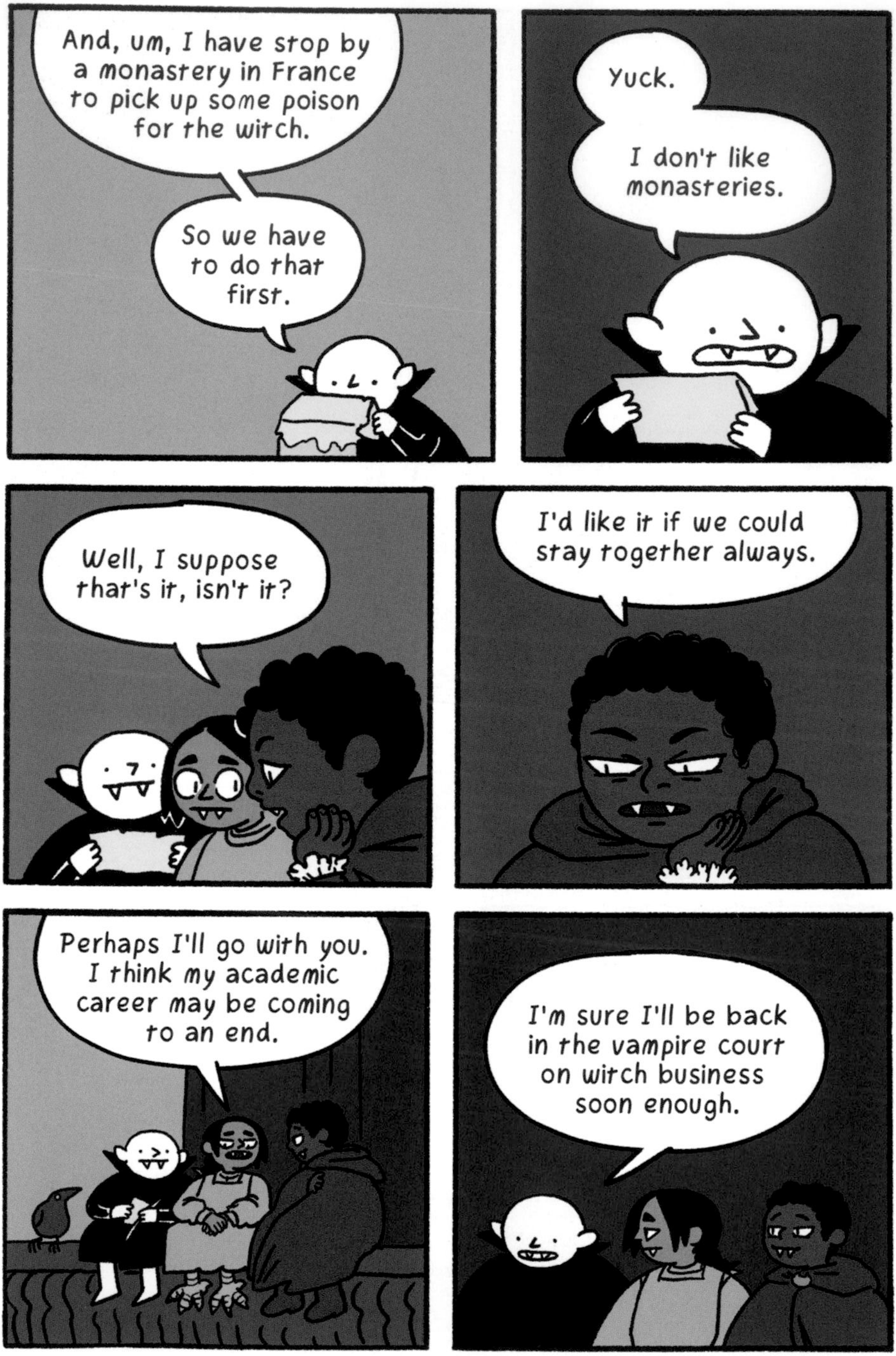
And, um, I have stop by a monastery in France to pick up some poison for the witch.
So we have to do that first.
Yuck.
I don't like monasteries.
Well, I suppose that's it, isn't it?
I'd like it if we could stay together always.
Perhaps I'll go with you. I think my academic career may be coming to an end.
I'm sure I'll be back in the vampire court on witch business soon enough.

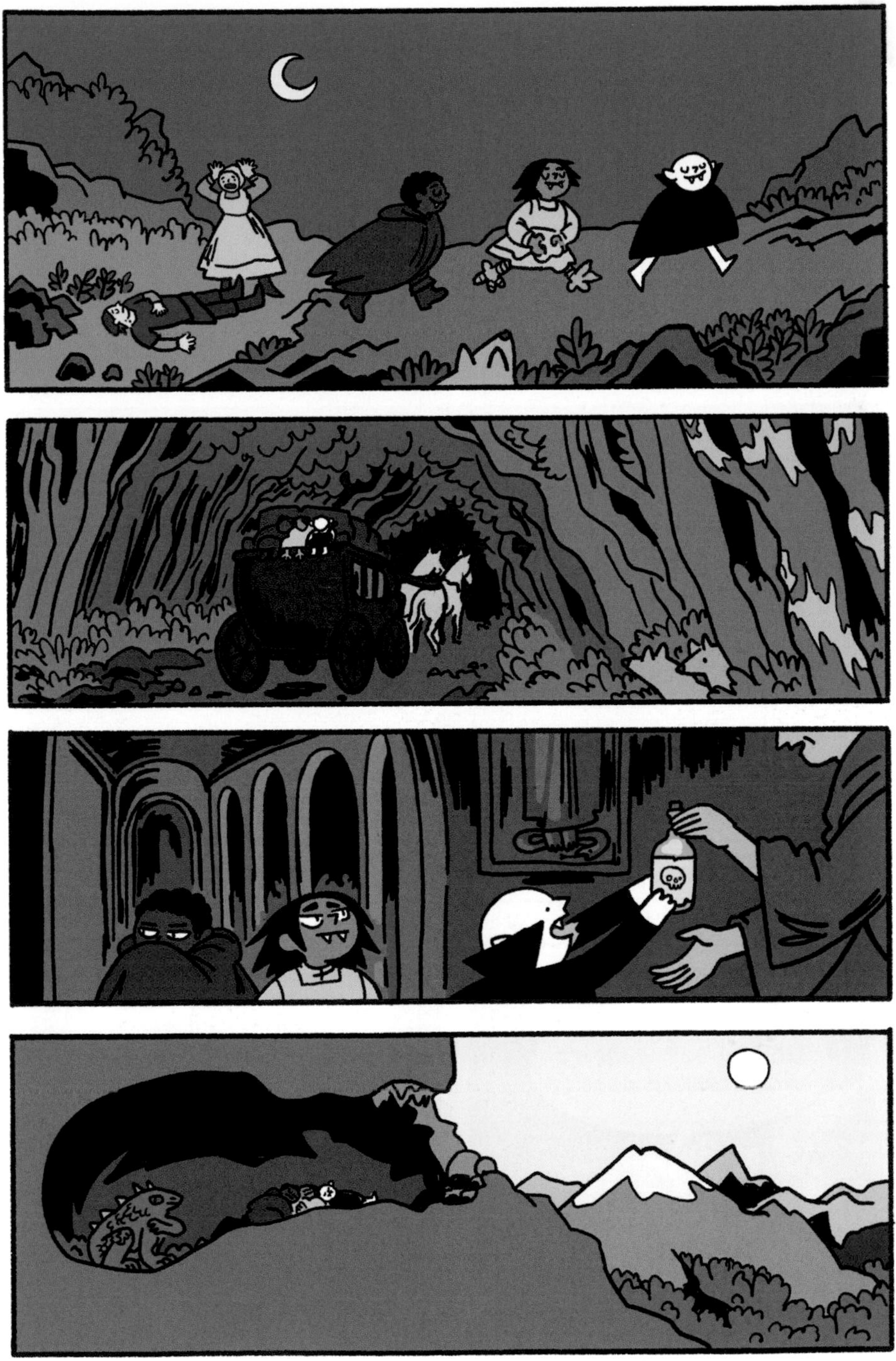

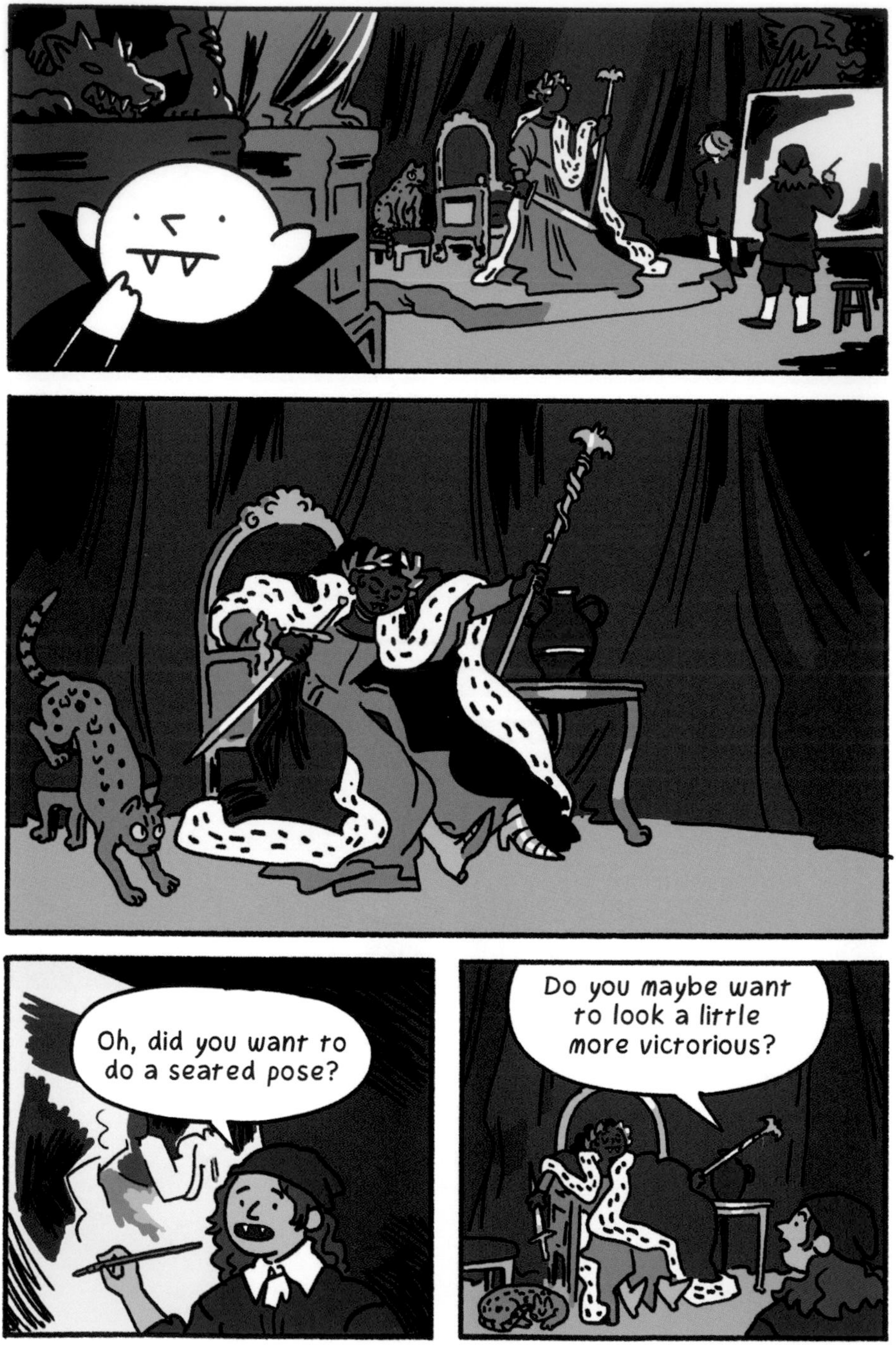
Oh, did you want to do a seated pose?
Do you maybe want to look a little more victorious?

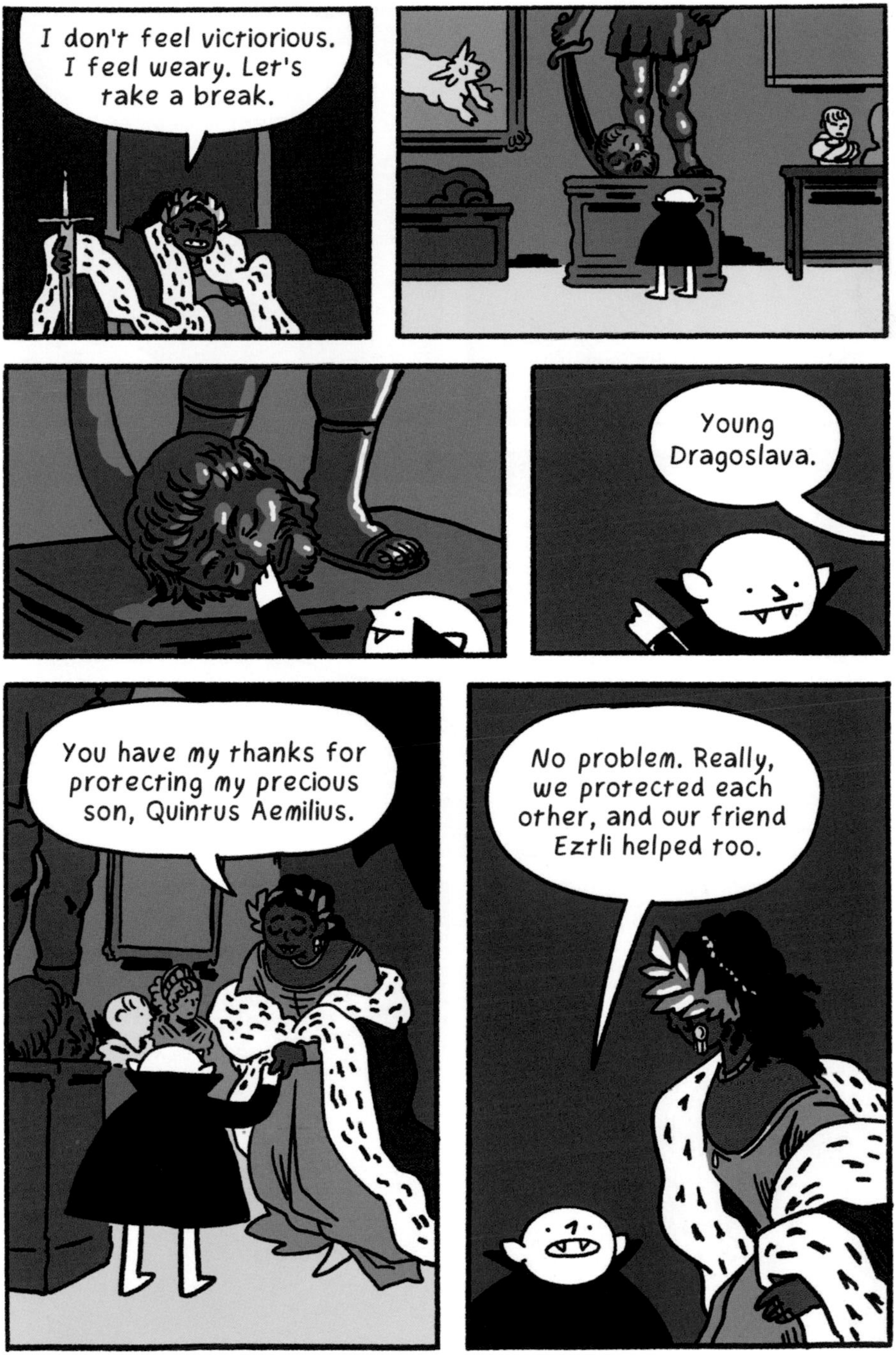
I don't feel victriorious. I feel weary. Let's take a break.
Young Dragoslava.
You have my thanks for protecting my precious son, Quintus Aemilius.
No problem. Really, we protected each other, and our friend Eztli helped too.

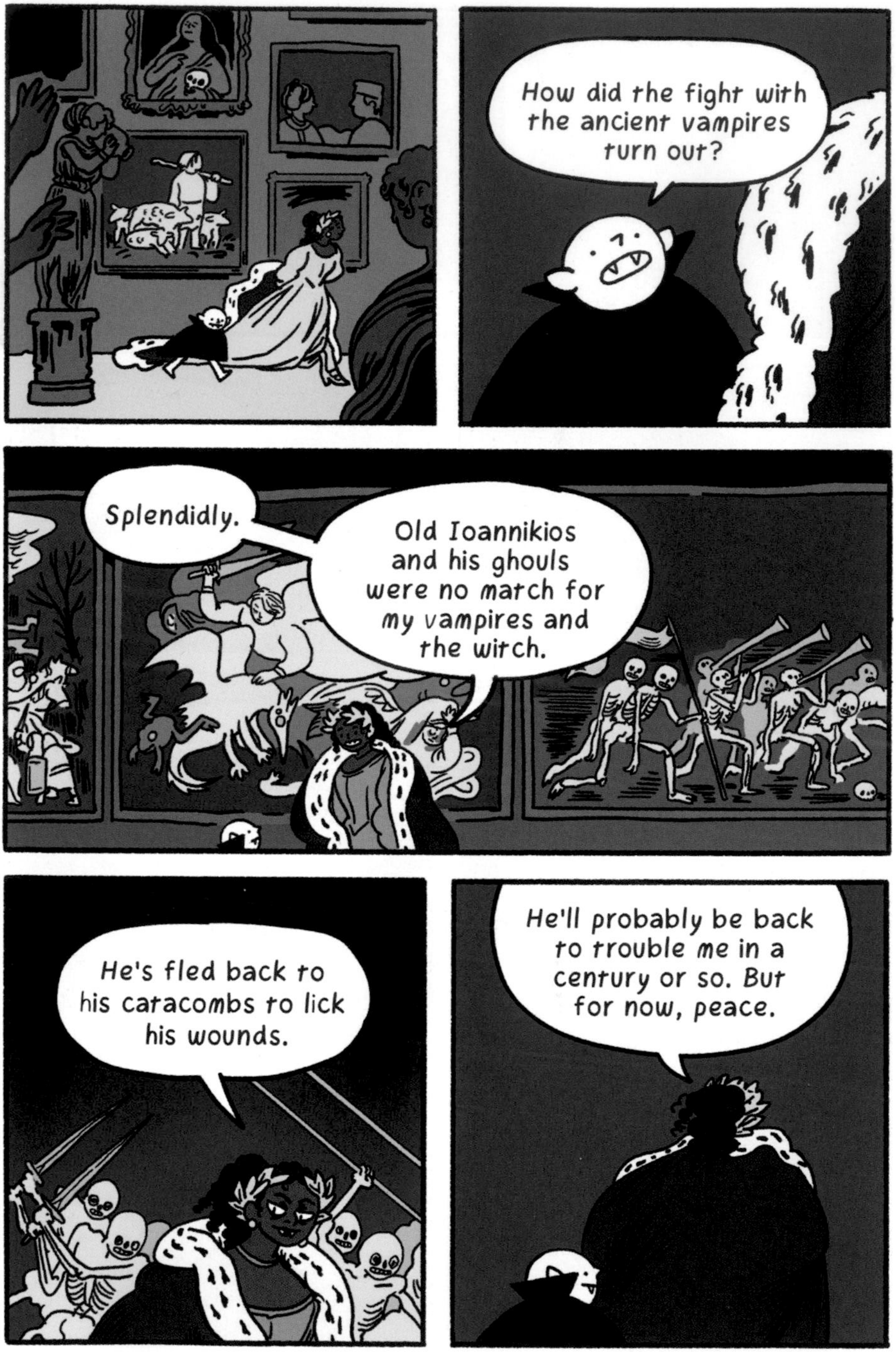
How did the fight with the ancient vampires turn out?
Splendidly.
Old Ioannikios and his ghouls were no match for my vampires and the witch.
He's fled back to his catacombs to lick his wounds.
He'll probably be back to trouble me in a century or so. But for now, peace.

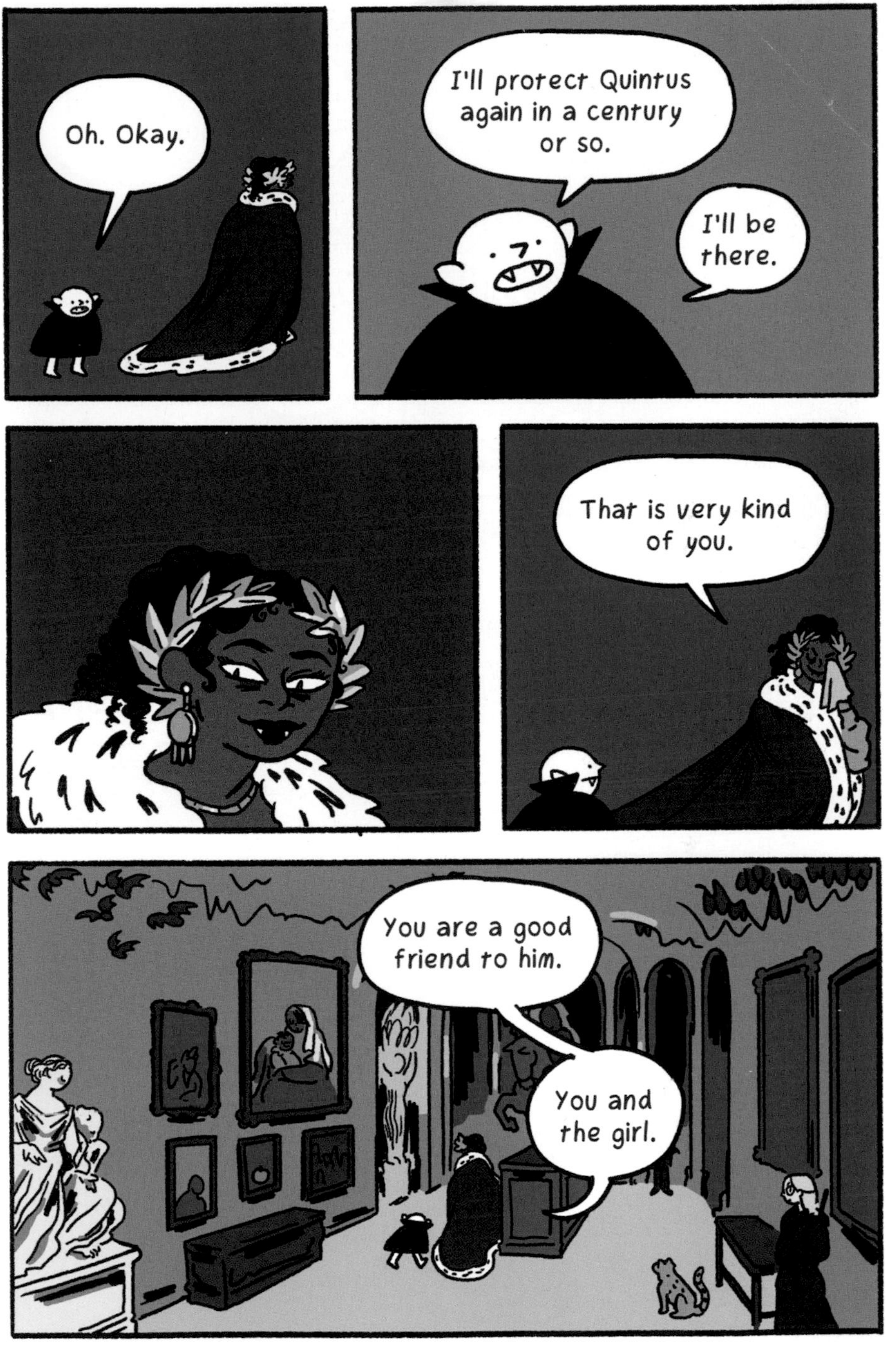
Oh. Okay.
I'll protect Quintus again in a century or so.
I'll be there.
That is very kind of you.
You are a good friend to him.
You and the girl.

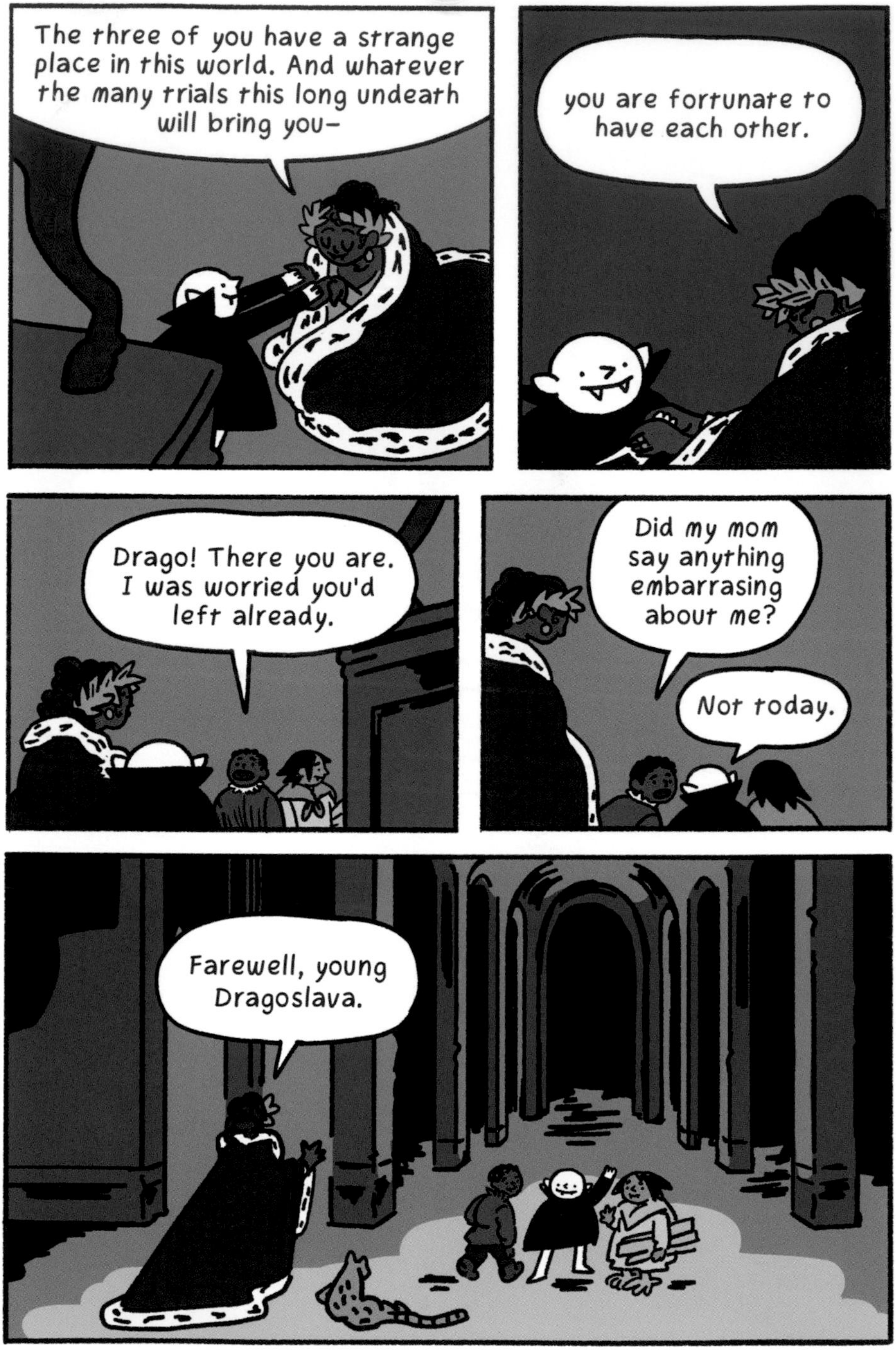
The three of you have a strange place in this world. And whatever the many trials this long undeath will bring you–
you are fortunate to have each other.
Drago! There you are. I was worried you'd left already.
Did my mom say anything embarrasing about me?
Not today.
Farewell, young Dragoslava.

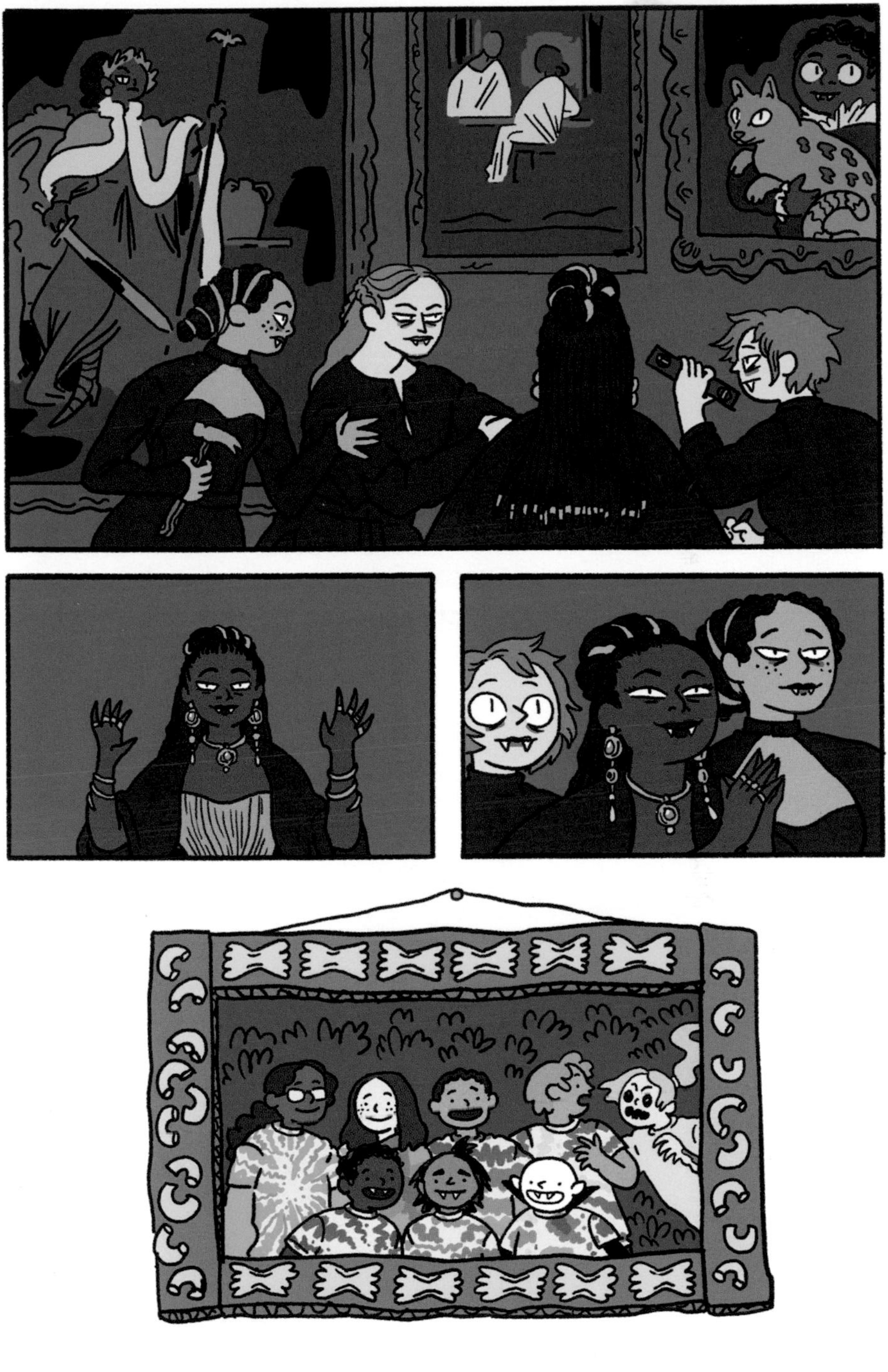

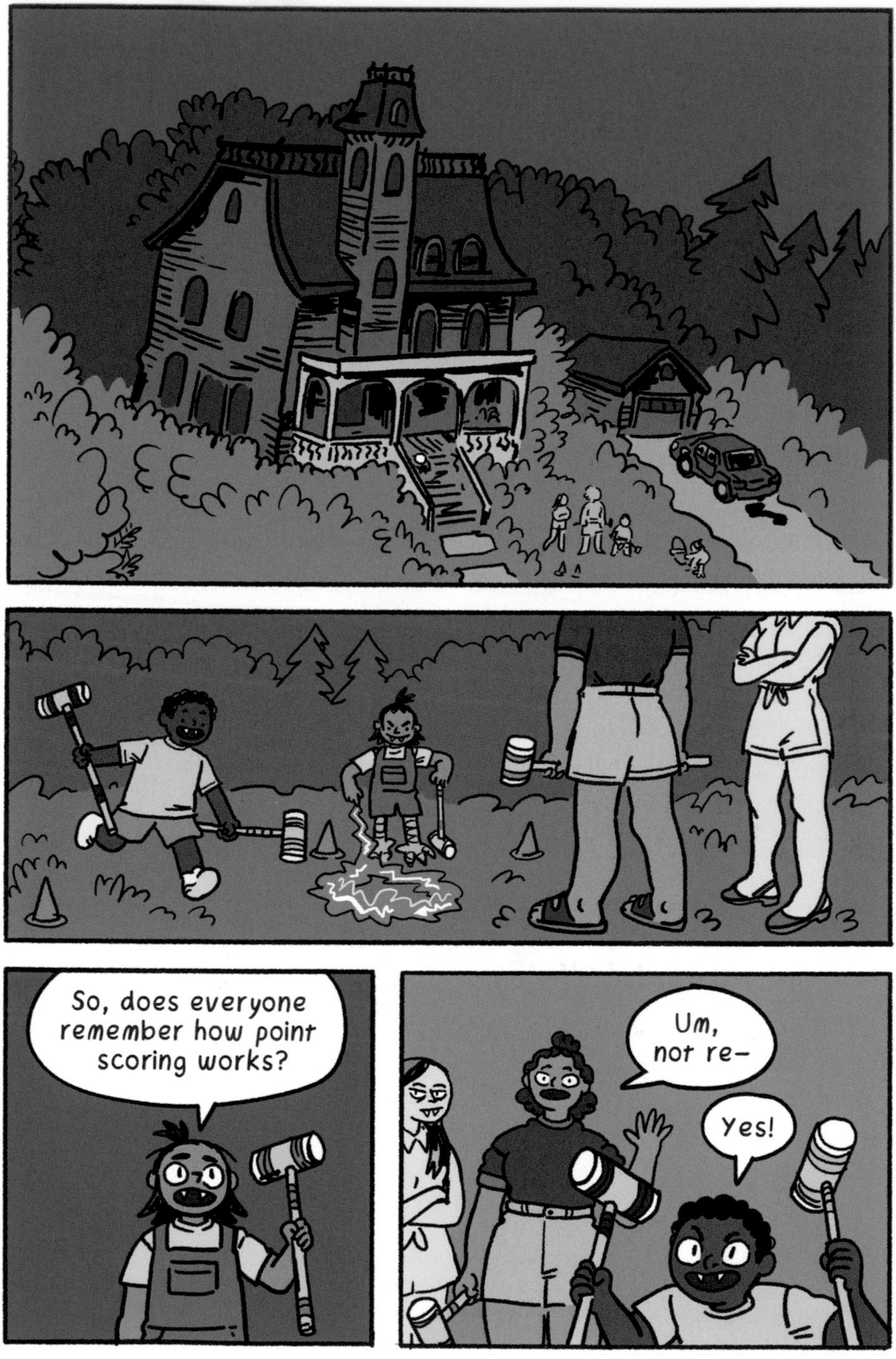
So, does everyone remember how point scoring works?
Um, not re–
Yes!

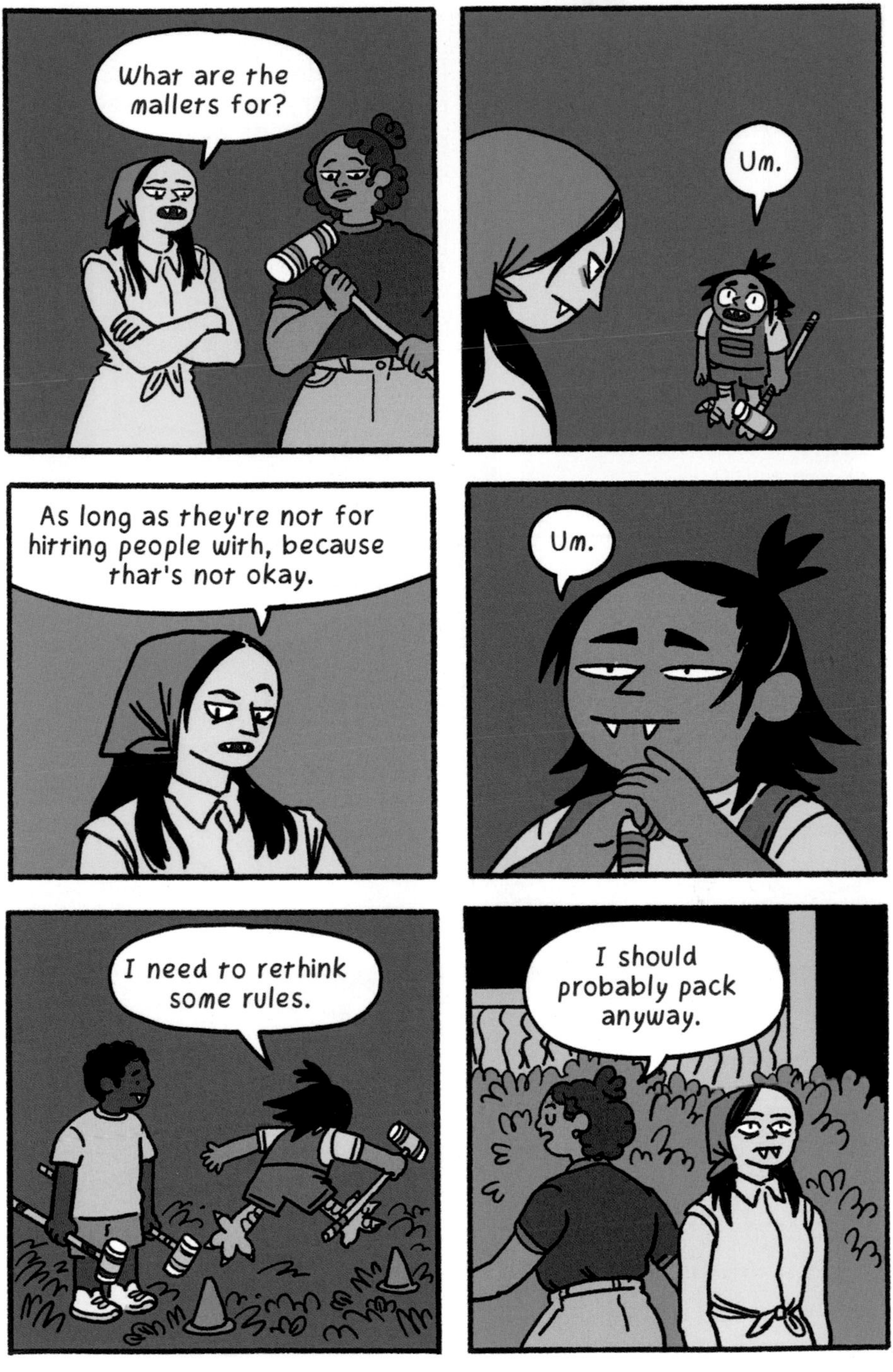
What are the mallets for?
Um.
As long as they're not for hitting people with, because that's not okay.
Um.
I need to rethink some rules.
I should probably pack anyway.

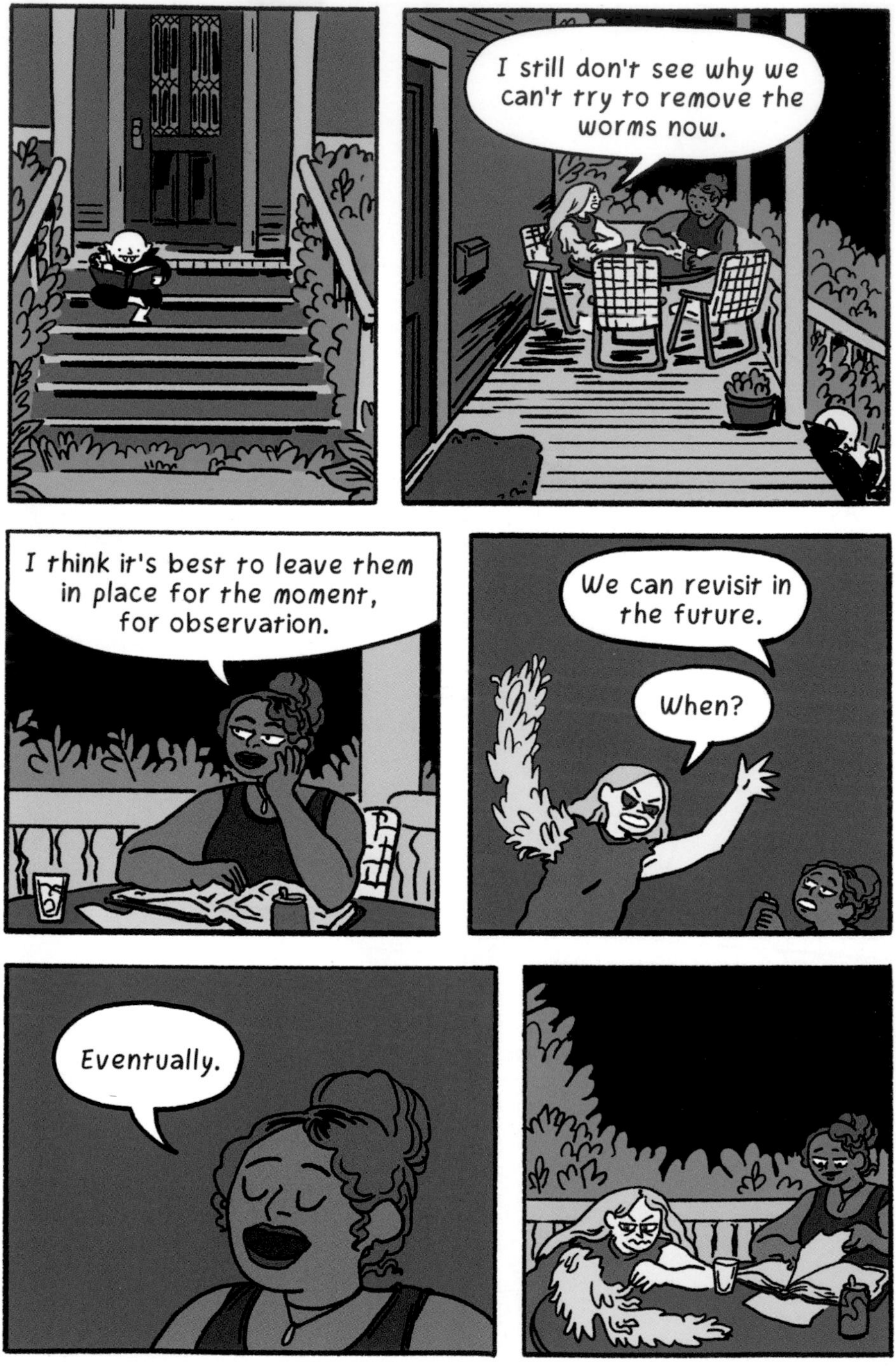
I still don't see why we can't try to remove the worms now.
I think it's best to leave them in place for the moment, for observation.
We can revisit in the future.
When?
Eventually.

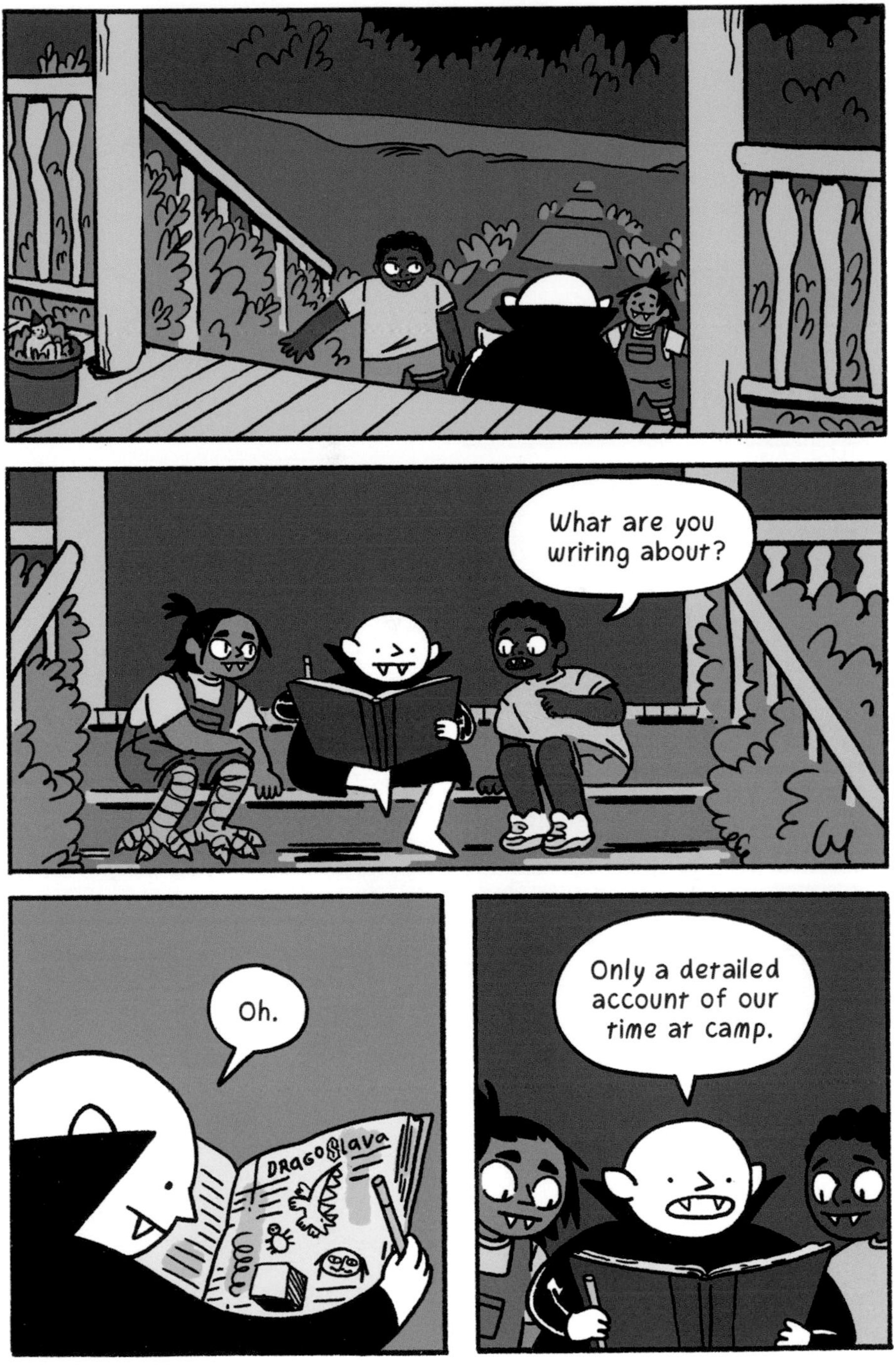
What are you writing about?
Oh.
DRAGOSlava
Only a detailed account of our time at camp.

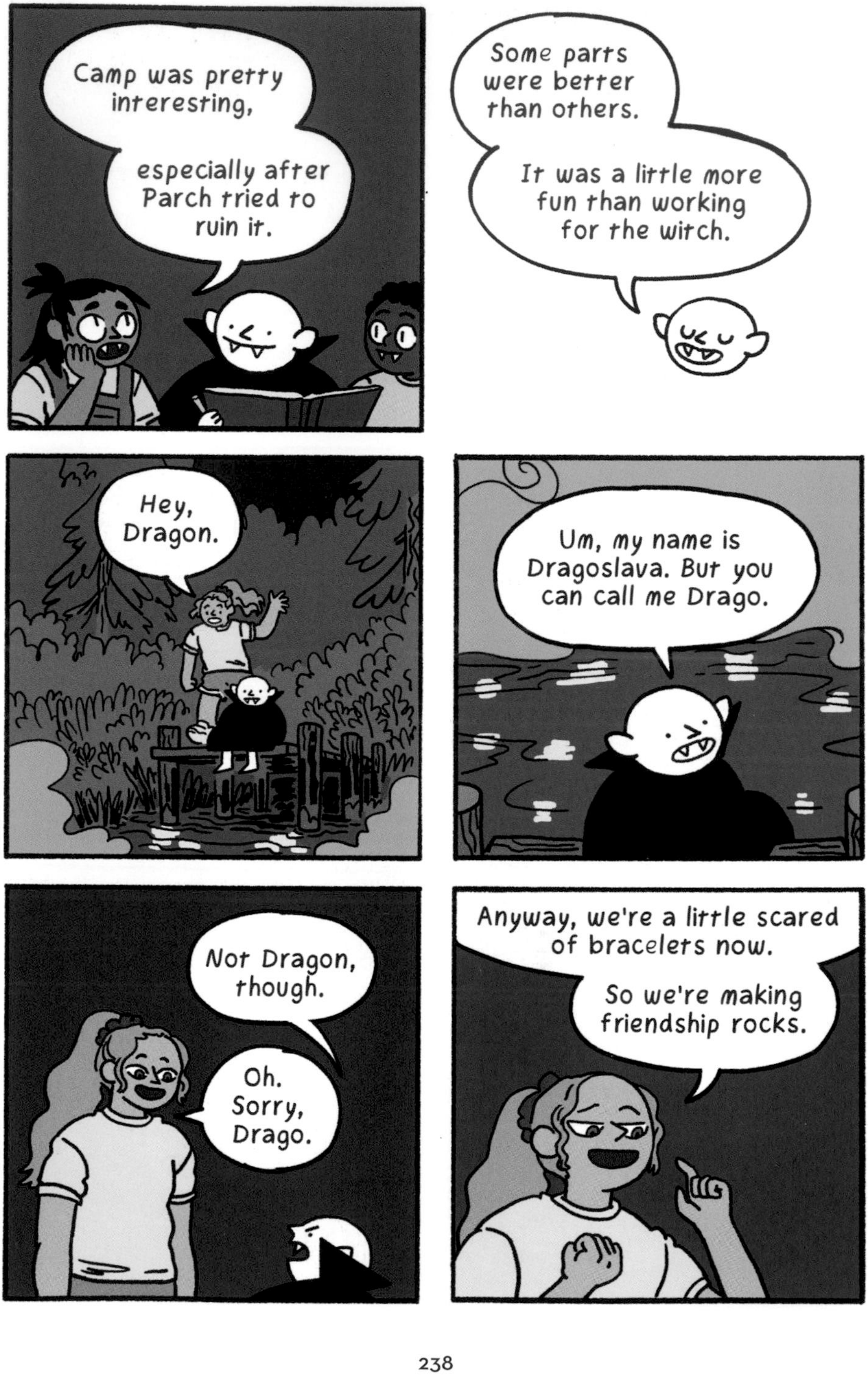
Camp was pretty interesting,
especially after Parch tried to ruin it.
Some parts were better than others.
It was a little more fun than working for the witch.
Hey, Dragon.
Um, my name is Dragoslava. But you can call me Drago.
Not Dragon, though.
Oh. Sorry, Drago.
Anyway, we're a little scared of bracelets now.
So we're making friendship rocks.

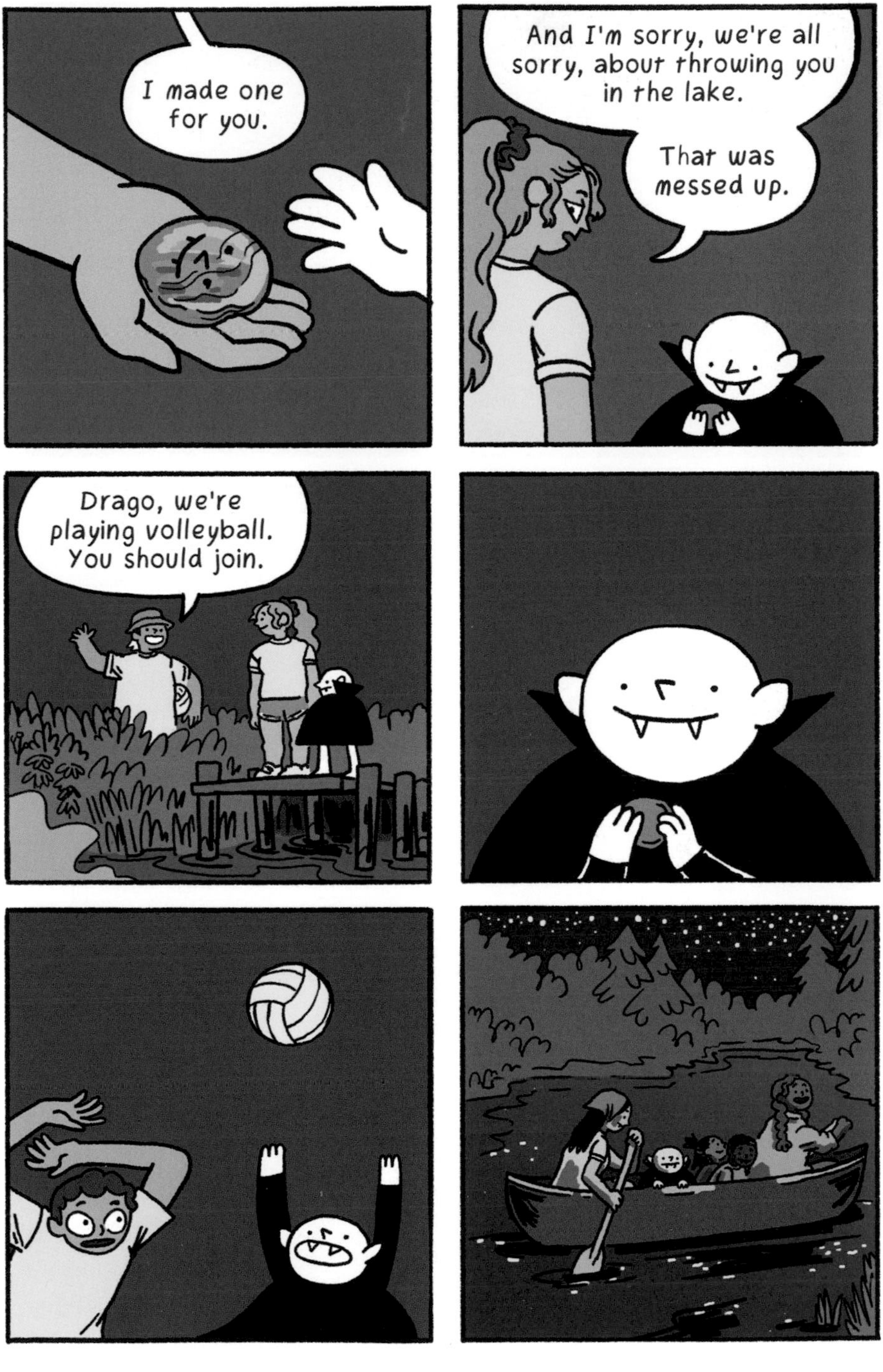
I made one for you.
And I'm sorry, we're all sorry, about throwing you in the lake.
That was messed up.
Drago, we're playing volleyball. You should join.

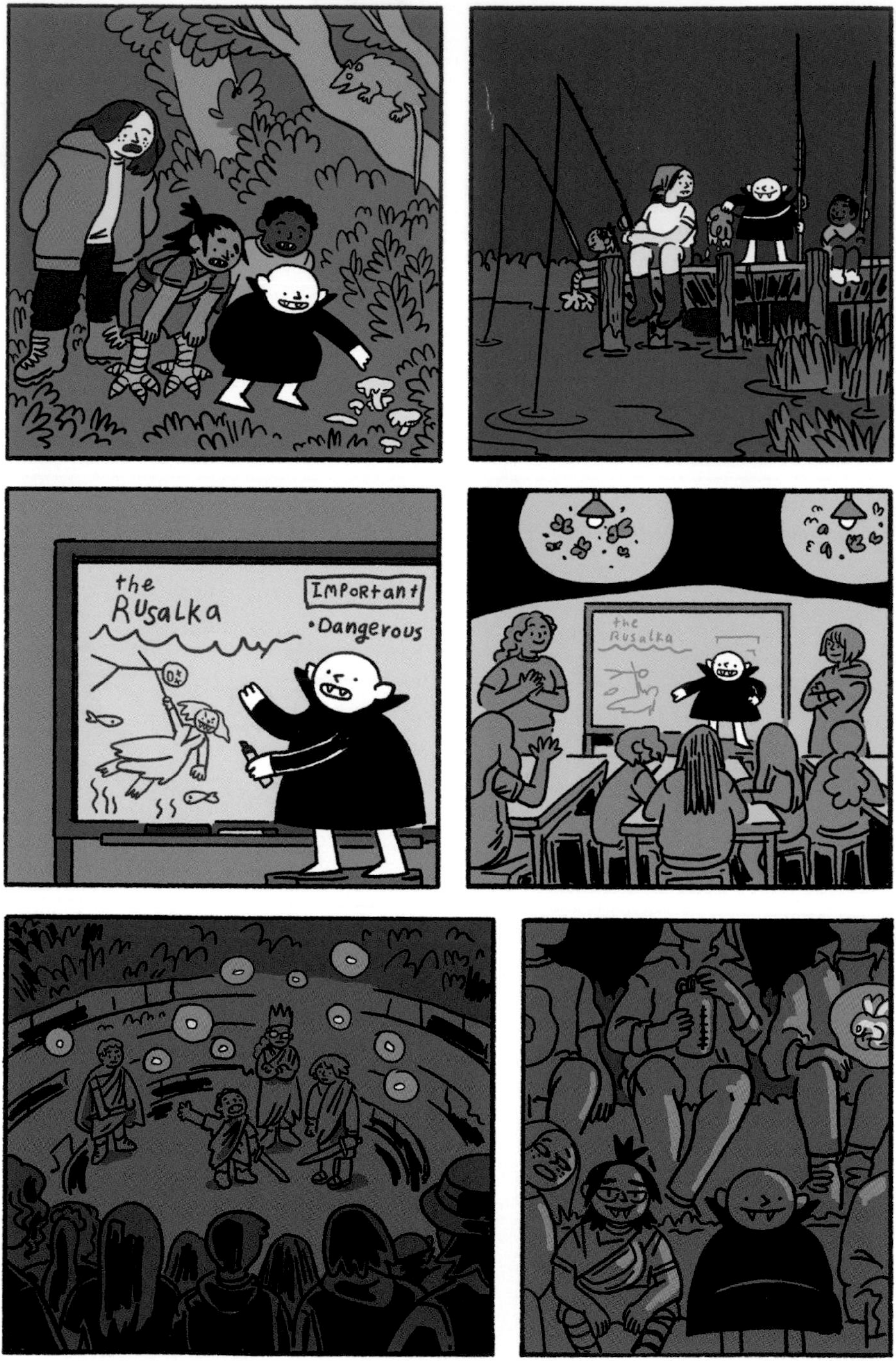
the
Rusalka
Important
•Dangerous
the
Rusalka

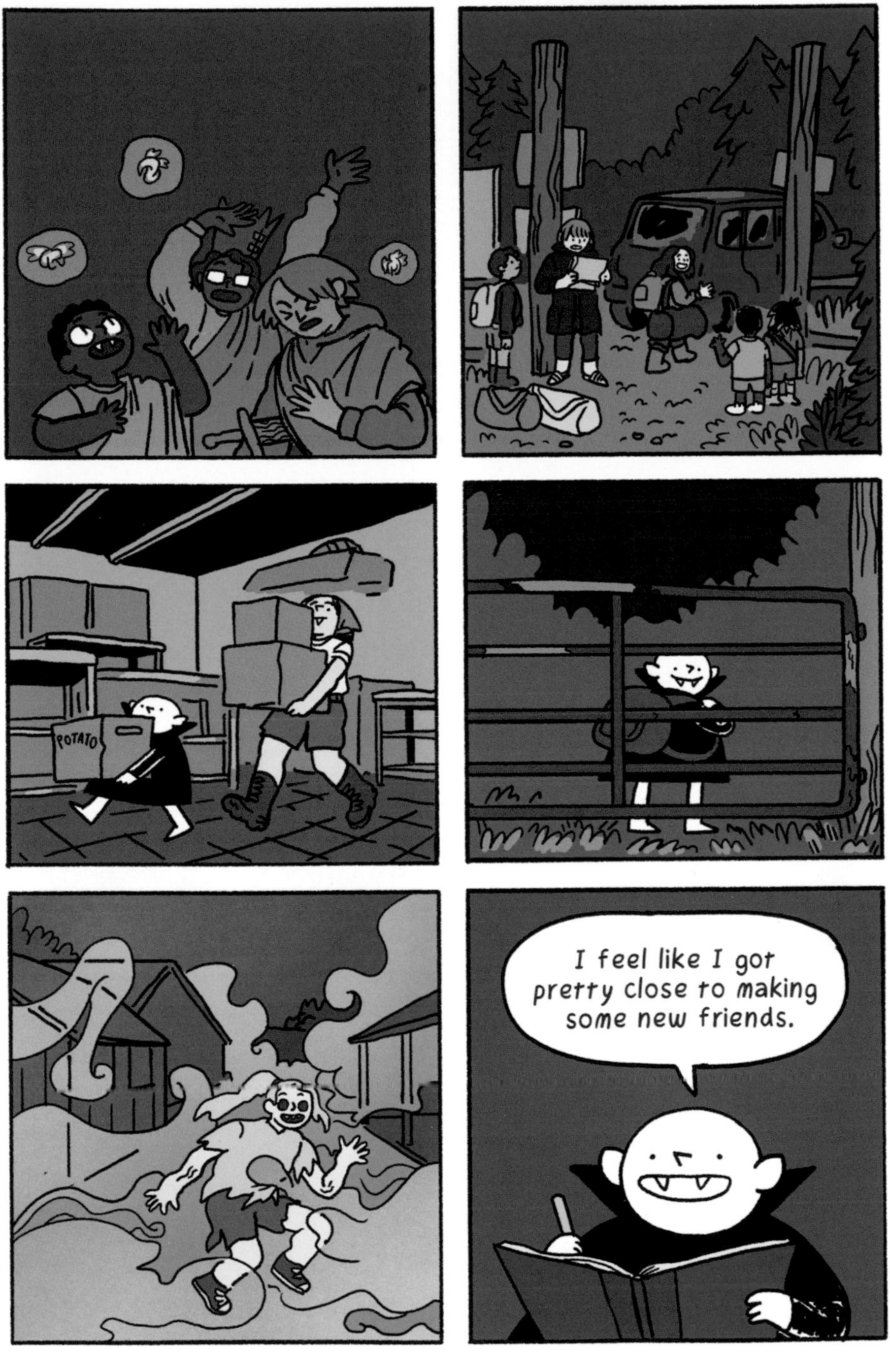
POTATO
I feel like I got pretty close to making some new friends.

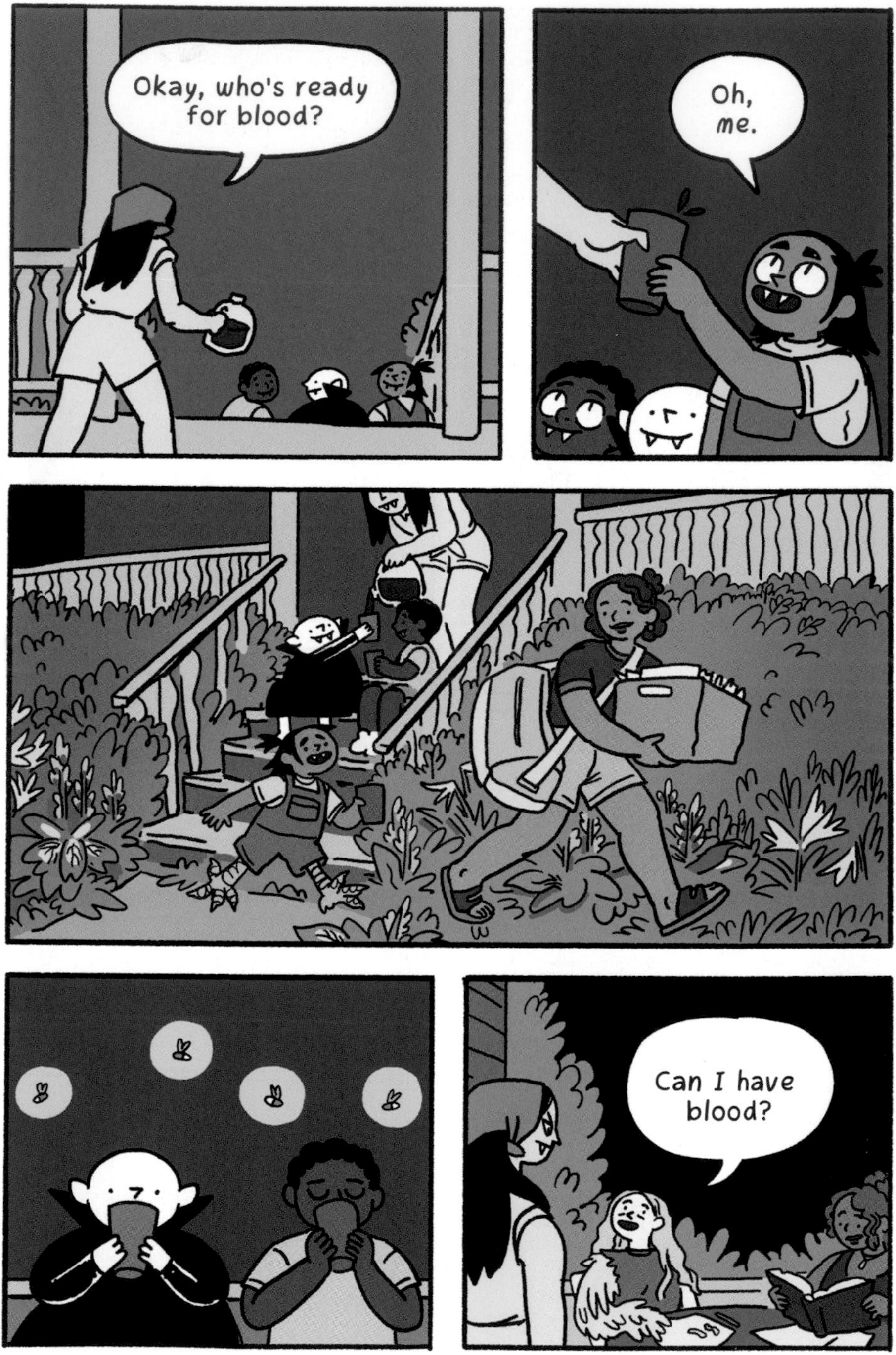
Okay, who's ready for blood?
Oh, me.
Can I have blood?

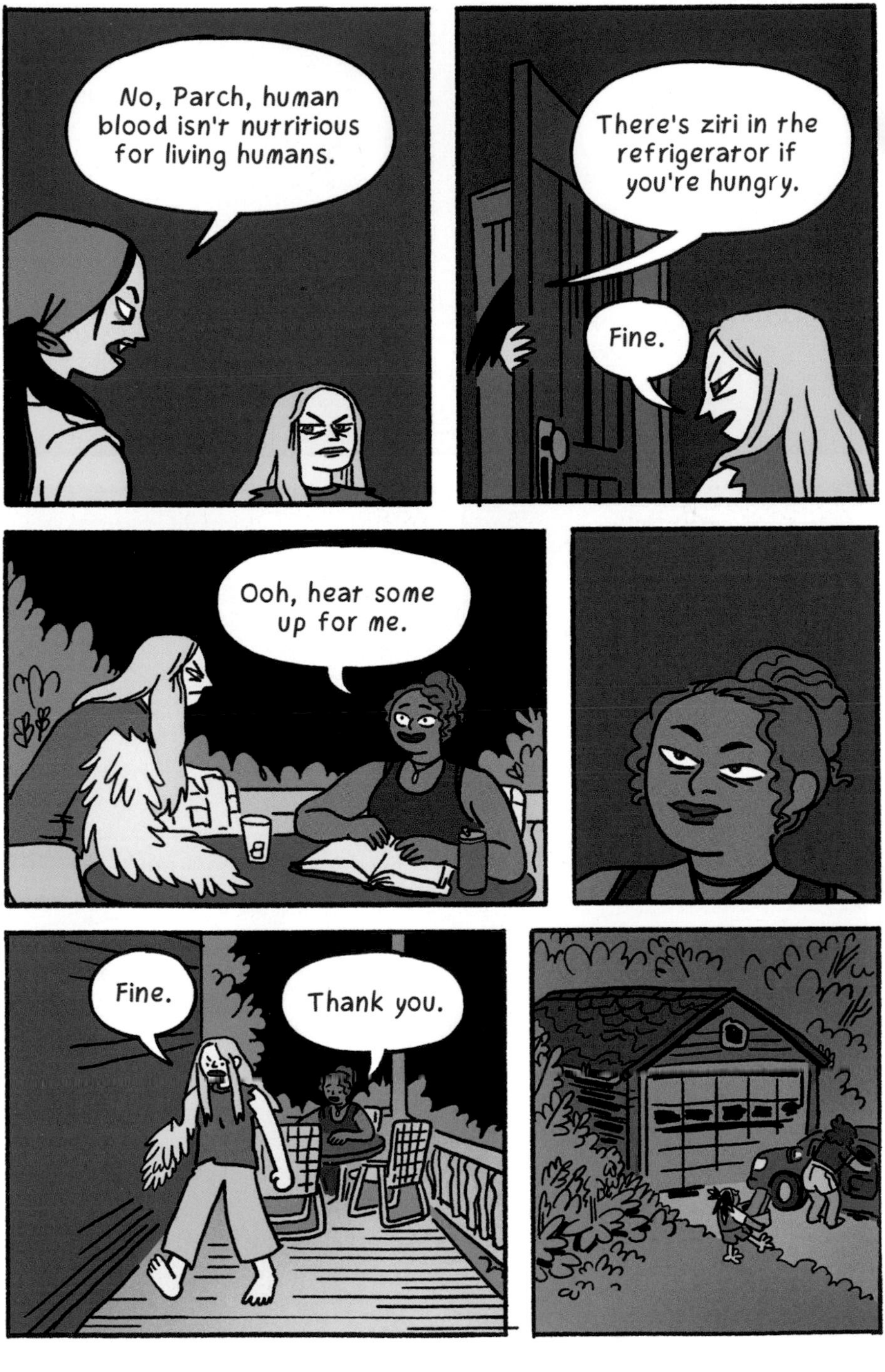
No, Parch, human blood isn't nutritious for living humans.
There's ziti in the refrigerator if you're hungry.
Fine.
Ooh, heat some up for me.
Fine.
Thank you.

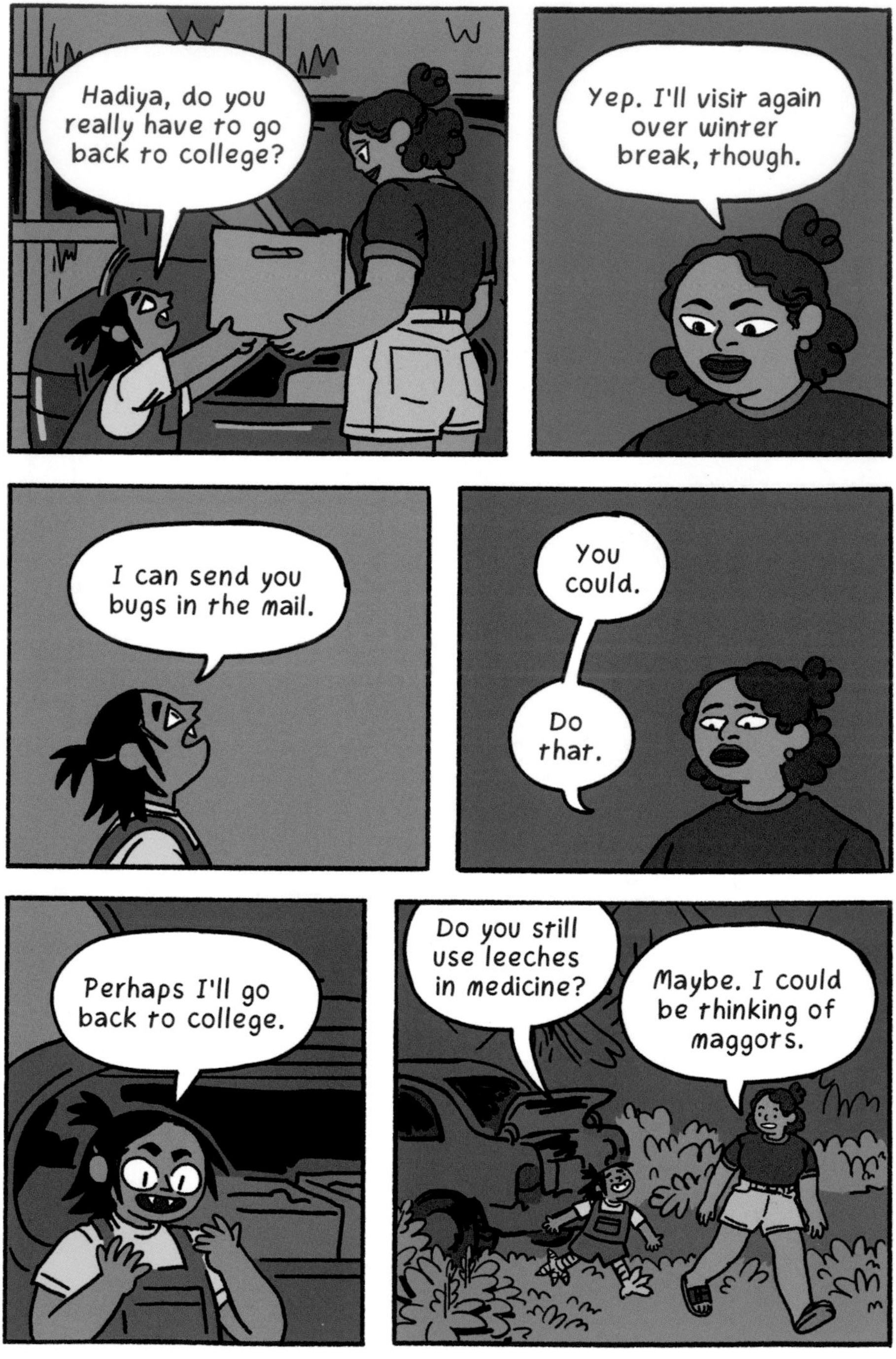
Hadiya, do you really have to go back to college?
Yep. I'll visit again over winter break, though.
I can send you bugs in the mail.
You could.
Do that.
Perhaps I'll go back to college.
Do you still use leeches in medicine?
Maybe. I could be thinking of maggots.

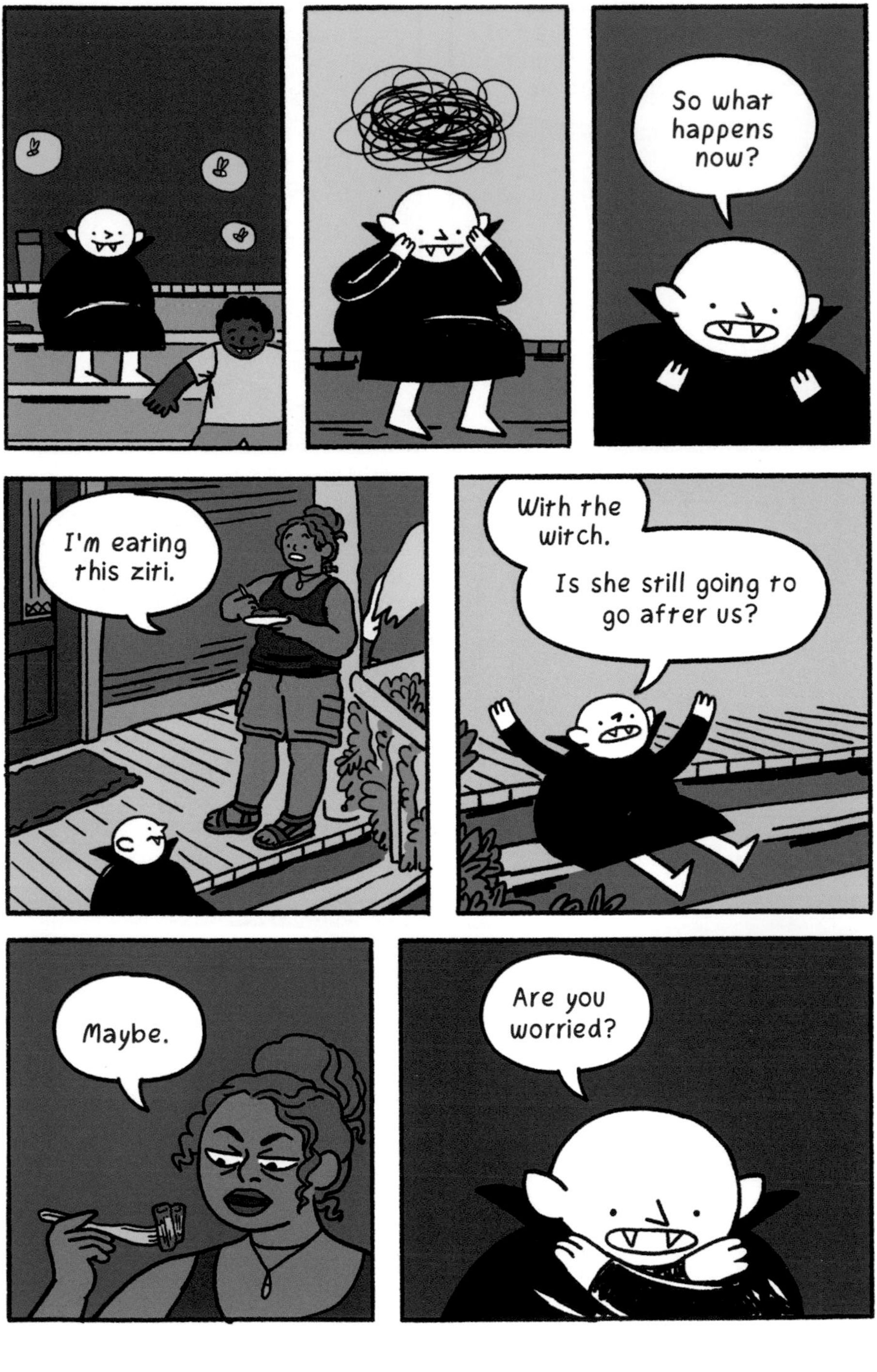
So what happens now?
I'm eating this ziti.
With the witch.
Is she still going to go after us?
Maybe.
Are you worried?

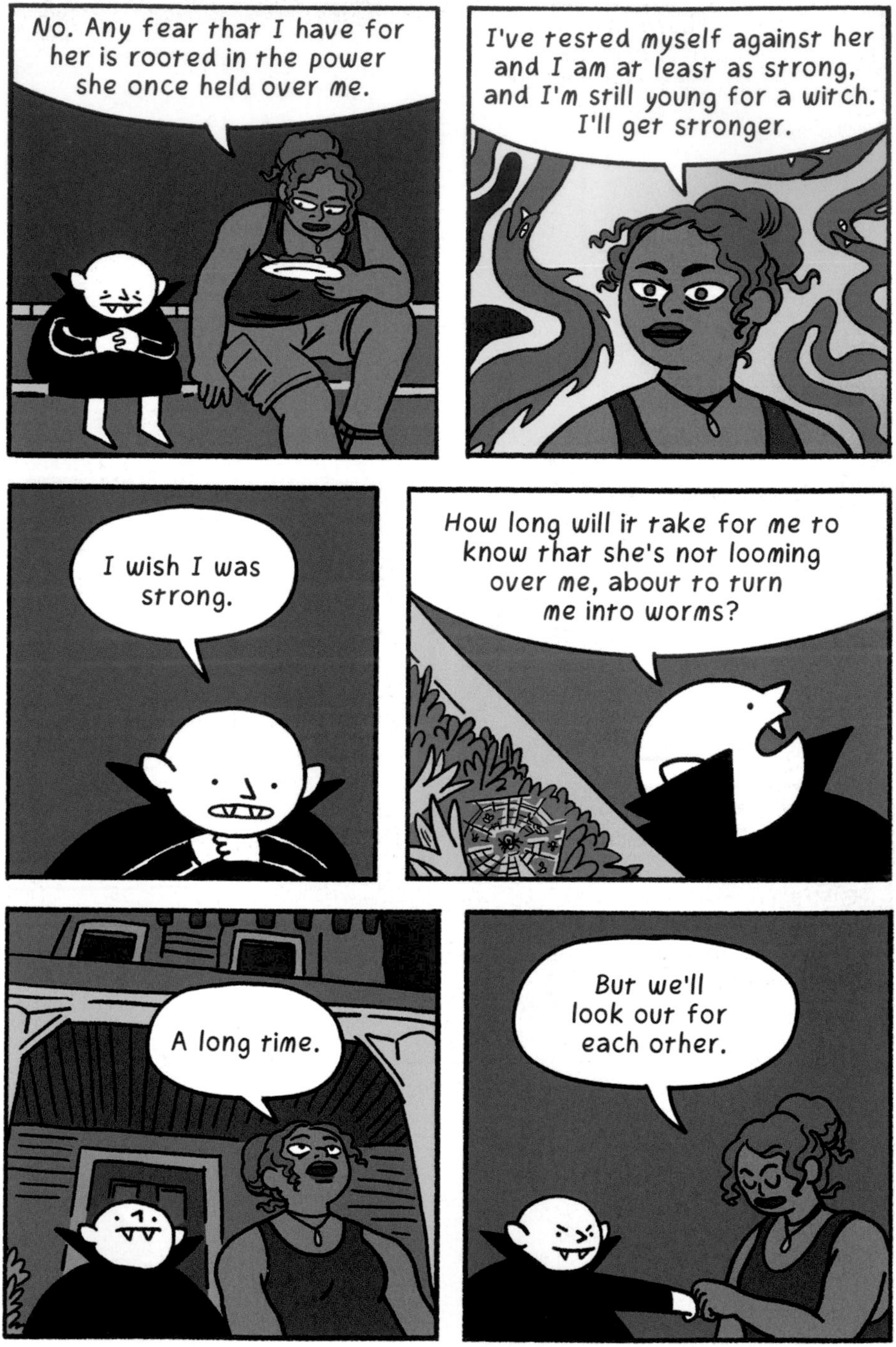
No. Any fear that I have for her is rooted in the power she once held over me.
I've tested myself against her and I am at least as strong, and I'm still young for a witch. I'll get stronger.
I wish I was strong.
How long will it take for me to know that she's not looming over me, about to turn me into worms?
A long time.
But we'll look out for each other.

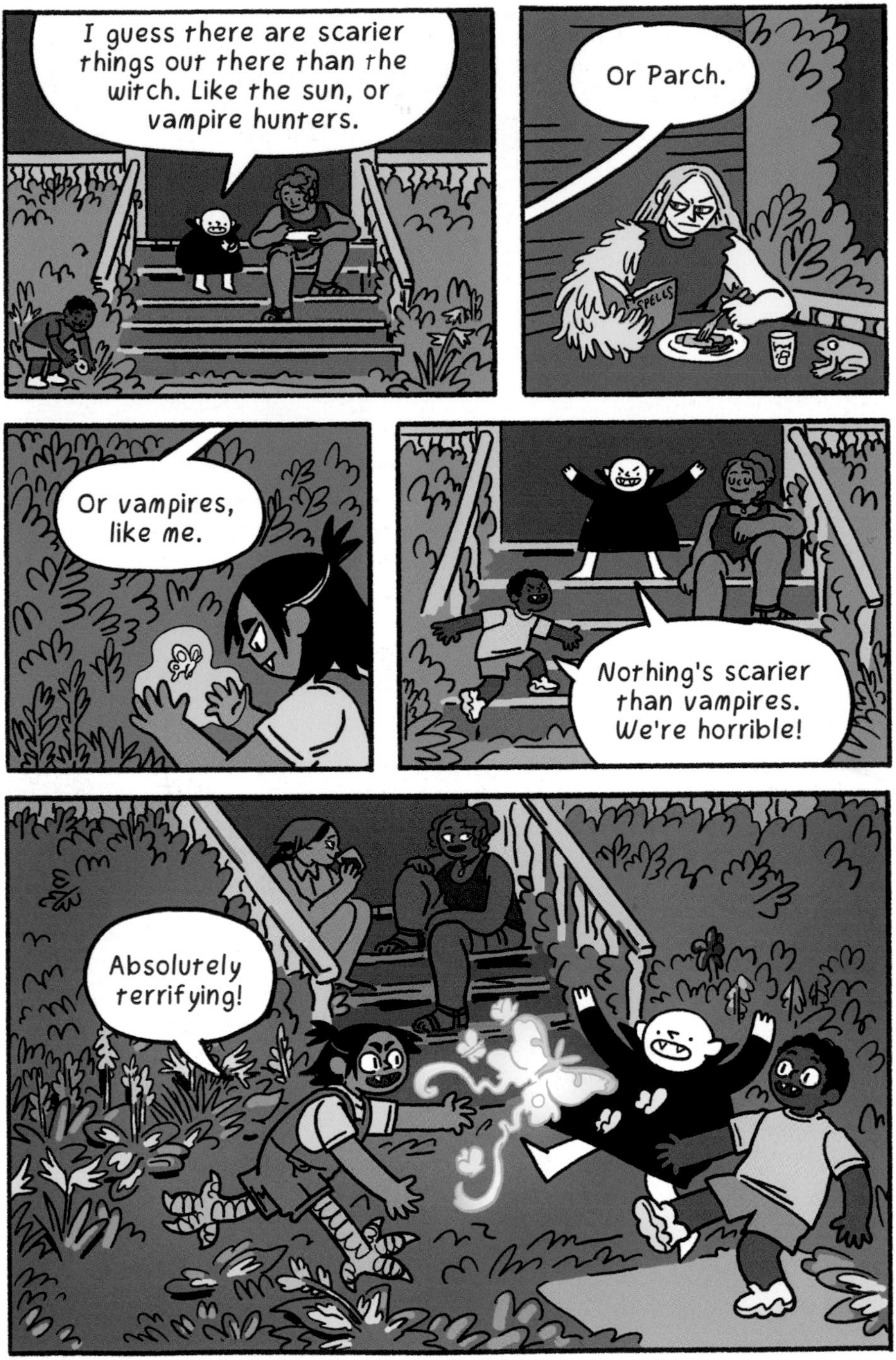
I guess there are scarier things out there than the witch. Like the sun, or vampire hunters.
Or Parch.
SPELLS
Or vampires, like me.
Nothing's scarier than vampires. We're horrible!
Absolutely terrifying!

Many thanks to my flatters,
Spencer Amundson
and **Ezra Mattes.**

Thanks to my editor,
Alyssa Miele,
who helped shape a better
and stronger story.

Thanks to everyone else
at HarperCollins who worked
to make this book exist.

Thanks to my
wonderful agent,
Linda Camacho.

Finally, thanks to the friends,
enemies, and almost-friends
from summer camp
in the distant past.

DEVELOPMENTAL SKETCHES

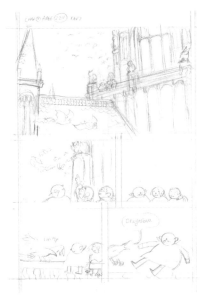

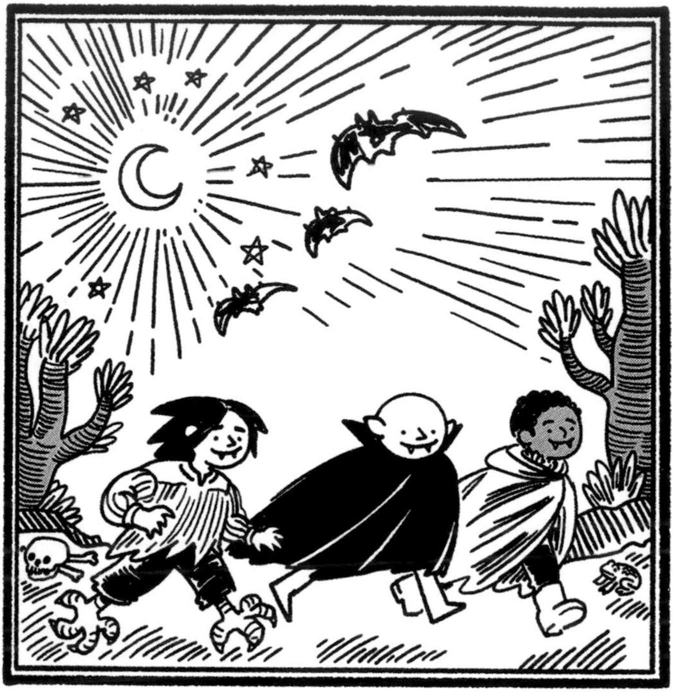

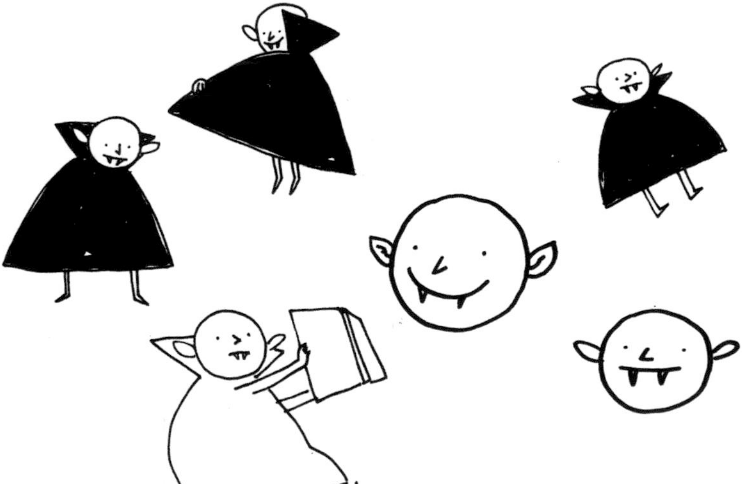